Once a Ranger

David watched Justin walk to the pretzel stand, taking his eyes off his son for no more than a few seconds as the line advanced a few steps to the carousel. Suddenly, as he turned to look back at Justin, he was knocked off his feet. David was taken by surprise, but he reacted fast, his hands reaching out to break his fall against a low iron railing. He spun toward the person who had knocked him down. Trying to get up, he yelled, "Jesus, man. What the hell . . ." He trailed off as he spotted Justin and then a man who looked like he was trying to grab the boy. "Justin!" David yelled as loudly as he could.

Justin turned to look at his father. "Daddy!" screamed Justin, terrified by seeing his father down on his knees.

Something animal stirred within David. Not in the last thirty years had so much adrenaline surged in his blood. Springing upright, in one fluid motion he lunged catlike toward his assailant. Hooking his foot under the man's leg, David simultaneously grabbed his open leather jacket and spun the heavier man down and hard toward the iron rail. The man's back slammed into the short rail, knocking the wind out of him. His jacket opened when he hit the metal, and David saw the massive 9mm automatic in the man's shoulder holster. *Who are you? Leave Justin and me alone,* he thought frantically.

David watched as Justin was lifted by the other man, kicking and screaming but unable to pull free. "Don't touch my boy!" David cried as the assailant started to carry Justin away.

ONCE A RANGER

Stan Johnson

Dear Sheldon,

Happy 78th!

I hope you enjoy the read.

Best.

Stan J[illegible]

A SIGNET BOOK

SIGNET
Published by New American Library, a division of
Penguin Group (USA) Inc., 375 Hudson Street,
New York, New York 10014, U.S.A.
Penguin Books Ltd, 80 Strand,
London WC2R 0RL, England
Penguin Books Australia Ltd, 250 Camberwell Road,
Camberwell, Victoria 3124, Australia
Penguin Books Canada Ltd, 10 Alcorn Avenue,
Toronto, Ontario, Canada M4V 3B2
Penguin Books (N.Z.) Ltd, Cnr Rosedale and Airborne Roads,
Albany, Auckland 1310, New Zealand

Penguin Books Ltd, Registered Offices:
80 Strand, London WC2R 0RL, England

First published by Signet, an imprint of New American Library,
a division of Penguin Group (USA) Inc.

First Printing, September 2003
10 9 8 7 6 5 4 3 2 1

Printed in the United States of America

PUBLISHER'S NOTE
This is a work of fiction. Names, characters, places, and incidents either are the product of the author's imagination or are used fictitiously, and any resemblance to actual persons, living or dead, business establishments, events, or locales is entirely coincidental.

Nora, my lover, cowriter, best friend, and wife

ACKNOWLEDGMENTS

This book would not have been possible without the patience and the editing skills of my wife, Nora. She was patient with me as I spent countless hours writing on weekends and evenings, and as I drifted off in the middle of conversations as thoughts came to me about the story, my mind lost somewhere in the pages of this novel. Moreover, when no one really believed in me, Nora was there to urge me on. I am lucky. Then, when the manuscript was on its third version and I could no longer edit my own work, Nora applied her keen editing skills to this novel, improving on it with great diplomacy and tact. Not one single major argument ensued! I am grateful for her.

My thanks to Gordon Cucullu, lieutenant colonel (retired), former Airborne Ranger, and Green Beret who is now a llama rancher, journalist, TV commentator, novelist, and my friend. Gordon's comments on my manuscript were of great help, not just on the Ranger-related scenes, but on many other aspects as well.

I owe my knowledge of airplanes to my late father-in-law, Al Hirschberger, World War II navy fighter pilot who flew Hellcats off the carrier *Hornet* in the South Pacific and who still flew his own plane until his death in September 2001, and my brother-in-law, Danny, also an accomplished pilot.

Thanks to the computer guys at my law firm and at Control Risks Group, an international security consulting company that is a client of mine, for teaching me the fundamentals of computer hacking.

Considerable literary license was taken with respect to

the FBI, DEA, and CIA. The antagonists within those agencies in this novel are purely fictional and not intended to detract from the hard work and dedication of federal agents who put their lives on the line in the drug wars. Likewise with respect to the people of Colombia, who suffer from, and battle against, the cocaine industry more than anyone else. Much is said in the United States in a derogatory way about Colombia, but we in this country should remember that Americans who purchase cocaine are as much at fault as those who sell it.

Few writers these days can publish without the support of a literary agent who goes to bat for him or her. I am no exception. My agent, Michael Carlisle, believed in me and championed my work. Without him, you would not be reading this novel. The same is true for Doug Grad, senior editor at New American Library. As he edited my manuscript, Doug seemed to get into my head and sense the passion and excitement that I was trying to convey. His edits were insightful, laser sharp, and always polite.

Finally, thanks to my three children, my day-to-day inspiration and joy.

Chapter 1

Washington, D.C., October 16, 1999

"Amy! Hi," Linda Ross said cheerfully when she and Debbie, her daughter, saw their friends. It was a brilliant Saturday afternoon despite the autumn chill in the air, and the two friends were grateful that they had decided on the playground. Linda approached the bench near the sandbox where Amy's daughter, Carrie, was playing. Debbie quickly bolted from her mother's side to join her playmate.

"Linda, how are you? Did you bring the pictures? I went to every magazine store in the neighborhood, and I couldn't find a copy of that issue. I can't believe I didn't get it when it first came out. It was so hectic, with Carrie having the flu and Mark getting sick."

"Don't be silly. I'm glad everyone's better. And I brought you your very own copy," Linda said, pulling a fresh *Washington Weekly* out of her bag and handing it to Amy. "Page seventeen."

"Linda, these pictures . . . she's gorgeous! Debbie has a radiance about her. I wasn't sure a photo could capture it, but these are great. She's so photogenic. Look at that smile."

"Thanks," said Linda, letting out a relieved breath. She never knew with other parents whether Debbie's exceptional looks would evoke jealousy or admiration. "I think she looks like a little movie star . . . but I might not be objective," she said with a chuckle.

Neither of the two mothers noticed the forest-green Dodge Caravan parked across the street. The occupants were not interested in the women. Their boss wanted Debbie.

Manuel, the leader, sat in the passenger seat surveying the playground intently. He was smartly dressed in a blue blazer, light blue shirt, tan pants, and brown Hush Puppies, giving the impression of an executive outfitted for casual Friday. His protégé, Joaquin, sat behind him, next to the sliding door. Joaquin was also well dressed in light olive khakis, a dark green shirt, and a light brown leather jacket that suited his muscular frame and dark good looks and also hid his 9mm Beretta and heavy silencer. Hector sat next to Joaquin on the middle seat, nervous and fidgety, ready to spring open the sliding door once their prey was snared and slide it shut as the van drove away. He was dressed in designer jeans, a plaid shirt, and an oversize denim jacket that concealed his Tek-9 machine pistol. Raymond, the only *gringo* in the van, sat in the driver's seat, tall and blond, with the steel blue eyes of a killer.

Manuel's boss, the *patrón*, had seen Debbie's photo in the *Washington Weekly* four weeks earlier. He wanted the little "poodle," as he called her, for his own, like picking a puppy out of a window. Manuel felt a shudder of resentment against the *patrón*. The days not spent fighting to establish the new drug cartel's operations in New York infuriated him. The collection of these children was a dangerous distraction, an obsession that the boss should control. *He's sick*, Manuel told himself for the tenth time that afternoon, *but he's the patrón. And he wants the girl.* And, as Manuel knew all too well, no one denied the *patrón* what he wanted.

At Manuel's signal, Joaquin stepped out of the van to stretch his legs and to get a better view of the layout. He scanned the playground and the surrounding area, searching for any sign of police. Finding none, he nodded slightly toward the van. On cue, Manuel began to walk slowly through the park, seating himself on a bench outside the playground within several feet of a sign that said ONLY ADULTS ACCOMPANYING CHILDREN UNDER 12 ALLOWED. He calmly opened the *Washington Post* and pretended to read, his back to the playground. Behind him, he heard the laughter of children and the conversation of two women.

"How's it going at school?" Amy asked Linda.

"Okay, but frustrating. Not so much the students. The kids are fine and I really like teaching Spanish and coaching the track team, but school politics are a pain in the ass."

Manuel listened intently to confirm that he had the right victim. The article in the *Washington Weekly* had mentioned that Debbie's mother, an African-American woman who was something of a track star in college, was a single parent who juggled raising Debbie, teaching and coaching. So far, so good.

"Are you thinking about pursuing the modeling offer?" Amy asked.

Bingo, Manuel said to himself.

"I don't know. I'm not sure how Debbie feels about it, and I won't push her. She's actually a little shy. You know, the weather was chilly that day and they didn't want her to wear a sweater with some of the outfits. She was a trooper, and performed without complaining, but I'm not sure that's such a great message for a young girl. And besides, look what we got out of it. Ten copies of the *Washington Weekly* and a family cold," she said with a laugh.

In fact, Linda was very proud of her daughter. Debbie had modeled the designer clothes with a poise well beyond her six years. Even the photographer had taken time out to tell Linda how extraordinary Debbie was: large brown melt-your-heart eyes, flawless chocolate complexion, a toothpaste-commercial smile, and dark brown hair that fell into soft curls framing her perfect oval face. Tall for her age, she had a lean, athletic body, very much like her mother. The magazine issue was out no more than ten days before Linda received seven unsolicited offers for Debbie to model. Linda's salary as an adjunct professor at a community college paid the mortgage, and kept mother and daughter well fed and clothed, but there wasn't a lot left over at the end of the month. The idea of Debbie's earning money for college appealed to Linda.

Manuel checked his watch. It was nearing the agreed-upon time. He folded his newspaper and set it down on the bench. That was the signal. The in-line skater approached, right on schedule. Joaquin casually reached inside his jacket for his Beretta and thumbed the safety selector, wondering idly if he would have to hit one or both of the mothers.

The in-line skater's good, Joaquin thought as he watched the drama unfold. He was a messenger from K Street who for five hundred dollars had agreed to "play a trick on some friends." The messenger thought the idea was crazy, but, what the hell, five hundred dollars was a lot of deliveries. He timed his fall precisely, appearing to avoid crashing into Manuel, who was by now inside the playground. The skater tumbled at the feet of the two women, letting out a howl.

Both women, startled, jumped up to render assistance. The young man moaned pitifully and grasped his knee. "It's broken, oh, no, please help," he cried. "My knee's broken."

As the man approached, Debbie saw him step into the sandbox but had no sense of danger. He looked like a nice man and he smiled kindly at her. She smiled back as he crouched down next to her. As he placed his hands under her armpits and lifted her up, though, she became confused and afraid. *Why is he picking me up?* It occurred to her that he must be a friend of her mom's. She was about to ask why he was putting the strange-smelling handkerchief on her nose when she passed out.

The trick was to move quickly, but not to run or do anything else that would draw attention. Without breaking stride, Manuel walked out of the playground with Debbie in his arms, and headed toward the van.

In the playground, Carrie, realizing that something was terribly wrong, began to shout. "Debbie! Debbie, come back. Where are you going?" she cried.

Alarmed, Linda looked up, still kneeling over the fallen skater. It took her several seconds to grasp the situation. Then a panicked gasp escaped from her lips. She sprang to her feet and began to run. "Debbie!" she screamed. "He's taking my baby!"

The young Rollerblader abruptly stopped his charade as he began to understand what was happening. Seeing Joaquin approach him, he blurted out, "Hey, man. What's goin' down here? I didn't sign up for none of this shit." Joaquin's Beretta spat two silenced 9mm rounds into the young man's chest. He casually stepped over the messenger's body and walked away nonchalantly, his weapon back in his jacket, out of sight.

Manuel jumped into the van and Hector slid the door partly closed. Raymond wheeled the vehicle around the corner, and, without slowing, Hector retracted the door and Joaquin jumped in. The van shot away, its passengers oblivious to the calls of the mother left behind.

"This one will be pleasing to my uncle," Manuel announced, covering Debbie with a blanket. "She'll sleep. Remember, don't speed or weave in and out of traffic. No one pays attention to a safe driver," he cautioned Raymond.

The van turned the corner and was lost from sight. "Call the police," Linda screamed. "Call the police!" Her child had been stolen in front of her very eyes and taken into the abyss of some unknown horror.

Chapter 2

New York City, February 4, 2000

Every few steps, the six-year-old boy skipped unexpectedly, tugging sharply at his father's left arm as they walked, hand in hand, down Central Park West on their way to the boy's school. Time was, the man told himself, a six-year-old pulling on his arm wouldn't have hurt. His buddies tried to convince him and themselves that cold weather aggravated their war injuries, but he wasn't so sure. There had been a lot of cold winters in the last thirty-two years, and this was the first time he recalled feeling pain.

"Daddy, can you skip backwards?" Justin Craig asked his father.

"Well, I haven't done it in a while." They stopped at an intersection, waiting for the light to change. "I suppose I still could," the investment banker added somewhat defensively. He was tired. He and his colleagues at Lanham, Klein & Barnes were locked in yet another takeover battle on behalf of their client. Between an endless conference call and reading documents e-mailed to him after eleven P.M., David Craig had been up most of the night. To make matters worse, unlike most of the engagements they handled, this one had not gone well. As he walked down the street, he was more focused on his defeat than on the fine art of skipping backward.

"Well, Mr. Craig, what are you going to do in school today?" his father asked, trying to change the subject as they crossed Seventieth Street.

"Daddy, you know it's Friday. On Friday we have

music with Mr. Paparelli." The boy paused. "And what about skipping backwards?" he persisted. "Could you show me now? Sean says that baseball players skip backwards sometimes, when they go to the outfield. But he doesn't know how to do it. Please, Daddy. Just once."

"Justin, that's enough. We're not going to do it now. We'll do it tomorrow," he said with a practiced tone of finality.

David Craig usually enjoyed his son's questions. He loved everything about his boy from the day he had popped his head into this world to the first few years when they were a loving family, through the agonizing final days of his wife's battle with breast cancer two and a half years earlier, to this very morning. He spent a lot of time with Justin, more than a lot of other dads with less demanding jobs. They had a live-in nanny who pulled double duty when David traveled on business, and on the all-too-many nights when he worked late at the office. But it was not the same as having another parent, not the same as when Cindy was alive. "By the way, isn't that Sean and Bobby and their mothers up ahead?" David asked, nodding his head toward four people half a block in front of them, hoping that this would divert Justin's attention.

Without saying a word, Justin let go of his father's hand and ran down the sidewalk to catch up with his classmates. As Justin ran, his golden curls poured from under his woolen sock hat. *Damn, Justin needs a haircut big-time,* David thought, running his fingers through his own hair and realizing that he needed one too. For the last few months his hairstylist had been trying to convince him to grow his thick brown hair, now tempered by a shock of gray at the hairline and temples, but David had resisted, content with the low-maintenance cut he had favored for years. At six-one and 185 pounds, David was still quite handsome. With his deep blue eyes and strong jaw, he was often told he resembled Jack Kennedy. David's one personal indulgence, regular workouts at the gym, kept him looking fit, and enabled him to at least try to keep up with his six-year-old son.

"Martha . . . Liz . . . how are you?" David asked cordially. He sniffed, then breathed deeply. One of them was wearing the same perfume that Jenny Benson, his colleague at LKB, wore. He wasn't sure what brand it was, but he liked it. It reminded him of a sea breeze.

"Great," Martha announced for both of them. "David, I saw Justin's picture in *New York Next* magazine. He looked terrific."

"Yeah, real star quality," Liz said. "You ought to have him model," she added with a too-loud laugh.

Justin was a beautiful child. Perfect proportions. He had his mother's creamy porcelain skin and curly blond hair as well as her ready, genuine smile. But most striking were his deep blue eyes. David's eyes.

One of the other parents at school had suggested that Justin model along with her daughter. A new, expensive line of children's wear was to be featured in the magazine, and they needed young models. The woman had persisted, as had Justin, who thought it would be fun to be in a magazine, and finally David acquiesced. The pictures were stunning. Within days of publication, David had been besieged with calls from agents trying to sign Justin for this or that TV show or movie. Yet David wanted no part of it. Justin had a lot more going for him than his looks.

Just then Justin slammed into him at full gallop to give him the requisite hug and kiss in front of the large red school doors. David knelt down to hug Justin.

"So today's music day," David said, his hands on Justin's shoulders. "Remember, music tames the beast inside us," he admonished, raising his index finger in front of Justin's face with mock seriousness. He was rewarded with the same lion's roar Justin gave him every Friday morning when David said this, producing the same hearty laugh from David. Within seconds Justin and the other boys had flown inside. David turned to Martha and Liz. "See you," he said as he saw a cab approach out of the corner of his eye, the light on the roof indicating it was available. He ran for the cab and opened the door. "Wall Street, please."

* * *

A dark green Dodge Caravan pulled away from the curb across the street from the school and wheeled into heavy traffic.

"I don't like it," Manuel said. "Look around. This street's a trap. Under construction, heavy traffic. Too many cops directing traffic. It's even worse in the morning with all the rich *gringos* bringing their kids to school," he added as much to himself as the others. "But the *patrón* wants this one bad. Calls him the little 'cocker spaniel.' Says this boy and the girl in Stamford will complete the 'kennel.' Let's get out of the city and snatch the girl today. It's easier in the 'burbs."

Joaquin shrugged. Do it here, do it there. Whatever Manuel decided was good enough for him. "What about Central Park? Maybe he'll take the kid there tomorrow. The weather's supposed to be good."

"More unpredictable than the school, but it'd give us room to work," Manuel agreed pensively. "Could work," he added after a pause.

"Daddy . . . Daddy . . . *Daddeee!*" Lisa demanded. Her father was preoccupied with the grocery list his wife, Anne, had scribbled on a notepad.

"What is it?" he answered, distracted, fumbling with the bothersome reading glasses that he had begun wearing the week before, annoyed with Anne's fine print. *Why*, he wondered, *couldn't she just write "milk" instead of "2 percent, check the dates," or "mayonnaise" instead of "low-fat mayonnaise (check the expiration date)"? Isn't life complicated enough?* he thought. He succeeded in keeping five-year-old Lisa quiet through the produce and dairy section by letting her load the cart, but her attention evaporated somewhere in the cereal aisle.

"Why aren't you listening to me?" She placed her hands on her hips and tossed her curly light brown hair in a gesture that reminded her father, Sid, of Shirley Temple. "Can I go out front and ride the little car and the horse?" asked Lisa, with a smile she hoped her daddy would find impossible to refuse.

"Not until we get to the checkout lanes, honey. But then you can take two rides," he said, handing her four quarters, hoping that the gesture would placate her for a few moments. "It's getting dark out. Just wait until we get close to the windows so I can watch, okay?" he said, his mind on the label, trying to make sure the cream cheese was both low-fat and low-sodium.

"Okay. Great, Daddy. Are you ready now?" she asked, already starting the equivalent of the backseat-of-the-car-during-a-long-trip mantra "Are we almost there?"

Ten minutes and thirty questions later, they reached the lines for the cashiers. "Can I ride now, Daddy? Please? You promised."

"Yeah, but stay where I can see you," Sid replied warily.

"Okay," shouted Lisa without turning her head. She ran through the automatic doorway, almost slamming into the slower-moving glass. She couldn't wait to ride the pink-and-yellow horse and the black-and-white car remotely resembling the Batmobile.

Lisa excitedly mounted the painted horse and slid two quarters into the coin slot. Before the horse even started to move, she was riding through the sky, enjoying her make-believe world. She wasn't troubled when she saw two men standing nearby, looking at her. She smiled at them without giving any thought to the many times her parents had warned her not to talk to strangers. It was the same captivating smile that the camera crew had caught with stunning clarity for the *Suburban Times,* which two months earlier had shown her modeling winter clothes for a children's shop in Greenwich. *Everybody smiles at me*, she thought as her horse rocked her gently. *I'm the most beautiful girl, just like Daddy says.* She looked over her shoulder through the window to see if she could spot her daddy inside the store.

Sid's head bobbed and his neck stretched as he tried to keep an eye on Lisa through the window, though his view was repeatedly blocked as the Friday-evening crowd left the store pushing carts heaped with groceries.

He and everyone else in the front of the Grand Union were suddenly startled when an entire display of Snapple soft drinks collapsed, almost crushing a twenty-something Hispanic man—or maybe the man was Middle Eastern, perhaps Greek, Sid and others later thought—who subsequently could not be found. Young men in white aprons ran about frantically trying to contain the broken glass, rolling bottles, and the growing puddle of tea and fruit juice cascading over the floor of the busy store.

Sid couldn't have had his eyes off Lisa for more than twenty seconds. Yet when he looked for her through the window, she was gone. He ran out the door, his eyes darting this way and that over the parking lot. He didn't notice the forest-green Dodge Caravan with four men in it as the van left the parking lot in the direction of I-95. All he knew was that his Lisa was nowhere to be seen. She had vanished.

Seconds later, panic-stricken and ashen-faced, Sid raced back into the store. "Call the police," Sid tried to shout, but his lungs would permit only an aerated gasp. "Someone call the police. My little girl's gone," he said as his speech gained some measure of power. "Oh, please help." His voice cracked. "My girl's gone."

Anne arrived within minutes of Sid's call. Her car still running in the parking lot, she shook her husband angrily in denial, yet facing the horrible truth, simultaneously blaming him and hugging him, a tornado of emotions. She couldn't talk at first. In her mind's eye she saw flashes of her angel, her baby, and already feared the worst. Her tears clogged her throat, choking her. She wished she would strangle and die. She knew the stats. She had read about them in the paper, seen them on TV. Within hours, in most instances, kidnapped children were sexually abused and then brutally murdered. Few were ever found alive. It was her worst fear, a nightmare she had not shared with Sid. Slowly she recovered, demanding of the police answers that they did not have.

The detective's notebook filled rapidly with "eyewitness" statements, but he'd been around long enough to know that most of them were useless. Other than that it was a young, dark-complexioned man who suspiciously knocked over the Snapple display and then disappeared, there wasn't much to work with. A middle-aged woman stated that she thought that a Middle Eastern man near the Snapple display had knocked it over deliberately and then fled the store. One man in the parking lot thought he'd seen a man taking a child—boy or girl, he wasn't sure—to a dark-colored van, but he didn't get a good look at him. That same man mistakenly, but convincingly, insisted the van was a gray Plymouth Voyager.

"We'll need a recent photo of Lisa," the detective managed after almost an hour. "Mrs. Waldron, we'll put your daughter's picture on the Internet, and see what the local TV stations can do to help," the detective said gently, closing his notebook softly as if to reflect the solemnity of the situation.

Chapter 3

David jumped between the closing doors of the elevator at 9:17:36 on his digital watch, nearly knocking over his partner, Jake Barnes. He pushed "34," his floor and the floor where the nine-o'clock meeting was taking place. To David's chagrin, he and Barnes were alone.

"The Consolidated Hosts meeting started at nine," Jake Barnes said testily. "I was called at home at one o'clock this morning and asked to attend. Your people said you were going to be there, so I begged off. This is one pissed-off client, David. Why in hell are you late?"

"Family obligation," David responded, not trying to conceal his annoyance with Barnes's attitude. *Fuck off,* he wanted to tell him. *My net worth may be a fraction of yours. But I didn't inherit anything from my dad and I'm still worth millions.*

"You can afford a baby-sitter, David. Consolidated's spitting mad about losing the bid for Kimberly Games. They're making noises about using Morgan for their next deal."

"They won't. But they deserve to be pissed. We didn't see the Dutch company out there and we misjudged its buying power. We should've had better intelligence. I'll make it clear that it won't happen again, and it won't. And besides, the CFO's a good buddy. I'll hold on to them as a client."

"Well, even if what you say is right, we got no success fee from them on this deal. That cost us forty mil," Barnes snapped.

David had learned long ago that any weakness could be used against you on the Street, particularly by your so-called colleagues. Old man Barnes never had liked him, and after a couple recent deals had unraveled, Barnes wanted him out, which David resented intensely. He had made enough money in the eighties and nineties to retire and do anything he wanted, and clearly his heart was no longer at LKB. Each hour he spent with its demanding clients was an hour away from Justin. But he stayed, and he wasn't sure why. Perhaps the challenge of winning still gave him a thrill.

"Say, Jake. Do you think Bernie Williams skips backward when he goes out to center field?" David asked.

"I've no idea what you're talking about," Jake responded with a *harrumph*.

"Didn't think you would," David muttered under his breath as he got off at the thirty-fourth floor.

"Hey, Rosa," he said cheerfully to his secretary. "Everything okay?" he asked as he walked quickly into his office, throwing his coat over his desk chair.

"You're in trouble," she said with her slight Dominican accent and a playful wag of her index finger.

"I'm always in trouble," he conceded, as he straightened his hair with his fingers and made a mental note to set up appointments for his and Justin's haircuts.

"Is Justin okay?" Rosa asked warmly. She had three kids and seven grandchildren.

"He's great," David answered. "Say, do you know how to skip backward?"

"Sure," she replied simply, as if it were a stupid question.

After making a quick pit stop in the men's room, David joined the others in the large, well-appointed conference room. He made the rounds, shaking everyone's hand, apologizing to Consolidated Hosts' chairman and other officers, including his buddy the CFO, for being late. Jenny Benson stood before the assembly giving a PowerPoint demonstration about future acquisitions that were available to Consolidated Hosts. She persuasively explained why LKB was the best investment bank to make those acquisitions happen, despite the screwup with Kimberly Games, for which she had already taken the heat before David arrived.

David poured himself a cup of coffee and sat quietly, grateful for Jenny's having taken command in his absence. She continued with her presentation, repressing an urge to address only David.

David had no need to repress his urge to look at her. She was the speaker. He was expected to look at her. He wasn't expected to mentally undress her, but that was what he was doing.

Despite the fact that she had slept only three hours, Jenny looked great. She was tall and trim, her body kept firm by a rigorous running and swimming regimen. A peaches-and-cream complexion, framed by her shoulder-length reddish-brown hair, set off her emerald green eyes. They were mischievous, brimming with intelligence. She looked younger than her thirty-eight years, easily passing for her early thirties, although when she spoke she had the confidence of a more mature woman.

David and Jenny had worked together for fourteen years. They had met at the University of North Carolina at Chapel Hill, where he interviewed her for a position the spring before she completed her program, a combined MBA/computer science degree. They had worked together briefly when she first started, in David's mergers and acquisitions department. She rotated off to investment banking for a few years as part of her training and did a stint in the London office for three years. She then came back to David's M&A group and stayed. At thirty-four, she had made partner and was considered a rising star.

Jenny had just one problem with her career at LKB: She was in love with David Craig. She had been attracted to him from the beginning, but didn't act on it. At least, not during the interview. She had tried a mild come-on during her second year at LKB, but he didn't notice, or pretended he didn't.

Their relationship had changed about a year after Cindy's death. They began to talk more, especially on the long and frequent plane trips. Over time, the conversations became more relaxed, more personal. But each time, on arriving at their destination, they would taxi off to the same hotel and go to their separate rooms. Until Chicago.

Chicago, David thought as he stared at her at the end of the long conference table, finding himself getting aroused at the thought of their recent trip. They had flown into O'Hare earlier in the week for meetings with a potential client, arriving at the hotel off Michigan Avenue only to find that a computer glitch had overbooked every room. One of their fellow travelers, a lawyer, as David recalled, had called the Hilton in suburban Naperville and found that it had rooms.

They wearily threw their overnight bags in the trunk of the only cab they could find. Two men climbed in front with the driver. Three men and Jenny squeezed together in the backseat. Jenny sat on David's lap, her arm around the back of his neck, her hand coming to rest on his right shoulder. His left arm was around her waist, under her open coat, firm against her brown silk blouse. He put his right hand on her knee. She made no protest. David and Jenny, as well as the man next to them, his elbow in her back, shifted, each trying to settle into a space that was simply too small. Her head was pressed to the ceiling. She held it there for a few minutes until her neck hurt, said, "The hell with it," and rested her head on David's shoulder, letting herself slide downward a few inches. As she slid down, his hand remained stationary, her thigh coming to rest in the gentle squeeze of his right hand.

They sat like that for a few moments, exchanging nervous conversation like two high school kids. She held her purse to her stomach, partially on his lap, until it was uncomfortable. She shifted again, and with her left hand she placed the purse on the ledge behind David's head, twisting her body as she did so, her breast pressed firmly against his cheek for an instant. It was enough for David, or rather not enough. She settled back into her prior position for a moment.

"My wallet's in my jacket pocket," he whispered after a moment or two. "It's uncomfortable and I can't reach it. Could you put it in your purse?"

Jenny understood full well that his wallet was just fine where it was, but welcomed the offer. She reached her hand under his suit jacket, stroking his strong chest before she removed the wallet from the breast pocket; then, twisting around to reach her purse, she took time with the zipper, placing the wallet inside, closing the bag. Again she pressed her breast against his cheek, this time lingering for a moment and exhaling, with her lips brushing the top of his head. Finally she twisted back around and placed her head on his shoulder, his right hand still on her thigh. After about a minute she raised her head to look into his deep blue eyes, a few inches from hers. He did not look away. Without taking her eyes from his, she kissed him gently on the lips, ignoring the two strangers next to them.

They booked one of the last rooms at the Hilton, making no pretense of taking two rooms. Jenny's secretary would note two days later that Jenny didn't have a hotel bill on her expense voucher and spread the gossip around LKB, but it didn't matter. David fumbled with the card key to their room, opening the door between kisses, Jenny pulling on his tie. They didn't tear each other's clothes off. After all, they did have meetings the next day. But they unbuttoned, unzipped, and tugged hurriedly, as if the moment might disappear.

Soon their bodies were touching, skin on skin, her back to the wall as he kissed her naked breasts, descending in a slow-motion tease, his lips and tongue working their way down her belly until he found her wetness, eliciting cries of pleasure. He rose, pressing his hard body against hers, his erection firm against her stomach. She led him over to the bed and gently pushed him down. He lay on his back on the bedspread. She knelt down and climbed on top of him. She made love to him the way she had imagined for years, she on top, he enjoying the view, driving both of them to climax.

"What do you think of that, David?" the chairman of

Consolidated Hosts asked, referring to something Jenny had said in response to a question David hadn't heard. David had no clue, momentarily startled to see that Jenny had her clothes on. He reached for his reading glasses as gracefully as he could, taking his time, stalling. He fumbled for an answer, then responded with an aplomb that made Jenny want to kiss him. The other LKB bankers wanted to laugh, impressed with his bullshit skills, tricks of the trade honed during his twenty-five years on the Street. Thereafter the meeting droned on like countless others before, sliding into a superb lunch in the executive dining room. LKB kept Consolidated Hosts as a client, just as David had promised.

Jenny and David walked down the hall back to his office. He stepped aside to let her go in first, greeting Rosa, who noticed a slight blush on his cheeks. He closed the door behind him. When she heard the metallic click of the dead bolt behind the door, Rosa smiled, understanding immediately what was happening. *Mr. Craig has a girlfriend*, she sang to herself. *It's about time*.

As soon as he closed the door, Jenny flung her arms around his neck. His hands began caressing her back, pulling her to him, their lips reveling in each other's warmth. *God*, he thought. *I shouldn't be doing this. This is so unlike you, David,* he continued to tell himself as he unbuttoned her blouse and she removed his tie. *This is so goddamned indiscreet*, he warned himself as he removed her skirt and she unzipped his pants. He hoped the sun was glaring on his windows. Otherwise the people in the insurance company across the street were getting a pretty good show. *To hell with 'em,* he decided as he slid the papers, stapler, tape dispenser, and everything else that was on the end of his large desk onto the floor. This time he was on top, which was just fine with Jenny.

Afterward they hurriedly straightened up, putting their clothes back on.

"How do I look?" Jenny asked as she brushed her hair and applied lipstick.

"Like the fee we'd get on a hundred-billion-dollar takeover," David said.

"Seriously," she insisted. "Do I look all right? You can't open that door until I don't look like I just climbed out of the sack."

"Then I'll never open the door, not after that." David smiled tenderly. "How does an old guy like me get a hot babe like you?" he asked only half in jest.

"Well, by looking at me the way you did back in the conference room."

"Was it so obvious?"

"To me it was."

"Guess it'll be hard to keep our relationship a secret around here."

"And what might that relationship be?"

"I'm not sure," he answered truthfully. "Can I take some time and get back to you on that?" He hadn't intended to sound so serious, and suddenly he was embarrassed. "It's more . . . a lot more . . . than an affair, at least it is to me. I want you to know that. But I'm not ready to pick out the wedding song yet. I mean . . . I guess you're not either . . . well . . . I mean . . . I guess I need some time."

Jenny looked at her watch, unable to suppress an ear-to-ear smile. "Okay, time's up."

They both laughed, each enjoying the smart banter and relieved that their growing feelings for the other seemed to be mutual.

"Let's have dinner tomorrow night. I'm coming into the office at five o'clock or so. Justin will be with me. He can play on the computer while I clean up some stuff, and then we'll go out to eat, the three of us. That is, if you're free," he added, hoping he wasn't taking too much for granted, studying her eyes jealously to see if she had other plans. "We can have an informal Italian dinner. Let the two of you get to know each other."

"Sounds great to me for three reasons," she said cryptically, kissing him on the cheek.

"Three?" he asked, wondering what she meant.

"One, you don't have another date. Two, I get to

spend some time with Justin. Three . . . I guess I'm more than just a good lay," she said, raising her eyebrows slightly.

He hesitated for a few seconds, his deep blue eyes fixed on her emerald ones. "Right on all three counts. Leave here by, say, six-thirty?"

Jenny smiled at David, realizing once again what a good man she had finally found. She loved the fact that he was so devoted to Justin. It was one of the many things that made him so appealing to her. "Actually, it will be great to get to know you better, too," she said. "Not that I haven't picked up a few things from listening to your end of phone conversations over the last fourteen years."

"Yeah?" he asked, his eyebrows rising. "What have you learned about me?"

"Well, not really that much." She reflected, slouching in the club chair across from his desk, suddenly unsure whether she should continue. "Truth is, I've learned more about you in the last three days than I have since I've known you. For one, I know about Ripcord and what you did," she led off.

"How on earth?" he asked, surprised.

"Well, it wasn't really all that difficult to figure out. You often use military terms. That's not common on the Street. Most bankers, lawyers, and the others in our circles here in New York never served in the military. I always thought it was some affectation that you picked up from your father or someone—"

"I didn't have a father," David interjected, trying to hide the pain in his voice but not succeeding.

"Oh, David, I'm sorry. . . ." She trailed off for a moment, sensing that he needed to compose himself. He nodded, indicating that she should continue. "Okay, back to the military terms. You'll say 'throw a grenade in their foxhole,' when someone else would say 'throw a wrench in their works,' or 'fire in the hole' when you've thrown the other side a zinger. On the weekends, when you bring Justin to the office, I've heard you call him 'troop' or 'trooper.' I've seen him tease you by saluting you with his left hand. How many kids in Manhattan would know that's a sign of dissing someone in the military?

"Then, in Chicago," she continued, "in the shower, when I asked you about the scars, you simply said, 'In the army, during the war.' You didn't want me to pursue it, so I didn't. But I went on the computer and looked up your name in the *Toledo Blade* during the three-year period after your high school graduation and found the story—stories, I should say."

Jenny reflected for a moment, trying to find the right words. She decided that there was no subtle way to ask. "My God, David. You have the Congressional Medal of Honor. The Medal of Honor," she repeated to herself, not him. "And no one on the Street, no one at LKB even knows about it. I wasn't sure you'd really been in the army." She wanted to say more, but couldn't. People at the firm had known him for twenty-five years, yet he hadn't shared this critical aspect of himself with any of them. She understood intuitively why. Men on the Street had all gone to expensive prep schools and had gotten deferments to attend Ivy League schools. Like all wars, Vietnam was fought by the blue-collar guys, young, uneducated men like David from the streets of towns like Toledo. His education and refinement had come later, after the war, at Ohio State, then at Wharton. "It's thirty-two years ago tomorrow, isn't it?" she asked in a whisper, knowing the answer, but wanting him to know that she was aware of the details, all of them.

"From the day we lifted the siege . . . yeah," he said, staring at the top of his desk, numb, reliving the battle in his mind's eye. "It started in the early morning of January thirtieth, 1968. The Tet Offensive. We—that is, my Ranger squad—had only landed on Ripcord two days earlier. They hit us with everything imaginable. It lasted seven days. We lifted it late afternoon . . . around seventeen hundred hours, on February fifth. Thirty-two years ago tomorrow." The topic was painful to him, and it showed.

"Are you able to talk about it?" she asked.

"It's hard enough to think about it, let alone talk about it," David answered slowly, staring at the palms of his hands. "Each time my mind drifts back to Ripcord, I see men blown to pieces—boys, really—blood flowing in rivers, agonizing pain and death. The thoughts bring back the smells. Blood and cordite embedded in my nostrils. It never leaves me. I used to wake up in the middle of the night in a cold sweat two or three times a week. It's now down to once a month or so. I still see Billy's face as they dragged him away. I wake up seeing—" David stopped and swallowed hard, fighting back the images in his mind.

"It's good to talk about it, David. I want to know about it. About you."

"I'll tell you about it someday. Promise. But don't worry too much. I talk about it with the other guys from my Ranger squad. We've stayed close—very close—over the years. We get together once a year to go skydiving, and we talk on the phone. We go to weddings, graduations, baptisms . . . and some funerals. But even we don't discuss it too much."

"Will you talk to Billy and the others over the weekend?" she asked.

He paused, studying her. "Yes," he said simply. "I'll talk to Billy tomorrow morning. Do you know the names of the other guys from my squad?" he asked, not sure if he was comfortable with her having delved into what he had kept private for so many years.

"No. The articles I read didn't give the names of the men in your squad. I only know the name Billy Dunn because the article said you saved his life," she explained, a tear working its way down her cheek as she thought about how much this man had gone through, and how courageous he was. As he looked at the loving expression on her face, David realized that it was okay, that it was more than okay. For the first time in as long as he could remember he had met someone other than his Ranger friends with whom he could let down his guard.

"Well, I want you to know the names of the others,

and I want you to meet them. I know they'll like you. There's Eric Randall. He works with the CIA. A real character, an acquired taste, but a great friend. Frank Lopez is a fisherman. Runs a small fleet of trawlers out of San Diego. Matthew Rice. Matthew—never Matt—sells insurance. A real ladies' man, never married. Not sure I want you to meet him." He smiled. "And Billy, who's still in the army. He's now a major general. Jack Heed, helicopter pilot—he wasn't part of our squad, but he saved us in a firefight before Ripcord and we never forgot it. We call him Happy Jack. Always happy-go-lucky."

"So," Jenny said after a long pause, standing up and walking around to David's side of the desk.

He swiveled around on his chair so that he faced her. Then, still sitting, he put his arms around her waist and pulled her close. "I suggest that we finish our work for the day."

She kissed him gently on the head. "Talk to Billy, Eric, Frank, and Matthew tomorrow. And let's have a great dinner tomorrow night. The three of us."

Jenny sat in her office, the door closed, staring out the window into the darkness of a chilly evening. It was five-forty and she had twenty minutes to kill before her conference call. She thought about returning the stack of phone messages, of checking her e-mail, but decided to reread the newspaper and magazine articles about Fire Support Base Ripcord that she had uncovered. Some of the articles were detailed accounts from men who had survived the siege, including Eric Randall and Matthew Rice, whose names she now recognized. Several articles were based on the one interview David gave, an interview with the *Toledo Blade*.

She leaned forward in her chair, rereading the printout of an interview with a young specialist 4 named Billy Dunn.

The Viet Cong, and the North Vietnamese regulars, had a practice of dragging a captured GI into the jungle. They'd string him up against a tree and cut off strips of his skin, cutting off fingers, slowly castrating him . . . all within earshot of the other GIs. The screams of the GI were supposed to get his buddies within the perimeter to come to his aid, where the other VC were waiting. That's just what the VC wanted, an ambush. So guys on the compound could either run into a trap or listen to the screams, screams that would penetrate your ears, no matter how tightly you covered them.

Toward the end of the second day of the Tet Offensive, a mortar round landed near enough to me to throw me off my feet. I'll never know why, but I only had minor injuries from the blast. I was stunned for a few moments and lost my helmet. I really don't know what happened next. My buddies later told me that a VC whacked me over the head with a pipe. Others say it was his AK47. I'll never know for sure, but it knocked me out. Next thing I remember was being pulled into the jungle, trying to resist as five or six of them dragged me down a dirt incline toward the tree line. They kept hitting me over the head. I remember thinking that I'd rather die right then and there than be tortured and used as bait to lure my buddies into an ambush. I guess I blacked out for a bit.

We must have been thirty feet into the bush when David came out of nowhere, bayonet fixed, slashing, shooting, butting with his rifle, fighting all of them. I was still too stunned to do much of anything but watch. The fight couldn't have lasted more than a few seconds. David killed the last VC with his bare hands. Grabbed the guy by the head, from behind, and snapped his neck, roaring like an enraged ape. I still remember the sound of the VC's neck breaking. David threw me over his shoulder and somehow we made it back to the compound. VC were shooting at us. Our own guys were shooting at them. It's amazing we didn't get killed.

Jenny rose from her desk and walked over to her window, barely noticing the traffic below, pondering the triviality of her own life against the backdrop of war, friendship, and sacrifice at a level she had never experienced. She returned to her desk and once again read David's interview in the *Toledo Blade* a week after President Nixon pinned the Congressional Medal of Honor on him in a private ceremony in the White House, just before David went off to Ohio State on a scholarship and the GI Bill.

We'd just come back from a mission in Laos. They should've sent us to division headquarters at Nha Trang, but instead they stuck us on top of a hill, a fire support base called Ripcord. We hadn't been there a day when the VC hit. Afterwards, we learned it was part of the big Tet Offensive.

They tried to overrun us. Actually, by the second day they did and we were in very deep trouble. We called in for air support, but couldn't get it. VCs were hitting friendlies all over the country. So we were on our own.

On the afternoon of the second day it suddenly occurred to me: No one left alive outranked me. So I figured that I must be in charge. The general—who was pretty safe back in Nha Trang, you understand—was so moved by our situation that he promoted me to second lieutenant on the spot, over the mike. He told me, in no uncertain terms, that we were to hold Ripcord *at all costs*.

I can tell you that the VC were not at all impressed by my promotion. They went for broke. They hit us with everything they had: rockets, mortars, artillery, recoilless rifles, machine guns, grenades, you name it. That's when they tried to take Billy. All of us got hit, several times. Most of the GIs on the hill were dead or dying. A few, including my Ranger team, could still function. For the past day our cannon cockers—artillery men . . . anyway, the few who were left—had depressed their howitzers and fired right into the enemy's faces. We hit them with all kinds of stuff. Killed so many it wasn't even a massacre. It was something else I can't really describe. But soon the artillery guys were out of ammo. So were most of us infantry types. I realized we didn't have a lot of options. If we surrendered, they'd kill us. If we kept fighting in a defensive mode, they'd kill us. I thought about it for a minute and decided, What the hell, we might as well attack.

We distributed what ammo we had left. Remember, by this time most of the guys were dead and the rest of us were hit once, twice, or more. But I believe you have to play the hand you're dealt, and I think my men understood that. So I told 'em to fix bayonets. I thought some of those guys would refuse, but no one did. After several human-wave attacks from the VC, with everyone left alive suffering from multiple wounds, the new lieutenant—that's me—tells 'em to fix bayonets. But the GIs did it. No moans. No protests. Just courage . . . and the sound of bayonets clicking in unison on the business end of our M16 rifles. Together we did the one thing the enemy didn't expect: We attacked like wild men, yelling and screaming. An old fashioned bayonet charge! We caught the VC totally off guard.

In the end, we did exactly what the general ordered. We held Ripcord *at all costs.* We held it with our last bullets, bayonets, and finally . . . our bare hands. But we lost a lot of good men on that godforsaken hill. . . .

Tears flowing down her cheeks, Jenny set down the interview with David and turned to another article. She read slowly, surprising herself with the sound of her own voice as she read out loud.

. . . act of Congress. It is awarded this fourth day of September, the year of our Lord one thousand nine hundred and sixty-nine, to 2d Lt. David Samuel Craig . . . for action in combat with enemy ground forces . . . against overwhelming odds . . . in defense of his unit . . . in disregard for his own safety . . .

displayed extreme heroism and self-sacrifice . . . while wounded several times. . . .

She blew her nose and continued.

. . . shot in the chest with small-arms fire . . . despite multiple shrapnel wounds to the back and legs . . . clubbed and bayoneted several times . . . 2d Lt. Craig . . . in total disregard for his own safety . . . rushed into the jungle and rescued SP4 William Dunn . . . killing all six enemy soldiers . . . carried SP4 Dunn to safety under heavy enemy fire . . . and continued to command . . . for display of intrepidity and gallantry in defense of Fire Support Base Ripcord . . . for action above and beyond the call of duty, is hereby awarded the Medal of Honor.

For several minutes after finishing the article, Jenny sat at her desk and wondered what had made David go after Billy. Was it a snap decision that could have been decided differently on a different day, or was it something ingrained deep within David that made him risk his life for another soldier?

She was sitting there, lost in thought, when the phone rang, announcing the conference call. It was scheduled to last no more than an hour, but she knew that with the three teams of attorneys it would drag on longer. She listened to the bankers and lawyers introduce themselves and their respective clients, thinking how unimportant all this was.

Chapter 4

At seven-forty-five, Justin climbed into his daddy's bed with his Game Boy, playing it close enough to David's ear to wake him. "Daddy. Come on. It's morning. *Pokémon* is coming on."

"Your daddy isn't home," David said in a deep voice, hiding under his covers. "This is Darth Vader."

"We're not playing *Star Wars* today. We're playing *Star Trek*," exclaimed Justin. At that very moment a bundle of pure energy from the Jardasian Sector exploded on top of David at warp speed, jumping on the former Darth Vader, now Spock. Others might have recognized the bundle of energy as Justin Craig, but David, a.k.a. Daddy, recently returned from the Tarantula Nebula, recognized him instantly as Captain Kirk, commander of the starship *Enterprise* on his way to boldly go where no man—

"Beam me up, Scotty. Oh, Scotty. Beam me up now!" David laughed as he grabbed Justin to tickle him.

"Daddy. Are we going to the carousel today? I want to be Robin Hood on his horse to save Maid Marian."

David grabbed Justin and tickled him again as he threw a blanket over his son. "Well, I thought you were Captain Kirk," exclaimed David, never ceasing to be amazed at how quickly Justin could morph into another being. "They opened the carousel for the weekend, but I didn't know that Captain Kirk liked to ride horses."

David got out of bed and started to walk to the bathroom when Justin interrupted. "Ah, Daddy, it's not fair. Come tickle me more. Pretend you can't see me," he said as he "hid" under David's blanket. David obliged and then picked up Justin by placing his hands under Justin's armpits, forearms straight with his palms facing each other, and, walking like a robot, said, "I am Robbie, the Robot. I have been sent to this planet called Earth to instruct you to go to your room, take a bath, and change your clothes while I make breakfast. What would this earthling like for breakfast?"

"This earthling would like Honey Nut Cheerios," responded Justin in perfect "robot-speak," as he wiggled free and ran to his room.

While David prepared the bath, it took Justin four commands from Darth Vader to take his pajamas off. Another four to get in the tub. *Twenty minutes of peace*, David thought, knowing that Justin would be occupied in the tub for about that length of time. Just enough time for coffee and part of the morning *Times,* he thought. He was still on the front page and only halfway through his coffee when the phone rang. "Hello?"

"Hey, David, it's Billy. How are you? This a good time?"

"Always, Ranger. Great to hear from you. How are Faith and the girls?"

"Everyone is fine. Faith and I drove out to Pittsburgh three weeks ago to take them back to college from Christmas break. They're doing well in school. I wish they'd stayed in the dormitory for another year, but they say I'm old-fashioned. How's Justin?"

"I'll get him. Hey, Justin," David shouted, his hand cupped over the speaker. "Uncle Billy's on the phone."

Justin was in the living room in a flash, wrapped in a towel, ripping the phone out of David's hand. "Uncle Billy! Hi. When are you gonna let me ride in a real tank, like you promised? I've got a toy tank that's really cool. It shoots fire out the cannon when you push a button. Well, not real fire. Pretend fire. Almost like real," Justin continued so fast that Billy, laughing at the other end, couldn't get in a word.

"Hello, Justin," Billy said while Justin caught his breath. "If you can convince your dad to bring you to North Carolina to visit, I think I might be able to find a tank somewhere that you can ride in. But we won't be shooting out any fire. Just takin' a ride."

"Oh, man. Supercool," Justin yelped. "Daddy, Uncle Billy says we should go to North Carolina so we can ride in a tank with him. Can we go there today? Please? We haven't seen Uncle Billy and Aunt Faith in . . . in . . . forever."

"Well, we can't go today. Maybe we can find a time to visit them this summer when you're off from school. Say good-bye to Uncle Billy and let me talk to him."

"Thanks a lot, pal," David scoffed at Billy lightheartedly after Justin handed him the phone. "Now I'm a war criminal for not flying to North Carolina this afternoon," he laughed. "Say," he said after a brief pause. "Why are you going to North Carolina?"

"Well, I'm being promoted and assigned to Fort Bragg to command the Eighteenth Airborne Corps."

"Holy shit, Billy." David sat forward on the edge of his chair. "This is wonderful news. Your third star. And . . . my God . . . the Eighteenth Airborne Corps! The prize every combat arms officer in the army dreams of. That's fantastic! When are you being sworn in? Justin and I will be there."

"Next month. The date's not yet certain. Depends on the president's schedule. He wants to make a big deal of it with the press. You sure you can make it?"

"Billy, nothing could stop us from being there. Say, by the way, when I say we'll be there, I think it means that three of us will be there."

"Okay, Ranger, give it up. Something you want to tell me?"

"Yes, I have some great news. I met a wonderful woman. Jenny Benson. Actually, we have worked together for a long time, but things finally clicked. This could be the real thing. In fact, I feel like she's the one."

"Outstanding, Lieutenant Craig. It's high time you started following the orders of a superior ranking officer," Billy exclaimed delightedly. "Faith will be really happy to hear that. And . . ." He paused, not knowing whether to say it but deciding to take a chance. "You know that Cindy would like it too."

"Yeah. You're right. She would. And it's time for me to start living again," said David, no longer feeling guilty.

"Good, so let's get together for the promotion ceremony."

"It's a date. I wouldn't miss it for anything."

The two hung up, promising to see each other at the promotion and change-in-command ceremony at Bragg. *Commander of the Eighteenth Airborne Corps*, David thought proudly of his friend who was more like the brother he had never had. The phone rang two more times before David could start to get Justin ready to go to the park. First Matthew Rice and then Frank Lopez called, each to share their camaraderie, nostalgia, and nightmares with David. He knew that Eric Randall was "away," no doubt on some secret CIA mission that would not permit him to call. The bonds had been reaffirmed with each of them, or would be within a day or two, just as the five of them had done each February for the past thirty-two years.

"Hey, soldier? Ready to head over to the carousel and mount up?" said David to Justin.

"Airborne, sir," said Justin, locking his heels and snapping a respectable salute as David had taught him to do.

"All the way," said David to his most beloved little soldier. "You know, Sergeant Craig, you shouldn't say 'Airborne' when you climb on a horse. You should say 'Gary Owen and Glory!' "

"What's 'Gary Own Nenn and Gory,' Daddy?"

"Gary Owen and Glory," corrected David with mock sternness. "Something the Cav . . . the guys who used to ride horses before they got smart and invented helicopters . . . used to say when I was in the army. It was a long, long time ago, before you were born."

"Even before the dinosaurs?" asked Justin.

"Well, not quite, but close."

Justin got his shoes and coat on quickly while David watched, wondering why Justin couldn't get ready that fast on school days.

Manuel and Hector turned left up Central Park West to follow Justin and David. They walked to Seventy-third Street and crossed the avenue to rendezvous with Joaquin, who had walked toward them from the opposite direction.

"What do you think, *jefe*?" Joaquin asked.

"Be prepared, my friends," Manuel said, always cautious, concerned about the danger of the back-to-back kidnappings. "If he takes the *chico* to the park, there will be many people and much confusion, like last night in the supermarket. When the time comes, we'll use this to our advantage."

"*Sí. Chévere,*" Joaquin said quietly. He liked action, and these operations provided a good rush. It didn't matter if he was knocking off somebody who was moving into their drug turf or kidnapping some rich gringo's kid, all of which were necessary steps if he was going to rise in Belalcazar's cartel. He slowly put his right hand into his jacket and eased the Beretta from its holster, nonchalantly checking the slide action. Satisfied, he let the slide close with a reassuring clink. His fingers patted his pockets where he kept the extra ammo clips. *Muy bien,* he thought. *Let's get this cocker spaniel in the bag for the patrón's kennel.*

Manuel pulled out his cellular phone to give instructions to Raymond in the van. The pickup instructions and meeting places were coded and prearranged. Then Manuel turned to the two others. "When I put on my sunglasses and immediately take them off, that's the signal to snatch the *chico. Comprende?*"

"*Sí, jefe,*" Joaquin and Hector responded.

Father and son crossed Central Park West at Seventy-second Street and made their way through Strawberry Fields, heading east into the park. As they walked along the loop, it appeared as if all of New York had come out to enjoy the short reprieve from winter. Daredevil bicycle riders shouted warnings and an occasional obscenity at slower-pedaling riders and pedestrians. In-line skaters sped by, swinging their arms, looking like participants in a futuristic gladiatorial contest.

"Listen, can you hear the carousel?" David asked as they turned down the path just south of Sheep's Meadow. They passed the deserted softball fields, with spotty patches of brown grass and windblown trash accumulated against the backstops. David smiled as he recalled smacking the ball at last summer's mixed softball league. Justin had sat on the team bench and cheered him on as David sped around second base, only to be tagged out at third. "Wanna play tee ball this spring, troop?" David asked.

"Okay," Justin responded, indifferent to something so far away as spring. "Are we almost there, Daddy?"

"Almost." There was a line at the snack bar, and as soon as they passed a large rock outcropping, David saw that there was a long line for the carousel, too. "Looks like a line, troop," he said. *New York,* he thought. *You gotta wait in line for everything.*

"That's okay, Daddy. We'll have to buy lots of tickets so we can just stay on again and again."

"Oh, is that the solution? We'll just buy ten tickets so we can stay on—"

"Five times," Justin interrupted.

"How'd you get so smart?" David asked as he reached over to tickle Justin's chest. "There'll be no more studying math. You're getting too smart. Even smarter than me. And nobody's allowed to be smarter than me," he said in his Darth Vader voice.

They stood in the ticket holders' line, three people wide and at least thirty feet long. Justin raised his voice over the loud music of the carousel. "Daddy, can I take my coat off?" he asked as he unzipped his jacket and began to take it off.

"No way, José," David answered. "You've just gotten over a cold, and it's not as warm as it seems. See, I'm keeping my coat on," he said, closing the second button from the top of his green-and-tan hunting jacket for emphasis.

It was easy enough for Manuel to spot David's jacket in the crowd as he made his way past the carousel and walked halfway up a nearby grassy hill, choosing a tree with a waist-high fork in it for cover. *Perfect field of fire,* he said to himself. With habits born of experience, he checked the positioning of his men and scanned the area for police. It appeared clear, except for the throngs of people. *Okay, we'll use the crowds to our advantage.* He studied the boy's father. Six feet, he guessed, and surprisingly trim, but clearly middle-aged. *Just another out-of-shape gringo desk jockey*, Manuel thought. *He'll be no match for Joaquin.*

Manuel reached into his jacket pocket for his phone. "Let's have lunch at the Plaza Hotel," he said. Raymond, still idling the Dodge Caravan on West Seventy-second Street, slowly turned south down Central Park West toward Columbus Circle. *Raymond ought to have sufficient time, even in Saturday traffic, to station himself near the Plaza,* Manuel thought.

Manuel put his sunglasses on and immediately took them off. Joaquin moved on cue. Hector reached into his jacket and put his hand on his Beretta.

"Daddy, can I get a pretzel? I'm hungry," Justin announced.

"Okay," David said, reaching into his pocket for his wallet. "I'll be here in line. You get the pretzel and come right back."

David watched Justin walk to the pretzel stand, taking his eyes off his son for no more than a few seconds as the line progressed and he needed to advance a few steps. Suddenly, as he turned to look back at Justin, he was knocked off his feet by a big man. David was taken by surprise, but he reacted fast, his hands reaching out to break his fall against a low iron railing. His right knee slammed hard against the concrete. He spun toward the person who had knocked him down. Trying to get up, he yelled, "Jesus, man. What the hell . . ." He trailed off as he spotted Justin and then a man who looked like he was trying to grab the boy. "Justin!" David yelled as loudly as he could.

Justin turned to look at his father. "Daddy," screamed Justin, terrified by seeing his father down on his knees.

Something animal stirred within David. Not in the last thirty years had so much adrenaline surged in his blood. Springing upright, in one fluid motion he lunged catlike toward his assailant. Hooking his foot under the man's left leg, David simultaneously grabbed his open leather jacket and spun the heavier man down and hard toward the iron rail. The man's back slammed into the short rail, knocking the wind out of him. Joaquin's jacket opened when he hit the metal, and David saw the massive 9mm automatic in his shoulder holster. *Who are you? Leave Justin and me alone,* he thought frantically.

David watched as Justin was lifted by the other man, kicking and screaming but unable to pull free. "Don't touch my boy!" David cried as the assailant started to carry Justin away.

Hector pulled out his large automatic and fired two shots into the crowd, hitting one woman in the leg and another in the shoulder. The shots achieved the desired effect, immediately scattering the terrorized crowd. The two women were thrown to the ground, screaming and bleeding.

From his post, Manuel saw that something had gone wrong. Very wrong. The boy's father reacted too quickly. In addition, two fathers began to go to Justin's aid, unwittingly running directly toward Manuel's sure aim. Rather than kill them, Manuel dropped both of them with his 9mm with a shot in each man's leg, their screams of pain designed to cause more terror than the presence of two lifeless bodies. Any resistance left in the crowd was now gone. Some parents grabbed their children and ran with them. Others pushed their young ones to the ground and covered them with their bodies. Manuel's eyes darted through the crowd, searching for Joaquin and the boy's father, but he found it hard to see them through the mass of people.

Kill or be killed, David's inner voice ordered. *Hurt my boy, and I'll kill you a thousand times.* David, former Airborne Ranger, hero of Fire Support Base Ripcord, counterattacked. He lunged for Joaquin again. The younger man, winded, struggled for his Beretta. David's hand shot forward, his forefinger and middle finger penetrating deep into Joaquin's eye sockets. Joaquin squealed in pain. As Joaquin's neck arched back, David's fist slammed into his exposed throat. The blow nearly crushed Joaquin's larynx. He fell to the ground, temporarily blinded and gasping for air.

Grabbing Joaquin's Beretta from his holster, David frantically looked through the crowd, not seeing Justin or the man who had just taken him. *Save Justin. Kill that bastard.* He pushed his way through the crowd, shouting, "He's got my son! Out of the way! He's got my son!" Some in the crowd saw the gun in his hand and froze, blocking David's path. He shoved them away, knocking them to the ground.

Hector continued to run, carrying Justin toward the tunnel to the east of the carousel. As he turned to see David coming after him, he ran square into a heavyset man who was running the other way with his baby. The collision knocked both men down. Recovering quickly, Hector flung Justin to the asphalt as if the boy were so much garbage. Jumping to his feet, he scanned the crowd for David.

David found Hector just as Hector saw him. David dropped to one knee, raised the Beretta, and took aim. Hector shot first but missed, firing high. The 9mm bullet whined off the pretzel stand. David's mind blocked out all else around him. During that frozen second, all was silence. All of his concentration was focused on the fear in Hector's brown eyes, like the fear he had seen in the eyes of the Viet Cong he had killed many years ago. He squeezed the trigger gently, the way he had been trained. He remembered to aim low, the powerful kick of the weapon in his hands enough to raise the trajectory a few inches even at close range. David let loose with three shots from the Beretta, each sounding like a cannon in his ears.

The first bullet hit Hector in the abdomen, the second in the chest, exiting through his back, severing two vertebrae, and killing him instantly. The third shot went wide as David looked up from the automatic to see if the first two shots had hit, a mistake he was warned against in Ranger School.

David raced toward Justin, not realizing there was a third shooter. He didn't see Manuel taking aim near a tree on the small incline at his nine-o'clock. Manuel fired four times. The first bullet hit David in the left shoulder, spinning him partway around. The second round hit him in the left side as he spun, breaking his three lowest ribs. The force of the impact picked David off his feet and threw him to the ground. The next two shots went wide. Manuel thought he heard the dull thud of David's head and torso hitting the hard asphalt. David went down and stayed there, the Beretta lying a few inches away.

Manuel didn't wait to see if David and his own men were dead. He assumed they were. His mission was to get the Craig boy and take him back to the boss in Colombia. That was all that mattered. Manuel grabbed Justin as he tried to crawl toward his father, shrieking, "Daddy, Daddy, Daddy," lips trembling, almost hysterical. "Don't die, Daddy. Don't die."

The boy was more solid than Manuel had expected, heavier than the girls he had kidnapped for the boss. And this time there was no chloroform to silence the child. The chloroformed handkerchief was in a plastic vial in Hector's coat pocket, and there was no time to get it.

"Let go of me," Justin screamed, struggling against Manuel's firm grasp. Justin struck him square in the eye, startling the seasoned killer, and wiggled free for a moment. The boy's wildly kicking feet then caught Manuel in the groin hard enough to nearly make his knees buckle. Now thoroughly enraged, Manuel backhanded Justin and sent him sprawling across the asphalt, knocking him out. He flung Justin's limp body over his shoulder and started to run without looking back.

The area surrounding the carousel looked like a war zone. Blood flowed onto the asphalt as children and adults alike screamed and searched for loved ones, hoping that their own families had been spared. In the confusion, Joaquin Garavito struggled to his feet, his vision a blur. Clutching his throat, he staggered away from the chaos and made his way to safety, the swelling in his throat nearly cutting off his air.

David remained motionless for a few seconds, pretending to be dead, gathering his strength for the next move. His mind raced. *Why Justin? Do I have enemies who'd do this to us?* Rage built within, giving him strength. He inched toward the Beretta. He grabbed it and rose as fast as his muscles could overcome the pain in his ribs and shoulder. His breath was short. He felt the pain in his side, the blood streaming down his hip.

David turned just in time to see Justin being carried through the tunnel. Grasping the Beretta firmly, he thought, *Nine millimeter, ten-shot clip. I fired three times. Seven left*, he calculated. He hobbled forward. Bystanders who saw the gun in his hand shrieked again, thinking he was the killer. He wanted to tell them he wasn't, but he didn't have time. He made his way through the tunnel as fast as he could, oblivious to the dark blood seeping through his shirt and jacket.

Despite the loud music of the carousel and the other noise of Central Park, two mounted policemen on the loop on the other side of the softball diamonds heard the distinctive *pop-pop-pop* of gunfire and called in the first alarm, before galloping to where they thought they had heard the shooting. "Central Park. Suspected gunshots. Near the carousel."

Within minutes the call was out from the nearby precinct headquarters to every cop in and around Central Park. "All units respond. Shooting in progress, several victims down, multiple shots fired. Use extreme caution."

Although they responded quickly, by the time the two mounted policemen reached the carousel, Manuel and Justin were midway down the hill from the Dairy toward Wollman Rink. Once again Manuel was surprised by how heavy Justin was. Manuel's left arm was already aching. He put away the Beretta and shifted Justin to his right arm. *Run like hell before the police come,* he told himself.

David reached the top of the hill in front of the Dairy, only to see Manuel and Justin round a large stone at the base of the hill. They seemed to be heading toward either Fifth Avenue or Central Park South; David couldn't be sure. If he guessed wrong, Justin would be gone, maybe forever. He tried desperately to get his legs to move faster, but the pain in his ribs denied him the strength he needed. *Ignore the pain*, he angrily ordered himself.

Manuel grabbed his phone, hoping the line was still open. It wasn't. He stopped and pressed the number "1" for the speed dial. The call didn't go through. He laid Justin down on a large rock where the path forked, one path toward the lake, the other up to the loop. As he redialed, he studied his options. He could follow the loop to the Plaza Hotel, running the risk of getting there before Raymond, or even worse, meeting up with the throngs of cops who were no doubt converging on the carousel. He decided to take the path that skirted the lake. He pressed the speed dial again. "Answer, goddamn it! Answer!" he yelled.

"Yes," Raymond finally responded. "I'm at Columbus Circle. Traffic's impossible."

"I have an emergency appointment at the Plaza, right now!" Manuel growled, giving the code for "All hell's breaking loose." "Be there!"

He slapped the phone back into his jacket pocket and hefted Justin onto his shoulder. Justin's fifty-five pounds felt like a hundred at this point. Sirens howled from several directions around the park, getting closer. *Shit*, thought Manuel, *if they catch me I'm looking at the death penalty. But, Christ, I'd rather be caught and die in the chair than go back to the patrón empty-handed. He'll feed me to the sharks for sure.*

David pushed ahead, now only a hundred yards behind Justin and the man who wanted to take his boy from him. He stared straight ahead up the path leading toward the lake and Fifty-ninth Street. The Beretta seemed double its weight. No one noticed his expensive clothing or his well-shaven face. They saw only a bleeding man carrying a very large gun. At the sight of him, some scattered. Others just stood screaming as he limped past them. David summoned his last reserves of strength. He knew that the kidnapper would soon be lost in the crowds around the Grand Army Plaza.

Fire burned Manuel's lungs as he ran up the steep steps leading to the Plaza. He burst onto the sidewalk, shaking with fatigue, Justin still draped over his shoulder. He looked frantically up and down the choked street for the van. *Come on, Raymond, you stupid fucking gringo. Come on!*

Manuel was getting desperate. Raymond and the van were nowhere to be seen and this *chico* was going wild again. Justin had just come to and was screaming and thrashing at him. Passersby looked at Manuel suspiciously. He shrugged and raised his eyebrows as if to indicate that Justin was throwing a tantrum. *Slow down,* he warned himself. *But if this fucking chico kicks me in the balls one more time, screw the boss. I'll kill the little shit.*

Two blocks west, Raymond beat on the steering wheel in frustration, stuck in traffic. Behind him, the wailing sirens of emergency vehicles futilely demanded that traffic clear and give them the right of way.

Manuel, carrying Justin, began to cross Fifty-ninth Street amidst the shouts and honking by frustrated drivers. He stood in the middle of the street for an instant and turned behind him to see if anyone had followed. A large delivery truck blocked his view of Central Park. "Get the fuck out of the road," a man in the passenger side of the truck yelled.

As David reached the top of the steps that led to the Grand Army Plaza, he was horrified by the chaos. The sidewalks were teaming with pedestrians taking advantage of the break in the weather. Horse-drawn carriages were parked tightly near the curb. Cars and trucks blocked his view.

Suddenly David spotted them. Justin was held high above the crowd, his telltale blond curls and his bright blue winter coat standing out like a beacon. With Manuel holding Justin, David didn't dare shoot. He limped into the street, dodging cars, ignoring the screech of brakes, rapidly closing the distance between them.

As Manuel turned to look for Raymond, he saw the gun drop a fraction of a second before David slammed it into his head. With lightning-quick reflexes, Manuel moved slightly and deflected the impact. The blow still hit with enough force to knock him and Justin to the dung-covered asphalt. The near-miss propelled David forward hard onto the street, the Beretta sliding across the pavement under a carriage. *You won't get another chance,* David raged within himself as he leaped at Manuel. He went immediately for the kill.

Manuel panicked when he saw that the man was the boy's father. He fought for his life, shocked by the fierceness of the *gringo* they had so underestimated. Meanwhile, Justin rolled into the path of a large Boar's Head cold cuts delivery truck. The driver avoided him only by veering to the right, overturning a carriage and sending the horse rearing high into the air.

David slammed Manuel's head against the pavement with his good right arm while he tried vainly to protect his vulnerable left side from the pounding by the frantic Colombian.

Manuel fought to disengage himself from this maniac long enough to pull his automatic and shoot him. He kept pounding David's wounded left side, seeing pain reflected in the man's eyes.

The frightened horses bucked forward. A driver who had joined the crowd watching the fight in the street heard a clattering of hooves and turned too late. "Stop, damn it," he shouted helplessly as a terrified horse over-ran him.

Hooves the size of dinner plates slashed through the air, bouncing sparks off the roadway from steel shoes. David heard the horse bray and looked up in time to see a horse and carriage bearing down directly above a helpless Justin, sitting sobbing in the street.

"No!" David shouted, pushing Manuel aside and lunging for Justin. He wrapped his son in his good right arm and rolled hard, just avoiding the stampeding horse.

Through the traffic, Raymond could see only a crowd and two or more men fighting. He abandoned the vehicle in heavy traffic and ran toward the Plaza Hotel.

Manuel, gasping for breath, jerked himself to his knees and began searching for the gun David had dropped. Sweat stung his eyes, partially closed by David's repeated pummeling. His hand grasped the Beretta. *You die now, gringo bastard!*

David fell hard on Manuel, both men crashing to the ground. For a second Manuel's gun hand was pinned beneath their writhing bodies. David, long past thinking of anything but survival, was losing blood and strength rapidly. He knew the other man was much younger and could outlast him. *End it now,* he thought.

With one swift move he whipped his good right arm around Manuel's neck and tightened his grip. Ignoring the pain in his left shoulder, he grabbed Manuel's hair in his left fist. He half rose, knees firmly planted against Manuel's lower back, and, with a primal roar that arose from his gut, thrust upward with his right arm and twisted left with his left hand. Even over the screams of the crowd and the incessant wail of sirens, he heard the satisfying pop of Manuel's neck. The Colombian's body convulsed for a few seconds and then went limp, his head hanging over David's right arm, his neck broken. David held him for an instant, making sure he was dead. He then let the body fall to the asphalt.

Is it over? David wondered, his eyes tearing, his lips trembling, looking over to where he had last seen Justin, and coming to the terrible realization that Justin wasn't there. There was no sign of him. David stumbled toward the spot where he had last seen his boy, turning in every direction, searching desperately. "Justin!" he shouted over and over. On instinct, he spun around toward the Plaza Hotel and caught a glimpse of Justin being carried by a white man with blond hair rounding the Fifty-eighth Street side of the hotel. In the instant it took him to react, a burly NYPD patrolman who had no idea that David was the father and not the assailant, slammed David to the ground. David, taken by surprise, momentarily passed out from the blow, long enough for the cops to cuff him. Long enough for Raymond to make his getaway down Fifty-eighth Street, through traffic to the subway.

Chapter 5

Jenny had arrived at her office a little before noon and had worked over five hours straight. She turned from the computer monitor, rubbing her eyes, which were irritated and watering from staring at her screen too long. She wiped them with a tissue and looked around the office, noticing the digital clock on the radiator. It was 5:15 P.M. David and Justin would show up soon. She made a quick trip to the ladies' room to comb her hair and add a touch of lipstick.

At five-forty-five she walked down the hall to see if David and Justin had arrived. The lights were still out in his office, so she returned to her desk and continued to work. When she hadn't heard anything from him by six-thirty, she was troubled and annoyed. When the clock struck seven, annoyance turned to concern. *What could have happened to them?* she wondered.

At seven-fifteen, she called down to the security guard in the lobby to see if David was somewhere else in the building. He wasn't. At seven-thirty she called his home, only to get his answering machine. By eight o'clock Jenny was hurt, angry, and worried. She turned off her computer, grabbed her coat, went to the elevator, and signed out in the lobby, thoroughly pissed off at David for not calling, yet harboring some hope that he'd have a good explanation for not meeting her.

She hailed a cab and hopped in. She was in no mood for chitchat. Yet the cabbie had spent all day with uncommunicative passengers and was eager to talk to the pretty woman in the backseat.

"Wild day in Central Park. They say that crime's down, but I don't believe it. Gettin' so a man can't take his kid to the park without somebody tryin' to kill him. Serves these guys right, though," the driver continued. "They picked on the wrong man today. Still got the boy, but the father made 'em pay for it."

Jenny, who was slouched in her seat looking out the window, shifted her position so she could look at the man's eyes in the rearview mirror. "Oh," she said, still only half listening, but trying to be civil.

"You didn't hear the news? Guy was in Central Park today with his boy. Bunch of thugs kidnapped the boy. Only six years old. Police don't really know much. Press reports are still coming outta Bellevue."

"When did it happen?" Jenny asked, slightly more interested.

"I think it happened 'round noon, one o'clock. Sumpin' like that. But they fucked with— 'Scuze me, lady; I get carried away. They messed with the wrong guy. On the radio they say the guy's a Vietnam vet."

Jenny sat forward, stunned, her seat belt preventing her from leaning closer to the driver. Her hands dug into the Plexiglas divider in the cab as she leaned forward to hear him.

"The father killed two of the bad guys. But he took a beatin'. They shot him in the chest, and—"

"Did you get the man's name?" she interrupted.

"No idea, ma'am. But get this. The man takes some bullets in the chest—Bellevue wouldn't say how many—and still chases down the third guy who's carryin' away the boy. Father catches him right in front of the Plaza Hotel and breaks his neck. Took his head damn near off. But while the father is takin' this man down, a fourth kidnapper comes along and nabs the boy. Been all over the radio and TV. Surprised you didn't hear about it. Well, you heard it first from me," the cabbie announced proudly.

"Driver, I think I know that man and his son. Take me to Bellevue now. Please hurry. Get me to Bellevue."

The driver turned to look at her directly, probing to see if she was pulling a prank on him. The answer stared him in the face.

"Yes, ma'am. I'll get you there right away." The cab lurched forward in the bumper-to-bumper traffic, nearing Houston Street. *Small world*, he thought.

Jenny ran into the crowded emergency room, which was filled with the pandemonium of a Saturday night. People who had been beaten, shot, and knifed filled the place. Drug addicts and homeless schizophrenics were clamoring for assistance. Jenny, looking fresh even though she had worked all day, stood out like a rose in a junkyard. She immediately drew the attention of two young medical students.

"Can I help you?" asked a tall, dark-haired attendant.

"Yes. I believe that a very good friend of mine was brought here earlier today. Someone shot him and kidnapped his boy. I'm told by a cabdriver that they brought—"

"'Scuze me," interrupted the blond student. "You must mean that Craig fellow. Brought him in about one o'clock today. I wasn't on duty, but I know he's been in the OR."

Jenny barely heard anything after the word *Craig*. She was shocked. So it *was* David. *What if he dies?* She trembled visibly and burst into tears, covering her mouth instinctively as she gasped for air.

"Miss, if you're family or a friend, I'll get you in touch with the doctors," said the dark-haired one, no longer flirting. "No one can see Mr. Craig yet. Doctor's orders. I'd take you there myself, but I can't," he said, gesturing at all the people in the ER. "I'll get someone from Transport to take you to his treating physician. Believe me, you'll never find it on your own in this maze."

Jenny and the attendant walked down a long hallway, where she was introduced to a middle-aged man from Transport. "The area up ahead is the auditorium. FBI, DEA, and NYPD are all over this incident with your friend," he said a few moments later. "Press is everywhere, too. Might want to avoid 'em."

"Why the DEA?" Jenny asked, puzzled. Kidnapping was a federal offense, jurisdiction of the FBI. But why, she wondered, was the Drug Enforcement Agency involved?

" 'Cause of the drug cartel. You know the kidnappers were part of the cartel, don't you?"

Jenny stopped cold, staring at the man, eyes wide in disbelief.

They approached the area near the auditorium. Media crews were assembled in front of the entrance. Thick television cables crossed the hallway into the front door of the auditorium, like so many snakes leading to their nest. She approached cautiously, as if something dangerous might be inside. Through the open back door, she observed a police officer in uniform and a man in a blue pin-striped suit standing at the podium fielding questions from journalists. The bright lights made the two men appear ghostlike. The excitement in the air was palpable, but the session seemed to be winding down. Many of the press had been in the auditorium since midafternoon, when word of the violence in Central Park had flashed around the city.

Dr. Ben Horowitz, chief of surgery at Bellevue Hospital, stepped out into the hallway after briefing the press.

"Are you David's doctor?" Jenny asked with trepidation.

"Ben Horowitz," he said, extending his hand. "Are you related to Mr. Craig?" he asked gently.

"Jenny Benson," she answered, shaking his hand. "We work together at Lanham, Klein and Barnes. He and his son, Justin, and I were to have dinner tonight after meeting at the office. When he didn't show up, I started for home and the cabdriver told me . . ." She couldn't finish the sentence.

Dr. Horowitz put his arm around her protectively. "Mr. Craig took a couple of bullets."

"Is he . . . okay?" Jenny stammered.

"We expect that he's going to recover fully. He's resting after the surgery. Everything went well."

"The bullets?"

"The one that hit him in the shoulder went right through him. Lucky man. The one that hit his ribs was pretty clean too. Three ribs broken, but it could have been a lot worse. Don't know of many men who could have taken bullets in the shoulder and ribs, run several hundred yards, and still managed to kill another man. Some nasty scars. Add 'em to his collection, if you know what I mean," he added, wanting to know how well this woman knew his patient.

Jenny nodded somberly. "You'd have to know David," she said, sensing that the tall doctor had developed a genuine respect for David, and liking him for it. "He did the same in Vietnam. They gave him the Congressional for almost the exact same thing."

"The Medal of Honor," Horowitz exclaimed loudly, impressed. He had never met anyone who had been awarded the nation's highest honor. "That's really something."

The doctor's voice caught the attention of a reporter from the *Daily News*. "Doc, did you say Craig has the Congressional Medal of Honor?" the aggressive man interrupted. "Do you know David Craig?" he demanded, turning to Jenny. "Are you part of his family? Girlfriend?" The reporter quickly motioned to his photographer to get a picture of the sexy woman dressed in black denim pants, a charcoal-gray mock turtleneck sweater, and a black leather biker jacket.

Jenny scowled at the photographer, who responded by taking yet another shot before Dr. Horowitz could intervene. The doctor invited her to leave by taking her elbow and motioning with a movement of his head that she should go down the hall to the right.

Inside the conference room, the chief of police of New York, two NYPD detectives, a representative of the mayor's office, three representatives of the FBI, and two representatives of the DEA debated the evidence. The

NYPD had recognized Manuel Ramos immediately. Hector Rojas had taken more effort, but within two hours his identity was also confirmed. They still had not figured out who the man at the carousel was. So far there was only one picture of him, caught in the background of a photo taken by a parent seconds before the attack on David at the carousel, but the angle wasn't good and it didn't give them much to work with. Although everyone agreed that Ramos and Rojas were Colombians and part of a drug cartel, the FBI and DEA agents were trying to convince the NYPD that they were with the Cali cartel, and some of the NYPD present were skeptical. The more difficult part, however, was tying the Colombians to the kidnapping of the son of a wealthy investment banker who had no criminal record.

"Look, kidnapping is outside the normal scope of activities of a Colombian drug gang, at least in the United States," Patrick Evans from the DEA asserted. "They're routine in Colombia, but they're generally tied to Colombian politics or a vendetta within a cartel. Kidnappings are a way of punishing a skimmer or some other disloyal capo."

"I agree," Robert Harrison from the FBI added authoritatively. "In the U.S., the Colombians are content to sell their cocaine and reap huge profits. They don't need ransom. They have more money than they can safely launder. But . . . they don't hesitate to punish disloyal subordinates."

The group of law-enforcement officials quickly agreed that it was safe to say that David Craig was not connected with Colombian politics, which left the alternative of some sort of vendetta or punishment. Everyone in the room questioned whether Craig was somehow connected to the drug ring.

Aaron McCormick left his office at the Drug Enforcement Agency at nine-twenty P.M. in a decidedly unpleasant mood. He had spent twelve-hour days every day for the last two weeks reviewing reports from covert agents in South America, preparing his closed-door briefing to the DEA's Congressional Oversight Committee. The committee had demanded a report across the board on the DEA's operations in South America, including budgets and top-secret covert plans. As the chief of operations, he alone within the DEA knew the whole picture, which was exactly how he wanted it. Not even the director was privy to the full set of detailed covert operations. Information was power in Washington, and McCormick jealously protected his domain. He had planned to spend all of Saturday and Sunday polishing up the finishing touches of the briefing, but the kidnapping in New York, carried by CNN as he ate a late lunch at his desk, had nearly given him a heart attack.

At twenty past five the next morning McCormick wheeled his car into the parking lot of a diner on Seminary Road in Alexandria. It was still dark out and the restaurant was nearly empty. Only two booths were occupied, each by elderly couples who sat in silence, sipping coffee and reading the papers.

As the waitress approached him at the entrance, McCormick glanced to the stack of newspapers on the shelf and was immediately shocked and upset with what he saw. He picked up the *Washington Post,* fixated on the large, color photograph on the front page of David Craig at the very moment he broke Manuel's neck, his mouth wide open in a primal roar as he broke the neck of the monster who had tried to take his boy. An amateur photographer who was at the Plaza at the time of the kidnapping had captured the grisly scenes with professional clarity. Like the *Post,* every major newspaper in the world carried the dramatic photos. McCormick scanned down the article and hurriedly turned to page three to read the rest of it and to see if there were more photos. To McCormick's horror, there were three. One image captured Manuel's lifeless head draped over David's arm. Another frame showed David crying out at the instant he realized that his boy had disappeared. The third caught the force of the patrolman's tackle as he and David crashed to the pavement.

"Sir. Uh, sir. Would you like the counter or a booth?"

the waitress asked after pausing a brief moment for McCormick to lift his head from behind the paper.

"Uh, yes. I mean a booth. . . . The one in the corner would be fine."

Gerald Warren entered the diner at exactly six A.M., spotted McCormick, and quickly walked toward him, indicating to the waitress that he was joining the man seated at the far booth.

McCormick noticed that Warren's tall, gaunt frame was slumped slightly more than usual. *On the sauce again,* McCormick thought with contempt. *Probably tied one on last night.*

"You called the meeting," Warren stated coldly. He nodded to the waitress, who waved a coffeepot, raising her eyebrows to see if he wanted some.

McCormick slid the main section of the *Post* across the table, turning it so Warren could see the picture. Warren's eyes went wide as he fixed on the photo. He set down his cup without looking at it, spilling some coffee on the table. He fumbled in his pocket for his reading glasses but his eyes remained glued to the article. After a moment, he turned to page three and continued to regard the pictures and scan the text. When finished, he folded the paper and moved it to the side, his face ashen.

"Look, you and I know Coffee's behind this, so let's not pretend otherwise," McCormick began, using their code name for Belalcazar. "The other kidnappings were discreet. No way to tie them back to Coffee. But this one went wrong. Very wrong. They did no homework on the father. Totally miscalculated. Now the whole world knows about this kidnapping. And worse, that it's connected to one of the drug cartels. Fortunately they don't know which one—yet. I sent Harrison and Evans to New York yesterday. They've taken control of the FBI's and DEA's investigations and will steer them in the right direction. But if we don't act quickly, the heat's going to be turned up so high on Coffee, he's going to burn. We've got to act immediately."

"I wish there was something we could do to get him

to stop this," the CIA man said. He did not care at all about the kids, but was very concerned about marines hitting the beaches of Colombia if the American people found out about the kidnappings. He couldn't even meet alimony payments, let alone child support, without Coffee's gratuities, wire transfers to secret offshore accounts and thick envelopes of cash.

"I know. We've got to persuade Coffee that he has enough kids for his family, 'puppies for his kennel,' as he says. We both know he's a psycho . . . got this dynasty thing . . . the kids have to worship him. But what the hell, we're all used to dealing with narcissists and sociopaths here in Washington," McCormick said, not aware that Warren thought he fit that description. "But we'll worry about that later." He paused so the waitress could take their order. "First we have to deal with this guy Craig," he instructed after the waitress left. "I've taken care of the FBI and DEA. Both agencies will be convinced, if they aren't already, that Craig's tied up with the Cali cartel. Steer 'em toward Cali. I need you to do the same within the CIA," he said.

Gerald Warren simply nodded.

Sebastian de Belalcazar was furious. He paced back and forth from the patio to his office, where his secretary tried desperately to reach Raymond Shannon to see what had gone wrong the day before in Central Park.

"Ms. Cuervas. If you can't do your job, I'll get someone who can," he said calmly, his eyes piercing hers, communicating the threat.

"I've tried all the usual places in New York, but only people we can trust, Señor Belalcazar, and only people who know the code. No one knows where he and the boy are. He must have gone into hiding."

Belalcazar had watched the fiasco on television. The first time he saw his nephew Manuel dead in David Craig's arms, his neck broken, he had bolted out of his chair. As CNN covered the story through the night and into Sunday morning he just sat staring at the screen, his eyes ablaze, intent on the loss of his trusted nephew, the only remaining member of his family, the son of his deceased sister. To make matters worse, Joaquin Garavito, a valued lieutenant on the rise within the cartel, was missing.

Why? Belalcazar thought as he walked in the garden outside his office overlooking the Pacific Ocean, chain-smoking. *Why didn't we know the boy's father was a war hero in the U.S. Army? And a highly decorated hero at that. Manuel was supposed to have done his homework. This stupidity runs the risk of exposing us,* he acknowledged to himself. As he thought about the blunder his lips pursed and his chin grew tight, indicators to all who knew him that he was very, very angry.

A few moments later the phone rang, startling his MIS director. Yolanda Cuervas grabbed the phone so quickly that she interrupted the first ring. "Raymond. We've been looking all over for you. The boss wants—"

Belalcazar abruptly grabbed the phone from her hand, hitting her in the lip and hurting her. "Tell me what happened to the delivery boys. But don't forget we're on the phone," he ordered, barely able to control his rage. "Where's my puppy?"

"Boss, I wasn't with them when they first went to the pet store. My job was to park the car. I only know what everyone else knows. The dog's owner decided not to sell it and put up a big stink. I rescued the puppy at the last moment. He's on his way to you now. Joaquin is with him."

Chapter 6

David regained consciousness in his hospital room, his eyes opening slowly as he adjusted to the morphine-filled stupor. As he stared at the squares of acoustic ceiling tiles, the harsh lights hurt his eyes. He shifted in his bed and was rewarded with sharp splinters of pain in his left shoulder and side. Everything came back to him at once. He glanced at the IV drip feeding glucose and antibiotics into his left arm, thinking that it was all for nothing if Justin was gone.

David had never felt so devoid of hope in his life. He had known death in the war. He had known sorrow and emptiness during Cindy's illness. But this was a gray-black bubble of pressure weighing down on him. He felt himself sinking into an abyss, powerless to do anything about it. *Please don't hurt him,* he thought as he drifted back to sleep.

"How long have I been out?" David whispered hoarsely to the doctor leaning over him and checking his vital signs.

"You were brought in three days ago," Dr. Horowitz gently informed him.

"Three days!" David exclaimed, trying to sit up, but prevented by a stabbing pain. "Any word about my son?"

"Nothing that I know of. Sorry," he added, looking compassionately at David. "Papers say the authorities haven't received any ransom notes or even any clues. I asked some of the police officers if there was anything they'd heard, but so far, nothing. I'm terribly sorry. I have children of my own. I think I know a little of what you're going through."

"Thanks, Doc. Then you understand that I have to get out of here as soon as possible. Give me a damage report."

"You got hit hard, but you're strong and very lucky. One bullet hit your left rib, third from the bottom. Shattered it into the two ribs just below it, breaking them as well. The force was directed downward. Had it gone up or inward, the ribs would have punctured a lung, or worse. The other bullet went through your shoulder. Straight through. Tore the hell out of your muscles but didn't hit anything major. You need to be monitored. If you take it easy and do what we tell you, we'll get you out of here in three, possibly four more days. Now, I want you to get some rest. Anyway, you don't want to walk out of here just yet and confront the press hounds encamped in the lobby."

"The what?" David asked, surprised.

"Newspapers, TV, and all that. When at least four men from a drug cartel kidnap a boy, and the father, a former war hero, kills or seriously injures three of 'em, that's front-page stuff."

David stared at the talkative doctor, unable to believe what he had just heard. "Drug cartel? What . . . who are these people?"

Now it was Dr. Horowitz's turn to stare at David, probing to see if he was telling the truth or just a good actor. The press was portraying him as either Mr. Clean the good father or Mr. Greed the money launderer.

"I'll leave that for the FBI to answer," responded Dr. Horowitz. "All I know is what I read in the papers. Sorry about the disclosure of your war record. Your friend Jenny mentioned it to me. I spoke too loudly and one of the reporters overheard. Jenny told me later that you don't like to talk about it," he added as he started to leave the room.

"Doc, where's Jenny now?"

"I'll get her in to see you. Not supposed to. FBI says no one is to see you until they talk to you. But I think we can get around that. Leave that to me."

"Thanks, Doc. Thanks for everything," said David as Dr. Horowitz reached the door.

"Don't thank me. Thank Marvin Williams, the EMS paramedic who brought you here. He fought with the cops to take you in fast. Said you were mumbling for a medic, calling for reinforcements. I know Marvin. Good man. Also a Vietnam vet. Told me he knew you were a veteran just by your vocabulary. You may owe him your life. You were losing blood fast."

David tried to raise his head to ask more about the paramedic, only to be informed abruptly by his rib cage that he was in no condition to move. *FBI? Drug cartel? Christ. Where is Justin? Who are these people?* He fell asleep once again, his mind racked with the agonizing thought that his son was out there somewhere in the hands of madmen.

David awoke after a little more than two hours. As his eyes fluttered open, his vision blurred from the painkillers, the first thing he saw was Jenny staring down at him. Her red hair cascaded onto her shoulders, framing her creamy-smooth complexion. The harsh ceiling light behind her made the outer strands of her hair look gold, like a halo. She looked like an angel. Her emerald eyes, moist with emotion, shone more brightly than usual. Her smile was radiant, though tentative, her lips quivering slightly, as if she were wanting to speak, but could find no words. She held a small vase of irises and daffodils, David's favorite flowers. "I understand that the Feds can't get in to see you, but Dr. Horowitz let me in. . . ." Her voice trailed off as she looked at him to see if he was happy to see her. He was. She leaned over and kissed him gently on the lips, wanting to hug him tightly, but afraid she would hurt him. She began to retreat, but David insisted on more kisses.

"Who did this to us?" David asked after a long pause, his voice raspy and fatigued.

"Feds say it's the Cali drug cartel from Colombia. They say the two men you killed are part of the cartel. NYPD agrees. Doesn't make sense, I know," she added, motioning for David to stay calm as he tried to sit up and protest.

"Any word about Justin?" David asked, his voice cracking.

"Nothing. A black hole. No communication at all. NYPD ordered a citywide APB on Justin on Saturday afternoon . . . but there's been nothing."

"What's all this about drug cartels, FBI, the press? Jenny, what the hell's going on?"

"There's a lot going on. I've been pumping the cops and doctors around here, on top of what's in the papers. The kidnappers were definitely with some Colombian drug gang. Nobody seems to know why they'd kidnap Justin, but there are lots of theories. DEA and FBI agents have implied . . . well . . . more than implied . . . that you must have been involved in the drug business—"

"That's absurd," David interrupted. "You know me—"

"Of course I do, David," Jenny cut him off. "Look, I've taken the liberty to get Billy Dunn's number from Rosa. I've been on the phone with him and your other Ranger buddies. We all know you. But listen. We have to deal with the accusations," she implored.

David pushed his head back deeper into his pillow, angry and wanting to fight.

"David," Jenny said gently, "the FBI and DEA are all over this. There's even some mention of the CIA. The NYPD is in it as well. The FBI and the NYPD interviewed people from LKB, even clients. They went to our partners' homes. They've already interviewed people in your co-op. I was questioned for three hours this morning by the FBI and DEA together, and separately by the NYPD. The police went pretty easy on me, so maybe they went easy on the others as well, but the Feds were brutal. They're asking all sorts of questions about you. David, it's not pretty. They're planting thoughts in people's minds. Like they're setting you up. LKB's falling for it. You know Wall Street. They're all self-promoting assholes with no loyalty. They're already distancing themselves from you, saying, 'Well, you never know . . . maybe he was dealing on the side,' and stuff like that. I got calls from our partners, insinuating the worst. Jake Barnes called and left me a nasty message while I was with the DEA and FBI. I didn't even bother to call him back. It's bad. Even your 'friend,' Herb Klein, is running for cover." She stopped to let that sink in, sorry that she had to tell David all this.

The pain of betrayal showed on his face. The lack of loyalty, though, was only secondary. What pained him the most was the appalling lack of concern about Justin. "Fuck 'em. Fuck 'em all. I don't give a shit about LKB. I want out of here. I have to find Justin."

"You're right. Justin is all that matters. I've already flooded the Internet with his picture. I got the NYPD to send his picture out to every police force in the country. We have rough sketches of the man who carried Justin away from the Plaza. White man. Tall. Chiseled face. Blond hair. But nothing more than that. I'm doing everything I can. Believe me."

"I do. You know I do."

"There's something big coming down from Washington in all this," Jenny added, trying to explain to David something that she herself had yet to understand. "People flying in from the FBI. DEA. Not relying on the NYPD." Jenny rubbed her hands together nervously. "David," Jenny said slowly, "the press says I'm in with you in the drug traffic. 'Red-haired bombshell may be a runner for David Craig's drug operations.' Hell, David, they don't even have to say I'm running drugs. All they have to do is say that I *may* be connected with a drug ring and all my so-called friends run for cover. I don't give a rat's ass about the publicity. But the more I'm suspected, the less help I'm going to get from the NYPD and the missing-children sites on the Internet. You know how it works. Too many kidnappings. Police in other towns will focus first on kids from 'good families,' not from a wealthy banker they think has run some money-laundering scheme for the drug lords. We have a serious problem. We have to get the truth out to the press."

"Let's do it," he said decisively.

For a moment the two were silent, each trying to grapple with the enormity of what they were facing: Justin gone, a drug cartel involved, the FBI and DEA suspecting David, the press smearing them . . . David was the first to break the silence. "I'll talk to the press," David said angrily, his eyes like two burning coals. "Here I am laid up in the hospital, my son kidnapped by God knows what kind of psychopaths, and these goddamn bureaucrats from Washington and the press can only think of coming after me!" He tried to rise up in his bed despite the pain.

"David," Jenny cautioned, "I'm with you, and we're going to come out fighting."

David looked down at the catheter in his left arm and then looked at the room around him. He wanted to jump out of bed and get to work. "What about Billy and the others?"

"They want to be here with you. They were worried about your safety, but I told them about the army of cops stationed at the hospital. They want to stand in front of the TV cameras and back you up. But . . . we talked about it. We agreed they'd stay put for now. I convinced them to sit tight until we know what we're doing."

David looked at Jenny, probing deep into her eyes. He knew she was right. Something big was happening. He nodded slowly to her.

"David," Jenny said, noticing his severe fatigue and gently touching his face, "try to get some rest. Try to eat. You need your strength. We have to keep our heads clear. It's going to get rough."

Reporters had swarmed over Lanham, Klein & Barnes as early as the morning after the kidnapping. At first they wanted to know more about the Vietnam hero who had almost saved his boy in Central Park. As word from the FBI and DEA leaked that David Craig might be tied to the drug cartels, the press smelled a better story. They turned against him as quickly as they had made him a hero. They launched a veritable siege on LKB's headquarters, waiting at the main entrance, cameras, microphones, and notepads in hand, ready to ambush those willing to challenge their barricade.

LKB's partners met early that morning and made contingency plans. The last thing they wanted to do was talk to the press about an LKB partner and the drug cartels. The partners arranged to meet with their clients elsewhere, in hotels, lawyers' offices, and partners' homes. Some clients accepted the inconvenience. Many others politely informed LKB that they would do the transaction at hand with another investment bank. Such were loyalties on Wall Street. LKB's partners watched as tens of millions of dollars in fees slipped through their fingers.

"Whether he's part of this drug cartel or not," said Ben Lanham to Jake Barnes and Herb Klein behind closed doors in Lanham's private, pearwood-paneled office, "we'll have to get rid of him. We can't afford to lose our clients to the competition for the sake of one man."

"I agree," Jake Barnes said, needing no prodding to fire a partner he didn't like in the first place.

"How can we vote David out of the partnership at a time like this?" Klein pleaded. "We have no proof at all that he's involved in drugs, his boy has been brutally kidnapped, and David, our partner, lies in the hospital. Hell, he may be dying, for all we know."

"How do we do it? It's easy. We call a meeting of the partners and vote him the hell out." Jake Barnes snorted. "He gets his capital account back and that's it. He's costing us a fucking fortune each day in lost business. He's been a weak performer for the last few years anyway. Spends too much time with his boy. Hell, we all have families. I have families from each of my marriages, and I don't spend nearly as much time with all of them combined as he does with one child," he snapped.

"Let me talk to David before we take any action," Klein pleaded.

"Herb, we don't have time," Ben Lanham countered. "Jake's right. We're losing too much money each day. Hell, Craig may be in the hospital, unable to talk to you, for days. I say we call the meeting and vote him out."

"Done," said Barnes.

"You have the votes on me. I won't vote against you in front of the other partners," Herb Klein acquiesced. "Call your meeting, but for the record, I think this stinks."

"One more thing," Jake Barnes added firmly, ignoring Klein. "Jenny Benson has to go too."

"Agreed," Ben Lanham said flatly.

Chapter 7

During the two days since David had regained consciousness, he had gone from the depths of depression to an anger-filled rebound. During the first day he cried himself to sleep, waking up in a drenched hospital gown and sheets from nightmares too horrible to fully recall. Images of his son being brutalized tormented him. He repeatedly asked himself if there was anything he could have done to prevent Justin's kidnapping. *I should've killed the bastard sooner,* he thought.

Jenny's access to David was restricted. Only with the help of Dr. Horowitz did she manage to visit him a second time. She was shocked by his appearance. He reclined in his bed with several newspapers on his lap, watching CNN. His bloodshot eyes were glazed over, underlined in dark, puffy circles indicative of sleepless nights. He looked ten years older than he had just two days earlier. His face was ashen. The lines on his face were more pronounced, darker, his anger palpable. The skin on his unshaven chin was taut, his jaw muscles visible as he clenched his teeth. He looked as if he might throw something through the TV.

After a long pause, Jenny decided to tell David what was going on at LKB. At first she dropped her eyes, staring at the floor, hesitant, concerned that he might not be up to it. "David, the rumor is that you—we—are going to be kicked out of the partnership. It's just a rumor at this point, but it's pretty strong. Could happen as early as tomorrow."

"Doesn't surprise me. Fuck 'em. I don't care," he said instantly, prepared to sever twenty-five years with LKB in the few seconds it took him to utter the words. "I can't work anyway. My job is to do whatever I can for Justin. Let the bastards throw me out. They'd prefer that I resign, but I won't give 'em the satisfaction. No. I'll make them vote and throw me out." He paused, thinking about Jenny, staring deep into her eyes. "What about you, Jenny? You've worked so hard and were on the rise. I'm sorry I got you into this."

"Screw 'em. Let's work on getting Justin back," she responded. In fact, she had anticipated the question and had had time to think it through. The decision had not come easily. Throughout her adult life, she had spent all her energies on her career. She had made partner at LKB a year earlier than her peers and was the youngest woman ever appointed. She made a lot of money. She had been on a trajectory that could have possibly led to her being the first chairwoman of LKB one day. But within seventy-two hours, fourteen years of work had been derailed. She was David's "biker girl." His "darker side." His "runner." After the events of the past few days, she'd go nowhere within LKB, or any other major investment bank. In essence, she had made her decision in Chicago. She'd stay by the man she loved.

At two o'clock, David walked to the podium from the side entrance of the Bellevue auditorium. He was dressed in a double-breasted navy blue pin-striped Christian Dior suit, with modest cuff links and a red tie. David winced from the glare of the bright TV lights and the continuous flashes of the cameras. He sought out Jenny in the front row and took comfort from the smile she gave him.

"May I have your attention, please?" David began, acutely aware that the TV cameras were broadcasting him nationwide. "On Saturday, February fifth, my son, Justin, and I went for a walk in Central Park. My son was kidnapped. I wasn't able to stop it." David paused to collect himself, his voice faltering. "It was a terrifying experience that I wish upon no parent." He looked around the auditorium to see the reaction of the press, but the lights and flashing strobes blinded him. He saw only a white glare. "I don't know who took Justin. I don't know why they kidnapped him. I'm informed by representatives of the Drug Enforcement Agency—the DEA—and the FBI that they believe that these men are connected to the Cali drug cartel. But I see no sign that the FBI is pursuing the kidnappers. Instead they appear to be more interested in going after me than in finding Justin. Some of you in the press, certain radio stations and newspapers in particular, have said I'm involved in the drug cartel and have stated that the kidnapping of my son is somehow an act of vengeance . . . or punishment . . . for my having done something to offend the drug lords.

"I'm here to tell you—and make sure you cover this in your articles and broadcasts," he added, his voice growing stronger, "that nothing could be farther from the truth. I have never used, sold, possessed, imported, or otherwise been involved with drugs. I am willing to take a lie-detector test to prove my innocence and answer any question the authorities wish to pose to me. Any question.

"As I said," David continued, no longer bothering to look at the index cards he had prepared, his voice now more somber, "I don't know who these men are or why they have kidnapped my Justin. I only know that they are very dangerous people and that my son is out there somewhere alone, afraid and in need of his daddy. Justin," he said as his voice cracked again and his eyes filled with tears. He pulled a handkerchief from his pocket and wiped his eyes amidst the flashes. "I don't suppose you are watching this on TV, but if . . . if by some miracle you are, I want you to know this: I am coming for you. I will bring you home. No matter how terrible the bad men who took you from me treat you, just hold on and remember that I will find you."

He wiped his eyes again and looked to Jenny for comfort. Despite the bright lights, he could see her sitting in the front row beaming with pride. David steeled his nerves once again and continued.

"I also have a message for the people who took Justin. I have done nothing to harm you. I don't even know who you are. I cannot imagine what I might have done to deserve this nightmare. But if I have inadvertently offended someone, Justin Craig, a six-year-old, is totally innocent. Let him go. If it's me you want, come get me." His voice was now defiant, threatening. "Give me back Justin," he implored. "Return him to me unharmed," he said, his eyes fixed on the TV cameras, "and I will let this go. I will not pursue you. But"— his finger jabbed at the cameras—"keep my son away from me, and I will find him. Harm one hair on his head and I will hunt you down. No matter how well you hide your tracks, no matter how far away you are, no matter how long it takes, I will find you. And when I find you, there will be no mercy," he vowed, slamming his fist on the podium. David stopped, visibly shaken by his own words.

Millions of day-time viewers across the United States saw a beaten but defiant father hell-bent on saving his boy. Several tens of millions more would watch the press conference on the evening news.

"I'll now take your quest—" he added, only to be cut off by scores of people shouting, competing to pose the first question.

"Mr. Craig," a bellicose woman in the third row cried out, grabbing David's attention and receiving a nod of his head toward her. "Do you think your boy is still alive and, if so, do you think he has been harmed?"

David stood motionless, incredulous. "Ma'am," he said, trying to control himself, his hands planted firmly on the edges of the podium, "I thought I made myself clear. I don't know who took my son, or why they took him. I don't know why they wanted Justin. I pray that they have the human decency and good sense not to harm him. But I know no more than you." He terminated the encounter with her with a turn of his head toward a tall man with very curly red hair who stood several rows back.

"I have children, Mr. Craig," the journalist said, trying to sound compassionate despite the fact that he was shouting. "I understand the pain you must be going through. How do you intend to find your boy?"

"Thank you. I'm relieved to know that some of you understand the tremendous stress and anxiety that I am going through. Frankly, when I read stories of kidnappings in the papers prior to my own ordeal, my heart went out to the parents, but I didn't fully appreciate their pain," he said, his voice cracking yet again. "The pain that a parent suffers in this situation . . . is quite literally unbearable." He stopped to collect himself. "How will I find Justin? I don't know. I don't know. We've begun to circulate photos of him to all the missing-children's organizations and law-enforcement agencies around the country. Photos have been disseminated on the Internet. How will I find my boy? I ask the American people to help me. He's out there somewhere. Someone will spot him. If you do, please, please tell your local law-enforcement authorities immediately."

"Mr. Craig. Mr. Craig, over here," a pale, middle-aged male reporter urged, capturing David's attention. "You mentioned that the DEA and FBI are more interested in 'going after you' than finding Justin. What do you mean by that? Can you elaborate?"

"My son and I were attacked in Central Park by three heavily armed men in broad daylight in front of hundreds of people, and then he was taken from me in front of the Plaza Hotel. I don't know the kidnappers or the person or persons behind them. The DEA and the FBI say that the assailants were involved with a drug cartel. Rather than use the information the authorities have about these criminals to help find my son, the authorities have shifted their attention to finding a connection between me and the criminals. It makes no sense. As they try to make connections that don't exist, precious time is being lost, time they could be using to find Justin."

"Will you be cooperating with law-enforcement agencies in their investigation of you?" a reporter shouted from the back of the room.

"Of course. I said that I will do everything to assist

the DEA, FBI, NYPD, and any other law-enforcement agency that wants to talk to me. The sooner the better."

"Why are they out to get you, Mr. Craig? Some of the reports describe you as paranoid. How do you respond to those allegations?" another reporter interjected.

"I don't know why they're out for me. All I know is that from the moment Justin was taken, law-enforcement officials have focused on me and, through innuendo and direct lies, spread stories about my alleged drug involvement and illicit connections. These lies have no basis in reality, but they have diverted attention from the kidnapping and the monsters who took Justin. When we find these animals, we find Justin."

Maj. Gen. Billy Dunn and his wife, Faith, watched the press conference from their comfortable home within the compound at Fort Meyer in Arlington, Virginia, near the Pentagon. Dunn was in transition between assignments, slightly easing his workload, and he had decided to rush home to watch the hastily called press conference with his wife.

Eric Randall watched it from a convenience store/gas station where he had stopped to buy cigarettes, mesmerized by his friend's face as it suddenly appeared on the TV behind the counter.

Matthew Rice watched with the woman to whom he had moments before sold a life insurance policy and then bedded, bounding off her couch stark naked as he ran to turn up the volume on the TV.

Frank Lopez, his wife, Eugenia, and his visiting daughter and son-in-law all watched from the crowded living room of their middle-class home in San Diego. He was now grateful for the storm that had prevented him from setting out to sea that morning.

Jack Heed watched David on the TV from his skydiving club in Borrego Springs, irritating his customers with the delay.

David had no sooner headed off the stage than Eric

was punching Billy's phone number into his cell phone as he walked to his car. "Not bad, hey, Billy?"

"Yeah. Bad guys took a beatin' today," Billy responded.

"He certainly slammed one over the net at the geeks at the DEA and FBI," Eric agreed. "And he's absolutely right. They're spending more time and energy trying to nail David than they are going after the bastards who took Justin." Eric snorted, never one to mince words.

"Anything on your research?"

"Not yet. Let me plug away. I'll stop by your place after dinner tonight."

Eric was the assistant deputy for operations at the CIA and, as such, also served as chairman of the National HUMINT Requirements Tasking Center. In the latter capacity, he coordinated human source intelligence, or old-fashioned spies, among all U.S. government agencies. He was the first to admit that the HUMINT position sounded more important than it was. The United States had cut way back on spies in recent years, favoring electronic and satellite surveillance instead.

Within hours of Justin's kidnapping, Eric had set in motion a personal inquiry within the government to see if anyone could come up with information about the drug cartels and why they would want to kidnap the son of a wealthy New York investment banker. Eric vowed to his friends to put the government at full throttle to dig for information.

The boy sat sullenly in the large playroom overlooking the lawn and the ocean beyond while the other children played. He was the most recent to arrive on Belalcazar's island. Of the five children, he was the least acclimated. He was still feeling the aftereffects of the drugs he had been given during the long, circuitous flight from New York to the Isla Gorgona. Jet lag disoriented him all the more.

"He's not playing like the others," said Sebastian de Belalcazar, more to himself than to his beautiful and much younger wife, Milana. They stood in the doorway of the playroom watching the nanny play with the children.

"It's been like that with the others, you know," she said to her husband. "He'll come around. They've all been like that. It takes them a while to get used to us, the other children, and the new surroundings."

"He seems different. Angry. The others were scared in their new surroundings. But he's defiant. I like that. We can channel his anger. The others are smart, particularly Lidia," he added, referring to the Spanish name his wife had given to Debbie Ross. "But this boy may be smarter, more alert. I'll name him José, after my brother. He, too, was smart and headstrong."

"Yes. It's a good choice," she responded quickly, careful not to disagree with him.

Belalcazar turned toward his study, followed by his ever-present bodyguards, Emilio and Alberto. He had permitted himself a few minutes to look in on his expanded "family" after watching a very upsetting press conference unfold on CNN. He now had to get back to business. They walked along the second-floor veranda overlooking the enclosed central courtyard, a large blue marble fountain bubbling hypnotically amidst the bougainvillea, azaleas, perfectly manicured miniature hedges, and closely clipped grass. The sun poured into the courtyard on a cloudless day, casting shafts of light through the mathematically precise columns of stone and wood.

"Joaquin will be in my office in fifteen minutes," Belalcazar ordered calmly, almost in a whisper, without turning to look at his bodyguards.

"*Sí, patrón*," Alberto responded crisply.

Belalcazar sat on a cushioned lawn chair, the azure-colored silk adorned with faint tan symbols of a conquistador's helmet, on his patio outside his office, and sipped Colombian espresso. The weather was hot, but the breeze from the Pacific cooled his chest under his custom-made silk shirt. A large blue umbrella protected him from the fierce tropical sun. Still, he needed his extra-dark sunglasses to shield his eyes from the bombardment of ultraviolet rays as he looked out over the Pacific Ocean. The cigarette he held between his nicotine-stained fingers was his twenty-fourth today, and it was not yet four o'clock P.M. A persistent, hacking cough betrayed his addiction. His legs were crossed at the knees and he leaned forward, hunched over as if someone were sitting on his shoulders. He was of medium build, and his wiry gray-black hair was combed straight back, accentuating his receding hairline.

Joaquin rounded the corner of the hacienda, running up the hill, careful not to keep the *patrón* waiting. "*Sí, jefe*," he said, standing in front of Belalcazar under the umbrella, panting slightly from the run up the hill. In respect for Belalcazar, he removed his dark glasses, revealing his still badly bruised eyes.

"Sit down. We need to talk," Belalcazar instructed, pointing to the chair next to him at his right. He lit another cigarette, sucking in slowly twice. A cloud of smoke lingered briefly, then disappeared in the breeze. Joaquin noted the honor of being offered a seat. The gesture was not lost on Emilio. With the loss of Manuel, Joaquin was rapidly ascending to the role of heir apparent, or more a long interregnum, until one of the children could take over. "I watched Señor Craig's press conference on CNN. He was very persuasive. He asked the press and the American people to help him find his boy. He boldly challenged the American government, especially the FBI and DEA, to find his son. Emilio taped the press conference. You must study it. Study this man. He is formidable. He is smart, rich, and may have powerful allies in the Congress. New York investment bankers are known to be influential in Washington," he added, pausing to light another cigarette even though the prior cigarette lay only half-consumed in a large ashtray in front of him.

"We must learn all we can about him. I will personally research his past, his daily movements. I will go to New York and take care of him myself," Joaquin said, his voice still raspy from the injury David had inflicted on his throat.

"No. It would be too dangerous. You must disappear for a few months. You are too well known to the American authorities now. We know they have a photo of you. It was taken at the carousel. Our people have managed to keep it from being published. But you can be sure the New York police have seen it. You will stay here and learn the business," he added. He pulled a long drag on his Marlboro and snuffed out the cigarette in the overflowing ashtray. "But you are right that Craig must die. You will call McCormick. Carefully. He and you must be on safe phones. You will tell him to kill David Craig. Quickly."

Aaron McCormick was at his desk at DEA headquarters when David gave his press conference. Alerted to the impromptu event by a call from Robert Harrison in New York, he had canceled his meetings, told his secretary to hold his calls, and flipped on MSNBC. He was impressed with David's media-savvy performance. For a person with no experience in speaking before the press, Craig had handled himself well. *Very well,* thought McCormick.

The press conference would have its intended effect. It was a frightening thought. Public opinion would shift in David's favor. *Those whores in Congress.* If public opinion shifted in favor of Craig, Congress was sure to be close behind. McCormick's real concern was that the parents of the other two American children might catch on to the common thread in all three kidnappings—the magazine pictures of the children. So far he had been successful in diverting attention away from the kidnapping to Craig himself. This press conference could change that. If David Craig were to be perceived by the public as a victim, and the parents of the other children were able to establish the linkage to Belalcazar, the next step could easily be a public demand for action. Real heat would be brought to bear on Belalcazar. The president would send in the marines, in this case with the willing help of the Colombian Army.

McCormick couldn't afford for Belalcazar to go down. He had worked too hard and sacrificed too much to allow his benefactor to destroy himself with this obsession over his dynasty. McCormick acknowledged to himself, and even to Warren, that Belalcazar was a madman. But he bestowed his riches generously on those whose services he needed, not the least of whom was Aaron McCormick. Millions in offshore accounts. *No*, thought McCormick as he shut off the TV with a tap on the remote control. *I can't let him go down. Craig has to be hammered, fast.*

Chapter 8

Eric Randall struggled out of bed after yet another night of inadequate sleep. At five feet, six inches tall and 195 pounds, he was overweight. He never exercised. He smoked heavily—two packs a day—and drank moderately to excessively every night. His 'Nam buddies, as he called them, worried about his health. He had recently had a gall bladder operation that had healed well. But the smoking, drinking, and lack of exercise had taken their toll. On top of that, he had a high-stress job, and felt the loneliness of being a bachelor with no contact with his two kids from his first and only marriage. His was a perfect profile for a heart attack. Every year he and his Vietnam buddies got together for their reunion and skydiving at Happy Jack's Jump Club in the Borrego Desert of California. David, Matthew, Billy, and Frank would fret over his condition and urge him not to make the jumps, to exercise, to go easy on the booze. And, most of all, to quit smoking. His response was to light up, blow smoke in their faces, put on his chute, and yell "Airborne, sir!" He made every jump, although over drinks in the evening near the fireplace he'd acknowledge that he'd landed harder than the others.

This morning Eric had no idea how he was going to find Justin's kidnappers or the bureaucrats who seemed to be setting David up, but he decided that the best way to start was to call in sick with the flu, fix some very strong coffee, read the *Washington Post*, and watch the news. Three doughnuts, four cups of coffee, four cigarettes, and an hour later he had read all there was to read about David in the paper and had heard about all there was to hear for the moment on TV. He rose, went to the bathroom, showered, and returned to the living room to return a call left on his message machine the night before. It was from coast guard Lt. Comdr. Bruce Jetwell.

Jetwell served as the coast guard's representative on the HUMINT committee. *What the hell,* Eric thought, *Bruce called me, so I owe him a call. Convenient place to start, and, so far, the coast guard doesn't seem to be concerned with David.* Eric gave seven staccato taps on his phone with his middle finger and was greeted by a cheerful female voice saying, "Office of Coast Guard Intelligence. How may I direct your call?"

Overly cheery people drive me nuts, Eric griped to himself. *Don't people like that ever just say "Hello"?* "Hi. Good morning to you. Lt. Comdr. Jetwell, please," Eric said with exaggerated glee.

"Yes. One moment while I direct your call," was the annoying response.

"Jetwell here," the lieutenant commander said a moment later as he picked up the phone with a gruff tone of voice more to Eric's liking.

"Bruce. Hi, Eric Randall here. You called me last night at home. Sorry I didn't get back to you, but I got home late. What's up?"

"Nothing real serious, but I thought I'd seek your help in handling Karen York. You saw her the other day during the meeting. I think there's a navy versus coast guard thing with her. She also seems hung up over her being a commander and me being a lieutenant commander. You know what I mean. All over my ass on the illegal immigrants, and damn near everything else. You're the chairman of the committee, so I thought maybe you could help. She's bright as hell, Eric. And she's making me look like an ass. Twisting every word I say. I've only got one more shot at making commander. I can't afford to blow this HUMINT assignment. I thought I'd enlist you to help rein her in before the next meeting."

"I'll try. I'll come up with some excuse to meet with

her in private and see what I can do. You know, God and country and all that. I'll work on her."

"Thanks. I appreciate it."

"Hey. While I've got you on the phone, I got a question for you. Nothing comes free." Eric laughed, trying to sound casual.

"Shoot. What can I do for you?"

"What do you know about the Cali cartel? Is it as broken up and on the rocks as some say, or is it still a force?"

"Funny you ask," Jetwell responded. "You know Jeff Sparks at State? We were talking about the cartels just a couple weeks ago. He described the Cali cartel like the carnival game where you smack a mole back into its hole by slamming it with a hammer only to see it rise up in another hole. He said the Cali cartel had suffered losses but that different people kept popping up to continue the cocaine business. Why do you want to know? It's a bit off your beaten path."

"Just curious. I read about that banker in New York. Papers think he's tied to the Cali cartel, but I thought they were flat on their backs."

"Mess, isn't it? That guy must have fucked over the cartel big-time for them to go after his son like that," Jetwell said. Eric grimaced on the other end of the line. "But Sparks knows this stuff well. He used to be assigned to our embassy in Bogotá. Give him a call. I'm sure he could answer your questions."

"Well, it's not that big a deal. Next time I see him at a committee meeting I'll ask him if I think of it."

Eric hung up the phone and walked to the bathroom to relieve himself of way too much coffee. Returning to his kitchen, he flipped open his frayed address book, found Sparks's office number, and quickly tapped it into the tiny keyboard on his phone.

Sparks had recently joined the HUMINT committee. Eric had seen him at only two meetings, but was impressed with his command of terrorist activities, electronic espionage, the proliferation of nuclear materials by former Soviet scientists and military personnel, and the other topics of concern to the committee. The trick in approaching Sparks, Eric thought, was to go at the topic from an angle oblique enough to allow Sparks to believe that he had come up with the idea.

"Jeff. Hi, this is Eric Randall from the agency. How are you?" Eric said, sounding very official.

"I'm good, Eric. How are you?" Jeff answered guardedly.

"Say, I was on the phone with Bruce Jetwell of the coast guard and we were talking about expanding some of the geographic scope of the committee. Can't talk over the phone because I'm not on a secure line. I'm gonna be at State on another matter at eleven o'clock this morning," he lied. "Thought we could grab a bite to eat, if you're free."

"So happens, my twelve o'clock's been postponed. Love to have lunch at, say, noon. Where shall we meet?"

"I'll come to your office and we can go from there. I know my way around the halls well enough to find you. See you at noon." *Not a bad start,* Eric said to himself, a smile creeping across his face.

Dressing in a conservative blue suit, he cursed himself for the thousandth time as he struggled into his suit pants. He closed the door to his small apartment, went down the stairs, and started up his five-year-old Ford Taurus. It was still in fairly good shape despite a dented fender that he hadn't repaired since he had backed into a truck one night a year earlier after too many scotches. The most distinctive feature about the car was the pungent smell of cigarette smoke. The ashtray was full of ashes and butts, but emptying it would have had little effect. The smell was in the carpet and the fabric of the seats. Eric instinctively began to light a cigarette as he let the car idle for a moment on this cold February morning. He was annoyed with himself for lighting up and stubbed the cigarette out in the overfilled ashtray. *Maybe I can go a whole day without smoking,* he thought. *I'm not going to help David find Justin if I die from a heart attack.* He removed the ashtray, opened the door to the car, walked over to a garbage can, and emptied it. He started to walk back to the car, but stopped, reached into his pocket, and pulled out a nearly full pack of Marlboros, then returned to the garbage and threw away the cigarettes as well. He sighed. *If only I could get rid of my ex-wife like that.*

Eric drove across the Potomac to State Department headquarters. He was feeling rather proud of himself for not smoking in the car. He parked the car in the State Department parking lot after showing his CIA ID and pass to the guard.

"Hi. I'm Eric Randall here to see Mr. Sparks," Eric said with uncharacteristic charm to Sparks's secretary.

Sparks heard Randall's voice and came out to greet him. They engaged in idle chitchat as they walked down the hall and took the elevator up to the eighth-floor dining room. Eric, taking Jeff's lead, declined any wine. He devoured his sourdough roll as if it were the nicotine his body begged for.

"Let me get to the point of why I asked to meet, Jeff," Eric said quietly, his mouth still half-full of bread. "The HUMINT committee's focused on terrorism mostly, as you know. Al Qaeda, bin Laden, Hamas, Hezbollah, the Libyans, the Russian Mafia and start-up operations in countries from the former Soviet Union, the possibility of cyberterrorism; you know the picture. North Korean missiles. But we've had very little focus on South America." He leaned forward and spoke even more softly for emphasis and to make sure that no one could hear him. "We've got no idea, really, of whether drug cartels or others in South America are linked to the terrorists around the world. We haven't really gotten into the question of whether some of their vast amounts of cash finds its way into the pockets of the terrorists."

"I agree," Sparks said readily. "But how does that involve me?"

"Jetwell tells me you were assigned to Bogotá for several years and that you know Colombia like the back of your hand. Now, you don't have to tell me whether you're in special ops here at State. It's really none of my business. But," he said with a lilt and a smile, "it is interesting to me that someone of your caliber and skills was assigned by State to Bogotá instead, of say, Damascus or Beirut."

Sparks said nothing—poker face. "So, tell me how my having been in Colombia is of interest to you."

"Well. I'd like for you to take the lead on the committee to refocus some—not all . . . just some—of our efforts on the drug cartels, and to know whether you think there's any link between the Cali and Medellín cartels and any of the terrorists we're tracking."

"I'd be happy to do that. I can tell you for sure that State would have no problem with my sharing what we know and don't know about the cartels," he said, relieved that this was all he was being asked to do. "Shall I give you an overview now?"

"Please," Eric responded as the waiter served lunch.

Jeff paused for the waiter to leave and then resumed the conversation. "First of all . . ." Twenty minutes later he concluded his lecture.

"Any link between the members of these cartels and terrorists outside Colombia?" Eric asked, not really caring about the answer but eager to continue the fiction that the purpose of this lunch was to discuss such a link.

"No. Not really. Not that we know of. The members of these cartels for the most part have only been interested in the accumulation of money and power within a particular organization that comes with it. So at least we at State haven't seen any evidence of a link with the terrorists we're tracking. But let me finish my first point."

"Of course," Eric said as he watched his lunch partner, pleased that he hadn't aroused suspicions.

"You have to keep in mind that there are formidable groups of drug dealers totally outside of these more famous cartels. Some of these people could harbor ambitions of political power. One in particular comes to mind." He paused to take a bite of his chicken breast.

"Who's that?" Eric asked with genuine interest.

"A relatively new cartel's been formed in the Valle del Cauca, north of Cali. Headed by a man who used to be part of the Cali cartel, but who broke away a number of years ago. He's largely responsible for Cali's current disarray. Incredible ego. He couldn't get along with any of the other members, so he killed many of them and terrorized the rest. Name's Sebastian de Belalcazar." He paused again to take a sip of water.

"Never heard of him," Eric said.

"Not many people in the U.S. have," Sparks responded. "He's a mean son of a bitch. Totally ruthless. Megalomaniac. Has many high-ranking members of the Colombian National Defense Force, the National Police, the politicians, the judges, and others in his pay. He's said to worship the Spanish conquistadors for their breaking the backs of the Indian nations and establishing their empires. In fact, Sebastian de Belalcazar isn't his real name. No one knows his real name. The real Sebastian de Belalcazar was a Spanish conquistador, a lieutenant of Pizarro. While Pizarro was off crushing the Incas in Peru, Belalcazar was crushing the Paez Indians and others in Colombia, or Neuva Granada, as it was then called. The real Belalcazar founded Cali, Popayan, and other cities in the Valle del Cauca region. There's a small village not far from Cali named after him. Rumors are that the modern-day Belalcazar comes from that village and that's where he got the idea to take the conquistador's name. He himself's a mix of Indian and Spanish, but it's the Spanish he admires. He's said to harbor ambitions of establishing his own empire. Now, whether that means a real empire in the physical sense or whether that means a business empire, we don't really know."

"How come nobody's bumped him off?" Eric asked, his mouth half-full of chicken Milanese.

"Oh, they've tried. But he's shrewd. He got to them first." Sparks paused to take another bite.

"Lots of nuts out there. Some around here too," Eric said, gesturing around the room with a smile.

"I haven't seen too many nuts like Belalcazar around this room." Sparks laughed. "Well, maybe some over in Langley," he admitted. "No, this one's real sick. Sort of like a Kim Il Sung, turning the whole of North Korea into a cult designed to worship him. Call him the Great Leader. Couldn't get enough adulation. Like Stalin, Mao, Hitler. All pretty much the same profile in that regard. Well, apparently Belalcazar's cut from the same cloth. His employees are trained to worship him. He's not just their boss. He's their god. Any sign of skepticism of his knowledge or judgment or, worse yet, any sign of disrespect, results in death."

"Nice guy," Eric said sarcastically. "Wonder why nobody's heard of him if he's such a megalomaniac. Seems like he'd seek the limelight."

"Well, he is known in Colombia, just not here. I sent several memoranda around about him, as well as several dozen other drug lords, but no one ever seemed to pick up on Belalcazar."

"What do you mean, 'no one ever seemed to pick up on him'?" Eric pressed, knowing that Sparks had chosen his words deliberately to solicit the question.

"I can't fully explain it. Customs showed some interest. Coast guard seemed interested too, but their interest waned. But the DEA, FBI, and CIA showed no interest whatsoever. For my money, it seems they didn't want to hear about him or the lesser-known organizations. The institutional focus has always been, and remains, on the two principal cartels. Bizarre, if you ask me."

"Well, that's why I'm asking. But getting back to the point, do you see any connection . . . that there's any tangible connection between the drug lords and terrorists—outside Colombia, that is?" Eric asked, continuing the pretext for the lunch.

"Not yet. But I'd be happy to keep an eye out on this and report to the HUMINT committee, if you'd like. We at State would also appreciate any info the Agency can give us on this point. You folks are supposed to be more adept at this sort of thing than us."

"I'd be happy to share whatever I dig up." Eric smiled, meaning what he said. "By the way, don't assume we at the Agency know what the hell we're doing out there. You spec ops types in State do this stuff just as well, if not better. But don't ever tell anyone I said that. I'll deny it under oath."

Half an hour later Eric eased the car past the security barriers of the State Department parking lot and headed toward Langley. *Not a bad start*, he thought, absentmindedly looking for a cigarette.

Chapter 9

Linda Ross sat in her small kitchen staring out the window, lingering over a cup of coffee that had turned cold an hour earlier. Her leave of absence from the college was over and she had returned to work, sort of. On her third day back, she had called in sick, claiming to be down with the flu, struggling with her depression instead. Time does not cure all ills. There are diseases of the heart for which it is not even remotely therapeutic. The passage of four months had not even begun to heal the loss of her only child. Linda wondered if four years might cure her, but then dismissed the thought.

She pored over the articles in the *Washington Post* about the kidnapping of Justin Craig, just as she read every article she could find about missing children. *Too many articles. Too many children.* Her heart went out to a small boy in New York, as if he had been her next-door neighbor. She felt the intense pain she knew his father felt. She had seen part of his press conference. There was no ambiguity for her. No equivocation like that expressed by the *Washington Post*. She pushed herself away from the table slowly to get a hot cup of coffee as she continued to read. As she was half-out of her chair, a line in the article caught her eye. She let out a gasp.

> One day, he was a father who had everything—money, career, and a wonderful son. A bright, blond, curly-haired boy of six, Justin Craig was considered so cute that *New York Next* magazine featured him wearing a new line of clothing just weeks before his

kidnapping. His photos were a sensation. Modeling offers descended upon him, but his father rejected all of them. The father did not want the publicity. Then one day he was gone without a trace, the boy's father left with only the photographs. The father's reputation as a respected banker is suddenly in ruin amid accusations of drug trafficking and money laundering.

Linda Ross fell back into her chair, hyperventilating, furious with herself. Debbie, too, had been featured in a magazine. She, too, had been a sensation. Offers from talent agencies had poured in after the photos appeared in the *Washington Weekly. Why didn't I make that connection?* she wondered. *How many of the thousands of children who are kidnapped each year in America had previously been featured in the press? There are pedophiles out there. Maybe the same one took Debbie and the boy in New York. The photos are a connection,* she reasoned.

She reread the articles about Justin Craig and his controversial father, noting the father's place of business in New York. She hadn't heard of Lanham, Klein & Barnes, but she was sure they would have a listed phone number. Within two minutes she was ringing up the general number of LKB given by the Information operator in New York.

"Lanham, Klein and Barnes," the receptionist responded politely. "How may I direct your call?"

"Mr. David Craig, please," Linda said, her voice filled with anticipation.

"Mr. Craig's calls are being forwarded to a special operator. I'll connect you," the receptionist said as she made the connection before Linda could respond.

"You have reached a dedicated phone line for Mr. David Craig," the monotone tape-recorded voice announced. "If you are a representative of the press, please be advised that Mr. Craig is handling his communications with the press and law-enforcement agencies directly and not through Lanham, Klein and Barnes. If you are a client of the firm, we ask that you call the other partners working on your matters, or if you wish you may call Mr. Jake Barnes through our general number. He will be happy to take care of your needs. Thank you for calling Lanham, Klein and Barnes." The recording ended, leaving Linda with no additional numbers to press, no human to contact.

Linda sat back in her chair, thinking desperately how she might reach David Craig. Reaching the Benson lady, she thought, would be equally difficult. She picked up the phone again and redialed the general number of Lanham, Klein & Barnes, this time asking for Mr. Jake Barnes's secretary.

"I'll connect your call. One moment please," a polite baritone male voice responded.

"This is Margaret. How may I help you?" Jake Barnes's secretary answered, noting that the call had come to her direct line, not to one of her boss's lines.

"I'm sorry. Your receptionist gave me the wrong extension. I'm trying to reach my sister-in-law, who works for Mr. Craig. Could you connect me, please?"

"I'm sorry, but you need to call a special line to reach Mr. Craig," Margaret responded.

"That's the problem. I lost my sister-in-law's direct phone number and I can't get through to her by calling Mr. Craig's line. I'm sure you understand. With all the calls going to him, I can't possibly get through to—"

"I understand," Margaret interrupted. "I'm not supposed to, but I'll put you through."

A few seconds later, the voice of Rosa Hernandez answered. "Norma?" she asked, referring to her only sister-in-law.

"No, my name is Linda Ross. I may have some information helpful to Mr. Craig about his son. Please don't hang up. My daughter was kidnapped—" Linda Ross interjected as fast as she could.

"Leave me a number. He'll reach you," Rosa interrupted quickly, mindful that her phone might be tapped and the call traced.

Rosa quickly noted the number and put down the phone, already thinking she'd have to exercise caution in getting the message to David, and figuring out the most discreet way to contact him.

Linda slumped back in her chair, relieved to have done something, some positive act. She stayed by the phone the rest of the day and into the night, praying that the New York banker would call her.

"No. I'm not gonna go to sleep. I hate this place. And I hate you."

"Justin . . . José," Stephanie Wagner, the American nanny, corrected herself. "You'd better never let your mommy and daddy hear talk like that! After all they've done for you."

"They're not my mommy and daddy. My mommy died. My daddy's in New York. He's gonna come get me. You wait. He's gonna be angry at you."

This one's impossible, she said to herself. "Justin," she said, lowering her voice, composing herself, "I know you're not happy. But let me tell you something: Your new daddy loves you. He really does. He wants you to have lots of fun here. He likes to play with you on his boat."

"I hate his boat. I hate him. He stinks. He smells yucky," Justin screamed, not knowing how to describe the combination of nicotine and coffee breath. "I don't like him and I don't like you. You're . . . you're . . . a . . . a fat idiot," he stammered, then stomped out of the room, only to be picked up by Emilio and taken back into the room. Justin sulked into the corner, his decisive blue eyes zeroing in on Emilio.

"Their father's gonna take 'em fishing now," Emilio informed Stephanie, but not addressing her directly, his eyes scanning the playroom. Jaime and Francisco were playing with a toy garage, lost in fascination with the elevators that took cars and trucks from the ground level to the second level so they could slide them down the ramp back to where they started. Sofia, born Lisa Waldron, seemed content playing by herself with Barbie and Ken dolls. Lidia, known as Debbie to her birth mother, alternated between Sofia, playing the roll of Sleeping

Beauty Barbie, and tending to Justin. She had liked him from the beginning, which was just a few days ago. He had been nice to her. And they both hated Belalcazar, the man they were supposed to call Daddy. Emilio noted that Lidia tried to console Justin—José—by handing him a Ken doll.

"I don't wanna go on any stupid boat with that stinky man. And I don't wanna go with you," Justin shouted. "I wanna go home. You just wait. My daddy's gonna hit you," he threatened Emilio.

"Get the little *bastardo* and the other kids down to the dock now," Emilio whispered to the nanny, the expression on his face leaving no doubt to anyone in the room that he wanted to slap Justin. "Five minutes," he snapped, and left the playroom.

Justin hated his new home. He was confused, lonely, and terrified. He could not understand a word his new "brothers" Francisco and Jaime spoke. Belalcazar and his wife had "adopted" the two Hispanic boys before him. Justin now shared a bedroom with them. Sofia—Lisa Waldron—wasn't nice, he thought, and she was a big tattletale. Anything that one of the other children did was quickly reported to Ms. Stephanie, whom he didn't like either. He disliked Milana Escheverria, Belalcazar's third wife, more. She was very pretty, but he thought her smile looked fake. Most of all, however, he hated Belalcazar. He hated his crusty skin. He hated his smell. His breath. And those dark, menacing eyes. The only person on the island whom he liked was Debbie. She alone seemed to understand him.

As they walked down the steps from the hacienda to the marina, led by Stephanie Wagner, Debbie reached out and held Justin's hand. His first reaction was to withdraw from her grip. But he didn't. He looked at her, his eyes apprehensive, distrusting. She smiled at him. He smiled back.

"I'm from Washington," she whispered. "My mom's a teacher."

"I live in New York. My mommy died when I was little. I live with my dad. He's a banker."

"What's a banker?" she asked, perplexed, twisting her neck and head as if to make the point.

"My daddy says he helps people buy companies."

"Oh."

Rosa thought for a moment, wondering which phone she could use. Making her decision, she took the elevator to the thirty-fifth floor and entered an empty conference room, closing the door behind her. She quickly tapped in David's home number. On the third ring she heard David's voice. "Call me on extension four-nine-three-eight in exactly thirty minutes," she said quickly, and hung up the phone.

Jenny saw the worried look on David's face as he put down the phone on the coffee table in his living room. "Don't say anything," she cautioned, grabbing a notepad and quickly scratching out a message.

Assume your phones are tapped, Jenny wrote quickly, and turned the pad toward David long enough for him to read it. *This place is probably bugged. Let's not signal any moves to the Feds,* she wrote hurriedly. *Who was it on the phone?*

David was silent as he contemplated the enormity of what Jenny was telling him. He was now a virtual prisoner wherever he went. *Rosa,* David scribbled as Jenny moved to sit next to him. *She wants me to call her at the office, but not at her extension.* After a long pause, David added, *Let's get a cab. We'll go to Moynihan's.*

Who's Moynihan? Jenny quickly jotted on the pad.

It's a restaurant on Nineteenth Street and Tenth Avenue. I know the manager. He'll let us use his office.

Jenny nodded and raised her eyebrows as if to say, *Very smart.* David was up against the ropes, but he wasn't down for the count.

David explained his situation to Sean, the restaurant manager. "Sean, I want you to know that—"

"Don't say a thing," Sean interrupted. "I've spent too many evenin's with you to even think you could do what they're sayin'," he intoned in his lilting Irish brogue.

"I'm just terribly sorry about your boy, David. Justin's such a wonderful lad. My wife is also praying for him. Use the phone as long as you want. Stay as long as you want, too. Just happy to help. The office is in the basement. Can I bring you down something to eat?"

"No, thanks," David quickly responded.

"Yes. We need food," Jenny countermanded, not needing a reminder that it was late in the afternoon and they hadn't eaten lunch. "Two salads, two stews. You decide, please. We're going to need our energy." She smiled at the manager. "Thanks."

"The lady's right, David. I'll bring 'em down myself. Make yourselves at home."

Linda Ross had dozed off to sleep on her living room couch, restless despite months of sleep deprivation, her cordless phone at her side as always. The first ring of the phone woke her; the second ignited her. As always, she fantasized that the call was from Debbie, saying that she was on her way home.

"Hello. This is Linda Ross," she answered, her voice shaky.

David breathed deeply, trying to compose himself. He didn't know whether the call would result in a notice of Justin's death, a ransom demand, a press inquiry, or just some psycho having a good time. "This is David Craig. I believe you called," he stated tentatively.

"Oh, yes. Yes," Linda said, excited. "Mr. Craig," she said, gathering her composure, "I called because my daughter, too, was recently kidnapped. Taken from me in a playground here in Washington last October. I know this may not be much, but in reading about you and your boy in the papers I noticed that he was recently featured in a magazine, *New York Next,* I think it said. Well, my little girl, Debbie, also six years old, was featured in a magazine, the *Washington Weekly*. Like your son, just a few weeks before she was taken from me. Like I said, I don't know if this means anything, but there may be some connection."

David was perplexed, pondering what he had just

been told. "I'm not sure, Ms. Ross. This is so out of the blue. Did . . . uh . . . did the kidnapping of your girl have anything to do with drugs?"

"With drugs?" Linda asked, surprised.

"If you've read about my situation, you know the people who kidnapped my boy are part of a Colombian drug cartel. Nobody—least of all me—knows why. I think you know what they're saying about me. I assure you that—"

"You don't need to explain to me, Mr. Craig. I saw you on TV. I crossed the line over to the living dead the day they took my Debbie. I can almost see the pain in your eyes as we speak. You want your boy. I want my girl. I don't know if there is a connection between them. I'm grasping for straws. But maybe . . . just maybe there is."

"Ms. Ross, I'm going to put you on the speaker so my friend, Jenny Benson, can hear you as well. Jenny's—"

"I know who she is," Linda interrupted. "It's okay. Go ahead."

"Okay. Let me fill Jenny in on what we've just discussed." David told Jenny what Linda Ross had just said. Jenny picked up on the conversation immediately, her mind on fire, excited about the possibility of their first real lead.

"Do you have a description of the people who kidnapped your girl?" Jenny asked.

"Of course. I see them in my mind's eye every minute of the day and night. Hispanic, all three of them. Athletic. Well dressed. Clean shaven. One husky, but not fat. A strong man. The two others were of medium build."

"Dear God," Jenny exclaimed.

"Ms. Ross," David said, his voice filled with urgency, "your description is awfully close to describing the three men who attacked Justin and me in Central Park. I presume you saw the photo of the man I killed in front of the Plaza Hotel. Did you recognize him?"

"No. I saw the pictures, but I can't say that the man you killed was the man who took Debbie."

"The FBI and the New York police haven't released

any photos of the other assailants. I'm not sure why. But if we can get you pictures, it may help us. We'll call you back in a little bit," David said, hanging up the phone abruptly.

"David. Thousands of kids get kidnapped each year in the U.S. I guess it's the same in other countries as well. But how many six-year-olds have their pictures in a magazine and then get kidnapped by three Hispanic men whose descriptions sound like the men who attacked you in the park? It's all too strange. Do you think this Ross woman is legit?" Jenny questioned.

"She might be a total fraud. A cruel extortion hoax. Who knows? She might know what they look like because she's one of them. If that's the case, my meeting her could be dangerous," David added.

"Who said anything about *you* meeting her?" Jenny exclaimed.

"I'll go to D.C. and sound her out," David responded. "Jenny, this is all we've got. We can't leave any stone unturned."

"I agree. But you're not going. I am. You've got to stay visible in New York. You head off to D.C. and meet this woman, and you'll draw the paparazzi to her. If she's legit, the press will scare the hell out of her. No, you stay here and serve as a decoy for me."

"Jenny, I can't let you get in harm's way," David said tenderly.

"Don't worry about me. I don't plan to walk into her living room and announce myself. I was thinking of something more like having her walk into Billy Dunn's living room with a tank sitting in his front yard for protection. That make sense to you? Your buddies want to help, David. Lean on them."

"Okay," he answered, acknowledging that she was right.

"Now, how do you plan to get the pictures?" Jenny asked as Sean brought them a bottle of water and two salads.

"Sean," said David, a light flashing in his mind. "I need to ask you a real big favor."

"You want me to go kill the others?" Sean asked, a mischievous smile spreading across his youthful face. Sean was at least forty, but with his lanky build, thick red hair, and boyish good looks, he could easily pass for ten years younger. "I'll get the IRA on 'em, David," he added playfully.

"Not quite, but you're close. Here's what I need you to do. . . ."

Five minutes later, David finished explaining his plan to Sean and asked Sean if he would be willing to help. Sean enthusiastically accepted.

It was Jenny's turn. "Now I have a smaller favor, Sean," Jenny said. "I need to have a hair colorist come here to cut and dye my hair. She—or he—needs to be discreet. It's short notice, so please tell her or him there's a very nice tip—say . . . five hundred dollars plus the regular fee. She—or he—has to be someone who can be trusted to keep this absolutely quiet."

"No problem. Hate to see that hair changed, but I know several good people. They come for the weddin's, you know. For that kind of tip, one of them will come. I got one lady in mind. Real trustworthy."

"Final thing, Sean," David added. "Can you get a case of your best Irish whiskey?"

"Quite a thirst there, Mr. Craig." Sean chuckled.

"It's not for us. I want to send it to a man who helped me out that day in Central Park. EMS paramedic. His name's Marvin Williams. Dr. Horowitz gave me his number and address," David added, scribbling the name and address down for Sean.

Billy and Faith Dunn greeted Jenny with open arms. They were surprised to see that she looked so different from her photos in the press and on TV. She had looked young and beautiful in her long reddish hair and biker jacket. But with her short blond hair, red lipstick, and heavy makeup, she looked like a twenty-three-year-old rock star even in her cashmere coat and pant suit. Despite the hour, they sat and talked about the events of the past week for almost two hours.

Jenny woke at nine-thirty, showered, and put back on her clothes from the day before, surprised that Faith had washed her underwear and had given her silk blouse a light ironing. When she heard Billy's booming voice as Eric entered, she came down the stairs quickly, eager to meet Eric and get to work.

Eric and Billy couldn't help but notice her beauty as she raced down the stairs. Eric was the first to speak. "I won't say that I'm surprised to see how pretty you are, 'cause that'd sound trite, patronizing, and sexist . . . which I admit I am. But I'll say that I am delighted that an old, worn-down guy like David can still attract a beautiful woman. Not for David's sake, mind you. I say that because there's still hope for me."

"You're kind," she said as she gave them both a hug and a kiss. "I know that David thinks the world of you two and your other buddies from Ripcord. He's got nowhere else to turn for help, so I guess we're it," she said expectantly.

"He's got it," said Eric.

Billy nodded in agreement. "Let's talk. Ms. Ross—if that's really her name—shows up in half an hour."

The phone rang at ten-twenty-five, the MPs at the main gate informing Major General Dunn that they had cleared Ms. Ross, as ordered. She was on her way, walking.

"I'm Billy Dunn," he said as he opened the door for Linda Ross and invited her in.

"I'm Linda Ross. I'm here to see Ms. Benson," she stammered, nonplussed by Major General Dunn's stature and the salad of medals across his chest.

"Please come in. I'll introduce you," he added as she stepped into the large living room. "My wife, Faith. Jenny Benson, with whom you've spoken. This is Eric Randall. Eric and I are friends of David Craig. You requested a meeting with David. We're standing in for him."

Jenny studied Linda carefully, not the way attractive women study each other to size up the competition, but the way a gladiator might study another warrior. Friend or foe? Linda was casually dressed in a long down coat, under which she wore a black turtleneck, khaki pants, and running shoes. Her simple jewelry and light makeup complemented her short hair. She had a perfect runner's body, despite the fact that she had not worked out or eaten a decent meal since the day before Debbie was kidnapped. The pain showed in her eyes, and that made Jenny believe Linda's story almost immediately.

Two identical couches faced each other, separated by a glass-covered brass coffee table. Billy motioned for Linda to take a seat at the end of one couch, and Jenny sat at the other end, shifting toward Linda so she could observe her more directly. Eric raised his open palms as if to say, *You called the meeting.* Jenny said nothing, but gave a faint smile to encourage Linda to start.

"My daughter . . . Debbie . . . was kidnapped here in D.C. . . . in a playground at the park last October—right in front of me. You can check out the newspaper articles and the official police files. If I had been as keen an observer of events then as I am now, I might've been able to protect her," she said in a monotone.

"It is a terrible thing, Ms. Ross," Jenny said kindly. "I'm not a parent, but I see the effect Justin's kidnapping is having on David. I've got something to show you. You must promise, though, not to tell anyone. I'm not supposed to have these," she added as she studied Linda Ross's eyes carefully.

"Look. If you've got something that might help me locate my Debbie, I promise not to tell anyone. I'll do anything to find her. Anything."

Eric and Billy studied Linda intensely, their eyes like cutting instruments.

"I've got photos of the two men David killed in Central Park and the one that he wounded. Of course, the pictures of the man David killed near the Plaza hit the press, but the other men's photos weren't released. A friend of ours got them from the police yesterday evening. Why they weren't given to the press is beyond me. But here they are," she said as she handed them to Linda.

Linda looked at the photo of Hector Rojas cooling on a slab at the New York City morgue and studied it carefully for a moment or two. "Sorry. I don't recognize him." She next looked at the photo of Manuel Ramos. She studied this one longer. The picture was also taken by the NYPD at the morgue. "He might be the one who carried Debbie away. I only saw him from the side and rear. It's very hard to say," she said sorrowfully.

"What about this one?" Jenny said, handing Linda the picture of Joaquin Garavito.

Linda gasped as she saw the photo and instantly said, "He's the one who shot the Rollerblader! I'm sure. That's him!" she exclaimed, her voice rising as she slid back into her chair, staring at the photo in amazement. "Do you know anything about this man?" Linda asked. "Do you know his name?"

"As far as we know, no one knows his name. Unless the police, the FBI, and the DEA are lying, they don't know him either. We can try the NYPD," Jenny said, looking to Eric, then to Billy for confirmation, "because at this point I don't trust the FBI or DEA."

"Linda," Billy added, "Jenny's right. Eric and I have known David for thirty-three years, since we were first assigned to the same unit the day we arrived in 'Nam. We served together that whole year. Do you know how David got his Congressional Medal of Honor the papers talk about so much? He got it saving my life. David's not just *like* family to Faith, our children, and me. He *is* family. We know him like we know ourselves. He's as straight an arrow as they come. These charges are wrong. Period."

"I believe you," she said. "And I believe him. But how can the government be so wrong about this?"

"We don't know. But we aim to find out," Eric responded, his voice resolute, his expression determined. Billy and Jenny nodded their heads in agreement.

The four sat in silence. Now it was Linda's turn to study the group. "Mr. Craig's going to try to find his boy, isn't he?" she exclaimed finally. "He's rich and smart and he's got great friends in high places," she added looking around the coffee table. "You're going to help him, aren't you?" She paused for several moments. "If he finds his boy, my girl might be with him. I want to help. Please. I want to be a part of whatever it is that you're going to do."

Jenny looked at Billy. He nodded ever so slightly. Eric did the same.

"For better or worse, Linda, you're in," Billy said, his voice weighted by the magnitude of the task. "Except at this point, we're not sure exactly in what."

Jenny and Linda sat on one couch. Eric sat across from them, a coffee mug in his hand. His feet rested on the coffee table. Faith had left to attend a church meeting that couldn't be canceled.

Eric reached for a pack of cigarettes in his shirt pocket, earning a disapproving frown from Billy. "How many times do I have to ask you to stop smoking?"

Eric slid the pack back into his pocket, blushing slightly with embarrassment.

Jenny and Linda observed the two men with amusement. There was something endearing about the relationship between them. They understood and cared for each other. The bond between them was as strong as a steel cable.

Outwardly the two men were as different as could be. One black, one white. One tall and trim, the other short and overweight. Billy exuded a polished, yet relaxed presence. He rarely lost his temper and was known to be exceptionally fair and reasonable. Just underneath his easygoing demeanor, however, was a highly intelligent man of strong ambition and determination, capable of a sharp elbow beneath the net. As an African-American, he had worked twice as hard as his white counterparts in the army to get to a position that was coveted by all. He was also his own toughest critic; perhaps that was what pushed him to his greatest achievements in his career. Eric was a classic what-you-see-is-what-you-get kind of guy. Frumpy. Rumpled. Very bright. No bullshit. What they shared was an admiration for each other's strengths, and a tolerance of each other's weaknesses.

Eric put his mug down with a clang that made everyone look up. He slouched back into the soft couch, covering his eyes with his hands and pushing his glasses to the top of his balding head in one smooth motion. "We've got to find a way to get inside the FBI and the DEA. They're the ones leading this witch-hunt against David. If only we could get inside their heads," he wished out loud, his eyes still covered.

"I can hack into their files," Jenny announced matter-of-factly.

"What?" Billy asked.

"I can hack into their files," she repeated, a thin smile forming on her lips.

Eric leaned forward, adjusting his glasses as they fell almost in place. "Goddamn," Eric said emphatically. It was actually the second word that came to mind, as he was biting his tongue in deference to the women.

"Jenny," Billy said softly, trying not to sound judgmental, "don't you think we have enough problems? David tells me you're a crackerjack with the computer, but he's already accused of drug trafficking and money laundering. Let Eric do his thing, and you behave," he said half joking, half pleading.

"Well . . ." Jenny said, smiling in mock disappointment and raising her hands up in surrender. "I'll do legitimate research to see what I can find. As in 'legal.' Okay?"

Billy shook his head and dropped the subject. He didn't believe a word she said. He paused, then added, "What the four of us have to do is come up with a plan of battle. But first we have to find out who we attack."

Chapter 10

The UH1H helicopter, better known as a Huey, raced across the waters lying between the west coast of Colombia and the Isla Gorgona. As the shoreline behind them grew more faint, the side gunners, Belalcazar's bodyguards, pulled in their 7.62mm M60 machine guns and slid the side panels shut. Their day's work was done. With only eleven minutes to go before touchdown, according to flight plan, Nick Field permitted himself to relax a little. He sat back in his seat, tension spilling off his shoulders, allowing the muscles of his back to loosen. He watched the evening sun dip into the Pacific, the horizon squeezing the sun's hues from the burning globe, splashing them across an azure sky and a glimmering sea. It was a gigantic painting on an Earth-size canvas.

Field cast a quick glance to his rear, where Sebastian de Belalcazar sat in his plush seat, which had been removed from a commercial airliner's first-class section and installed in the helicopter when the carpeting and paneling had been added. Nick had not liked the additional weight, but Belalcazar was not about to sit on canvas stretched between aluminum piping like a common soldier.

As he approached the compound, Field gazed at the hacienda and its well-manicured lawns. He never ceased to marvel at its beauty. His eyes fixed on the upper helipad, approximately two hundred feet south of the main house, and he cringed. He really didn't like Belalcazar's most recent whim of having the kids and the women at the pad, where they were instructed to wave admiringly as if the helicopter were a chariot bringing a god to earth.

He didn't concern himself with where the children came from. Like others on the island, he never questioned the party line—that they had been abandoned and lovingly adopted by Belalcazar and his sultry new wife to give them a decent home. Having ferried each of them to the island and having seen their drugged and panic-stricken eyes, Field supposed otherwise, but kept it to himself.

The kids; Belalcazar's trophy wife, Milana; and the American nanny, Stephanie, Nick's sometime bunkmate, all stood at the northern edge of the helipad, not quite directly opposite the wind direction, but close enough. All that was Belalcazar's problem anyway. His problem was crosswinds. The helipad, like the main house, was on the top of the crest and was thus buffeted by the strong winds off the Pacific.

Judging from the wind sock, the wind was holding steady. But "steady" winds were a trap. Experienced pilots like Nick Field knew that. One gust of fifteen knots from 230 degrees could easily push the heavy chopper in the direction of the women and the children waiting reverentially for "Papa." Field had raised the point with Stephanie. She, in turn, had raised it with Milana, who had swiftly put an end to such insubordination. Her husband wanted them at that particular spot, where no shrubs obscured their view of the helicopter as it appeared out of the east. End of discussion. Nick was no lover of kids, but he worried how long Belalcazar would make him suffer on the reefs if he dropped the Huey on them. *One of these days I'm gonna plop this damn thing right on top the little buttheads. They're all just trophies for the sick bastard,* he thought angrily as he slowed a few hundred yards off the east side of the island and made his approach.

Field pulled back slightly on the stick and eased the chopper up to 160 feet. The pad was 130 feet above sea level, and Nick wanted to come in just above it and set the chopper down quickly, without jolting his passenger.

As he gained altitude, he saw the sunset on the other side of the island and was rewarded with a bright flash of sunlight in his eyes, despite his dark aviator glasses. Shifting to avoid the glare, he noticed that the bright orange wind sock was more agitated. "Shit," he said out loud, his copilot also aware of the increased danger. They each instinctively sat straighter in their seats, their bodies tense, adrenaline now shooting through their veins.

Field watched the wind sock, his altimeter, and the helipad simultaneously. The orange wind sock was a fifteen-knot sock, designed to be fully extended, perpendicular to the ground, at a steady fifteen knots. It was now flapping wildly, indicating that the wind was stronger than its capacity. He guessed that the gusts were at twenty knots. *A storm must be brewing to the southwest,* he concluded.

The kids were now buffeted by the strong rotor wash of the helicopter, straining to keep their watery eyes open, but not daring to turn their gazes away. The noise scared them, but they stood dutifully. Nick Field inched the Huey slightly to the left to compensate for the increased wind. Then the wind sock relaxed just a bit. He compensated again, bringing the chopper down on the pad only slightly harder than he had intended.

The two bodyguards immediately slid open the right panel, jumped to the tarmac before the blades had even begun to slow, stood at attention, and waited for Belalcazar to step out regally to be greeted by the squinting, teary-eyed kids. It was the turn of Lidia, alias Debbie, to hand a bouquet of fresh-cut flowers to Papa and to be the first to kiss him. Her kiss was perfunctory, the way a reluctant but polite girl might kiss an old family friend. José, né Justin, was next, as he had been instructed. He stepped forward against the wind, standing on his toes as the older man stooped to accept the kiss. Justin closed his eyes and pursed his lips, as if to make sure no part of the older man's parched skin could penetrate his own. Belalcazar saw the look and sensed the child's fear. He turned to the other kids. *The Craig boy is still very frightened,* thought Belalcazar. *Very well. Fear begets respect.*

As Belalcazar bent over to receive Justin's kiss, Nick Field noticed a quick glance from Milana to Ernesto Rojas, Belalcazar's chief of security. Nick had had plenty of affairs in his life, and knew instantly what the eye contact between Milana and Ernesto meant. *God help you two if the patrón sees that,* he thought, and wanted to tell them, but knew better than to get involved.

David hadn't slept at all. He had tired of pacing the floor during the night and couldn't force himself to watch TV, other than a brief look at CNN to see if there was any news about Justin. There wasn't. At precisely three-forty-seven A.M., he recalled, he shut off the television, silencing the droning voice. After two hours of lying in bed, he crawled from under the covers with a curse and wandered from the living room, to the kitchen, to the guest bedroom, back to his bedroom. Every room except Justin's. There were too many things, memories turned into ghosts, in Justin's room. He knew he was nearing his breaking point. He felt it in the constant dryness in his nostrils and throat, the raspiness of his voice. He couldn't breathe. Something in his chest wouldn't let it expand normally. His heart wasn't functioning properly. His cardiovascular system had always been strong, possibly the result of his swimming regimen. Now there was just pain, as if his heart were being slowly ripped from his chest.

His body hurt. His rib cage was still bandaged and painful. His left shoulder muscles throbbed with each movement. The bruises were healing, but not as rapidly as they would if he could make his way to the pool and do some slow laps. He tried to force breakfast down, but couldn't. He struggled through a shower and a shave. He hoped the third cup of coffee he poured for himself would revive him.

The harsh ring of the building's intercom reverberated through the living room, startling him. He picked up the phone, hoping that Jenny was in the lobby. Yet he knew that it wasn't her. Eduardo, the doorman, would have sent her up without calling.

"Mr. Craig. Good morning," Eduardo said. "There's someone here to see you. A Mr. Matthew Rice," he added, reading the name on the business card just handed to him.

"Let me talk to him," David responded suspiciously. Matthew lived in Santa Monica and had been urged by Jenny and Billy to stay put. This person might be a reporter, faking a name to get access, or worse.

"David, it's me, Matthew. Thought you might need some company. I'm coming up." He handed the phone back to the doorman without waiting for David to respond.

Eduardo put his ear to the phone for a second, got David's okay, and gave the visitor instructions.

David waited near the elevator, eager to see his friend. Matthew had simply decided to ignore Jenny, Billy, and the others and come to New York. That was Matthew's way. "Better to ask forgiveness than permission," he was fond of saying.

Matthew Rice, formerly Private First Class Rice, Airborne Ranger, survivor of the siege of Fire Support Base Ripcord, hugged David in the hallway in front of the elevator.

"Look, pal, I know you, Billy, and Jenny didn't want me to get involved in this just yet," Matthew began to explain. "Something about staying away so we don't get dragged into the shit. Billy's playing the curmudgeon role, telling me and Frank to stay on the West Coast and chill, but that's not me, man. You know that. You're in trouble; I'm in trouble. Besides, thought you might like some company," he proclaimed as he picked up his suitcases and followed David down the hall to the apartment. David closed the door behind him.

"Brought my bags," Matthew announced as he scooted the suitcases away from the door with a shove of his foot. "Thought I'd sleep on the couch. Sing you some lullabies." He smiled, the best Hollywood teeth money could buy framed by his olive tan.

"Well, I sure need something to help me sleep," David

said frankly. "And I sure could use the company. . . . God, it's great to see you, Matthew." He gestured to the ceiling to let Matthew know he thought the apartment was bugged. Matthew's wink indicated that he understood. "Do the wolves out front know you're here to see me? Did they hear you talking to Eduardo? Wouldn't want your picture splashed on the front pages. Next thing you know, they'll have you as my male companion, with Jenny as my beard." He feebly tried to laugh.

"No. Some jerk stuck a mike in my face and asked me if I was here to see you. Told him my sister lives here."

"Sit down," David said warmly, gesturing to the couch near the fireplace. "Christ, it's good to see you," David said again, his face animated for the first time in days.

"I'm sorry about Justin. God, I'm sorry. Any news?" Matthew observed that David looked ten years older than the last time he'd seen him.

David shook his head slowly. Large tears broke through David's defenses, skirting his nose, the salty liquid stinging his parched lips. He wiped his face dry and hoped he could contain further tears.

"What's coming down, buddy?" Matthew asked compassionately. "What's all this shit about drugs?"

David pressed his index finger to his lips to silence Matthew. He grabbed a pen and a small notepad and wrote a message. They should speak cryptically, if at all. David scribbled out a note and slid it across the coffee table. *They now know your name,* it read.

Matthew took the pad and pen from David's hands and scribbled his own note. *Couldn't give a rat's ass.* It was one of Matthew's favorite expressions. Matthew looked around the room and silently gave the FBI the finger.

Two FBI agents across the street in a closed van couldn't see him flip the bird, but they knew the conversation had abruptly stopped, which in their experience usually signaled that written notes were being passed. Few people were able to maintain one conversation while writing another one. They had Matthew's name. They also had a clear photo of him as he got out of his cab in front of David's building. The FBI's powerful computers in the basement of the Hoover Building in Washington were already spitting out the names and photos of every Matthew Rice on file. There were fifty-four Matthew Rices in the FBI data banks. Of them, thirteen had criminal records, three for drug-related offenses. Within minutes the computers would print all this out, together with matched photographs, addresses, and other vitals. But never having been arrested, Ripcord's Matthew Rice was off the radar screens of law-enforcement agencies around the country, like the vast majority of Americans.

"How long can you stay?" David asked, feeling that the question was harmless enough for the FBI to hear. The expression on his face told Matthew at once that David hoped it would be a long time.

"I'll stay as long as you need me. The business is pretty much on autopilot. Got a young man helping me these days. He can do the follow-up on my accounts. I'm here for the duration," he said with a smile as he reached across the coffee table to gently slap David's knee.

"Thanks," David said simply. "Thanks for coming. You look like you could use a shower and a shave," he said as he rose from the couch and reached for the suitcases. "Christ. What's in here?" David exclaimed as he picked up the heavy cases, nearly pulling his back out. "You must have paid a small fortune in overweight baggage for the plane trip."

"I drove," Matthew whispered with a smile, indicating to David with a wave of his hand that the topic of driving was not to be pursued out loud. "Picked up some things along the way for you. Just got you some gifts I thought you could use," Matthew added, gesturing toward the ceiling and placing his index finger over his lips to tell David that he didn't want others to hear. The two men walked to the guest room down the hall past Justin's room. David placed the heavy suitcases on the bed and Matthew opened them. He watched with pride and amusement as David stared silently at the small arsenal. A disassembled M16 assault rifle, two 9mm automatic pistols, a MAC-10 machine pistol, and enough ammo magazines for each weapon to hold off an invasion. "Thought you might need these to entertain any guests who might stop by," Matthew said, grinning broadly and displaying his flawless white teeth.

Now it made sense to David. Matthew had driven across the country because he never could have transported the weapons on an airplane. His friend was concerned that the assassins might come back to get him in his apartment. Then the thought hit him: Matthew had set aside his business and taken the risk of multiple felony convictions for the purchase and transportation of illegal weapons across the continent. He feared for David's life, and would fight side by side if the enemy came.

Matthew sensed that David didn't know what to do next, so he gently hugged him for a few seconds, patting him on the back. "Oh, by the way, your doorman gave me something to give to you."

He reached into his coat pocket and pulled out a plain white envelope. David grabbed the envelope like a starving predator snatching his first meal in weeks. Momentarily embarrassed by his own behavior, David mumbled an apology. He quickly opened it, his heart pounding in his ears. Was it a clue? A ransom note?

Dear Mr. Craig:

My name is Sidney Waldron. Last week, the night before your son was kidnapped, my daughter, Lisa, was taken from me while we shopped at the local Grand Union. I know that many people probably tell you that they know how you feel and express their condolences. They, of course, cannot truly know how you feel. I, however, do. Please accept my most sincere sympathies. I never saw the kidnappers who took my daughter, but some bystanders thought that they might have been Hispanic. I know from the press coverage that some of the men who took your boy were also Hispanic. That may just be a coincidence.

But there is one thing in common with the kidnapping of Lisa and your boy that is certain. My wife read in the paper that your boy's pictures were in *New York Next* magazine several weeks before his abduction. Lisa's photos were in the *Suburban Times* two months before her disappearance. The police told us that they didn't believe the photo shoots were related to the kidnapping. They said many children are in magazines and nothing happens to them. Other children are kidnapped who weren't pictured in the press. But my wife and I believe that there may be a connection. Both your son and our daughter are beautiful. We believe that perhaps someone, some very evil person, saw the photos of these two wonderful children and then stole them from us.

This may lead nowhere, but we must explore this with you. My wife and I are in Manhattan today. Our cell phone number is listed at the bottom of the note. Please call us when you get this message. We can come to your home, if that is easier for you. You can reach us on that cell number at any time, day or night.

Please do not think this is a prank. No one who has ever lost a child could joke about it. Please call.

Sincerely,

Sidney Waldron

David looked up and said, "Matthew, read this." David handed the letter to Matthew. Picking up the phone, he rapidly punched in Sidney Waldron's cell number. "Mr. Waldron. This is David Craig. I got your message. Can you please come to my home now? Thank you," he said, hanging up, not giving a damn that the FBI was listening to his conversation.

Two FBI agents sitting in the Triple C Custom Cabinets Corporation van on Seventy-second Street straightened up as they heard the phone conversation.

"Who's Waldron?" one asked the other.

"No clue, but listen up and we're gonna find out." During the course of the next two hours they recorded the entire conversation between the Waldrons, Craig, and Rice.

"Sounds pretty convincing," one agent said to the other. He took his headphones off and began to massage his sore ears. "Listening to them, it's hard to imagine Craig's guilty, unless he knows he's being bugged and this is all for show."

"The whole thing is weird, if you ask me," the shorter man replied as he, too, removed his headphones. "Something about him just doesn't fit the pattern."

"Oh, well, that's for the higher-ups. Our job is to report the facts and let our bosses sift through them."

"Yeah. I'll get this to Harrison right away."

Eric Randall sat at his desk and looked at the stack of phone messages. He separated the urgent from the merely politic into two piles. He spent a little over an hour returning the urgent messages and, growing impatient, another half hour making calls dictated by protocol, which was never his strong suit. He began to place another call, grumbled to himself, put down the receiver, and began scratching out notes on a pad.

Of the members of the HUMINT committee, Eric had already spoken to Jetwell at the coast guard, Sparks at State, and Patterson at the FBI. Doris Shaw from the NSA and Karen York from the navy had also willingly provided whatever information they had, but they added little to Eric's real inquiry. Wang at the army had furnished a great deal of economic information about the cartels and drug sales, which was of no use to Eric, and then had pointed him to Terry O'Neal at the DEA, with whom Eric had made a lunch appointment for later that day. As Eric scribbled on his pad, he hoped O'Neal could help him, because he was running out of people to contact, and also running out of time.

Terry O'Neal was sitting back in the booth when Eric arrived, ten minutes late, slightly wrinkled, apologetic. He dropped his reading glasses on the floor as he picked up the menu, drawing a laugh from the good-natured O'Neal. In the nineteen months O'Neal had served as the DEA's representative on the HUMINT committee, O'Neal and Randall had been friendly but had never socialized. O'Neal was now curious as to what had motivated Eric to buy him lunch. Eric went through the same routine he had with the others, feigning interest in a possible connection between terrorists and the drug lords, but diverting attention to the latter at the earliest opportunity.

"But I don't get it," Eric persisted after O'Neal had told him much of what he had to say. "What you seem to be saying is that the DEA comes across a new drug lord who's so powerful that he's killing off the leaders of his old cartel. Guy's so rich and power-hungry that he might be the principal moneyman behind the FARC's insurgency," he added for emphasis, referring to the Spanish acronym for the Revolutionary Armed Forces of Colombia, a rebel group controlling a third of the country, "and you and others within the DEA are being told that he's a nothing. Concentrate on Cali and Medellín. It doesn't make sense."

"Yeah . . . basically," O'Neal responded as he covered his mouth with his fist to suppress a burp. "The Medellín guys are flat out on their asses. Those whom the elite Army Search Block didn't eliminate have been killed by the Cali cartel or by other Medellín members. Belalcazar got most of those who remained. Same for the Cali cartel. The Search Block got some. Rival factions within the cartel itself killed off some, and Belalcazar pretty much slaughtered the rest."

Eric took his elbows off the table and sat back to let the waitress place a cup of coffee in front of him. "Do you believe he has linked up with Marulanda and is financing him?" Eric asked, referring to the leader of the FARC.

"Some signs of it, but no proof. Though I suspect he is. If not, it would be inconsistent with what we know of his personality." O'Neal paused to take a sip of coffee. "Megalomaniac. Said to fashion himself as a modern-day conquistador."

"What kind of person is he? Is he married? Kids in line to take over the business?" Eric asked nonchalantly.

"No kids. First two wives were infertile. At least that's the macho spin. He's probably impotent."

"Kind of like Henry the Eighth, huh?" Eric interjected with a smile. "Of course, we all know that Henry was the problem. Bad sperm, low count, poor morphology, and all that stuff," Eric added.

"Yeah, probably right," O'Neal agreed, not mentioning that he and his wife were having trouble getting pregnant and that he too knew all the buzzwords from the fertility doctors. "But apparently Belalcazar's got a hot new wife. Time will tell."

"By the way," Eric continued as he penned in the tip and signed the credit card slip, "how come you know so much about this guy?"

"Hell, I've written at least two dozen reports about him and many other Colombian, Peruvian, and Mexican drug lords. He's just one of them. But he happens to be a survivor and a dominant player. Shit, I bet I've used up a good part of the storage capacity on the DEA's computers writing these research reports that go nowhere. And I'm not the only one within the DEA to have done the same and gotten the same result."

Eric nodded sympathetically, trying to appear nonchalant.

"Incidentally," O'Neal began to ask as they stepped into the parking lot and the February wind began to bite at them, "I thought you wanted to talk about the drug lords and the Middle Eastern terrorists?"

"Hey, that's okay. We'll do it another time," Eric responded, now distracted as he pondered what all of this could mean and what any of it had to do with the kidnapping of David's son.

Gerald Warren of the CIA sat on the bench opposite Aaron McCormick in a booth in the back of the restaurant. Something was wrong, Warren sensed immediately. "What's up, Aaron?" Warren asked nervously.

"Harrison and Evans tell me agents from the Bureau recorded a conversation in Craig's home between Craig and the parents of the Stamford girl. Can't remember her name. Not important. Craig told the girl's parents—the Waldrons . . . that's it . . . Waldrons," he corrected himself, "that he's been in touch with the Ross woman. They're focusing on the magazine pictures. The link to Coffee is about to blow," he declared. "According to the tapes, Craig wants the Waldrons and Ross to go public with this. Hold another goddamn press conference."

"What are you . . . er . . . we . . . going to do about it?" Warren asked, not really wanting to know the answer.

"I'll take care of Craig," McCormick said without skipping a beat, his voice as cold as ice. "You need to go see Coffee. You need to talk to him. Tell him that you and I want him to stop the kidnapping thing. Can't have that conversation over the phone. Make it clear to him that we don't give a shit about the kids. That's his personal business. But he's got to know that if Craig, the Waldrons, or Ross convince the public that some Colombian drug lord is stealing their six-year-olds and make the connection to Coffee, America will invade his little island paradise."

As McCormick left the restaurant, he saw Robert Harrison pacing by McCormick's car.

"You wanted to see me?" asked Harrison, towering over the smaller man from the DEA.

"This Craig fellow?" McCormick asked as he casually opened his door.

"Yes?" Harrison asked simply.

"Kill him. Do it fast. Make it look like he went after you. Twenty-four hours. No more."

Chapter 11

At two o'clock the following day, the Waldrons, Linda Ross, and David Craig stepped out of David's apartment building, Eduardo holding the door for them as their eyes adjusted to the bright sun on the blustery February afternoon. David guessed there were thirty members of the press milling about. He took a deep breath to steady his nerves and let it out slowly.

"Ladies and gentlemen," David began, beginning with the script he had prepared, "we would like to thank you for coming out on this cold afternoon." The wind blew his hair over his forehead. "I would like to introduce to you Sid and Anne Waldron of Stamford, Connecticut, and Ms. Linda Ross of Washington, D.C. The four of us have come together because we are bound by a terrible common experience. We are all the parents of kidnapped children. The night before my son was taken from me, Sidney and Anne's daughter, Lisa, was kidnapped in Stamford while she and her father were shopping at a grocery store. Linda's daughter, Debbie, was kidnapped last October in Washington while she played in front of her mother in a playground. As you know, my boy, Justin, was kidnapped seven days ago in front of the Plaza Hotel.

"These are not missing children. They're not runaways. These children were violently taken by dangerous men. We can't tell you that the men who kidnapped my boy are the same as those who kidnapped Lisa Waldron. But we can with absolute certainty tell you that the men who kidnapped Debbie Ross are the same men who kidnapped my son." David paused.

"I obtained photographs of the man who assaulted me at the carousel in Central Park who later escaped. Ms. Ross has identified him as the killer who murdered a young man in a playground while her daughter was being kidnapped." He paused again to let it sink in. "The killer identified by Ms. Ross and the man that I fought in front of the Plaza Hotel also fit the description given by several eyewitnesses of the men who wrenched Lisa Waldron from her family.

"What, you may ask, do these three children or these parents have in common that would cause these young children to be kidnapped by the same terrible villains?" David took a long breath, letting the question hang. He brushed his hair back from his forehead and continued, cameras clicking. "The fact is that as we stand here before you today, we do not know the answer. But we can tell you that shortly before they were kidnapped, each of our children were featured in photographic spreads in prominent, respected magazines. In Lisa Waldron's case it was *Suburban Times*. Debbie Ross was featured in the *Washington Weekly*. Justin was in *New York Next*. Copies of these magazine articles and the photos will be made available for all of you.

"In each case," David continued, "within weeks of the publication of the magazines, our children were violently taken from us. We don't know why," he said, his voice now unsteady and growing softer. "We simply don't know why. It's as if some terrible person were 'shopping' for beautiful children out of a macabre catalog. From the law-enforcement agencies, we know that these people are somehow tied to the drug gangs. In the case of the kidnapping of my son, we have been told that the assailants are known to be associated with Colombian drug organizations.

"Many of you in the press have latched onto the drug connection, and have presumed without a shred of evidence that I must have been involved in the drug traffic . . . that Justin's kidnapping was an act of revenge against me. Nothing could be farther from the truth. I reiterate that I have never had anything whatsoever to do with drugs and I never will. But . . . if you don't believe me, believe the Waldrons and Ms. Ross. They have no connection to the drug trade, and yet in Debbie Ross's case we know that the same people took her daughter." David had to stop. The emotions swelling within him were surfacing. Sid Waldron reached out to hold his left elbow to show support.

David breathed deeply, deciding that it was pointless to hide his efforts to regain composure. "We do not know who these terrible people are. We don't know why they've done this. We only know that we want our children back." He clenched his jaw and squinted. Linda Ross sobbed openly, and Anne Waldron's head involuntarily sank against her husband's shoulder. "We won't rest until we find our children. We will hunt these men down and we will get our children back. We ask for the help of all Americans. If you see any of our children, please, please notify the nearest law-enforcement agency. Please help us. We want our children back."

"Hey, partner. Pretty good stuff, don't ya think?" one FBI agent said to the other inside the van. "I gotta say they came across pretty damn credible."

"Yeah. I know . . . but we got something happenin' upstairs, chief," the agent said hurriedly. "Our Mr. Craig is going out for dinner tonight. The others are going back to Stamford and D.C. Looks like they're leaving now."

"Okay. Rock 'n' roll. Better let Harrison know on a real-time basis. He's on his way up from D.C. Said we can reach him on his cell phone," the senior agent ordered.

"Will do." He tapped in the number of Harrison's cell phone. Harrison answered instantly, listening intensely. The agent was silent for a few moments as he digested Harrison's instructions. "Harrison wants a man posted at all exits of Craig's building, service doors included," he said. "When Craig goes out to dinner, he's to be followed. Harrison will arrive in the city at about five o'clock and will be part of the stakeout team tonight."

"Fuck me big-time! This is a strange one," the senior

agent said as much to himself as his fellow agent. "A deputy assistant director participating in a stakeout like one of us grunts. All right." He shrugged. "Let's get Foster over to watch the service entrance 'round back. He's the youngest agent on duty. Let him stand out in the cold."

At six-fifteen sharp, Marvin Williams maneuvered the heavy EMS vehicle west onto Seventy-third Street through sluggish traffic and pulled in front of the service entrance of the large prewar building. David and Matthew walked briskly to the boxy red-and-white ambulance, the rear doors swung open and quickly closed behind them, and the vehicle pulled away without ever having fully come to a stop. David was determined to spend the evening dining with his guests, and the press was definitely not invited. While he was successful in avoiding the press, he was less fortunate with the FBI. Marvin's ambulance blocked the view of Special Agent Foster, who stood shivering across the street in the shadows, but the activity did not go unnoticed.

"Foster here," he reported into the mouthpiece. "EMS Vehicle Number two-fifty-seven heading west on Seventy-third Street has just picked up one or more persons. Cannot . . . repeat . . . cannot verify who got into the vehicle."

"Roger that," responded one of the agents in the van. "Stay put. We'll get a car to follow the van. Good work. Stay warm."

"Good evening, Mr. Craig. Great to see you again," Marvin Williams greeted David as he drove down Broadway. "You sure look better now than you did on the way to Bellevue that day."

"Thanks, Marvin. It's good to finally meet you, too," David responded. "Thanks for the help. Ben Horowitz says you might have saved my life. Maybe I'll get to thank you properly over dinner without all the press watching what sticks to our teeth and how many times we use the john. And please call me David."

"Then David it is. And thanks for the booze. That was mighty nice. Smooth stuff. I generally go for Jim Beam. Jameson's a bit large for my budget."

"Meet Matthew Rice," David added belatedly. "Matthew and I were in the army together. He's one of my oldest and dearest friends. Came here to New York to help me through all this."

Mathew said, "Honored to meet you, Marvin. I can never thank you enough for what you did for my buddy here."

"Hey, it's my job, man," Marvin responded, giving Matthew a big smile as he maneuvered through traffic. "By the way," he added, "my turn to apologize for the lack of intros. This here," he said, motioning to the man who had opened the rear doors for them, "is my brother-in-law, Michael. He's going to watch this baby while we eat," he explained.

Twenty minutes later they arrived at Moynihan's. It was a gloomy New York winter night, the windchill lowering the temperature to single digits. The chill made the mellow golden light filtering through the windows of the Irish country–style inn all the more inviting.

"Good evening, David," Sean greeted him in his lilting Irish brogue, arms warmly extended. "And good evening to you, gentlemen." He shook each of their hands. "When you get in, go quickly to your left, through the first dining room and past the sliding doors. That's your room for the evening. The drapes and blinds are drawn on the windows. You'll be completely private here," he assured them. "Anyway, it's only six-forty. The crowd won't come in for another hour or so."

The brass sconces and warm fire sent light caroming off highly polished copper pots and an impressive collection of Waterford crystal, undulating light and shadows, warming icy bones. The flickering light from the large hearth in the rear danced around the room.

They walked through the large room to the left of the bar area. An elderly couple sitting in a booth toward the back of the room paid no attention to them. An attractive young waitress gulping down dinner before the start of an evening's work noticed Matthew. She would be assigned to the private party, and the thought of serving the strikingly handsome man gave her a rush. Matthew, surveying the room for signs of FBI plants, caught her looking him up and down. He unconsciously placed his right hand inside his jacket. Feeling the Sig Sauer 9mm comforted him.

"Sir, we have a confirm that the suspect was in the EMS vehicle. We got a visual on him at eighteen-forty hours. He, Rice, and the driver of the vehicle went into Moynihan's on Nineteenth Street and Tenth Avenue," the tailing FBI agent reported mechanically from the dark blue Caprice that had followed the EMS vehicle to the restaurant.

"Roger that," the control agent responded. "You're to stay put. Repeat. Stay put. Deputy Assistant Director Harrison is on his way. He has taken direct charge of the operation. You're to follow his instructions. Out," the control agent ordered curtly.

Dr. Ben Horowitz, chief of surgery at Bellevue Hospital, arrived a few minutes after the others.

"Ben," said David, giving him a hug. "Thanks for coming. This is my friend Matthew Rice." Matthew shook hands affectionately with the doctor he knew had befriended David. "You already know Marvin."

"Yes," Ben Horowitz responded with a wry smile. "Marvin and I see entirely too much of each other." He shook Marvin's hand.

"Say, we're already into our first drink," said David. "You've got some catch-up ball to play. What's your pleasure?"

"I'm on good behavior tonight. I've got surgery in the morning. But I will have a nice sherry if you've got one," he said to the cute young waitress.

"Yes, sir, will do. I'll bring it straightaway," she said as she curtsied and smiled, her eyes on Matthew.

"Matthew, I don't know how you do it," David said. "You're only two years younger than me, and you've got this girl young enough to be your daughter flirting with you. Mind your manners, though. She's probably Sean's niece. He'll cut your balls off if you allow this to go beyond flirting." David laughed. Matthew and Ben Horowitz noted the laugh, glad to see David taking advantage of the evening's brief diversion. Everyone in the room studiously avoided any discussion of Justin and the recent events. They ordered another round of drinks, Matthew paying particular attention to the young waitress's rear as she left the room.

Harrison and Evans parked their car directly behind the blue Caprice on Tenth Avenue across from the restaurant. The two FBI agents had kept the engine running. The agent sitting behind the wheel saw Harrison in the side-view mirror and rolled his window down halfway as Harrison got out of the car. In deference to Harrison's rank, he decided that he had better get out of the car. He started to open the door, but Harrison, walking quickly, blocked it from opening.

"No need to get out in the cold. Please stay seated," Harrison stated firmly as he put on a pair of black leather gloves. "You the only agents here?" he inquired as he glanced up and down Tenth Avenue.

"Yes, sir," the agent responded, mentally noting in the rearview mirror that the DEA agent, whose name he didn't know, was oddly standing behind the Caprice, to the right, as if he expected trouble from him and his partner.

"Good," Harrison replied simply as he slid his hand into his suit jacket and quickly removed an automatic from his pocket. The silencer at the end of the long barrel was no more than three inches from the agent's temple when Harrison gently squeezed. The man's eyes went wide. With a hideous spit from the silencer, the bullet blew out the back of his head. The agent sitting on the passenger side had no time to react as Harrison placed two rounds into his chest. The first round tore through his heart, plowed a tunnel through his right lung, and exited below the shoulder blade, lodging in the door. The second round entered the left side of the man's chest with a *pap,* hitting a rib and sending bone and metal fragments spiraling throughout his torso.

Harrison stood erect, glanced over to Evans, and nodded, signaling that the job had been done. Cars raced by on Tenth Avenue, but there were no pedestrians on this frigid night.

Harrison placed the weapon back into his coat pocket, next to another 9mm in his holster. He opened the door, careful not to touch the dead driver for fear of leaving clothing fragments, reached in, and pressed the automatic window control to roll the window back up. He then turned the ignition off, left the keys in place, closed the door, and stepped back. It was a very professional hit. Later, forensic analysts at the FBI would conclude that the shots were delivered through an open door and would not even guess that the window had been rolled up after the slayings. Harrison smiled to himself. No witnesses. No one to report later that he and Evans had gone into the restaurant not to arrest but to assassinate. Harrison withdrew his weapon and detached the silencer, keeping his gloves on to avoid any prints. As he turned to face Evans he tossed the heavy piece of metal down a storm drain with a loud *chink-a-chink* until it and its sound disappeared in the netherworld.

The attractive young waitress placed the drinks around the table and quickly exited the private room, casting one more glance at Matthew before she slid the double doors closed behind her.

"No need to close them," Matthew said with his most seductive smile spreading across his tanned face. "I need to find the men's room. Perhaps you can point the way?"

"Certainly," the waitress responded. "I'll point you in the right direction, and then I'll get everyone their menus."

Matthew started to close the doors behind him, but Sean stopped him gently. "I'll get that," the manager said. "I want to tell you our specials for the evening. You'll be right back?"

"Just going for a pit stop," Matthew responded somewhat sheepishly. He closely followed the young woman toward the rear of the dining room.

Evans opened the heavy wooden door to the quaint Irish restaurant, his eyes darting in all directions to get the lay of the land. Harrison closed the door behind him. There were a few patrons at the bar, but no one paid attention as the two men entered. The bartender was crouching behind the bar, searching for something in a cabinet. Waitresses milled about, preparing tables for the rush that was sure to start soon.

"May I help you, gentlemen?" the smiling hostess asked, her brogue exaggerated for effect. "My! You are brave to be out in the cold without overcoats."

"We're here to join the Craig party," Evans said without a smile.

"Is he expecting you, sir?" she responded, perplexed. She hadn't prepared for two extra dinner guests in the private party.

Sensing her concern, Harrison said, "We can't stay long. We're just going to have a quick drink. David's our close personal friend from the office," he explained.

"Very well. This way, please," she answered with a smile, relieved that she hadn't made a mistake.

Evans and Harrison surveyed all around as they entered the front dining room. The double sliding doors to the private space were directly ahead. They noticed an elderly couple in a booth. They also noticed a bald, rotund man wedged into another booth eagerly attacking what appeared to be a large plate of beef stew. A tall, trim, dark-complected man in a suit was following a waitress toward the rear of the restaurant.

Evans and Harrison slid their hands into their unbuttoned suit jackets as they made their way across the room. Their Beretta 9mm automatics' safety selector switches had already been set in the fire mode.

There was something about the sound of their shoes on the wooden planks that arrested Matthew's attention. The sound was too purposeful, the heels of the heavy wing tips echoing like jackboots. Men in a hurry. *Soldiers!* An alarm sounded within him. He instinctively reached for his weapon as he twisted toward the threat.

The two government agents had already withdrawn their automatics, holding them against their chests to conceal them. As the hostess slid the doors to the private room open, Evans noticed a movement to his right and rear. From the corner of his eye, he saw Matthew rotate in their direction, but couldn't see the gun coming out of Matthew's holster. Evans spun slowly, gripping his weapon firmly.

"VC!" Matthew roared to David. His left hand gripped his right wrist as he dropped automatically to one knee. Standing no more than twenty feet apart, Evans and Rice fired. Evans's shot missed Matthew's head by an inch, but slammed into the young waitress's spinal column in the small of her back, severing it instantly. She was thrown off her feet into the booth where the elderly couple were finishing their desserts.

Matthew fired a split second later. His aim was true. The impact of the bullet lifted Evans off his feet as it drilled a hole the size of a dime through his sternum and blew a wound out of his back the size of a baseball. He fell hard against the wall, slamming into the hostess.

Harrison spun toward a now-kneeling Matthew and fired. His shot clipped the wood table, splintering the wood into Matthew's eyes, blinding him as he dove to his right, landing hard on the chair next to him. The hostess screamed and began to run, knocking into Harrison. He placed the barrel of the automatic against her belly and squeezed, tossing her aside like a used towel.

Increasingly desperate, Harrison pushed his way into the private dining room, stumbling over the dying hostess. He took a wild shot at David, who was coming around the long table straight for him with nothing but a table knife in his hand. Sean ran frantically toward the open doors. He was stopped by the bullet meant for David, which hit him full in the chest. Oddly, he didn't immediately fall back or forward. The momentum of his forward movement checked the force of the bullet's impact. He stood, statuelike, for a split second, mouth open, took one step forward, then fell flat on his face.

Harrison tried to shoot once more, but David was on top of him, going for his throat with the knife. His other hand pushed Harrison's wrist aside just as Harrison pressed the gun to David's chest and squeezed the trigger. The bullet whizzed past Marvin Williams's nose, striking Dr. Horowitz above the ear. He was dead before his knees hit the floor.

David tried to slam his right knee into the more powerful Harrison, but the maneuver left his right leg in the air, and Harrison deflected the blow by knocking David's left leg from under him with a simple judo move. David fell to the floor, his eyes fixed on the assailant's weapon. He watched in horror as Harrison aimed at his head to finish off the kill. Then David heard three very loud pops, and Harrison's chest exploded. The blood and gore spattered on David as Harrison fell on him.

Matthew Rice's mission in coming to New York was to protect his fellow Ranger. He had not failed.

"You all right?" Matthew screamed at David as he pushed the dead man off him. David nodded as he struggled to rise to his feet. "Who are these people?" Matthew yelled.

"Who's hit? Who . . ." David stammered as he saw Sean facedown on the floor, his back a bloody pulp. The hostess moaned as the life drained from her. "Doc. Can you get to this woman?" David mumbled to Ben Horowitz, not realizing that the doctor was no longer of this world.

"David, we gotta get out of here," Matthew ordered. "Come on!" he urged as he grabbed David under the arm and helped him up.

David looked around the private dining room in disbelief, leaning against the door frame for support. His entire body felt like it was convulsing. It was all he could do to force himself erect. His eyes welled up with tears when he saw Ben Horowitz sitting on the backs of his feet, pressed against the wall, a stream of blood leading down the green-and-white wallpaper, stopping where his head had come to rest. Marvin Williams was struggling to his feet. David turned to survey the public dining room. The young waitress was lying on the table where the two elderly patrons huddled, crying uncontrollably.

David looked down at the body of the first assassin Matthew had killed. He had landed on his back, leaving his unbuttoned jacket lying open. Matthew and David saw it at the same time and froze. Patrick Evans's DEA ID badge stood out like a beacon in the dimly lit room. David turned to his left and gazed down on the second assassin lying facedown on the floor, the back of the killer's suit jacket torn in three neat circles the size of dimes. David dropped to his knees and turned the large man over. Reaching into his pocket, he pulled out a leather folder containing an FBI badge. Robert Harrison.

"David, Matthew's right," Marvin said as he examined the hostess to see if there was any life left. "We gotta get the fuck out of Dodge—now. I mean *now*!" Marvin yelled in terror. "These bastards, badges or not, didn't come in here to make an arrest. They came to kill you . . . and us."

David was stunned by all the murder victims. "Where do we go? We've got nowhere to go," he mumbled.

"Follow me," Williams said as he gently closed the hostess's eyes and stood up. "I know where."

The bar area was empty. The beer- and whiskey-drinking patrons, as well as the bartenders and waitresses, had bolted for the back door at the opening of the salvo. As they reached the front door, David turned to gaze at the war zone behind them. "A trail of death," David muttered to himself. "Everywhere I go. Clear away from me," he warned Matthew and Marvin, his voice firmer. "Marvin, you're not involved in this. You did nothing wrong. Call nine-one-one and get your medics over here to help these people. Stay away from me."

"Ain't no way to help these people. They're dead. You haven't done anything wrong either. Let's get the hell outta here and make tracks."

David shot a glance at Matthew as if to urge him to leave and protect himself.

"Let's just get the fuck outta here . . . now," Matthew snapped as he opened the door and stepped into the cold night air.

"Where are we going?"

"Just get in. I'll figure this out as we go," Marvin answered as he picked up his pace toward the EMS van.

Chapter 12

Marvin had formulated his plan as they made their way out of Manhattan and through the Lincoln Tunnel. David and Matthew at first were opposed, since it was too risky to Marvin. But he persisted.

Marvin's brother-in-law maneuvered the EMS vehicle into the tight driveway on a side street off Kennedy Boulevard in Jersey City. Once inside the small apartment on the ground floor, David and Matthew washed the blood off themselves as best they could. Marvin explained the circumstances to his sister. She had had her run-ins with the law in her wilder days and was no fan of the police, but it took some talking to get her over the multiple-murder rap the two white guys messing up her bathroom were facing.

Matthew and David returned to the small living room. "Can I use your phone?" Matthew asked blandly, as if he wanted to order in a pizza.

"So here's the plan," Marvin continued, nodding to Matthew, somewhat bewildered by his request. "You take my sister's car to Baltimore. Leave it with my mom. That'll get you out of the New York area, unless they got roadblocks set up on the turnpike. If you move fast enough, there probably won't be any roadblocks and you'll be in Baltimore by midnight. That's the best I can do for you. From there, you're on your own. I suggest you find out who your real friends are and go to them for help."

David was about to respond when Matthew interjected. He had been standing in the doorway listening to Marvin after he had made his brief phone call. "We'll take the car to Baltimore. We'll pay you for it. I have money," he said, patting his pocket. Before leaving for dinner, he had stuffed in his pockets $22,000 of the $47,000 he had packed in his suitcase. "From there we'll link up with some people I know. We can go deep undercover for a while."

David stared at a still-life painting on the wall for several moments, lost in thought, while Marvin and his sister rejected Matthew's offer of payment. Finally he said, "Marvin, you have to tell the police that you were in the men's room when the shooting started. You saw nothing. Matthew and I held you at gunpoint and made you drive us to Hoboken. Tell 'em you think we got on the PATH train. Yeah," he confirmed to himself. "That's the safest story."

"Bullshit, man. I'll tell them the God's honest truth. That these motherfuckers came in loaded for bear and tried to kill you," Marvin responded, furious at the dead assassins and the unknown forces behind them.

"Do that," David said calmly, "and you'll be a dead man in twenty-four hours. They'll kill you for sure. Tell 'em Matthew and I are murderers, that we attacked Harrison and Evans, and they'll know you're lying. That you know the truth. They'll kill you just the same. I've left enough death in my wake. Trust me on this. This is the only way for you to stay alive."

As both an investment bank and a commercial bank, LKB was unique on Wall Street. It could take deposits and lend money like any other commercial bank, and underwrite securities like investment banks. As such, LKB was regulated by a horde of governmental agencies, both federal and state. LKB's computers "talked" with those of each of the regulatory agencies constantly during the course of each day. As the computer geek-in-chief, Jonathan Bernstein not only knew LKB's passwords to the agencies' computers; he and two LKB partners comprised the committee that had devised them. The partners, who were selected from the pool of all junior partners, rotated in and out of this assignment for three-month stints. Since most paid little attention to security and passwords while they were on rotation, Jonathan was, in effect, the password security committee. Jenny had discovered this during the first day of her rotation on the committee four years earlier, just after making partner. Unlike her fellow junior partners, though, she was very interested in the details.

As a computer jock in her own right, Jenny held her own with Jonathan. They became fast friends. Jonathan and the other geeks in the basement enjoyed her flair and rapid-fire banter, quasi-sexual in tenor. They also enjoyed, as they openly admitted, her legs. She, in turn, admired Jonathan's sheer brilliance on the computer. While she was very good with a PC, Jonathan was a virtuoso on the Crays and SPARCs.

Tonight Jonathan and Jenny sat in front of his extra-large monitor and began their assault on the DEA. After a little more than two hours of painstaking hacking through the systems of a number of federal agencies and departments, overriding security mechanisms, and tricking the slower government computers into divulging passwords, they made their way into the DEA's central server and gained root access. But after another hour of navigation within the DEA's servers, the two intruders were stymied.

"Zippo," he exclaimed. "Are you sure your friend got the poop straight about this? There's damn little about any Belalcazar in these files. *Nada!*"

"Are you a hundred percent sure we're in?" Jenny asked, frustrated. "Eric's contact at the DEA said he and others clogged the DEA's servers with reports of Belalcazar and other drug barons. But there's nothing but meaningless, tangential references to him."

"Of course I'm sure we're fully in. I am the superuser," Jonathan said defensively. "Like great sex, Jenny, we are all the way in, baby," he added, using their standard banter. "I'm equally sure we'd better get out too. Unlike great sex, it's not a good idea to linger."

"Okay, okay," she acquiesced. "Let's see what they've got at the CIA," she said anxiously.

"First we raid the DEA files. Now the CIA. Any other systems you want hacked on this fine evening?"

"State Department and FBI."

Jonathan stood, stretched, and announced that he needed some coffee. Jenny nodded without looking up. After fetching two cups, Jonathan returned, locked the door behind him, and took his seat. He took a sip of the hot coffee. Jenny's sat untouched.

After a little more than an hour, he pulled his hands away from the keyboard and said with a grin, "I spy with my eye the most famous spy agency in the world. Guess what I spy."

"I spy the CIA," Jenny responded, continuing the child's game that Jonathan had initiated several years earlier. But Jenny wasn't enjoying this. Her muscles ached, her eyes burned, and her throat and skin were dry from the heated air swirling about her. She wanted to call David, but didn't dare run the risk of his phone being tapped.

Another two hours and twenty minutes later, they had still found nothing of significance in either the CIA's or the FBI's computer files regarding Belalcazar. Jonathan was tired and wanted to go home.

"Doesn't make sense, does it, Jon? It's as if Belalcazar doesn't exist," Jenny said to herself as much as to her partner in crime as she slouched in her chair, pressing her temples with her index fingers to ward off a headache she felt rapidly coming on. After a long pause, she sat erect in her chair. "Hey, Jonny boy. What if the files, the important stuff, were deleted?"

"Could be," he allowed.

"If the files were deleted, we'll override the delete commands. Hell, we're the superuser. We should be able to retrieve them," she said, vastly understating the task at hand. "That's if we're good enough," she added, challenging his ego.

"Screw you. We're good enough. We're also bone tired. 'I wanna go home, let me go home,' " he sang, badly, from the Beach Boys' "Sloop John B."

"Let's just go back to the DEA and see if files were

deleted. Just the DEA," Jenny pleaded. "We know from Eric that O'Neal's files should be there. We'll leave the other agencies for tomorrow night. Promise."

Several hours later, Jonathan exited the DEA's most sensitive files and watched as the downloaded materials spewed out of his high-speed printer. "We did it, pal," he said. "Your perseverance and my sheer brilliance have done it once again," he said with a seemingly endless yawn and a lame high five.

"Yeah. The old team is still in form," she responded, weakly slapping his outstretched hand. "I'll have to read the hard copy of O'Neal's report, but on the screen it looks like it doesn't tell us anything more than what O'Neal has already told Eric. These two other reports may add something, maybe not. But—"

"But," he interrupted, wanting her to know that he too was a sleuth, "at least we know that the files on this drug honcho were systematically deleted. Someone tried to eliminate the information, at least the heavy stuff, on this *narcotraficante*," he said with a poor attempt at a Spanish accent.

"Yes, Tonto." She grabbed the last page as it printed out. "Let's go back to your place and sleep on that. I'm beat. Tomorrow's another day . . . except that it started five hours ago," she noted as she looked at the clock on Jonathan's desk. *Wonder how David's evening went?*

Aaron McCormick watched the late-night news from his home in Alexandria. He was as jubilant as he ever permitted himself to be. The events in New York had not gone as planned. They had gone far, far better. The execution of David Craig would have ultimately caused some within the FBI and NYPD to question the circumstances that led to his killing. Now he was a murderer on the run, leaving behind the unforeseen bonus of automatic weapons and wads of cash in his apartment. The loss of Evans and Harrison was a blow to McCormick's organization, but they knew too much anyway and were also becoming too costly. They could easily be replaced.

* * *

The police investigation was relatively straightforward. The private dining room that was the scene of the carnage was neatly booked in the name of David Craig in the restaurant's reservation ledger. Six people were lying dead. David Craig wasn't among them. Moreover, two of the dead were federal agents. The bodies of the two FBI agents growing cold in the Caprice across the street were found within the half hour and added to the list of murders. David's fingerprints were soon confirmed on one of the drinking glasses and on a table knife found on the floor near Harrison's body.

An NYPD SWAT team raided David's home within an hour. The cache of automatic weapons and $25,000 in cash that they found in a suitcase confirmed their suspicions. David and Matthew were up to their eyeballs in guns and cash, leaving no other conclusion but that the stories of David's drug involvement were true. By ten P.M., the local and national late-night news carried the grisly details of the massacre and the discovery of the weapons and cash in David's apartment. By midnight, David Craig and Matthew Rice were on the FBI's Most Wanted list. A New York area-wide manhunt was already under way.

The drive in the borrowed Saturn down the New Jersey Turnpike, through Delaware and across Maryland, to Baltimore, had been uneventful, except for the one New Jersey state police car that passed them near exit 9. Matthew, who drove, had noticed the police car in the rearview mirror coming up fast from behind them and had had a major anxiety attack, shared by David, but the two policemen inside the car paid no attention as they sped by with other things on their minds.

Matthew and David listened to the radio, surfing channels for reports of the shootout. As they crossed the Delaware state line, the radio reported the raid on David's apartment and the seizure of the cash and weapons. David hadn't known about the cash. Matthew apologized for inadvertently setting David up, but David hushed him. It didn't matter. What had shocked him and Matthew was the execution of the two FBI agents outside the restaurant. Those murders were now being blamed on them.

They parked in front of Marvin's mother's home, as planned. They left the keys in her mailbox, walked a hundred yards up the street, and climbed into Billy Dunn's van. Billy sat behind the wheel, waiting to take his friends to his home as he and Matthew had agreed during the phone call Matthew had placed from Marvin's sister's home in Jersey City. The conversation had been brief and to the point. Matthew had given Billy a quick description of what had happened at the restaurant and told Billy what he wanted to do. Billy had processed the data quickly enough. His Ranger buddies were in combat. He agreed on the spot, painfully aware that the simple word *yes* could end his military career and send him to jail.

Jonathan ran up the three flights of stairs with more energy than he knew he had. His small frame, 135 pounds on a heavy day, seemed to fly as if propelled by an updraft. He fumbled to get his keys, dropping both the *New York Times* and the *Daily News* from under his left arm as he finally inserted the key and opened the door.

"Wake up, Jenny," he shouted. "We've got big trouble. Real big trouble."

Jenny struggled to sit up on the couch. Her eyes were heavy and puffy from too little sleep. Her hair looked like it had been caught in a blender. Her first thought upon hearing the words *we've got trouble* was that their hacking had been detected. She rubbed her eyes and looked sheepishly at Jonathan. "Did we get caught?"

"Not us, pal. Not us," Jonathan shot back. "But your friend David is in deep shit. Look at this," he said, his voice uncharacteristically grave. He handed the *Daily News* to her.

Jenny sat up straight, instantly alert as she read the large headline: *Ranger Rampage* and in smaller print, *Four Federal Officers Murdered; Four Others Dead.* Next to the headline was a picture of David, which she recognized as the file photo maintained by LKB.

Jenny set the paper down on the coffee table and stared blankly into space. She wanted and needed coffee, but was unable to persuade her legs to get up.

"It's not true. It can't be," she insisted, trying to convince both of them. "It's impossible. What the hell's happening to our world, Jon? What's going on?"

"Don't know, Jenny. But I know he didn't kill the men in the car. David might have killed the agents in the restaurant if things just got terribly confused. But there's no way he killed the agents in the car."

"And the part about his holding the EMS paramedic at gunpoint and forcing him to take them to Hoboken. David wouldn't have held Marvin Williams hostage. Hell, he befriended David. David invited him to dinner to thank him for his help. But why would the paramedic lie? I don't get it, Jon. It's just not coming to me. He'd never shoot Ben Horowitz. And Sean! Christ. David and Sean were friends. David would never kill them and the two women, Jon. Never. Not under any circumstances. Goddamn it! It just doesn't make sense . . . unless . . ."

"Yeah, Jenny? What you got, pal? Think it through."

"Unless the government agents were out to kill David," she said to herself slowly. "And something went wrong for them. Like Matthew's being there. Christ, maybe Matthew stopped them. Took one of their guns. And people got caught in the cross-fire."

Shit. What do I know? Nothing. Goddamn it! Where was I? Sitting in a fucking basement playing with a computer again when the man I love is out on the streets being shot at . . . Could I be wrong about him? Jenny wondered. *Is it possible that I really don't know him? Could he be a schizo capable of fooling everyone? Leading a double life? No. It can't be. He's not that good an actor. And I'm not that big a fool.*

"I'll make a big pot of very strong coffee. It'll help. Take a shower to clear your head. Then we'll think this through," Jonathan urged.

While Jonathan made coffee and toast, Jenny took a long shower. She let the hot water pour over her head. It felt good, but it didn't wash away the confusion. Her mind continued to race as she slowly toweled herself dry and put on the clothes Faith had purchased for her at the PX—corduroy cargo pants and a loose-fitting sweater. Some dark brown lipstick to go along with her short-clipped blond hair and she was just another funky New Yorker, no resemblance to the photos in the papers. According to the *Times,* FBI officials were looking for her to question her. She, too, was a wanted person now. She, too, must go deeper into hiding.

Jonathan poured the dark coffee and placed the mug next to the toast that he had amply covered with grape jelly, hoping Jenny didn't notice that his hands were trembling slightly as the gravity of the situation—and the dangerous implications of his own involvement—started to sink in. He urged her to sit. "I've got an idea. I'll call in sick for the day. Got the flu or something. I'll stay with you. We'll work this out."

"Can you help me get out of town? I think I know where they went. I'm going to join them. I need your help. I can't get around as easily as you can. If I'm recognized, the FBI will tail me . . ."

"I guess I could rent a car. You could lie on the floor in the backseat and I'd take you wherever you want to go," Jonathan offered.

"I know where they'll go. But," she added after a long pause, "I don't want to leave just yet. Can you go to the office today, and tonight if necessary, and get back on the computers?"

"Yeah, sure. Why?"

"You're the greatest friend, Jon. I don't know how I'll ever repay you for all this," she said, taking his hands into her own.

"I'm sure I'll think of something, Jenny," he responded, smiling. *How come I never get the girl?* he wondered. "But for now let's just put it on your tab."

"Okay, I owe you. Can you get into the phone company's servers?"

"Never have, but don't see why not. Gotta be easier than the CIA." He chuckled nervously.

"Good. Here's what we need to do." She explained her concern. He took mental notes, once again impressed with her brilliant strategic planning.

"Bring 'em down, Jon. All the way down . . . the long-distance records. You can't fail. And one more thing; can you . . ." She told him precisely what she wanted him to do as she read her handwritten notations in her address book. He carefully wrote the information on an old steno pad. When they finished verifying that Jonathan had recorded every company and bank account accurately, he lifted his mug to hers and they clanked noisily, a toast to aggression.

"One more thing, Jon. Can you find out who in the DEA deleted the files? If so, maybe we can get a message to someone in the government we trust."

"You're one tough lady," he said, smiling at her affectionately. "One very tough lady."

Chapter 13

Billy walked into his kitchen at five-forty-five P.M. He wore his dress greens. His uniform jacket, bedecked with ribbons, including the Distinguished Service Cross, Combat Infantrymen's Badge, and "Master Blaster" jump wings, hung over his shoulder. A yellow-and-black embroidered Ranger tab was neatly sewn on the left shoulder of the jacket. He took off his garrison cap, with his general-grade "Scrambled Eggs" on the bill. He pulled a bottle of Sam Adams ale from the fridge as Faith came from the living room to greet him, followed closely by Jenny.

"How was your day?" Faith asked as she kissed him on the cheek.

"Lousy." He took a long gulp of his one allotted beer for the evening. "Now there's a sight for sore eyes. You okay?"

"I feel better now that I'm here," Jenny said with a grin.

"Did your buddy go back to New York?"

"Yes. He dropped me off and headed right back. He can help us better from New York."

"Good, we can use all the help we can get. Great to have you here," he whispered. "David really needs you. He's about to go over the edge," he added softly. "Well," said Billy to all as he untied his thin black army tie and walked into the living room, where Eric and Matthew sat on one couch and David sat opposite them on another. "Let's get down to business. What's for dinner?" he asked, looking over his shoulder at Faith.

"Soup in mugs and finger food so we can eat and talk here in the living room," she replied.

"Perfect," he said, slowly savoring the beer. "Eric. Do you have anything for us?" he asked, pulling up the club chair at the end of the coffee table.

"Not much. I met with all of the HUMINT committee members. O'Neal's given us the most useful info so far. He's given me a verbal of his report, but his computer has mysteriously crashed and he's trying to re-create his files. Unfortunately, he left on a business trip yesterday. I won't be able to get a copy of the reports till he gets back.

"We know that at least one person, Harrison, within the FBI and one, Evans, within the DEA are—were—really bad guys. And, thanks to Buffalo Bill Rice here," he said, grinning affectionately at Matthew, "they're both very dead, leading the whole goddamn world to think that David and Matthew wasted these two good government employees in cold blood, which leads us to all be gathered 'round this table." Eric took a good-sized swallow, more a gulp, of his Jack Daniel's and continued. "What we don't know is why they tried to kill David or who they were really working for. Are there more bad guys left in the agencies? Finally, while we don't know for sure—a hundred percent sure—that Harrison and Evans were in cahoots with the druggies, we're pretty damn sure."

"David. You have anything to add?" Billy asked gently, observing his friend with concern. David looked thinner and more drawn than Billy could ever remember seeing him. His eyes were outlined by deep circles, his complexion ashen.

"Well," David stammered, "I'm not sure I have anything."

"Can I say something?" Jenny asked as she pulled a document from the manila file folder resting on her lap. "Here's a copy of O'Neal's report."

"How in the hell . . . ?" Eric blurted out, straightening in his chair.

"Bear with me, and I'll tell you," she said more calmly

than she felt. "A friend of mine and I hacked into the DEA's computer system Thursday night. At the very time you two were going through your hell at Moynihan's," she explained, looking at Matthew and David, "we spent the night working our way into the DEA. At first, we couldn't find anything of substance about Belalcazar. Zippo! Except tangential references to him. Then it occurred to us to check to see if any files were deleted. Sure enough, several files regarding Belalcazar had been, O'Neal's with them. So we overrode the delete commands and re-created the files. It took some time, but it worked. We downloaded them, printed them out, and, well, here they are," she said as she patted the thick file folder on her lap. "Not just O'Neal's, but two reports by a woman named Crawford and one by a man named Katz. After we downloaded the files, we redeleted them and put everything back in its place, so to speak. They'll never know we were feeling around in their underwear."

"Son of a bitch," Eric said, pronouncing slowly for emphasis.

"Damn impressive work," Matthew chimed in.

"Hold on," she said. "I'm not finished. Eric, you just said you weren't sure whether there are other bad guys left in the agencies after Harrison and Evans. There are," she confirmed. "I lay low in my buddy's apartment yesterday, but he went back into the DEA's files to see what he could find. Katz mentioned Belalcazar in another memo filed two days ago. It was deleted yesterday." She paused to let that sink in. Harrison and Evans had died Thursday night, but someone within the DEA was still deleting files relating to Belalcazar on Friday.

"And what do these reports say about this Belalcazar?" Billy asked, eager to get to the details, as he was trained to do.

"Until yesterday, the most detailed information is that in O'Neal's memo. It's completely consistent with what O'Neal told Eric. Belalcazar's a megalomaniac who may very well be succeeding in taking over the entire cocaine business, and perhaps even the government, of Colombia. He's reported to talk in terms of legacy, dynasty, and that sort of thing, but has no children of his own. Then comes the zinger," she said, sitting forward, animated. "This guy Katz—the one who filed a report two days ago, the one that was deleted yesterday—says, in a totally offhanded way, a non sequitur in the context of his memo, that there are rumors within the Cali cartel, or what remains of it, that Belalcazar has adopted several kids. His enemies in Cali apparently, according to the rumors Katz cites, joke that the guy couldn't get a hard-on with his first two wives. Number three isn't doing the trick either. He's giving up and adopting. According to the rumors cited in Katz's report, there are several children, some of whom are North Americans."

Everyone in the room sat still, mesmerized by what Jenny had just said. "You sure about this, Jenny?" David asked, desperation in his voice.

"All I know is what I've read. But think about it. Harrison and Evans are dead, but someone's still hiding information about Belalcazar. On top of that, Katz says this nut job has adopted kids from Mexico, Venezuela, and the U.S. How does a drug baron legitimately adopt children? Hell, as a single woman investment banker, I couldn't adopt. Something's not right."

"Jenny's onto something big here," Faith said.

"Where does he live?" David asked, his voice firm for the first time in the past two days.

"He's rumored to have at least six homes, but the main one is on the Isla Gorgona, a small island off the west coast of Colombia," Jenny responded, eager to finish her briefing. "Katz's report says nothing about where the 'adopted' children are. I've done some research on the island. I have one not-so-good map, but no real descriptions. Apparently it was used as a prison at some point in time. I started to do the research on the Internet last night in New York, but didn't get too far before I had to leave to come here. A lot of the stuff is, I think, in Spanish, so I'll need your help, Matthew."

He nodded.

"Good. We can work on that tonight. The PC upstairs is connected to the Net. It'll work just fine."

"My God, Jenny. Damn good work. It's the best lead we have," David said, looking lovingly into Jenny's eyes, momentarily forgetting that the others were in the room. Then he added pensively, "No . . . it's the only lead we have. We gotta pursue it."

"Any thoughts as to how we do that, other than Jenny and I learning more about the island?" Matthew asked, looking around the coffee table for suggestions.

"I can get to an ex-DAS agent in Bogotá," Eric responded, reaching for a sandwich. "DAS is a Colombian army unit. Man's named Pablo Santiago. Sparks at State told me about him. He was part of the elite Search Block unit until he lost an eye in the final battle with Escobar back in ninety-three. In fact, he's the one who killed Escobar. Took early retirement after that. No doubt helped him stay alive," Eric continued. "I'll get to him through Sparks. Probably only speaks Spanish, but Matthew could handle that. Let me work on that end."

"Jenny. Outstanding work. May I see that map of the island?" Billy asked, pointing to the manila file folder on her lap. He studied the map carefully in silence. "I'll see if I can improve on it."

The Huey approached the island from the east at ninety-five mph just two hundred feet off the water. It was dusk, and the hills of the Isla Gorgona blocked the sun setting in the west. The brilliant hues splashed across the sky. But Nick Field wasn't interested in the colors dancing before him. His eyes were riveted to the water and his altimeter. He had made the trip hundreds of times, but they were late tonight, his boss delayed in meetings at one of his cocaine-processing plants in Popayan on the mainland. Field didn't like flying at night, and two hundred feet between him and the water was not what he considered a good margin of error. He was eager for a touchdown before it got darker.

As he passed over the marina and the guards on patrol

along the breakwater, his eyes shot down to the lower helipad to his left; he badly wished he could land there instead. He continued toward the upper helipad. He could see their faces clearly now. Milana was smiling and waving as if her husband were an astronaut returning from Mars instead of a drug baron coming home for the evening. The wind pressed Milana's white cotton dress against her voluptuous body, and Nick couldn't help but be jealous of Ernesto.

She yelled something at the children over the roar of the jet engine and the whoosh of the rotor wash a few feet above her. The children saluted their new father in unison. One of the boys managed to give a pretty good salute, Field observed. What caught his attention mostly, though, was the left-handed salute given by the latest boy to arrive, the boy they called José. Nick Field had noted before that the boy was left-handed, but still lefties didn't give left-handed salutes, and this boy's father was an ex-army man, according to CNN. He found the thought amusing. *Is this kid dissing the patrón?* Field wondered if Belalcazar noticed it.

Linda Ross took the bus from the FBI's headquarters after her third "interview," as they called it. She was exasperated and felt violated. The FBI had first questioned her at five-thirty A.M. on the morning after the killings in the restaurant. Then the DEA later that day, and now the FBI was back again this afternoon.

She had given them no new information. She had none, as she had repeatedly told them. She did not know where David Craig was. She had met him on only one occasion, the day of the press conference, just hours before he became America's Most Wanted. The agents from the two federal agencies did not learn anything material during the first two sessions. The third was even less fruitful.

Linda, however, learned a great deal during the third session. David's apartment had, in fact, been bugged. That was clear from the questions the federal agents asked about conversations that she, David, and the Waldrons had had in David's apartment. It confirmed that her decision during the first two interviews not to tell the agents about her meetings with Jenny, Billy, and Eric was the right thing to do. She didn't trust the agents. She wasn't sure why. At first she had made the decision to withhold that information more from a gut feeling than anything else. She had recalled the sincerity and intensity of David and his friends as they desperately tried to figure out who could have taken the boy they all referred to as "our Justin." They were as desperate to find Justin as she was to find Debbie. They were also the only people who could help her.

She got off the bus several blocks before her regular stop. She walked in the brisk wind, letting the tiny snowflakes fall on her face, grateful for the cold, wet caress. She entered her building. She walked up six flights of stairs, preferring the physical exertion to the ease of the elevator. She made herself a pot of very strong tea and sat down at her kitchen table. The first few sips burned her lips and tongue, but she was indifferent. After a few more sips, she set down her cup and quietly opened the front door of her apartment, closed the door slowly behind her, and walked three more flights of stairs up to her friend's apartment. She knocked on the door. After greeting her, Linda posed the question on her mind, got the answer she wanted, and made the phone call she knew she had to make, a call she couldn't risk making from her own apartment. She asked the biggest favor she had ever asked her friend, explaining that it might help find Debbie. Her friend, holding a baby in her arm and trying to keep up with an energetic toddler at the same time, gave her a kiss on the cheek and whispered an anticipated, yet very much appreciated, "You got it."

Linda's spirits rose a notch as she walked down the stairs to her apartment, opening the unlocked door as quietly as she could and closing it gently behind her. She finished her now-tepid tea, knowing that it might be the last cup of tea she drank in her own home for a long time.

* * *

"What do you mean, 'we've got nothing'?" Dennis Rakovic, twenty-year veteran of the FBI and agent in charge of the Craig file, said to the five men sitting red-faced in the conference room of the Hoover Building. "You mean I gotta report to the wolves in the press corps that after two days we've got absolutely no fucking clue where Craig and Rice are? That we have our fingers so far up our asses we can't even locate the Benson woman? Fuck me," he nearly spit at the other agents. "No," he corrected himself after a momentary pause. "Fuck you! Fuck all of you," Rakovic yelled as he slapped the table loudly. "I want the effort redoubled. I want more agents on the case. I want to find these agent-killers and I want it done fast. They can't just have disappeared," he continued, becoming more agitated. "Check out Craig's friends at his office. Check out his social friends. His doormen. His fucking dry cleaner. Where do we stand on his Rolodex file?"

"Kept everything personal on his Palm Pilot . . . must have it with him. His secretary has only his business numbers. We're checking them, but so far there's nothing."

"Have we checked frequently called incoming and outgoing numbers on his phones?"

"Got a problem there, sir," an agent at the table reported haltingly, afraid of the repercussions that would follow. "Verizon computer records are intact for local calls. Lots of calls between Craig and the Benson lady, both at Craig's office and his home. Not much else of use. Problem's with AT and T, LKB's long-distance carrier. Craig used it at his home as well. Strange glitch in the computer system erased all long-distance records. The techies are trying to reconstruct the data in the servers, but they're having a devil of a time. We gotta look over Craig's long-distance calls using the hard copies. But we're having a tough time locating them as well. You can imagine the billions of monthly bills in AT and T's storage facilities. Literally tons of paper shipped off to warehouses and forgotten. But we're working on it.

Once we locate the files, we're gonna need a lot of people assigned to the case."

"The computers lost only Craig's files?" the suspicious agent in charge asked.

"Oh, no, sir. Computer glitch destroyed all computer records of calls along the eastern seaboard from Virginia to Maine. Massive system failure."

"Any signs of foul play?"

"None, sir. AT and T computer techies can't figure it out. But so far it looks like a legitimate meltdown."

"David, look at this." The information Jenny had just gathered on the Internet seemed useful. Isla Gorgona had in fact been a prison during the period known as La Violencia in the late fifties and throughout the sixties. It was a natural prison, much like the infamous Devil's Island of French lore. It was a small island, only nine kilometers long north to south and 2.5 kilometers wide east to west, located fifty-five kilometers off the west coast of Colombia as the seagull flies, but more like one hundred kilometers from Buenaventura, the nearest port. The island itself, Jenny noted, from the air looked like a whale heading northeast, its tail fin flipping slightly to the west. It was patrolled by some of the most shark-infested waters in the world and, to make matters worse, was for the most part a dense rain forest populated by at least fifteen different species of snakes, one in particular, a member of the coral snake family, being extremely poisonous.

The island was discovered by Francisco Pizarro, the famous conquistador who subjugated the Incas. According to legend, snakes killed so many of his men during his one and only stay on the island that he named the island after the Gorgons, three-winged monsters in Greek mythology who had live snakes for hair. Crocodiles presently inhabited at least one of the ponds in the southern part of the island. Beyond this historical and geographical data, the research had also uncovered a reference to a magazine article written about the island by an ex-prisoner who did an exposé on the horrors committed during La Violencia.

"So why do you think Belalcazar has a home on Isla Gorgona?" David asked after he finished reading. "The place sounds awful. Sharks, snakes, crocs. And he doesn't sound like a person who builds a home based on great sunrises and sunsets," he reasoned. "The place sounds like a natural fortress. Probably near impossible for his enemies in the other cartels to get to him."

"Pizarro," Jenny exclaimed, slapping the printout. "Conquistador stuff. Remember O'Neal's memo? He mentions that Belalcazar fashions himself as a modern conquistador. Katz's brief says the same thing. Sparks, the State Department rep on the HUMINT committee, said so too in his conversation with Eric. Belalcazar has another home in a small town named Belalcazar. Crawford's report states that he's believed to have been born in that town. If you put them together, you get the facts that he was born in this small, no doubt dirt-poor village named after a Spanish conquistador. Later on, when he's rich, he has several homes, probably a magnificent one in his hometown. But he builds an estate on an island discovered by the greatest conquistador, Pizarro, and that is his palace . . . his lair. Don't know if there's any truth to that psychoanalysis . . . but it sounds good. He's living out his fantasies, or delusions. . . ."

"Could well be," Faith responded, looking up from her newspaper for a moment and nodding. "Sounds like you're on the right track to—" She stopped abruptly, staring wide-eyed at page four of the Metropolitan section. "My God," she gasped. She had the full attention of everyone in the room. "What are the names of the three people who wrote the DEA reports . . . the ones you just mentioned?"

"O'Neal, Eric's contact," Jenny answered, alarmed and on the edge of her chair. "And a woman named Crawford. Dianne is her first name . . . I think. The other is Maurice Katz. Why?"

"They're dead," Faith said, her voice incredulous. "They and two government pilots flying for the DEA went down in Chesapeake Bay yesterday morning on their way to New York on government business. It's right here," she added as she handed the paper to Matthew, the person nearest to her.

Matthew read the article and then put it down angrily on the table between David and Jenny. The two of them read it next. If there had been any doubt as to whether the villains within the DEA were still alive, any doubt that the deletion of Katz's report was a coincidence, those doubts were now erased, as were the lives of the three persons within the DEA who had tracked Colombian drug lords the most closely.

They sat silently, trying to regain their composure. The enormity of the forces they confronted, forces whose names they did not know, and whose faces they could not see, was overwhelming.

The silence was broken by a loud ring of the phone. Faith rose and answered. She listened for several seconds, her expression serious, her eyes intensely focused. "Let me get a pad and pen," she said as the other sets of eyes in the kitchen watched her. She jotted down the number given to her by the person at the other end and placed the phone down in its cradle without another word.

"It's Linda Ross. She wants to meet us," Faith said, unclear how the others would react.

"Let's do it," David said. "How about tomorrow morning?"

"Sure," Matthew said, "we could do it after we pick up Frank."

"Frank!" David exclaimed. "I can't let more people become involved in this. What the hell do you think you're doing, Matthew? You want the whole Ripcord team dead or something?"

"Cram it, David," Matthew ordered, more fiercely than he intended. "We couldn't keep him away any longer. He'll be here tomorrow."

"Why do you have to go? The police or the FBI can do it. They can't all be corrupt."

"If David even thinks he knows where Justin is, he's going to go charging in there to get him. That's the way he is. And if that happens, I have to go with him," Billy said patiently to Faith. The small light on the nightstand dimly lit their bedroom.

"Isn't that why we have police? Why do you all have to be so macho? You're middle-aged men. You haven't been in combat for over thirty years. And it's not just the danger I worry about, Billy. You know, you—we—have worked so hard to get where we're at. The Eighteenth Airborne Corps, Billy. The Eighteenth! The best combat command in the army. A black man at the head of the Airborne Corps! We've spent our whole lives working at this, following procedures, kissing butts, politely smiling at racist jokes at the O club for fear of offending some redneck officer and his wife. Climbing up the ladder. We're now at the top. The very top, Billy. You go off playing G.I. Joe outside official channels, you'll throw it all away."

"Faith, I owe it to David," Billy responded. As he caressed his wife's cheek, he realized that she was crying. "It's not just that he saved my life. He's my friend. From our first day together in Vietnam, that first night in the unit together, just off the plane, he's been my dearest friend. I'm not telling you anything new, baby. We're like brothers. I can't let him put himself in harm's way alone. And we all know that he can't just dial nine-one-one and get the cops or the Feds to rescue Justin. They—whoever *they* are—will kill him."

"I love David, too. And I love Justin. But I love you more, and I love our life together. I just don't want you getting shot, or arrested and drummed out of the corps. We don't really know where Justin is, except maybe on that island where that whack-job of a drug baron *may*—and that's a big *may*—have some children. But if we do get more information, promise me that you'll try to figure out some way to get him back to safety without you throwing everything away."

"If we're not sure where he is, I'm not going anywhere. I'm not going to do anything rash or stupid. I'm far too cautious a man to do that. But, if we know for sure where he is . . . well . . ." Billy paused to study Faith's eyes, looking at least for acquiescence. "I'll be right at his side."

"Okay." She sighed, turning off the light and pulling herself close to her husband, wondering how many more nights they had together. "If we know for sure. One hundred percent. Then you go get him," she said, knowing she had no choice.

Chapter 14

A trim Hispanic man stepped off the plane, thanking the flight attendant as he walked past her, and headed up the ramp to the arrival lounge at Dulles International Airport. He carried little baggage and was dressed casually. He looked as if he might be in his late fifties. His face was deeply tanned, weathered and coarse. His thick curly hair was salt-and-pepper, graying at the temples. He was fit, someone who worked hard outdoors. His hands were callused and chapped, scratched in several places. They were strong hands—they looked as if they could crush another man's hand merely by shaking it. He walked purposefully toward the exit. He stepped out into the frigid air and glanced around, searching for a certain vehicle. He spotted it and waved, a smile forming on his lips. The van pulled up and he climbed in, sitting next to the driver. He gave her a kiss on her cheek. "Great to see you, Faith."

"Great to see you too, Frank," she said affectionately to Frank Lopez as she put the van in gear and drove away. "David's not happy to see you get involved in this," she warned him after inquiring about his family. "He'll get over it. As for the rest of us, we're damn happy you're here. And I think we all agree that we can use your help." She smiled, knowing that he had traveled across the country for just that reason.

"You need a tough old commercial fisherman?"

"We do," she responded, looking at the merging traffic as she came down the ramp onto the highway. "We need all the help we can get, including Linda Ross, the mother of the girl who was kidnapped here in D.C. She's joining us tonight. We're going to pick her up at the Lincoln Memorial subway station on the way."

He remained silent the rest of the trip from Dulles to Fort Meyer as Faith explained the events and discussions of the past few days.

The friends' first moments together were what they were every year when they played paratroopers at Happy Jack's: Backslapping and warm embraces. Matthew saw Frank more often than the others, since they both lived in southern California, but even for them it had been four months. Frank looked older and they noted it, not thinking that they, too, had put another year behind them. Frank had ended any discussion with David about his staying out of the fray before the discussion even began. A simple statement that he was in for the duration coupled with his penetrating stare and David was silenced.

"Say, where's Billy?" Frank asked.

Faith shifted uncomfortably. "He said he had to go do something. He should be back soon."

A half hour later, Billy walked into the kitchen and tossed his garrison cap on the counter, not hanging it on the doorknob as was his custom, catching Faith's eye as she stood next to the stove. "Hi, honey," he said, giving her a peck on the cheek in a way that let her understand that his mind was miles away. "Frank here?" he asked in the military voice he had promised Faith so many times to leave at the office.

"Yes, sir," she responded to remind him that she was not his subordinate officer, but he was already in the living room by the time she spoke.

"Listen up. All of you," he commanded, looking around the room at his friends. "We may have something to help us. I've got some pictures of Isla Gorgona. Let's spread 'em out on the kitchen table," he continued, waving a large manila envelope in his hand and causing a stampede to the kitchen.

"These photos are aerial shots taken two days ago from a satellite. Don't ask me how I got 'em. Let's just say that I cashed in some old chips," Billy explained as he looked at the first photo. "The pictures are grainy. I was told they would be. We can't get a resolution greater than point five meters. From there we'd have to get digital enhancement, and that I don't know how to do. I ran out of chips just getting the satellite to be repositioned for a few moments." He then laid the first of twenty black-and-white, 8 by 10 photos in front of the thunderstruck group leaning over the table. "Oh, I see my friend included a CD," Billy observed, spilling the contents of the envelope on the table. "I guess that's for any digital enhancement we can come up with. Okay, let's take 'em in the order we're supposed to. This one was taken at 14:59:30 Zulu, or Greenwich mean time. That would mean . . . let me do this right . . . 09:59:30 local time in Colombia.

"This is apparently the whole island and the Isla Gorgonilla off to the southwest," he said, pointing to the two islands. "The number twenty-five here in the corner means that the picture has a resolution of twenty-five meters, meaning it can pick out objects twenty-five meters across. Here's the compound on the north end of the island"—he indicated with his index finger—"where the prison used to be."

Jenny excused herself and walked out of the kitchen. She flew up the stairs to the room she and David were sharing, turned on the computer, waited impatiently for it to boot up, and made her Internet connection. Once on-line, she rapidly typed in Jonathan Bernstein's e-mail address at LKB and a cryptic message. She was rewarded instantly with a message back saying, *No prob. Gimme two. Luv.* She left the computer on and raced back downstairs, catching her breath as she approached the kitchen.

"Here," Billy continued, placing the third photo next to the second. "This one's closer in. Resolution of twenty meters." He set down photos four through eight. Fifteen meters. "These appear to be reefs," Billy said with some hesitation, pointing to dark spots at various places in the waters east of the larger island. "I don't have much experience looking at aerial shots of this type," he admitted. "So don't let me make all the conclusions."

He placed photos nine through eleven on the table. "Ten-meter image. Some smaller buildings."

"Helipad," David noted, jabbing at a circle near what appeared to be a small port. "And these are the breakwaters," he continued excitedly.

"Is that a swimming pool?" Eric strained to see, pointing to a rectangular shape between the large structure, presumably the drug lord's mansion, and another circle that caught the attention of David, Billy, Eric, Frank, and Matthew.

"Looks like another helipad. Might be a chopper on a pad," Matthew was the first to observe. "It's not really clear."

"There's a chopper on the pad," Frank confirmed with certainty, pointing to the round configuration. "But why's it so fuzzy? Chopper's blurrier than the pool and the house."

"Blades are moving," Billy and David responded, almost at the same time.

"Number twelve. Five-meter resolution. Looks like a lighthouse," Billy noted, his thick index finger moving slowly across the photo as the others looked on with rapt attention.

"That's right," Frank said, his spirits elevated. "The article in the magazine describes the old lighthouse that doubled as a watchtower for the prison. It's right where the article said it was."

"This one's a one-meter image," Billy said as he placed the next photo on the table. "Look," he said, his voice rising. "People . . . here . . . between the swimming pool and the mansion."

"People are either waiting for the helicopter to take off, or it has just landed and they're greeting someone," David said, completing Billy's thought. "Let's see the next one."

"Looks like someone has come out of the house . . . walking toward the pad," Eric said as they looked at the next frame. "Hard to tell. It's too blurry."

"I think you're right," Faith exclaimed.

The room was charged with excitement. The .5-meter images were a clear improvement over the other photos, but the resolution was still too grainy to identify people. They reviewed the next few frames, taken seconds apart. The person who had left the large structure was now "walking" haltingly, like a character in an old silent movie, as the group moved more quickly through the next few frames.

"Two people following him, off to the right and the left," Eric noted.

"Bodyguards, is my guess," Matthew ventured.

"Belalcazar," David spit. "That's got to be him. He's going to his personal helicopter, and those are his guards."

"It's a Huey," Billy noted. "I'd recognize that shape anywhere. Even from this altitude."

The next few photos made it clear that the lone figure followed by the two others was in fact going to the Huey. He climbed into the chopper in picture number fourteen. The two men following him disappeared in photo number fifteen, presumably having followed him into the helicopter.

"I think these are kids," Linda said, squinting and pointing to several figures between two taller figures. "Maybe these two are adults," she added, pointing her slender index finger at two figures. "Women . . . I think."

Billy put down the next frame. Number sixteen. The Huey had moved slightly. It was lifting off the pad. "Chopper's leaving," he said dryly as he put down numbers nineteen and twenty.

David immediately slid his chair over to position himself in front of the two remaining pictures, his face inches from them, obscuring them from the view of most of the others around the table. He pressed his face closer yet to the photos, adjusting his reading glasses as they slid down the bridge of his nose, studying the photos. Then he slid his chair back, his face betraying his frustration and despair. The pictures were far too grainy to distinguish the faces. "Son of a bitch," he snapped. "I can't tell. Can we enhance the images?" David asked, turning to Jenny.

"They're very blurry. We'll need the best enhancement software there is. I'll see what I can find."

More waiting. Collective frustration permeated the Dunn residence. Linda Ross left the kitchen, not wanting the others to see her tears. Faith took off after her, guiding her to a couch in the living room. Jenny stood next to the chair where David sat. He leaned his head against her stomach, his eyes fixed on the last two, nearly identical photos, as if by staring at them long enough he could make them clearer. The others left David and Jenny in the kitchen and returned to the living room. After several minutes David and Jenny joined them. The scene in the living room reminded Jenny of her father's wake.

Billy and Eric tried their best to bolster the team. For the next half hour they discussed plans to get more information, but time was their worst enemy. Their luck in hiding from the FBI could not hold out.

Jenny, who had repeatedly checked her watch, excused herself and went up the stairs slowly. After less than three minutes, she flew back down the stairs, startling the others as she raced to the kitchen. She grabbed the CD on the table near the photos and ran back through the living room.

"We've got digital enhancement," she shouted gleefully.

"Christ in heaven," Eric shouted as he took off after her. David was already climbing the stairs, taking the steps three at a time like Jenny, paying no heed to the stampede behind him.

Jenny sat in front of the computer. She anxiously fumbled the compact disc, uncharacteristically clumsy as she placed it in its cradle. Her hands trembled as she slid the cradle into the hard drive. "The software was e-mailed to me and is downloading. I started the process before I came back downstairs. It'll still take a few minutes. Let's all try to keep calm," she said excitedly.

"Where did you get the software?" David asked, not sure where this was going, and not trusting the emotional roller coaster he was on.

"Don't ask," Jenny instructed. "My buddy in New York got it for me."

"Okay, but where did he get it?" Eric asked, as ever pressing the inquiry.

"Well, you can get this stuff from a number of places," Jenny responded evasively. "For example, there is commercial software available . . ." Before she could finish, the software finished downloading and an FBI warning appeared on the screen not unlike the warning at the beginning of a home video, except this warning announced that the software was the property of the FBI itself. "Oops," she said with a nervous smile. "Guess that answers that."

"How did you do that?" Matthew asked, amazed.

"Look. My friend in New York didn't have time to go shopping at the local computer store, and I wanted to make sure we got the very best—"

"You did great," David interrupted. "Let's see what this stuff can do."

"Okay. It might be slow. A Pentium Three may have a hard time pushing this stuff through the pipeline," she cautioned as she typed and clicked. She pulled up picture number twenty and tapped the enter key with a loud *pap*.

The grainy image didn't appear to change at first. Jenny wished they were all in LKB's basement using the Crays or the SPARC stations instead of this home PC. *We'd have this image crystal-clear in seconds,* she thought. The room was silent.

Slowly, very slowly, the image began to clarify. After what seemed like an eternity, David placed his index finger on the screen and said, "I think they're saluting. They're sending this guy off with a salute. Look here."

All eyes were on the screen, waiting for the answer.

Suddenly David saw it. His heart leaped, lodging in his throat. His lungs spasmed, gulping for air so fast that the surprise caused a sharp pain to his ribs. By reflex, his hands clamped down on his chest. He gasped several times, his eyes streaming with tears. He tried to talk but the words wouldn't flow. "It's . . ." He sobbed, now out of control. Within a few seconds he was able to stammer, "It's Justin. He's saluting with his left . . ." It would be several minutes before he could speak coherently. By then Justin was coming into focus on the screen, as were Debbie and the other children.

Linda gasped when Debbie's face began to appear on the screen. Like David, she experienced a spasm of her lungs. It felt as if her lungs had conspired to push her heart through her throat, choking her in the process. Unlike David, though, she didn't have a chair to prop her up. She would have collapsed to the floor were it not for the fact that Eric maneuvered himself behind her in time to catch her. When she was finally able to breathe, she found herself crying hysterically, tears of joy and pain so intense it hurt.

"That's Lisa Waldron," David stammered, pointing to the girl standing to Justin's right.

"Who are the other two boys?" Jenny asked, her voice a whisper, as if there were a need for reverence.

"Don't know," David whispered in return. "That sick son of a bitch took them all. He just plucked them away, all of them. . . ." He tried to continue, but slumped yet further into his chair, emotionally drained, his eyes still glued to the monitor.

Matthew retrieved a chair from his bedroom and returned, helping Eric seat Linda as close to Debbie's picture as possible. Eric sat heavily on the end of the bed next to Faith, both shaking their heads in disbelief. Frank and Matthew stepped back, their emotions also running wild. Billy stood immobile, his arms folded, his pipe gently cupped in his right hand, his gaze fixed on Justin. He made no effort to wipe the tears that slid silently through the stubble of whiskers on his chin. He turned slowly to Faith. Their eyes connected, sending and receiving complex communications as silently and as thoroughly as satellites, each recalling their bedtime conversation, acknowledging what Justin's image on the screen meant, Faith accepting Billy's decision.

"Let's go downstairs," Billy suggested after several minutes, breaking the silence that permeated the bedroom like a thick fog. "We have work to do. And we don't have much time," he cautioned, his military mind racing to develop a plan.

"I want to stay here near the screen," David said, still staring at Justin.

"Me too," Linda added.

"Let me print out a couple pictures and we'll take them downstairs," Jenny offered.

After two copies were made, everyone descended to the first floor, huddling around the coffee table in the living room. There was a quiet expectancy as each contemplated what this latest development meant.

Linda was the first to speak. She turned to look at David, her face tense. "What do we do about it? What are you going to do?" she asked, posing the question parent-to-parent, as if the others in the room didn't exist.

David's eyes roamed from Linda to the others in the room. "I'm going to go get him. I'm going to bring my boy home."

Matthew jumped on that. "What do you mean '*I'm* gonna go get him'? *You* are not going to do anything. *We* are going to go get Justin and Debbie. *We.* Get that? I haven't come all across this country to kill two rogue federal agents, to get myself on the FBI's Most Wanted list, to just walk away from some maniac who has kidnapped a boy I consider my nephew. No fucking way! We do this together."

"I can't let you do that, Matthew. I can't ask you to put yourself in that danger."

Billy shook his head hard, as if to toss the offending words off. "I can hardly believe my ears. Let me ask you a question," he said softly. "When I was pulled into the jungle in 'Nam, how long did you have to think about it? Two . . . maybe three seconds? It doesn't matter," he said, putting his face closer to David's. "What matters is that you had to decide whether to save yourself or come after me. You made a choice to rescue me. Without you, I wouldn't be here," he said, placing his right palm against his chest, his voice rising. "Faith and I would not have our beautiful children. I owe it all to you, David. Everything. How many times do you think I've thought about that over all those years? Try several times a day. Faith and I have discussed this. We've agreed that if we could find him, I'd go with you. Justin's the son I never had. I love him. And you, David Samuel Craig, are my brother. You will not tell me you're going it alone. You will not deny me the privilege of accompanying you into this battle."

"I'm sorry . . . I didn't mean—"

"You're the boy's father," Eric interrupted, "but . . . like Billy said . . . we're family. You can't shut us out. Justin's a part of every one of us. Hell, my own kids won't see me. The only people I have are in this room. I've got nothing but you guys. These madmen took Justin. They tried to kill you. If you're going to that island, I'm going too."

"David," Frank said when his turn came, his deep voice calm, "you have no chance to get on and off that island by yourself. You'd end up dead, with Justin lost forever. We won't let you do that. We've watched him grow. He's part of our lives. I feel he's my son, too. In all the years I've known you, you have never asked anything of me. Maybe there was never anything I could do for you before. But I've asked you for your help. When I needed money 'cause the insurance didn't cover all the storm damage to my boats, I went to you. When I needed money for the kids' college, you loaned me money and wouldn't let me pay you back. I wasn't too proud to ask, and you were good enough to give. Now . . . you need me and everyone else in this room to even have a chance of getting the kids off that island. Even with all of us, there'll be hell to pay."

David looked at Frank, not in defiance or refusal, but

in quiet appreciation. All of his war buddies, not the invincible kids they were thirty-plus years ago, but middle-aged men with families and careers, were prepared to do battle again to save his son. He looked at Frank, then at Billy, Matthew, and Eric. "I don't want you to go to war again," he said slowly, his voice filled with pain. "But you're right. All of you. I have no choice. I need you on this."

"I'm going too," Linda blurted out. "My daughter's on that island. I'm going."

"And you're not leaving me here to get arrested by the FBI while you guys go off and do the 'man' thing," Jenny protested, anticipating David's resistance. "I can help. I'll figure out some way to help. I'm not staying here. Period."

"Jenny, that's crazy. It could be—no . . . it *will* be dangerous," David corrected himself. "I can't let you go."

"It's not up to you, David. I'm part of the team. And I'm going."

"Well, I can't go with you. And Billy has made it clear that he'd go to the ends of the earth with you, army career or not, danger or not," Faith said stoically. "I have to be here for our daughters in case something happens and you old fools get yourselves killed. I do have one request, though. No, make it two. One is that you be careful. The other is that when you find those people . . . the men who took the children . . . you take no prisoners."

Chapter 15

Billy taped two maps that he had "borrowed" from the army to the wall near the large dining table, one of Isla Gorgona and the other of its smaller neighbor, Isla Gorgonilla.

"No easy way on or off," Matthew noted, the first to state what the others were thinking. "The map's not clear about this, but the article written by the ex-prisoner is explicit: The west side of the island is a sheer cliff ranging from eighty to one hundred twenty feet high, with the prevailing currents coming in from the open Pacific and the waves smashing against the cliffs. An approach from the west is impossible. As for the east . . . well . . . any boat approaching from the east would be spotted miles away."

"Any boat leaving from Buenaventura, the nearest port on the mainland, would be tagged by Belalcazar's men. They'd call ahead to warn the island guards, if they didn't kill us on the spot," Frank said. "I could get my trawler in, but it'd take a long time to get there."

Jenny didn't look at the others as they spoke. She focused on the map, deep in thought.

Billy was fixed on the map too. "Only four ways to get on the island. Boat, seaplane, helicopter—"

". . . or parachute," Jenny said, completing his thought.

"Right," Billy said as he cast an admiring glance her way. "The approach by boat's difficult. There are no doubt lots of armed guards on that island. Judging by the size of what looks like a barracks in the photos, there must be at least thirty. The hacienda will be heavily protected, all approaches patrolled. There must be an element of surprise. We have to catch them totally off guard."

"Same problem with a seaplane or a floatplane," Frank added.

"They'd be worse," Billy corrected. "We'd need more than one, unless we could find a big one. The bigger the plane, the harder it'd be to achieve surprise. It'd be difficult enough to charter a boat without Belalcazar knowing about it. One or two planes would be impossible."

"Well, helicopters are out," Eric added. "Might just as well drop leaflets letting them know we're on our way."

"Which means we have to parachute," David concluded, ready to put on his gear and jump.

"But that's not so easy either," Billy cautioned. He shuffled through the satellite reconnaissance photos and separated the first picture, a twenty-five-meter image that looked as if it had been taken from 35,000 feet, roughly the altitude commercial aircraft fly. He then selected a five-meter image of the island. It looked as if it was taken from ten thousand feet. Another was of a clarity that suggested it was taken from half that distance. All of the photos were grainy. "Jenny can enhance these pictures later, but I don't think it'll affect this point. I don't see any drop zones except on the lawn surrounding the hacienda. That's a possibility. Could also land on the roof of the hacienda itself. Some of us are accurate enough with chutes to pull that off, providing the wind is calm . . . and there's enough moonlight to see." He paused to reflect. "We would have to go in at night, no matter where we landed, especially if we land on the lawn or on the roof." His voice trailed off as he tried to work out the details of each option.

"Yeah, but the roof's small. Looks like there's a courtyard in the middle. Like a square doughnut," Eric observed.

"But land in the jungle, and we have to make our way through snake-infested jungle as thick as we saw back in 'Nam," Matthew cautioned.

"And we'd be toting heavy backpacks of food, water,

ammunition, and weapons," David added, the first to mention weapons.

"And we're not kids anymore," Billy noted. "I'd even have serious reservations sending in the young men and women from the Eighty-second Airborne, unless there was just no other choice. This is an extremely difficult mission."

No one spoke for a minute or two, picking at their food, sipping water or coffee, and trying to formulate a plan. Jenny was the first to come close to succeeding.

"Do you think they'd hear or see the plane if it dropped us off from, say, seventy-five hundred feet?" she asked Billy, but turning to David as well. "Even if we find a place to drop, if they hear us coming in we'd lose the element of surprise," she reasoned, surprising everyone except David with how fast she was picking up on battle tactics.

"I thought about that," Billy responded. "A low-flying plane could be seen or heard and send the guards into instant alert. We'd have to drop from much higher. Free-fall to two thousand feet or so and pop the chutes."

"A night HALO jump?" Matthew asked, his voice betraying his alarm. After receiving a tug on his arm from Linda, he explained that it was military jargon for a high-altitude, low-opening parachute drop. From the sound of his voice, she got the message that it was no cakewalk. "I'd bet you're probably the only one in this room who has done a HALO jump, day *or* night," Matthew continued as he stared at Billy.

"You'd lose that bet," Billy said solemnly. "I've never done it. That's for young soldiers. Not me."

"I've done it," Jenny said. "Twice. For fun on weekends. I've been skydiving since I was in college. Normally we'd jump from ten thousand to twelve thousand feet. But twice I jumped from just above twenty thousand and didn't pop the chute until two thousand feet. It was fantastic. But then I didn't do it at night. I wasn't carrying water, food, or weapons. I wasn't landing in shark-infested waters or a jungle. And nobody was shooting at me."

Billy spun his spoon in his coffee cup, making a little whirlpool, his eyes fixed on the movement. "There's no other way to do it," he announced. "Just no other way. But I think we'd get by with a jump from fourteen thousand or fifteen thousand feet. They couldn't hear the plane at that altitude. We'd jump as far away from the island as the wind permits. Here's how I see it," he said, rising from his chair to stand next to the maps. "Four of us will jump from the lowest altitude possible, depending on the weather conditions. I think I can get my hands on the equipment. We land in the water here," he said, pointing to a spot on the east coast of the island, approximately midway north to south. "We'll land in the water as close to the shore as possible, well within the reefs. If there's a small beach, then all the better. The reefs will offer some protection from the waves if the seas are heavy from the east. They also may keep out the sharks. Let's hope for that," he added seriously. "We'll be about three miles from the compound on the northern tip of the island. That's far enough for them not to see us, even on a clear night. Once we're down, we'll head by raft up the coast until we get within a thousand yards or so of the compound. Two of us will head inland and attack from the south. Two will take a raft and make a wide loop to the east, far enough out of sight of the compound and the guards patrolling the breakwaters, and circle back to land from the north. The trick is to hit them just before first light. We'll need the right kind of weapons."

"Who jumps, and what do the rest of us do?" Linda asked, knowing that she could not make the jump.

"Four parachute in," Billy responded. "The others fly to Colombia. Go to Buenaventura and charter—or steal—a boat and come rescue us within forty-five minutes of our attack," Billy responded, pursing his lips at the complexity of the mission. "My candidates for the jump are David, Matthew, Jenny, and me.

"Frank," Billy stated before Frank could protest, "you could make the jump as well as the rest of us, but we need you on the boat. Any boat you get is likely to be a pile of junk. We'd need you to skipper and be the mechanic. Eric, you're in no condition to do a jump and then tromp through the jungles. Sorry. But you'll be on the boat," he said authoritatively, taking command of the operation. "Linda, it's pretty clear that Isla Gorgona isn't a good place to learn how to skydive." He smiled. "You speak Spanish well. It'll come in handy on the mainland."

"Perhaps we can get Santiago to join us," Eric proposed, indicating that he wouldn't contest his assigned role. "He might want to add Belalcazar to his collection of late drug lords. I'll get his number and call him."

"Great," Billy responded. "We're going to need all the help we can get," he said as he returned to his chair, his mind already beginning to puzzle over the next set of logistical and tactical concerns.

"What about the Waldrons?" David asked. "Their daughter's on the island."

"Well," Billy began, exhaling loudly as if to let everyone know that he was making this up as he went. "I presume they've never skydived. I don't know if they speak Spanish. I have no idea if they have experience with weapons. What do they add?" No one had a ready response.

"Excuse me," Jenny said after a few moments. "I have to go upstairs," she said as she rose from her chair. "I'll be right back." She walked up the stairs slowly, picking up the pace as she entered her and David's bedroom. She sat in front of the computer, grateful that it was still on. The screen saver saying *Women Rule* bounced slowly from one side of the screen to the other. Once again she put in Jonathan's e-mail address at LKB and typed in *N$N,* the code they had agreed upon back in Brooklyn for "need money now," and clicked on the send button.

"Happy Jack will probably do it," David conceded in response to a comment from Billy that Jenny didn't hear as she returned to the living room. "But his plane doesn't have the range. It's good for the local jumps. But here we're talking about a trip that's approximately six thousand miles, with the four of us, our gear, Jack, and maybe a copilot as well. He'd need a bigger, faster plane."

"What about the gear and hardware?" Frank asked.

"Normally we could buy a hell of a lot of it," Billy answered. "Hell. Folks who collect guns buy a lot of the weapons we would need, and anyone can buy a hand-held global positioning system receiver."

"You forget that two of us are fugitives, and the rest of you soon will be," Matthew said soberly.

"I know that. Well, if we can get down to Bragg, I think I can get us some gear there. Won't be easy, but maybe I can cash in some more chips. Let me work on that," he added as he sought to recall who he knew at Fort Bragg.

"Excuse me; I'll be right back," Jenny whispered as she rose and turned to go upstairs. No one noticed the spring in her step. She checked her e-mail. There it was. Jonathan had responded with the agreed-upon code: *$2BD2,* the code for "money to be delivered tomorrow." Very pleased, she hurried down the steps to join the others.

In her absence, the conversation had turned to the boat and the related logistics of getting Frank, Eric, and Linda to Colombia, linking them up with Pablo Santiago, if he would in fact join them, and then getting them to Buenaventura and on a boat without their being detected.

"Our chances of being detected by Belalcazar's men is high. Very high," Frank explained to Linda so she would understand the full danger.

"I think that our good general here," Eric said with a gesture to Billy, "understands that we'll be detected. We're decoys, right, Billy?"

"You are," Billy admitted. "I won't deny that. Belalcazar and his men must think we're coming at them from the mainland. Otherwise they might figure out that we'll parachute in. But this is *not* a sacrificial diversion. I wouldn't do that with my soldiers and I certainly won't do that with you. This operation has to be credible and well planned to get you safely to the island with the boat and then to get us all to Panama."

"What about money?" Frank asked. "We'll need money for air tickets to Colombia. Money to charter a boat. Big-time money to buy or even charter a plane. Money to get us to Jack's place, if that's what we intend to do. I hate to be the one to say this, but we need money that I personally don't have. My money's tied up in fishing boats. I could borrow some, but not enough to make even a small dent."

"Frank's got a good point," Eric agreed. "If I cashed in everything I owned, I could probably contribute something like forty-two cents. My ex owns everything else."

"I can get us about fifty thousand dollars," Billy said, casting a glance at Faith. The two lived comfortably, but college for their two girls was costing them a minor fortune, and they had little cash to spare.

"And I emptied my money market and checking accounts before I left Santa Monica," Matthew commiserated with the others. "I have twenty-two thousand in cash. The other twenty-five thousand was confiscated by the goddamned FBI."

"My accounts are frozen," David said.

"My assets are totally illiquid. The FBI isn't going to let me get anywhere near them. But money's not going to be such a problem," Jenny added, causing everyone to turn to her.

"What do you mean?" David asked, surprised.

"Well, you see, after that horrible night at the restaurant, a buddy of mine and I set up some offshore companies and foreign bank accounts for each company in the Cayman Islands, Gibraltar, Cyprus, and Panama. I just thought it was a good measure of caution in case you needed to free up some money. I made contingency arrangements to get the money in your accounts wire-transferred to these banks in the name of the offshore companies. I just went upstairs to send an e-mail and then back to verify that the transfers were being done. By my guess, you'll have about four-point-two million in the Cayman company's corporate account in Panama by tomorrow. The rest will go to other accounts in Cyprus and the Cayman Islands."

"How in the name of God can you do that?" Faith asked, as amazed as the others.

"Well, it's not exactly legal, of course." Jenny smiled nervously. "My friend and I . . . well, make that my friend at this point . . . hacked into the bank's computers and instructed them to override the freeze order and to transfer the money out. The money's routed to various offshore accounts in havens that guard bank secrecy at all costs. Yes, this is the same technique money launderers use. David's banks and the FBI will never trace them. Well, at least it'll take them a long time. They won't even know the money's missing for a few days. My guess is that it would take them months to track down the final destination of the money."

Jenny looked at her friends, who in turn stared at her as though she were some sort of wizard. "Well, come on, guys. We need the money," she stated defensively with a shrug and a modest smile. "We also need someone's—my suggestion is Eric's—bank account information so we can transfer some money to us here."

"You are one tough bitch," David said admiringly. He laughed and squeezed her. "You are one very tough bitch," he repeated, as everyone laughed in relief.

Chapter 16

"Jack? Hi, this is Eric. I need to have a long conversation with you later today, buddy, but I can't talk now. Give me a number where I can reach you in about three hours, say, at noon my time, nine o'clock your time, but not your home or office." Eric wrote the number down on a small piece of paper and put it in his wallet. "Don't ask," Eric instructed as Jack began to ask the obvious questions. Eric hung up the pay phone outside the convenience store several miles from his apartment. It would be the one call he would make to Jack's home.

Eric drove to Fredericksburg, Virginia, outside what he figured was the NSA's normal listening area around Washington. After driving around the town for a few minutes, he found what he was looking for, an enclosed phone booth, the old-fashioned kind that protects from the wind. He quickly parked and stepped into the booth, closing the folding door behind him. He opened three rolls of quarters and put them on the small stainless-steel counter. He then dialed the number Jack had given him and began to drop quarters into the slot. Twenty-two dollars later he had brought Jack up to speed on the plan, enlisted his support, and discussed weight and range requirements. The two agreed that the next communication to Jack would be from Billy. Eric would be leaving for Colombia shortly and would be out of touch. They bade each other farewell and good luck. Eric then drove at a correct fifty-five to sixty miles per hour back to his home.

On Monday afternoon, Eric drove to a bank he seldom frequented but where he maintained a very modest checking account that he had never disclosed to his ex-wife, and withdrew the $200,000 that Jonathan had arranged to wire-transfer to him from Cyprus. It had taken some convincing on Eric's part for the bank to release that much cash at one time, but after presenting his CIA identification badge with his picture on it and a plea to keep the matter quiet as a matter of national security, the bank manager had acquiesced. Stifling an urge to laugh, Eric had stuffed the cash in his bag, walked out of the bank, and driven to his home. As planned, Linda and Frank were in his apartment when he returned, ready and waiting with their carry-on bags at their feet.

Their plan was to drive to Houston and catch a plane to Mexico City. From there they would fly to Bogotá and link up with Pablo Santiago, who had readily agreed to help when Eric called him, and the Waldrons. After much debate in the two days since the delivery of the satellite photos, it had been decided to make the Waldrons part of the team that would go to Buenaventura. Linda had been assigned the task of getting in touch with them and had reported back that the Waldrons were, to say the least, willing. The drive to Houston would take about twenty-four hours. It would be grueling, but it would delay anyone tracking them. A flight out of Dulles would be too easy for the Feds. A nonobvious airport as their point of departure could throw the Feds off a day or two, perhaps. It would buy them time they increasingly felt they needed.

"You have a booger in your nose."

"Do not," Justin said angrily. Lisa, now called Sofia, annoyed him. Knowing that she annoyed him, she tried all the harder to get under his skin. "You're jealous 'cause Stephanie likes me better," he teased, setting aside for the moment that he really didn't like the nanny.

"Where do you live?" Lisa asked him.

"New York City. I'm going back when my daddy comes. Do you live in New York?" Justin forgot that she had already said she lived in Stamford, wherever that was.

"How many times do I have to tell you?" she responded, irritated. "I live on Shippan Point. My mommy and daddy love me. They're coming to get me tomorrow," she insisted.

"My dad's coming next week," Justin retorted, confusing himself as to whether it was true.

"My mom's coming too," Debbie said, fearful she'd be left behind when Lisa's and Justin's parents took them home.

"And you *do* have a booger in your nose," Lisa teased.

"You're a jerk," he said defiantly, his voice rising. Stephanie heard him and scolded him.

"You don't have a booger in your nose," Debbie whispered kindly.

Major General Billy Dunn boarded the army Cessna at Fort Belvoir south of Washington for the hour-long flight to Fort Bragg, North Carolina, where in two weeks' time he was scheduled to take command of the army's most elite corps, fully 40 percent of the army's combat strength.

Once there, he made an all-important phone call. "Top, I'm looking forward to working with you. It's been a long time," Billy said. "I'm here early on personal matters. As you know, the change-in-command ceremony is two weeks from tomorrow. But still, I want to get a jump on things and get the lay of the land. See where my DZs are, if you will."

He hadn't been particularly close to Ralph Webster, the man who was now the command sergeant major of the XVIII Airborne Corps. They had worked together at Fort Riley, where Billy had saved him from a court-martial and an abrupt demotion from sergeant to private E-1. Webster had been drinking while on duty and had nearly directed artillery on his own men by mistake while out on maneuvers on the plains of western Kansas. Billy would have drummed him out of the army in a New York minute, but Webster had pleaded, promising to overcome his alcohol problem and put his family life back together. He did put the alcohol behind him and saved his marriage, keeping his wife and three children. With the monkey off his back, he had become an extraordinary soldier and served as Billy's first sergeant, his Top, when they later served together in Germany. Webster had risen to become the highest ranking enlisted man in the XVIII Airborne Corps, but to Billy he was still his Top.

"Sir, my pleasure. It's an honor to serve under you again," the sergeant major responded truthfully. "Where can I meet you, sir?"

"Let's meet in front of Womack Hospital and just take a walk. I'll be in civvies, but don't bother to change."

The two men greeted each other warmly in front of the hospital. Active-duty soldiers and their families, as well as retired personnel and their dependents, went in and out of the hospital, too busy with their own lives to notice them.

"Good to see you, sir," the command sergeant major said genuinely.

"Top," Billy began, "I want to tell you a story." His career was effectively over the day he had decided to harbor David and Matthew. The course of action he was about to embark on would not only end his army career; it could land him in jail, if it didn't kill him first. As much as he loved David and Justin, it was a tough decision. Commander of the XVIII Airborne Corps! Finally within his grasp after all these years, yet he had decided to turn away from it all. "Please just listen to me until I'm finished," he said as they started their walk west on Normandy Road. "When I'm finished with my story, I'm going to ask you to do me a very big favor. If you can't or won't do me that favor for whatever reason, I'll understand and won't hold it against you. But if you can't, or won't, then I'll ask you to do me a smaller favor, and that's to forget this conversation ever took place."

"Yes, sir," Webster replied cautiously, not having the slightest idea what the general was about to disclose.

The two men walked for an hour in the dark, avoiding

the crowded areas, sticking to roads where there were few pedestrians. Billy did all the talking, with Top posing a question or two here and there.

"So you see, Top, not only do I not have a choice about this, I *want* to help David Craig. This madman has his son. The man who saved my life at Ripcord is now faced with the possibility of going onto that island by himself or with the only friends who will help him. I'm going, Top. And I'm going real soon."

Webster said nothing as they continued to walk slowly in the cold. As he stood under a street lamp at the corner of Normandy Road and Bastogne, he had no doubt about the magnitude of General Dunn's decision and request. He also realized that a major chip, earned by the general many years earlier, was about to be cashed in. Command Sergeant Major Webster didn't know the cost to him, but he assumed it would be high, and he knew he would pay it.

"Sir," he said as he pulled out his wallet, "I've got three kids. Two daughters and a boy. They're all grown up now. You helped me hold my marriage together back at Riley. Without that I probably wouldn't have watched them grow up, and wouldn't be enjoying my five grandchildren. My oldest girl's second daughter, Brenda—here she is," he added, handing a wallet-size photo to General Dunn, "she's six and she has leukemia, sir. My son-in-law's a spec-four. They're stationed at Fort Gordon, so they're not far away. Susan and I get down to see them as often as we can. Brenda's been through treatment at the army hospitals and they've been great. My daughter and her husband couldn't have afforded it on the outside, sir. But it doesn't look like she's gonna make it. Maybe just a few months left." He paused to wipe the tears from his eyes. "Christ," he said, gathering his strength. "When I think about someone kidnappin' my little Brenda . . . well . . . can't even think about it."

The Top sniffled and cleared his throat. He didn't want to break down in front of the general. He resumed walking, holding the picture of his granddaughter in his hand. Billy followed his lead and walked alongside him.

"You know the army, sir," Webster continued, regaining his composure. "We grunts don't take to anyone who injures a child. Kidnap a kid and we lock 'n' load. Then you consider that the boy's father's got the Congressional. That's quite a combination, sir. You gimme the word, sir, and I'll put together a reinforced rifle company of volunteers by tomorrow morning. Gimme two days and I'll get the air force over at Pope to take us there in C141s."

"Thanks, Top," Billy said placing his arm briefly around Webster's shoulder, as much to thank him as to comfort him. "But you know I can't ask for volunteers. I need your help in another way, though. I need transportation on army aircraft. To San Diego, or as near as you can get me and three others. Nobody can know about it. We can't be listed on the passenger logs. I know it's against regulations, but that's the way it has to be."

"I think I can swing it, sir. If a command sergeant major can't pull that off, nobody can."

"I'm not done yet," Billy cautioned. "I need gear for four for a parachute drop—we'll jump from fifteen thousand feet or so—complete with a four-person raft, EPIRBs, and the whole works. I'll also need hardware. Grenades, night-vision goggles, the latest in telecom gear, GPS, sidearms, and anything else you can suggest."

"What about rifles, sir? You didn't say anything about rifles."

"Well, I was getting to that, Top," Billy whispered as they reached the intersection of Normandy and Ardennes Road. "I don't just need rifles. I need four M16A2/M203s."

"Jeez, sir. That's a lot of firepower. We normally have only one grenade launcher per squad. From what you tell me, it sounds like all of you will be toting them. Sir, that's a pretty tall order. Let me see what I can do and get back to you."

"No time, Top. You know how these things unfold. There's never enough time. I need them and the transportation in the air by this time tomorrow." He checked his watch and confirmed with Webster, "Nineteen hundred hours. I need the plane off the tarmac at nineteen hundred hours."

"Sir, I know what Craig means to you. Fact that he's got the Congressional means a lot to me. Fact that the bad guys got his boy . . . well, sir, that says it all. I'll do what I can." He paused and looked directly into Billy's eyes. "Airborne, sir!" he added with a crisp salute.

"All the way."

Faith slowed to a stop as she approached the MPs at the gate until they recognized her behind the wheel and snapped to attention. She pulled the U-Haul van into the driveway of the large Federal-style house that she and Billy had called home for the past three years. She and her fugitives loaded the vehicle with the small bags of clothing and toiletries they carried, the PC that Jenny had insisted be carted out and destroyed, and an old living room couch that belonged to the army. It was a crime to steal the furniture, Faith acknowledged to herself, but the interior of the old and deteriorating house was scheduled to be gutted and refurbished upon their departure, before the next general-grade officer could move in. She figured the army wouldn't miss the furniture it was going to destroy anyway, and in the scope of things, this was the least of their crimes. At two-fifteen P.M., with Jenny, David, and Matthew seated behind her in the truck, Faith left Fort Meyer for the last time.

"Has anyone gone through these boxes?" asked an FBI agent recently assigned to the Craig file.

"Don't think so. We've been so understaffed it's ridiculous. Dig in. You find anything, you let me know."

"Sir, could I talk to you?" the agent said, knocking on his boss's door less than three hours after he opened the first box of materials removed from David Craig's home and stored at the regional office for safekeeping. "I've sifted through the cases and found some interesting stuff. Don't know why we haven't thought about this, but Craig was in the war—"

"We know that," the older agent cut him off. "Hell, that's been in the friggin' newspapers."

"Yeah, I know that, sir. But he's got war buddies."

"What?" the overworked and irritable senior agent groused.

"War buddies. Appears he stays in touch with them fairly often. Still, don't have phone records so we don't know how often they talk, but it looks like he meets them once a year or so. Lots of photos of them at reunions somewhere in the desert. They're skydivers. Looks like they meet once a year and jump from airplanes. I think we should follow up on it."

"Fercrisakes," the older agent said, expelling air through his teeth loudly. "You're right. Christ, don't know what the hell we've been thinking. Get on it. Fast. Get two agents to help you track them down."

The crime scene had been sealed off. The restaurant remained closed as forensic studies continued and the owner made plans for renovations. Two uniformed policemen kept guard in front of Moynihan's to make sure no one tampered with evidence or looted the restaurant.

Two dogged NYPD detectives remained stubbornly at the scene despite the late hour and the freezing temperature. Det. Malcolm Kitt jogged quickly across Tenth Avenue, too cold from the brisk wind to wait for the WALK sign. He approached his colleague, who, flashlight in hand, had been examining the area where the two FBI agents had been killed in their car.

"Don't know about you, Mickey, but I'm stumped. I don't get it," he added, waving his arm across the street to the restaurant.

"Me neither," Det. Mickey Connelly responded. "I don't understand how they did it. Craig and Rice whack Harrison and Evans and then just saunter across Tenth Avenue and ice these two guys in their car?"

"Maybe there were others."

"Possible," Connelly admitted. "Let's walk the scene again."

Chapter 17

Jack Heed was thrilled. Eric had told him the plan. It was up to him to do the rest. He hadn't been so excited in years, maybe not since he had jockeyed a Huey in the war. This wasn't a routine excursion for his weekend customers. These were friends who knew his wife and children. Friends who needed help as badly now as they had back in Laos when he pulled them out of a nasty firefight. It had taken him all of a few seconds to volunteer. He consulted his wife, Claudia, briefly outlining the situation and hoping she would agree with his decision. "Go get the boy," she said in her native Spanish. And that was that.

Happy Jack plunged into the project, canceling all other appointments under the pretext of being ill. He pulled out his charts of Mexico, Central America, and Colombia and made a rough sketch of a flight plan, calculating weight and fuel requirements. His Cessna wouldn't do the trick. He needed a plane with greater range. Eric had said that there would be four adults and about five hundred pounds of gear. Eric okayed a copilot, saying money wasn't a concern. Jack offered the copilot's slot to his friend Chris. He accepted on the spot, happy to have the extra cash.

Jack contacted several aircraft brokers in southern California. After considering his options, he settled on a 1996 Beech King Air B200 down at Brown Field, just south of San Diego. The owner was a prominent lawyer in San Diego, who frequently chartered the plane. He was also a bandit. The going rate for the plane was between $1.6 to $1.7 million, depending upon its condition.

The lawyer, sensing Jack's urgency, opened at $2 million. Jack countered with $1.8 million, which was accepted without further negotiation. Jack was content that he had stayed within the range of Eric's instructions: "Whatever it takes." He simply asked for the lawyer's wire-transfer instructions, which were provided.

Jack and Chris immediately left Chris's mobile home and drove to Brown Field with their preferred mechanic to inspect the King Air. Pleased with the inspection, they were back at Chris's place within a few hours, drinking iced tea and waiting for the phone to ring.

Faith pulled off Highway 95 just south of Richmond at a large truck stop. After filling up the tank of the U-Haul at the self-service island and paying cash, she eased the vehicle as close to the outside phones as she could.

Jenny slid open the side door, dialed a number and deposited several quarters. The information Jack conveyed was short: $1.8 million for the owner of the plane and $25,000 to Chris's account. Jack would accept no money for himself. After writing down the wire-transfer instructions, Jenny put down the phone, called Jonathan back in New York, and gave him the same information, except that she added $50,000 to Jack's account just in case.

Within seconds of putting down the phone, Jonathan was tapping his keyboard to convey those same instructions to a bank in Panama City. The transfer would take twenty-four hours.

With the phone call successfully completed, the next stop was to dispose of the computer as planned. Faith pulled up next to a Dumpster behind the truck stop. Jenny jumped out and threw parts of the dismantled hard drive away. The other components of the PC were to be tossed into three different Dumpsters several miles apart. No trace of Jenny's end of her e-mails to Jonathan would be left behind.

Jack was already driving south on Route 79 from Warner Springs toward Julian. He stopped by the B-and-B to check in on Claudia, not wanting to use his cell phone. He parked on the steep hill and entered the kitchen through the rear door. Claudia ran to him, worry written across her face. "What is it?" he asked, fearing the worst.

"The FBI called about forty-five minutes ago. I wanted to call you, but you said not to use the phones."

"What did they want?" he asked, agitated.

"They wanted to talk to you. I told them you were away on business. I told them you took some fishermen to Canada."

"Did you tell them where in Canada?"

"No. I told them I didn't know."

"Great work. I gotta go," he said as he darted up the stairs. He quickly packed his small travel bag with toiletries and extra clothes, adding his .357 Smith & Wesson revolver and an extra box of ammunition. He almost knocked Claudia off her feet as he pushed the swinging door into the kitchen, once again ignoring the *Open Slowly* sign.

"Claudia, listen carefully. They'll be here soon. They'll find my plane at Borrego Springs. If they ask, tell 'em you think I chartered a bigger plane for the trip to Canada. Otherwise, just play dumb. You don't know anything. I'll sleep on the floor at Chris's place tonight. Don't call or come to see me." He kissed her passionately and embraced her as he always did before a long flight. This one was different, though, and their bodies lingered together a few extra moments. As they separated, he ran his fingers through her short, lustrous black hair and, gently touching his fingertips to her lips, told her that he loved her.

A few moments later, he was heading south on Route 79 on his way to Brown Field. As he passed the turnoff to Route 20 at the Cuyamaca Reservation, he saw a late-model navy blue Caprice coming north up the hill with two white males in the front seat. He quickly pulled his handkerchief from his shirt pocket and hid his face in it, faking a sneeze as the two FBI agents passed him. He was soon at Brown Field on the Mexican border. After he and the lawyer's mechanic made sure the plane was ready, there was nothing more he could do but wait for the wire transfer in the morning. He bought the maps he needed and headed for Chris's home. His heart raced with each mile. He hadn't had this much fun since 'Nam.

At five-fifteen P.M., Faith steered the U-Haul van between the dividers that separated the Burger King parking lot and the Holiday Inn so that she didn't have to pass the hotel's office. The front right wheel and then the rear right wheel thumped over the six-inch-high concrete bars, jolting the three passengers in the back of the van. Faith saw the Ford Taurus that Billy told her he would rent. It was parked under a lamppost. The green-and-white National Car Rental bumper sticker partially covered with an army bumper sticker confirmed that it was Billy's car. She parked the van close to the Taurus, gave two quick taps on the horn, and stepped out into the well-lit parking lot. Billy appeared on the second-floor walkway. Within seconds they were all in the room.

"Now listen up," Billy instructed. "I spoke to Jack an hour ago. The FBI's on to him. They called Claudia and then came out to the B-and-B. Claudia's telling 'em she doesn't know where he is. His plane's at Borrego Springs." He paused, realizing that he might need to fill in the gaps for Jenny. "That's where he's got his jump club. He's staying with a friend. Guy named Chris. He'll copilot for us. The new plane's ready to go when the owner gets his money. Hopefully, that's tomorrow morning." He looked around the room to see if anyone had any questions or comments.

"I've prevailed upon an old friend of mine to get the four of us on an army flight to Fort Huachuca in Arizona. It leaves in less than two hours. The same friend is trying to get us the gear we'll need, but I can't say at this moment that we'll have all or any of what we want. We'll just play it by ear. If need be, we'll buy what we need in Kingman, Arizona, or some other place. Matthew knows where to buy this stuff. It'll take time and money if we have to do that, but I guess Jenny can get us the money."

Jenny looked at Billy knowingly. "I've arranged for Jack and Chris to have some extra cash—fifty thousand dollars—in case we need it."

"I figured as much when Jack told me you were wiring more than he asked for. Good move," Billy approved.

Faith was fighting back her tears. She kissed her husband of twenty-six years, the father of their two girls, and she tried to stay strong for him. She then kissed David and Matthew and embraced Jenny as though they, too, had been lifelong friends. She followed them down to the parking lot and watched them pile into the car.

"Airborne," Billy said. He gave her one last loving smile as he stood, one foot in the car, the other foot planted on the asphalt. He sat down, put on his seat belt, and closed the door behind him.

"All the way," she whispered. "All the way."

Billy was careful to stay just under the speed limit as he drove north on the All American Freeway from central Fayetteville to Fort Bragg. He drove to Honeywell Road and turned right as Webster had suggested. He continued on Honeywell Road until he saw the Hardee's and turned into the parking lot, mindful to turn his directional signal on and drive slowly. He was sweating heavily despite the cool winter air of central North Carolina. He didn't want to show his anxiety to David, Jenny, and Matthew, and he was grateful that they could not see the beads of sweat running down his neck. Had he dared to discuss his apprehension with the others, he would have discovered that they, too, were dripping with sweat.

As agreed, Webster was sitting in his red Mercury Sable, driver's-side window down, parking lights on. Billy backed the rental car into the space next to his as the two men exchanged glances. Billy slid his long frame from behind the wheel with some difficulty, closed the door behind him, and sat next to the command sergeant major in his car.

"How'd we do, Top?"

"We got most of what you wanted, sir," he responded. "Got you on a flight out of Simmons that leaves in just under an hour. It's too risky to try to take you out of Pope. I don't know the air force types well enough to trust them on this one, sir, so you'll fly out of Simmons Army Airfield. The command sergeant major of the Eighteenth Weather Squadron and I are good friends. Go way back. He's worked some miracles for us," Webster continued, breathing rapidly. "It hasn't been easy, sir, but here's the plan. You need to get into your fatigues. I've got a set for you in case you didn't bring yours. The unit patches, rank, everything are sewn on, so don't worry 'bout a thing. We knew you were incoming as the new CO, so we had all that ready anyway. Your companions," he added, indicating David, Jenny, and Matthew, who watched silently from the other car, "will have to travel in uniform, too. I matched the sizes best I could from what you told me. I made up their names and ranks, and they all have travel orders in case someone asks, which I doubt they will under the circumstances.

"I've got a van over at Simmons parked next to a hangar. You'll change in the van. Flight's leaving for Fort Huachuca, stopping at Fort Polk along the way to pick up documents and refuel. There'll be a pilot and a copilot, both warrant officers. They've been told your group's top-secret and that none of you will be listed on the passenger manifest. The weight of your gear will also be off the books. They know your name, sir. I had to tell 'em that, or else I wouldn't have gotten to first base with 'em," he said as he looked at General Dunn for approbation and found it in a knowing nod.

"If anyone's nosing around, I'll throw up enough bureaucratic roadblocks to get you a couple of weeks or so, sir. Can't promise much more than that. Oh, sir," Webster added after a pause, "the pilots aren't dumb, and your people are front-page news. They'll recognize them. Don't worry 'bout it. They ferry around all sorts of people and they're accustomed to keeping their lips sealed. There won't be any security breaches. Ever."

"What about the hardware, Top?"

"Sir, if I can get to that in just a moment, I'll give you the full rundown." This was his show and he'd play it his way. "Now, here's the story when you get to Huachuca. The flight ends there. This is a regularly scheduled flight, so nothin' in the flight plan will be out of the ordinary. Can't get you any farther than that. But I've got a good buddy there, sir. His name's Marcus Sears. Master sergeant. He'll meet you at Libby Field. You're scheduled to land at Libby a little after oh-three-hundred hours. He'll be there with a rented truck or van. He'll spend a couple of hours with you in the desert to familiarize you with the weapons. After that, you're on your own . . . and . . . oh, sir," the Top added. "Marcus laid out cash. Used a false ID. He's tight on money. Several kids . . . you know. If you could reimburse him in cash when you hit Libby, he'd appreciate it. Maybe give him a little extra for staying up all night . . . takin' a risk . . . if you know what I mean?"

"Will do, Top. It's not a problem. Now, how about the gear?"

"I got you four M16A2/M203s and enough ammo to take on an enemy battalion, like you wanted. Your guys Craig and Rice will be familiar with the M16 side of that weapon. The A2 isn't quite fully automatic like the M16A1s they used in 'Nam. As you know, the A2s shoot in one-round or three-round bursts to cut back on wild firing. Otherwise, they're pretty much the same as your friends used before. You'll need to give 'em a refresher course and give the lady whatever training you have time for. The three of 'em will need instruction on the M203. Marcus will show 'em. They'll pick up on it fast. As you know, sir, the M203's easy to use. Laser sights and night-vision scopes. It'll blast the hell outta anything within three hundred meters. Believe me, they won't need much training."

"Okay, Top. What else do we have?" Billy asked, his voice betraying his eagerness.

"I've got all the jump gear, chutes, EPIRBs, Zodiac raft, jump helmets with night-vision goggles and altimeter warning devices. I also got you tac vests, camouflage watch/compasses, greasepaint, rations, water, water purification pills, canteens, load-bearing equipment . . . the works. You each get a Glock 35. It comes with a laser finder and with clip-on tactical illuminator flashlight."

"What about explosives?"

"You've got four antipersonnel grenades for each of you for tossing where you're too close to use the launchers. You've also got C4 plastic explosives and detonators."

"Commo?"

"Good stuff in this department, sir. It's all in the helmet. Each of you will have receivers and mikes. All you have to do is whisper."

"Great job, Top. I can't thank you enough. If the shit hits the fan and the Feds are coming down on you for this, denounce me and say you had nothing to do with it. Or tell 'em I blackmailed you or something."

"Already got it scripted, sir. I'll tell 'em that you assured me I'll be command sergeant major of the army when you become army chief of staff." He laughed, though actually he thought the idea not all that crazy. "One more thing, sir. I know you and Mr. Craig did that bayonet charge back at Ripcord. I highly recommend against that. You'll find Special Forces daggers on your LBE vests, and I've got extras to strap on your legs, but I suggest that you shoot from a distance. Daggers are too close for comfort. Gotta boogie, sir," he added, looking at his watch.

Billy looked at his watch and nodded, thanking Webster for the help. He stepped out of Webster's car and joined David and the others. As he turned the ignition key, he said to his three coconspirators, "We're good to go. Plane leaves at nineteen hundred hours."

They drove south on Bragg Boulevard. Billy followed Top closely to Simmons Army Airfield as he briefed David, Jenny, and Matthew on his conversation with Webster. The command sergeant major parked his car to the left of an olive-drab army van, motioning with his left arm out the window for Billy to park to the rear of the vehicle. Billy turned off the ignition. He and the others got out quickly and headed toward the two open rear doors of the van, where a soldier who appeared to be in his early twenties sat nonchalantly on the bed of the vehicle, his legs dangling out the back as he smoked a cigarette.

The staff sergeant climbed down from the driver's seat of the van as the SP4 made his way around the front of the vehicle. Each saluted Webster briskly. Billy was in his civilian clothing, and they had no idea who he was. "Where's the gear?" Webster asked.

"It's all on board, sealed in crates and fastened down as you said," the staff sergeant responded dutifully. "I checked the contents against the list," he added, handing over the only copy of the manifest that the Top had handwritten. "Here are the keys to the crates."

"Good work. You guys take a walk and come back in fifteen," he ordered. Webster pointed to the army fatigue uniforms heaped in four neat piles on the bed of the van. Next to each pile was a pair of immaculately polished black jump boots. "I'd suggest you change in the ladies' room, ma'am," Webster said apologetically to Jenny, "except that it's at the other end of the field. If you want to change separately, you can change in the van while the men change out here."

"Don't bother. I'll change here. The cold wind will do me good," she said matter-of-factly.

"Well, ma'am, at least I can give you some privacy," Webster said, turning away from her, surprised she had already removed her shoes and was unzipping her jeans like her male companions.

"Don't worry, Top. You saw more skin at the beach last summer than you'll see here," David said with a laugh.

"Don't be so sure." Jenny giggled. "I might have to take my bra off if they've given me an olive-drab one in this pile," she said to him as she fumbled through her stack of fatigues. She stood in her sweater and panties behind the van, convinced herself that an olive-drab bra had not been provided, and quickly slid into the fatigue pants, then removed her sweater and replaced it with the fatigue shirt. "Pretty good fit," she admitted. "I didn't know the army was so fashion-conscious. Who gave them my size?"

"The general did." Webster nodded with a grin as he motioned to Billy.

"So how'd you know my size?" she asked Billy, suppressing a laugh.

"Years of observation and fantasy," he answered with a smile. "David and Matthew have taught me well."

"You look great," David whispered in her ear.

" 'Scuze me. What rank are you?" she asked, not knowing what the stripes on his collar meant.

"I'm Sergeant Major Duffy. And you're Staff Sergeant Walker," he said, bending closer to read the fictitious name sewn on her right breast pocket, "and thus my subordinate. So you'll submit."

"I'll gladly submit, Mr. Sergeant Major, sir," she responded with her Chapel Hill accent and as good a salute as she could muster. "But not because you outrank me," she added with an inviting smile that would have led somewhere serious under different circumstances.

"Sorry to ruin the party. But you folks gotta go now," Webster interrupted. "The uniforms seem to fit all of you well enough. Sears will have another set for each of you when you hit Huachuca."

"You guys are amazing," Jenny said, impressed with army efficiency. She took two quick steps toward Webster and kissed him gently on the cheek. "Kissing's probably not the right protocol, but what the hell?"

"Quite all right with me, miss, but this here is nothin'. We moved half a million men and women to the Middle East in a few months in Desert Shield. If I can't get four good people to southern Arizona overnight, then I ain't for shit, 'scuze the expression, as a command sergeant major." He grinned. "All of you, please, listen up. Take all your civilian clothes with you on the plane. Put 'em in this duffel bag," he instructed, holding up the olive-drab duffel bag in his hand.

"Don't leave anything behind. Toss the bag somewhere between Huachuca and wherever you're going."

The two soldiers returned exactly fifteen minutes after they had departed. Webster instructed the SP4 to take the wheel of Billy's rental car. "General, my man here will drive your car back to the hotel and leave the keys under the front bumper. And, sir, I'll let your wife know where the keys are."

"Son," Billy called out as the SP4 started to walk toward the car. "There's a U-Haul van in front of my wife's hotel room. Room two-forty. There's an old couch inside. Could you please get the key from my wife, dump the couch somewhere, and then drop the van off at the nearest U-Haul? I'd appreciate it," he said earnestly, hoping no questions would be asked.

"No problem, sir," the young man responded with a salute. "Happy to help."

Billy turned to Webster. "Thanks, Top. Well done," he said as he patted him on the shoulder. "You've taken great risks to do what you have done. I'll never forget it."

"My pleasure, sir. Good luck findin' the boy." He looked to David and stepped toward him. "Mr. Craig?" he asked, his voice tentative until he saw the warmth in David's eyes. "I know what you did at Ripcord. What all of you did. And I'm honored to meet you." He sought the right words to say, but couldn't find them. "Airborne, sir." He locked his heels and saluted.

"All the way," David responded with the best salute he had delivered in three decades. "Thanks for all you've done."

Without saying another word, they made their way quickly to the plane. Billy, Jenny, and Matthew closed their fatigue jackets against the cold wind whipped by the turning propellers of the twin-engine turboprop. David kept his open, grateful for the blasts of cold air against his chest. It felt good to be out of the prisonlike confines of his apartment and the Dunns' house, and finally doing something.

Jenny looked for Webster through the porthole window next to her seat. He was long gone. The plane taxied across the tarmac to the runway, the engines revved to full power, shuddering until the pilot released the brakes. The plane lurched forward, reaching airspeed within a few moments, and lifted off the tarmac 2,300 feet later. Within seconds, the landing gear was raised and the plane began its rapid ascent to 21,000 feet, where it would stay until shortly before its first scheduled touchdown at Fort Polk in west-central Louisiana.

"Folks," the pilot announced over the speaker system, "we've got water, sandwiches and fruit for you in the fridge. There's also a Thermos of coffee. Help yourselves. Flight attendants are on strike." He laughed at his own joke, one he probably used on every flight. "You'll have to serve yourselves. Feel free to use the latrine, but please keep your seat belts on when you're seated. We expect turbulence over Georgia, and there's a storm brewin' over Mississippi. Might get rough."

"Okay," Billy said after the pilot finished. "Somebody get the sandwiches. We'll eat as we work. I spent a few hours today with the aerial reconnaissance people at the Eighty-second Airborne Division. I told 'em I needed help with a training exercise and they seemed to buy it. I gave them the digital enhancements that Jenny made for us of all the photos, and they've helped me analyze them. Recon people are trained at picking things out of aerial photos. Go light on the coffee. We'll work two hours, then sleep.

"If there are no objections," he said, looking primarily at David, "as the senior officer present, I'll be in command. Only one of us can be in charge, and I've got the most experience. If we're going to find Justin and get our asses off that island alive, we'll have to be the best-oiled commando team a bunch of aging farts and a banker lady can be. We're gonna go up against forces that are superior in number. We'll most likely have superior weaponry. But we still gotta catch 'em by surprise and knock 'em on their asses before they know what hit 'em. We'll synchronize to the second. We'll kick ass and take names . . . or . . . we'll fail."

"You're in command, General," David said without hesitation. "And we won't fail."

Chapter 18

The flight from Simmons Army Airfield to Fort Polk was as turbulent as the pilot had warned. The small plane bounced roughly on the strong air currents over Georgia and Mississippi. The passengers ate their sandwiches and fruit. No one drank coffee. The problem was not how to stay awake, but how to force themselves to sleep.

Billy laid out four of the digitally enhanced photos taken by the spy satellite. He first pointed out to the others the most obvious structures. The large hacienda in the center west of the compound. The hacienda's placement permitted a large field of fire for the defenders from an attack from the east, but little or no field of fire against an attack from the west near the cliffs. One helipad was near the marina, at the end of the southern breakwater. The boats in the marina were visible, as was what appeared to be a large repair shed at the intersection of the northern breakwater and the land. Another helipad was up the hill near the hacienda. The two appeared to be separated by a swimming pool. Directly north of the hacienda was the old lighthouse that had served as a guard tower when the compound was a prison. Now it appeared to serve as a radio tower as well. The recon experts agreed with Billy: The long building near the lighthouse was probably a barracks. A square building near the barracks appeared to be a mess hall.

"Now for the hard part," Billy said after each had an opportunity to study the four pictures. He took the last bite of his sandwich and a long drink of water. "Recon folks say that these are fuel tanks." He indicated with the eraser end of his pencil. "One is no doubt for the helicopters. The other is for the boats. We think the third is diesel to fuel the compound's generators. We don't need to get too bogged down in what kind of fuel is in which tank. We're gonna blow the hell outta all three of 'em."

Billy took another long drink and emptied the bottle of water. "We are assuming that this black box that separates the end of the breakwater from the helipad is a machine gun bunker." He indicated, again using the pencil as his pointer. "This bunker can direct fire at any vessel approaching from the southeast or east toward the marina. But it's blind to the west and northwest. It might be blind to the southwest as well, but we can't count on it. This black dot," he continued, "near the upper helipad, is also a bunker. It appears to be blind to the northwest due to the slope of the hill into which it is dug, but it commands a field of fire that covers the entire southern edge of the compound. Anything coming out of the jungle that they can see is mincemeat.

"By the way, this line that runs down the hill from the high point on the western edge of the island down to the sea on the eastern side appears to be a fence. Probably electrified to keep out intruders like us. Might also be designed to keep out all those nasty animals like snakes and caimans. Now back to the bunker. It also commands the entire lawn east of the hacienda and can easily reach the marina. We have to assume they're equipped with thirty-caliber machine guns, possibly even fifty-caliber. This dot over here northeast of the hacienda and thirty meters or so due east of what we think is the mess hall is another bunker. It has a clear field of fire over the entire marina and any approach to the marina from the northeast."

"It's like the Maginot Line," David observed. "Fixed fortifications facing in one direction. They're all blind to the west."

"Don't forget the lighthouse," Matthew cautioned. "It has three-hundred-and-sixty-degree vision. With sniper rifles and a nice machine gun, it can reach everything on the compound."

"The lighthouse is a problem," Billy acknowledged. "As for an approach from the west, keep in mind that the waves at the base of the cliffs, which are themselves formidable, are ten to fifteen feet high. We'd be smashed to bits if we tried to come from the west. Besides, folks, I don't know about you, but I'm a little too old to climb eighty-foot cliffs. That's for young people."

"Speak for yourself," Matthew responded.

"You wanna climb that cliff?" David joined in as he elbowed Matthew.

"No fucking way!"

"Okay, back to work," Billy said as the plane began to bounce heavily in the storm above central Mississippi. "Note that this little structure near the northern edge of the island but slightly to the east down near the marina"—he indicated with the pencil—"looks like a kennel. So, in addition to fixed fortifications, we can expect dog patrols. The guards will have some sort of assault weapon. My guess is M16s or AK47s. It's hard to see, but there are little dots all around the compound. Recon people think that they're light posts. They think that this place is lit up at night like Broadway. Makes sense. Any good security system would have plenty of lights. Also lots of cameras and motion detectors."

"What about electricity?" David asked as he continued to study the photos. "Do the recon guys agree with us that this large box between the lighthouse and the barracks is the main generator?"

Billy nodded. "Yep. And they agree that this box near the fuel tanks is the backup generator."

"What about guards and sandbag bunkers on the roofs of the buildings?" Matthew asked. "I don't see any."

"It looks like the roof's very sloped. Can't tell for sure, but that's my hunch. Steeply slanted tile roofs would make it damn near impossible for skydivers to land on them. Given the cleverness of the way this place is laid out, the recon guys don't think the designer would've missed that trick."

"So what's the plan?" Jenny asked.

"Okay. Pretty much as we discussed back at my place the other night, but with a few refinements," he said as the plane began to descend to Fort Polk. "We'll land off the eastern shore midway down the island and make our way north by raft as far as we can, just like we discussed. When we get a few hundred meters south of the marina, two of us will go ashore. That will be me and Matthew. I'll cross the island and attack from the west at the edge of the cliff. My job will be to take out the bunker near the higher helipad and then rush across the lawn to take out the bunker just north of the hacienda. Matthew will hug the eastern shore and take out the fuel tanks. Blowing the tanks should also take out the backup generator and the bunker nearby. Putting the backup generator and the bunker so near the tanks is a design defect in the security system, probably one of their few oversights. We'll take any breaks we can get. We'll deal with roving patrols as we encounter them. The grenade launchers are going to get a workout.

"After we're dropped off south of the compound, David and Jenny will take the raft and head far enough out to sea to stay out of the lights along the breakwater. You two will circle back to the northern edge of the island, staying clear of the bunker and the kennel. Remember the former prisoner who wrote the magazine article. He said there are large rocks at the very tip of the island that protect against the waves from the west, creating a small eddy in the current immediately to the east of those rocks. The photos show the rocks, but we'll have to take his word about the eddy. You'll land in that eddy, make your way up the edge of the cliffs to the main power generator, place your C4 charges on the generator and tower, and get the hell away from the blasts. You then run like hell for the hacienda. I'll cover the barracks with my grenade launcher after I take out the northeast bunker."

"What makes you so sure that the guards in the lighthouse won't see David and Jenny?" Matthew asked.

"We'll just have to hope that they're not expecting

any visitors coming from the north," Billy said, as if to say, *What the hell else can we do?* "As soon as the men in the lighthouse are taken out and the barracks is ablaze, the three of us will hightail it to the hacienda and look for Justin. I don't have any plans once we get inside the hacienda other than to guess that people sleep upstairs, not on the ground floor. We'll have to play it by ear from there."

"So what am I doing after I take out the south bunker and blow the fuel tanks?" Matthew asked.

"You race like a son of a bitch to the northern end of the marina and take out that bunker. You then secure the entire marina, killing anyone and everyone who might stop Frank, Eric, and the others from getting the rescue boat to us. They'll show up at dawn. We have to be ready to jump on the boat and get the hell out of there."

"No problem," Matthew responded matter-of-factly but with an exaggerated shrug, trying to add some levity to the situation and earning a smile from the other three. "So Frank and the cavalry will simply show up on time and ferry us out of danger after the four of us have taken on Belalcazar's entire security detail?"

"Do you have another plan?" Billy asked.

"It's a good plan, Billy," David said protectively. "It's not only a good plan. It's the only plan."

"We all know it's a dangerous mission and it's risky," Billy said somberly as the plane descended toward Fort Polk. "We all know that if there is a way, this is it. We'll rehearse the hell out of it from here on in. Overwhelming firepower, surprise, and determination are our strengths," he said as the plane touched down at Fort Polk. "And fatigue is our enemy. We sleep from here to Huachuca, and then we take turns sleeping in the van or truck from Huachuca to the strip where we meet Jack. Think and sleep. That's our job for the next forty-eight hours or so. Then all hell breaks loose."

"So you tell me they're all missing! One's called in sick, and no one can find him, even though he's some honcho at the CIA. A fisherman disappears. A charter pilot goes off to Canada without a flight plan and he can't be contacted. It's all bullshit. Too much coincidence. But a fucking two-star general who's about to take over the entire airborne operations of the U.S. Army in two weeks takes an emergency 'family' leave and he can't be reached! The army doesn't allow a goddamn lieutenant to be unreachable, let alone a fucking general," Agent Rakovic screamed at the men around the conference table, where they assembled twice daily in the Hoover Building. It was the end of another frustrating day on the Craig case, and Rakovic was exasperated. "Now, what the hell would happen if we were to go to war tonight? Are you telling me that the Eighteenth Airborne Corps doesn't know where its next commander is?"

"Sir," a young agent dared to interject, "he's on emergency leave and between assignments. He's not due to take over the Eighteenth for another two weeks."

"Shut up, for Christ sake," the senior agent yelled. "Call the fucking army chief of staff himself and have the army find Dunn. Kick some ass over at CIA and find Randall. Now, what's the story on this Happy Jack character?"

"Well, sir," a lanky agent looking much younger than his thirty years volunteered, "his plane's still on the tarmac outside his jump club. His wife says he chartered another plane and flew to Canada. Very little way to check that out, sir. Borrego Springs airport's an uncontrolled field. No FAA monitoring. No control tower. Just a private strip. Planes come and go all the time. Even if you have a flight plan, there's nobody to register it with at these fields."

"How many airstrips are there like this?" Rakovic snapped, amazed that people could still fly around the country without being monitored.

"Hundreds, maybe thousands."

As the plane began its descent over the Arizona desert, David looked over at Jenny, who slept in the rear-facing seat in front of him. His faced hers. He thought about how much he loved her and how little chance he had had to express it. Their years of admiration from a distance, growing attachment, intimate conversations on business trips. Chicago. And then terror. They had made love several times at the Dunns', but with the exception of the last night, he was tense and preoccupied. As he watched her sleep, he longed to feel her pressed against him. He knew at that moment that if they survived the coming battle, he'd ask her to marry him.

"What are you looking at?" she asked from underneath her army cap.

"The person I love," he said quietly.

"Me too," she said as she sat up. "But what were you thinking?"

"Actually, I thought you were sleeping and I was mentally taking your clothes off. You have a problem with that, Staff Sergeant?"

"Yes, First Sergeant. I do. I'd rather you took them off for real." She smiled. She removed her cap and ran her fingers through her short blond hair and then put her cap back on, this time on the top of her head instead of over her face.

"Keep it clean over there," Matthew joked. "Billy and I are supervising you lovebirds. Nobody gets naked on a U.S. Army plane. They only do that in the navy."

"Did any of you get any sleep?" Billy asked, receiving three resounding nos as the answer.

"I did think a lot," David added. "So I didn't disobey your order in full, General, sir," he quipped, surprising even himself with how far his spirits had bounced back. "I thought about Jenny's breaking into the banks' computers and transferring my money out, sending it through cyberspace to banks in unsavory places all over the world. Damn, she already controls all my money and she's not even my wife yet."

"Well, well, Mr. Craig," Jenny quickly said. "I don't believe that you have asked for my hand."

"Christ, David," Matthew enjoined, "you have a way

with words. Don't believe I've ever heard anyone propose quite that way."

"What would you know about marriage proposals, Rice?" Billy interjected. "You probably can't even spell the word."

"So . . . will you?" David asked, ignoring the others' banter.

"Will I what?" Jenny asked tentatively.

"Marry me when all this is over."

She nodded, momentarily speechless.

"Say yes now and I'll throw in Hawaii with Justin over spring break," he added.

"Deal," she said, smiling, extending her hand to shake his.

"Deal." He took her hand in his and kissed it. Matthew and Billy clapped and cheered. Jenny leaned forward to kiss David on the lips. "Wait!" he said with mock seriousness. Everyone was suddenly silent. "First we have to negotiate the prenup."

"Prenup, my ass. I already have your money!" she said, drawing howls of laughter from them all.

"I don't know about you folks," Billy interrupted as the plane slowed to a halt on the tarmac. "I got a car waiting for me," he added, looking out the window. A tall, good-looking African-American NCO was standing next to a National Car Rental van. Billy opened the door to the plane and let the steps down carefully. "You go ahead and get out. I'll slide the gear to you."

Matthew was closest to the door and was the first to disembark. He shook hands with the NCO, noting that the name on his jacket was Sears, but didn't volunteer either his own real name or the one sewn on his fatigue jacket.

Webster, back at Bragg, hadn't told Sears who the passengers were, so he did a double take when he saw David. His eyes quickly shifted to Jenny, and he recognized her instantly despite her military uniform and change of hair. "Holy shit," he exclaimed involuntarily. David, Jenny, and Matthew winced. *Damn the evening news,* David thought. Like almost everyone else in the army, Sears had paid particular attention to the kidnapping and its aftermath. Craig had the Congressional. Nothing focused the attention of army lifers more than someone with the Congressional Medal of Honor. Like many NCOs, Sears had read about the bayonet charge and was generally familiar with David's having saved Billy Dunn, a black man. As with many other black NCOs, the fact that a white man had risked his life to save a black man back in 1968 struck a chord. David was already golden in Sears's book.

Billy slid the last crate out the door. David and Matthew carried them to the van. Billy yelled a heartfelt thank-you to the two pilots, who had remained in their seats, despite their eagerness to get to their quarters and catch a couple hours' sleep.

"Sir, as far as the world knows, we never saw you. Neither you nor your pals were ever on our plane," the pilot said as he gave a short salute and a wink. He knew exactly who his passengers were. Billy returned the salute and backed down the steps, glad to put his feet on the ground. The cool night air refreshed him. He glanced at his watch: 0245. More than fifteen minutes ahead of schedule. Libby Field seemed as empty as the desert surrounding Fort Huachuca. The full moon was bright and the sky clear. He was grateful for the moonlight. They'd need it in the desert in just a few minutes.

Sears saw the face, then the two stars and then the name Dunn sewn in black thread on the right vest pocket of the fatigue jacket. He recognized Billy immediately. Billy had been featured in *Soldier* magazine just the month before as the first black general assigned to command the XVIII Airborne Corps. Sears locked his heels and saluted. He studied the general intensely. Then it came to him. He glanced toward David. The man who saved Billy Dunn. *Now I get it*, he said to himself. *The Craig boy. They're goin' to get him.*

Billy read Sears's thoughts. He nodded in simple acknowledgment. "So, you see . . . we gotta move quickly.

Show us what you can in three hours. After that, we'll study the manuals and make do from there."

The four comrades in arms piled into the back of the enclosed van while Sears slid behind the wheel. He drove for twenty minutes to the army range in the desert. The space was so vast, and the hour so early, they could have fired off howitzers and no one would have heard them. To be safe, Sears drove farther into the range, behind a small mountain and down into a large gully, where the sound would be muffled. By 0327 hours, they had removed the M16A2/M203s, using the headlights from the van as well as the moonlight to set up a makeshift classroom.

David and Matthew were in need of a refresher course. Jenny needed the 101. Sears went through the basics: how to load an M16 magazine, chamber a round, click from safety to the single-round mode, then to the three-round mode. Sears walked them through the paces. He and Billy set targets up at fifty, one hundred, and two hundred meters down range, then returned to the threesome and instructed them how to use the night-vision scope on the M16. Within seconds the distinctive *pop, pop, pop* of the M16s reverberated in the desert.

The feel of the rifle, the power of the kick, the smell of cordite reminded the three men of times long ago. Strangely, it was a feeling they hadn't realized they had missed. It felt good to be shooting. Together again. Jenny, too, found satisfaction from the power she held in her hands. She liked the smell of gunpowder. The kick of the discharge against her shoulder felt oddly reassuring. After they each had hit their targets with some regularity, Sears called a halt. Time to move on.

Sears went to the van and pulled out the four jump helmets. "Now, folks, these here helmets are gonna be a bit strange for you. They're deluxe jump helmets. We don't normally use 'em. They're too fancy for us grunts, but Webster said he picked 'em out special for you. So here they are. They're several things rolled into one.

They're supposed to make bullets bounce off your head. They're also commo gear. They've got speakers and receivers so you can talk to each other, with a range of several hundred meters, dependin' on the weather and terrain. They've also got a night-vision goggle. Also, this here thing that looks like a Game Boy stuck in the side of your helmet is an audio altimeter warning device. You program it to warn you up to three times as you're free-fallin' and it tells you your altitude. Say you program it for ten thousand feet. It'll set off a loud beep when you hit the ten thousand-foot mark. Let's say your next warnin' is five thousand feet. It'll beep when you hit five thousand. If you programmed the final warning level at two thousand feet, it'll beep again at 2,000 feet. But that's your last warnin'. Pull your ripcord when you hear the third beep. By the way, you each have AADs—automatic activation devices. It'll pull your cord for you, just in case you panic or pass out. General Dunn, sir, if it's okay with you, I'll set your altimeter warning devices for ten thousand, seven thousand five hundred, and two thousand feet, and the AADs for fifteen hundred when we're done. But I'm gettin' ahead of myself . . ."

By 0430, they had each fired several grenades from the M203 grenade launchers. They found it quite simple, not unlike a shotgun. Insert a round in the chamber, aim, fire, and out came a 40mm grenade. "Don't really have to hit your target with it. Close counts in horseshoes and grenades." Sears laughed. "The forty-millimeter grenade has a casualty radius of seven meters, or about twenty-three feet. If your target is inside the casualty radius, he is shredded wheat."

Billy had qualified with each weapon less than two years before as part of his required training. After taking several refresher shots with the M16 and two shots with the M203 grenade launcher, he returned to the van to ready the other weapons and gear. He removed the four Glock 35 9mm automatics from the crate and attached tactical illuminators—military talk for flashlights. The night-vision goggle provided to each of them on the helmet covered their left eye only, and could be flipped up and out of the way with a brush of the hand. The tactical illuminator would not be necessary, or even helpful, if the night-vision goggle was down. At close range and in a rapidly moving situation, the night-vision goggle was a detriment, better to be flipped up away from the eye so that both eyes could watch for any movement visible in the glare of the flashlight attached to the bottom of the short barrel of the automatic. The goggle and the tactical illuminator took some time to get accustomed to, as did the laser finder.

Once he had loaded two ten-shot clips and placed one in the Glock, Billy flipped the night-vision goggle down over his left eye. The scene before him looked like daytime, except for the strange, greenish-yellow hue the goggle gave to the desert. He found a small cactus about twenty meters away, clicked on the laser finder, and pointed the red dot at the unsuspecting plant. He squeezed off three shots, paused, fired three more times, paused, and emptied the magazine. He walked to the cactus and studied the holes. Five bullets had found their target in a ten-inch radius. *Not bad*, he thought, *but not great.* He repeated the exercise on a different part of the cactus and was pleased that seven rounds had found their mark in an eight-inch pattern. He repeated it again. Seven rounds in an eight-inch circle. *It'll have to do,* he said to himself. *Just hope the bad guys are nice enough to sit still like that cactus and not shoot back.*

Satisfied with his own proficiency, he joined Sears and the others and walked them through the paces with the 9mm automatics. Jenny had fired a pistol twice at a dude ranch in Montana, which was the extent of her prior experience with guns. She followed instructions carefully and squeezed the trigger rather than jerking it. She fired three rounds, trying to keep the weapon from climbing after each kick. She paused, as instructed, lowering the automatic and focusing her eyes on the target, and squeezed off another three rounds. She then repeated the exercise. After twenty minutes, Sears pronounced the session over. "You'll have to make do with this. Just remember the cardinal rule. It's like the sailors' expression: If you can't tie good knots, tie lots of 'em. Well, pretty much the same. If you can't get a clean shot at the enemy, shoot a lot. Put enough lead on the bastards so they can't shoot back. One of the pieces of lead you're flingin' might just hit 'em.

"One more thing. Listen up, folks," he said, holding a block of what looked like a small brick of Play-Doh. "This is C4 plastic explosive. It's really very simple. Stick the plastic on whatever surface you wanna destroy, insert the detonator needle in the plastic explosive, and stick the timer on the surface of whatever you wanna destroy or even on the plastic. Figure out how much time you need to get the hell outta Dodge and set the timer, turning the dial like you'd set your washing machine or clothes dryer. And then run like hell. Sports fans, this here shit'll surprise you. It's not your grandma's C4. The stuff you used back in 'Nam's like firecrackers compared to this. Get the hell away from it before it blows."

At 0600 hours they packed up. The approaching sunlight began to turn the night into a dull, smoky gray dawn. By 0630 hours, they dropped Sears in front of his home. Matthew reimbursed him for the van and handed him a wad of cash. "It's fifteen thousand, Sergeant," Matthew said.

Shocked by the generosity, Sears mumbled, "Thank you, sir." He saluted Billy and shook the hands of Jenny, Matthew, and David. "Good luck, sir," he said to David, saluting, gazing at the Medal of Honor winner in awe. "God be with you and your son."

David returned the salute and bade him farewell.

Chapter 19

"Boss, can we talk to you for a minute?"

Capt. Angelo Ferraro saw two of his senior detectives at the door and waved them in. "What's up?" Ferraro nodded to his assistant, who took the cue and left to tend to other matters at precinct headquarters.

They exchanged glances. Det. Malcolm Kitt leaned forward. "It's the Craig shooting. Me and Mickey been talkin' 'bout it. We've been over the scene again and again and we just don't get it."

"The Feds took that case away from us. You guys don't have enough to do? You need extra work?" Ferraro gestured toward his overflowing in-basket and a stack of police reports in front of him.

Ferraro's mind drifted off to Craig and Rice and memories of a war that refused to leave his consciousness. He, too, had experienced the brutality of the Tet Offensive of '68. He had been assigned to Special Forces Detachment B-42, an Operation Phoenix recon unit in IV Corps. While Craig and Rice were slugging it out up north at Ripcord, Ferraro's outfit was fighting at Chau Phu on the Cambodian border near the Mekong River. "Doesn't get any deeper in shit than at Ripcord," Ferraro muttered to himself. He hadn't wanted to accept Craig's dealing in drugs or Craig's and Rice's guilt in the murders at the restaurant, but, he acknowledged, stranger things had happened.

The two detectives looked at each other, wondering what their boss would say. "Chief, cut us some slack on a couple other cases and let us check this out more,"

Kitt pleaded. "Something stinks, but we're not sure what. We need more time."

Ferraro nodded slowly, his thoughts still thirty-plus years and twelve thousand miles away. "Okay, I'll put Bartlet and Figueroa on the Gualdoni hit. They can also take the murder of the real estate magnate off your hands. Craig's record at Ripcord means a lot to me. He deserves a thorough investigation by us, not just the FBI. Now get the fuck out of here and let me tend to this mountain of paperwork."

The bank didn't open until nine A.M. Pacific Coast time. Most of the staff didn't effectively start until fifteen to thirty minutes later. A young woman in charge of wire transfers wandered over to the coffee machine. She hadn't slept much the night before. A single mother with money worries and a sick four-year-old with strep throat, she had spent the night taking her child's temperature, administering amoxicillin, Tylenol, and Motrin, and praying to God that she was doing it right. She finished half her cup of coffee and was working on a muffin when the phone rang. She yawned deeply.

The lawyer's secretary had been extremely annoying the day before, insisting she be notified the minute a wire transfer in the amount of $1.8 million arrived. *I'm supporting two people on a salary of thirty-two thousand a year, and this bitch is worried about her boss collectin' a fortune.* She assured the lawyer's pushy assistant that the money had not yet arrived, though she hadn't turned on her computer. The banker promised to call the very moment the transfer was confirmed. She put down the phone and slowly finished her coffee and muffin and then went to the ladies' room, taking her time to comb her hair, redo her makeup, and reapply some lipstick. She returned to her desk and called her mother to see how her little boy was doing. At nine-forty-five, she turned on her computer and called her sister in San Diego. They were talking while the computer booted up. After fifteen minutes she glanced at the clock on her desk, said good-bye to her sister, and turned to her computer screen.

At just after noon, Billy pulled into a gas station on I-8 just south of El Centro, California. The tank was almost empty, and he had been sweating it out. He should have filled the tank back in Yuma, Arizona, but Yuma was an army town, and he didn't want to run the risk of someone recognizing him. He filled the tank at the self-service island and paid the attendant in cash. He then placed a short call to Chris, the copilot, got directions to his home, and gave their estimated time of arrival.

"They're gonna be here 'round four-thirty," Chris informed Jack, yelling into the phone so Jack could hear him over the loud music in the diner from the jukebox playing just a few feet from where Jack sat. "Think you'll have the plane by then?" he asked nervously.

"Hope so," Jack said in a low voice, hoping Chris could hear him. "Plane's in great shape. All we need is the wire transfer. Things are getting pretty hot. I spoke to Eddie in Escondido. FBI's been there asking about me. They're nosing around the airports and brokers to see if I chartered a plane to fly some guys to Canada. They haven't been down here to Brown Field yet, but it won't take 'em long. As soon as I get the clearance to take the plane, I'm gonna boogie out of here up to Warner Springs."

"By the way, Jack, did you get the wire transfer from your buddies?"

"Yep. Bank gave it to me in cash. Prettiest wad of money you ever saw." He laughed. "I've got your twenty-five K and plenty extra for the trip down," he assured Chris, who he knew was down to his last few dollars.

"Sir, can I talk to you in private?" the lanky FBI agent asked the older agent.

Agent Rakovic was lost in thought as he stared out

the window at traffic on Pennsylvania Avenue. "Yeah, what's it now? Have we determined that everyone he ever knew is now missing?" he asked gruffly.

"Well, sir, not exactly. This time it's money. I got a call from Pace Bank in New York just a few minutes ago, and they tell me that the money in Craig's account with Pace is missing."

"Whadda ya mean, 'missing'?" Rakovic asked as he leaned forward in his chair.

"Just that, sir. Someone's transferred all of the money out of Craig's account. The bank can't tell just yet who did it, or where the money went. All they know is that it was transferred yesterday morning. They think someone raided the bank's computer and emptied the account. Pretty damn slick, if that's what they did."

"Pretty damn slick! Is that all you have to say? Pretty damn slick! You mean Craig now has . . . How much was in that account?"

"Four point two million, according to the bank." The younger agent cringed, knowing his boss would hit the roof. "Bank says he stayed liquid and just had this pile of cash sitting in a money market account. Now it's gone."

"Do we know where the money was transferred?" Rakovic moaned.

"The bank doesn't know. The instructions were coded and they're trying to sort all that out. It's a mess. They left a virus or two behind, like land mines, so that when the bank tries to follow the computer trail, sniffers spot the bank instructions and then delete them or send them down false paths. Real clever hacking job. All the bank really knows is that the money's gone."

"Holy shit." Rakovic slumped into his chair. "You mean that we've been counting on this guy going broke and he now may have more than four million bucks offshore?"

"Not exactly," the other agent answered, nervously shifting his weight from one foot to the other. "We're checking with Craig's other banks. He's a rich man. I assume that if in fact he did get his money out of Pace, he might have done the same at his other banks. We're checking on that."

"I want our best forensic computer experts in the country in those banks by tomorrow morning. Fly 'em in. I want to know how this was done and who did it. Goddamn it!" Rakovic paused to think, running his finger across his lips as he concentrated. "Are we a hundred percent sure they haven't left the country?"

"Passports have been canceled. All airlines and shipping lines have been notified."

"What about that joker who runs the skydiving club? The one with the dumb-ass name. Doesn't he fly small aircraft?"

"Happy Jack Heed? We're stumped on that one, sir. His wife's holdin' to her story. She says he took some customers to Canada. According to her, he's due back in two or three days."

"What about the general's wife?"

"Maintains she doesn't know where he is. We located her at a hotel just outside Fort Bragg. We're sure she's lying, so we're working on her. She's one tough cookie, though. We can't count on much from her."

Rakovic looked worried. "Bragg's an airborne unit. Have we checked the flights out of the army fields? Interviewed the pilots?"

"Yes, sir. Army and air force. No sign of the general or Craig. Nothing."

Pablo Santiago sat behind the wheel of his battered 1988 Ford station wagon in the parking lot adjacent to the Puente Aéreo passenger terminal. The Ford had seen better days. Its paint was flat and chipped. Large rust spots dotted the hood, fenders, and body. The side panels at the bottom of each door were nearly rusted through. Half of the right front fender was missing. The seats were split, the dirty yellow foam cushion oozing through the vinyl. The air conditioner had died an ignoble death several months earlier, a useless piece of equipment carried around by the nearly spent motor. Pablo noticed the concern registered on the faces of his

American guests and the furtive glances they cast at each other when they first saw the vehicle.

"Don't worry, my friends." He smiled. "This car could take us all the way to Buenos Aires. She's been with me through thick and thin."

"Yeah, but she hasn't been through anything with us, so we're not quite so loyal." Eric grunted.

"Maybe there's some way to rent a car," suggested Linda more diplomatically.

"We may need to buy a car," Pablo said seriously.

"Then let's buy one. We need a reliable car—with an air conditioner," Eric said.

"Better save your money for the weapons we'll buy in Manizales." Pablo laughed. He watched the Americans wipe the sweat from their brows. "Relax. I've rented a van from Avis. It's on the Avenida Fifteen in the city. So we have to go into the Centro. Otherwise, we'd head northeast directly toward Manizales and avoid Bogotá altogether." He started the car and backed it out of its parking space. As he drove to the pay booth at the exit of the parking lot, the car shimmied from poor wheel alignment, coughing and sputtering, sounding as if there were no muffler at all. "Thank God for Avis." Pablo roared with laughter as he rushed into the stream of traffic on the *autopista*. His passengers nodded warily, not really getting the joke.

Pablo handled the transaction with the clerk at Avis, paying in cash from money Eric had given him on the ride from the airport, while the Americans remained sweltering in the station wagon parked down the street. The midafternoon sun beat relentlessly down on the roof and through the windows. The heat from the concrete below combined with it to cook them like a convection oven. Thirty minutes later, Pablo pulled a shiny tan Ford Windstar minivan in front of his station wagon and stepped out, beaming, clearly proud of his acquisition. At forty-eight, he was athletic and well proportioned, still quite attractive. His most distinctive feature was the patch covering his left eye, giving him the appearance of a soldier of fortune. The deep furrows on his face and his salt-and-pepper hair, mostly gray at the temples, only added to his allure. His teeth were heavily stained from copious amounts of strong Colombian coffee.

Pablo wore off-white, loose-fitting linen pants and an even looser red-and-blue linen shirt that hung over his belt. Except for the patch, at first glance he seemed to be dressed casually and comfortably, like many other middle-aged Colombian men. However, a keen observer would have noticed a slight bulge under his shirt when the wind blew against him, revealing the vague outline of his Sig Sauer automatic. That observer might also notice that his shoes were not loose-fitting, basket-weave loafers like those worn by most of his countrymen. Instead he wore laced shoes with rubber soles for running. Shoes that had saved his life more than once.

The Americans knew how he had lost his left eye. As a member of the elite Search Block of the DAS, he had been a member of the team back in December of 1993 that found Pablo Escobar after a 499-day search. Bloodied from an explosion of dynamite that would later require the removal of his eye, Pablo Santiago had nevertheless pressed on in the battle for control of the drug lord's stronghold in Medellín. It was Santiago who personally riddled Escobar with lead and witnessed his death. Afterward, he had retired from the DAS, a hero to law-abiding Colombians, but an avowed enemy of the drug barons, and a marked man.

Santiago had survived several attempts on his life, but his loved ones weren't so fortunate. He had lost his entire family in the drug wars. His father and brother, who were also members of the DAS, were killed in September of 1989, when a huge truck bomb vaporized the DAS headquarters in Bogotá in a blast so powerful it damaged buildings twenty blocks away. Several years before, his mother and one sister were killed in the crossfire of rival drug gangs on the streets of Bogotá. Then his wife and only son were kidnapped and brutally murdered in June of 1996 in retaliation for Escobar's death. His face revealed his pain and fury when he talked of the drug lords. His good eye, clear chestnut, glistened with intensity and hatred that few men knew. He despised the drug barons for killing his family and destroying his country. Not surprisingly, he had jumped at the opportunity to take on Sebastian de Belalcazar and his henchmen.

The van was equipped with two large Thule luggage containers on top, as Pablo had requested. He also had the foresight to bring a large ice chest filled with bottled water. He and Frank moved the heavy chest from the station wagon to the back of the van, while the others quickly placed their carry-on bags in the luggage containers. All other storage space in the van, including the legroom in front of and under the seats, would be needed for the weapons they'd soon purchase. Pablo made one last trip to his car and returned to the van carrying a midsize white bag with a large red cross on either side. All eyes in the van stared at the first-aid bag, an ominous reminder that this was not a vacation jaunt.

Ernesto Rojas watched the Huey lift off the helipad to ferry Belalcazar to the mainland, pretending to check on the motion detectors and other security apparatus. Emilio Piña, Belalcazar's primary bodyguard, and his second bodyguard, Alberto Reyes, were still on a mission with Nick Field somewhere on the mainland and were not expected to return until early the next morning. It was an opportunity he and Milana couldn't pass up. Ernesto waited a half hour before he carefully meandered from the marina up the hill to the hacienda. He entered Belalcazar's home through the kitchen and made his way up the steps to the second-floor veranda. Two maids noted his presence and discreetly disappeared to the ground floor. He knocked gently three times on the heavy oak door to her bedroom and opened it slowly.

Milana was waiting for him. He was the only man who addressed the desires of her twenty-eight-year-old womanhood, and it had been weeks since they had been together. She was dressed in a long, sheer nightgown. Her jet-black hair descended over her shoulders midway down her back. Her firm breasts stood out and their erect nipples were visible through the gown, exciting him. Her perfume was sweet, almost as sweet as the mischievous smile she gave him as he locked the door behind him. He approached her slowly, his passion-filled eyes locked on hers. He smoothly slid his arm around her slim waist and gently pulled her against him. He placed his hand tenderly against her cheek and drew her face to his, kissing her passionately.

He whispered to her, telling her how much he had missed her and what he was going to do for her, how he was going to do it, and how many times. She became immensely aroused when he talked to her like that. He didn't want to climax early. That was the mistake of young, foolish men. He was old enough to keep calm. First he would work her to a feverish pitch and make her explode with pleasure. Then and only then would he satisfy himself.

On fire, Milana returned his kisses, nearly inhaling his tongue. Her leg wrapped around his, pressing herself against him through his khaki pants. He shifted their entwined bodies around so that her back was against the heavy door and he began to nibble on her ear and neck, sliding his right hand gently from her buttocks to her breast, exploring its fullness. He played skillfully with her nipple, teasing more than squeezing. He whispered to her that he was going to go down on her, but as he raised her arms and slid off her gown, his lips first lingered on her breasts, arousing her further. He retreated one step, keeping his eyes firmly locked on her black eyes and long black lashes. He removed his shirt with deliberate care, then his pants, stripping for her, letting her eyes feast first on his muscular arms and chest, then downward to his powerful erection. He stepped closer to her. He kissed her mouth slowly and deeply and began his descent down the nape of her neck and breasts. By the time his mouth reached her womanhood she was moaning with pleasure, begging him to take her. Within minutes she was screaming for more.

* * *

After a few turns through the crowded streets and a near accident with a bus driven by what Frank was certain was a maniac, Pablo navigated them north on the Avenida Caracas to Avenida 81 toward Medellín. Traffic was heavy at first, and it took them the better part of an hour to reach the outskirts of Bogotá. It began to thin out as they approached the village of Mosquera, and became downright manageable as they reached the small town of Madrid, except for the express buses and trucks that tailgated and passed the Windstar on the two-lane highway that twisted down the mountains toward the valley formed by the Río Magdalena.

When it became clear to Pablo that Frank had the driving under control, he broke the silence in the van. "So, my friend Eric, you told me you want to go to Buenaventura. I will take you there. You told me that you want machine guns and grenades. We will buy them on the black market in Manizales. Now, tell me what we shall do when we get to Buenaventura with all these machine guns and grenades."

"Well, our plan," Eric began as he glanced at Linda sitting to his left and to Anne and Sid behind him, "is that when we get to Buenaventura, we talk to people about chartering a boat, telling everyone who will listen that we want to go fishing. Our guess is that no one will believe us. Our guess is also that Belalcazar's men will know who we are, or think they know who we are. But we're decoys, you see. We're the mock invasion force. As I said, the real assault will take place from the air. More on that in a minute. Anne and Sid here," he said, pointing over his shoulder, keeping his gaze on Pablo, who now sat sideways in the front passenger seat, his head turned to face Eric directly, "look enough like Jenny and David that perhaps—if we get lucky—Belalcazar's men will think they are Jenny and David. Anne's dyed her hair to look like Jenny's used to. Sid's cut his hair so he looks as much like David as possible. We keep them out of view as much as we can. We refer to them as Jenny and David.

"Our guess is that Belalcazar's men will know who we are the minute we start nosing around the port for a vessel. Which is what we want, so long as they think we're David, Jenny, Eric, Frank, and Linda. And, of course, you. You add weight, and they know who you are. Your presence will drive home the point that we're here to rescue the children, and to kill Belalcazar. While we're playing the decoy role, others, including the real David and Jenny, will parachute onto Isla Gorgona and rescue the kids. That's where the ticker-tape parade, cushy job, naked women, and so on come in."

"Naked *men*," Linda corrected. "And I get my daughter back." She smiled wanly.

"And we get back our Lisa," added Sid somberly, speaking up for the first time. He and Anne sat together, hands clasped tightly, making no effort to hide their growing anxiety.

"By the way," Frank interjected. He kept his eyes on the road as yet another express bus passed him in a no-passing stretch. "You left out a key part. We in fact do acquire a boat, whether by legitimate charter or whether we steal one. That's where I come in. I captain fishing boats for a living. We take the boat to the island, pick up the children and our friends, and head for Panama."

"Sounds a bit simple, but it's all we have," Eric added, immediately regretting how negative he sounded.

"How many people will attack the island from the air?" Pablo asked, still trying to fit the pieces of the puzzle together.

"Four," Eric responded simply, wishing he could say there were more.

"It's not very many," Pablo observed quickly, his tone indicating concern about the number. "I hope they have a sound plan and very good weapons. There'll be many well-armed security guards on the island. Your friends will need more than a good plan. They'll need good luck."

"The question I have," Eric said, "is whether Belalcazar will try to kill us in Buenaventura or let us get on the boat first, thinking he can kill us when we try to land on the island. He'll know we're in Buenaventura as soon as we step on the dock."

"My friend, he'll know you're in Colombia the moment we start buying machine guns in Manizales, if he doesn't already know," Pablo said, clearly speaking from experience. "If he knows already, he could have any one of these trucks or buses run us off a mountain road. Or he could have a truck pull in front of us, open up the back doors, and put a rocket-propelled grenade through the windshield. My guess—and it's only that, a guess—is that he doesn't know you're here yet. At least, so far I haven't seen any signs that we are being followed . . . and we're still alive," he added with a smile.

"So," said Linda, "when we get to Manizales and start shopping at the local Kmart for machine guns, he'll know we're here for sure and track us."

"Let's take that as a given," Eric said.

"Okay. We assume that. What do you think he'll do?" she asked as Frank slowed in heavy traffic caused by the military checkpoint at the Río Magdalena crossing. Pablo turned toward the traffic and verified their location, satisfied that it appeared to be a routine stop.

"I think he'll let us get on a boat . . . uh-huh. Yes . . . he'll decide which boat we get on. He'll then let us land on his beautiful little island and then feed us to the sharks. That will be his way of thinking. It's more sadistic that way. It is said that he feeds his enemies to the sharks on the reefs off his island. They say he ties them to a water-ski rope behind a fast boat, drags them across the shallow reefs to cut their flesh into bloody strips, and then drags them out to deeper water, where the sharks can feast on them while his victims are still alive," Pablo informed the Americans, observing that his words had the desired chilling effect.

"Of course, that's if he doesn't know your buddies are dropping from the sky," Pablo added after some reflection. "If he knows they're coming, he'll focus on killing them first and won't let us get on the boat in Buenaventura. He'll kill us there instead," he said matter-of-factly.

"So if they start shooting at us in Buenaventura, there's a good chance the others have already failed," Frank reasoned.

"That's what I think. But I could be completely wrong. He may know nothing about them and wipe us out in Manizales just to be done with it," Pablo concluded without emotion, turning his body to face the front of the car and the approaching foot soldiers at the checkpoint.

"Charming thoughts," Sid Waldron managed to get out. He, too, was perspiring heavily. "You're not very reassuring."

"I'm alive because I'm a pessimist, and I don't turn away from truth. People who are in denial, as your psychiatrists are fond of saying, don't live very long in Colombia. See the truth and deal with it."

"Then what's the plan in Manizales if they start shooting at us?" Linda asked. "We don't have anything to fight back with."

"Well, I've got a .38 revolver in each of my socks," Pablo informed her. "And I've got my automatic under my shirt. I'll give the .38s to Frank and Eric when we get past this checkpoint. I'll keep the automatic. It's not much, but it's all we have. If they start shooting . . . well, we shoot back," he said, concluding the discussion with a wave of his hand.

Two boorish-looking soldiers approached outside Frank's window, demanding identification. Pablo handed his DAS (retired) card to the one standing closest to the window. The soldier studied the card, stared at Pablo for a long moment, locked his heels, and saluted. It wasn't often that a soldier from a small town in the Andes got to see a national hero in person. The soldier waved them on with a brisk salute.

Nick Field brought the chopper in low over the marina toward the lower helipad and set it down gently, immediately cutting power, the rotors slowing overhead. Emilio, Alberto, and Joaquin exited the Huey and began their ascent to the hacienda. They had made good time on the return flight and were eager to shower and change clothes after their grueling journey across Colombia and back ferrying Stinger missiles and other weapons to the FARC, the leading rebel group seeking to overthrow the Colombian government.

As he wearily climbed the steep steps toward the hacienda, Joaquin noticed that the camera attached to the wall of the cantina, designed to scan the western wall of the barracks and the entrance to the tower, was broken. It would have to be repaired before nightfall.

Joaquin entered the hacienda, followed immediately by the two bodyguards. He went directly to Ernesto's office, where the island's electronic security and surveillance monitors were located. He entered the small room filled with twelve computer monitors, ten of which were currently scanning the compound. Two were broken. The monitors played to an empty room. Joaquin picked up the intercom and demanded the whereabouts of Ernesto, puzzled by the evasive responses he received. He stepped out of the room, his brow furrowed. Centrally located camera monitors inoperative. The whereabouts of the chief of security unknown. *Unthinkable.* He nervously touched his automatic sidearm for reassurance. He looked around the courtyard as if an answer might be lurking there. Something was not right. Emilio and Alberto sensed Joaquin's concern, and immediately Emilio withdrew an automatic from his shoulder holster. Alberto followed, and Joaquin did the same.

At the top of the stairs stood a maid's cart, not unlike that seen in the halls of every hotel in the world. Of the four maids who tended to the daily cleaning of the immaculate hacienda, none were present. The cart stood unattended, as if someone had frightened them away. With a wave of his automatic, Joaquin motioned for Emilio and Alberto to check the ground floor for signs of danger. They fanned out along the archway, checking each room, finding the four maids busily cleaning on the ground floor. The maids seemed surprised, almost embarrassed to see the bodyguards, and in response to their questions professed to not know where Ernesto was. The two bodyguards quickly reported back to Joaquin that the ground floor was clear, which left the second floor. They looked to one another and then to the top of the stairs. On three, Emilio and Alberto darted across the courtyard and quickly ascended the staircase nearest Belalcazar's office, while Joaquin bounded up the stairs nearest the security room, weapons at the ready.

Joaquin placed his ear to the door of the American nanny's bedroom on the northwestern corner of the hacienda but heard nothing. He moved stealthily down the hall toward the children's playroom and opened the door. The children and Stephanie Wagner were playing. The large classroom on the southwest corner of the hacienda was empty. Emilio and Alberto had checked the rooms on the south side of the house, including Belalcazar's bedroom. All clear. Only one room left.

The three men converged on Milana's bedroom, pausing outside the thick door to her room. Inside, they heard the unmistakable sound of passionate lovemaking. With a nod from Joaquin, the three men stepped back and pointed their weapons at the bolt. Each fired several rounds. Emilio kicked the door open and dove into the bedroom, landing on his knees, his automatic expertly pointing in the direction of the bed. Alberto stepped inside and rapidly moved to his left, his weapon ready. A fraction of a second later Joaquin entered the room to see a stunned, and completely naked Milana de Belalcazar lying beneath Ernesto Rojas, her long, trim legs wrapped around him, he still firmly lodged inside her.

Chapter 20

Jack Heed was happy-go-lucky by nature. His blue eyes had a playful sparkle to them more common to a child than a middle-aged man. He was quick to joke, and to take a joke, and his smile stretched from ear to ear, contagious to all who met him.

It was David who had given him his nickname. Born John Charles Heed, he had been known as Jack since childhood, until one hot day in Vietnam in January of 1968, when he had flown through a hail of enemy fire to pluck David and his fellow Rangers out of a heavy firefight. He had landed his Huey in an opening in the jungle cleared by several artillery rounds and had asked with his big smile if anyone wanted to go to China Beach for the weekend. As bullets bounced off the sturdy Huey and Jack snatched the outmanned Ranger team from its pursuers, he had given the Viet Cong the finger. "What are you so damn happy about?" David had asked him as they reached safety at three thousand feet. "We didn't get killed," he said with a laugh. David dubbed him Happy Jack on the spot. From that moment on, the name stuck. After Vietnam, he put it to good commercial use, naming his flight school and skydiving club Happy Jack's Flight School and Happy Jack's Jump Club. The names were catchy and helped attract the weekend pilots and skydivers.

But as Happy Jack paced the concrete floor of the hangar at Brown Field, he was decidedly not happy. Something had gone wrong at the lawyer's bank, and the receipt of the wire transfer had been delayed. The soft black leather pilot's briefcase he clenched in his left hand bulged with more cash than he had ever seen, but that was Chris's money and the extra money Jenny had sent for the flight to Colombia, nowhere near the cash he needed to purchase the airplane.

Jack had struck up a nice rapport with the mechanic who took care of the King Air, and he allowed Jack to stock the small refrigerator, store his bags aft in the plane, place his charts and other gear in the cockpit, and otherwise ready the craft for takeoff. But despite the good relationship and bantering, the mechanic was not about to let Jack take the airplane without confirmation from the owner's secretary that the money had been received by the bank. All that was needed was a phone call.

Jack paced in front of the immaculately clean white-and-green, twin-engine King Air. The immense hangar door was up. The warm breeze off the tarmac drifted in from the Pacific. He looked out at the small, two-seater forest-green helicopters of the U.S. Border Patrol, a unit of the Immigration and Naturalization Service. Five of the helicopters sat idle in front of the Border Patrol's office and hangar, only two hundred yards from where he stood. He saw the chopper pilots milling about, service automatics strapped to their waists, readying themselves for yet another day's futile battle against the illegal immigrants flooding across the nearby Mexican border. He knew some of the pilots and wasn't eager to be seen by them.

He saw a dark blue Caprice turn into the parking lot in front of the Border Patrol office. It glided into a parking space reserved for official use. He instinctively retracted deeper into the hangar. The driver and the passenger promptly climbed out of the Caprice. They were white, tall, and trim; wore dark blue suits, white shirts, and dark ties; and had short hair. Jack wondered why they just didn't print FBI in ten-inch letters on their backs. He had no way of knowing whether they were looking for him or meeting with Border Patrol officials on other matters, but he wasn't taking chances.

"Any word from the lawyer's secretary?" Jack asked

the mechanic as the man returned from a nearby Quonset hut.

"She says she still hasn't received confirmation from his bank. . . . Now, there's a real bitch for you," the mechanic complained. "Talks to ya like you're a real piece o' shit. I'd like her to talk like that to me in person. I'd plant my size-eleven shoe so far up her ass she'd choke on it."

Jack paused, the frown marks on his forehead deepening as he reflected. "Do we know what bank they use? If she's talking like that to you, she's probably just as bitchy to the people at the bank. Maybe I oughta call 'em and sweet-talk 'em. Catch more flies with honey than vinegar, and all that." He chuckled nervously.

"Sure. She said they were waitin' for word from Pacific Capital, but I don't know the branch or who the person is at the bank," the mechanic responded, eager to help Jack get on his way and get out of there himself.

"Let's call the secretary and see if we can talk her into givin' us the name of the person at the bank. I'll call the bank myself," Happy Jack offered with a forced smile as he took the first few steps toward the Quonset hut where the pay phones were located. He wasn't about to use his cell phone. He placed his ball cap over his bald head. Only the white-gray hair at his temples, sides, and back showed. As a result of a nasty chopper crash back in Vietnam, he walked with a limp and favored his left leg slightly. He tried to minimize the limp as he walked across the field, afraid his gait would be noticed by the Border Patrol pilots.

They reached the hut and walked in. Jack was sweating, though the air conditioner whirled away, cooling the hut to sixty-five degrees. He punched in the numbers on the pay phone as the mechanic read them to him. His voice was sugar-sweet as he charmed the secretary with a story of how his daughter was sick and he needed to pick her up in Idaho and get her back home to a hospital. Armed with the name and phone number of the woman at the bank, he quickly dropped two quarters into the coin slot and tapped the number into the keyboard, missing a number the first time and having to try again before he got through. The mechanic stood by, quietly chuckling as Jack charmed the woman at the bank with the same story, his voice smooth as honey.

Jack himself was surprised how effective he was over the phone. "Thank you, ma'am. 'Preciate your help. If you could call the lady at the lawyer's office right now, I'd be ever so grateful. Thanks again," he concluded after she promised she'd take care of it immediately.

"Let's wait a few minutes, and then we'll call the lawyer's secretary," Jack said nervously, expecting the FBI to burst into the Quonset hut any minute. "Got any coffee 'round here?"

Happy Jack watched through a small window of the Quonset hut as one of the Border Patrol choppers took off, ascending into the moist haze drifting in off the Pacific. Other pilots were milling about. There was no sign of the two FBI agents. Jack let three minutes more go by. He turned toward the phone just as a young pilot stepped in front of him and deposited a quarter. Jack's heart pounded. He felt his breathing speed up. He decided that, if needed, he'd yank the phone out of the young man's hand and take it away from him, but he decided to wait a minute or so. The commotion would draw attention to him that he couldn't afford.

The pilot was apparently calling his girlfriend, trying to make up for something he said the night before. After several minutes his lover must have accepted the apology, because the pilot spoke about meeting her later at a nearby bar. "I love you, too," he whispered into the phone, blushing, slightly embarrassed in front of the others in the room. He reached in the pocket of his jeans, presumably for another quarter.

"Sir, hate to interrupt you, but I've got an emergency call. It'll just take a minute," Happy Jack said as he nearly knocked the young man over and grabbed the phone. He slid a quarter into the coin slot and began tapping the keyboard with sharp jabs. The young pilot mumbled something like "Chill out, old man," which under different circumstances Jack would have found amusing.

Jack tried to make his voice as sweet as he had before but wasn't quite as successful. "That's great," he said to the secretary. "We've taken care of all the papers and we'll register with the FAA. Yes, ma'am. Thank you. Could you tell your mechanic here so that he hears it from you?" he asked the woman, who by now was almost civil. Jack handed the phone to the mechanic, who listened for a few seconds and put down the phone.

"Good to go," he announced to Jack, giving the thumbs-up.

Jack clutched his briefcase tighter and made his way toward the door closest to the hangars. The distance from the Quonset hut to the plane was about seventy-five feet. He hoped he could make it without a Border Patrol pilot noticing him. He pulled the visor of the ball cap down over his forehead and kept his face down as he walked quickly. The mechanic followed.

As Jack walked, he opened the briefcase and slid his hand in to grab a few of the hundred-dollar bills. He crumpled what felt like five of the bills in his right pants pocket and flipped the cover of the briefcase back into position, buckling it as he walked. That accomplished, he allowed himself a stealthy glance in the direction of the Border Patrol office. Two pilots were descending the concrete steps that led from the office to the glistening tarmac. One of the men stopped at the base of the steps and stared in his direction, obviously studying his movement. Only then did he realize that he had forgotten to control his limp.

Jack could feel his pulse quickening. He made an effort to minimize his limp, but he knew it was too late. The pilot had recognized him. Jack walked faster, trying to stay calm, surveying the scene out of the corner of his eye. The one who recognized him remained at the base of the steps, while the other continued to walk toward the chopper. A government mechanic was inspecting the helicopter and paid no attention to the pilots or Jack.

Jack wanted to run, but he didn't dare. He self-consciously placed each foot forward, trying to lessen the distance between himself and the plane, still trying to minimize his limp. It reminded him of a nightmare he used to have as a child: He was running from first base to second base after hitting the ball, his legs moving in slow motion. He couldn't make it to second base running at full speed. The more he ran, the farther second base moved away from him.

The Border Patrol pilot who didn't know him suddenly turned to his colleague who remained on the steps, extending his arms out from his sides, palms up, asking his copilot, "What gives?" Jack couldn't hear the response, but the excited gesturing in his direction made his heart beat even faster.

For a moment the pilot stood still. He had just come from a meeting with two FBI agents who were inquiring about Jack Heed, and claiming that he had some connection to the killing of two federal agents in New York. The agents had described him—six-foot-two, strong build, walked with a limp. He was shocked that within five minutes of that conversation, the very man the FBI was looking for appeared to be a mere two hundred yards from the Border Patrol office.

Jack approached the corner of the hangar. He turned to look back at the pilot, forgoing the previous effort to be nonchalant. The ID was already made, he reasoned, and the only viable plan now was to get the hell away from Brown Field as fast as possible. He ran the remaining few yards to the plane.

He pulled the five hundred-dollar bills from his pocket and slapped them into the hands of the mechanic, quickly thanking him without waiting for a response. He ran to the left side of the plane, banging his head on the top of the frame of the small door as he jumped inside. He shrugged off the pain, pulled the door shut with the drop cord, twisted the locking mechanism, and dashed for the cockpit. No preflight check today. He'd have to rely on the mechanic. He started the right engine and automatically fastened his seat belt and harness. Through the cockpit window, he saw the mechanic duck under the plane to remove the yellow triangular chocks that prevented the plane's wheels from rolling forward. As soon as he saw the mechanic step clear of the plane, he started the left engine and began to inch forward, not waiting for the left engine's rpms to catch up with the right engine. The resulting imbalance of torque caused the plane to shiver slightly, but he knew he could handle it. Jack raced the powerful Pratt & Whitney 850-horsepower engines to full power, released his foot off the brakes, and was rewarded with a forward thrust that propelled the sleek craft out of the hangar. Within seconds the King Air had traveled three hundred feet from the hangar, heading away from the Border Patrol office toward the runway. He got on the radio with the control tower.

Unlike Warner Springs and Borrego Springs, where Jack regularly flew, Brown Field had air-traffic controllers. He had flown out of Brown Field hundreds of times and was familiar with most of them.

Meanwhile, the FBI agents and the pilots were running from the Border Patrol office to the hangar. They spotted the King Air just as it sped across the field toward the runway. Realizing that they were too late to stop Jack on the ground, they abruptly halted. One agent reached for his cell phone, while the other sprinted back to the Border Patrol office. The two Border Patrol pilots ran toward their chopper, where the mechanic was still tinkering with its electronics. They all had the same objective; to reach the control tower and stop the King Air from lifting off.

Jack couldn't see the activity behind him, but he knew he had to get in the air and put serious distance between him and Brown Field. The King Air B200 could cruise at speeds up to 338 mph and easily outrun the Border Patrol helicopters, but no plane could outrun a radio or radar. He had to get to Warner Springs, spend no more than five minutes on the ground, get his passengers and their gear on board, and head south to Mexico as fast as the plane would permit. But to do all that he had to first get in the air. For that he needed the help of the control tower. He could simply take off without the tower, but he was too experienced a pilot to ignore the risk of a collision with another plane, even under the urgent circumstances.

"Hey, this is Jack Heed in King Air November one-five-zero-two Golf," he barked into the speaker inches from his mouth. "Repeat: November one-five-zero-two Golf. Can you get me in the air on a priority basis? Who do I have the pleasure of dealing with?"

"Don Anton," was the loud response through the headset. "What's the rush? Wife having another baby?" The two men knew each other well. Anton was an experienced skydiver and occasionally jumped from Happy Jack's plane over the Borrego Desert.

"Got a sick kid up in Idaho . . . need to get her back here to a hospital."

"Christ, Happy Jack. I can see you from here," Anton exclaimed as he watched the King Air taxi toward the runway at least three times faster than permitted. "Better slow down or you'll take off on the taxi run." Anton laughed. "Don't they have hospitals in Idaho?"

"Not one with the specialists she needs. Gotta get her back here to La Jolla. I need immediate clearance, man."

"You got it." Anton instructed the three pilots queued up on the tarmac in front of Jack to let him proceed. He immediately zoomed past them to the front of the line.

Jack slowed slightly to turn the plane onto the runway, revved the combined seventeen-hundred-horsepower of the turbo engines at full power, released the breaks, and catapulted down the runway toward the Pacific Ocean. As the plane reached airspeed at one hundred mph, Jack pulled gently back on the yoke. The flaps pointed downward and lifted the King Air rapidly into the air less than a third of the distance down the eight thousand-foot runway. He immediately retracted the landing gear to cut drag on the plane's speed and maintained the engines at full power.

Anton watched enviously as the B200 shot down the runway and began to climb. "Nifty piece of equipment," he muttered to himself as he reached for the phone, now ringing loudly, that connected the Border Patrol office directly with the tower.

"Jack," Anton spoke into the mouthpiece seconds later. "Must be some sort of mixup, buddy, but Border Patrol says the FBI's lookin' for you and wants you to come back. They wanted me to stop you from takin' off, but that's just a tad late, since you've already done that." He laughed. "Turn it around and come back. You can clear this up with the Feds and get on your way."

Happy Jack heard the words, but did not respond. He had no more intention of returning to Brown Field than he'd had of obeying orders back in Vietnam not to go into the bush to save his Ranger buddies. His friends needed him in Warner Springs in a few minutes. He'd be there. Failure was not an option.

He found Highway 117 and followed it west. He was soon flying south of Imperial Beach Naval Air Station, taking pains not to fly directly over it. He reached the ocean at Imperial Beach State Park, descended to fifty feet above the Pacific, covered fifteen miles in less than four minutes, and banked north. He would head north to Encinitas, cut east-northeast over Escondido, continue east-northeast over Mount Palomar, then bank due east toward Warner Springs and Borrego Springs. He'd have to land into the wind and take off into the wind, which right now was out of the west at seven knots. He switched to the frequency he and Chris had agreed to use and said, "ETA in twenty from east. Five on the ground. Max!" He shut off the transmission, not waiting for Chris to respond from the radio in his mobile home.

"He's not answering," the air-traffic controller explained in amazement to the Border Patrol official and the FBI. "I don't get it. He's descended out of radar level somewhere out over the Pacific. Might've gone down . . . No . . . we don't have a flight plan." He heard a click and checked to see if the callers were still on the line. He concluded they weren't, hung up, and tried to refocus on his business of getting planes up in the air and bringing them down safely.

At the first crackling of the radio in Chris's tiny bedroom in his mobile home, Billy, David, Jenny, and Matthew jumped. They had arrived three hours earlier, expecting Happy Jack to be waiting for them on the Warner Springs strip. There was no way of knowing what was detaining him, but there were numerous possibilities, and none of them were good. When the message that he'd be there in twenty minutes finally came through, they scrambled to the door. Happy Jack's warning that they'd have only five minutes on the ground meant he was being followed. It would take ten minutes to get the van down Hot Springs Mountain to the strip at Warner Springs.

The FBI agents tried desperately to scramble navy fighters from the U.S. Naval Air Station located on North Island in San Diego Harbor, but interdepartmental cooperation being what it was, there were too many bureaucratic hoops to jump through for the FBI to get F-18s in the air. They had better luck with the air-traffic controller at the naval air station. There, powerful radar picked up the small plane skimming one hundred feet above the surface of the Pacific and began to track Jack's flight. As Jack approached the coast off Encinitas, he ascended to three thousand feet and banked east-northeast toward Escondido. He knew he couldn't skim the ground over southern California because there were too many high-tension wires and radio-transmission towers. He was also aware that at the higher altitude it would be easy for the navy to track him. He was right. Within minutes the navy air-traffic controller, the Border Patrol helicopters, and the FBI on the ground were on the radio urging him to land and surrender. He gave no response, and hoped to God that Chris and the others would be at Warner Springs on time.

Two Border Patrol helicopters were put in the air and headed north on orders to intercept the B200 if it landed anywhere near San Diego. They were still due east of San Diego, near LaCresta, when the control tower at the naval air station informed them that Jack had banked east-northeast and was heading for Escondido. One helicopter veered off to the northeast, heading for Borrego Springs on the assumption that Happy Jack might be headed to his regular airstrip. The other continued north to cover a number of smaller airstrips located at Mesa Grande, Warner Springs, and Rincon. If Happy Jack overflew all of those airfields, it meant the King Air was headed well out of the range of the small helicopters and would have to be pursued by other means.

Chris raced the van down the steep road leading from his home on the west side of Hot Springs Mountain to Route 79. He wore gloves to make sure he left no fingerprints. The FBI might find tiny fragments of hair and establish a DNA portrait of him, but he wasn't about to make their job easy. The others remained out of sight in the back of the van, bouncing uncomfortably as the wheels sank into foot-deep potholes caused by heavy snows and rains earlier that winter. The tension was palpable. They were minutes away from either a clean escape toward Colombia and Justin, or imprisonment.

They reached Route 79 twelve minutes after leaving the mobile home. Chris made a mental note that they were running late. It would take them another two minutes to get to the airstrip. Jack was coming in from the west, but would need to circle east and land into the wind, he calculated. Chris planned to park the van at the extreme eastern end of the runway.

The Warner Springs airstrip was just that, a strip of asphalt used primarily by the glider school housed in the small corrugated sheet metal building adjacent to the strip. The field was surrounded by scrub brush and a few trees, and nothing else. The owners of the school, who were friends of Chris's, had taken the day off to attend a glider and experimental aircraft show at the convention center in San Diego, which was why Chris and Jack had chosen Warner Springs. The fewer witnesses the better.

The operations office sat in a narrow gravel parking lot. Chris drove the van over one of the horizontal wooden telephone poles bordering the lot to prevent vehicles from driving onto the airstrip. Jenny, David, Billy, and Matthew were thrown from the crates that served as their seats as the front wheels and then the rear wheels climbed over the thick pine pole and landed with a thud. Chris sped across the tarmac and brought the van to a halt at the eastern end of the runway. He jumped out, telling the passengers to remain inside, and immediately began to search the skies for signs of the twin-engine King Air.

"Looks like he's not going to land in Ramona," the navy air-traffic controller announced into the wire microphone attached to his headset.

"Roger that," said the civilian air-traffic controller at the airfield in Ramona, who had joined in the hunt. "He's headin' east. My bet's Warner Springs, if he's gonna land in these parts at all. Can't really tell what the hell he's up to."

"You keep on track for Borrego Springs," one Border Patrol helicopter pilot said to the pilot of the other chopper. "I'll head for Warner Springs."

"Roger. Better get the FBI movin' on the ground to both places. If he flies by heading east, we'll lose him. He's too fast for us. If he lands at Borrego Springs or Warner Springs, we'll get him—if he stays on the ground long enough."

Two FBI vehicles, each with two heavily armed agents, were dispatched from the regional office in San Diego and sped east on Valley Freeway heading toward Interstate 8, and Route 79 to Julian. "If Heed's with Craig, remember that Craig's dangerous," an agent warned the Border Patrol pilots, who by now were well ahead of them over El Capitan Reservoir. "He killed four federal agents in New York. Consider him armed and extremely dangerous," he continued. "We're far behind you, but two cars from the county sheriff's office are just south of Julian. Don't—repeat—don't attempt an arrest without backup from the sheriff or us if we get there in time," the agent ordered above the roar of the engine and the *whoop-whoop-whoop* of the siren.

Jack adjusted the frequency of the radio one more time and caught the tail end of the conversation between the FBI agents and the helicopter pilots. The adrenaline rush he had experienced since leaving Brown Field ratcheted up several more notches. *It's gonna be tight,* he told himself, grinning from ear to ear. *Just like in 'Nam.* He scanned the horizon to his east and located the silhouette of Hot Springs Mountain in the light of the approaching dusk, east and slightly north of the Warner Springs airfield. He knew the terrain and the airfield well. His altitude was 4,100 feet. The Warner Springs airstrip was 2,885 feet above sea level. Normally he'd need to begin his descent within the next few minutes if he expected to circle over Warner Springs and land from the east. Instead he climbed rapidly to 7,600 feet as if he were going to fly over Hot Springs Mountain. The feint had its desired effect, as he heard the navy air controller and the civilian air controller in Ramona bark to the air and ground forces converging on him that he was headed over Hot Springs Mountain toward Borrego Springs in the desert due east of Warner Springs. Two county sheriff's cars heading toward Julian on Route 79 turned right on Route 78 in the direction of Borrego Springs. Jack hoped the diversion would gain him a few desperately needed minutes.

After reaching 7,600 feet, Jack continued at that altitude for only a few seconds before standing the plane on its right wing and diving toward Warner Springs like a fighter going in for a strafing run. The wing-over maneuver had often been used by pilots in World War II, but few contemporary pilots had the skill or the guts to try it. The King Air stood on its right wing, lost lift, and immediately began to slip downward to the right, even as Jack pushed the yoke forward, accelerating as he dove. His airspeed over the ground reached 325 mph, and for a moment he was weightless. The briefcase on the copilot's seat to his right floated across the cockpit and landed on his lap, as did a pencil and a small notepad.

The air-traffic controller at the naval air station watched Jack's dive on the radar screen with a mix of surprise and admiration. "The guy's got balls, I'll say that for him," the man said as much to himself as to his colleagues who watched the screen with him. "Warner Springs," he yelled into his mouthpiece. "He's landin' at Warner Springs. Divert—repeat—divert to Warner Springs," he screamed at the sheriff's cars rushing east on Route 78, nearing Borrego Springs. The two well-trained drivers conferred on their radios. One continued on Route 78 to connect with San Felipe Road, where he would head north, preserving the ability to quickly get to either Warner Springs or Borrego Springs. The other slammed on his brakes and turned around. Within seconds that car was speeding west on Route 78, heading back toward Julian and Warner Springs.

Jack's immediate problem was speed. Far too much speed. To land safely and bring the plane to a halt on the three-thousand-foot runway, the King Air could hit the tarmac at no more than 125 mph. He flattened out the plane after diving as much as he dared, chopping the power to flight idle. He then looped around south of the airfield and flew over the strip, heading due north. In the dim light of dusk, he saw a van making its way across the parking lot and onto the tarmac. He knew it was his copilot and passengers. As soon as he overflew the field, he executed another wing-over maneuver wide to his right and then lined up with the runway at 270 degrees.

Dusk was setting in. Chris had the good sense to keep the van's lights on bright and pointed down the runway, allowing Jack to see where the scrub brush ended and the tarmac began. The lights of the van, plus the altimeter readings, were sufficient for an experienced pilot to make the landing, but it wasn't for the faint of heart.

The wheels of the King Air hit the asphalt harder than Jack expected. The plane leaped into the air several feet and bounced twice before settling, still speeding down the short runway. Jack stood on the brakes, engines in reverse thrust at full power. The plane shimmied and groaned, protesting the harsh treatment. Jack didn't look at the airspeed indicator. His eyes were fixed on the end of the runway, visible in the plane's headlights. "Come on, baby, slow down," he coaxed the plane. "Slow down for me and I'll never do that to you again. Promise."

The King Air slowed, but not rapidly enough. Jack pressed the brake pedals to the floor so hard his calves began to cramp, mindful that he ran the risk of burning the brakes out completely. His efforts paid off: 115 mph . . . 95 mph . . . 75 mph . . . the airspeed indicator read. He continued the reverse thrust of the engines. Finally, with one hundred feet remaining on the runway, the airspeed indicator read 20 mph.

Jack turned and taxied back to the eastern end of the runway at 35 mph. Once there, he turned the aircraft around and idled the engines as he brought it to a complete stop. He immediately unhooked his seat belt and harness and moved to the back of the plane to open the door. Chris, standing on the tarmac opposite the door, caught the door as it fell toward him. He nearly flew into the cabin. Billy and Matthew were already carrying a large crate from the van to the plane, moving as quickly as the weight of the crate would allow. David and Jenny were offloading another crate from the van.

Jack raced back to the cockpit, followed by Chris. Chris sat in the copilot's seat to the right and began checking all instruments, readying for takeoff. Jack revved the engines at full power and clamped his feet down hard on the brakes. The plane began to vibrate from the competing forces, and for a moment it seemed that the aircraft might explode.

Within three minutes, the crates and bags were loaded. The four passengers scrambled over the gear into position. As soon as Billy, the last person to climb on board, was in, Jack released the brakes, even though the door was still down. The plane shot forward just as Billy pulled hard on the drop cord connected to the door, causing him to lose his grasp of the cord as he fell toward the rear of the cabin. David jumped toward the door and grabbed the latch. As the lock sealed the door, the plane was already speeding down the runway at 65 mph.

The Border Patrol choppers were approaching from the south only five hundred feet above the ground, traveling at 100 mph, two miles south of Warner Springs, when the pilots saw both the King Air speeding down the strip and the van with its doors wide open, its headlights illuminating the strip. They increased speed, trying to head off the plane. Sensing that their efforts would be futile, the pilots screamed into their radios for Jack to stop and barked orders to the sheriff's cars racing toward the airstrip, only a half a minute away, to move it. The pilots in the lead helicopter watched with frustration as the King Air gained speed on the runway, its westerly course perpendicular to the northerly path of the helicopter. The copilot of the lead chopper lowered his window and readied his service automatic to fire.

The King Air was now going 80 mph midway down the runway, each of its 850-horsepower engines straining as Jack and Chris demanded the maximum from them. They carried a full load of six adults and an estimated four hundred pounds of weapons, ammunition, parachutes, and other gear. The engines groaned and the plane shook. Every ounce of aluminum and steel in the aircraft seemed to strain to get off the ground. As he reached airspeed at 100 mph, Jack pulled back gently on the yoke. Everyone in the King Air felt its wheels lift off the tarmac. Their momentary sigh of relief was interrupted as two 9mm bullets slammed into the fuselage and entered the cabin with loud metallic *zaps*. One bullet slightly grazed the heel of Billy's boot and lodged into the floor. The other bullet missed the passengers altogether and pierced a crate of military gear, causing no real damage.

The second chopper was now in position over the airstrip. Its copilot fired several shots at the King Air, but they missed. Both helicopters roared over the plane, banked left, and turned for another pass.

With well over four hundred feet to go on the runway, the powerful Pratt & Whitney PT6A engines did their magic and lifted the B200 several feet off the asphalt, rapidly gaining speed. By the time the plane was twenty feet above the grassy meadow west of the strip, Chris had raised the landing gear and the plane was rapidly distancing itself from the slower helicopters.

Jack began banking to the north as soon as he reached an altitude of one hundred feet. The aircraft, now traveling at 165 mph, engines humming, rolled gently to the right. The radar systems tracking them were located in San Diego and Ramona to the west, and the only way to lose them would be to get behind Hot Springs Mountain. Pilot and copilot continued putting distance between their craft and the Border Patrol helicopters, heading northwest toward Mount Palomar, then due north just before reaching the observatory. Chris spotted the sparse lights of the small town of Cahuilla at their three o'clock. They banked ninety degrees to the east and headed for the equally small town of Anza, then banked again, this time to the southeast, and descended into the Borrego Valley.

They made good time to the Mexican border, crossing at Tierra del Sol a few minutes later. By the time the navy and the FBI coordinated with Mexican authorities, the small craft would be skimming the Gulf of California between Baja and the mainland at five hundred feet, with a comfortable cruising speed of 250 mph, out of site of radar and of no great interest to the Mexican government. The plane could go faster, but Jack and Chris wanted to conserve fuel. There were 3,040 miles remaining to their destination in Panama, and another 664 miles for the round trip from Panama to Isla Gorgona.

Chapter 21

"Cap'n, we need to talk to you when you have a minute," Malcolm Kitt pleaded as Captain Ferraro chatted with three rookie cops near the coffee machine in the rear of the open bay.

"What have you got?"

"Can't say right here," Detective Connelly said nervously, glancing at the young cops in uniform, whose eyes lit up at the thought of hearing precinct gossip. Ferraro and Connelly stepped aside a few paces. "It's the Craig shooting, sir," Connelly whispered. "We think we've got something."

"Okay. Excuse me, gents," the captain said to the young men. "Let's go to my office," he ordered Kitt and Connelly.

Kitt closed the door while Connelly moved to the white board and erased stray marks on it. Quickly he sketched the layout of the crime scene. "Here's Tenth Avenue; this is where the Fibbie tail parked. Here's the restaurant. This is Nineteenth Street. This is the car that Harrison and Evans drove."

"Now, boss, let us walk you through this, okay?" Kitt pointed to the board. "The tail car with two Fibbie agents follows Craig and Rice to the inn. They report to Harrison. Now, what are two senior FBI and DEA guys doin' screwin' 'round New York acting on their own?"

"How do you know that for sure?" Ferraro interrupted.

"Boss, where's the backup? You gonna tell me that these senior agents are gonna make a bust by themselves? No way! And if they were in a hurry they're not gonna at least use the men in the tail car? Remember, the FBI didn't even get notified till our guys ID'd the stiffs. No way does it make sense."

"Not standard procedure," Ferraro allowed.

"Sometime after the tail car is parked, Harrison and Evans pull up and park here." Detective Connelly made a mark with a felt-tip pen on the white board behind the mark designating the surveillance car. "Harrison and Evans go into the restaurant. Alone. Then the shit hits the fan. Bullets everywhere, people running. At this point we're supposed to believe that the suspects—Craig, Rice, or both, right?—came outta the restaurant, casually walked over to the tail car, and iced the two Fibbies. What, were they asleep? The door or window of the car hadda be open, 'cause there were no shots fired through the glass. And the windows were rolled up, 'cause it's freezing out. Two very senior agents go in alone on the bust and these guys stay outside and don't help or call in? Then all hell breaks loose and they continue to sit on their asses in the car? And to top it off, they're so out of it that the bad guys can prance up to their car, open the door, and whack 'em without any resistance?"

Ferraro sat back in his chair, intrigued. "Okay. Okay. How do you two see it goin' down?"

Encouraged, Detective Kitt pointed to the board. "The brass from D.C. pulled in behind the first car. Suppose one of them comes up to it and gets recognized. So the agent opens the door. Or rolls down the window. Don't matter. Then the brass—Harrison or Evans—ices them. Hell, they're relaxed. Not expectin' anything. Then—"

"Wait a minute!" Ferraro exploded. "You expect me to believe that a high-ranking FBI agent, or the DEA agent, whacked these two men? You're thinking they were bent?"

"It's the only way it makes sense, boss, that these two guys in the car don't react when the heavies go into the restaurant and a gunfight starts. They hadda be dead already." Detective Connelly looked to Detective Kitt, who nodded. "Suppose that Craig and Rice weren't the ones who started the gunfight. Suppose the Washington brass went into the restaurant intending to take out Craig and his friends. To cover their tracks, they take out the surveillance team first—can always blame it on Craig afterward—and then go into the restaurant. Only instead of a clean hit, they walk right into a shit storm and get killed themselves. Then Craig goes out the back. Hell, he might not have even known the Fibbie team was outside. It sounds crazy, but it holds together."

The police captain digested that for a long moment. "This is some heavy shit. You're gonna have to get solid evidence to back it. What about forensics?" he asked after a long pause, rubbing his chin, deep in thought. "Can we ID which gun took out which victim?"

"Brick wall, boss," Kitt said. "We tried to talk to Doc Bardez but he told us to take a hike. Says the FBI took all the evidence and put a muzzle on him."

"I seem to recall that our guys were on the case first," Ferraro thought out loud. "Took the FBI how long to get the evidence from Bardez?"

"One, maybe two days," Connelly offered. The detectives exchanged glances, nodded and shrugged. "Yeah, two days . . . max."

Ferraro chuckled. "I've known that cranky little bastard for twenty years. If Luis Bardez had that evidence for forty-eight hours, he's got all the data squirreled away somewhere." He sat forward, his elbows planted solidly on his desk. "Okay, you two did a good job. Here's my orders. You do nothing. Say nothing. Indicate nothing to anyone outside this room about this. Not friends, wives, girlfriends, not even your mothers. Clear? No hints, innuendos, nothing. I'm gonna see my old pal Luis and dig out what I can."

The mood at the dinner table in the large baronial dining room was tense, but the children did not know why. The two chairs at either end of the large table reserved for Belalcazar and Milana were empty. Stephanie sat with the children. She seemed preoccupied and spoke little. The servants were wary and nervous. Like young deer picking up on the instinctive fear of the adults, the children sensed something was wrong. Although their favorite chicken-rice soup, along with mild sausages and noodles, were served, they barely touched their food.

"Why's everybody so quiet?" Justin asked, breaking the rules by speaking in English.

Stephanie didn't hear him at first. She was lost in her thoughts, nervously stirring her soup with a spoon. She wondered how she had come from a working-class neighborhood in Indianapolis to live on this beautiful but bizarre island. She wondered how she had spent an entire year on the island without realizing how truly evil her boss was.

Belalcazar had returned by helicopter a little before seven. Stephanie and the children had greeted him at the helipad as per his standing orders, but Milana was not present. Stephanie, like everyone else on the island except the children, knew why: The boss's bodyguards had caught her in bed with Ernesto, and had immediately confined them to different quarters. As soon as Belalcazar entered his office, he was informed of the reason for her absence. Stephanie had not been in the office when the boss gave his instructions on how the matter should be dealt with, but she rapidly learned what he said. According to her source, he had simply instructed that Milana would be fed to the sharks along the reef in the morning. As for Ernesto, he was to be tied to a large anthill a few hundred meters south of the compound, near the eastern shore of the island, and fed to the ants alive. Stephanie couldn't get either image out of her mind as she stared into her soup, not hearing the question that Justin had posed.

The two boys sitting on either side of Justin didn't understand English and didn't fully understand what he'd asked, but they each had a pretty good idea. Lisa and Debbie understood, as was clear from the knowing glances they gave Justin from across the table, encouraging him to probe further.

"Stephanie," Justin insisted, "why's everybody acting

so strange?" He still did not get an answer. He asked again, raising his voice, and finally got her attention. She looked at him across the table sadly, as if she wanted to tell him something but couldn't.

The absence of a response frightened Justin and the others. He looked at the other children at the table and then looked dejectedly down at his plate. "I hate this place. I wanna go home," he said, sobbing, surprised and embarrassed that he couldn't hold back his tears.

"Me, too," Stephanie mumbled as she continued to run her spoon through the now cold soup. "Me, too."

The deputy director for operations was important enough to merit an official car to pick him up at the Puente Aéreo passenger terminal at Aeropuerto El Dorado in Bogotá and escort him to his hotel. Donald Norquist, the CIA station chief in Bogotá, had initially thought that a driver and two guards would be sufficient to satisfy protocol, but at the last moment decided he'd better meet Warren at the airport in person. Norquist didn't like Warren, and on the few occasions they had met, he had struggled hard not to show it. Going through the ritual of meeting his so-called superior at the airport and pretending to be flattered that the pompous drunk had honored him with an unexplained and unnecessary visit would take a great amount of self-control. He surmised that this latest "fact-finding mission" was an effort to make it appear that Warren was actually doing something on the drug front and about the devastating civil war waging in Colombia. Norquist wondered who was being fooled by this charade.

As they climbed into the armored Chevy Suburban for the drive to central Bogotá, Warren informed the local CIA man that he had come to Bogotá to get the lay of the land on the escalating civil war. He professed to be particularly interested in the rumor that the rebels had Stinger missiles.

So that's the official explanation, the station chief thought. He nodded but said nothing for several minutes as the car made its way through heavy traffic on the

Autopista El Dorado toward the Centro and the U.S. Embassy. Warren, who didn't appear ill, broke the silence, announcing that he was not feeling well and needed to go to his hotel to rest. "Cancel the briefing meetings," he ordered. "I might be coming down with the flu. I'm going to hit the rack and see if I can nip this in the bud."

"Too bad. I hope you feel better. If you're up to it, I'll take you up to Santander province tomorrow, where you can see the fighting firsthand," Norquist volunteered, struggling hard not to smile. He knew that the last thing Warren wanted was to drag himself into a one-horse backcountry village and run the risk of getting shot. He also knew that Warren was almost certainly not sick, but laying the groundwork so he could be holed up in his hotel room and get laid and drunk.

It was Warren's turn to nod but say nothing, not sure if the station chief was pulling his leg. Warren checked into the Hotel Quesada and was given VIP treatment through the check-in process and quickly whisked to a suite on the top floor facing the rear of the hotel, away from the noisy streets below. He noted with approval that the suite was located next to the freight elevator. Belalcazar's men had planned well, he thought, no doubt with a combination of bribes and threats. What he didn't know was that Belalcazar owned the Hotel Quesada, which was named after the Spanish conquistador who founded Santa Fe de Bogotá, and that his every move was being watched.

Within twenty minutes of his arrival, Nick Field knocked on the door. The two men took the service elevator to the ground level, exited the building through the rear kitchen door, and jumped into the car that was waiting in the alley behind the hotel. Forty-five minutes later, Field's copilot strapped Warren into Belalcazar's first-class airline seat in the rear of the Huey and the chopper lifted off from the remote pad in Sibate, south of Bogotá, and headed for Isla Gorgona.

* * *

Tension ran high within the King Air until they reached the waters of the Gulf of California, one hundred miles south of the U.S. border. Jenny studied the faces of the three men with whom she had traveled across the United States and with whom she was soon to go to war. She swallowed hard as she thought about how much each of them had sacrificed to be sitting where they were just now, and how much they might sacrifice in the coming hours.

Billy tried to make light of the bullet that had nearly taken off the heel of his boot, but he was clearly shaken. Jenny was unnerved by his reaction. She had assumed that a tough old soldier like him would not be fazed by a near miss. Matthew inspected the two bullet holes in the ceiling of the cabin. He, too, looked traumatized, she thought. The sweat rings under his arms were visible, as was the band of sweat on his army-fatigue ball cap, his right knee shaking rhythmically.

Jack handed the controls over to Chris, informing him that he was going to the toilet in the rear of the plane. On the way, he, too, studied the bullet holes, noting their location and their angle of entry. He struggled to recall the configuration of the King Air B200. There appeared to be no damage to the plane's hydraulics or electronics. There were no fuel lines on the top of the fuselage. His initial conclusion was that while the bullet holes would create some drag and slow them down marginally, they had done no serious damage. He exhaled with an audible "Whew" and yelled, "Hot damn" as loud as he could.

"Say," he said, crouching next to Jenny, holding her armrest for balance. "I don't normally say this to beautiful women the first time I meet them." His face was only a few inches from hers. "But you look like you just saw a ghost." He laughed. "What did you do to this here girl, David?" he asked, slapping him on the knee.

"Hey, I'm proud to look as bad as the rest of you," Jenny answered, appreciative of Jack's efforts to lift the spirits in the cabin.

"Not as bad as the rest of us," David intervened. "I'd take you any day or night over our pilot here," he said, releasing his seat belt.

Jack understood the gesture. He swiveled toward David and the two hugged each other, both kneeling on the floor. These men, David's war buddies, were the father and brothers David had never had. As they hurtled through the air at 250 mph, five hundred feet off the water in the small bullet-riddled aircraft, Jenny was once again struck by the love between them.

"Sorry about Justin, good buddy," she heard Jack whisper in David's ear. "We'll get him back. You just keep yourself together. Keep focused, man."

Jack hugged Billy and Matthew with equal intensity, long, hard embraces. He then looked around the small cabin with a quizzical look that caught Jenny off guard, but didn't appear to faze the others. "Damn," he snapped. "What's that foul odor?" he asked in a huff. He sniffed several times and said, "Christ, that's me. Plum forgot I was makin' my way to the head to clean out my pants," he deadpanned, while the other men laughed, releasing more tension. Jenny caught on a few seconds later and joined in.

"You'll have to forgive Jack," David explained with a smile. "He's like Peter Pan. He'll never grow up."

"Anybody want some bottled water?" Jack asked as he returned from the toilet.

"I'll get it," Billy interjected. "You probably didn't wash your hands."

"I did. Yesterday morning. Just before breakfast."

Jack then clasped his hands together. "Okay, guys, here's the flight plan. We gotta go about twenty-one hundred miles along the coast of the Mexican mainland. We're east of Baja goin' straight down the Gulf of Mexico, huggin' the mainland shore so we can keep the lights from the shore in view. We may be below U.S. radar, may even be below Mexican radar. But just in case, we're gonna pretend to land at a couple spots while we're still pretty far north. Plan's to get down to fifty feet or so off the water as we approach one or two of the uncontrolled fields along the way. The ones we got in mind have mountains immediately to the north, so we'll be temporarily out of view from radar back in the U.S. We'll take advantage of that and continue southeast behind the mountains and hopefully lose them entirely. In case the first try doesn't work, we'll do it again farther south. Of course, we won't know what really works until we're either shot down or we clear the Guatemalan border.

"There are a couple of uncontrolled airstrips in Panama just over the Costa Rican border where we should be able to get fuel," he continued. "Should be able to clean up, eat a good square meal, and get some rest there. From either of those airfields, Isla Gorgona is about three hundred and fifty miles south-southeast. I'll work on the exact flight plan as we go, but three hundred and fifty miles is about right. In this rocket ship," he said as he looked around the plane, "we'll get you from the airstrip in Panama to Isla Gorgona in about two hours, taking into account the fact that I'm gonna slow down just a bit before I push your sorry asses out that door." He laughed as he pointed to the rear.

"Okay. Now, my job's to fly this plane. Your job's to eat dinner and sleep. There are cold sandwiches and soup in the fridge and a microwave in the rear. I packed the food and drinks early this morning back at Brown Field. Should still be fine. Eat and get some sleep," he ordered. "But . . . not before we have a toast. Matthew, Billy, you're the closest to the bar."

Billy and Matthew filled five glasses with ice and poured a hefty amount of Jack Daniel's in four of them, a small portion for Jack's glass.

Jack was suddenly, uncharacteristically serious. "To be with you guys under these circumstances is my privilege and honor. To know that you've risked everything to save Justin makes me proud that you're my dear buddies. I love you guys . . ." He wanted to say more, but his words clogged in his throat. His right hand quivered, the ice softly clinking. The others had never seen the happy-go-lucky, devil-may-care Jack Heed so emotional.

He recovered somewhat, raised his glass to his eye level, and said simply, "For Justin. Everything for Justin."

The cabin was silent. The only sound was the din of the engines and the slight whistle from the wind rushing over the bullet holes in the fuselage. Even those sounds seemed muffled. They all raised their glasses in unison. "For Justin."

Chapter 22

Frank drove.

Linda tried to sleep but couldn't. Pablo appeared to be asleep, at least viewed from her angle from the second row of seats in the van. She studied the others. Eric also seemed to be sleeping. She turned to look behind her to see the Waldrons wide-awake, each staring ahead like lifeless mannequins. Linda knew the look. She herself had worn that look countless times since Debbie's abduction. It hadn't been till that morning, just a few days ago, in the home of Billy and Faith Dunn, that she had started to feel again.

Now she was cruising down a highway in Colombia. Within the next forty-eight hours she would either be reunited with her Debbie or she would die. The personal danger meant little to her. If her daughter was lost, death would be merciful, no matter how the angel of darkness delivered her. She wondered if the Waldrons were thinking the same thing.

At first, neither Anne nor Sid noticed that Linda was watching them. After a few minutes Sid's eye caught hers, startling him. In the darkness of the van, lit only by the quick rush of headlights coming toward them, her eyes stood out prominently, creating an eerie catlike image.

Linda and the Waldrons began to share their fears with each other, lamenting the fact that the three of them had so little to add in terms of military training. Eric sat sideways in his seat, his eyes fixed on Linda. He had been listening to her conversation with the Waldrons, not sleeping. *There is something about this woman that is so compelling,* he thought, an appeal that went far beyond her physical attributes, although, admittedly, he was struck by her beauty the first time he had seen her in Billy and Faith's living room. She was intelligent, strong, and genuine. Here she was in the middle of Colombia willing to risk anything for her child.

Eric hadn't had a relationship with a woman in a long time. When and why his marriage fell apart was now a blur in his mind. It was sometime before his son was fourteen and his daughter was twelve. Sometime before his ex had taken up with her boss, and moved with her lover and the kids to Florida when the company relocated. Although he had seen the children on holidays when he wasn't working, and for a week each summer when they were willing, he was never really close to them after the move. That was almost five years ago. It was his biggest regret. "This is what we have to do," Eric heard Linda tell the Waldrons. "Follow these men. Go find our daughters. Nothing else matters."

"That's right," Eric unintentionally said aloud.

Linda quickly turned to him, surprised to see that he was awake and looking at her. "I thought you were asleep."

"Can't sleep." He sat up in his seat and turned to nod to the Waldrons. "Too many things on my mind. Couldn't help but listen to your conversation. We're all scared," he allowed. "But we're here for the children. Nothing matters but the kids. I should know. God knows I don't miss my ex . . ." he added bitterly, "but I shouldn't have let her turn the kids against me. Almost as much my fault as hers . . . almost . . ." he added, more candidly than he intended.

"So why aren't you home trying to win 'em back instead of down here trying to save Justin and two children you don't even know?" Linda asked kindly.

"Because David needs me. Then you came along. You looked so desperate that morning at Billy's."

Linda nodded, but said nothing.

"You were ready to put your hands into molten steel if you thought it'd lead you to Debbie. It was inspirational. Christ," he said, "none of us has been in combat since we were kids, over thirty years ago. Hell, now we're old farts. Pretty damned improbable bunch of commandos, if you ask me. And, by the way, none of you is more afraid than I am, or Frank or Pablo. You don't get used to it. Believe me, when the shit hits the fan—and it will—you'll have an overwhelming desire to run away. Don't. You'd be letting down your daughters and yourselves. You've come this far because you're strong and you love your kids. Remember that, and you'll know what to do."

Linda smiled at him affectionately, grateful for his effort to shore them up. Behind Eric's gruffness and sarcasm lay a heart of gold, something his Vietnam buddies had discovered three decades earlier. She was beginning to see it, too.

"Do you think David and the others are scared, too?" Anne wondered out loud.

Frank laughed. "Ever jump out of a plane at night?" His voice boomed from the driver's seat. "It's like jumpin' down a dark elevator shaft, only much farther. You bet they're scared."

Pablo laughed. He had never skydived. He found the idea of jumping out of an airplane bizarre.

"Yeah," Eric continued. "They're up there in the air somewhere," he said as he pointed to the dark sky. "If all goes well, they're somewhere over Mexico, checking their charts, examining their equipment, finalizing their plans. And when Jack opens the door to the plane and the wind rushes in like a speeding freight train, they'll want to tie themselves to their seats. But they won't. They'll jump. They'll jump for the kids. They'll jump because Linda's right. Nothing else matters."

Agent Rakovic was more depressed than angry, although there was still enough anger in him to make the small conference room in the Hoover Building feel crowded. The other five FBI agents sat quietly as the head of the task force read the two-page summary of the status of the manhunt, watching his eyes narrow to slits. When he finished reading, Rakovic studied the other agents as if he were deciding which one to execute first.

"You mean to tell me that I have to go downstairs and once again face the press with not one shred of positive news. Nothing! It's fucking unbelievable. Not only do I not have any good spin on this, it's a goddamn debacle. Somehow, I gotta tell 'em that even though we had full manpower assigned to the case, Craig, Rice, and all their buddies slipped through our fingers and flew to Mexico. Is that what I should tell 'em?" he challenged the agent who had the misfortune of sitting closest to him.

"Sir, we don't know that all those people were in the plane."

"Great. I can stand in front of the press and tell 'em we still have no fucking idea where all these people are, but that they may have been on that plane." Rakovic paused to reflect. "So what do we know? We know that a van was rented near Fort Huachuca, Arizona, by a person who has been dead for two years. We know that the vehicle ended up on a remote airstrip in California, the same strip that this Heed fellow landed on for a few minutes and then took off from in the direction of Mexico. . . ."

A brief knock on the door of the small conference room interrupted the briefing. A woman in her late twenties entered the room and sat at a seat as far away from her boss as possible.

"Sir," she said flatly, "we've got positive ID in the van. Craig's, Benson's, Dunn's, and Rice's prints are all over it. They made no effort to hide 'em. There was a fifth person. The driver. He wore gloves. Don't know who he is. We're looking for clothing and DNA samples, but that'll take a little longer. So we know that they're all in Mexico. Navy radar and Mexican radar indicated that they may have landed around Ortiz, just south of Hermosillo. We're working on that with the Mexican national police, and this time they appear to be cooperating."

" 'Appear' is probably the operative word there," Rakovic snapped. "Is there anything else I need to know before the media roasts my ass again?"

"Well, sir. There is one more piece of information."

"Get on with it," Rakovic barked.

"It's the Waldrons and the Ross lady, sir. The three people who appeared with Craig at the press conference the day he popped Harrison."

"What about 'em?"

"They're missing, too."

Jonathan Bernstein delegated LKB's systems upgrade to consultants he had brought in on special hire, an expense the investment bank could easily afford, and assigned two junior technicians who worked for him to handle the research that the new head of mergers and acquisitions wanted done immediately. He then closeted himself in his small office and set out to do the task that was really on his mind. Using the same methods and skills that Jenny and he had previously used to hack into the DEA, he set out to find out who had deleted the files of O'Neal, Katz, and Crawford relating to Belalcazar.

"So who is this jerk?" he asked himself several hours later. He stood, went down the hall to relieve himself of the six cups of coffee he had consumed, then returned to his computer and began to check the personnel records of the DEA.

"Holy shit," he exclaimed. He had expected to find that a junior person within the DEA was behind the deletions. Instead he saw the face of Aaron McCormick, director of operations, number two man at the Drug Enforcement Agency. He wished he could call Jenny to share the news. He wondered how he would get this message to Washington and to whom he would send it.

From the street, the gun shop resembled a fort; inside it looked like the lumberyard it once was. There were no doors or storefront windows, only a thick stucco wall, its dull orange paint chipped and peeling, and a large gated archway wide enough for a small truck to enter.

The building looked as if it had been there for hundreds of years. Even the graffiti looked ancient. Behind the gates was once a brightly tiled courtyard, now mostly gravel and broken tile, weeds sprouting at the edges of the walls and other less-trafficked places. To the left of the courtyard was a chest-high wooden counter, behind which was a closed door that Pablo presumed led to some type of office. Beyond the courtyard was the former lumberyard. A large open shaft stood three stories high, covered by a corrugated tin roof. On either side of the central space were three open wooden platforms, reached only by the rough-hewn ladders that leaned against them. One ladder led from the ground floor to the second platform. Another led from the second level to the third. Heavy hemp ropes connected to large pulleys dangling from the beams at the top of the warehouse were used to raise and lower the heavy crates of weapons and ammunition.

The plan was for Pablo to enter the store first and begin the discussions. Frank and Linda would join him if he signaled them. Eric would guard the van. Sid and Anne, alias David and Jenny, would stay out of sight as much as possible. Frank drove past the depot. He didn't like what he saw. Once inside the courtyard, Pablo would be trapped, easy prey for an unscrupulous arms merchant and his henchmen.

Pablo didn't like it either. But he had no choice. He steeled his nerves, walked under the archway, and asked the first worker he saw for the owner. Within a few minutes, a short, fat, unkempt man shuffled toward him from the rear of the arms depot. As he approached, Pablo noted that the man smelled like a urinal that hadn't been flushed in days. The stubble on his round face descended over his treble chin and merged with the hair on his chest. He had no neck. His filthy sleeveless undershirt was too short by several inches, revealing a hairy belly that hung over his thick leather belt. Yet the man's eyes were clear and they sized up Pablo intensely.

Pablo began the conversation with pleasantries, hoping to establish as much of a rapport as possible, given the fact that the fat man would have no qualms about killing him on a word from Belalcazar. He hadn't fully explained his strategy to the others in the van, partly because he was sure they wouldn't have liked it. But it was, after all, his country, and to a great extent his show, so he decided to play things his way. Within the first few minutes of banter with the merchant, Pablo told him what he needed: six Czech-made AK47 assault rifles, two thousand rounds of ammunition, extra magazines, cleaning rods and oil, and night-vision goggles. He also inquired about the condition of the roads to Buenaventura, leading to a conversation that revealed, as was Pablo's intent, that he was on his way to the port city. He didn't volunteer why he needed weapons to go to a port city as far removed from the fighting between the army and the insurgents as any town in Colombia, and the merchant, who had his suspicions, didn't ask. They haggled over the price of the cache of arms, Pablo finally agreeing to $8,000, which was high. In fact, he knew the price was absurd, but if it were to be believed that he was traveling with the rich investment banker from New York, he'd have to demonstrate his ample supply of greenbacks. The merchant assured Pablo that the weapons would be ready in a few minutes, and he snapped a command in an incomprehensible local accent to two of the peasant workers, who dutifully began to fill the order.

The arms dealer excused himself on the pretext of having to call his importer, and retreated behind the counter and into the office that Pablo had noted when he first entered the courtyard, closing the door behind him. Pablo had no doubt that the merchant really was making a phone call, and he believed that the call was to Belalcazar's people. They would determine whether one of the merchant's goons would cut Pablo down with an Uzi right here and now, or let him buy his armaments and go on his way.

Pablo stood on the gravel in the courtyard facing the chest-high wooden counter that separated the merchant's office from the courtyard. The acrid smell of an overflowing ashtray stung his nostrils. He pushed it to the end of the counter. The wall behind the counter was covered from floor to ceiling with clippings from porno magazines, a collage of hundreds of breasts, buttocks, and female genitalia. He pretended to study the pictures, feigning interest and planning his next move. The only space on the wall not covered by the clippings was a small window that allowed some light into the office. The window was closed. A tattered yellow curtain on the inside of the window shielded the merchant from view. In the reflection of the glass, he saw a man on the roof across the courtyard watching him, and felt extremely vulnerable. He couldn't see the weapon pointed at him, but he was sure that there was one. Sweat began to drip down his back.

After keeping Pablo waiting for approximately five minutes, the merchant emerged from his office and stood behind the counter. "You will excuse me, I hope. I had a very important call with my importer that was previously scheduled. I'm sure you understand that. We must keep up our inventory. Demand is very high these days, and supplies are short," he apologized unconvincingly.

Pablo relaxed ever so slightly. The fat man was continuing his harangue over prices just in case Pablo decided he wanted more firepower and gadgets. That was a good sign. Whoever had been on the other end of that phone call had given him the go-ahead to make the sale.

Within a few minutes the workers were lowering the crates with the pulleys and ropes. They lowered a long wooden crate and four smaller wooden boxes. One of the men also carried a cloth bag containing night-vision goggles, and a large paper bag, the contents of which were unclear. The workers opened the crates and Pablo was allowed to inspect the six AK47s. He carefully checked the mechanism of one rifle, chambered an imaginary round, and pulled the trigger, listening carefully to the metallic click. He did the same with the other five rifles. He then examined the 7.62mm ammunition that filled the four smaller wooden crates. Everything appeared to be in order. The paper bag contained empty ammunition magazines for the AK47s. The night-vision goggles seemed to be working, although Pablo had no desire to test them out in the darker recesses of the former lumberyard, especially without a loaded assault rifle.

Pablo cast an appreciative smile at the merchant. "Now, one more thing," he said matter-of-factly. "I need six Berettas, model ninety-two, with ammo and spare magazines. With laser finders and tac lights."

"Ah, but these are very expensive. They'll cost you two thousand dollars each," the dealer hissed through the spaces between his darkly stained teeth.

"Include five hundred rounds of ammo and thirty clips and we've got a deal," Pablo said, poker-faced.

The merchant nodded to the same two employees, and again they climbed up the ladders to the storage areas. It took them ten minutes to return. Again, Pablo carefully inspected the weapons. He chambered a nonexistent round, turned on the laser finder, pointed the weapon into the dark end of the warehouse, illuminated a thick support beam with the red dot, and clicked the trigger. He repeated the same exercise with each Beretta and was satisfied. Before paying, he walked the few paces toward the sidewalk. He stood under the stone-and-stucco archway and looked up and down the street. Spotting the van, he motioned to Frank to pull up closer to the archway, but to remain in the street. He turned to walk back to the counter, reaching into his pockets and pulling out bands of hundred-dollar bills, each neatly wrapped in folds of $2,000. When he got to the counter, he rapidly counted out the hundred-dollar bills and pushed the $20,000 pile across the counter. The dealer grinned broadly as he opened a drawer on his side of the counter and swept the pile of cash toward him, letting the greenbacks fall into the drawer.

The two workers lifted the crates and bags and carried them under the archway toward the waiting van. Pablo opened the rear door, removed the large ice chest, and motioned to the two men that they should pile the lethal cargo in the space he had cleared. Approaching the van, the workers stared through the tinted window to get a better look at the occupants. Sid and Anne partially covered their faces, as they had rehearsed. As the two men loaded the cargo into the rear of the van, they sought to get a better look at Sid and Anne, but were not able to see their faces directly. Pablo closed the door and gave each man a two-hundred-dollar tip. He then carried the ice chest to the sliding door on the right side of the van, passed it to Eric, and jumped in the front passenger seat, and they drove away.

"That was easy," Frank said as he glanced at Pablo, his disbelief apparent in his tone. "Six assault weapons, six Berettas, and enough ammo to take on a battalion, just like that," he continued as he snapped his fingers.

"Guess that means they'll lead us to the slaughter in Buenaventura," Eric added.

"Or on the island," Pablo said matter-of-factly. "When we get out of Manizales, I'll call some friends in Pereira. We can buy more guns and ammo there. We'll junk these weapons when we get there."

"What?" Linda exclaimed. "Throw 'em away?"

"They're probably rigged to jam on us, or the ammo's bad. We can't trust them."

"So why'd we buy 'em?" she persisted.

"Misinformation and insurance," Frank ventured.

"*Sí*," Pablo offered pensively as he searched the road behind the van to see if they were being followed. "We paid a lot of money for what we are supposed to think are weapons in excellent condition. Let's hope they buy that. We also let them know who we are and where we're going. Let's hope they buy that as well. If all goes well, they think David and Jenny are in this van. They also think, we hope, that we'll storm Buenaventura brandishing useless assault rifles and ammo. A ship captain will agree to take us to Isla Gorgona. And then he'll take us to our death. I believe they know who I am. I saw it in the arms dealer's eyes. So they know you're not just a bunch of *gringos* rambling around Colombia looking for somebody to shoot. You see"—he pointed to Frank—"I have given you credibility. I saw how the two workers looked at Sid and Anne," he said as he turned to the rear of the van, studying them as well as the traffic behind them. "I believe they reported back that you are David and Jenny. They believe that in part, I hope, because the rich *gringo* banker would recruit someone like me, offering me large sums of money to add Belalcazar's head to my collection. At least that's what we hope they think." He paused to reflect, watching Frank ease the van down the ramp onto the expressway leading south to Cali. "Now we'll do something they don't expect. We'll get good weapons and ammo in Pereira. Let's then hope that we catch them off guard in Buenaventura. We're taking long shots, but it's all we have."

Chapter 23

Sebastian de Belalcazar was at his desk at six A.M., watching CNN and studying reports of his varied enterprises. An elderly Paez Indian woman from Belalcazar, their native village, who had served him his meals for over twenty years, set the coffee on the large baroque desk in his office, just to his right, the way he liked it. He had always amazed her with his ability to concentrate, but this morning was exceptional. Despite the screams that every soul on the compound could hear through the night from Milana Escheverria as she was bound to a tree, awaiting her execution on the reef, and despite the slow and horrible death of Ernesto Rojas, Belalcazar appeared rested.

The word from the four soldiers who had been assigned to shackle Ernesto to the anthill was that all that was left of him were his bones. The ants had devoured everything in the fourteen hours since he had been strapped to the hill, each guard holding a rope tied to one of his limbs, then tying the ropes to nearby trees. No matter which way the strong Ernesto pulled, he was trapped. The soldiers had watched the ants from a distance with powerful halogen flashlights. Ernesto, who had been their friend, had begged for them to shoot him, but they were under orders not to do so. They watched him die, apparently of a heart attack, approximately forty-five minutes after the ants swarmed over him.

Stephanie Wagner hadn't slept. Her eyes were visibly puffy despite her attempt to conceal the dark circles under extra makeup. Milana's screams during the night had kept her awake. Closing the windows helped only marginally. She struggled hard to keep the image of the anthill and the coming execution of Milana on the reef out of her mind, but it was impossible. She imagined herself a helicopter pilot, starting the powerful engine, the blades rotating above her, flying herself all the way back to Indianapolis, and into the arms of her parents, who still lived in the blue-collar neighborhood where she and her brothers and sisters had grown up. Stephanie wanted out.

After the children finished their breakfast, Stephanie ushered them up the large, imposing staircase to the second floor, pushing them inside the large playroom and closing the door while a servant closed the windows. Stephanie ran to the CD player and put on a disc of Colombian children's songs, turning up the volume as loud as the children could tolerate.

She stood by the window, staring at the vast waters of the Pacific. Despite the closed windows and doors and the loud music, Stephanie thought she heard a scream. *Maybe it's just my nerves,* she tried to convince herself. *Maybe I imagined it.* She had fought back her fear and horror so far that morning and maintained some composure, but at that moment she lost it, collapsing into a high-backed chair next to the window, covering her face with her hands, hoping the children wouldn't notice her sobs.

After a few moments Justin walked over to Stephanie and placed his hand on her shoulder. "My daddy's comin' to take me home. You can come too," he said gently, even protectively. Despite his distrust of and anger at Belalcazar and Milana and their strange island, he had started to like Stephanie and to sense that she was somehow different from the other adults here.

Stephanie looked at Justin, the tears pouring down her face, her mouth disfigured with grief. She knew who his daddy was, and what his daddy had done in Central Park. She had overheard Joaquin telling Emilio in the courtyard the day before how much he hated Justin's father and how he would kill him the next time he had the chance. It was clear to Stephanie that Joaquin's machismo was all bluster—he clearly feared Justin's father and believed him to be a dangerous man. She looked at Justin, wondering if somehow what he was saying might be true, that David Craig would come and rescue his boy.

"It's true," Justin announced, returning her gaze with equal intensity. "My daddy said that he'd never leave me. He'll come. I know it." Stephanie wondered how he could be so sure, having lost that level of confidence long ago in her youth.

"My mommy's coming, too," Debbie interjected, startling Justin, who didn't realize she was standing just inches away. "She's really, really strong and can do anything. She's coming tomorrow."

God, I hope that's true, Stephanie admitted to herself.

At nine o'clock, Alberto descended the steps from the hacienda. He placed two fingers in his mouth, and with a shrill whistle he summoned the three men designated to assist him in the next execution.

Milana was a nearly lifeless lump of flesh. She bore no resemblance to the glamorous beauty of the day before. Her hands were several inches above her head, cuffed to a hook embedded in a tree, giving her arms barely enough slack to permit her to rest one hip on the damp ground. Her off-white dress was filthy, her hair snarled, her complexion ghostly. Her arms were drained of blood, devoid of feeling. Her beautiful face was swollen and bruised as a result of the struggle she had put up before being shackled to the tree.

Alberto retrieved a small key from his shirt pocket and removed the cuff from her left wrist, then her right. Gravity pulled her body to the ground without resistance. She moaned grotesquely from somewhere deep within. She opened her puffy eyelids slightly. Alberto stood above her, the bright sun in the eastern sky behind him. In the glint of the sunlight, a halolike glow formed around his head. She thought he was Ernesto, her lover. She involuntarily stretched her still-voluptuous lips to form a thin smile, earning a sharp kick to her solar plexus from Alberto's heavy boot.

Alberto grabbed her lifeless right wrist, while another guard grabbed her left arm. They began to drag her down the hill toward the docks, bringing Milana back to the terrible reality that she was soon to die. She was being dragged toward the boat that would deliver her, alive, to the sharks. Despite her pain and exhaustion, she let out a scream that was heard throughout the compound. The screams continued until they could no longer be heard over the powerful twin engines of the cigarette boat as it gracefully glided over the still blue waters of the marina through the narrow opening formed by the breakwaters, and headed in the direction of the reefs.

The meeting was all business. Joaquin had been instructed to brief the *patrón* on the status of the Colombian civil war and Belalcazar's plans to engineer the FARC's overthrow of the government. Joaquin had just returned from a series of meetings in the Norte de Santander province northeast of Bogotá, where he had engaged in a type of shuttle diplomacy between the ELN and the FARC, trying to unite their forces against the army in the battle for control of Colombia. The introduction of Stinger missiles, paid for and delivered by Belalcazar to the FARC, had given the FARC an even greater military edge over the ELN than it already had. The growing power of the FARC relative to the ELN and the Colombian army allowed Belalcazar to increase his leverage over both factions, and eased his ability to unite them under his behind-the-scenes control. If events unfolded according to plan, he would soon have effective control over all of Colombia, an empire larger than that of any single Spanish conquistador except Cortés. That Belalcazar was pleased with the report was evidenced by a gentle pat on Joaquin's forearm, a rare display of affection.

Inside the boss's office, the distinctive *pop, pop, pop* sound of the Huey was at first faint, almost imperceptible, then grew louder as the helicopter approached the island from the east. Gerald Warren stepped out of the helicopter and walked briskly toward the hacienda. He had been there before and knew the way.

"You have requested this meeting," Belalcazar said sharply in passable English to the associate director of intelligence.

Warren was puzzled by the icy tone. In their prior encounters Belalcazar had never been what one could call warm, but he had not been this abrupt. Something was bothering the drug lord. *Perhaps he knows,* Warren thought, *that I'm here to talk about the children.*

"Señor Belalcazar," Warren began ceremoniously, "our cooperation has netted us great benefits, and we wish to continue to prosper together. My colleague, Aaron McCormick, has asked me to visit with you to discuss matters of mutual concern," he continued in his official language and tone. "We believe we have been of great assistance in helping you overtake your rivals. Soon your operations will have control of all the east coast, and you can consolidate and expand from that base." Warren stopped, waiting for some reaction from Belalcazar, but there was none, and he continued. "We—Mr. McCormick and I—wish to continue to assist you. However," he said, pausing for effect, "we've run into a big snag over the kidna . . . er, adoptions. McCormick asked me to visit with you to make sure you understand the situation in the United States at present—"

"We have run into some problems, and we have made some foolish mistakes," Belalcazar interrupted. "You and Mr. McCormick have compounded our mistakes with those of your own. We all have lessons to learn from these events," he said evenly, signaling to Warren that he was unwilling to let him take the lead. "We did not study this Craig man in advance. We did not do our 'homework,' as you say. That stupid mistake cost me my nephew, some good men on the ground, and almost cost me Mr. Garavito here—" he added with a gesture toward Joaquin.

"The underlying problem, sir, if I might add," Warren interrupted, something few dared do, "is the children.

We understand the desire of you and your wife to adopt children. The first two adoptions in the U.S. were fine. Nothing could tie them back to your organization. But the Craig matter, that's a different story. We've kept all official inquiries pointed at your rival organizations," he said confidently, straightening himself in his chair. "And I believe we've contained this matter. Craig will soon be arrested, along with the woman. He will be prosecuted and convicted, possibly executed, for the killing of the government agents. That will put an end to that unfortunate episode. We can then get back to business as usual. We must, however, have your assurances that there will be no more . . . er, American adoptions. They're too risky. If the American public were ever to get wind of that aspect of your . . . life," he stammered, "Congress would demand military intervention. And there would be nothing we could do about that. We couldn't contain it."

Belalcazar said nothing for a few moments. He stared at Warren intensely, his eyes locked on the arrogant Yankee official who had the nerve to talk to him with so little respect. "You say you have contained the 'Craig matter,' as you call it. Who will arrest him and his friends now that they have fled your country?" he asked, the edge in his voice now razor-sharp. Warren looked surprised. Noting the puzzled look on Warren's face, Belalcazar explained. "It was on CNN this morning. Craig and the woman and several others were spotted near San Diego and flew to Mexico in a private airplane."

"I had no idea. As you know, I traveled through the night and have not been able to catch up on the news," Warren responded defensively. "But if they're in Mexico, we'll get the Mexican government to hand them over to us. This is actually good news. It further inculpates Craig. He'll never be acquitted after this."

"But he is no longer in Mexico, Mr. Warren," Belalcazar retorted sarcastically. "He and his friends are in Colombia. My people in Manizales identified them. They were buying machine guns. They said they were on their way to Buenaventura, but that may have been a ruse. If they show up in Buenaventura looking for a boat ride, they will get it." He laughed at his own joke.

"Are you sure it's them?" Warren asked incredulously, unable to hide his disbelief. "How'd they get to Colombia so fast?" he blurted out. *And how did Craig learn that his kid is in Colombia?* he thought nervously.

"Our people identified Craig and the Benson woman. There's a black woman with them. Maybe the woman at the press conference, Lidia's mother. The others appear to be his army friends, judging from their age and description. The black general isn't with them. He may be traveling separately, or he may be with the man known as Rice. Craig's traveling with Pablo Santiago, the man who killed Pablo Escobar. Somehow Craig has joined forces with him. We believe they're looking for a way to invade our island and take the children."

Belalcazar looked at Joaquin Garavito and nodded, indicating that he should take over. "Señor Belalcazar's right," Joaquin continued dutifully. "We've made mistakes about Craig which we will not make again. But you have made mistakes about him too. You and Mr. McCormick failed to keep them from learning about us. You assured us that you had covered all this within your government. But somehow they have learned who we are and where we live. They're clever people. But we are more clever. We've laid a trap for them. We will let them come to our island, and then we will kill them. We don't need you for this. They're in our country now, and we will deal with them in our way." He smiled. "They could be here as early as tomorrow, but most likely they'll come sometime in the next forty-eight to seventy-two hours. We will be ready for them. Then you can go back to Washington and continue to work for us."

"And the children?" Warren persisted against all common sense.

"This is of no concern to you," Joaquin admonished, his tone rising. "There are some matters—our larger plans for your country—that we need to discuss later today. Matters where we can use your and Mr. McCormick's help. Matters for which we will pay you very well.

"But right now we have other, more urgent things to do. If you'll excuse us for a few hours, we would be most grateful," he said politely. "Perhaps you would like to go fishing off the reefs. The fishing is good there. Our cigarette boat, made in America, should have returned by now from a run it made earlier."

"Of course," Warren responded, his mind focused on the words *we will pay you very well.* "I enjoy fishing."

"But first call Mr. McCormick," Joaquin instructed.

"Well . . . yes, sure. I'll do that."

"I need a favor," NYPD Capt. Angelo Ferraro announced as he sprinkled Parmesan cheese over his plate of ravioli.

"Why else would you ask me to lunch?" Dr. Luis Bardez looked over bifocals. Ferraro noted that his gray eyes were more red-rimmed than usual. *He looks like hell,* Ferraro thought. *One of these days the job's going to kill him if he doesn't slow down.* Bardez was known for the long hours he kept in the crime lab and his devotion to—some said obsession with—his work.

"Luis, I hear you had the evidence on that hit last week on Tenth Avenue. Multiple shooting. FBI and DEA officers killed. Bystanders killed. Remember it?"

"How could I forget? Your guys did everything but run buffalo across the crime scene. Angelo, can't you tell your boys to be more careful? What a mess they made."

"Don't change the subject."

"Hey, the Feds took over the case. I've got enough to do, so what the hell—let them do the forensics." Dr. Bardez twirled his fork into his spoon and loaded his mouth with spaghetti. He grunted approval.

"Luis, don't bullshit me. I know you. You're the best. You had the evidence for, what . . . one, maybe two days? I need to know what you found." Ferraro sat back, waiting.

Doc Bardez mumbled through his pasta, reaching into

his rumpled jacket and extracting a folded sheaf of paper. "Mmmm."

Ferraro lunged forward in excitement. "How in the hell did you know this was what I wanted?"

"You guys think you're the only ones who can work a crime scene? Your detectives' asking me yesterday about the case got me thinking. I went back, pulled out the raw data that I'd set aside, and processed the evidence. Something that I didn't do at first."

"What did you find?"

"This is not dynamite, Angelo. This is nitro!"

"Tell me."

"Like I said, I collected all this info quickly—figured the Feds would take it off my hands—but just put it on the shelf. Until your guys called. Anyway, I about crapped when I put it together. Look at this chart," the doctor said as he unfolded a hand-drawn matrix on the table. "Each of these vertical columns represents a gun. Weapon one, a Glock, is Harrison's. Two, a Beretta, is also Harrison's. He fired the Beretta in the restaurant. The Glock was in his suit pocket. Evans's is three. We never found weapon four, just the bullets from it that killed Evans and Harrison. Now, over here on the left, the horizontal rows, is who got iced by which gun. See these two names? Those are the agents found in the FBI car outside the restaurant."

"Got it," Ferraro said, tracing his finger over the chart. "Gun one fired the bullets that killed them . . . and that weapon was found on Harrison. Jesus Christ, Luis. Are you sure? That means Harrison killed his own people?"

"Either that or Rice—or Craig—took Harrison's Glock after he was down, walked out of the restaurant and killed these two agents, then walked back inside, held Harrison's hand on the weapon to impart his prints, and then put it in Harrison's suit coat. My guess is that Harrison intended to plant the Glock on Craig's dead body, fingering him for the deaths of the two agents. Otherwise it doesn't compute with me."

"It didn't with my guys either." Ferraro reached for the report, but Dr. Bardez withdrew it.

"What are you going to do with it?"

Ferraro thought. "Well, you've got to figure if we know this, the FBI crime lab knows it, too, right?"

Dr. Bardez nodded. "If the real evidence ever made it to the lab."

"Right, okay . . . but assume the lab has it. Or assume some rogues within the Bureau trashed it . . . or someone in the lab has been turned . . . it means that either the FBI is on the track of something and isn't telling us—always a possibility. Or—and this is the part that scares me, Luis—that someone high up in the Bureau is crooked and is calling the shots. I'm gonna find out. But I'm gonna need that chart."

Chapter 24

The main highway, Route 25, runs north–south through the valley formed by the Río Magdalena between Cordillera Central to the east and Cordillera Occidental to the west. Frank exited the highway at Marsella and headed southeast on the secondary road through the rolling hills and coffee plantations to Pereira. The van approached the town from the northwest, followed the buses to the bus terminal, and then drove south on Carrera 13 to the Avenida 30 de Agosto, following the directions given to Pablo by his friend. The Avenida led to the airport, but they didn't need to drive that far south. Soon they found Calle 26 and arrived at their destination on schedule. The auto-repair shop would have been hard to miss. It was more a junkyard than a body shop. The ample lots to either side of the stucco-fronted building, painted cobalt blue with canary-yellow trim, were strewn with wrecked and rusting cars jacked up on cinder blocks. What appeared to be hundreds of engines, transmissions, car seats, and mufflers were lying in piles of various sizes throughout the site.

Frank eased the van into the lot, just missing a large, mangy dog. The mutt wandered off, annoyed with the vehicle that had interrupted its siesta. Frank cut the engine and Pablo stepped out of the van. Linda looked at her watch: two-thirteen. The sun bore down mercilessly on the yard, reflecting off chrome auto parts and the sheet-metal roof of the building.

Pablo looked around for signs of his friend, but saw no one. He knocked hard on the front door, but there was no answer, so he tried the door. It was unlocked.

He entered cautiously, his hand ready to reach for his Beretta. There was no one in the front room, which was unusual. Then he heard people shouting, a television blaring, and immediately understood: football. Cali was playing Bogotá. Pablo was one of the few Colombians not obsessed with soccer and one of the few Colombians who could have forgotten today's game. He walked quickly toward the screen door to the rear of the shed and, peering out, saw his friend with several other men, women, and children seated under a large tree, cooled by the shade, huddled around a small TV.

Pablo's friend, Hector, finally noticed him, jumping off the small aluminum chair and apologizing for his inattentiveness. He embraced Pablo with enthusiasm, kissing him on both cheeks. Hector's wife and children also rose and embraced him. The two men who worked the yard for Hector rose respectfully and nodded their greetings, but maintained a discreet distance as Pablo and Hector spoke in hushed tones.

"Would you and your friends like coffee?" Hector asked.

"No. Thank you. We don't have time. Have you been successful?"

"Yes," Hector answered simply. "It will be expensive, but it will be waiting for us in Tulua. I will go with you that far and make sure that you're taken care of."

"Can we go now?" Pablo asked politely, but it was clear to Hector that it was not a question. "Also, I must ask you a great favor. We will compensate you well, but it is still a favor." Pablo looked attentively at his former colleague in the Search Block. "We need you and one of your men to come with us to Buenaventura. You'll need to drive your own car. Our van will be spotted the moment we drive into town, so you need to go to the port first and check out everything for us. You pick a boat for us to charter or hijack and report back to us. Then you return to your family. There will be bloodshed, but that will not be your problem. We will deal with it. Can you help us?"

"Yes, my friend, of course," Hector answered after a

few seconds' pause. "Where are the weapons and ammo you bought in Manizales?"

"In the back of the van," Pablo answered with a gesture toward the front of the building. "Take them. If you can fix the weapons, so much the better."

"I will take them as my brokerage commission." Hector laughed.

"We'll pay you and your friend each five-thousand dollars for guiding us to the boat in Buenaventura," Pablo added.

"Well, this is a good day. I see my old friend. I get some free rifles and automatics that maybe I can sell. And I pick up some extra cash."

"Now, if you could get Cali to beat Bogotá, it would be a perfect day." Pablo chuckled, relieved that Hector had agreed to help.

"Don't expect miracles," Hector cautioned with a throaty laugh as he headed to the rear to recruit one of his workers and to tell his wife that he would not be back until midmorning the next day. He packed no overnight bag or gear other than an automatic pistol that he slid under his belt and covered with his loose-fitting shirt and five fully loaded ammo clips, which he shoved into the pockets of his jeans. "I'm ready," he told Pablo. "Juan will meet us around front."

Happy Jack had never ceased being amazed by the Global Positioning System. In the old days, he reflected, a pilot had to locate visible markers on the ground—highways, buildings, radio towers, and the like—and then try to figure out where he was. Alternatively, a pilot could establish radio contact with a local ground station and have the ground crew guide him to the airfield. With the satellite-directed GPS, he didn't need to do either. He and Chris knew where they were within meters. They were now over the Pacific, exactly 49.3 miles due south of the Burica Peninsula, a thin finger of land divided roughly down the middle by a low ridge that formed the border between Costa Rica and Panama. There were several airports on the Panamanian side of the border, ranging in quality from paved runways with control towers to grass strips in the low-lying jungles. The major airport in the area was Enrique Malek International, but to call it *international* was a stretch. The next most sophisticated airport in the sector was the strip at Puerto Armuelles. It was also shamelessly labeled *international,* a notion that made Happy Jack laugh out loud. Nevertheless, they would avoid both airports and select the remote airstrip at Progreso. They would over fly it once, maybe twice. If it wasn't what they were looking for, they'd fly on to El Hato, a strip at five thousand feet altitude in the jungles near the Chriqui volcano. All they needed was a grass strip and fuel tanks—the more isolated the better.

Chris confirmed their location, then verified the GPS coordinates for Progreso and read them to Jack, who banked smoothly to their left and headed north at 180 mph. They maintained an altitude of five hundred feet until they reached the Panamanian coast, exactly 12.4 miles east of Puerto Armuelles. They then climbed to two thousand feet. Within four minutes of reaching land they were over the airstrip at Progreso. It looked perfect. The grass strip appeared to be well maintained and recently mowed. Chris pointed out a red tractor with a large mower behind it. It was parked next to a small freshly painted operations building. Large letters spelled out PROGRESO on the roof. A hexagon with a dot in the middle painted on the roof indicated that the airport's radio was a VHF omni-range. Chris raised his eyebrows and nodded to Jack, indicating that he was impressed. The outline of a single-engine airplane was painted in white on the concrete pad next to a fuel tank, signaling that a pilot wishing to refuel should park his plane on the pad in the direction shown. There were three small shacks bordering the single-lane road that led to the village of Progreso, about a half mile away from the strip. Barring a change in circumstances on the ground, it would be their base of operations for the next twelve hours. The digital clock on the instrument panel read 1409 hours.

As soon as the wheels touched the grass airstrip, Jack reversed the props and was rewarded with a comforting *whoosh* and the gentle pressure of the straps of his shoulder harness against his chest as the plane slowed. The ride down the grass runway was bumpy, but the sturdy landing gear withstood the jolts easily, and the King Air came to halt well before the 3,000-foot strip ended abruptly down a deep, vine-filled ravine. He turned the plane around and taxied at 15 mph back to the operations building at midfield.

The proprietor of the Progreso airport came out to greet them. A slender man, his thin mustache neatly trimmed, he seemed no more than thirty years old. He was dressed in well-pressed, tan khaki pants and a white, short-sleeved polo shirt separated by an expensive braided leather belt. The words *Aeropuerto Progreso* and the same symbol of an airplane that decorated the concrete pad near the fuel tank were embroidered on the left breast of his shirt right above the name *Raul,* and also on his white baseball cap. Jack saw that the man seemed to focus on the King Air's call numbers.

"He's no slouch," Jack muttered to Chris as he continued to idle the engines just in case they needed to flee on a moment's notice. "Stay here. I'll go talk to him."

Chris nodded.

Jack and Raul shook hands and exchanged pleasantries. Jack began by speaking Spanish, but soon learned that Raul also spoke English. He had studied at Emory Riddle University, the same school Jack graduated from, which seemed to put the young man at ease.

"My name's Jack Heed," he said, extending his hand, wondering if he should have given a different name.

"I know," Raul said simply, shaking Jack's hand. "My name's Raul. Raul Noriega. Not related to our former dictator, who now sits in your prison." He laughed. "But my family name is Noriega."

"How do you know who I am?"

"I watch CNN," he responded ironically, as if to say, "Civilization doesn't stop at the Rio Grande." "Your FBI thinks you landed in Mexico. At least that's what they're telling the public. It seems you've come a lot farther south than they think," he added admiringly. "You can tell Mr. Craig that I have no reason to do him harm," he said truthfully, looking over to the King Air. "I have a wife and two small children, also boys. I wish him well and I hope he can save his son. Actually, I think we can help each other." For the next few minutes he outlined his impromptu plan, fleshing out the details as they came to him.

"I think I can sell that," Jack said after a brief pause.

The two men laughed heartily, shaking hands and slapping each other on the back.

"I guess things are going well," Jenny observed as she pressed her nose against the porthole window of the plane, turning to Billy, Matthew, and David as they, too, peered through the small portholes. All of them wondered what Jack and the well-dressed man found so funny.

Joaquin wasn't pleased with the state of their defenses. The Ranger-turned–investment banker was most likely on his way to Isla Gorgona, and Joaquin needed Ernesto's knowledge of the security system. Almost any of the guards could watch the surveillance screens in the security office, but only Ernesto knew how to make the necessary repairs, although it was clear that his mind had been elsewhere during the last few weeks. The broken camera on the side of the cantina remained out of order. More significantly, many of the functioning cameras were known to fail even in the slightest rain. Several of the electronic sensors along the trails in the jungle south of the wall were malfunctioning, reporting false positives, or not reporting at all. Mines and most of the motion detectors had been removed so that the sensors could be repaired, and hadn't yet been replaced.

Joaquin walked the grounds like a general inspecting his troops. Weapons that did not pass inspection were ordered cleaned. Fines were meted out to guards who didn't know their defensive positions. Gardeners were ordered to stop their makeover of the grounds so they could clip branches and bushes that obstructed possible fields of fire, leaving partially dug holes and mounds of dirt and stone for retaining walls lying about. The three cigarette boats were inspected by the mechanics and their fuel tanks filled to capacity. The two smaller boats were docked in the marina in their usual slips, while the third, the *Pizarro,* newer and more powerful, was hidden in a bunkerlike garage at the end of the marina. The electronic motor and gear that raised and lowered the heavily armored garage door was inspected and oiled, as was the M60 machine gun mounted on the vessel. Joaquin made the strategic decision to keep the children in their rooms for the time being. Not by coincidence, the children's and Belalcazar's bedrooms, situated on the upper floor of the hacienda, were considered the most secure. If, by chance, Craig or his friends were to make it to the hacienda, they'd have many obstacles to face before they were anywhere near the children or the *patrón*.

They didn't knock. They barged in and stood in front of his desk, each wearing a cheek-splitting grin. "We'll discuss your lack of decorum later. It's late . . . very late. I wanna go home. Okay, what've you got?"

With a flourish, Detective Kitt pulled a plastic bag with an evidence tag on it from his jacket. "Boss, we did like you said. Went back and shook down the crime scene, especially where the FBI car was parked. Check this out."

"Son of a bitch," Ferraro said slowly as he held the bag containing an innocuous-looking steel tube. "Where'd you find it?"

"Well, you know what they say. Shit seeks its level," Detective Connelly said, pointing to his partner, then looking at the silencer in the bag.

Kitt's grin grew broader. "While Mickey and his crew were crawling around on all fours near the gas station and auto-body shop, I had some of the uniforms open the drain covering and look around with flashlights. That silencer was supposed to be in the Hudson by now. It got hung up on an outcropping."

"You guys did good," Ferraro said. "Get this over to Doc Bardez. Tell him where you found it and ask him to run ballistics on it. Tell him to stand by for a meeting with the commissioner."

Tulua looked to Linda and the others pretty much like the other small towns they had been through. A large church or cathedral, a few small parks, overcrowded buses careening down narrow streets, nearly hitting the throngs of pedestrians crossing anywhere they pleased. Children played in the streets.

Linda drove, closely tailing the rear end of Hector's car, an old Nissan, lest she lose him in traffic. Hector circled the plaza in front of the church, but didn't slow down as he continued toward the industrial sector south of the town. When he reached the southern outskirts of Tulua, he slowed in front of a series of squat, cinder-block, single-story buildings. Some bore the names of the companies housed behind their windowless facades. Oddly, there were no doors facing the road. One building had a large beer advertisement on the roof. Hector made a sharp turn into one of the alleyways between two of the buildings, almost hitting a telephone pole that partially blocked the narrow passageway. Linda followed, slowing almost to a stop to avoid the pole.

Hector turned right when he reached the gravel lot behind the buildings and swung around in a wide loop, parking the Nissan next to a late-model, dark blue Ford Econoline 350 that was parked facing out from one of the buildings, its rear bumper a few feet away from a heavy metal door. Next to the Econoline was an older-model large Chevy van that appeared ready for the junkyard. Linda parked next to Hector. Within a few seconds two men stepped out of the building and embraced Hector. The three of them spoke quickly, their flying arms animating the discussion. Pablo joined them, nodding frequently in agreement. Linda could hear Pablo mention David Craig several times, nodding his head toward the van, where she sat behind the wheel. She made out a word here and there, but was unable to follow the conversation. After several minutes Pablo disappeared into the cab of the Ford Econoline and emerged a few minutes later. He then peered into the Chevy van, taking inventory of whatever it was inside that caught his attention. After a brief pause he walked toward the van where the Americans waited, jumped into the side door, and explained.

"They got what I asked for. They also want us to buy these two vans," Pablo said, motioning to the Ford and the Chevy, "and take them instead of this van," he continued, tapping the rented Ford with the palm of his hand. "They're right about one thing: We can't use this van. We'll be spotted by Belalcazar's men even before we get through Buga. I agreed to their terms. They've done a good job for us on short notice, and this is no time to bargain. Hector will drive his car and go first to Buenaventura. His friend Juan will be next in the Chevy. We'll follow in the blue Ford, but first we'll make a stop in the woods, where we can familiarize ourselves with the weapons. We must move quickly. Time is running out."

Hector was the first to leave the small parking lot, exiting through the narrow alleyway as quickly as he had entered. Juan pulled the old Chevy van out of the lot slowly, staying behind Hector. Linda started up the Ford and initially followed Juan. Pablo gave her directions as they drove and the old Chevy dropped out of sight. The others sat uncomfortably in the dark, sweltering van, each wondering what would happen in the coming hours. Pablo was deep in thought.

Eric broke the silence. "So, Mr. Santiago, what gives?"

"Sorry," Pablo said, shaking his head to clear his thoughts. "Hector's going ahead in his faster car to Buenaventura. Juan's heading there too, only more slowly. While they scout for us, we'll get some practice with the

M16s. You and Frank know how to use them, but the ladies and Sid need instruction. We also have two Czech grenade launchers. Two of us will carry them along with our M16s. And we have Beretta 9mm automatics, but I hope we won't get so close that we have to use them."

"Okay, but what's in the Chevy?" Eric asked, sensing there was more to the plan.

"Dynamite. It's full of dynamite. Fourteen hundred kilos."

"Three thousand pounds of dynamite!" Sid exclaimed, quickly doing the rough math. "What are we going to blow up?"

"I don't know," Pablo responded quickly as he placed his finger over his lips as if someone might overhear the conversation. "Hector will blow the hell out of something to serve as a diversion. It worked for us back in Medellín. Except that the explosion was too close. Should've been farther away," he added, running his fingers over his patch. "This time I hope Hector explodes the dynamite farther away."

"Could I speak to the director, please?"

"Who may I say is calling?" the secretary of the director of the FBI inquired.

"Police Commissioner Ressin, NYPD. Jimmy and I grew up together in Queens. I need to see him tomorrow morning."

"I'm sorry sir, but his schedule is booked solid tomorrow starting at eight A.M. sharp."

"Fine," the commissioner snapped. "Tell him that I'll meet him at his home tomorrow morning at six. I know the address. Tell him that it is very, very important. I'll bring the bagels so he and Christine don't have to bother."

"Yes, sir. I'll pass on the message."

"Oh, yeah. Almost forgot. Capt. Angelo Ferraro of the NYPD will be with me."

Jack climbed into the plane and squatted in the doorway, keeping his eyes on Raul, who remained on the tarmac approximately fifty feet away. Jack explained the deal that the owner of the airport proposed. He would extend his hospitality to the band of Americans. They could remain at the airport for a day and use the shower and the kitchen, such as they were. Raul would bring them food from the village. They would have complete privacy and he would say nothing to the authorities. In exchange, he would be allowed to tape an interview with them for his radio station and they would let him take two pictures. The tape would not be aired nor the pictures released until twenty-four hours after their departure. Jack liked the deal, and assumed everyone else in the plane would too. After all, he reasoned, after twenty-four hours the publicity wouldn't hurt, and they needed a base of operations. When he finished, he was surprised that the others were unconvinced.

"You mean he's telling us he won't turn us in if we give him publicity rights?" Billy asked skeptically.

"Yeah. Sounds like what he's saying," Matthew ventured.

"Well, folks," Jack urged, "we can either take this deal, as is, or we can kill Raul and stay here and use the place, or move on to a better airport. I don't know about you all, but the deal's lookin' pretty good to me."

"I don't trust him," Billy explained. "Why does a man who appears to be a successful, law-abiding citizen risk going to jail for a bunch of fugitives who, for all he knows, may just be murderers?" Billy asked.

"I pretty much asked him the same question," Jack answered.

"I think he watched CNN and decided he doesn't buy into the government's BS," Jack ventured. "He's a businessman tryin' to promote himself. He's willin' to take a risk. Could be a real coup for his radio station. Also—and I really believe this—he's a father with two boys. I think he felt some kinship with David as he watched him on CNN."

As he had done so many times before in boardrooms over the years, David looked at Jenny for guidance. Until a few weeks ago, each had earned a very good livelihood reading people and negotiating tough deals on Wall Street. Long before they were lovers, they were partners who relied on each other's instincts. She nodded in agreement with his unspoken question.

"Jack's right," David began. "We need this place. We'll take the deal. But he doesn't leave our sight. We'll take away his cell phone if he's got one. He doesn't go near a phone or shortwave. He doesn't pee without one of us present." He paused to think. "We'll take him with us. If he wants a story, he can watch us jump. Jack and Chris will fly back here and keep an eye on him for another twenty-four hours. Then, one way or the other, it won't matter what he does."

"Right on time, as usual. You must have left pretty damn early." The FBI director laughed as he opened the front door of his house in Bethesda at six A.M. and let in his old friend, Frank Ressin, now the police commissioner of the City of New York, and the detective who traveled with him.

"Came down last night. Brought real bagels from home," he added, holding up a plastic bag. "We have to talk, Jimmy. The captain here has a lot to tell you."

"Come into the kitchen. Coffee's ready."

Ferraro explained what Detectives Kitt and Connelly had uncovered, showed the director Doc Bardez's findings, and then slid the evidence bag containing the silencer across the breakfast table.

"So, Jimmy. You've got some bad apples in the Bureau and the DEA," the NYPD police commissioner concluded, taking the words from Ferraro's mouth.

Chapter 25

Hector prepared to drive across the Puente El Piñal, the only bridge from the mainland to Isla Cascajal, the island on which the port city of Buenaventura was located. The structure crossed the narrow, rapidly flowing tidal channel. The checkpoint on the near side of the bridge looked the same as the hundreds of army checkpoints along the highways and back roads of Colombia. Men in uniform, toting assault weapons, examined identification cards and questioned the drivers and passengers of the vehicles. Concrete barriers were strategically placed to require all vehicles to maneuver around them slowly. A sandbag revetment three hundred feet away on the far side of the bridge barely concealed a .50-caliber machine gun powerful enough to penetrate an armored personnel carrier at that range. But this checkpoint was actually different. The uniforms that the soldiers wore did not bear their names, nor did the soldiers bear regimental patches on their left shoulders like soldiers of the Colombian army. These were men of a different, private army. They were Belalcazar's soldiers. Buenaventura was his town.

Hector slowed the Nissan to a crawl. When the soldiers approached, he flashed his ID card and was allowed to pass without incident. A little over two hours later, Juan drove the Chevy van, heavily loaded with dynamite, across the same bridge past the same soldiers. He, too, was allowed to cross without inspection.

A half hour later, Hector met the Econoline at the second-to-last intersection before the checkpoint on the Puente El Piñal. Frank was driving, and Linda sat in the passenger seat. Hector, who was on foot, approached from the passenger side, opened the door, and slid in next to Linda, edging her to the left and leaving her door slightly open. He instructed Frank to approach the bridge slowly. There would be three soldiers on the right side of the structure, he explained. They had been paid well and would let the van pass. Sid and Anne now understood why Pablo had broken the overhead light. It didn't go on when Hector opened the door, allowing those in the rear to hide in the darkness.

Frank eased the van forward. The two-lane, simple-truss bridge hadn't been painted in years, and the orange paint chips that remained were surrounded by deep rust blisters caused by the salt air. The steel superstructure ascended about three stories above the roadbed. Two strings of light were affixed to the rusty girders about twenty feet above the pitted asphalt surface. More than half the bulbs were burned out or broken, but even in the dim light Linda and Frank saw six soldiers milling about on either end of the bridge. Three were standing at the midpoint looking over the side rail.

Eric, Pablo, and the Waldrons squatted in the darkness, Sid and Eric facing the rear, ready to shoot anyone who tried to open the rear doors, Pablo and Anne facing the front and the right side door, ready to do the same. Pablo strained to see what lay ahead as they edged forward. There was no traffic at this hour, something Pablo found odd. He had never been to Buenaventura, but he had read much about it. In addition to its busy port, it was known for its seedy *salsatecas*, where salsa music blared from dusk to sunrise and where the *aguardiente* flowed in torrents down the gullets of thirsty seamen, truck drivers, Belalcazar's soldiers, and the whores who serviced them. At ten-fifteen P.M., Pablo thought, the Puente El Piñal should be a snarling traffic jam.

When they reached the bridge, Hector swung the right-side door of the cab fully open and stepped down, while Pablo retreated farther into the shadows in the cabin, straining his ears to hear the conversation between Hector and the soldiers. Within a minute Hector was back in the van, resuming his position next to Linda, the door slightly ajar. He motioned for Frank to cross the bridge, just as one of the soldiers waved them on. Frank drove at no more than 5 mph across the two-hundred-foot expanse, maneuvering around the concrete barriers. Within several minutes, they were on Isla Cascajal, angling northwest at each Y intersection down nearly deserted streets, with Hector giving directions.

"This place looks dead," Frank observed, directing his comment to Hector in Spanish. "I'd have thought a port city would be jumpin'." He nearly missed a small street that Hector belatedly told him to take.

"All that happens on the other side of the island," Hector explained. "That's where you find the *salsatecas*, the bar fights and shoot-outs that you read about. That's why we're heading in the opposite direction," he continued in Spanish that everyone but Eric and the Waldrons understood.

Eric saw Pablo shift his position and reach for something in one of the crates. He thought he saw him place something in his pocket, but in the darkness of the van he couldn't tell for sure. Pablo inched closer to Eric and placed his lips against Eric's ear.

"When we stop, I'll jump out the side door. Tell Frank to drive away as fast as possible. Something's very wrong," Pablo whispered.

Eric turned his eyes toward Pablo's good eye, now only a few inches from his. Pablo's expression was deadly serious. He was worried, and his fear was contagious. Eric was already sweating profusely from the heat and the tension of crossing the bridge. Now his heart was racing too. Oddly, he had no desire for a cigarette or a drink. He cursed himself for being so out of shape and feared that it might cost him his life if he needed to run. He gripped the M16 more tightly. The weapon had served him well thirty-two years ago. He hoped he could still use it half as well.

Pablo tilted his head, silently asking if Eric understood. Eric nodded in return. The Waldrons saw the exchange of glances between the two men in the darkness but didn't know what to make of it.

Pablo shifted back to his position near the sliding door immediately behind Hector. Eric continued to guard the rear door with Sid, but he kept casting glances over his shoulder toward Hector. His skittishness infected Sid and Anne, who instinctively moved closer together.

Frank continued to drive down the narrow road Hector had directed him to take. They passed a stretch lined with single-story corrugated-metal buildings. A few had signs, but Frank doubted that the activities that took place behind the walls had anything to do with the businesses advertised. They reached an opening at the end of the narrow road. On the far side of the clearing, two hundred yards away, the port's single pier stretched east to west for 1.3 miles. Ahead, to Frank's right, he saw the Chevy van parked in the right angle formed by two tall concrete walls, the remains of a former coal bin, with Hector's Nissan parked directly behind the Chevy. To Frank's left, a large crane, used for loading containers and other heavy cargo, loomed eerily above the roof of a warehouse. Powerful lights mounted on one hundred-foot poles placed every one hundred yards along the pier lit the port like a football field at night, harsh white light beyond which was total darkness.

When the Econoline came into view, Juan stood up straight and acknowledged them with a fully extended wave of his right arm. Pablo was immediately disturbed. The gesture was too energetic, too staged, perhaps a signal to others. He studied the situation unfolding before them. Through Frank's side window he saw two medium-sized container ships berthed along the pier, their bows pointed to the west toward the Bay of Buenaventura and the Pacific Ocean. A large trawler was tied to the wharf, close to the Chevy van. Pablo assumed that the trawler was the ship designated to take them to Isla Gorgona.

Juan was the only person in sight. Pablo scanned the Nissan and the Chevy. The van filled with dynamite should have been on the opposite side of the island. His mouth was dry, his throat like charcoal. Despite the grip he maintained on his Beretta, his hand was cold. It was something he had never understood about himself. Unlike others, when he was faced with danger his palms didn't sweat. They became cool. Now they were icy.

Frank slowed the van to a halt near the Nissan. Pablo shot a lightning-fast glance at Eric, but didn't wait for a response. As Hector jumped from the front seat of the van, Pablo slid the side door open and placed the business end of his Beretta firmly against the base of Hector's neck. Juan's eyes went wide with surprise. As Juan reached for the weapon under his shirt, Pablo withdrew the Beretta from Hector's neck, sliding it off the top of Hector's right shoulder, and fired twice from only ten feet away. The first bullet caught Juan in the lower abdomen, the second squarely in the chest, as the large-caliber weapon kicked Pablo's hand in the air. Juan was lifted off his feet. His head struck the side of the Chevy as his lifeless body came to rest at the base of the left rear wheel.

The moment Pablo made his move, Eric yelled to Frank to gun the engine and get the hell out. Frank wasn't completely caught off guard, his instinct, too, telling him something was terribly wrong. Still, it took him a split second to react. As he stomped on the accelerator, he was startled by the sound of the two shots, more like howitzers shattering the still of the night. The van lurched forward toward the pier and the water below. Trying desperately to maintain control, Frank turned the wheel hard to the left. His right foot bore down on the gas pedal so hard his calf muscles began to cramp. Glancing into his side-view mirror, Frank saw Pablo and Hector, who were like brothers only hours before, standing face-to-face, each preparing to destroy the other.

In the back of the van, Eric, Anne, and Sid were thrown toward the rear from the rapid acceleration. Sid crashed against the left rear door, his head hammering hard against the metal. He nearly lost consciousness but managed to recover enough to turn toward the front, resting his back flush against the door. Anne, who was more forward in the cabin, fell toward the center and landed facedown, her nose bloodied. Eric, too, was thrust backward, but he had anticipated the movement and steadied himself by grabbing a handle.

Pablo studied his old friend. Hector's eyes were wide, full of shame and fear. Shame at his betrayal of his former Search Block comrade. Fear for his impending death.

"Was it for retirement money? Or were you always with Belalcazar?" Pablo asked, his voice resigned.

"For retirement," Hector responded truthfully. "I was a good Search Block member. I was loyal to our cause. But Pablo, as you know, our retirement is meager. We starve while inflation increases. My family is large and we are poor. I needed the money."

"And we were to die for this money?" Pablo asked, his voice showing no emotion.

"Forgive me, my friend," Hector responded, his eyes now on the ground.

Were it not for the patch on his left eye and his limited peripheral vision, Pablo would have seen them coming. But he did not. Several men, Belalcazar's soldiers, had been watching through small darkened windows in the nearby warehouse. At the instant Frank pounded his foot to the gas pedal and the Econoline shot forward, Belalcazar's foot soldiers emerged from their hiding place, each carrying an AK47 assault rifle or a Belgian FN P-90 machine gun.

One soldier, the same man who had ushered Hector across the bridge, motioned with his hand for one group of soldiers to go after the van, while he and two other soldiers ran toward Pablo and Hector. After only a few paces, the lead soldier stopped and extended his left arm, indicating that the others should hold back. "He's mine," he whispered as he dropped to one knee and raised his AK47. He squeezed the trigger twice and was rewarded with the sight of the legendary Pablo Santiago thrown to the ground.

The first bullet hit Pablo in his left kidney and exited

through his stomach. The second tore through his left shoulder, nearly severing his arm. The impact threw him several feet to his right, slamming him to the ground hard on his back. Hector, who had seen the soldiers coming, retracted his automatic pistol from under his shirt, spun toward Pablo, and stopped, statuelike, his body pitching slightly forward. There were two small holes in his chest. He looked down to study them, a strange fascination in his eyes. He wondered how Pablo had done it. He couldn't see the golf ball–size holes in his back. It didn't matter. He crashed facedown on the gravel, his arms helpless to break the fall.

The soldiers turned abruptly away from Pablo and Hector and, along with the other soldiers, opened fire on the blue van as it raced along the pier. Three shots slammed into the rear of the vehicle, one against the bottom half of the bumper, ricocheting harmlessly into the gravel. Two other shots hit their mark. One pierced the left rear door with a hideous dull sound somewhere between a *zap* and a *thud*, traversed the length of the cabin, grazed Frank's right shoulder, and ripped a hole in the windshield three inches in diameter. The third pierced the right rear door with the same sound as the other bullets, but was followed by a thicker, more muffled sound as it bore a hole in Sid's vertebral column, pierced his right ventricle, and lodged against his sternum. He slumped forward and died without a sound.

Pablo wondered if he was already dead, but concluded that the sound of rifle shots, the distinctive popping sound of AK47 rounds, could only mean that he was not yet in heaven. His body was largely numb. The former hero of the Search Block knew enough about dying to know that the absence of pain in his abdomen, despite the large pool of blood gathering, was not a good sign. He rolled slightly to his left and was punished by excruciating pain in his shoulder. Pablo looked quizzically at his left arm and wondered how it was still attached. He struggled to reach into his right pants pocket, fumbling several times, pausing between each effort. Finally he grasped the grenade and wiggled it free, praying that he would have the strength to remove the pin. Pablo placed the pin in his teeth and pulled hard. His hand flung away from his face and hit the gravel below. The pin remained in his teeth. He raised his hand and threw the grenade with a backward flip of his wrist toward the dynamite-filled Chevy. The grenade bounced twice, coming to rest a foot behind the bumper. As if in a dream, Pablo saw the grenade explode. It was a hero's last act. As the white heat flashed over him, a brilliant light engulfed him. For an instant, he thought he saw Jesus.

The grenade exploded first, then the van's fuel tank, and then more than three thousand pounds of dynamite, the sequence so rapid it appeared as one blast. The right angles of the concrete walls that in times past formed the coal bin directed the energy of the explosion southwest, toward the warehouses and shantytown. The warehouse that had hid the soldiers was the first to disappear. Its corrugated-aluminum shell, loosely attached to a thin steel frame, shredded and blew in a southwesterly direction at several hundred miles per hour. Within milliseconds, neighboring warehouses disappeared, hurling tiny shards of metal through the air at the speed of sound, lancing through anything in their path. Belalcazar's foot soldiers seemed to vaporize, like puffs from a cigarette in a strong wind. The lead soldier, the one who was so proud to have shot Pablo Santiago, was closest to the impact. The other soldiers near him were next. Their loved ones would find no trace. They ceased to exist.

Frank wasn't sure what was happening. Although a mile away, the force of the blast overcame the Econoline at more than 200 mph, swallowing all oxygen in its path, numbing human consciousness. Life was momentarily suspended. All sound was snuffed out by the rush of the wind. Particles of buildings, gravel, and other debris sped past the vehicle. As the impact lifted the rear wheels off the ground and the vehicle tilted to the left, Frank uselessly tried to steer. The van turned sideways, then twisted upon itself like a bucking bull in a rodeo, landing on its left side. Up front, Linda's and Frank's seat belts held them in place. Eric, Anne, and what remained of

Sid were not so fortunate, tumbling in the rear cabin. The vehicle slid on its left side for more than two hundred feet, steel against gravel, heating the driver's side red-hot. Finally the Ford came to rest, still on its side. It was less than two hundred feet from the point where the main pier ended, giving way to a six-hundred-foot slip, cut at an angle perpendicular to the pier.

The explosion destroyed everything within half a mile to the west and within three-quarters of a mile to the southwest. Partygoers on the southwest of the small island, the red-light district of Isla Cascajal, were knocked off their feet. Windows were blown out. Roofs were torn away. Alcohol-impaired sailors, truck drivers, fishermen, and their scantily clad women of the night fell to the floors of the bars and whorehouses, as much in fright as from the blast itself. They lay on their backs, staring in disbelief at the moon and stars, hanging like ceiling decorations above them, through gaping holes in the roofs.

The trawler berthed nearest the blast was rid of its upper decks, had broken loose of its lines, and was taking on water rapidly through plates of steel separated at their rivets. Belalcazar's soldiers on the trawler, who were ready to pounce on the Americans and Santiago once they boarded, were sinking with the vessel.

An eerie silence descended upon the island. The survivors remained in whatever position the explosion had left them, fingers searching for wounds they hoped they would not find. It would take a full ten minutes for those with minor injuries to begin to fathom what had happened. For others it would take much longer. Many would never understand as their lifeblood drained from them.

Linda regained consciousness first. Her eyes fluttered open, instinctively trying to focus and regain the moisture they had lost in the heat of the explosion. As her mind cleared, Linda realized that she hung from her seat belt on the passenger side of the overturned van, gravity pulling her toward Frank, who remained behind the wheel, pressed against the hot door, motionless. She moved her head cautiously, verifying that her neck wasn't broken. Linda worked her feet, then her legs. Her arms responded, but felt more like wiggly globs of her daughter's Play-Doh. Her fingers ached.

Linda called out to Frank and saw him begin to move, his eyes opening with a start. *Thank God he's alive,* she thought. "Are you okay?" she asked in a hoarse whisper, to which he nodded. "We have to get out of here. Now," Linda urged, knowing she had to make the first move. She forced her hand under her hip toward the buckle of the seat belt and tried to press the release button. It didn't work. *Try again. You can do it; you must do it,* the former track star coached herself. She grasped the buckle and squeezed harder, this time rewarded with a metallic click, a *swoosh* as the belt retracted across her stomach and chest.

Oddly, the impact of Linda's body falling against Frank's, accompanied by the sound of his own voice as he registered the pain, comforted him, confirming he was still alive.

Linda maneuvered herself over Frank's seat and came to rest on top of Eric, who was unconscious, his face oddly peaceful. She gasped, thinking he was dead. She placed her ear on his chest and heard his heartbeat. Linda cradled him in her arms and kissed him gently on the forehead, praying. After several moments Eric groaned and moved slightly. She continued to hold him, rocking him like a baby, uttering gentle words, coaxing him back to consciousness.

Frank freed himself of his seat belt and struggled over the bucket seat, trying to make his way to the back of the van. He stumbled in the darkness, accidentally kneeing Sid in the groin, and instinctively apologized. There was no response, even though the pain had to be excruciating, Frank thought as he reached the rear doors. What was the left door was now on bottom, the right door on top. The bottom door opened easily enough and slammed flat on the gravel with a *thud.* The top door wouldn't stay in position. He had no energy to fight it and let it dangle.

Crouching as low as his aching body would permit, Frank slid through the open door. He knelt uncomfortably on the hard gravel, and tried to grasp what had happened. The scene before him was one of devastation, like the aftermath of a tornado. All electric power was out, the only light coming from a half moon shining peacefully in the slightly overcast sky.

Pablo, Frank thought. *Pablo exploded the dynamite.* The two cranes closest to the blast were bent over, their necks broken, hanging in the opposite direction of the explosion. The third crane, the one in the middle of the pier, was intact, but the operator's cab had been torn from its bolts and lay smashed at the foot of the superstructure. Everything near the explosion was destroyed. He figured he was still alive because the van had rolled with the blast, rather than offering resistance. Frank's mind functioned in small, linear thoughts. *Get everyone away from the van. Find a boat. Get out of Buenaventura.*

Frank heard Eric's voice. He reached into the van, grabbed Sid by both feet, and pulled him out faceup, laying him flat on the gravel. He knelt down and stuck his head through the opening again, barely able to make out Anne's crumpled form. He placed his hands firmly in her armpits, braced his back, and pulled her through the opening, noting that she was breathing and beginning to stir. As he placed Anne on the gravel next to her husband, she planted her elbow on the ground, raising herself up for an instant, and then collapsed on her back. Her face was bloody from the injury to her nose, but she began to wipe the blood off with her sleeve. It was a good sign, Frank thought. She'd live.

Eric crawled on his hands and knees through the opening, followed by Linda. She, too, crawled, but her movements were deliberate, decisive, as if she knew that she, along with Frank, had the laboring oar. Linda, too, took a few seconds to survey the scene, then turned on her knee, lowered her head, and crawled back into the van, pulling out everything she could get her hands on and sliding things out of the vehicle, calling to Frank for help. M16s. Ammo boxes. Grenade launchers. Pablo's white bag with the red cross on each side. She turned to Frank, who was stacking the weapons on the gravel, and said, "Let's get the hell out of here."

Anne was now sitting up, her eyes open, holding her forehead and fighting valiantly with an excruciating headache that distorted her senses. Eric indicated with a wave of his hand that he was okay, coming to slowly, but okay. Frank and Linda knelt beside Sid, seeking signs of life. There were none. No breath. No pulse. Nothing. Outwardly there seemed to be nothing wrong. He lay on his back, his face placid. Frank turned him over gently and grimaced. There was a large circle of blood in the middle of his back, a gaping hole a half inch in diameter. He glanced at Linda, then at the holes in the left rear door of the van, and he recalled the bullet that had pierced the windshield, the one that had grazed him. Sid was dead. Frank, Linda, and Eric exchanged knowing glances as Frank and Linda turned him over again so that his face was up.

Despite being disoriented, Anne understood, rousing instantly to full consciousness, dragging herself to Sid's side. She held him by the shoulders and shook him gently, at first saying nothing, then whispering, "Don't die, baby. Don't die, baby," over and over. Denial gave way to reality, bursting the dam. Anne broke down sobbing as she lay across her husband, as if to shield him from the evil that had already claimed his life.

Frank nodded to Linda, signaling that they had to move. He grabbed an M16, chambered a round, and flicked the toggle switch. He passed an M16 to Eric, who did the same. Eric stood guard near the van, checking all approaches for signs of danger. Linda tried to comfort Anne.

Frank ran to the west toward the end of the pier, about two hundred feet from where the van had finally come to rest. In the dim moonlight, under patchy clouds, he saw the slip Pablo had described to him. It was, as Pablo had said, over six hundred feet long, and slightly more than one hundred feet wide. In the darkness Frank couldn't tell how deep it was, but he remembered Pablo telling him it was thirty feet from the top of the pier to the surface of the water. The slip was used for transient vessels too small to take up valuable wharf space along the primary pier. Frank ran away from the slip toward the smaller docks, where Pablo had said the shrimp boats and trawlers docked. He ran for no more than a few seconds when a man toting an AK47 appeared from what seemed like thin air.

"Hola, mi amigo," the man said to Frank. "What the hell was that?" he asked in Spanish.

Frank, whose first language was Spanish, shrugged, but said nothing as he approached the man, wondering if his Americanized accent would betray him. Frank studied him as they each stepped closer, probing for signs of vulnerability, thinking that he might be drunk or still in shock from the blast. The soldier, who was neither drunk nor in shock, strained his eyes in the semi-darkness to see if he recognized Frank and then stopped at the top of a long stone staircase that descended to a narrow stone pier. The staircase had no railing on the side that faced the slip. Frank continued to approach slowly until they stood only a few feet apart.

"You all right, man? That was one fuckin' blast."

"I'm okay," Frank responded simply. "How 'bout you? Were you down there?" he asked, doing his best to imitate a Colombian accent and pointing to a trawler docked in the slip.

"Yeah. But not in that old fishin' boat. We were in the *patrón*'s personal boat." He turned to point to what appeared in the dim light to be a white cigarette boat, a Sea Ray, Frank recognized.

Suddenly the soldier's eyebrows narrowed. Belalcazar's soldier leaned forward slightly to get a better look at this stranger. Frank, in turn, stiffened involuntarily. *It's my accent*, he thought.

"What's the code word for the night?" the Colombian asked.

"This," Frank responded with an upward swing of his M16. The soldier recoiled, but it was too late. The hard plastic butt of the rifle caught him under his jawbone, hurling him off the top of the stairs. He hit the narrow pier thirty feet below with a *crack* as his skull hit stone, his AK47 falling at his side with a metallic clatter.

Frank quickly moved away from the stairs, looking for any sign of more soldiers. He waited a few seconds, his M16 ready for anyone who would have him for a target. Seeing no one, he sprinted as fast as his legs would carry him back to the van, shouting to Eric to pack up and move out. Linda was still trying to comfort Anne, who continued to hold Sid.

"Anne, we gotta get the hell outta here. I just killed one of the bad guys. It won't take long for his buddies to find him. Sid's dead. We've gotta move now," Frank commanded as he hefted a crate filled with rocket propelled grenades on his shoulder, holding his M16 in his other hand, ready to fire it like a pistol. Eric slid the shoulder strap of Pablo's first-aid bag over his right shoulder and then hoisted the other RPG crate over his left. Like Frank, he held his M16 in his right hand, ready to fire at will.

"I can't leave him," Anne said to Linda.

"He's dead and we can't take him with us," Eric said harshly as he followed Frank, panting as he transported the heavy crate to wherever it was Frank had determined to stash them.

His words wounded Anne. She stared at Linda, as if imploring her to explain the madness.

"It's time to go, Anne," Linda said soothingly. "Sid would want you to. Lisa needs you. Debbie needs me. And they need us alive."

Anne was still sobbing softly as Linda rose to her feet. She continued to cry as Linda picked up an M16 and strapped it over her neck and shoulder. Linda tried to pick up two of the ammo boxes, but found them too heavy. She let one plop to the ground. She placed her hands on the rope straps attached at either end of one wood crate and began to follow Frank and Eric, bracing the crate on her right hip to take the pressure off her back. "Anne," Linda said for the last time, "I'm going to get my daughter." She turned away, struggling under the weight of the crate.

Anne watched Linda disappear into the darkness. She crawled over to a medium-sized bag that she had been told contained the extra ammo magazines for the M16s. Anne placed it around her shoulder and neck, did the same with an M16, and rose to her feet. She looked at Sid one last time. His face was tranquil.

"Good-bye, Sid," she whispered. "I've got to find Lisa. Forgive me." She stooped to grab the rope handles of the ammo crate that Linda had left behind, hoisted it to her shoulder, and tried to catch up with Linda.

Eric returned to the van, leaving Frank at the top of the stairs. He met Linda midway. He was breathing heavily, sweating profusely, and silently cursing himself for being so out of shape. The heat and the humidity were getting to him. Eric felt like throwing up. He relieved Linda of the ammo crate and accompanied her back to Frank. He then half ran to Anne, intercepting her in the darkness. He grabbed one rope handle with his left hand, freeing up his right hand for the M16. Anne held the other handle with her right. Together they ran to the stairs, keeping their heads down, neither exchanging a word. He gasped for every breath. Anne wondered if Eric was going to have a heart attack.

Frank had managed to pry open one of the RPG crates with a flat piece of steel. He attached a pointed grenade to the business end of the launcher. "Eric. Here," he said, handing the long grenade launcher to him, his voice dry, his fear evident. "Hold this position. You've got a two hundred-degree angle of fire. Hold 'em, buddy," he added, gripping Eric's arm as if it might be their last moments together. "Anne, stay with Eric. He'll tell you what to do. Linda, you go down the pier so that you're just above the white boat down there," he instructed. "I'm going on the boat. Belalcazar's soldiers are on board. Don't know how many. Stay low."

Frank began a measured descent down the stone

stairs, hugging the high stone wall to his right for support, careful not to trip. Linda crouched and sprinted the three hundred feet she needed to be above the vessel. She dropped to the ground on her belly, the M16 held tightly in her hands. She edged forward a few inches and pointed the weapon into the darkness of the slip, dismayed by how difficult it was to make out shapes in the dim moonlight.

Eric and Anne squatted at the top of the stairs. They descended three steps and sat, pointing their M16s east and south. The grenade launcher lay flat on the first step, out of the field of fire, ready. Eric gulped for air, his chest rising and falling rapidly. He had an overwhelming desire to drink cold water. *If I make it out of here, I'm gonna lose thirty pounds and stop smoking,* he promised himself.

"Bad guys at one o'clock," he said in a harsh whisper to Anne. "They're over there," he added, pointing to them in case Anne did not understand. "Coming from those shrimp boats. Three of them. Behind that pile of rubble," he whispered, referring to what was a shed a few minutes before. He paused to breathe. Anne stared at him. He was pale, as white as the moon. "They're not after us . . . least not yet. Don't shoot till I tell you," he gasped.

Anne nodded, as if to say she wouldn't think of doing otherwise. "Over there! More over there," she blurted out in a low tone, pointing to something Eric couldn't see.

"Where?" Eric snapped, again in a harsh whisper.

"At . . . eleven o'clock," she stammered.

"Good . . . good . . . I got 'em," he acknowledged as his eyes darted to his eleven-o'clock. "Keep an eye on 'em. Watch for others." Just then a burst of gunfire from behind him nearly lifted him off the steps.

Frank had toggled the selector switch on the M16A2 rifle to the three-round-burst mode. As he approached the long white boat, he spotted a soldier twisting into position to fire on him. His rifle was already raised.

Frank squeezed the trigger twice, firing two three-round bursts, but it sounded like more. The man catapulted off the stone pier to a watery grave.

After a brief pause, several more shots were fired, this time by Linda. A soldier had appeared on the bow of the Sea Ray, attempting to catch Frank by surprise. Silhouetted against the white gel coat of the new boat, he formed a perfect target for Linda. Like Frank, she had placed the selector switch on the three-round mode, the way she had been instructed earlier that day. Thoughts of Debbie, alone and frightened, gave her strength. She squeezed her index finger gently against the trigger and repeated the action three more times in rapid succession. A total of twelve rounds spat from the powerful assault rifle, but she couldn't tell how many of the bullets hit the man. She heard several of the deadly *plap* sounds of bullets tearing into the man's torso. The other shots splashed the water, followed by the dead soldier. Strangely, she felt a fierce pride swell within her.

All hell broke loose on Eric and Anne's perimeter. The four men Anne had spotted responded clumsily, first running in the direction of the gunfire, but they were met by a hail of bullets from Eric's M16. He killed one and wounded another. The soldiers retreated behind a four-foot cinder-block wall approximately two hundred yards away. Eric directed Anne to put her M16 in single-shot mode and to aim at the wall. She quickly began popping off a round every two seconds. At first her aim was poor. The bullets hit low and harmlessly into the ground. In a few seconds, though, her aim became steadier and the cinder blocks began to disintegrate, pinning down the three remaining soldiers. By the time twenty of the rounds had chipped at the wall, the soldiers behind it were scrambling for better cover. The sight of the men running gave her strength. She hoped Sid was watching.

A light rain began to fall, obscuring the moonlight.

At the same time Anne was firing on the group at eleven o'clock, Eric was doing the same with the soldiers at his one-o'clock, but with much less success. His targets were better trained. Two took cover, lying prone behind the scrap heap formed by a collapsed shed, while another fanned out toward Eric's two-o'clock, taking cover behind a tree. The men behind the shed didn't have a good line of sight; nor did Eric have a good shot at them. But the single soldier at Eric's two-o'clock had a clear line of fire. The former Ranger chose to ignore the men behind the shed and trained his sights on the tree. His strategy was simple. He toggled his selector switch from the single-shot mode to the three-round mode. If the man moved, Eric would spray a couple of three-round bursts his way and hope at least one would find its mark, or at least keep him pinned down. Within seconds the man rounded the large tree, his assault rifle firing away. Then he wildly spun around from three M16 rounds in the chest.

In the meantime, Frank's heart had leaped to his throat when Linda fired at the man on the bow. He hadn't seen him. She had saved his life. Frank swallowed hard, took a deep breath, and sprinted the distance to the stern of the boat. The familiar sound of M16 rounds popping behind him could only mean that Eric and Anne were under attack. He crouched on the stone pier next to the open deck and cockpit. He swung his left leg over the gunwale, then his entire body, rolling on his chest on the rear deck. He low-crawled on his elbows and knees, pointing his M16 at the open door of the cockpit that led below deck. It was risky, but he had no choice. Frank rose, strapped his M16 over his shoulder, and removed his Beretta. Rapidly, but methodically, he searched the berth, the stateroom, the heads, and every possible hiding place. After a few moments it became clear he was alone.

Frank raced back up the steps to the cockpit. He noted that the boat was a Sea Ray 630 DA, America's fastest performance cruiser, resembling a cigarette boat as much as a pleasure cruiser. He turned the key in the ignition, providing enough juice to check the instrument panel. He found what he wanted: full fuel tanks. He darted aft past the seating area and with one easy leap was back on the stone pier. "Linda, we're all clear! Get down here!" he shouted, not thinking that there was no way down the thirty-foot-high wall other than the stairs where Anne and Eric were fighting for their lives.

Frank bounded up the steps behind Eric and Anne and knelt on one knee behind them, several steps below the surface of the wharf. "Anne," he shouted, passing one of the ammo crates to her. "Take this and go to the white boat now. Get ready to cast off. Now. Go now," he urged, seeing her hesitate. Anne scooted down a few steps, keeping her head low, took a deep breath, stood, and started down the stairs.

"Linda's trapped up there on the pier!" Eric screamed to Frank over the roar of gunfire. "We gotta get her off there and down to the boat." He turned, rose, and emptied his clip in the direction of the wrecked shed. "She'll have to jump into the water at the end of the berth. Go help her. I'll cover. I've only got one more magazine. Let's boogie."

Frank strapped Pablo's first-aid bag and the satchel of empty magazines over his shoulders, grabbed the unopened RPG crate and the remaining ammo crate, and disappeared down the dark steps, calling to Linda.

She needed no prodding. She understood her precarious position. She couldn't advance to the steps where Eric was taking fire. She couldn't jump thirty feet to the stone pier without breaking an ankle or worse. And she couldn't remain in her exposed position. She swiveled again on the ground and crawled like a lizard away from the firefight toward the juncture of the long wharf and the slip below. She reached the edge formed by the slip and the wharf and sucked in her breath as she looked down at the thirty-foot drop into dark, ominous waters. A large container ship was berthed alongside the wharf, its bow pointing menacingly at the very spot where she would have to jump. In order to clear the end of the stone pier, she would have to make an Olympic-quality long jump.

Linda retreated about twenty-five feet, stood, took three deep breaths, pumped her legs several times, and sprinted toward the point where the slip and the wharf met as fast as her legs would allow. She gained speed with each thrust of her legs, the M16 in her hand keeping stroke with her free hand. As she ran, she concentrated on the concrete edge of the pier. Her eyes were ablaze with determination. When her right foot touched the edge of the pier she gave out a loud grunt and sprang forward, her legs still running in midair, her arms splaying to give her balance, as she hurtled toward the dark waters below. She cleared the stone pier by several feet and plunged deep into the water, struggling not to let go of her rifle. Within seconds she rose to the surface and sidestroked to the stone pier with one arm, keeping her M16 out of the water with the other.

Eric inched his head above the top step. Bullets instantly whizzed by, just missing him. Several more of Belalcazar's soldiers were joining the fight, dark shadows moving in the patchy moonlight that filtered through the passing rain clouds. He was outnumbered and outgunned. He could hold for only a few more seconds. He put the M16 in single-shot mode, raised it above his head, and began to squeeze off rounds in the direction of the soldiers. He had no expectation of hitting anyone. He only wanted to pin them down for a few more seconds. He turned his head back down the berth behind him and saw Linda and Anne running along the narrow stone pier, approaching the white boat.

"Time to go. Go . . . go . . . go," he muttered as he emptied his magazine at random in the direction of his attackers. He grabbed the grenade launcher in one hand, the M16 in the other, nearly flying down the steps.

Linda, dripping wet from her dive into the water, untied the starboard foreline, placed her M16 on the deck, and grabbed a stanchion. She braced the rubber soles of her wet shoes against the stone pier and pushed the vessel with all her strength, forcing the bow from the pier as she swung herself over the starboard lifeline. She crashed to the foredeck, unharmed. At the same time Anne tended to the aft lines while Frank started the twin engines with a roar that surprised him. He edged the vessel forward slowly even as Anne climbed over the starboard aft gunwale.

Eric struggled down the stone pier, desperately trying to gain speed. When he was close enough to the vessel, he jumped, placing his right foot on the gunwale, and allowed himself to fall flat on the semicircular cushion that covered the engines. Frank had been watching every move that Eric made and gunned the engines as Eric was still midair on his way toward the engine cover. No one was prepared for the boat's power. Frank was pulled backward, but held on to the wheel for balance. Linda slid on the bow, grabbing a stanchion to brace herself. Anne fell to the deck, as did Eric.

Several bullets hit the stone pier to Frank's right, bright sparks shooting up into the darkness. A thumbnail-size hunk of lead hit the instrument panel to his left, destroying the depth finder. Another put a three-inch hole in the windshield, nearly taking Frank's ear with it. Linda took a bullet to her left forearm. It was only a scratch, but it scared the hell out of her. Frank jammed the throttle forward as far as it would go: The combined 2,150-horsepower of the twin engines catapulted the sixty-three-foot-long vessel forward. Rain began to fall.

The Sea Ray gained speed and raced alongside the stone pier just a few feet away. As the sleek vessel reached the point where the opening of the slip met the edge of the long wharf, it was already beginning to plane and rapidly accelerate.

Eric placed the rocket launcher on his right shoulder and aimed it at the top of the stairs, where Belalcazar's soldiers stood firing at the boat. Bracing himself with his legs spread apart, he squeezed the trigger. His aim was high and the fireball, clearly visible, streamed directly toward the soldiers. It would have made contact had two soldiers not dropped to the ground. The fireball passed over them into the darkness. Eric cursed himself, but the shot had the desired effect. The boat was now in the main channel, going 40 mph and rapidly gaining speed. They had made their escape.

After making her way back to the aft seating area, Linda sat clutching her M16 like a security blanket, her clothes and hair dripping wet, her arm bleeding slightly. Her eyes found Eric's. He was breathing heavily, trying to ease the pounding in his chest. He loaded a fresh magazine into his M16, the rifle shaking slightly in his hands. Linda, too, shook as she tried to steady herself, moving slowly across the boat and sitting next to him, her left hip touching his right. She put the M16 safety on and placed it on the deck between the seat and her heels. She slid her left arm under his and placed her head on his shoulder. They sat together silently, oblivious to the now-hard rain.

Anne sat in a semicircular seat immediately behind Frank. Her rifle rested on her thighs, its barrel pointed starboard, her left hand resting on the forestock, her right hand on the rifle butt. The rain pelted her. She looked back at the wharf and the large seagoing vessels, her mind an emotional swirl of guilt and hope: guilt for leaving her husband behind, unburied; hope that she would find Lisa and give meaning to Sid's death.

They rapidly distanced themselves from the port, the moon obscured by passing clouds. Unlike the others, there was no rest for Frank. While the others began to recover, he was still very busy watching the channel for buoys and markers. Squinting in the rain, his eyes shifted from the channel to the compass and back again. He maintained their course due west at 270 degrees. He had memorized the chart Pablo had given him during the trek from Bogotá to Buenaventura. They were to head due west until they spotted a large buoy with both a light and a bell, which would signal that they had reached open waters. From there, Isla Gorgona was southeast at 225 degrees, less than a two-hour run at their current speed. Frank glanced quickly at the digital clock on the instrument panel. He didn't believe it possible: 10:57:14. Only forty-two minutes had elapsed since they had crossed the Puente El Piñal and driven onto Isla Cascajal.

Frank kept his eyes on the channel and the compass as he struggled to figure out their schedule. They were early. He hadn't expected to embark before two o'clock. He also hadn't anticipated taking such a fast vessel. At their present speed of 52 mph, he calculated, they would reach Isla Gorgona before one o'clock, more than four hours ahead of schedule. He decided to maintain their current speed until they reached the safety of the open Pacific. From there he would hand the helm over to one of the others. That would give him time to find any charts aboard, study the GPS, plot a course, and decide what to do about the timing problem.

His eyes darted back to the clock. It still did not seem possible that they had been on the island only forty-two minutes. It seemed like several hours had passed since he drove past the soldiers on the bridge. Pablo and Sid were dead. He and Eric had tasted combat again, after what seemed like a million years. Anne and Linda had tasted it for the first time. Linda had killed at least one man, and in so doing had saved his life. Anne, too, had held up well, even in the face of her husband's death. His first thought was to be surprised, but it hit him that the women were fighting for their children. For the first time since meeting them, he decided he'd trust them in combat.

Chapter 26

Spreading ponchos and blankets on the ground under a banyan tree near the airport's operations office, they disassembled, cleaned, reassembled, and tested each weapon. A half moon hung brightly in the night sky, obscured occasionally by scattered clouds. Several yellow lights dangled from electrical wires clamped to the lower branches. The yellow light cast a surreal glow on the commandos encamped underneath. A sweet breeze wafted westerly from the ocean, mingling the scent of salt air and jungle.

David found himself pleasantly absorbed in the task, his attention focused, his hands occupied. The solvent and gunsmith's oil had a familiar feel. His brain welcomed the long-forgotten smells, like a lost friendship rekindled. The sound of metal sliding smoothly against metal, then slamming true into a receiver, was gratifying. He became lost in the details, blessed for the moment with a need to focus on small parts and the interconnectivity of these terrible, yet magnificent weapons. David glanced up and caught Billy's eye. The general, voluntarily performing the work of an enlisted man, winked and flashed a knowing grin. For a moment, in the blink of an eye, they were young again. Rangers about to embark on a mission.

David watched his friends. Their bent posture reflected the weight on their backs and their lack of conditioning. *Hope we don't run out of gas.* He hopped twice in place and shrugged his shoulders, letting the equipment settle in. It felt right. He strapped on the chute. *Was it this heavy in 'Nam?* His knees felt as though he were carrying two hundred pounds. *Damn.* He mopped his brow with his shirtsleeve. David methodically clipped stainless-steel snaps over D rings. He pulled straps snug and S-folded the excess into elastic retaining loops. Recalling the lessons he had been taught in jump school, he did a half squat and pulled sharply on his diagonal straps, tightening the rig across his chest and back. When he stood straight, the parachute straps dug deep into his shoulders and groin. *It hurts. Must be right.*

The clean, crisp nylon and chemical smells that characterized all skydiving gear filled his nostrils, imparting a familiar feeling of security. He had been trained to trust his equipment and to trust his training. It was all coming back. He picked up his reserve chute, hefted it, and buckled it swiftly into place. Old habits died hard.

Like a snake sheds its skin, so the civilian identity, built up for so many years with so much effort, sloughed off the old Rangers. Tactical procedures long buried suddenly resurfaced. Most important, thought processes shifted subtly from those of civilians to those of soldiers. Jenny was caught up in it too. It showed in the resolve on her face, the steel in her eyes, the way she enjoyed the snugness of the harness, the sheer pleasure of cocking her M16. David knew, watching his comrades, that the old ways were back. There would be no hesitancy, no fumbling on this operation. And when the enemy was trapped, there would be no quarter for the kidnappers. By the time Billy began his jumpmaster check, the metamorphosis was complete. The team was ready mentally for the cruel reality that awaited them on the beaches and in the jungles of Isla Gorgona.

"Jack's gonna swing forty miles wide to the west of the island," Billy said loudly to the others, even though they had been over this time and again since leaving Bragg. "We'll go thirty miles south of the island and loop back around, heading north. We'll jump from fourteen thousand feet or more, depending on the weather. Your Pro-Dytter altimeters in your helmets have been set to beep in your ear first at ten thousand feet, again at seventy-five hundred feet, and for the third and final time at two thousand feet. That's when you rip the cord.

"I'm carrying the rubber raft and the collapsible oars," Billy continued. "I'll be the low man, the first out. You will follow me, one, two, three. Each of our helmets has an IR strobe light on the back, as do our belts. Use your night-vision goggle to find it. Keep your eyes fixed on the east side of the island. If the commo gear works right, we'll be able to talk to each other all the way down.

"Remember: The jungle's too thick. Land in the water just a few feet from the shore, as close to me as possible . . . but don't land on me. Turn the strobe off as soon as you hit the water. We don't want to announce our presence prematurely.

"We've been over this. Keep the layout of the island and the northern end of the compound in your mind's eye. Remember what Jenny said: From the sky, the island looks like a whale heading northeast. There's a slight bulge on the whale's breast. That's our DZ, just off the bump on the whale's breast, in the water. We'll go over the plan again on the plane. Any questions?" There were none. "Let's take a walk, stretch our muscles, try to relax. We lift off in two hours, at midnight."

The plane was now stripped of its seats. The room was needed for the paratroopers and their bulky gear, which was laid out on ponchos under the banyan tree in four neat piles. After a while Billy distributed the greasepaint. The four commandos first applied it to themselves, then checked each other to make sure that every spot on their faces, necks, ears, and hands were covered.

Liftoff was scheduled for midnight. At eleven-thirty, Raul took a picture of the commandos in front of the King Air. Next, Happy Jack snapped a shot of the others with Raul, again with the airplane in the background.

David approached Raul and said, "We've decided you should stay behind. There's no reason to expose you to the risks we're taking. We think we can trust you," David added.

"Go with God," Raul said firmly. "He will help you find your boy."

At eleven-fifty-six, Jack sat in the pilot's seat, snapped his seat belt and shoulder harness, and taxied to the eastern end of the runway. At twelve-oh-one, he revved the engines to full throttle, released the foot brakes, and the plane disappeared into the night sky.

Anne took over from Frank after they passed the light and bell due west of the Bay of Buenaventura and turned south to the open sea. When she told him during the drive from Bogotá that she had grown up boating on Long Island Sound, he was skeptical. *I was wrong to underestimate this woman*, he thought as he admired the way she steered the sixty-three-foot vessel over the swells. He went below deck and studied the nautical charts he found at the navigation station. Within a few minutes he was back on deck, discussing plans with Anne. They set course at 215 degrees on the compass, south southwest, throttling back to 25 mph. The waves were long, deep rollers plowing directly into the bow, the product of a storm to the southwest. The Sea Ray crested, and Anne expertly surfed down the south side of each wave at a thirty-degree angle, reversing the angle, east and west, with each alternate roller, taking no risk of cracking the hull.

They had plenty of time to get to Isla Gorgona, more time than any of them wanted. Frank checked the charts again and confirmed their position on the GPS. He determined that their best option under the circumstances was to head to Punta Ortiz and hide in the mangrove swamps near Isla Carauma and rest. While it wasn't the closest point on the mainland to Isla Gorgona, it was close enough, and the swamps would provide some cover.

Eric and Linda explored the cabin below deck, careful to draw the curtains over the tiny portholes before turning on the lights. Each had seen pictures of boats like this in magazines, but neither had ever been on board one. The galley was a state-of-the-art kitchen equipped with a convection oven, a Sub-Zero refrigerator, and a rack filled with fine wine. The salon next to the galley was furnished with plush leather seats and couches. An entertainment center covered the entire wall opposite the galley. While Eric contemplated emptying the fridge, Linda discovered the stateroom, a beautifully decorated bedroom in the bow larger than her bedroom in Washington. The master head was about the size of the bathroom in her home, but then hers didn't have gold-plated Moen fixtures or handmade ceramic tiles. Thick Egyptian cotton towels filled the closet. She was surprised to find a laundry closet, complete with a washer and dryer.

"Would you like to make an offer?" Eric asked as he caught up with her.

"Couldn't afford the mooring charges." She held on to him and a door handle as the boat crested on a long rolling wave and Anne surfed down the backside at a sharp angle.

"Well, you see, it's preowned, and it has some bullet holes, so the price has very recently gone down a lot." He laughed. Anne surfed down the next roller at an opposite angle and it was Eric's turn to grab on to Linda. He was happy to hold her, and even happier that she didn't seem to mind.

"Do you think there's enough water for all of us to shower?" she asked hopefully.

"If we shower together," he teased, "oughtta be. This boat's designed to carry more than four people, so the holding tank must be big. The real question is whether it's full. Judging from how well the fridge and the wine rack are stocked, my guess is there's plenty."

"Then we can all wash our clothes and shower. We stink."

"Well, speak for yourself." He laughed.

"Trust me." She smiled. "This should be a group effort. We *all* stink."

"Okay, but let's talk to Frank and Anne first. We've got enough time for each of us to clean up, eat, and maybe even get some sleep." He placed his hand on the small of her back and ushered her aft toward the stairs leading to the cockpit.

"This boat's a floating palace," Eric announced as Linda and he reached the bridge. "Plenty of food, showers, beds. Even a laundry."

"Let's divide up into two groups," Frank said simply, feeling the exhaustion the others had experienced earlier. "If you two can hang in for another two hours, Anne and I will sleep for two hours. I'll be on duty when we get to Punta Ortiz. There may be some tricky reefs to maneuver, so I should be at the helm when we get there. I'll need Anne with me. From here to Punta Ortiz it's straight sailing. I've programmed the GPS to give us the way points. It'll tell you within a yard or two whether you're on course. When you get to here"—he indicated the point on the lighted screen with his finger—you'll be one mile off Punta Ortiz. That's when you need to wake us up."

Eric took the helm, while Linda familiarized herself with the GPS and the other instruments on the panel. They didn't say anything for a few minutes, letting their eyes adjust to the moonlight on the waves and the pale green and orange lights of the instrument panel. He was the first to speak.

"I sense you like me," he said awkwardly. "But I don't know why. I mean . . . why a beautiful young woman like you"—he struggled for the words—"might like an overweight guy who smokes and drinks too much . . . who's got a cue ball for a head . . . and who's—"

". . . older?" she interrupted, a sexy smile spreading across her face.

"All of the above." He smiled back.

"Maybe because you're just about the most genuine man I've ever met. And there are only four other men on earth who are as self-sacrificing as you." She slid her hip along the edge of the instrument panel, stepping sideways a few inches closer to him.

"You're losing me."

"See, that's what I mean. You don't know what I'm

talking about, do you? The four other men are Billy, Matthew, Frank, and Happy Jack. You're all risking your lives to save someone else's child," she said, placing her hand over his. She stepped closer and kissed him on the cheek.

"Not just 'someone else's child,' " he said softly, almost a whisper. "David Craig's boy . . . and your girl."

"You love David, don't you?"

"Well, you see, he risked his life for us on more than one occasion, and what he did to save Billy was . . . well, above and beyond. The rest of us know he'd have done it for us, too."

She kissed him again, this time brushing his lips. "I rest my case."

"Hey, watch it. I'm trying to keep this boat on course," he said with mock seriousness. "And it's not as easy as I make it look." Emboldened by her frankness, he slid one arm around her waist and pulled her to him, keeping a hand on the wheel, and kissed her on the lips more firmly than she had kissed him, withdrawing to maneuver the boat down a large swell. "You didn't really answer my question," he teased after a brief pause, keeping his eyes on the compass and the waves.

"You mean about being mature and the . . . um . . . thinning hair? Hey, I like older men. They have more experience," she laughed. "As for the balding head . . . I think it's sexy, but if you don't like it you should just shave it all off. Beats wearing a toupee," she said with a giggle.

He joined in the laughter. "Christ, no toupees. Couldn't handle *that*! Never thought of going the full Kojak, though. And hey, when we get home, I am going to cut way back on the drinking, eliminate the fat, and join the gym."

"What about the cigarettes?"

"Now, there you've crossed the line," he said, trying to appear serious. "Do me a favor. There's a carton of cigarettes on the shelf near the entertainment center."

"I know. I saw them," she responded cautiously.

"Toss 'em overboard."

* * *

Happy Jack removed his earphones, unbuckled his seat belt and harness, and left the controls to Chris. "Listen up." The four soldiers shifted from one uncomfortable position to another, tight straps digging into shoulders and groins.

"In just a few minutes we're gonna be approaching Isla Gorgona," Jack announced. "According to the airline communications we're monitoring, there's a storm off the coast of Ecuador. It hasn't moved in almost twenty hours, so it doesn't look like it's migratin' this far north. Best we can make out, the winds on the surface around the island are fifteen to twenty knots. We don't have any marine reports. But a storm that's been parked that long has to be kickin' up rollers. I've been lookin' at a chart book I brought along. Prevailin' currents along the coast of Ecuador and Colombia are south-to-north at about one and one-half knots. Not fast, but steady. The combination of current, wind, and storm all pushin' in the same direction should be producin' some of the longest and deepest rollers you can imagine."

"How are the visuals?" Billy asked.

"Scattered clouds. We're at fourteen thousand feet now. The clouds are below us, but we can't tell at what altitude. Maybe some scattered showers. Half moon. Not bad. Not bad at all. You should have good visuals most of the way down."

"It's now zero-one-forty-six hours on my watch," Billy said. "Everyone still in sync?"

The others checked their watches and nodded.

David, Jenny, Matthew, and Billy felt the plane bank left. They had reached the southernmost point in their journey. The King Air decelerated as they approached the island. Jack unlocked the door and let it drop down. At 120 mph, the rush of the air was deafening—and intimidating. The wind immediately filled the cabin, causing everything that wasn't nailed down to flap noisily. Chris slowed to 110 mph.

David had jumped from airplanes since Army Jump

School at Fort Benning, just before going to Vietnam. He had continued to jump at annual reunions at Happy Jack's, and from time to time with Jenny and others from LKB in upstate New York. But it never got any easier. Before each jump, particularly night jumps, at the very moment when the door was first opened, when there was no turning back, his stomach muscles tightened, his throat became parched, and his hands turned sweaty. This time was not any different. He suspected that the others experienced the same thing, except perhaps Billy, who had undergone the rigors of jumpmaster school, where all fear was purged.

Billy tested his commo gear once more, adjusting the speaker attached to his helmet so that it almost touched his lips. The others did the same. "David, copy?"

"Good . . . to . . . go," David answered.

"Matthew?"

"Loud and clear."

"Jenny?"

"Ready."

"David," Billy said, "your speaker's crackling."

"I know," David responded. "I heard it too." Matthew and Jenny nodded, indicating that they, too, had heard the static. "Nothing we can do about it now. If it breaks down, we'll communicate through Jenny's. Let's go. We're having breakfast with Justin."

Billy shuffled to the door with his main chute on his back, his reserve chute on his chest, and his rucksack hanging from his web gear from his front belt line to his knees. The rucksack was heavy with extra 5.56mm ammo magazines for the M16, plastic explosives and detonators, flashlights, extra batteries, a compass, a small first-aid kit, an updated version of a foxhole shovel, one long rope with a grappling hook, heavy-duty wire cutters, and a poncho. The weight was in addition to the two canteens on his belt, handheld grenades attached to rings on his web gear on his chest, sixteen 40mm fragmentation grenades attached to his belt for the grenade launcher, the Beretta 9mm automatic pistol he carried in a holster on his right hip, a bayonet held upside down on the web gear at his left breast, another knife in his right boot, and his helmet, boots, and clothing. There was no place to carry the inflatable raft other than strapped to the outside of his right leg. It made for very difficult walking.

"David," Billy shouted, "follow me." He switched on the two battery-operated IR lights on his back. "Jenny, you're next. Matthew, you're after Jenny." He paused, looked at the blackness through the open doorway, and glanced at Jack, who nodded. He turned away and fell headfirst, propelling himself forward with a thrust from his legs to clear the steps. David followed immediately, then Jenny and Matthew.

Billy guessed that the scattered clouds below him were at about six thousand feet. The half moon was high above him, now somewhat to the west, lighting the ocean like a dull mirror, and at this distance making the two small islands below resemble black holes. One, Isla Gorgona, was shaped, as Jenny had said, like a whale swimming northeast, its tail flipping westward. To its southwest was a much smaller piece of land that looked like a seahorse.

"David, Jenny, Matthew. You there?" Billy yelled into his commo gear.

"Roger," they said in unison. Matthew's and Jenny's responses were clear. David's crackled with static, hardly audible.

The Pro-Dytter audio altimeter attached to the right side of Billy's helmet beeped loudly, indicating that he had just crossed the ten thousand-foot mark. A split second later the altimeters in David's, Jenny's, and Matthew's helmets beeped, in that order.

"Can you see my lights?" Billy yelled, fighting to overcome the whooshing sound in his ears as the speed of his descent now reached 100 mph.

"Roger. And I . . . visual . . . you," David's voice crackled, now cutting in and out. "You're clear . . . water, but not . . . island."

"Roger," Jenny said. "David's saying we have you visually when you're silhouetted against the water, even without the IRs. We lose you against the background of the island. Not a problem. Keep the IRs on."

"Roger that," Matthew chimed in.

The second altimeter warning beeped. They were now at seventy-five hundred feet and rushing toward earth at 125 mph. Billy disappeared in a passing rain cloud. The others lost sight of his IRs. Then they, too, passed through the cloud. Once again, the two IRs on Billy's back below David, Jenny, and Matthew were clear through the goggles, despite the rain that the cloud dumped on them.

"DZ in sight," Billy yelled excitedly. "Watch for the small bulge in the island at my eleven-o'clock. Follow me in."

The altimeter beeped once more. The final warning: two thousand feet. Billy's heart raced. He pulled the cord on the main chute. The wing chute unfurled, exiting the bag on his back from the left to right, marginally slowing his fall. Still, the opening shock was tremendous. The chute opened with a crackle, followed by a distant *pop*, like a gunshot. Billy was propelled forward in a wide swinging motion. Then he hung vertically under the wing chute, facing north, the island in sight. Four chutes in line, the northernmost lowest, descended silently toward the drop zone.

There are five distinct peaks on a low ridge of mountains that run along the center of Isla Gorgona. The highest, Cerro de la Trinidad, near dead center of the island, rises to a little over one thousand feet above sea level. With the moon now slightly to the west, the mountains and thick jungle cast a shadow on the water east of the island about three hundred feet into the sea. Billy guided his chute northward, four hundred feet above the water, parallel to the jungle along the eastern shore. He pulled on the guidelines, gently tugging to his left and right, to hold the chute on course.

As Billy descended, the water turned from a dull silver to a jet-black mass. He was reminded of the fact that he had impressed on the others: The human eye had no depth perception in the darkness. He saw some reflection of the moon off the water farther out to sea, but it was of little help near the tree line. Suddenly, feeling very stupid, he realized he had forgotten to pull down his night-vision goggle. Billy immediately took his left hand off the guideline and dropped the goggle into place. Just a hundred feet above the water, he struggled to adjust to the pale greenish light, to process what his left eye was reporting to him. On the eastern shore of the island, the reef generally ran along a relatively straight line about three hundred to four hundred feet offshore and was about forty or fifty feet wide. Between the reef and the shoreline, the depth of the water generally was no greater than eight to nine feet, and often, closer to the tree line that substituted for a true beach, it was four to five feet deep. But the reef was not that predictable. Here, at the "breast" of the whale, the reef was one continuous belt, stretching from four hundred feet offshore nearly to the shore. Closer to the shoreline, it was only two to four feet below the surface.

In the pale green light of the night-vision goggle, Billy saw the ominous gray mass of the reef. He was only fifty feet above the water. "Pull up! Pull up! Land farther north. Reef! Reef!" he screamed into the speaker in his helmet. By pulling up on the lines, Billy was able to glide a few feet farther north before he hit the water, although he still landed hard on coral only three feet below the surface rather than on sand four or five feet below the surface, as anticipated. He tumbled forward, instinctively turning to his left to protect his right arm.

David heard Billy's frantic warning and pulled up on the guidelines. It gained him another forty feet, but he still didn't clear the reef. He, too, tumbled forward into the water, unable to control his fall.

Jenny and Matthew also heard the warning and pulled up on their lines. She gained a few feet of altitude and flew over Billy and David, off to their right, perhaps sixty feet, witnessing their plight. Through her night-vision goggle, she saw the clearing ahead where the bottom was pristine sand, just north of where the reef formed a jagged line southwest to northeast, and tried to maneuver herself to the clearing away from the ledge. She would have made it, but as she landed feet-first in the water, her head snapped back and hit the coral ledge just two feet below the surface. The helmet saved her life, but the impact was brutal. She blacked out. Her chute covered her like a shroud, as if to pronounce her dead.

Matthew intentionally veered right, to the east, to avoid Jenny. He landed directly on the reef line another fifty feet out to sea, the razor-sharp coral causing a deep ten-inch gash in his left lower leg.

Billy recovered from his fall. He had twisted his left ankle, cut his left elbow, and bruised his left shoulder, but he was fully functioning. He struggled to release himself from his chute without losing it. The raft inflated automatically, remaining tethered to his belt. He staggered to the shore, where the jungle and ocean met directly. Standing in the water, Billy placed his spare chute and his rucksack between two mangrove trees, still holding on to the wet chute. As soon as he had placed the other gear in the trees, he struggled to wad the chute together, his arms working furiously to pull the chute through the water. He couldn't let it float away. The current would take it directly to Belalcazar's marina, announcing their position. The raft drifted northward, stopping abruptly when the tether played out. Billy pulled hard on the cord and drew the raft to him, tying it to a tree.

David worked frantically to release his harness without losing his chute, as he, like Billy, understood that a chute discovered in the light of day would alert the enemy to their presence and prove fatal. He had no injuries that he could ascertain. As he scanned the waters where he thought Jenny had landed, his pulse pounded in his chest as he searched for and couldn't find her. Finally he saw her chute flat on the water, beginning to drift northward in the current into deeper water. It was snagged on something. He had to get to her fast. Releasing his chute, weapons bag, spare chute, and rucksack in four nearly simultaneous movements, David let them all drop in the shallow water and raced across the almost-flat reef as fast as his legs and the water would allow. His night-vision goggle over his left eye was still in place. As he approached Jenny, her head bobbed up and she gasped for air. She was struggling to hold on to the ledge of the reef two feet below the water, but the weight of the spare chute, rifle bag, and rucksack still strapped to her was pulling her down in six feet of water.

David stumbled as he neared her, his arm reaching out, but he had to get closer. He half crawled, half swam through the shallow water on top of the reef, as determined as he had ever been in his life. He lunged forward and grabbed the chin strap of her helmet as she was pulled backward into the darkness, her face dipping just below the surface. Latching onto the strap with one hand, David planted his other hand on the reef and pulled with all his strength. Her face emerged, her mouth hungrily taking in a breath. He swung his legs around, his boots slipping on the coral before they found an edge to hold on to. With his left hand on the chin strap of her helmet and his right hand squeezing her forearm, he again pulled with everything he had until Jenny arched out of the deep water, falling toward him and landing them both in a sitting position on the reef's ledge. She coughed up water and gasped for air, but she was alive.

Jenny's chute continued to drift northward, trying to pull her with it. Having no choice, David released her lines and let her chute drift away in the water, making a mental note that he would swim after it. Reaching under her spare chute, he pulled the ring that held it in place, releasing it almost at the same time as he stood, propping her up with his arm. He reached under her belt and unhooked the rucksack. Then he disconnected the rifle bag, which sank, coming to a rest against her knee in the shallow water. The spare chute started to float away, but he grabbed it and attached it to the rucksack. Her coughing stopped and her breathing became more regular. They looked at each other, but neither of them spoke.

A moment later, the silence was broken by Billy's frantic message. "David," he roared. "Matthew's in trouble. I'll get the chutes."

"Are you okay?" David asked as he put his hands on Jenny's shoulders. He didn't wait for a response. "Hold on to these," he told her as he dropped the rucksack and spare chute on her lap and ran, stumbled, and swam for Matthew.

It took David a full four minutes to reach him. The chute wanted to pull Matthew into the deeper water, but he was resisting defiantly. He pulled himself onto the reef and released the lines from his right hand, emptying the bucketlike chute. He let it drift limply in the waves, still held firmly in his hand, knowing what the consequences would be if it was lost. Blood flowed freely from the gash in his leg, immediately attracting the smaller fish whose home was the reef. So far the pain was bearable, but his nerve endings were not yet fully recording the sensation. He tried to retrieve the chute, to wad it up in his arms as he had been trained to do so long ago, but it was all he could do to hold on to it. His rifle bag stuck uncomfortably in his rib cage, but didn't cause real pain. His rucksack and reserve chute were deadweight, further draining his energy.

David almost fell on Matthew as he plunged into the shallow water, both of his hands grabbing the chute lines. Matthew immediately relaxed his grip and his hand fell back into the water. David pulled the lift lines with both hands, rapidly retracting the chute and folding it against himself.

David didn't have to ask Matthew if he was hurt. The night-vision goggles covering David's left eye highlighted Matthew's blood in the water, although the eerie green light made the blood swirling around his leg look more like squid ink, thick, dark, and ominous. "Can you walk?" David asked.

"I don't know. But let's get the fuck out of this water before a shark bites my goddamn ass off," Matthew said, trying to sound strong, but starting to feel the increasingly sharp pain.

"Okay, man." David released Matthew's rucksack from the front of his belt and slid his arms into the shoulder straps. He removed Matthew's rifle bag, holding it in his left hand. He took Matthew's left arm, wrapped it around his own shoulder, and held it there, hefting Matthew to his feet. Using David as a crutch, Matthew limped across the shallow reef back to where David had left Jenny.

Jenny had recovered enough to kneel in the water and put her rucksack on her back. Her head still pounded, but less than it had right after the impact, and she guessed that she had narrowly escaped a concussion, or worse. She was rising to her feet on the reef when David and Matthew approached. Together the three of them slowly made their way across the reef toward the shoreline where Billy had stashed his gear, and David's weapons bag and rucksack, in the trees.

David and Jenny helped Matthew to a narrow ledge of soil at the tree line, where they eased him into a semireclining position. David knelt beside Matthew, gently propping his injured leg on his own. Holding a penlight between his teeth, he searched his rucksack. He found his first-aid kit and handed it to Jenny. David proceeded to cut Matthew's pant leg to the knee, careful not to touch the painful wound. *Damn, it's deep. At least it's clean*, he thought, grateful for the salt water. Blood flowed from the cut downward toward the back of Matthew's calf and on David's pant leg.

"This is going to hurt like hell, man," David warned.

With Jenny's help, he took a sterile gauze pad and dried Matthew's leg around the wound so that the inch-wide surgical tape would adhere. Satisfied that the leg was as dry as it could be under the circumstances, he told Jenny to tear a foot-long piece of tape while he applied an antibacterial ointment to disinfect the wound. Using both hands, he held the wound together. Matthew grimaced but did not flinch. Following David's instructions, Jenny wrapped the strip of tape around Matthew's leg. They repeated the procedure three more times, placing the strips of tape approximately two inches apart. Jenny, working quickly and efficiently despite the throbbing pain in her head, retrieved a package of surgical wrap from the first-aid kit and began tightly wrapping Matthew's calf. When she finished, David taped the wrap with eight strips of tape that circled his leg from the knee down. Finally David replaced the wet fatigue pant leg that he had moments before slit with his knife over Matthew's calf and wrapped it with olive drab–colored cravats, completely covering the white bandage.

Billy returned fifteen minutes after he had taken off to retrieve David's and Jenny's chutes, which had floated northward in the wind and current toward the marina. He was breathing heavily, desperate to drink water from the canteens he had left hanging from his web gear in an overhanging branch. "I only got one main," he gasped, handing the loosely bundled gray chute to David. "The other main's gone. So's your reserve. I guess it's been a long time. We were taught to never let 'em get away from us."

David bridled at the reprimand and started to retort, and then stopped. Everybody was under tremendous stress. *Let it go*, he told himself.

"Let's hope to God the bad guys don't see 'em." Billy snorted as he tried to drink from his canteen and talk at the same time, the water streaming down his chin.

Glancing at his watch, David studied their situation. Matthew had suffered an injury that would slow him down. The injury might also get infected quickly in the jungle and turn gangrenous. Jenny had suffered a minor head injury, but seemed coherent and functioning. She was taking two Advil and handing out two for each of the others as David took inventory. Billy was fully combat ready, as was he. They had lost a main and a reserve chute. That loss wasn't an operational problem—they were going to discard the chutes in the jungle as soon as they landed—but rather a matter of security. The reserve chute, still wrapped tightly in its olive-drab pack, would float only half above the waterline and most likely wouldn't be seen. The off-white main chute would drift on the surface, however, and would be relatively easy to spot if it drifted to the marina. Their only hope was that the main would snag on a low-hanging branch or on the coral or sink.

David and Billy glanced at their watches simultaneously. "We gotta go," Billy said. "Matthew, can you make it?"

"Hell, yes," he snapped, rising to his feet in the shallow water, trying hard not to wince. He had taken three Advil and hoped they would soon start working. He raised his left hand melodramatically and with his right index finger pressed the illuminator on his watch with a flourish. Then, with a broad smile that he hoped would comfort his worried comrades, he called out, "Airborne! We're twenty-four minutes behind schedule. Let's hump."

Jenny and David quickly stashed the chutes under what rocks and logs they could find, while Billy assembled the four oars and put them in the four-man raft. Matthew practiced walking a few paces along the narrow beach and pronounced himself good as new despite the pain. The four soldiers removed their rifle/grenade launchers from their canvas bags, chambered a round in their rifles, and placed the selector switches on safe. Breaking into two-person teams, they checked each other's web gear, front and back, making sure everything was strapped tightly in position so that nothing would make noise or work its way loose.

Satisfied that everything was in as much order as it could be under the circumstances, they placed their rucksacks in the middle of the small raft, slung their weapons over their necks and shoulders, and boarded. Each gripped a paddle and began stabbing at the water, working their way north, the current and wind behind them.

Between them and the compound were two streams that would serve as markers. The first was a mile north, halfway to the marina. The second, the point where Billy and Matthew would insert into the jungle, was an eighth of a mile farther, perhaps less. They reached the first stream in twenty minutes, their arms growing tired, each of them needing no convincing that war was a young person's game.

They continued paddling to the second stream, landing on a five-foot shelf of a beach immediately south of where the stream met the ocean. Billy stepped out of the raft and steadied it as Matthew followed, weapons at the ready. They reached into the raft, retrieved their rucksacks, and laced their arms through the shoulder straps.

Billy checked the time—0259 hours. The hard rowing and favorable current had allowed them to pick up a few extra minutes, but they were still twenty minutes behind schedule. He looked seriously at his three comrades. "Let's hump," he said as he shook David's and Jenny's hands quickly.

"Good luck," Jenny and David said together as Matthew and Billy saluted. Then the two waded up the stream and disappeared into the darkness.

It began to rain. Jenny shifted to the position Matthew had just vacated, David front and left, she right and rear. They paddled out to sea, to the east beyond the reef fighting hard against the waves from the south that buffeted the small raft on Jenny's side. Just beyond the reef they were hammered by a particularly high wave that almost capsized the normally stable craft. David and Jenny paddled furiously. They had to put at least a quarter of a mile between them and the shore, or the current would push them too close to the marina. Their plan was to pass the marina a third of a mile offshore to avoid detection. The rain, if it lasted, might give them a margin of error, but they would not rely on it. Once past the marina, they would angle on a northwesterly vector toward an imaginary point an eighth of a mile north of the island and then approach from the north. Already their shoulders were aching. Still, they paddled with all their might. Failure was not an option.

As they ascended the shallow, wide stream, Billy took the point, ten yards ahead of Matthew, searching in the pale green light of his night-vision goggle for signs of any trails on the right bank that might run parallel to the eastern shore of the island. His rifle remained at the ready, selector switch on the three-round mode. Matthew followed, similarly armed, searching for trails and enemy soldiers.

"Matthew," Billy whispered into his mouthpiece after he had waded about one hundred yards up the stream. "How are you doing on that leg?"

"Hurts like a son of a bitch."

"Can you make it? This is pretty tough schlepping for me, and my legs are fine," Billy said.

"Well, you're an old fart," Matthew whispered back. "I'm only fifty."

"Go to hell. David . . . Jenny, what's your status?" Billy whispered into his microphone.

". . . arms . . . sore . . . just past . . . reef . . ." David's voice crackled. ". . . schedule . . ."

Jenny heard David say something. "What did you say?" she asked as she continued to paddle, trying not to break her rhythm.

"I told Billy that we're picking up on our schedule. Didn't you hear me?" David asked anxiously. They had known that David's commo gear wasn't functioning at 100 percent, but a complete communications blackout would be a serious obstacle that they hadn't planned on.

"Did Billy say something?" she asked, her voice and face showing her apprehension.

"Yeah. It came through garbled. He was checking on our status. Isn't your commo gear working?"

"Guess not," she said, alarmed. "Maybe the blow it took on the reef."

"Damn." David sighed. "We'll just have to make do with mine."

"Billy . . . illy . . . you hear . . . ?"

"You're breaking up. Can you hear me?" Billy said, his voice louder than he intended.

". . . hear . . . clearly," Billy heard David's voice in response.

"Did you say you hear me clearly?" Billy asked.

". . . aff . . . affirma . . . firmative," David repeated.

"Good. I'll do the talkin'. You just respond repeating 'affirmative' or 'negative,' " Billy instructed. "Speak only when spoken to so you save batteries or whatever's causing the problem. Is Jenny's commo working?"

". . . tive . . . neg . . . ," was all Billy could hear at the other end.

"Not a good sign," Matthew said glumly.

"Did all that come through loud and clear for you?" Billy whispered in his mouthpiece.

"Your part did," Matthew responded. "Guess we're gonna have to do this the old-fashioned way and just count on 'em to be where they're supposed to be at the right time."

"They'll be on time. I should have checked Jenny's systems after her fall," Billy scolded himself.

"Could you have fixed it?"

"Probably not. But I don't like surprises. Let's hoof it. We have a long way to go," Billy said, trying not to sound discouraged as he struggled upstream.

Chapter 27

News of the battle in Buenaventura and the hijacking of Belalcazar's speedy vessel had put the compound on full alert. The bright lights suspended from sixty-foot poles, palm trees, and nearly every corner of every building made it look as if a flare had gone off on the northern end of the island and forgotten to fall to earth. Throughout the compound, jittery soldiers wearing ponchos to ward off the rain paced under the lights, rifles or machine guns in hand, nervously looking for signs of activity along the electrified wall to the south of the compound and the marina to the east. Two men held tightly to chains, being pulled forward by strong Dobermans. Two guards occasionally peered over the cliffs to the west and northwest, but Joaquin believed that an approach from that direction would be sheer insanity. Likewise, Joaquin told the troops that between the cliffs and the minefield, an approach from the north was impossible. He had decided to concentrate his forces to the east and south near the marina, where Joaquin was sure the stolen vessel with its commandos would land. Guards patrolled the breakwaters. Powerful searchlights stabbed at the ocean in search of boats, penetrating two hundred yards into the darkness even in the rain.

They had discussed the plan again and again. Their chances of success all came down to electricity. Many of the great technological advances and most of the creature comforts developed during the twentieth century depended on electricity. Remove the electricity and everything shut down. Belalcazar's island was equally as dependent on electricity—if not more so—as the mainland. Without electricity, their radar, sirens, searchlights, motion detectors, closed-circuit television, and electrified fences were useless. The compound's bright lights gave Belalcazar's army an advantage against intruders. The plan was to shift those odds.

David and Jenny's first mission was to shut down the main electric generator, located between the guard tower and the barracks to the extreme north of the island. That mission had to be accomplished before Billy and Matthew could attack the compound from the south. Their first mission was to blow the three fuel tanks next to the backup generator, and that generator along with them.

"Speak softly. They may have sound as well as motion detectors out here," Billy reminded Matthew. "Let's try to raise David and Jenny and see where they're at." After several attempts to get through to David or Jenny, though, there was no response, not even static.

"Shit," Matthew exclaimed. "They might be able to hear us, but can't talk back. We should've brought backup radios."

"I know. I relied too much on this fancy commo gear," Billy admitted, annoyed at himself. "Let's keep moving. They'll bring down the lights. That will be the signal. Like you said, we'll do it the old-fashioned way. Let's keep thinking like David would and keep talking to each other."

"That's easy enough. David will take down that generator if he has to do it with his fingernails."

"I should peel off here and head up the hills."

"Good luck, Billy," Matthew said, squeezing his hand. "See you at the compound."

"Yeah, but talk to me on the commo."

The two men parted, Matthew making his way along the eastern trail, Billy cutting a path through the thick jungle up the steep hills.

David and Jenny rode the rollers like a bottlecap in a whirlpool. The tiny raft surfed down a twenty-foot roller, gaining speed, only to slow as it climbed the next large wave, stopping at the top, momentarily suspended on the peak, and then surfing down again, the high walls of water dwarfing them. David and Jenny paddled hard, not resting on the downward surf. They were gaining time. The strong northerly current allowed them to go much faster than they had anticipated.

Jenny looked at her watch. "I think we're back on schedule," she shouted over the wind and surf.

David said nothing, his paddle cutting through the water like a knife, mechanically, relentlessly. Suddenly he stopped paddling for a few seconds, rising onto his knees, his back straight, straining to see the compound and mark their position. The clouds that had been showering them with a light rain were passing, the half moon visible in the western sky. The brightly lit compound was at their nine-o'clock. He crouched back down low in the small rubber raft and continued rowing down one steep wave and up the next, keeping the compound off his left shoulder, increasingly to his rear. "Keep paddling. On the next wave we angle to the left forty-five degrees."

"Eric. Linda. Wake up," Anne insisted for the third time, finally deciding to shake them.

"Okay . . . okay," Linda responded groggily. Eric snored loudly until Linda shook him, softly at first, then more roughly.

"Christ," he moaned. "Can't possibly be time."

"Your clothes are clean. On the dresser. If you're awake, I'm going up on deck to help Frank. We're heading out now," Anne added just as Frank started the powerful engines.

Eric jumped out of bed, wearing nothing but a white bathrobe that might have belonged to Belalcazar. Linda did the same, wearing a matching robe that might have been Milana's, had things played out differently. They had pulled their two-hour shift on deck while Anne and Frank slept in their respective quarters. When they reached the designated spot on the GPS indicator, off Punta Ortiz, they had awakened Frank and Anne, showered separately, and crashed together on the queen-size bed in the master stateroom. They fell asleep almost instantly with their arms around each other, Linda's head on his shoulder, both too tired even to consider making love. They were asleep before Frank and Anne began to maneuver the boat into the mangrove swamps near Isla Carauma. It was now three-thirty A.M., and Frank was moving out of the swamp, on the way to Isla Gorgona.

In two minutes Eric and Linda were fully clothed and on deck.

"Aren't we leaving early?" Eric asked with concern.

"Yeah," Frank answered, keeping his eyes on the water and the GPS, and trying to make out the reef in the moonlight. "We're thirty minutes early. No particular reason. Just cautious. If the fireworks start early, I want to be three or four miles offshore so we can move in fast."

"Good idea," Eric said.

"Anne made coffee. How 'bout you get some?" Frank asked as the boat cleared the reef into the open, rolling sea. "Scattered clouds . . . half moon. Perfect morning for a fight."

While Billy laboriously trudged through the jungle, making his way through thick branches and tangled vines, Matthew followed a trail that, despite its twists and turns, essentially ran parallel to the eastern shore of the island. He crouched low, walking slowly, ready to fire, watching for any signs of the enemy through his night-vision goggle. Sharp needles of pain shot through his leg with each step. He took two more Advil, afraid to take anything stronger that might dull his senses. So far he had seen nothing, except a large monkey that he almost shot as it scampered up a tree. The monkey screeched loudly, piercing the silence. Matthew wondered if he was the only person who heard it.

A sound—a human sound, metal on metal—interrupted his thoughts. Matthew froze instantly. He waited for a few moments, then began to move forward slowly, peering through the goggle, probing for the enemy, scanning the path in front of him for any signs of land mines or trip wires. He saw nothing, and continued slowly up the narrow trail, one excruciating step at a time.

After bearing a course of 315 degrees, due northwest, until they were an eighth of a mile north of the island, David and Jenny adjusted course in the trough of a long roller and paddled due south on a compass reading of 180 degrees. Despite the monstrous waves that threatened to swallow the tiny craft, the storm that originated somewhere far off to the south of the island had been a godsend. Now, in the lee of the island, the waves were smaller, but more frequent, which required as much effort from Jenny and David as had the larger rollers minutes ago. David glanced quickly at his watch. "We've picked up our lost time. We're eight minutes ahead of schedule. Let's keep up the pace, though. We may need those eight minutes later," he added, sounding more optimistic than he had since jumping from the King Air.

"Aye-aye, Cap'n," Jenny answered, exhausted, but finally believing they might make it to the shore.

"How you holdin' up?" he asked, panting as once again his paddle dug deep into the black water.

"My shoulders no longer have pain. I'm past that. And to tell you the truth, I hate this fucking ocean. You know"—she gasped between strokes—"I've always had a phobia about water at night. After this is over, I only have one request."

"What's that?"

"The three of us—Justin, you, and me—we're gonna stay on dry land where there aren't any goddamn oceans."

"Okay, Omaha it is," he said as his oar sank deep into the water and he pulled.

As they approached the island, the sea became calmer. The island itself acted as a breakwater against the northerly winds and currents. But they were also approaching the Rocas del Horno, a string of sharp rocks on the northern tip of the island that posed a new challenge. The waters around them began to swirl with conflicting currents that pushed and pulled the rubber raft toward the jagged rocks. The largest one was a huge boulder, perhaps four hundred feet north of the island, standing about thirty feet out of the water and appearing to be about sixty feet wide, although, as with an iceberg, neither David nor Jenny could tell how far out it extended just below the surface. The other rocks were smaller but equally treacherous.

Jenny and David passed the largest boulder, after having been pushed by the currents to within a few yards of it. Only their adrenaline-reinforced paddling saved them from careening into the large rock. No more than five minutes passed from the moment when they cleared the monstrous black form to when they reached the northern tip of the island, but it seemed like a lifetime. The sea became eerily silent as they approached the compound. Jenny could hear her heart pounding in her chest. They searched for the slightest sign of movement of soldiers along the low cliff in front of them. For a few brief moments, when they were out of the shadows of the Rocas del Horno and visible from the lighted compound, they were totally vulnerable, and they knew it. One soldier with an assault rifle or a sniper in the guard tower could have ended their mission.

As the rubber raft neared the shore, David and Jenny jumped into the shallow water, one hand on their weapons and the other on the raft. They lifted it onto the narrow, rocky beach. They had landed.

The cliff along the narrow northern end of the island sloped down from a height of eighty feet. At the point where Jenny and David landed, the cliff was only twelve feet high. David led the way, heading east, head down, keeping below the crest. With each step to the east, the crest became lower and lower. After they had gone about fifty feet, they reached the point where the cliff, now a mere ledge, was only five feet high. David raised his head cautiously. Their plan was to hug the cliff line westward up the steep incline toward the barracks, the generator, the guard tower, and ultimately the hacienda.

The lights that flooded the compound elsewhere were not bright where they stood. There were no patrols. It was as if this part of the compound was of no importance to Belalcazar. For an instant David couldn't figure it out. Then it hit him like a sledgehammer. "Don't touch the top of the ledge," he whispered to Jenny urgently. "Mines. Land mines. This whole field in front of us is mined," he exclaimed in frustration.

"How can you tell?"

"No grass. Just fine gravel. Damn." He flipped down his night-vision goggle and scanned the area where the gravel met the edge of the cliff. "Four-inch gravel. It runs from the kennel," he said, pointing to the now-empty kennel perhaps seventy-five feet from where they stood. "Along the cliff. Looks like it goes south almost to the steps from the marina up to the barracks. Son of a bitch," he snapped, cursing himself for not thinking about it sooner.

He studied the compound, searching for a solution. They couldn't go east around the minefield because that would put them in front of the bunker near the marina and under the bright lights that they planned to extinguish. Going west was out of the question. With each step to the west, the cliff became higher and higher.

David looked at his watch—0449 hours. Four minutes ahead of schedule. Nineteen minutes ahead of time for lights-out. And a minefield separating them from Justin. He searched for a solution, but found nothing.

"What about the storm tunnel?" Jenny asked suddenly. "We can go through the storm drain. It comes out somewhere near the guard tower."

"What tunnel?"

"The tunnel the prisoner used to escape. You know. The guy who wrote the magazine article about his escape from here when it was a prison. The storm drain's somewhere between the tower and the barracks. The prisoners had to dig the tunnel. It empties to the north. I remember . . . the first thing the prisoner saw when he came out of the tunnel when he escaped were the Rocas del Horno."

"Jenny, I love you. Let's go." David followed her back down the beach from where they had just come, past the raft and farther along the base of the cliff, which was in the shadow of the lights of the compound. They used their night-vision goggles, but it was still hard to see up the cliff from the angle the narrow beach permitted. What looked like an opening could have just as easily been darker rock. They were growing more and more desperate as the precious time they had gained on the water slipped away.

"I think I see it," Jenny exclaimed after a few minutes, removing the goggle to see if it was more distinguishable in the light of the moon. "Look. Up there about twenty feet. Yeah. There's even a little water still coming out from the rain."

"Are you sure that's it?" David asked, not able to distinguish the area Jenny pointed to from any other dark patch of rock on the side of the cliff.

"Sure? No, but I'll climb up and take a look."

"Let's see if there's a better way," he said as he removed his Beretta from its holster and pointed the laser dot at the area. He rotated the red dot around the dark patch and then on it, and then back to the wall of the cliff. "That's it. Goddamn it. You're a genius."

"I know. But I'd rather be Batgirl at the moment," she said as she handed David her weapon and removed her rucksack and web gear. Jenny also took off her helmet, appreciating the breeze on her sweaty head. "I was pretty good at rock climbing when I was in college. Hope I can still do it."

David said nothing. The worried expression on his face said it for him. "Wait a second," he said excitedly as he fished in her rucksack and pulled out a long rope with a grappling hook at the end. "Here's the way to do this." He wrapped the rope around her waist several times, placing the hook on her belt in the small of her back. He boosted her up as far as he could, about eight feet with his arms extended above him. Jenny's fingers grasped onto the uneven cliff, and she ascended with surprising agility. Her toes slipped as she searched blindly for something for the tips of her boots to bite into, but her fingers held on the rocks as she pulled herself up one step at a time.

The most difficult part came when she reached the opening. Clinging onto the lip of a rock a few inches below the floor of the tunnel with her left hand, she thrust her right hand upward to the edge of the tunnel, nearly losing her hold altogether when one hand slipped. Catching the thin edge of a rock and holding, she grunted and strained as first her forearms, then her elbows, and then her shoulders cleared the ledge. At that point she knew she would make it. She probed with her fingers for the firmest, deepest lip of rock to hold on to and hoisted herself into the black hole, the inner side of her elbows burning as they pressed against the rock.

The tunnel was nearly round, about three feet in diameter, large enough to get through with their gear, small enough to send her into a claustrophobic panic. Hyperventilating, she swiveled within the confines of the space and poked her head out the opening, looking down at David. "I'll set the grappling hook," she said as she dropped the other end of the rope to him. "Send up the gear first."

David immediately stripped off his gear. One by one she raised their rucksacks, rifles, and other equipment up the rope and pushed them into the darkness of the tunnel behind her. When that was done, it was David's turn. She didn't try to pull him up. He'd have to hoist his 185 pounds up the cliff by himself. She pushed their equipment deeper into the tunnel and retreated farther into the darkness to make room for him. She placed both hands on the top of the hook and pressed down with all her weight to hold the hook in place.

The rope tightened. After a moment or two she saw his fingers in the moonlight as he grasped the lower rim of the tunnel. Like Jenny, David measured his progress by the distance he was able to move his arms past the ledge. First his forearms, then his elbows, then his upper arms were over. Like Jenny, he ignored the pain to the inside of his elbows as he hoisted himself up. There was no other way to do it. Next his head cleared, then his chest and stomach. They were in.

Matthew crept along the trail silently, freezing the instant he saw them in the faint green light of his night-vision goggle. Two men, soldiers in Belalcazar's army, were positioned behind a low log revetment on the left side of the trail no more than sixty feet away. He could see their weapons resting on the top log of the barrier. He pointed his M16 directly at them, ready to kill, but hesitated, wondering what he should do. He couldn't get past them on the trail. He couldn't go through the jungle. He'd make too much noise, unless he retreated one hundred or more feet and then made a wide sweep around them in the jungle. But that would take too much time, especially given the pain in his leg. He couldn't wait. *David and Jenny will be putting the lights out in a few minutes*, he told himself. In the pale yellow-green light of his goggle, Matthew noticed a trip wire across the trail about two inches above the ground, protecting the revetment against attack.

One soldier raised a small radio phone to his ear, yawning as he did so. He said something in Spanish, but Matthew couldn't make out what it was. As Matthew pondered how he would get past the two guards, the other soldier slowly raised a large pair of night-vision binoculars to his eyes. Matthew's dilemma was immediately resolved. Although he was off to the side of the trail, he was fully exposed. His rifle was already aimed at the soldier with the binoculars, the selector switch in single-shot mode. The mouth of Belalcazar's soldier dropped when he discovered the rifle pointed at him, but only for a moment. The 5.56mm bullet left the muzzle of the M16A2 at more than a thousand feet per second, piercing the man's eye and exiting the back of his skull before he even knew what happened. The second guard never saw Matthew. Nor did he hear gunfire. He did, however, see the second flash from Matthew's barrel, but his brain had no time to record the event before it exploded.

Matthew limped toward the bodies, careful to step over the trip wire, trying to ignore the pain in his leg. He grabbed the radio that was still held firmly in the soldier's hand, waiting for someone to talk, not daring to speak first. He continued to limp up the trail toward the compound, searching for the enemy, watching for any sign of mines, struggling to get himself to his designated position.

"What the hell was that?" a voice questioned in Spanish from the speaker of the handheld radio.

"It was a monkey. It was stupid. Sorry. I shot a monkey. Guess I'm too nervous," Matthew responded in Spanish, trying to disguise his accent.

"Pedro, you're a goddamned idiot," the voice yelled back. "I'll dock your ass a full month's pay for that. Now pay attention and stop shooting the fucking monkeys. You nearly had everyone around the marina down there."

"Sorry," Matthew responded simply, trying to keep his conversation to the minimum lest his accent betray him. He turned the radio off and tossed it into the jungle. "Billy," he whispered into his speaker. "Did you hear that?"

"Yes. What the hell happened?"

"I whacked two of them. One of 'em saw me in his night-vision binoculars. Had no choice. Hope it doesn't turn all hell loose before we're ready."

"Who were you talking to?"

"I grabbed the dead man's radio and told his commander that I shot a monkey. I think he believed me," Matthew stated. "Where are you now?"

"I'm nearing the top of the hill, close to the fence. I can see the lights through the jungle. I'll be in position in five," Billy responded confidently. "Where are you?"

"Still on this trail. I'm making good time now," he said, trying to sound upbeat despite the throbbing in his leg. "I'll be in position in five as well. Good luck, man. Airborne."

"All the way," Billy whispered as he silently cut through the underbrush, praying that they hadn't been discovered.

"You go first," Jenny insisted.

"How can I get around you in this space?" David asked, wondering why Jenny was suddenly acting so strange.

"Please, I'll make room. I'm claustrophobic. You go first and I'll follow. I just can't go first into a dark tunnel of this size."

"Okay, okay, I'll go first," he relented. He, too, felt uncomfortable in narrow, dark enclosures, but now was not the time to come clean on that score. He squeezed past her, banging his head on the side of the tunnel, grateful for the helmet despite its communications failure. "I'm gonna put my penlight on and hold it in my teeth. I'll shine it against the wall so you can see too. My guess is that we've got about a hundred and fifty feet to go. It's gonna be steep. We'll ascend about fifty feet."

"Got it," she acknowledged simply as she put her gloves on and strapped her weapon over her head and shoulders.

Within a minute they were inching through the narrow tunnel. They picked up their rucksacks and plopped them in front of them two or three feet as quietly as they could, and then crawled forward, trying unsuccessfully not to scrape their knees and hands, repeating the maneuver again and again. Jenny illuminated her watch. "David. We're eight minutes late. Hurry."

Chapter 28

Frank held the Sea Ray as steady as he could in the rollers, keeping the bow pointed southward in the direction of the waves, careful to descend at an angle to avoid cracking the hull. They were three miles offshore, and dared not get closer. The lights of the compound were visible even without the powerful binoculars Eric held to his eyes.

"Can you see anything?" Anne asked.

"The lights are still on," Eric said, as much to himself as to the others.

"Get ready to move. They'll turn 'em off soon," Frank said confidently.

"What's happening on your end?" Billy asked, whispering into his commo mike.

"All kinds of shit happenin' here," Matthew responded nervously in a low tone. "I'm in the underbrush maybe fifteen feet from the fence. I can't see everything, but I can hear that something's goin' on out on the southern breakwater. I'm gonna edge closer to see what I can pick up. What's your situation?"

"I'm ten feet away from the fence," Billy guessed. "Jungle's so thick they can't see me, and I can't see much either. These guys are a noisy bunch, though. I can hear them shouting. Must be five or six up here. How many down there?"

"More," Matthew whispered. "Fifteen. Possibly twenty . . . oh, shit," he exclaimed. "They found David's chute. Goddamn thing floated right up to the breakwater. They're pullin' it out now, tryin' to figure out what it is. I can see the breakwater clearly from where I am," Matthew whispered softly as he low-crawled on his belly and peered under a large leaf only three feet from the fence and the water's edge. "The fence doesn't go all the way to the water. Guess that'd be a problem with electricity. I have an unobstructed view of the southern breakwater. Gotta talk real low now. Can you hear me?"

"Barely, but okay."

"Won't take 'em long to figure it out. In a minute or two they'll know we're out here. Shit's gonna hit the fan real soon," Matthew said, his voice barely audible. "Well, add to that," he added after a brief pause, "some guy's on the radio and looking out in my direction. Guess he's the one I spoke to on the radio. Yeah, gotta be him. He's gettin' all worked up because nobody's answering."

"Once they put two and two together, they'll send out a patrol in force. Where the hell are David and Jenny?"

"Billy," Matthew whispered excitedly, looking through the night-vision scope on his M16. "The bastard David injured at the carousel in Central Park . . . the guy we got the picture of . . . he's here. He just arrived on the breakwater—no more than one hundred feet from me. Looks like he's in charge. He's talkin' to the men who pulled the chute out of the water and givin' instructions. People are starting to run. Whole bunch of guards coming down the hill from the direction of the barracks. Ten to fifteen more. Must be thirty total. Oh, shit . . . they've got dogs. My ass is cooked. Time to rumble, man. Time to rumble."

"I hear you, good buddy," Billy said. "When you give me the word, I'll blow a hole in the fence up here with a grenade and run out shooting. I've got plenty of targets up here to deal with. That may distract them."

"Awful lot of bad guys down here. Maybe I can fry 'em when I blow the tanks."

"Do you have a clean shot at the tanks?"

"I can hit two of 'em from here with the grenade launcher once I shimmy around the opening between the water and the fence. I only need to blow one of 'em.

The others will explode with it . . . I hope. Question is whether the tanks are thick enough to resist an antipersonnel grenade. Maybe I'll pump a few rounds at a spot on one of them with the M16 and then try to hit that spot with a grenade."

"Matthew. If you get a shot at that son of a bitch from the carousel, take his head off."

"Roger that."

David turned the penlight off and placed it in his shirt pocket. They had reached the end of the tunnel. Three tiny slits of light filtered through the drain cover four feet above the floor of the tunnel. He rose carefully, slipping on the mud but steadying himself with his hands on the sides of the now-vertical drain shaft. He pressed his ear against the drain cover, listening for the voices or footsteps of any nearby soldiers. He heard nothing. Bracing his feet as firmly as he could, he pushed up on the drain cover gently. It didn't move. He nearly panicked at the thought that it might be bolted or welded shut. He tried again. No half measure this time. He pushed with all his strength. The cover nearly flew off the drain, clanking softly as he sought to buffer its fall with his shoulder. He slid the cover to the side as quietly as he could, lowered himself back down the shaft and peeked his head out, the Beretta ready to fire.

The draincover was partly concealed by low shrubbery, no doubt by a dutiful gardener trying to preserve the esthetic beauty of the grounds. David wanted to kiss that man. He studied their position through the shrubs. The barracks were about forty feet to the south of the opening. The generator was about the same distance to the north. The guard tower was up the hill another sixty to seventy-five feet on the other side of the generator. While the eastern side of the generator was in the shadows, the white guard tower was awash in bright lights.

David ducked back into the drain. "We're in," he whispered, and quickly briefed Jenny on where their position was vis-à-vis the other structures. He drank the remainder of his second canteen and discarded both of them. Jenny did the same. He hoisted his rucksack through the opening of the storm drain, carefully placed his Beretta next to it on the ground, and quickly hefted himself upward, his rifle hanging over his neck in front of him. Once clear of the drain, he immediately retrieved his Beretta, searching for the enemy. Jenny followed him out of the tunnel. They prepared their weapons and ran toward the generator.

To their relief, the generator was also concealed in part by low shrubbery. It stood six feet high, about as wide, and slightly longer. The diesel motor next to it was somewhat smaller. A pipe connected to the fuel tanks near the marina snaked through the ground to a pump connected to the diesel engine. The pump was covered by vegetation.

David and Jenny huddled on the dark side of the generator, out of view of the guard tower. Jenny searched through their rucksacks, quickly removing the C4 plastic explosives and detonators while David inched his way along the wall of the generator toward the light. He stuck out his head as far as he dared until he spotted the control panel. From the corner of his eye he saw men toting guns running toward the southeast corner of the compound, near Matthew's designated position. He prayed he and Jenny weren't too late.

David slithered on his belly toward the side of the generator that faced the steps leading from the marina to the hacienda and found the control panel. He crawled back to Jenny's position. "We won't need much C4 for this job. Just gimme a quarter pound, a cap, and a timer. We'll set the timer for forty-five seconds. While I set the plastic for the generator, rig your rucksack with all the plastic we have and set the timer for twenty seconds. That'll give us almost ten pounds of C4 for the tower. I don't know how much of this stuff we need, so screw it; use it all. Don't start the timer. I'll do that on the run just before we get to the tower. If I slow down to toss the sack in the door or for any reason, you just keep going."

Jenny nodded, the muscles in her jaw clenched tightly

like steel cables, her eyes determined. They exchanged knowing glances. David took the plastic explosive, blasting cap, and timer from her hands and low-crawled back to the control panel, affixing the plastic to the corner of the panel and inserting the thick needlelike cap into the plastic. Then, without any hesitation, he set the timer to forty-five seconds and pressed the button that started the clock ticking. He closed the door to the control panel and crawled away. As he rounded the corner of the generator, he grabbed Jenny's rucksack with his left hand and his weapon with his right and broke into a run, passing the opposite side of the generator and sprinting toward the open door at the base of the guard tower. Jenny sprinted on his heels.

The three guards in the tower were tired and distracted by the commotion along the breakwater. One held his binoculars to his eyes to see what was going on, while another spoke loudly to someone on the radio. The third halfheartedly watched the compound, hoping it was all some sort of drill that would pass so he could close his eyes. Ironically, he was the one who saw the movement below, although he almost missed it. Two figures, faces painted black, were running toward the base of the tower from the direction of the barracks and the generator. He reacted slowly, initially wondering whether this was part of the exercise that had captured the attention of his fellow soldiers.

"They found a parachute along the breakwater," the soldier with the radio reported to the others in the tower. "Two men on the eastern trail aren't responding to the radio. Joaquin thinks there might be enemy in the jungle. He wants everyone to be on the lookout."

"Oh, shit," the third guard responded. "There they are," he yelled as he pointed his rifle at David and Jenny, who by then had disappeared at the base of the tower. He leaned out the open window and managed to squeeze off several rounds, but the two were already on the far side. The three guards quickly shifted to the other side of their perch and began to fire their sniper rifles at the attackers, now sprinting toward the hacienda. The last thing they saw was the larger one crumple to the ground and the smaller one stop, presumably to assist.

The shots were heard throughout the compound. Billy and Matthew heard them too, their hearts stopping. For a split second the compound was silent, heads turned in the direction of the tower.

The plastic explosives mounted on the generator and the C4 in the rucksack thrown inside the base of the tower ignited within a split second of each other. At that instant the lights throughout the compound went dark, and the flames at the base of the tower shot like a cannon up its interior at several hundred feet per second, incinerating the wooden staircase that wound around the inside of the tower like a corkscrew, blowing the conical tile roof and the three soldiers fifty feet into the air. Belalcazar's army was momentarily immobilized by the spectacle. A few of those running toward Matthew's position instinctively threw themselves to the ground and covered their ears, but for others it was too late. The shock wave from the blast reverberated throughout the compound. Every window on the north side of the hacienda was instantly blown out, as were most of the windows on the east side. The cantina, which was directly in the path of the blast coming from the open door of the tower, not only lost its windows but much of its roof as well. Every window on the west side of the barracks was obliterated. The tower shifted at its base with a grinding sound of stone on stone and brick on brick, and began to pitch down the slope to the east. It seemed to descend slowly, as if it were falling through water. Finally it crashed to the ground in one loud thud with fireballs visible at both ends. The giant cylinder imploded, extinguishing the fire within. The compound was now completely dark.

Three miles offshore, Frank, Anne, Linda, and Eric observed the fireball and the darkness that followed.

"Lights out!" Eric shouted.

"Hold on," Frank warned, not wasting any time as he gunned the engines, turning west on the backside of a large wave. The powerful Sea Ray leaped at his command.

Linda and Anne studied the darkness of Isla Gorgona, holding on to whatever railing or stanchion they could find for balance with one hand, their M16s in the other, their faces resolute, ready for battle.

"Hot damn," Billy nearly shouted into his speaker as the lights went dark and the hum of the electrified fence turned silent. "I knew they'd do it. What's your position, cowboy?"

"Feeling much better," Matthew whispered, still paying careful attention to the guards through his starlight scope.

"Good, 'cause in one second I'm blowin' my way through that fence. Watch your ass," Billy said. He removed a grenade from his web gear. He retreated into the jungle in order to be farther from the explosion and the deadly shrapnel that it would send flying in every direction. He tossed it at the fence as he dropped to the ground, blowing a jagged hole in the mesh several feet in diameter. He crawled on the ground through the jungle. Watching the enemy soldiers in his goggle, he began popping off the M16A2 in single-round mode, sending five of Belalcazar's soldiers and two of his Dobermans to hell in the order he found them. Three men went down, dead before they crumpled to the well-manicured lawn. Two others were wounded, but fumbled for their rifles. Billy killed them as he ran toward the bunker near the helipad.

Through the night-vision scope of his rifle, Matthew sought the man from the carousel but couldn't find him. Some of Belalcazar's soldiers had positioned themselves at the end of the breakwaters, anticipating an attack from the sea, knowing that Frank and the others had hijacked the *patrón*'s Sea Ray in Buenaventura. Others headed west, up the hill to where Billy was shooting, and being shot at. Matthew searched in his scope for a leader. Someone must be giving the orders. *Where are you, you bastard?* Finally Matthew saw him hunched down, AK47 assault rifle in hand. He was shouting, pointing this way and that, ordering men to their positions. As Matthew watched, Joaquin stood upright. Matthew took his shot. He saw his target spin into the water outside the breakwater at almost the exact spot where the chute had washed ashore. *That's for Justin.* But it wasn't a clean shot, and Matthew knew it. He cursed himself, aiming the rifle at the water, looking for the opportunity for another shot. It would have to come within the next few seconds, he told himself. His position was now revealed, and Belalcazar's soldiers would be throwing lead his way any moment.

Matthew put a .40mm grenade in the M203 grenade launcher and selected the three-round mode on the M16's selector switch. The lights on the compound came back on for an instant, as one of the soldiers made it to the backup generator next to the fuel tanks and turned it on. Matthew immediately fired three, three-round bursts at one of the tanks, keeping the shots in an eight-inch pattern. Using the M203, he then fired the grenade at the spot where the bulk of the M16 rounds had hit. The characteristic shotgun-like blast, more a thump, of the M203 was heard by all the soldiers in the southeastern quadrant of the compound.

The marine fuel tank exploded in a fire burst that shot a hundred feet in the air, immediately followed by the aviation fuel tank and then the diesel fuel tank. Those soldiers in Belalcazar's army who were closest to the tanks were killed instantly. Those on the very end of the south and north breakwaters were thrown into the water, some injured, some unharmed, except for the ringing in their ears. The backup generator, located only a few feet from the tanks, was destroyed.

"*Patrón,* we're under attack from all sides," Emilio said urgently as he entered Belalcazar's bedroom. "If you please, sir, I want to get you off the island," he pleaded as he ran to the window to see if the helicopter was damaged. In the moonlight, at least, it appeared to be intact. He reminded himself that Nick Field always tied the chopper down properly. "Alberto can fetch Field and get you off the island."

Belalcazar nodded in agreement and said, "And the children. If it's Craig who attacks us, and I believe it is, I'll make sure he doesn't get what he came for. Also, find that idiot Warren. We'll have to take him with us. We can't have a CIA official caught on this island, dead or alive," he ordered, recovering quickly from the shock. "Joaquin will stay behind to lead the defense. Alberto, you will stay behind to help him. If it is the last thing you do, kill David Craig."

"Yes, sir," Alberto responded obediently. "Now, sir, please get dressed quickly. I'll get Stephanie to help me with the *chicos*."

Alberto and Emilio had slept fully clothed, with their rubber-soled, ankle-high boots opened and ready to slip into at the side of their beds. Nick Field had done the same. When the first explosions woke him, he jumped out of bed, dressed and ready for action. He heard rifle shots. M16s. He knew their distinctive pop like the sound of his own voice. The moonlight lit the courtyard well enough, but it offered only hints of light under the covered archway that surrounded the courtyard on all four sides, and there were many places for intruders to hide. Nick made his way up the pitch-black stairs slowly. Alberto nearly knocked him backward down the steps as they collided.

"Damn it to hell, man. Watch where you're going," Nick whispered angrily.

"It's me. Alberto. We're going to take the *patrón*, the CIA man, and the kids off the island. Get the chopper ready."

Chapter 29

The force of the explosion caught David by surprise. He had no idea that the almost ten pounds of C4 could take down the tower. He recalled Sears's words back at Huachuca: "This isn't your grandma's C4."

David and Jenny had been spared the full impact of the explosion in part because the blast at the base of the tower was directed through the open door toward the cantina, the opposite direction from that they had taken. They were also spared because of the fall David had taken as the three guards in the tower shot at them right before the blast. David's left foot had slid in an eight-inch hole dug by a gardener who, under Joaquin's orders, had quit for the day, tending to other matters Joaquin considered more important. He had fallen with a thud, the wind knocked out of him. Just as Jenny knelt down to help him up, the thrust of the explosion flew over their heads.

Ironically, David's fall also saved them from running square into the fire of several soldiers who had come running around the northwest corner of the hacienda. Now they found themselves pinned between the soldiers taking cover behind the mansion and a large group of soldiers who had begun to run in their direction before the fuel tanks exploded.

The eruptions of the fuel tanks thinned the ranks of those soldiers closest to the tanks, but many survived. Twenty or more were now making their way in the moonlight toward David and Jenny's tenuous redoubt. David positioned himself behind a small mound of stone and soil left by the gardener, on his belly, facing the attackers coming from the marina. Jenny lay ready a few feet from him, partially protected by several large stones that were to serve as a retaining wall. Through his night-vision scope, David saw a group of soldiers coming toward him from the marina. Jenny saw them too. They fired their grenades at the onrushing soldiers, killing or wounding as many as half of them. They also taught those who survived a lesson in respect. The remaining soldiers wouldn't be so foolish again. They dispersed and began flanking motions, slowly, warily. One inexperienced soldier attacked wide to David and Jenny's left. David spotted him through the scope as he reloaded his M16 with a fresh magazine. He yelled to Jenny to watch behind her. She sent the young soldier to his maker with a burst of fire.

David and Jenny lay there, unable to advance to the hacienda, bullets whizzing over their heads or landing short, splattering them with mud. Their frustration with their position was stronger than the fear of their vulnerability. After coming thousands of miles to rescue Justin and the other children, they were pinned to the ground less than a hundred feet from the building where they expected to find him. They held off two squads of enemy soldiers, one to the east of the hacienda, one to the west, but, without any discussion, both knew that they couldn't remain in their present position too much longer. David wondered where Billy and Matthew were and prayed that Frank and the others on the boat would arrive soon.

Billy, too, had his problems. He encountered much more resistance than he had anticipated. He had estimated the guards' total troop strength on the island at about thirty men, based on the size of the barracks as seen in the digitally enhanced satellite photos. He now believed their strength was upward of forty-five men, and he cursed himself for underestimating the enemy. It could be a fatal mistake. He guessed Matthew had killed about eight soldiers when the fuel tanks exploded, and that David and Jenny had taken out somewhat fewer, but with the six he had killed, that still left more than twenty-five soldiers and very unfavorable odds. To make matters worse, there was no longer any element of surprise. From this point on the attackers would have to rely on the superior firepower of the grenade launchers and the tactical advantage of the night-vision scopes.

The fuel tanks, now three-foot stubs, continued to burn, spewing thick, acrid smoke across the compound, carried by a northerly wind that the wind sock at the helipad told him was at about ten knots per hour. But the marina itself didn't appear to have caught fire. That meant that only those soldiers nearest the fuel tanks were killed or wounded badly enough so that they no longer presented a threat, and that most of the soldiers who patrolled the southern breakwater, and all those on the northern breakwater, had survived. The odds made him shudder. He hoped to God that the reinforcements on the boat would arrive soon.

"Matthew," Billy yelled into his speaker. "What's the situation with the bunker at the foot of the breakwater?"

"Crispy critters," Matthew responded, panting hard as he reached the gate of the fence.

"Take out the bunker at the base of the northern breakwater. You've got to get across the compound, or Frank and the others will get cut to shreds when they come in with the boat. I'll take out the bunker up here," Billy added, already making his way toward the bunker, past the Huey on the helipad.

Matthew headed north as per the plan, cautiously watching for any signs of the enemy. He heard the dull thud of a grenade explode in close quarters. Out of the corner of his eye he saw the flash of fire burst from the opening. Billy had done his job. The bunker at the base of the helipad to the south of the hacienda was out of commission.

So far they had been lucky, but that was bound to change. *Where the hell are Frank and the other reinforcements?* Billy wondered. "Are you wearing your goggle?"

"No. I'm using my rifle scope."

"Flip down your goggle. You'll get a wider angle and you'll see what I see dead ahead of you."

Matthew complied and in the pale green light of the wide-angle lens, he saw the enemy soldiers, squirming on the ground under bushes and behind trees, intermittently firing their assault rifles on David and Jenny's position, as if taking turns, emptying their magazines, testing David and Jenny's defenses.

"Ready on the range?" Billy asked, his voice powerful, decisive, employing the jargon of an army range instructor.

"Ready on the right," Matthew called out crisply as he eased a .40mm grenade into the grenade launcher.

"On my count," Billy ordered. "One . . . two . . . three."

Two loud thumps resounded behind Belalcazar's soldiers, many turning in the direction of the sound just in time to die.

Thump, thump, two more grenades announced as they streamed into the air, exploding upon the impact of whatever it was that they hit. Screams of pain from those wounded followed the explosions. *Thump, thump.* Another two grenades resounded over the eastern lawn of the compound. Those soldiers who were not dead or too badly wounded to move ran, limped, or crawled down the hill toward the northern end of the marina, the last bastion of the compound available to them other than the hacienda itself.

In the predawn darkness, it took the two soldiers in the bunker at the top of the hill on the north side of the compound a moment or two to locate the area where the grenades were coming from. When they thought they found the attackers, they sprayed the general area with .30-caliber machine gun fire, forcing both Matthew and Billy to scramble for cover.

Billy took one shot with his grenade launcher. Again, the now-familiar thump announced that a grenade was tumbling through the air. It landed on the ground forty feet in front of the bunker, causing no more damage than a bit of mud and grass flying through the opening.

Matthew rose to get a better angle up the hill, hoping to skim the grenade inches off the ground. His shot was high, sending the grenade over the bunker to explode harmlessly behind it. Had the grenade flown higher, it would have landed close to David and Jenny. As Matthew ran for the cover of a decorative coral rock arrangement that the gardener had left unfinished, a .30-caliber bullet slammed into his left leg, just below the knee, splintering his tibia. He crumpled to the ground behind the decorative rocks, unable to repress an outcry of pain.

Billy didn't need the receiver in his helmet to tell him that Matthew was down. He heard the old-fashioned way the single shriek that Matthew uttered. David and Jenny heard it too, as did everyone on the eastern side of the compound, encouraging Belalcazar's soldiers to fight harder even as they retreated from Billy and Matthew toward the northern breakwater. Billy ran down the hill as fast as he could, given the distortion in his vision between his left eye and his uncovered right eye, which reported back images through the increasingly gray dawn. Spotting Matthew writhing in pain behind the rocks, he slid the last twenty feet on the wet grass and mud, bullets whizzing past him and in the mud around him.

"Where are you hit?" Billy started to ask, but found the answer on his own. Matthew's left leg, the same one injured on the reef, was nearly severed below the knee, hanging by the few muscles that remained. Billy immediately realized what Matthew already knew: Given the time it would take to get to Panama—if they could make it to Panama—there would be no way to save Matthew's leg. Billy also reached another conclusion that Matthew had come to a few seconds before: Between the powerful machine gun in the bunker and the defending troops rallying at the northern breakwater, they were trapped.

Matthew's scream had spurred David to action. Billy and Matthew's attack had broken the enemy's assault on their position, allowing Jenny to concentrate on the soldiers west of the hacienda and David to make his move. "Fire your grenades at the palm trees behind the house," he called out to Jenny. "The fragments will spray against the wall and force them back. I'm going for the bunker," he shouted, already several steps down the hill.

Jenny fired one grenade into a palm tree a few feet to the west of the hacienda, spewing tiny shrapnel against the backside of the residence, forcing the soldiers to retreat. She quickly reloaded and waited to fire again.

David silently approached the bunker from the rear and side, crouching low. He carefully placed his weapon on the ground, removed a hand grenade from his web gear, pulled the pin, and slid on his belly toward the opening. He tossed the grenade into the narrow opening with his left hand and crawled behind the bunker as fast as he could. Still, the concussion lifted him off the ground a few inches. With the bunker out of commission, Billy and Matthew were in less danger, but they continued to take rounds from the soldiers near the marina and the kennel. David fired one grenade in the direction of the soldiers, and Billy did the same.

With the immediate danger of the soldiers attacking from the eastern lawn momentarily eased, and with Jenny holding her own against the soldiers west of the hacienda, David allowed himself a brief moment to reflect on the bigger picture. The hacienda could not be taken until the soldiers near the northern breakwater and the kennel were eliminated. To make matters worse, the bunker at the base of the breakwater and the machine gun inside were undamaged. And those in the bunker, together with the men on the breakwaters themselves, could sink any boat Frank might try to maneuver into the marina, barring all escape. Again, defeat and death would result, unless he backtracked and eliminated the enemy strongholds. As a father, the realization that he would have to retreat from his position, that he would have to put more distance between himself and the hacienda where Justin was held captive, was devastating, but the Ranger in him knew that there was a job to be done first.

As he prepared to flank the remaining bunker, wishing

he could communicate with Billy and Matthew to coordinate the attack, a rocket that originated somewhere from the waters off the marina slammed into the area near the remaining bunker. The face of the battle was changed. Reinforcements had arrived.

While it seemed as if the battle had raged all night, only twelve minutes had transpired since David and Jenny had turned out the lights and brought the tower down in a ball of flame. In that time Frank had raced the boat toward the island as fast as the powerful rollers to his port would allow. As the vessel approached the marina, he cut speed rapidly and reversed the engines. Everyone was on deck, straining their eyes to identify any movement along the breakwater and in the marina itself. They were too far offshore to see Belalcazar's troops, but they knew the soldiers were there from the crackling sound of rifle fire that carried over the water.

As Frank held the boat steady, pointed south, into the waves, Eric attached a grenade to the end of the cumbersome Czech grenade launcher. The repeated thumps of the grenades fired by Billy and David—and the resulting explosions near the kennel—told him where Billy and David were firing. In the grayness of the predawn light, he made out the long, dark shape of the northern breakwater—barely, but enough to get his bearings. From the satellite pictures, he knew that the bunker was at the base of the breakwater. He aimed the grenade launcher at the location where he thought the bunker was, confirmed that Linda, Anne, and Frank were clear of the back blast, and fired. The fireball sailed low over the water as Eric watched, a surrealistic slow-motion action that mesmerized him and the others on the boat, as well as the two horrified men in the bunker. The grenade flew a few inches over the bunker and landed in the midst of the guards regrouping behind the bunker near the kennel. None of them saw it coming, nor would it have helped them if they had. Four of the soldiers died on impact. Several others were wounded, stunned by the attack from behind them.

Eric quickly reloaded as Frank gunned the engines to move farther out to sea, away from the men now firing back at them from the bunker. Linda and Anne sprayed the north and south breakwaters with bullets from their M16s, forcing the exposed soldiers to dive into the marina and swim to shore.

Billy left Matthew behind the relative protection of the rock formation and pressed the attack, using his grenades sparingly, firing three-round bursts from his M16A2 as he crouched and slowly approached the enemy. David did the same from the top of the lawn, while Jenny held the soldiers behind the hacienda at bay. Linda and Anne held their fire lest they give their position away, while Frank gunned the engines and moved back into position for Eric to fire from four hundred yards. Again the grenade raced across the water, just missing the narrow opening of the bunker, this time wide to the left, but once again killing enemy soldiers as it burst into thousands of pieces of shrapnel behind the bunker.

Everyone on the Sea Ray saw the red flashes of the .30-caliber machine gun, and heard the sound of large bullets hitting the water near them. Two of them, each the size of a thumb, slammed into the stern of the Sea Ray on the starboard side. The bullets pierced the gunwale several inches above the waterline, and clanked loudly into the starboard engine, cracking the block. Frank shut it down before a fire could start. They'd have to operate the Sea Ray on one engine. Anne hurried to stuff the holes with strips of towels.

The tide of battle had shifted in favor of the attackers, a fact that escaped neither them nor those of Belalcazar's soldiers huddled near the kennel. Only seven remained unharmed. Four more were wounded and in no position to run, but still fired their weapons. The thick, acrid smoke from the burning fuel tanks blew directly into their faces.

"Herd them on to the minefield," David shouted to Billy. "It's northwest of the kennel and up to the barracks along the cliff."

Billy understood instantly why David and Jenny had been late to destroy the generator. Their path of insertion was mined and they had been smart—or lucky—enough to detect it. He wondered how they had made it up the cliffs, but that was a question for another time. Billy flanked to his right toward a hangarlike structure near the base of the northern breakwater, reloading another thirty-round magazine as he ran. David flanked to his left near the cantina and pressed the attack. The wounded still firing their weapons were killed in successive three-round bursts from the M16s. Those who retreated were either shot or blown to pieces as they were forced onto the minefield. Billy sent the two men in the bunker to hell with a handheld grenade, and at that point the northern quadrant of the compound belonged to the attackers. The hacienda and the helipad, however, were still controlled by Belalcazar's men, a number of whom had retreated from the southern breakwater to the hacienda. And Belalcazar still had the children.

Stephanie Wagner helped the children get dressed. Wanting to delay, she gave the impression of being in a hurry, but buttoned each button and tied each lace as slowly as she dared. Alberto, joined by Emilio, shouted at her to take the kids in their pajamas.

Nick Field was no stranger to combat. He knew that the men in the bunker near the pad were dead. He, too, had heard the dull thud of the grenade exploding in the tight confines of the bunker and heard the crackle of M16 fire, sounds he had heard all too often back in Vietnam. As the fighting moved closer to the kennel and away from the helipad, he raced to the helicopter and began to untie the ropes that held the rotors in place and to unfasten the anchors that held the skids to the pad. *Thank God I'm a pilot and not a foot soldier,* he thought as he readied the Huey for their escape.

Frank chose not to enter the marina, fearing that they could be trapped within the narrow passageway between the long arms of the two breakwaters. Instead he powered the Sea Ray along the outside of the northern breakwater, where the water was almost as well protected from the southerly waves as they were inside the marina. As he approached the shore near the bunker, he reversed the one remaining engine and brought the sleek vessel to a dead halt twenty feet in front of the destroyed bunker. He turned the boat around, reversed the engine, and backed up toward the shore as far as he could, idling the engine at the last moment. He didn't have to signal to the others to disembark. Anne and Linda had already jumped into the shallow water as Eric stepped off the rear swim platform, right behind the two mothers. Frank gunned the left engine once again and moved the vessel a few hundred feet offshore to keep it safe.

Billy was soon knee-deep in the water, helping them to the shore, rapidly updating them on the situation. "Matthew's hit," Billy told them. "Left leg's gone. He can't walk and he may bleed to death. Anne, I'll show you where he is. You stay with him and stop the bleeding. Linda, follow me. We'll flank south around the pool and attack the hacienda from the south."

David appeared through the inky smoke from the fuel tanks. He greeted them with a nod. The tension was evident on his face, the sweat pouring down off his brow and slipping smoothly over his green-and-black greasepaint. "Jenny's on top of the hill by herself," he said panting. "She needs help. Eric, come with me."

As they huddled the compound was silent. No thumps from the grenade launcher. No pops from rifle fire. It was as if the billowing smoke from the fuel tanks had snuffed out all energy, all sound. As the first sunlight streaked the sky over the Andes to the east, the dawn seemed to add to the quiet.

Moments later the silence was broken by the sound of the Huey's jet engine. It caught Eric and David as they were about to run to help Jenny, and Anne, Linda, and Billy as they were rising from their huddle and setting off to find Matthew. They froze in their tracks. No one nodded to the others, or even exchanged glances. There was no need to. Helicopter turbines meant Belalcazar was taking the children off the island.

Linda was the first to break into a sprint. She sped from her position as if she were launching out of the starting block in a race. David and Eric were the next to charge through the wall of acrid, gummy smoke that hid the helicopter from view. Billy and Anne were also on the move.

Eric ran up the steps that would take him to Jenny, sweating in the humidity, hyperventilating from the exertion. Yet he surprised himself with the speed of his adrenaline-pumped legs as he took the steps two at a time, despite the weight of the Czech grenade launcher in his left hand, two extra grenades tucked under his belt, and the M16 in his right hand. While he raced to Jenny's aid, the others sprinted through the smoke and up the steep hill toward the helipad. As they cleared the other side of the forty-foot-thick wall of smoke, the helicopter was visible up the hill on the pad, beyond a large TV satellite dish. The Huey's blades were rotating faster and faster.

Billy was torn as to whether he should go to Matthew's aid or go to the children. He cursed himself for not having destroyed the Huey when he had had the chance just a few minutes earlier. He had been so intent on silently approaching the bunker near the pad that he had left the chopper intact. In retrospect, he should have destroyed the bunker and then doubled back to the pad, turning the Huey into a fireball with one grenade. Now he had to make a very difficult choice. *Matthew would want me to go for the children,* he thought. He flanked slightly to his left to get what he hoped would be a better shot at the helicopter, while the others stormed directly toward the pad.

Belalcazar was furious with his men. Soldiers huddled against the western wall of the hacienda, cowering from Jenny's grenade bursts—"Craig's whore," as Belalcazar called her. His men couldn't even see her around the corner of the mansion, let alone shoot at her. He threatened to kill them himself if they didn't attack, and, more fearful of his wrath than the enemy's grenade launcher, they obeyed. But with each attack Jenny countered, grenades exploding against nearby trees and the hacienda itself, killing or wounding as the sharp fragments cut into the soldiers at hundreds of feet per second. Another group of soldiers, still wet from their dive into the marina, straggled up the hill, past the helipad, and approached the patio. Belalcazar ordered them into the hacienda to fire on Jenny's position from the protection of the second floor. As Alberto pushed and prodded the children down the stairs, wet soldiers scrambled up the steps to take the high ground against Jenny.

Emilio was on the patio just outside Belalcazar's office, eyes darting in every direction for signs of danger. He peered around the corner of the hacienda, looking for the thumbs-up from Nick Field. When the long rotor blades of the Huey attained sufficient rpms, Nick gave the sign and Emilio began to usher the passengers toward the chopper. Alberto led the way, followed immediately by an agitated Gerald Warren. Belalcazar followed, with Emilio on his left, acting as a human shield. The children were next, first Lisa, then Justin, Francisco, Jaime, and Debbie. Stephanie Wagner was last. She had made up her mind that she wouldn't go with Belalcazar. She had determined to fling herself on the mercy of the attackers, but she had no idea how to carry out her plan.

As David ran across the lawn, trying to keep up with Linda, who was faster, he sized up the situation. Their field of fire was obstructed by a large satellite TV dish that stood between them and the chopper. In addition, Linda and Anne carried M16A1s, which weren't equipped with the powerful M203 grenade launcher. Although he could see only the tips of the rotating blades from his position behind a ridge in the lawn, from the speed of the rotors he knew that the helicopter would lift off momentarily. If they were going to take out the Huey, they had to do it now, while it was on the ground, and they had to do it before the children were too close. But where were the children? He couldn't see them.

"Billy, take the shot!" he roared. "Take the shot!"

Billy had already reached the same conclusion. He raced toward a small mound of soil the gardeners had left after digging a nearby hole. He leaped to the top of the mound. It gave him just enough additional height to see the cabin of the Huey from the rear. He could also see a line of people, some adults and some children, making their way from behind the hacienda toward the helipad. Already approaching the swimming pool, which was halfway from the hacienda to the pad, they were only a hundred feet from the Huey and soon would be dangerously close to the target. He gripped the grenade launcher, braced his feet, and fired just as his right foot slid on the loose soil. He had aimed for the fuselage of the Huey, but the shot went slightly high.

The grenade struck the swirling base of the rotors and exploded. Nick Field had no time to react. The grenade hit the rotors and jolted the Huey forward, sliding it on its skids a few feet across the concrete pad. The mass of the rotors forced much of the impact of the explosion downward into the fuselage, hurling molten metal fragments into the cockpit, killing the lone pilot before he even understood what had happened. The fuel tank exploded within seconds, and the Huey erupted in a fireball that sent large pieces of metal flying in all directions. Billy dove behind the dirt mound on which he stood. David, Linda, and Anne instinctively fell to the ground. Alberto Reyes, longtime bodyguard to Belalcazar, was less resourceful, and a shaft of metal pierced his skull, killing him instantly. Gerald Warren passed out and bled to death, his aorta severed by a twisted fragment of the helicopter's door. Emilio Piña was badly wounded, but he would live long enough to help the stunned, but unharmed, Belalcazar back into the hacienda.

The blast of the grenade frightened Stephanie Wagner, but it gave her the opening she needed. In a maneuver that was in part heroic and in part reflexive, she herded and pushed the five children into the swimming pool, jumping into the pool herself just as the helicopter exploded. Stephanie and the children were low in the water when shrapnel whizzed overhead.

Lisa Waldron had learned to swim early at the Stamford Yacht Club. She and Jaime, who was also a strong swimmer, rose to the surface, terrified and confused, but able to make it to the side of the pool and hang on. The other three children were not good swimmers. Francisco had fallen close to the edge of the pool near Stephanie. When he surfaced, coughing and frightened, but unharmed, she pushed him to the ledge, where he held on. Debbie hit her head on the side of the pool as she plunged into the water and sank like a rock. Stephanie had the presence of mind and strength to pull her up and heft her onto her side on the concrete walk. But she couldn't find Justin. She took in as much air as she could, went underwater, and searched the bottom of the pool, resurfacing empty-handed, gasping for air. Despite her growing hysteria she was about to go under again just as someone plunged into the water.

David, Linda, and Anne had charged toward the helipad seconds after the shrapnel from the Huey landed around them. From their angle down the incline, they couldn't see the children, but knew they were somewhere near the Huey when it exploded. As Linda and David crested the hill and reached a flat grassy area on the far side of the pool, they saw three children—two boys, one girl—clinging to the side of the pool at the opposite end. Another girl lay on her side on the concrete. David and Linda dropped their weapons on the run and sprinted, Linda realizing that the child on the concrete was her Debbie and rushing to her. David spotted another boy in deep water and dove in, reaching Justin as he was struggling below the surface in seven feet of water. Father took son into his arms, and together they burst to the surface, gasping for air.

Anne ran to Lisa, Jaime, and Francisco and pulled them out of the water. Linda determined that Debbie was not breathing but that she had a pulse. She held her panic in abeyance as she struggled to recall what she had learned in a first-aid course when she was pregnant. Then she began to administer artificial respiration. She slid her arm under the back of Debbie's neck to arch her head slightly, clamped the child's nostrils shut with her fingers, and blew air from her lungs into Debbie's. Linda repeated the procedure as she had been taught, wishing she had paid more attention in class, hoping she was doing it right.

After several repetitions, Debbie coughed, rolled to her side, and vomited, wondering whose arms were holding her and whose lips were kissing her cheeks and why the person was crying so uncontrollably.

Anne hugged and kissed Lisa, crying hysterically. She had her daughter back. Lisa stared blankly at her mother, wondering where on earth she had come from and why she had taken so long.

With Justin in his arms, David swam to the side of the pool and reluctantly lifted him onto the concrete, not wanting to let go even for a second. He then planted his own palms on the ledge of the pool and hoisted himself up and out. He took Justin into his arms again, hugging and kissing him, even as he ran with him back to the position where he had dropped his weapon. "Justin," he said softly, sobbing. "Justin, I love you. It's Daddy. I've come for you. I'm taking you home."

Justin smiled weakly and slumped his head onto David's shoulder, his body shutting down, overwhelmed by the events, needing rest.

Eric stopped his sprint up the stairs when he reached the point where the guard tower had fallen across the path, leaving a heap of crushed, charred brick and stone. He spotted two soldiers in a window on the second story of the hacienda, taking aim at Jenny. From their angle her stone redoubt offered no protection, and she didn't see them. Eric dropped to one knee, shifted the grenade launcher to his right hand, and fired just as one of the soldiers turned to see the rocket leave the launcher. The grenade hit the windowsill inches in front of the two soldiers, obliterating them and saving Jenny's life. The hacienda rocked from the blast. The room where the soldiers stood burst into flames.

Jenny swiveled on her belly to see who had fired the grenade, expecting to see David, already trying to figure out why there was no thump from his M203. She couldn't believe her eyes. "Eric," she yelled in jubilation. For the first time she realized that reinforcements had arrived.

"Jenny," he shouted. "Run for the helipad." Jenny needed no encouragement. She took off after Eric, catching up with him easily as he ran across the compound toward the others.

Billy reached Mathew within seconds after the Huey exploded, fearful that he'd find his friend unconscious, if not dead. To Billy's astonishment, Matthew was not only conscious, he was applying a tourniquet to his leg a few inches above his knee, using two cravats knotted together for extra length and twisting it with his bayonet scabbard, the bayonet still inside. Billy smiled for the first time since jumping from the King Air, thrilled to see Matthew alert and functioning. He quickly related to Matthew what was happening at the pool and asked him what he could do to make him more comfortable. Matthew dismissed Billy's offer with a flip of his wrist and a command to "Go help with the kids." Billy nodded, turned, and ran back up the hill toward the swimming pool.

Eric and Jenny ran up the steep incline just as David, carrying Justin, squatted to pick up his weapon. Eric and Jenny beamed, ear-to-ear smiles stretching across their faces, when they saw Justin in David's arms. They glanced over David's shoulders to see Linda and Anne on the other side of the pool, hugging and kissing the girls. A young woman whom they didn't know had just pulled herself out of the water and was calling out in Spanish to the two Hispanic boys they had seen on the computer screen. Stephanie Wagner urged the two boys to go with the Americans, praying that they'd take her too.

Eric ran to Linda and hugged her and Lisa, kissing both of them on the cheek. Tears flowed in torrents down Linda's face. "Who are you?" Eric demanded of Stephanie Wagner harshly.

"I was their nanny," she responded, breathing heavily between gasps for air, exhausted as much from fear as physical exertion. "I'm American . . . Indiana . . . I was hired to be a nanny . . . a teacher. I had no idea the kids were kidnapped before I got here. I've been as much a prisoner as them," she said truthfully.

"You pushed them into the pool?" Eric asked, surveying the scene around him.

Stephanie nodded.

"Smart," he said. "Get the kids to the boat. You're goin' home."

Eric surveyed the battleground. The grenade, the explosion of the Huey, and its aftermath had, surprisingly, left only three dead, and remarkably all of them were Belalcazar's people. His eyes were drawn to the bloodied body of a man that stood out for the fact that he had died in a dark blue business suit, rather than a soldier's uniform like the others. Eric's instinct was to avoid looking at the dead man's face, but he found himself doing so anyway. What he saw gave him the shock of his life. Mouth agape, he blinked several times to make sure he wasn't hallucinating.

Billy reached the pool in time to turn the second-floor corner room of the hacienda—space that had been the children's classroom—into a fireball with his M203. Soldiers who were taking aim at the distracted parents and children were incinerated without a second to spare. The distance from the poolside to the explosion was only eighty feet, twenty feet less than what was considered the minimum safe range to avoid the back blast. Billy knew that, but he had no choice. Bits of debris cut David's back, Stephanie's shoulder, and the back of Debbie's hand, adding to her hysteria and her mother's panic. A tiny piece of shrapnel grazed Jenny's scalp. No one was seriously injured, but the message was clear: Time to go.

"Get the kids out of here," Billy yelled as he popped another grenade into the launcher and gripped the forestock, his eyes studying the hacienda for any sign of movement.

"Let's get out of here," Eric yelled frantically, raising his M16 to fire at any soldiers in or near the hacienda. He decided not to wait for signs of movement. Instead, he began firing single bursts of M16 rounds at the various windows, at no particular targets, simply an announcement to Belalcazar's soldiers that he was all over them.

Under the protective M16 fire that Eric laid down on the hacienda and under Billy's protective watch with the grenade launcher, David made his decision. He looked once at Jenny, who nodded in the affirmative to the question that didn't need asking. He turned to Eric and Billy, who nodded in agreement. Billy tapped his chest once and pointed to David, indicating that he'd go with him. Eric nodded again, accepting Billy's decision. Eric's M16 continued to spit out rounds, shooting through the windows randomly, effectively keeping the unseen enemies at bay.

"Justin," David said gently but firmly, "go with Jenny and Uncle Eric to the boat. We're heading home today. I can't wait to play in your room," he said, really meaning it. "But first I have something I have to do. I'll meet you at the boat," he added, trying to hand Justin to Jenny.

Not surprisingly, Justin resisted, clinging to his father's neck, unwilling to let go, afraid of losing his daddy once again. David gently pried Justin's hands free as he dropped to his knees. David kissed Justin on the cheek and hugged him tightly, then tenderly tore himself away. "I'll always be with you. I'll never, ever leave you. Promise. Go with Jenny and Uncle Eric." He rose to his feet while Jenny put her arms around the boy. "I'll meet you on the boat. Promise."

Justin acquiesced, accepting Jenny's and Eric's hands,

his tearful eyes lingering on his dad. David watched them descend the hill and run toward the Sea Ray.

"Let's go," David said resolutely as he turned to Billy.

"I'll flank to the other side," Billy said as he loaded a fresh magazine into his M16.

"There are double doors just as you round the corner, at the top of the steps. There's another single door all the way to the right on the north face," David informed his friend.

"Give me one minute and then enter from the terrace in the back. There must be a door there."

They nodded to each other and ran to their positions.

Chapter 30

Matthew's shot had struck Joaquin in the head, but only grazed him, an inch above his right ear. The impact was powerful enough to knock him off his feet and down the outside of the breakwater. His head hit a rock and he fractured his left arm as he crashed hard on the large stones that formed the seawall. He lay unconscious at the water's edge, five feet below the top of the breakwater. He wasn't aware of anything until he came to with a splitting headache, awakening to the horrifying sight of eels slithering around his head, sucking up the blood dripping from his head wound. It was enough to jolt him to full consciousness. As he scrambled to safety, he was furious that not a single soldier had come to his assistance. All had given him up for dead.

He climbed to the top of the breakwater, holding on to the moss-covered rocks with one hand, his left arm dangling uselessly at his side. He knelt rather than stood, determined to keep his profile low to avoid another bullet. His vision was blurred from the blood and salt water, but he saw enough of the compound to know that the damage was devastating. The fuel tanks were still burning. The guard tower had vanished, spilled down the lawn near the cantina. Fires burned in the hacienda. The Huey, or rather the wreckage that remained, was still smoldering. Dead soldiers, some charred beyond recognition, lay on the grass; others floated facedown in the marina.

Like the other defenders on the island, Joaquin had grossly underestimated the power of the attackers. They had come from nowhere, yet they seemed to be everywhere. He had anticipated assault rifles and handguns, and maybe even one or two slow-to-reload grenade launchers like the one Eric used, not rapid-firing M203s. He had believed the defenders had the advantage at night. Instead the attackers were equipped with sophisticated night-vision goggles that had turned the advantage against him and his troops. Although he was one of several who had misjudged Craig's strengths, he was painfully aware that this was the second time that he had personally faced Craig and come up short.

He watched Eric and Linda run down the steep lawn to come to Matthew's assistance, but couldn't see all that transpired through the smoke. He didn't see Billy run in front of the hacienda, but he did see a man run along the south side and wondered if he had spotted David Craig. He assumed that he had. He also observed women, including Stephanie Wagner, leading the children through the dark tunnel of smoke and then running to a boat on the outside of the north breakwater.

Joaquin frowned as he recognized the boat. It infuriated him to think that the gringos had stolen his boat and were using it to escape from the island. It didn't bother him that the kids were escaping; he was glad to be rid of them. The children and the conquistador obsessions were Belalcazar's Achilles' heel, and Joaquin hated him for that. They would destroy Belalcazar, if they hadn't already, and jeopardize the cartel. In fact, he secretly welcomed Belalcazar's death and toyed with the idea of killing the *patrón* himself, if Craig didn't do it first. Belalcazar had outlived his usefulness, and once he was eliminated, Joaquin would be free to take over the cartel. He knew what to do, and how to carry it out.

Joaquin struggled to his feet. Keeping his head down, he walked as quickly as his injuries would permit. He staggered and swayed like a drunk man, but followed the south breakwater, unnoticed by the Americans. If he could find a weapon, he could get a shot at David Craig.

Billy entered the hacienda through the kitchen door, rejecting the double doors on the porch as too inviting, too dangerous. He crouched low, his eyes darting animal-like through the smoke for any sign of danger, moving quickly but cautiously across the room. As he approached the door that led from the kitchen to the covered inner walkway and the courtyard, he lay prone on the floor. He stuck his head out beyond the passageway, at ground level, searching for signs of the enemy along the archway on either side of his corner perch. He saw none. He scanned the two staircases leading to the second floor. One was to his left, near the double doors that he had chosen not to open. It looked clear. The other was more of a problem, his view obstructed by the stone columns that formed the archway. He had a fairly clear line of fire along the archway on the ground floor, but only a partial line of fire to the second-floor veranda across the courtyard.

Billy was surprised by how peaceful the courtyard seemed. The large fountain in the middle no longer bubbled water, there being no electricity to power the pumps, but it was undamaged, circled by colorful flowers and neatly trimmed miniature hedges. It reminded Billy of the Jardin du Luxembourg in Paris, which he and Faith had visited the summer before. The beauty of the courtyard stood in stark contrast to the surrounding devastation and the stench of charred bodies, cordite, and burning fuel that permeated the compound.

David entered the hacienda through Belalcazar's office slowly, trying not to step on the broken glass, but unable to avoid it. The glass crunched beneath his wet boots, which squished with each step.

Billy heard the footsteps down the archway to his right. Not willing to risk that they didn't belong to David, he inched forward on his belly through the doorway enough to cradle the forestock in his right hand so that he could fire his M16 with his left.

David, too, crouched low, poking his head through the door to the archway, his eyes searching the courtyard, the veranda, and the archway in front of him and to his left. His eyes found Billy's M16 and the wide hole of the grenade launcher pointed directly at him, leaving him breathless until he saw the weapon rise and Billy's look of relief. David duckwalked a few paces into the archway, approaching a staircase that led to the second-floor veranda.

David felt more than saw the soldier on the veranda above and to Billy's left. The tip of the barrel of the AK47 pointed no more than two inches through the railing. The man lay on his belly, the silhouette of his shoulders barely visible through the slats of the railing.

David dove forward under the staircase a fraction of a second before the 7.62mm rounds from the AK47 plowed into the concrete wall behind him. He fired back, bursts three rounds at a time clanking against the painted metal railing along the veranda, preventing the enemy soldier from firing effectively, but not neutralizing him.

Billy jumped to his feet and removed his last handheld grenade from his web gear. In one continuous motion he leaped into the courtyard, hooked the grenade with his right hand like a basketball player, dashed across the courtyard, and dove into the archway on the opposite side. The grenade exploded amid cries of pain from more than one enemy guard. The screams provided a valuable piece of intelligence. Billy now knew where at least several of Belalcazar's men were located, although they, too, were aware of his position. Ironically, while the soldiers didn't know that he no longer had any handheld grenades, and his grenade launcher was useless at this range, Billy was not aware that the guards who remained alive, huddled in the bedrooms above him, had had enough fighting and were contemplating surrender. A strange stalemate ensued, neither party in a position to attack, each waiting for the other to act.

David raced up the stairs. He turned right into the nearest door, prepared to fire the M16 at anything that moved. Soccer balls painted on powder-blue walls, model airplanes suspended from the ceiling, Spanish children's books on the shelves. Three twin-size beds with matching Pokémon bedspreads. Anger welled up in him. The bastard had made the boys' bedroom, the room where Justin had been imprisoned for nearly a month, look like a cheerful, cozy place, a macabre home away from home. As David looked around the room, the resolve that had wavered when father was reunited with son grew with his fury—the Ranger could not go home until Belalcazar was dead.

He moved to the next room, smashing in the door with his foot, the muzzle of his rifle ready to spit death at anyone in its sight. This room, smaller than the boys' room, was clearly that of an adult male. Pinups from porno magazines decorated the walls. The March issue of *Penthouse* lay on the nightstand next to the twin-size bed.

Next was a big corner room. David recalled that the two corner rooms facing the marina had small balconies, perhaps large enough for four adults to stand but not sit. *Belalcazar's bedroom*, he thought. His heart raced as he thought about the pain Belalcazar had caused him, Justin, and everyone around them. His eyes stung from the smoke of the burning helicopter that drifted in through the empty windowpanes. His pulse quickened as he sensed that Belalcazar was very near.

Taking a deep breath, David turned the knob and at the same instant kicked open the thick oak door with all his might, swinging his body through the door frame and jumping to his left several feet away from the door. Emilio, who sat on the floor with his back against the wall opposite David, fired at him twice. The bullets missed David, chipping two-inch conical holes in the concrete wall to David's right. David's M16 ripped Emilio's chest apart from less than fifteen feet away. The bolt of the M16 remained open as the last shell of the magazine fell noisily to the tile floor. Time to reload.

David turned to face Sebastian de Belalcazar. The bedroom was vast, perhaps forty feet long and twenty-five feet wide. Belalcazar stood at the side of a large Spanish baroque canopy bed, leaning against a matching night table for support. He appeared unarmed, hands at his sides, palms turned to David to show that he had no weapon. They stood approximately thirty feet apart, two sets of eyes locked on each other. For the first time since his early youth, Belalcazar's eyes registered fear. He recognized David from the newspaper and magazine pictures, and he knew from David's expression that David had no question who he was.

David pressed the button that released the empty magazine. It fell to the terra-cotta floor, where it bounced several times on the tile and broken glass. He calmly slid his right hand into the opening in his army fatigue shirt just above his belt and removed his last thirty-round magazine, inserting it until he heard and felt it click into its locking mechanism. He slapped it on the bottom with the butt of his palm to make sure it was securely in place and then chambered a round.

"Señor Craig, I have much money. I can compensate you and your friends well," he said in surprisingly good English.

David said nothing. He simply cradled the M16 chest-high and pointed the muzzle at Belalcazar.

"Mr. Craig. I want to assure you that neither I nor any of my people ever harmed José," he pleaded. "We have taken good care of him."

"Who?" David asked simply, his eyes and weapon still aimed at his enemy.

"Oh . . ." Belalcazar responded, more desperate, "he liked to be called José. I want to repeat that no one ever harmed your boy."

"You took him from me."

Belalcazar saw David's lips tremble and then saw them utter something. He would have heard David's voice stutter with emotion, but the words couldn't be heard over the deafening *brrripp* of the M16. David held his finger on the trigger until six three-round bursts tore into Belalcazar's abdomen and chest, lifting him onto the nightstand behind him, leaving the drug baron dead in a seated position. His eyes held the expression they had at the moment he realized that he was about to die, the moment he saw the animal look in David's eyes harden for the kill. David turned and walked away, picking up speed as he went down the stairs, finding Billy near the double doors.

"Did you get Belalcazar?" Billy asked. He had heard the shooting, but had no way of knowing who David had shot. "Is he dead?"

"Yeah."

"You sure?"

"Yeah. Let's go."

The two men bolted out the doors, jumped off the porch, and ran down the steps toward the breakwater and the boat that would take them home.

Billy slowed to let David be the first to wade through the water and climb onto the swim platform on the stern of the Sea Ray. David scrambled over the cushion that covered the engines, eager to hold Justin in his arms. His son had been in the boat no more than a few minutes, but he was already in a panic about his daddy. When the boy saw David run into the water, safe from harm, he broke from Jenny's arms and lunged at his father. The two collided and fell to the deck. David was on his knees, touching Justin's face and hair, kissing and hugging him. He studied his son, his hands softly probing to see if Justin was really there and unharmed. Frank gunned the one good engine of the Sea Ray as Billy was halfway on board. David tried to say something over the roar of the engine, but the words were choked by the stream of tears that cascaded down his cheeks. Justin uttered the word *Daddy* over and over as he clung to David.

Below deck, the tearful reunions between Linda and Debbie, and Anne and Lisa, mirrored that of Justin and David, as mothers and daughters held each other and cried for the time lost and celebrated the joy ahead. Stephanie held Francisco and Jaime, trying to comfort them and herself.

Eric, Billy, Frank, and Matthew exchanged proud glances, congratulating each other for a job well done, even as Eric and Billy ministered to Matthew's leg as best they could and gave him a shot of morphine from Pablo Santiago's first-aid kit.

But something was not right. Billy turned to see if there were any pursuers, surveying the compound and the marina for snipers. His military sense told him that they were not out of danger, not yet. At first he couldn't put his finger on it. Then he saw them.

"Stop," he yelled to Frank, as the Sea Ray began to plane and pick up speed, the one 1,075-horsepower engine being powerful enough for their purposes. Frank turned to see what was bothering Billy. "The cigarette boats. We gotta sink 'em. They're faster than us."

Eric, David, and Frank exchanged glances, acknowledging that Billy was right, but reluctant to go back. Frank reduced the speed further and turned the sleek vessel around. Linda and Anne rushed from below deck, alarmed by the change in course. As they approached the north breakwater, Billy and Eric made their decision as to how they would destroy the two cigarette boats. They could either enter the marina and use Jenny's handheld grenades from close up, or they could stay outside the marina and use the grenade launchers. Not much of a decision, really. Better to use the launchers and move on. If they missed the first time, they could shoot again. Billy took a quick inventory. Between them they still had ten .40mm grenades for the M203s, and Eric still had one for the Czech launcher.

"Let me take the first shot," Eric pleaded with a grin, like a child wanting to go first in a game. "I haven't hit a damn thing with this clunker," he said, referring to the missed shots in Buenaventura, and the bunker and the windowsill shot at the hacienda. "Damn good thing that 'close' counts in grenades."

Billy smiled. Frank laughed out loud. David motioned for Jenny to join him and Justin, and the three of them hugged each other. Justin recognized her from his daddy's office, but was a little suspicious of his daddy's affection for her.

Frank stopped the Sea Ray about two hundred yards north of the breakwater and turned it around so that

Eric could fire off the starboard side. Seeing Matthew dozing from the morphine, Billy and David took advantage of their being stopped to carry him below deck, laying him on the aftmost bed, where the ride would be smoother, gently elevating his leg on a pillow and placing pillows on either side of him lest he roll off the bed.

The two cigarette boats were about 250 yards away, each capable of traveling at 70 mph on smooth water. They glistened in the morning sun, one fire-engine red, the other canary yellow, in contrast to the smoking fuel tanks behind them. Eric stood and braced his feet, took aim at the red boat, and fired.

Everyone on deck watched the grenade arch toward its target. It hit the stern of the red boat a few inches left of center, igniting two forty-gallon fuel tanks. The explosion lifted the vessel fifteen feet out of the water, breaking it in two. Its flaming stern, heavy with two 350-horsepower motors, landed on the yellow boat next to it. There was a brief pause, perhaps three seconds, and then the yellow boat exploded as well.

" 'Bout time. And a twofer at that," Eric exclaimed proudly, feeling vindicated. He tossed the empty launcher into the sea.

"Let's get out of here," Billy ordered.

Joaquin Garavito had entered the hacienda as David and Billy ran to the marina. He stood in the archway listening for sounds of life, but heard none. Picking up an AK47 from a dead soldier, he stepped quickly and silently up the stairs and made his way cautiously to Belalcazar's bedroom, where he thought he had heard the most recent shooting. He entered the bedroom, ready to shoot, but found only dead men.

He stared first at Emilio, feeling some pity for him, a good soldier who died with his *patrón*. Then he turned his attention to Belalcazar, still seated on the nightstand, a death mask on his face. Joaquin walked over to the fallen leader and, with a poke from the barrel of his AK47, knocked the corpse to the floor. He had only contempt for Belalcazar and the obsession that had nearly brought the empire to ruin. Now that *he* was the *patrón*, this bedroom, the hacienda, the drug operations, the casinos, and the other businesses were all his for the taking. Sure, he would be challenged by others eager to split the cartel, but he'd kill them, kidnap their loved ones, and do whatever else it took to consolidate his power. He shouted for anyone left alive in the hacienda to report to him immediately.

In response to Joaquin's command, five guards, three of them still wet from swimming across the marina, assembled in the bedroom. Other than two maids, three cooks, and two gardeners who had hidden on the ground floor of the barracks during the battle, all those remaining alive on the island were now assembled before Joaquin Garavito. The soldiers coldly eyed Belalcazar's body, lying disgraced on the floor.

Joaquin stepped out onto the small balcony to survey his new compound just in time to observe the Americans on the Sea Ray leave to the north, stop, and return, as if they had forgotten something. He soon discovered what the Americans had forgotten as the two cigarette boats exploded. Joaquin smiled, then laughed as the Sea Ray turned and headed to sea, grateful to the Americans for helping him formulate his plan.

Joaquin turned to the guards, singling out the three who were wet, indicating that they should approach him. His own clothing and hair were beginning to dry, as was the blood on the side of his head. He briefly studied the men, wondering if they had been on the south breakwater, whether they were the cowards who had left him to die to save their own skins. "The *Americanos* are trying to escape in the Sea Ray. Go to the shed and launch the *Pizzaro*. You've run it before. I know you can handle it and its machine gun. The *Americanos* are vulnerable now. The *Pizzaro* is faster than the Sea Ray, and the damn gringos have nothing that can match the M60," he said, dropping his voice for a moment. "Now, get your sorry asses back in the water and go kill them," he threatened with a gesture of his AK47. They were running for the shed before he could say another word.

"You," he said dismissively to one of the two remaining soldiers. "Get me a pair of binoculars. I want to watch this."

The morning sun shined brightly on the glittering sea. The long, high rollers continued on their north–south path as they had through the night. With one engine out, and five children and one seriously wounded man on board, Frank took it easy, going no more than 20 mph, surfing down the waves diagonally to keep the ride as smooth as possible. The mood on the vessel was one of unparalleled joy, adults hugging children, embracing each other.

"We could use some champagne," Eric announced.

"Do you have any?" David asked, surprised, his arms around Justin, who was resting on his lap.

"Of course. The bar's well stocked. The fridge has several bottles of well-chilled white wine and champagne. Lots of beer, if you want that," Eric responded.

"Well, I could go for some champagne," Billy admitted.

"Airborne," Frank said enthusiastically.

"All the way," Jenny answered with a smile and a crisp salute, drawing a laugh from the former Rangers on board.

Eric went below deck with Linda and resurfaced with two bottles of Dom Pérignon and several glasses. He leaned against the hatchway for support as the Sea Ray rolled with a wave, facing his companions in the large open cockpit, Isla Gorgona growing smaller in the distance. As he started to open one of the bottles, something in the distance caught his eye. He strained to see what it was, hoping that it was a reflection off the water. As Eric's expression turned from jubilant to somber, the others became alarmed and turned to see what was behind them. At first they saw nothing. As the Sea Ray surfed down a roller, the wave they had just crested blocked their view. At the same time the red-and-white cigarette boat, the *Pizzaro,* was also in the trough of a wave. Neither crew could see the other.

"What is it?" David asked Eric, concerned.

"Don't know," Eric said, making no effort to hide his alarm. He continued to gaze off the stern of the Sea Ray, squinting in the sunlight. Frank eased the throttle forward gently, increasing speed by another 5 mph. Whatever it was, it wouldn't hurt to put more distance between them.

The Sea Ray crested on a roller at the instant that the cigarette boat did the same a third of a mile behind them.

"Holy shit," Eric blurted out. "Did you see that?"

"Son of a bitch," Billy answered. "Where in the hell did it come from?"

"Maybe Buenaventura," Frank offered, pushing the accelerator down further.

"No. I don't think so," Billy said, suddenly realizing their mistake. "The shed—or garage—near the breakwater. Damn it." He was furious at himself for the oversight. First the helicopter, now this. *How could I have forgotten the shed?*

Billy would have been even more furious had he known right then what the shed concealed. At forty-five feet, the *Pizzaro* was almost 50 percent longer than the cigarette boats destroyed in the marina, and with four five-hundred-horsepower outboard motors, it was faster than the Sea Ray.

As he watched through the binoculars from the balcony, Joaquin was proud of the reinforced hull, special-ordered at his insistence to take the pounding of high-speed racing on heavy waves. In a light chop, the *Pizzaro* could go 90 mph. On the heavy rollers, it would be slowed to 50 mph, perhaps 45 mph.

"Jenny," David said, dread in his voice. "Get the children to the front of the boat, flat on the floor, as far to the front of the boat as you can."

The adults tossed their glasses and the bottles of champagne overboard and scrambled for weapons, back in full battle mode. "Daddy, what's happening?" Justin cried, frightened by David's expression.

"Justin. Go below with Jenny," David ordered.

"I wanna stay with you." He started to cry.

"They're gaining on us," Billy warned.

"Justin," David said firmly, "this is not the time to argue. Get below deck with Jenny *now*." He lifted Justin into Jenny's arms. "Jenny, come back up. We need you and Linda on deck. Anne and Stephanie will stay with the kids."

Jenny carried Justin below deck, colliding with Linda, who was coming up to find out what the commotion was about.

"We're being chased, and they're gaining on us. We have to get the kids forward, on the floor, flat," Jenny said as she motioned Linda out of the way.

"My God!" Linda cried, and immediately followed Jenny.

Anne, Stephanie, Linda, and Jenny guided the children to the stateroom in the bow of the Sea Ray and made them lie at the base of the bed. Anne and Stephanie stayed with them, placing themselves aft of the children as human shields against any bullets that might come from the rear. Linda and Jenny raced back on deck, Jenny toting her M16A2/M203, Linda carrying Matthew's rifle/grenade launcher in her right hand and her own M16 in her left hand. She handed Matthew's weapon to Eric, knowing that he'd know how to use it better than she.

The Sea Ray crested, but they couldn't see the red-and-white *Pizarro*. They rose to the top of the next wave and caught a glimpse of the boat as it disappeared into a trough. The smaller, faster vessel was getting closer. Again the Sea Ray crested, this time in sync with its pursuer, and was strafed by the M60 machine gun. Frank was thrown against the instrument panel as he was hit, a bullet entering his left shoulder from the back and exiting his chest just under the collarbone, plowing into the instrument panel. David was grazed on the left hip, the impact strong enough to knock him down, but the wound was superficial. More rounds whizzed overhead. Yet others cracked into the overhead wind foil.

Wincing with pain and bleeding, Frank recovered

enough to hold the Sea Ray steady with his good arm as it surfed down the roller. The vessel crested and everyone on deck braced themselves for another strafing, but the *Pizarro* was in a trough and they were spared. Their situation was desperate. There was no way the Sea Ray, even operating with both engines, could outrun the swift cigarette boat. The pursuers also possessed a powerful machine gun. The superior firepower that the Americans had enjoyed during the battle on the island was now reversed.

A plan came to David instinctively, as the bayonet charge on Ripcord had more than thirty years earlier. He hadn't come this far to fail. *When faced with defeat and everything seems lost, attack.*

"Jenny, move the kids to the rear of the boat. Lay 'em flat in Matthew's room," he shouted. "Anne, find a life raft. If we go down, we'll put the kids in the raft."

"To the rear? Why would we . . . ?" Jenny began to ask, puzzled why they would move the children closer to the incoming machine gun fire.

"Bayonet charge," Billy and Eric interrupted in unison, realizing immediately what their former Ripcord commander was thinking. David nodded, and he, Billy, and Eric scrambled toward the gunwale, making their way along the sides of the vessel to reach the bow. The Rangers needed no explanation.

"Frank, you've got to hang on. Hold her steady in the trough. Don't crest if you can avoid it. On my command," David ordered. The determined expression on his injured friend's face told him that Frank was not about to give up.

Linda scrambled after Billy on the port side, holding on to the rail so as to avoid being tossed overboard. Below deck, Stephanie hurried with the children toward the rear of the Sea Ray, pushing and shoving them desperately. Anne searched frantically for a life raft.

The Sea Ray surfed down the roller much as it had on many waves during the past few hours. But this time, rather than surf down an angle thirty degrees off a northerly course, Frank eased up on the throttle and pulled the wheel hard into the wave in an effort to stay on the roller longer. The Sea Ray was almost parallel to the wave, its course off due east by only ten degrees. The slender vessel pitched hard to port, nearly throwing Jenny and David into the water as they crawled along the port side toward the bow. David almost lost his weapon as he grabbed on to the pulpit railing. Yet the course change kept the Sea Ray on the roller longer.

The three soldiers in the *Pizzaro* were confused when they lost track of the Sea Ray. Based on the pattern that was establishing itself, they figured that the Sea Ray would crest in sync with their boat every third or fourth wave. Five waves had gone by with no sign of the vessel. The Sea Ray was due to crest. When it did, they planned to finish it off and sink the troublesome children with it.

When Frank could no longer surf the wave and they were about to be swept sideways, he turned the Sea Ray into the roller and gunned the engine. The bow hit the crest and rose out of the water several feet, the wave rolling underneath the boat. The Sea Ray crashed hard on its hull and plowed into the next wave, the water rushing over the bow, almost washing everyone on the bow overboard. They held on to the railing, trying to find the cigarette boat as they crested the next wave, but not finding it. They picked up speed as the powerful diesel propelled the Sea Ray forward. The hull pounded on the water once more. Still, there was no sign of the cigarette boat.

Again they rose, and there it was. Linda was first to fire with her M16. She had no grenade launcher, so she fired three-round bursts as rapidly as the weapon would permit.

"Fire," roared David. He squeezed the trigger of the grenade launcher and was rewarded with the now-familiar thump.

Thump . . . thump . . . thump . . . Jenny, Billy, and Eric followed. They struggled to reload, sliding on the wet bow, grabbing for railings.

The Sea Ray crested, and again its hull rose out of the water and crashed violently. It cascaded down the roller and up the side of the next oncoming wave, making its way closer to the enemy, closer to the lethal M60 machine gun.

To the surprise of the crew on the Sea Ray, there was no incoming fire from the *Pizzaro*. The M60 was silent. Unbeknownst to the crew on the Sea Ray, the soldier who manned the machine gun was dead from the impact of a grenade that had grazed the side of the swift vessel and exploded. The soldier who had been working the gas gauges was pulling him away from the M60 over which he had slumped. The vessel was designed to be operated by three men, one to handle the wheel, one to control speed, and one to fire the weapon. The soldier who had operated the throttles was now struggling to work the M60, leaving the accelerator and the wheel to the driver. Both men cursed Joaquin for not giving them a fourth man.

"Fire," David yelled, but Billy had already fired. *Thump.*

Thump . . . thump . . . thump.

The Sea Ray crested again, pounding hard down the next wave. It rose high above the next roller, the bow suspended ten feet above the water, the five desperate people on its bow struggling to hold on and straining to see the cigarette boat. Their efforts were not in vain. As they watched, one of the grenades found its target. The cigarette boat exploded in a fireball, sending pieces of the vessel high into the air and then to the bottom of the sea, along with the remains of the three ill-fated soldiers.

Chapter 31

They reached the outer edge of the Gulf of Panama twelve hours later, Anne at the helm. Frank was below deck, like Matthew, in a morphine-induced sleep, checked on by their friends every few minutes. A half moon lit the evening sky between increasingly thick clouds. Wounds had been treated as best they could. The children had been fed, until seasickness proved that to be a bad idea. Those adults who could sleep, had, after a champagne toast to make up for the one that had been interrupted earlier.

Knowing their phone calls would be detected, alerting the FBI and the Panamanian National Police, they decided to place the calls they needed to make from the vessel's phone. First, a coded message to Happy Jack: "Grand Slam. Head home." Then Billy phoned Faith. Her cry of joy could be heard ten feet from the phone. The NSA's listening devices placed the vessel approximately sixty miles south-southeast of Panama City, and they passed that information on to the FBI.

David then made one final call.

"United States Embassy," the polite receptionist answered and then repeated in Spanish.

"I would like to talk to the FBI liaison office in Panama City. Can you give me the phone number?"

"I'll transfer you. One moment please."

"FBI. How may I help you?" yet another well-mannered clerk offered after a brief pause.

"My name is David Craig. I'd like to talk to your person in charge about surrendering. I and some of my colleagues are wanted for crimes that we did not commit, but we want to surrender and clean the slate."

"Excuse me?" the stunned clerk blurted out. "Who is this?"

"David Craig from New York. I'm on a boat approaching Panama City and I want to surrender to the FBI."

"Hold one moment, please." David heard an incredulous "Holy shit" as the man reached for the hold button.

"Who do I have the pleasure of talking to?" the agent on duty asked.

"This is David Craig. I am—was—an investment banker in New York. My son was kidnapped—"

"I know who you are, Mr. Craig," the agent interrupted. "We've been looking for you."

"I know. You don't need to look any further. We're going to head into the entrance of the Canal. The nautical charts that we have on board indicate that there are piers for smaller vessels off to our right just after we pass La Boca, but before we get to Puerto Balboa and the Canal itself. Unless we're delayed by vessels in front of us, we'll arrive at approximately zero-nine-thirty hours today. We will surrender peacefully. Every person on the vessel will be on the deck, including the kidnapped children we rescued in Colombia. We will be unarmed. Every weapon on board will be disassembled and taped to the foredeck in open view. We also have some information that we believe you will find very valuable."

"And what is this information that you think we'll find valuable?"

"I'll tell you that when we meet personally. And one other thing. We're alerting the local press, MSNBC, and CNN. They'll be watching us as we enter the port. If your men try to kill us like they did in the restaurant in New York, the whole world will see it."

Postcombat exhaustion hung over the vessel. Its crew had come far. Risked everything. Lost Sid and Pablo.

Matthew's leg was almost certainly inoperable; Frank was seriously wounded. Linda, David, and Jenny had suffered minor wounds. Everyone ached. Like the former Rangers' return from Vietnam, they weren't returning to a hero's welcome. There'd be no parades down the Canyon of Heroes. No accolades on the Senate floor. They were returning to prosecutors, ruined careers, unseen enemies. But they were returning with the greatest of all prizes.

Jenny and David sat on a comfortable seat near the engine cover, Justin asleep on David's lap under a blanket, his legs resting on Jenny. David gently ran his hand through Justin's hair as he stretched out his right leg on the bench to ease the pain in his hip. Each sipped a glass of very good California chardonnay, compliments of the late Belalcazar. Linda and Eric sat together, holding each other, each cradling a glass of wine in their free hands, Debbie asleep on Linda's lap. Billy sat to the side, pondering his and his friends' fate. Anne and Lisa slept together in the stateroom. Stephanie Wagner watched over the two boys.

Billy waited for a break in the conversation, not wanting to change the mood with topics more somber. After a few minutes there was an opening, a comfortable silence in which everyone seemed to be at ease in his own thoughts. "Eric," he said carefully, as if to ask permission to intrude.

"Yes."

"I hate to bring this up, but I've gotta ask you something." Billy paused tentatively.

"Go ahead," Eric encouraged.

"At the swimming pool. You recognized one of the bad guys. Didn't you?"

"Yeah," Eric said heavily. "I was waiting to tell you. Now's as good a time as any. He was CIA. Gerald Warren. Deputy Director for Operations, the DDO."

"The Deputy Director for Opearations of the CIA?" Jenny asked, astounded.

"Yeah . . . my direct boss," Eric added. The cockpit was quiet for several moments.

"So there it is. Belalcazar had friends—no doubt on the take—high up in the CIA. Where else?" David said more than asked, his eyes fixed on the half moon hanging in the night sky.

"We can be sure there are others," Billy ventured. Everyone on deck nodded and was silent. The only sounds were that of the motor, pushing them closer and closer to Panama and their fate, and the sound of the hull slapping the increasingly rough surf over and over again.

"So we made some very powerful enemies," Jenny added after a while.

"And so have they," David added slowly, his eyes turning to his companions.

"And so have they," Billy repeated for himself and the others.

"Do you think they have enough men?" Eric deadpanned to the others on deck. "Sorta gives the 'overwhelming force' doctrine a different twist."

"Well, we did take out Belalcazar's entire security force," Billy said as he watched the Panamanian and American helicopters circle overhead. The Sea Ray approached the docks, Anne skillfully steering toward a vacant pier. Snipers hung from helicopters and perched on rooftops nearby. Frogmen sat on the skids of the choppers, ready to drop into the water in case one of the fugitives were to make a swim for it. More than twenty Panamanian soldiers lined the docks, each heavily armed with assault rifles and an assortment of machine pistols. Two teams of machine gunners were ensconced behind makeshift sandbag revetments on the wharf, M60 machine gun barrels poking out ominously. As they approached, David noted a CNN vehicle, its camera crew on top. A rival MSNBC van and crew were also present.

"Put your hands in the air," the loudspeaker blared from one of the helicopters. "This is the FBI and the Panamanian National Police."

"Do as he says," David urged the others on the vessel.

"Everyone will raise their hands, except Anne, the lady at the helm," David said, speaking on the ship's cell phone to the FBI agent, hoping that his efforts to stay calm would encourage the FBI to do the same. "I'll keep my phone to my ear so I can stay on the line. As you can see, we're traveling with the children," David told the agent. "Any gunfire on your part will endanger them. I assure you that all weapons on the vessel are on the foredeck for you to see."

"I can see them," the agent observed from the wharf where he stood. "Looks like you had an arsenal. And, Mr. Craig, we don't shoot children. But one false move and your head will be removed. We have snipers focused directly on your forehead."

"Would you get one of the techies to come in for a moment?" a perplexed attorney general of the United States asked her secretary. "There's something strange on my monitor and I can't get it off."

Within minutes a computer specialist was at work on the AG's keyboard. "Well, ma'am, the people who sent this to you by e-mail must've figured out some way to make it your screen saver. It should be easy enough to remove." The techie reread the e-mail, no less amazed at its explosive contents than he was when he had first read it. He clicked through a series of screens on the attorney general's computer, found what he thought he was looking for, clicked again, and waited. The message remained. "Geez, whoever they are, it looks like they really wanted you to read this."

"I've read it, believe me. I'm not so much concerned about removing it as I am with finding out who sent it. Can we do that?"

"Unlikely, ma'am. Very unlikely."

"Please get me the director of the FBI. I need to see him immediately," the attorney general instructed her assistant as the technician gathered his things and began to leave.

"That's funny," the secretary responded. "He's on the

other line. He's in his car coming over to see you now. He says he must see you urgently."

Fifteen minutes later, the director of the FBI, the commissioner of the NYPD, and Capt. Ferraro finished their briefing.

"So add this to your growing pile of evidence," the attorney general said as she handed the printed e-mail message to the director. "I received it this morning."

"Holy shit," Angelo Ferraro exclaimed as he read the e-mail message. " 'Scuze me, ma'am. Didn't mean to say it out loud."

"Don't worry." She smiled. "Those are the exact words I used when I first read it. If whoever sent this is right, McCormick is not only taking money from a drug cartel, he is implicated in the deaths of a lot of people."

"We'll bring him in and squeeze him," the director said firmly, just as the attorney general's assistant handed him an urgent message. "Christ in heaven!" he shouted. "Craig and his friends, and the children, are heading into Balboa, Panama, now, and we've got an army down there ready to shoot them. Get me the FBI liaison office in Panama City," he said to the assistant. "Now, please."

"Tell them I want to talk to them this instant," the AG added as her assistant hesitated.

The head of the FBI's liaison office in Balboa, a young man assigned to a remote and usually unimportant post, was on the dock like all the agents assigned to Panama, as well as those agents flown in during the night. Amid the excitement, he almost didn't feel his cell phone vibrate against his waist. When he felt it, his first inclination was to ignore it, wondering what on earth could possess his secretary to bother him just as the Sea Ray, only 150 yards away, was approaching the dock. Repressing an urge, he shifted his service automatic from his right hand to his left and removed the cell phone from its holster. "Brammer, here. This had better be good," he added in an annoyed tone.

"This is the director of the FBI, Brammer. Repeat, I am the director. Is Rakovic there?"

"Yes, sir," the surprised young man answered, not sure if this was a hoax or something serious.

"Hand this phone to him now."

Brammer hurried over to Rakovic, who stood on the edge of the pier, concentrating on the Sea Ray, eager to arrest the agent killers and their accomplices. "Mr. Rakovic, sir. It's the director himself. At least he says he is," he added, handing the cell phone to the senior agent and hoping he wasn't being made a fool of.

Rakovic stared at Brammer for a moment, then put the piece to his ear. "If this is a joke, it's piss-poor timing."

"This is no joke," the director snapped. "Listen to me and listen real good . . ."

Brammer saw Rakovic's jaw drop and his shoulders slump. Moments later, Rakovic muttered a humble "Yes, sir," and handed the phone back to Brammer. "Bring me that bullhorn over there," he ordered the liaison officer. "Make it fast."

Yelling into the loudspeaker, Rakovic ordered all agents on the dock to stand down, to keep their weapons at the ready but to no longer point them at the Sea Ray. He also requested that the Panamanian National Police do the same. The Sea Ray was now only a few feet from the dock. Billy and Linda were preparing to toss the lines to the Panamanian police waiting near the slip.

"Mr. Craig," Rakovic shouted into the bullhorn. "I have ordered my men to stand down. You, Mr. Rice, and your other colleagues are no longer suspects. It appears that there has been a terrible mistake."

". . . so there you have it, Mr. President," the attorney general reported at the end of the hastily called meeting.

"We arrested McCormick earlier this afternoon," the FBI director added.

The president turned his gaze away from the attorney general and toward his chief of staff, then to his senior political adviser and then to the White House spokesperson. "So we've got a travesty of justice, and a front-page, in-our-face scandal . . . on top of everything else. Corruption within the FBI, DEA, and CIA. Not just the goddamn Russians or Chinese and the usual payments for spying, but payoffs by a drug lord. Christ! A fucking drug lord!" he said between his teeth as he rose and walked over to the window. He stared at the Rose Garden for several moments. "Okay, General Roach. What does the army recommend that we do with General Dunn?" he asked, then turned to the others in the Oval Office.

"Well, Mr. President, sir. The first rule of a Ranger is to never, ever fail his fellow Rangers. We demand that they make great sacrifices—even the supreme sacrifice—for their fellow Rangers, and for the country. We train them to be bold leaders. I don't know of anyone in the army who measures up to the task better than Billy Dunn."

"All right," the president commanded after a moment's reflection. "Let's do the right thing by these men and women. Full amnesty. All charges dropped. And let's put the right spin on this before the press eats us alive. We've purged the bad guys from our ranks, quickly and decisively. Craig, Dunn, and the others are American heroes."

Chapter 32

David glanced at Jenny, then at Billy, when Matthew arrived, surprised by Matthew's agility with his prosthesis as he made his way up the steps of the reviewing stand, but not at all surprised that he was with a beautiful woman, perhaps in her mid-thirties, arm in arm. It turned out she was his physical therapist, which gave them all a laugh.

Anne and Lisa Waldron had arrived with Eric, Linda, and Debbie and taken their assigned seats. Frank Lopez was healing rapidly, his weathered face only slightly thinner. His wife and children accompanied him, enjoying their father's celebrity status. Happy Jack, Claudia, and Chris had also flown in for the occasion. Marvin Williams chatted with Jenny. They had never met before and they hit it off immediately. Raul Noriega whispered in his wife's ear, translating English to Spanish, explaining who the different people were.

Jonathan Bernstein did not attend. Jenny initially urged him to come forward with the others and share in their fame, but he resisted. His role as the superuser required that he remain anonymous, and, after much discussion, she agreed. She, in turn, repeatedly denied having anything to do with the bank transfers of David's funds or any other computer hacking. None of the FBI agents believed her, but they were totally stumped and couldn't prove her involvement.

Jenny sat in the reviewing stand next to David, Justin on her lap. Justin had finally gotten his ride in a tank, an old M551 Sheridan, the afternoon before, accompanied by Lisa, Debbie, and Command Sergeant Major Webster—

"Top" to Billy and his friends. Justin couldn't stop saying "awesome" at dinner the night before at the Officers' Club, and now he was whispering a request for another ride, just as the president was about to pin a third star on the new commanding officer of the XVIII Airborne Corps.

The entire 82nd Airborne Division, headquartered at Bragg, was present, except for those units in Yugoslavia on peacekeeping missions, and one battalion training in the Sinai. The 75th Ranger Battalion, USASOC, save a company training in the jungles of Costa Rica, were also standing at attention, along with smaller units representing the 3rd Infantry (Mech.), the 10th Mountain, and the 101st Air Assault divisions, as well as a number of tenant units that comprised the XVIII.

Top had been to many promotion and change-in-command ceremonies, but none held the electricity in the air that was present today. Almost eighteen thousand soldiers were assembled on the vast parade ground. Civilians would most likely not have noticed it, for the troops stood in perfect formation, at parade rest, their hands clasped behind them, feet apart. But Top saw the slight movement in the troops standing in front of him. Necks strained ever so slightly to see the heroes of Ripcord and Isla Gorgona, particularly their new CO.

The press maneuvered their cameras to film the heroes and snap their pictures. The president dropped his prepared speech on policy matters, and spoke about the general and his friends. ". . . and so we are gathered to honor the leadership and courage of Lieutenant General Dunn . . . to entrust in him command of the army's finest units . . . and we are also here to praise him for his sacrifice and courage as a friend . . . and to praise those before you who risked everything—and I do mean everything—to save their children.

"General Roach informs me," the president continued, "that the cardinal rule of a Ranger is to never, ever fail a fellow Ranger. Knowing the risks to his life and career that he took, and knowing what General Dunn accomplished on Isla Gorgona, I know—and you know—that he will never, ever fail any of you assembled on this great parade ground. Never."

Faith and all of Billy's friends radiated pride as Billy formally took command of the XVIII Airborne Corps. He stepped up to the microphone. "Soldiers of the Eighteenth Airborne Corps, stand at attention," he ordered, and was rewarded with the muffled thunderclap of the heels of sixteen thousand pairs of leather jump boots locking together. He snapped to attention and saluted his men and women. "Airborne," he said proudly.

The soldiers standing before him immediately saluted and roared in unison, "All the way, sir."

Later, after the president's motorcade departed, Billy and his friends went to the Officers' Club for a private party, attended by the commanding generals and colonels of the units of the XVIII, their respective sergeants major, and the officers of Headquarters Company who would comprise Billy's staff. After the formal toasts were made by the chief of staff and the division commanders, David suggested a toast for his friends. Those not involved in the raid on the island distanced themselves out of respect, allowing them some measure of privacy in the large ballroom.

As waiters served the champagne, the friends gathered closer together. The conversation drifted from Billy's triumph, to David and Jenny's impending wedding, and then to Eric and Linda's search for an apartment. David told his friends that Justin had taken to calling Jenny "Mommy." Everyone noted that Jenny beamed with a radiance that was luminescent. Not long into the conversation, Jenny and David pulled Eric aside and renewed their sales pitch to convince him to join their new investment banking firm. Linda took the opportunity to spend a few moments alone with Anne to see how she and Lisa were doing.

"Shit, what do I know about investment banking? The only thing I know is that you make a lot of money and spend all your time on airplanes and cell phones," Eric noted with a wicked smile. His friends could tell he was interested, and knew that he had resigned from the CIA and needed a job.

"So what do you say?" David persisted. "You'll make a lot of money."

"Yeah, that could work." Eric grinned.

"Gentlemen," Jenny said, smiling, "I'll put my time in until November and then I'm taking off a few months. I need a sabbatical. You guys can cover for me for a while."

"Sabbatical, my ass," David said in mock seriousness. "We've got a new business to get up and running, and I plan on talking to a good number of LKB clients who Rosa tells me were very unhappy about our sudden departure."

Billy motioned to Command Sergeant Major Webster, who quickly crossed the room. "Top, you should be part of this," Billy said, handing him a glass of champagne. "Afterward, could you take this young soldier on another tank ride?" Billy asked, knowing the answer.

"Yes, sir. My pleasure."

"But wait. What's this stuff about extended time off in November?" David asked.

"Oh, I took the test this morning," Jenny said, her emerald eyes locked on his blue ones. "I'm pregnant. Justin is going to be a big brother."

David stared at Jenny for a moment, hardly believing the good news possible, his eyes glistening. "Outstanding news." He hugged her and gave her a long kiss. "Let's tell Justin. And let's toast to that."

David raised his glass and the room became silent. No one moved. Even the waiters stopped what they were doing and turned to David. "A toast to Lieutenant General Dunn, the finest soldier I have ever met. To the most amazing group of friends that any man could ever dream of having. To Anne and Linda. To Sid and Pablo, who paid the supreme sacrifice. To Top, Marvin, and Raul for all their wonderful help. To Jenny . . . to Jenny . . . partner, lover, fellow soldier, soon to be my wife, a mother to my son . . . and"—he looked at Jenny, who nodded—"she says it's okay for me to tell you this . . . soon to be the mother of my second child." David beamed as he motioned to Justin to come to his side. "And most of all, to the children."

Acclaim for Larry Niven and Jerry Pournelle

and

THE BURNING CITY

"Pournelle and Niven provide a full quota of invention, speculation, and adventure. Their characters leap vibrantly off the page."

—*Realms of Fantasy*

"Another absorbing book from [Niven and Pournelle] . . . bodes well for yet more of the collaborations."

—*Booklist*

"Niven and Pournelle are in fine form. . . ."

—*Locus*

"Vivid and unusual."

—*Kirkus Reviews*

Larry Niven

TALES OF KNOWN SPACE
THE INTEGRAL TREES
WORLD OF PTAVVS
RINGWORLD
PROTECTOR
THE SMOKE RING
N-SPACE
PLAYGROUNDS OF THE MIND
CRASHLANDER
FLATLANDER
THE RINGWORLD THRONE
DESTINY'S ROAD
RAINBOW MARS

Jerry Pournelle

JANISSARIES
HIGH JUSTICE
KING DAVID'S SPACESHIP
EXILES TO GLORY
RED HEROIN
PRINCE OF MERCENARIES
FALKENBERG'S LEGION
STARSWARM

Larry Niven & Jerry Pournelle

INFERNO
OATH OF FEALTY
THE MOTE IN GOD'S EYE
LUCIFER'S HAMMER
FOOTFALL
THE GRIPPING HAND
THE BURNING CITY
BURNING TOWER

Larry Niven & Steven Barnes

DREAM PARK
THE BARSOOM PROJECT
THE CALIFORNIA VOODOO GAME
DESCENT OF ANANSI
ACHILLES' CHOICE
SATURN'S RACE

Larry Niven, Jerry Pournelle & Steven Barnes

LEGACY OF HEOROT
BEOWULF'S CHILDREN

Larry Niven, Jerry Pournelle & Michael Flynn

FALLEN ANGELS

Jerry Pournelle & Roland Green

TRAN

Jerry Pournelle & S. M. Stirling

GO TELL THE SPARTANS
PRINCE OF SPARTA

Jerry Pournelle & Charles Sheffield

HIGHER EDUCATION

BURNING TOWER

LARRY NIVEN

&

JERRY POURNELLE

POCKET BOOKS

New York London Toronto Sydney

POCKET BOOKS, a division of Simon & Schuster, Inc.
1230 Avenue of the Americas, New York, NY 10020

Originally published in hardcover in 2005 by Pocket Books

ISBN-13: 978-0-7434-1692-4
ISBN-10: 0-7434-1692-9

This Pocket Books paperback edition October 2006

10 9 8 7 6 5 4 3 2 1

Cover art by Paul Youll; design by John Vairo, Jr.

Manufactured in the United States of America

Maps by Paul Pugliese

For Roberta and Marilyn

Cast of Characters

Tep's Town Basin

Lord Regapisk: Sandry's cousin, assigned to Fire Watch
Lord Sandry: Chief of the Fire Watch
Peacevoice Fullerman: Lordsman assigned to Fire Watch
Yangin-Atep: the fire god, now gone mythical
Strafreerit: a Lordkin of Serpent's Walk
Wanshig: Lordkin chieftain, "Lord" of Serpent's Walk, and brother of Whandall Feathersnake
Lord Witness Qirama: a judge
Glegron: Lordkin Fireman killed by fire
Bonwess: Chieftain of the band of Lordkin called Bull Pizzles
Shanda: Sandry's aunt, First Lady of Lordshills
Roni: Shanda's daughter
Quintana: Lord Chief Witness of Lordshills, Lord's Town, and Tep's Town
Chalker: Sandry's valet, a retired Peacevoice of the Lordsmen
Younglord Maydreo: an officer cadet
Toronexti: a Lordkin band; formerly tax collectors
Bordermaster (once Master Peacevoice) Waterman: Lordsman
Dibantot: a Lordkin of Serpent's Walk, guardian of the Fire Sale Inn

LORDSMAN YILER: spearman
SECKLERS: a Lordkin of Serpent's Walk
EGMATEL THE SAGE: a Wizard hired by the Lords Witness
WALE: apprentice to the Sage Egmatel
LADY WHALANI: Lord Sandry's mother
HENRY: a Lordsman guard

Bison Tribe and the Wagon Train

BURNING TOWER OF BISON TRIBE: daughter of Whandall Feathersnake and Willow

GREEN STONE: wagonmaster of the lesser Feathersnake Bison Tribe wagon train; younger son of Whandall Feathersnake and Willow; Burning Tower's older brother

NOTHING WAS SEEN (LURK): a bandit's child now adopted into Bison Tribe and a scout in the Feathersnake wagon train

TWISTED CLOUD OF BISON TRIBE: wagon train shaman; daughter of Hickamore, deceased, once shaman of the Bison Tribe wagon train

CLEVER SQUIRREL (SQUIRRELY): daughter of Twisted Cloud and the god Coyote

MOUSE WARRIOR OF BISON TRIBE: A wagon train guard officer

WHANDALL FEATHERSNAKE: master trader; born a Lordkin in Tep's Town, now a merchant prince of Bison Tribe; owner of the wagon train

WILLOW FEATHERSNAKE: born a kinless of Tep's Town, now Whandall's wife and mother of Green Stone and Burning Tower

Avalon

WHEEREEZZ: a mer wizard schoolmaster
CONAL: a wizard of Avalon
MORTH OF ATLANTIS: Atlantean wizard; refugee, formerly of Tep's Town and now resident in Carlem Marcle, a sea town far north of Tep's Town
COYOTE: a god

The Wagon Expedition

TREBATY, a Lordkin of Serpent's Walk
SECKLERS, a Lordkin of Serpent's Walk
YOUNGLORD MAYDREO
YOUNGLORD WHANE
FALLEN WOLF: of Bison Tribe
LEFT-HANDED HUMMINGBIRD: a god
SPIKE: a one-horn born as a kinless pony

Condigeo

PERGAMMON: Commodore of Condigeo
GRANTON: First Captain of Condigeo
PEARL, wife of First Captain Granton
GRANDIN: wife of Captain Wartin
LORD WITNESS QU'YUMA: Lady Shanda's husband and Roni's father; ambassador from Lordshills to Condigeo
BETTING MASTER CALAFI: of Bell's of Condigeo

TRAS PREETROR: a teller; onetime friend of Whandall Feathersnake
ARSHUR THE MAGNIFICENT: a Northern Barbarian
SPOTTED LIZARD OF THE HIGH TRAIL: a guide
JUNIOR WARMAN GUNDRIN of the Condigeo Marines: an officer cadet
LORDSMAN BANE

The Angie Queen

SAZIFF: captain
THE OARMASTER
FETHIWONG and THE GHOST: oarsmen
RAILILIEE: first mate

Crescent City

ZEPHANS MISHAGNOS: an Atlantean wizard
BUZZARD AT PLAY: Mayor of Crescent City; onetime shaman of the Road Runner wagon train
FUR SLIPPER: a shaman
JADE COIN: a money changer
RUSER OF LOW STREET: a jeweler
ERN: Wagonmaster of the Road Runner wagon train
BLACK STONE: proprietor of Black Stone Inn
LAUGHING ROCK: his daughter

Sunfall Crater

GREAT MISTRESS HAZEL SKY: Governor
CAPTAIN SAREG: of the Imperial Guard
REGLY: Chief of the Office of Imperial Gifts
THUNDERCLOUD: Chief of the Office of Rain
JARAVISK: Chief Apprentice in the Office of Rain
MANROOT: an Imperial Officer

Aztlan

FLENSEVAN THE JEWELER: brother and partner of Ruser of Low Street

Archpriests:

COYOTE
ROAD RUNNER
JAGUAR
PRIEST MANY NAMES
LEFT-HANDED HUMMINGBIRD
BIGHORN SHEEP
BISON WOMAN
MAMMOTH
PRAIRIE DOG

THE EMPEROR: the Almighty one, Son of the Sun
LADY ANNALUN: a talented courtesan
MOUNTAIN CAT: of Bison Tribe (resident at New Castle, present by sand painting)
DOENTIVAR: the Grandson of the Sun, heir to the Emperor

PINK RABBIT: son of Flensevan
EGRET: the stronger son of Flensevan

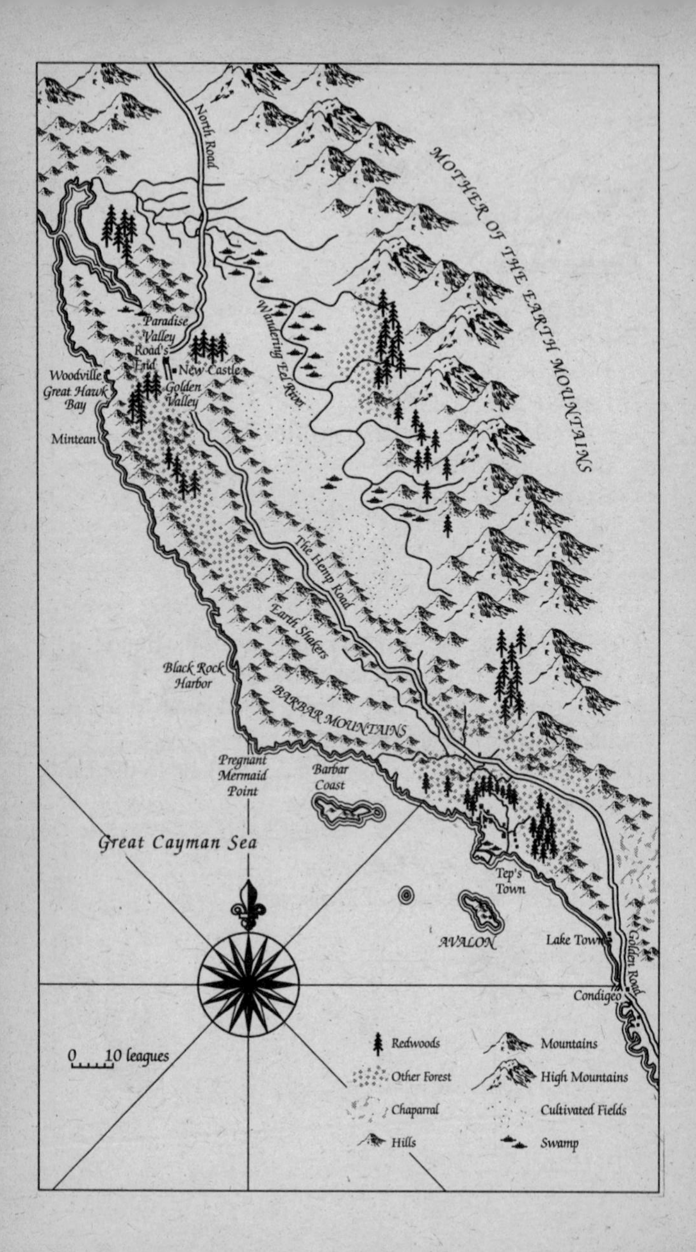
North Road
MOTHER OF THE EARTH MOUNTAINS
Paradise Valley
Road's End
New Castle
Woodville
Great Hawk Bay
Golden Valley
Wandering Eel River
Mintean
The Hemp Road
Earth Shakers
Black Rock Harbor
BARBAR MOUNTAINS
Pregnant Mermaid Point
Barbar Coast
Great Cayman Sea
Tep's Town
AVALON
Lake Town
Golden Road
Condigeo
0 10 leagues
Redwoods
Mountains
Other Forest
High Mountains
Chaparral
Cultivated Fields
Hills
Swamp

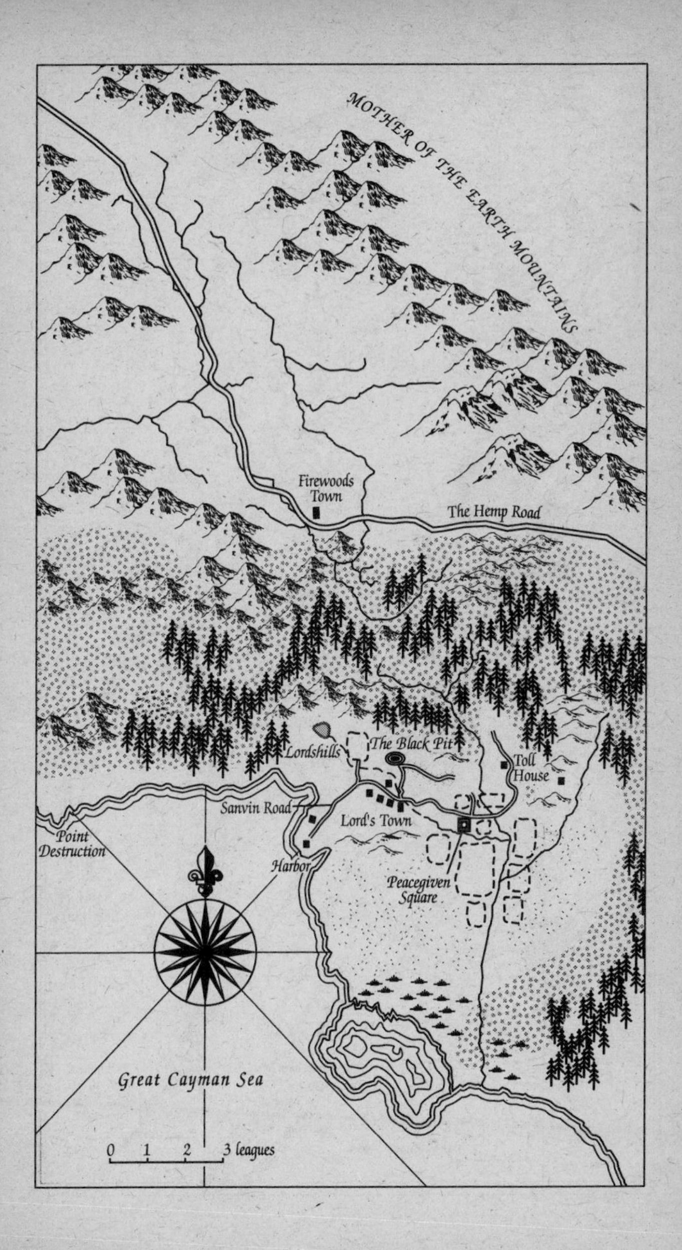
MOTHER OF THE EARTH MOUNTAINS
Firewoods Town
The Hemp Road
The Black Pit
Lordshills
Toll House
Sanvin Road
Lord's Town
Point Destruction
Harbor
Peacegiven Square
Great Cayman Sea
0 1 2 3 leagues

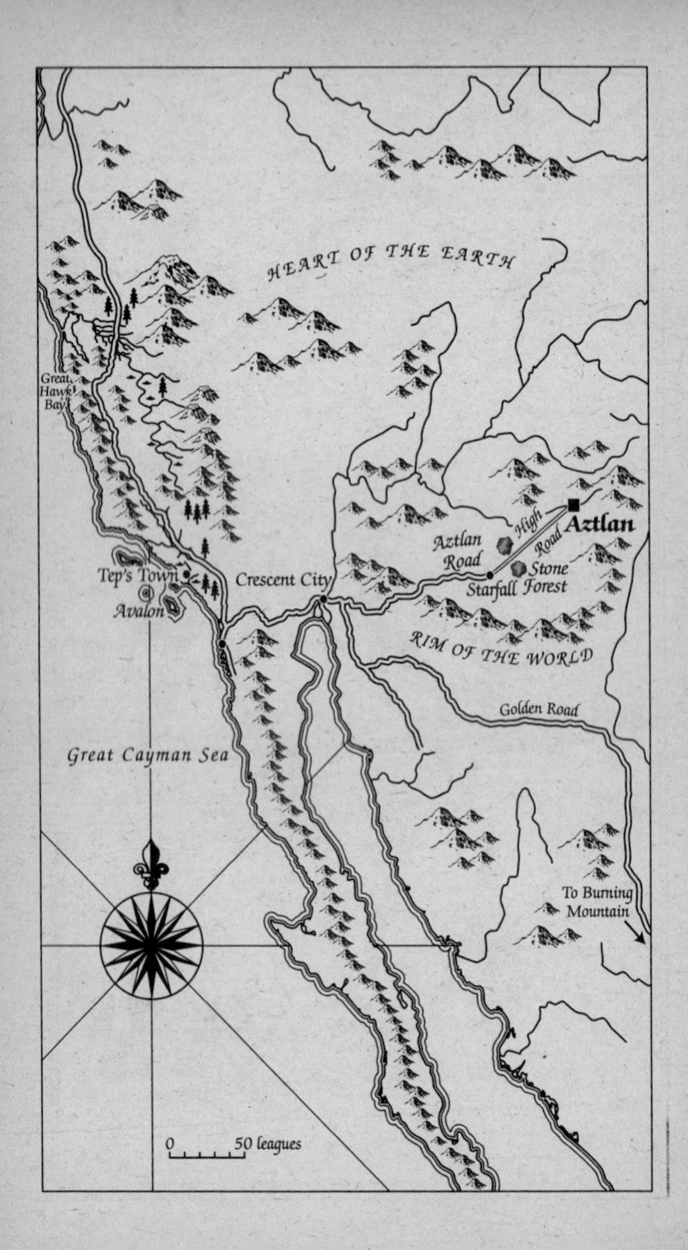
HEART OF THE EARTH
Great Hawk Bay
Aztlan
High Road
Aztlan Road
Stone
Starfall Forest
Tep's Town
Crescent City
Avalon
RIM OF THE WORLD
Golden Road
Great Cayman Sea
To Burning Mountain
0
50 leagues

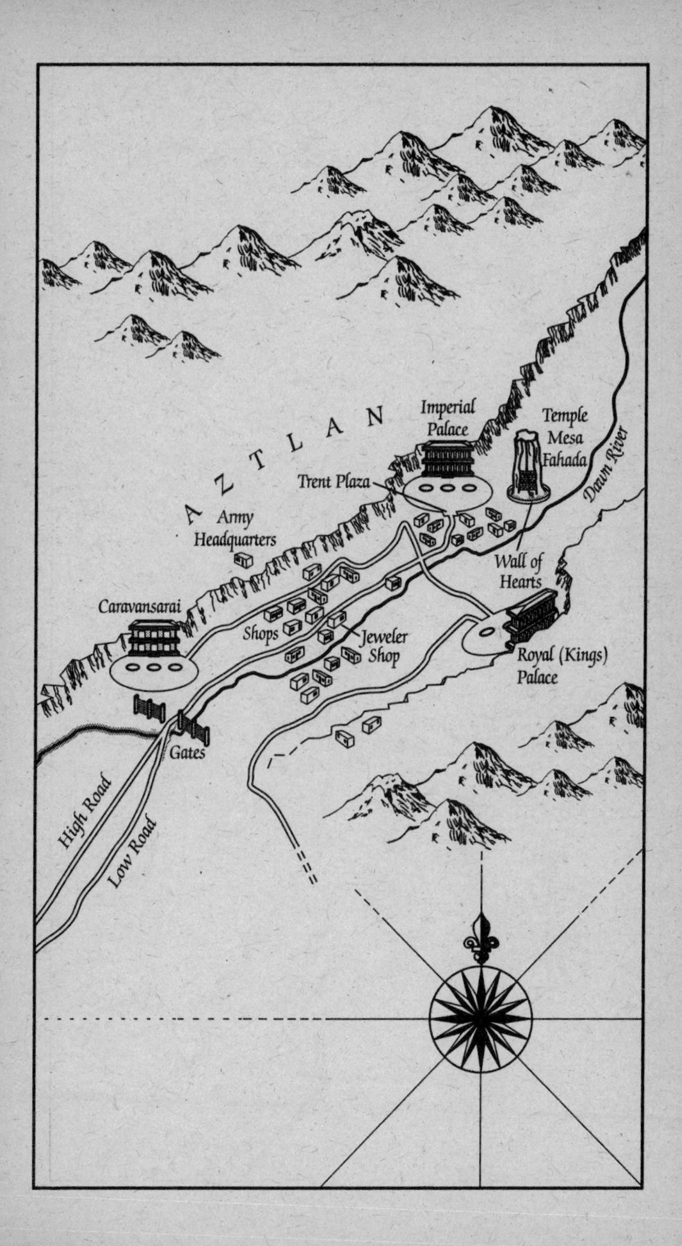
AZTLAN
Imperial Palace
Temple Mesa Fahada
Dawn River
Trent Plaza
Army Headquarters
Wall of Hearts
Caravansarai
Shops
Jeweler Shop
Royal (Kings) Palace
Gates
High Road
Low Road

BOOK ONE

TERROR BIRDS

Chapter One

Devil Wind

The hot wind was rising. Kinless called it a Devil Wind. Lord Regapisk had his doubts about devils, but any devil might have invented that wind. It was hot and dry and gusty and it was whipping fire into a frenzy. A dozen houses had already burned. They were only Bull Pizzle houses, not in the territory Regapisk was guarding, so they weren't his business. Five houses on the other side of the Darkman's Cup gorge were part of Serpent's Walk, but there was no way to save them. Regapisk's Firemen had tried, but no one would blame him for losing those houses.

They'd been able to loot the occupied houses before the fire got them. *Gather,* Regapisk thought, grinning. His Lordkin Firemen would call that "gathering." And if the Lords' Council asked him, Regapisk would say "salvage," but it was looting all the same.

Lord Regapisk coughed. The smoke was blowing across the canyon, thicker now, and the wind grew hotter. The fire was coming.

A chariot clattered up the road along the edge of the canyon. Regapisk turned with what he hoped was well disguised contempt. It wasn't that he didn't like his second cousin. Sandry was a likable boy. But he was younger than Regapisk, so recently a Younglord that he still answered to the lesser title, and yet he was put in charge here, while Lord Regapisk, fully a Lord for three years now, was assisting his young cousin.

He got lucky, Regapisk thought. *I was busy at the Harbor when the Congregation of Lords Witness decided to organize these Lordkin as Firemen. Cousin Sandry was available and I had other work.* One day it would be different; the Council would put Lord Regapisk in charge of all the fire brigades. Until then, Lord Regapisk nominally worked for his younger cousin—

"Hail, Cousin."

"Hail, Lord Regapisk," Sandry said formally.

His cousin always did that, used formal titles, when their Lordkin Firemen were around. Sometimes it drove Regapisk to distraction. What was the need for all that? But you had to admit, Sandry made a handsome figure, standing tall in his chariot, the reins held so loosely that it looked as if Sandry could guide the big horses by talking to them. Whatever else you thought about Lord Sandry, he knew horses. Loved them more than he did people.

The chariot was one of the larger war chariots, with room for two spearmen and the driver. It held only Sandry and a small kinless boy.

"Hail, Firemen," Sandry said. He waved to the four Lordkin who worked with Regapisk. The Firemen got to their feet and acknowledged Sandry's greeting with waves and a few muttered words. Sandry was popular with the Lordkin Firemen of Serpent's Walk, and this was wild enthusiasm compared with the way Lordkin usually acted around someone they worked for.

With, Lord Regapisk reminded himself. Lordkin worked *with* you. Even though both you and they knew that they were working for you. Lord Regapisk could understand that.

"I see we lost the houses on the other side of the Cup," Sandry said. "Too bad the wind came up like that."

"Yeah, we tried, but there just wasn't any way," Regapisk said.

Sandry nodded. "No use crying about it. But we have to stop the fire here," he said. "At this gorge, before the wind whips up and drives it across this road. We need a firebreak just here, and I can't spare you any more men." Sandry dismounted and looked across the canyon to the wall of flames. The wind was blowing it toward them, along with smoke and hot ashes. The fire hadn't gone down into the canyon yet, but that was a matter of minutes.

Lord Regapisk knew what a firebreak was. Peacevoice Fullerman had explained it when the Council put Regapisk into the fire brigade. It was one of the things fire brigade officers had to learn. "Won't have time with just four men," Regapisk said. He pointed to the rising flames. "Once it gets down into the canyon, it will be up here in moments."

Lord Sandry nodded. "I know, Lord Regapisk. We'll use a backfire."

Regapisk frowned. "You sure about that?"

"It's chancy, but it's the only thing we can do." Sandry inspected the gorge, then stooped down and picked up a handful of dust. He released the dust and watched it blow. "With this wind, I'd say about four paces, wouldn't you?"

"Four paces," Regapisk said. "Sounds about right."

"Good. Get torches and go four paces down the canyon. Light fires. When the fire burns here to the road, get through the ashes and go four more paces down and do it again. I doubt you'll have time to do it again after that, but if you can, do four more paces. I'm pretty sure an eight-pace firebreak will stop that fire, and I know a twelve-pace break will do it."

"Yeah, twelve paces will do it," Regapisk said. He looked down into the canyon, then across. The fire would start down into the canyon pretty soon. "This is going to be tricky—"

"Yes, so get started now. You understand—four paces, set fires and let it burn off, then four more. Start the second fire as soon as the first one burns off. And be careful; you don't want to get trapped between fires. Right?"

"Right."

"Good. I have to go. We've got more fires to the south. They'll be harder to stop because there's nothing like the canyon there. We're tearing down houses to build a firebreak. After this fire season, we're going to have to plan more firebreaks—"

"Sure."

"Good luck, then," Sandry said. He leaped into the

chariot and twitched the reins in one motion. The horses turned sharp left, turning the chariot around in its track on the road. "Git," Sandry said. The chariot clattered off, the kinless apprentice boy hanging on for life, but Sandry stood balanced in the chariot, just swaying with its motion.

He sure can drive, Lord Regapisk thought. He looked up. The fire was already closer to the canyon lip.

This was how the land lay:

Fire held the valley. The wind was blowing the fire uphill toward this road. The road was wide; it must have been a mammoth trail once. If the fire jumped the road, it might take a hundred houses before it burned out.

A year ago, fire would not burn indoors. An adobe exterior wouldn't burn either, then or now. Fighting a fire was easier when houses wouldn't burn.

But the fire god was dead, was myth, for most of a year now. Lord Regapisk felt he understood fire, fire under the new rules.

"Let's do it," Lord Regapisk said.

Lordkin Strafreerit asked, "Why do twice the work? Lord, let's just go eight paces down and light it off there."

Lord Regapisk thought about it. Later he remembered the way the other three were grinning. Now he didn't notice. "Good," he said.

Strafreerit measured off eight paces . . . odd paces, stepping long here, shorter here. What was he doing? He'd picked his place and was making his paces match, Lord Regapisk thought, but he didn't quite have the nerve to speak.

They spread out in a line through the brush. All together, they set off the fires, then stepped back in case the wind changed. But the wind held steady; the fire leaped upward in a great roar. Lord Regapisk waited until the flames died down and then followed the fire up the hill, stepping over the still-burning roots. The stalks and dried grass burned hot, but they burned out quickly—

The fire had jumped the road. Brush was burning on the other side.

Lord Regapisk yelled. "Help! It's jumped the gap!" He whirled off his cloak and began beating at the flames. Only when he'd clearly lost the battle did he wonder why he had no help.

Then he looked down across a ten-pace gap of black ash and saw his four Lordkin searching where the brush had burned away. They barely looked up at his yells. Then fire swept around them, and *that* got their attention. They ran.

Four houses were burning now. The fifth and sixth were just catching. Where was that misbegotten Lord? Regapisk was supposed to have backfired to make a firebreak! Sandry, moving at a careful run with a bucket in both arms, looked about him through smoke and red-and-yellow light.

Wanshig's Lordkin Firemen ran with buckets, splashing water all over themselves. One was caught in a sudden gust of flame; he doused himself with the bucket and ran with it still on his head. *Good move,* Sandry thought. Wanshig was yelling his head off. A few did hear: they converged on the eighth house and hurled their half-bucketsful at the roof.

No sign of Lord Regapisk.

He was torn between rage and fear for the do-nothing Lord and his men. Fire can sweep around and have you surrounded. Fire can take your mind. Fire can burn indoors—

But men did not obey Regapisk. If it was a talent, Regapisk didn't have it. Or it might be that the Lord expected too little of himself, and men saw that.

The wizard Morth of Atlantis had sunk Yangin-Atep the fire god into the tar. He was myth now, a myth that lived under the Black Pit: children were told to fear the fire god as well as the tar. You'd think Yangin-Atep's town would have fewer problems with fire!

And the Lordkin were holding it.

Take a moment, savor that: these were *Lordkin*. You couldn't make Lordkin work. They wouldn't be anywhere on time; they wouldn't get up if they were sleepy; wouldn't hoe grapes even to get wine, wouldn't carry anything but loot. But under attack, they'd be awake and sober in an instant.

Never mind that fire had been sacred to them once. Yangin-Atep's gift was that fires would not burn indoors. Now anything could burn, anytime.

Once thought, the logic was inescapable. Fighting a fire wasn't like farming or hauling or taking coins for goods and a smile, or any kind of mind-numbing kinless labor. Fire didn't keep regular hours. Firemen didn't take a salary; they took gifts from those whose houses they'd saved. Fire was an enemy worth facing. Saving a child from burning was a feat worth bragging about, and remembering in old age.

You could get Lordkin to fight a fire. You could even get Serpent's Walk Lordkin—Snakefeet—to fight fire in Grey Falcon—Dirty Bird—turf!

And Lordkin wouldn't kill Lordkin firefighters . . . unless in a turf war.

Of course these houses belonged to kinless. The eighth house belonged to Artisan, and he ran about screaming orders that didn't match Wanshig's until Wanshig's man clubbed him to the ground. Other kinless watched. Not all. Here came one running with a borrowed armful of empty buckets; maybe they'd make some progress now.

Sandry watched. The Lordkin were wasting effort, wearing themselves out where any officer could have steered them right. But they were learning, and they were winning. Eight houses were lost, collapsing in upon themselves, but the Snakefeet were containing the sparks.

A dozen stranger Lordkin ran in from under cover of the smoke. They threw rocks at Sandry's Firemen. Another band ran into a house and began carrying out goods. "I am possessed of Yangin-Atep!" one shouted. The others laughed. And more came out of the smoke. Some carried clubs. No knives were drawn yet, but any moment now . . .

This was the pity of it: Lordkin fighting a fire made a fine target for a rival band. There had never been anything stronger than truce between Serpent's Walk and Bull Pizzle, and usually there wasn't even that much peace. What would Wanshig do? Sandry raised a hand and waved, but nothing else. Wait for Wanshig. . . . Wanshig was the proud leader of Serpent's Walk—Lord of

Serpent's Walk in Lordkin parlance when the Lords weren't listening. He would accept help, but he'd never ask for it, and if help was offered when it wasn't needed, there could be trouble. Sandry hadn't been aware of all this when he took the assignment to build a Fire Brigade, but he'd learned.

And Wanshig was special. Wanshig was Burning Tower's uncle.

Burning Tower! He hadn't seen her in nearly a year, and still the memory was exciting. Long red-brown hair, deep brown eyes, slim legs dancing on a tightrope, perfect bare feet on the taut hemp line. She wasn't like any of the girls in Lordshills, not like any girl he'd ever known. And she would be coming back soon. . . . He shook his head. No time for this.

Wanshig threw his bucket and had his weapon in hand and was screaming warning as he leaped. A Pizzle ducked the bucket but not Wanshig's knife. Did Wanshig actually need help?

But when he counted thirty more Pizzles, Sandry knew this was a major raid, not just a group of Lordkin pretending this was a Burning, even though some carried torches and shouted of their possession by the fire god. The new chief of Bull Pizzle had to prove himself. This would be the way he did it.

Sandry frowned at the empty leather bow case on his chariot. He hadn't really expected to fight. There were two throwing spears in their larger quiver. *Have to do,* he thought. He raised both hands high in signal, then shouted: "The Fire Brigade is under the protection of the Lord's Witnesses! All not part of the Fire Brigade are ordered to leave this area immediately. This I command. I am Lord Sandry acting under the authority of Lord Chief Witness Quintana and the Lords of this city! Leave now or you will be killed."

Some of the Pizzles looked up, astonished, and a few turned to run. A dozen others, all shouting to Yangin-Atep, came on, throwing rocks and screaming challenges, and ten more moved into another house to gather.

"Peacevoice Tatters! Forward the guards!" Sandry commanded.

"Aye, My Lord!" The shout came from upwind. There was the clatter of hooves. Five chariots riding abreast came out of the smoke and fog. "Stand ready to throw! Throw!"

Spears arced from the chariots. They weren't throwing to kill, not yet, but two of the raiders went down. The others scattered.

Armored Lordsmen came from the shadows. Sandry smiled to himself. If those idiot Pizzles had thought to look, they'd have seen where Sandry kept his troopers, and they could have raided elsewhere. But would they? Or was there some crazy point of honor involved? Sandry didn't know. He knew more of the ways of the Lordkin than most Lords, but they were still a mystery. No one really understood the Lordkin.

The shouts of "Yangin-Atep" and "I am possessed!" quieted as the Pizzles realized they were trapped and defeated. For a moment Sandry thought of his options. If he killed them all, there would be trouble. Bull Pizzle wasn't as powerful as it used to be, but it was still large and powerful enough to challenge Serpent's Walk. A real war between Pizzles and Snakefeet would harm everyone. Most of his Fire Brigade would quit to go fight, and many of them would be killed, and he'd have to start all over again.

He raised his voice. "Evidently you did not hear! This area is under the protection of the Lord's Witnesses! I command you to leave this area at once. Do so now!"

The Pizzles looked at Sandry's men, then to Wanshig. Wanshig turned away contemptuously and began shouting orders to his Firemen. The bucket lines began to move again.

"Now, if you please!" Sandry shouted. "Troopers! Make ready!"

Spearmen in each chariot raised spears.

"Oh yeah, we didn't hear you before," a Pizzle shouted. "We're leaving!" They gathered their dead and wounded and left in a walk, their heads still high.

Sandry glanced over to Wanshig and got a grin. *Good,* Sandry thought. *Good.* Wanshig didn't really want a war either.

As the Pizzles were leaving, a chariot clattered out of the smoke from the north. Regapisk blocked the retreating Pizzles with his chariot. "Stand! You're taken!" he shouted. "Lord Sandry, I have them!"

There were three Snakefeet with Lord Regapisk, all clinging to his chariot, all looking blackened and the worse for wear. They'd been in smoke and ashes. And the Pizzles had dropped their dead, carefully set down their wounded. They hadn't drawn their knives. Not quite.

"Cancel that order!" Sandry shouted. "You are free to go. Now go! Lord Regapisk, a moment of your time, if you please . . ."

Chapter Two

Congregation of Witness

They had rebuilt the Registry Office on Peacegiven Square. The fountain in the center of the square gave out only a trickle of water, but it was working, and you couldn't see any grass growing up between the paving stones. There were two permanent market tents, each protected by an armed Lordkin who sat quietly without menacing the mostly kinless customers. Give it another year, and Peacegiven Square might be the center of town again, a neutral place for markets and trade and city administration. And that, Sandry thought, was all the doing of Whandall Feathersnake, master trader, Wagonmaster, a great man whose name and sign were known all along the Hemp Road—and once a Lordkin of Serpent's Walk. Brother of Wanshig. Burning Tower's father.

Inside was cool. They'd done a proper job of rebuilding the Registry Office. Light came from shafts built into the ceiling and reaching through the roof. The hearing room was paneled in redwood, with redwood benches, and a table for the Witnesses. When everyone was inside and seated, a clerk rapped on a connecting door.

Four Witnesses came out and sat in silence. They all wore their robes of office, and tight-fitting caps that hid their hair and ears so that it was impossible to know if they were Lordkin or kinless. A Witness Clerk came out with them. He concealed his ears too, but it was pretty obvious that he was kinless. The clerk looked around the room, then spoke loudly.

"We are ready. This Congregation of Witness is now in session. All those with matters of concern to the Lords Witness of this city draw nigh and you shall be heard! Lord Witness Qirama presiding. All stand."

Sandry was pleased to see that everyone did, without prodding. Lordkin were unpredictable. Qirama strode into the room at a dignified pace and took his place at the center of the big table.

Lord Witness Qirama was about ten years older than Sandry, a relative who as a Younglord had specialized in law rather than warfare or administration. He wore the cap of a Witness and also a hood, but it was clear enough that he was a Lord, neither Lordkin nor kinless. Sandry knew that two of the junior witnesses attending today were Younglords in training. Most Witnesses were kinless who handled routine business in the city, recording pacts between bandleaders and carrying decrees from Lordshills to the townspeople. Some Lordkin suspected this, but they could never be sure who the Witnesses were, and harming one was always sure death. The Younglords and hired Lordsmen saw to that.

A congregation of five Witnesses was unusual and showed this was an important session. Everything said would be attested to by all five, and no one would ever be able to dispute that record. *Get it right,* Sandry told himself. *Get it right.*

The clerk took a pose and spoke facing the crowd. "Lord Witness, we see Wanshig, Leader of Serpent's Walk, who approaches with a complaint for the Lords Witness. We see also Lords Regapisk and Sandry of Lordshills, who will speak to this matter. We see Bonwess, Chief of Bull Pizzles. Witnesses, the fees are paid."

All five Witnesses nodded. The clerk said, "Let Wanshig of Serpent's Walk come forward and speak."

Wanshig didn't look nervous. Most Lordkin put on a bluster when testifying to Witnesses. Most people in Tep's Town believed that Witnesses were wizards and had a way of knowing when you spoke truth and when you didn't—and that those caught in lies to Witnesses had a way of disappearing.

That last part was true enough. As a Younglord, Sandry had taken his turn in that duty, leading six Lordsmen to track down a Grey Falcon who had lied in an important matter. They'd sold the Dirty Bird to a ship owner, and if the man ever returned, he wasn't likely to say where he had been, for fear of being sent back.

"Lord Witness, I send this complaint to the Lords,"

Wanshig said clearly. "I say that the bad actions of Lord Regapisk have cost me one man dead, and two kinless, and four houses destroyed. I seek payment." Wanshig paused to allow the clerks to write what he had said. He'd been through this before.

Regapisk hadn't. He shouted, "Witness! This is not true."

Lord Witness Qirama regarded Regapisk coldly. "Lord, this is not a trial. We are here to take statements and record them. You will have your turn. Until then, you are requested to hold your peace."

Sandry shivered at the cold tones. If this story got back to the Council—*when* this story got back to the Council—cousin Regapisk was going to be in trouble, and there wasn't anything Sandry could do. He'd *had* to stop the man, stop him openly before two Lordkin bands, or face a war.

"Continue, Wanshig of Serpent's Walk," the Lord Witness said.

"Lord Witness, it was Lord Regapisk who allowed the fire to spread west of Darkman's Cup Canyon. It is there we lost four houses destroyed and three more damaged. Witnesses, you will hear statements from the kinless who lived in those houses, and the Lordkin who protected them, as to the value of those properties."

All five Witnesses nodded. "Say why you believe Lord Regapisk was responsible," Qirama said. "We understand there were Devil Winds that day, and many fires. Surely not all of them were the responsibility of Lord Regapisk."

"No, Lord Witness, only this one," Wanshig said. "Lord Regapisk set that fire himself! We have those who saw him do it. And when the fire flashed up, Fireman Glegron was trapped between the fires Lord Regapisk set and the blaze coming across the canyon from the east. Fireman Glegron was burned to death. Fireman Strafreerit was injured."

"Who saw Lord Regapisk set those fires?"

"Fireman Strafreerit, Witness. He and his brothers set torch to the chaparral on the orders of Lord Regapisk." The clerks scribbled madly.

"Lord Regapisk, do you dispute this?" the Lord Witness asked.

"Witnesses, I say only truth: I set the fire on orders from Lord Sandry, who was in charge!"

Now it was Sandry's turn to be regarded with that cold stare from under the black skullcap and hood. It was disconcerting. Of course it was supposed to be.

"Lord Witness, I ordered Lord Regapisk to set a backfire."

"Explain *backfire.*"

This had best be very clear, Sandry thought. "Witnesses, to prevent fires from spreading, you must have a firebreak, a line where nothing will burn, wide enough that flames cannot jump across it. The road along the west rim of Darkman's Cup Canyon is eleven paces wide. This is not enough to stop a large fire coming up the canyon, but if the fire could be slowed below the canyon rim, it might be. If we had twelve paces of cleared land below that canyon rim, the fire could not cross it. Even eight paces would very likely be enough in the wind I observed."

"You observed that wind yourself?"

"Yes, Lord," Sandry answered.

"And you base your opinion that eight paces cleared plus the road would be enough on your own expertise?"

"Yes, Lord Witness."

"Let the records show that Lord Sandry has been chief of the Fire Brigade from shortly after the end of the Time of Yangin-Atep, and no other has a claim to more expertise," Qirama intoned.

Aha, Sandry thought, and breathed easier. "Lord Regapisk had only four men, and I had no more to assign to him, so there would never have been time to clear that brush, to chop it and haul it away, for eight paces down or even four.

"So I ordered Lord Regapisk to go down the canyon four paces and start fires that would burn up to the road."

"Four paces," the Witness said. "But you said that would not be enough."

"No, but it would be dangerous to go farther before starting the backfire," Sandry said. "Go farther, the fire burns hotter; it would be moving fast enough to jump across the road. Go four paces down, let the fire burn out, then four more and do it again. But Lord Regapisk set those fires at least ten paces from the road, not the four I ordered. The fire jumped the road."

"Who says this?" the Witness demanded.

"Strafreerit, Witnesses," Wanshig said. "He was there and he saw it."

Strafreerit's head, neck, and arms were covered with clean gray cloth. Wanshig might have overdone that, covered clean skin, but Sandry saw blisters clearly under the edges. Strafreerit had been glaring hate at Lord Regapisk.

He said, "We set the fires where Lord Regapisk told us to. The fire whirled up and caught us while we were still in the brush, held by the fire we'd set! We ran through it. I lived because I knew better than to breathe, but Glegron, he breathed fire."

Lord Regapisk looked as if he had swallowed a toad. "Strafreerit is the one who told me to start it farther down!" he blurted.

Everyone turned to look at him. *Now he's done it,* Sandry thought. . . .

The Lord Witness was startled, then gravely amused. "Lord, were you under this Lordkin's orders?"

As often before, Regapisk knew he was in trouble, he just didn't understand what the problem was. "But it made sense! We all knew there wasn't time to set fires twice. If we set the fires eight paces down, we'd get our backfire. *Maybe* it wouldn't jump the road. It was our best chance. As for Glegron and Strafreerit and the others, what were they doing still in the brush? They had time to get out! They had time to help *me*!"

It was never Reggy's fault. Sandry felt old rage closing off his throat. He would have helped Reggy if he could. But Reggy had lost control of his troops, his Lordkin, and he didn't seem to know he'd admitted it. He faced the cold eyes of the Witnesses and waited for a cue.

"Wanshig of Serpent's Walk, have you more testimony to be heard by this congregation?"

They listened to one of Wanshig's kinless, a woman now homeless with four children. Two less agile kinless children had died in the flames. They heard the Serpent's Walk Lordkin who lived among those kinless and enforced Wanshig's orders against gathering there. They heard Wanshig testify to the value of the artisans who lived in those houses and how he had pledged to protect them from fire and theft to the best of his ability.

Which he did, Sandry thought. *Even so, he'll have lost a little of his reputation over this. And reputation is everything to a Lordkin chief.*

They heard of the misunderstanding that led to a Bull Pizzle raid, and how the Pizzles had departed carrying their dead and wounded when they understood that the Lords were present and had granted protection. Qirama was skillful enough to get that and no more on record, but then Regapisk had to say something.

"Lord Sandry took my chariot!"

So that story came out. The Witnesses demanded of Sandry why he had taken Regapisk's chariot by force. Sandry had no choice: he called Bonwess, the Pizzle boss this past year, and the Pizzle raider who had called for retreat. Both testified that the truce was holding, the misunderstanding had been adequately explained, until Lord Regapisk charged into a situation he knew nothing of, armed with three burned and exhausted Serpent men, five burned-out torches, and an overly sharp spear.

The sun was set before the gathering broke up.

Chapter Three

Aunt Shanda

Sandry woke in his own bed in his own house in Lordshills. Since he had become chief of the Fire Brigade, he usually stayed in an inn off Peacegiven Square, but yesterday had exhausted him, and after the Congregation of the Witnesses he'd had his men hitch fresh horses to his chariot and he rode home to bathe and sleep and be pampered by the servants. . . .

The house was quiet, the only sounds some activities in the kitchen. Sandry's mother was feeling her age and seldom left her suite on the east side of the house. She liked watching the sun come up. Sandry always went in to see her when he was in the house. She always knew who he was, but he didn't think she knew very many of the others who visited her, even her old friends. She'd been that way since Sandry's father died in a raging fury over some mistakes by the gardeners. His father had always been that way, in a rage one moment and then calm the next. It was one reason Sandry had learned early on to stay calm.

But a year ago Father had screamed at the gardeners, looked surprised at something, and fallen over. The Lordshills wizard hadn't been able to revive him. Shortly after that, Sandry's mother began her rapid decline.

Sandry's rooms led directly out to the back courtyard and the fountains. He stripped and plunged into the pool. He swam ten laps with rapid strokes, then climbed out to do stretches and exercises. The new Lord's wizard Tasquatamee had a young wife, Hela, who delighted in torturing people with new ways to sit and stand and twist, but he always felt better for it when he was done.

He heard giggles. "You're good at that!"

He looked up to see his cousin Roni looking over the wall. Roni was fifteen—no, sixteen—years old. Her father was Mother's brother. The thoughts came automatically to Sandry and always had. Lords thought about families.

When he was first assigned to build the Fire Brigade, it had shocked Sandry to find that the Lordkin often didn't know who their fathers were and never talked about family relationships. Sandry knew the exact degree of relationship of everyone in Lordshills.

Roni and he were closely enough related that they could not marry without the consent of the Lord Chief Witness—and that permission would be granted in an instant if requested—and Roni knew that too. They'd talked about it when they were younger.

"Mother says you're to come to tea this afternoon," Roni said.

It wasn't surprising that her mother knew he was at home this morning. Aunt Shanda knew everything. Of course as titular First Lady of Lordshills she was supposed to know everything. And she'd always taken a special interest in Sandry.

Sandry waved and climbed onto the small tower he'd had built by the pool so that he could see over the Lordshills wall. From there he had a good view of Tep's Town. No smoke other than a few smudges from yesterday's fires. There was no Devil Wind today, and fog covered the western part of what used to be called the Valley of Smokes before it became Tep's Town.

"No fires," Sandry said. "No big wind, so Wanshig can handle anything. Tell Aunt Shanda I'll be pleased to join her for tea." He hated to think what might have happened if the Devil Wind had still been blowing. Aunt Shanda didn't like disobedience.

Tea was in the garden, so it was easy to be on time. When Roni was much younger, the gate between the two courtyards had been locked, but it hadn't been for nearly two years. That thought had excited Sandry up until a year ago. It was a clear invitation. Sleep with Roni (when she's of age, of course), marry quickly, and be heir to all of Aunt Shanda's considerable holdings. . . .

"You might say a few words before you wolf down everything in sight," Aunt Shanda said.

"Oh. Sorry. I didn't eat much yesterday, and I got home too late for a real dinner, and—"

"They're saying in the guardhall that you were a real hero," Roni said. She had the usual banter in her voice. Sandry didn't think she was in love with him—he was sure she was not in love with him—but she still acted possessively, teased him as a young wife might. *Practicing,* Sandry thought.

That had never bothered him until a year ago, when he had met Burning Tower.

"So what happened at Congregation that they got the Lord Chief Witness out of bed to read it?" Shanda asked.

Aha. Aunt Shanda never missed an opportunity to get him together with Cousin Roni, but she usually had other purposes in mind when she invited him to tea. So here was one thing she didn't know. Yet. Quintana would tell her in due time. And Aunt Shanda would be pleased if she already knew. . . .

"Regapisk mucked up bad," Sandry said bluntly.

"You sound irked."

"Yes, ma'am, irked I am," Sandry said. "Three dead. Twenty houses burned. *My* reputation that I don't quite have yet. Irked."

"What did he do?"

And now he had to explain firebreaks and backfires, and Aunt Shanda would look at Roni, and Roni would ask questions, until both women understood as much as he did about the subject. *Thorough, that's Aunt Shanda. Thorough. And she's damned well raised her daughter to be just like her.*

Marriage to a girl like that could be frightening, but

then all of the girls Sandry might marry seemed a bit intimidating. Burning Tower frightened him too, but she was *different*. . . .

"And now you know about backfires, because you asked all the right questions," Sandry said. "You don't even notice yourselves doing it, do you? But Reggy can't ever admit he doesn't know something—" *Worse than that,* Sandry thought. "Reggy always knows more about it than you do, even if he never heard of it before."

"So his men got caught in the fire," Shanda said. "But what were they doing down there in the ravine with a fire coming?"

"Darkman's Cup, Aunt Shanda," but she still didn't understand. "Last year, when Whandall Feathersnake and Morth of Atlantis made myth of Yangin-Atep," Sandry said, "they had to lure the water sprite up to the Black Pit. It was chasing Morth, to drown him, but it wasn't strong enough to get there, so they threw raw gold along its path to give it strength. It came up Darkman's Cup. The gold dust will still be down in there. Reggy's men burned off the brush so they could look for gold."

Roni frowned. "Why would gold still be in there?"

"Disputed territory," Sandry said. "Snakefeet think it's their turf; the Bull Pizzles claim it too. Going in there to hunt would start a war. Maybe that's what brought the Pizzle raiders this time, I don't know. But Reggy's men would know there might be gold down there, and here was their chance."

"So it's not Reggy's fault?"

Sandry was just too tired to watch his mouth. "It's every bit his fault. He's a Lord. If he can't control four

Lordkin, he's no business pretending he can. If he doesn't understand a firebreak or a backfire, he can ask me! I was right there! He faked it, and I was harried. . . . I'm sorry, Aunt. I should have caught it. I *know* the fool."

Aunt Shanda was looking grim. "We had to get him away from the docks," she said.

"Yeah, he spends a lot of time with the mers," Sandry said. He was bone tired, now that his hunger was abated. Reggy wasn't any of his favorite people; he only knew what he heard in casual conversation. "I thought he liked it there, but Reggy said he wanted to join the Firemen."

Shanda nodded, jaw set, eyes distant. Presently she said, "He's been going to the docks since he was ten, but now he's a Lord, he acts like he's in charge, anywhere he goes. He gives orders to the longshoremen and the Water Rats and even the crews in port. Well, he's a Lord! Sometimes they obey! Then the overseers and captains complain to us. The Lord Harbor Master had a word with Lord Quintana, you know." Aunt Shanda's voice deepened, and the consonants were a little sharper: " 'If I catch him down here again, I won't care if he is Lady Shanda's cousin. I weary of untangling lines he's fouled. Get him away from me, Quintana, or I swear I'll feed him to the crabs myself.' Quintana's a good mimic. Quintana talking to *me,* as if it were *my* fault. He wanted Reggy as far from the harbor as he could get. I said—" Shanda broke off.

"You sent him to Peacegiven Square," Sandry guessed. "You wished him off on me. Three dead, twenty houses, and when they pay off Serpent's Walk, we'll be a thousand shells in the hole."

Roni was looking at him in something like fear. Aunt Shanda's jaw was set like a boulder. It began to dawn on Sandry that he'd said too much. But he was so damned tired, and there was still a lot to do. He poured more tea, and then gulped it.

Aunt Shanda looked up with a smile. *Change of subject coming,* Sandry thought, and he could guess what it was.

"Now that you're out of the Younglords and have your own command and everything . . ." Shanda said.

She didn't need to finish the sentence. It was time for him to think of marriage. He already had a house, now that his father was dead. And no one to manage it but a kinless overseer who had been his nurse.

"I've been busy setting up the Fire Brigade," Sandry protested.

"Yes, dear, but it's not as if you have to look far," Shanda said. "Or go to great pains at courtship."

That's for damn sure, Sandry thought. Roni was busy watching the cat watching the fishpond, that little half-smile almost hidden. And in a minute Aunt Shanda would send Roni on an errand, and—"I know, Aunt Shanda. But this really is a difficult assignment, and—" Too late.

"And I've heard tales," Aunt Shanda said. "Roni, please go get me a fresh lemon."

"Yes, Mother." Roni was gone in an instant.

"Now," Shanda said. "What's all this talk I hear of you pining after that half-Lordkin girl?"

For a moment he remembered. Long brown hair streaming behind her as she danced on a high wire. The flashing smile, her cheers during the battle with the Toronexti. . . . He caught himself. "I'm not pining."

"No, certainly not," Shanda said. "Do you think I didn't see the two of you together when the caravan was here?"

"She's Whandall Feathersnake's daughter, and you tell everyone you're an old friend of Whandall's," Sandry protested.

"Yes, she is Whandall's daughter, and yes, he is an old friend, and you know I have no prejudices, none at all. But her mother is kinless! And her father is Lordkin! And you know as well as I do what that means here in Tep's Town! How could you command the loyalty of Lordkin in the Fire Brigade if you married a girl with a kinless mother?"

At least, Sandry thought, *at least she's not hinting I ought to just keep her as a mistress. Not that I could. Whandall Feathersnake's daughter? There wouldn't be enough money to protect me from her brothers if I did that. I'd never be able to leave Lordshills.* "Aunt Shanda, her father is Whandall Feathersnake! Even Wanshig boasts that Whandall's his brother! *Brother,* right out loud, and him Lordkin! If I could—if I were fortunate enough to marry Burning Tower, I'd have more power than ever."

"In Serpent's Walk, dear. They'd still laugh at you everywhere else. And what of Roni?"

"Well," he said, too reasonably, "let's ask Roni."

She backed off from that. "Well, we'll see. And there are other girls if you don't like Roni. It would be a good match for both of you, but I know she can be formidable. We can talk about other girls here in Lordshills. But I'm afraid you'll have to forget that Feathersnake girl, Sandry. Just stop thinking about her. I remember when I was a little girl, I used to think Whandall might come back for me, but I got over that. You will too."

Mercifully, Roni came back with lemons before Shanda could say anything else.

Chapter Four

Fear and Foes

The inn at Peacegiven Square was beginning to seem like home. Sandry spent enough time there that he took a permanent room for himself and another for Chalker.

Chalker was something between a valet and a tutor. He had been a retired Peacevoice of the Lordsmen as long as Sandry could remember. After he retired he worked as valet to Sandry's father, but as he got older, he became Sandry's bodyguard, not that the children of Lords much needed bodyguards. That was an honorable position for a retired soldier.

Chalker had been born in Condigeo, or Blackmouth Bay, or Big Rock, depending on which version of his life story you believed. Certainly he had come to the harbor as a young man, married a local kinless girl, and joined the Lordsmen as a recruit while Sandry's father was a Younglord. Chalker's wife was long dead, and his own children were grown, gone to sea and never returned, and it seemed a kindness to let him continue in Sandry's service. What else would the old man do? Not that he seemed old, except late in the evenings, and not always then.

Breakfast at the Firesale Inn ran to the elaborate. It started as a tearoom the year before when Whandall Feathersnake's caravan set up market in the square, and then quickly grew to a full-size inn and restaurant, mostly inside but with three tables under a canopy facing on the square itself. Sandry sat at a table there when weather permitted.

The Feathersnake market had been out in the square. Just over to his right, they'd set up the poles for the tightwire, and Burning Tower had climbed up there to dance in a revealing green-and-orange costume made mostly of feathers. Her feet and ankles had been bare.

His reverie was interrupted by breakfast. There was a pretty kinless girl as breakfast waitress, but Chalker insisted on bringing Sandry's eggs on a toasted muffin, and a cup of dark tea he'd made himself.

Sandry sipped hot tea and smiled. "Thank you, Chalker."

"Welcome, sir. It's a good morning."

Which in fact it was. The sun had been up about two hours, and there was activity on the square. Kinless sweepers. A kinless artisan and his son were tinkering with the central fountain and muttering either curses or invocations when the flow didn't increase. A clothing shop next door was opening under the protection of a Lordkin guard.

"The Lordkin don't gather here now," Chalker said. "Like the old days. Maybe better, some ways."

Sandry automatically translated *gather* into *steal.* "Tell me about the old days."

"Well, there's old days and really old days," Chalker said. "Old days is before that year when they had two Burnings and the whole square and a lot more burned down."

Sandry nodded. He'd been about ten when that happened, and he'd heard the story often. The Lords had bought dragon bones in a cold iron box. Manna to power rain spells, Aunt Shanda said. And when they opened the box here in Peacegiven Square, the Lordkin went mad. A dozen were possessed of Yangin-Atep, and a dozen more thought they were or pretended to be. Fire and madness everywhere, and when it was done, Peacegiven Square and everything around it was ashes and soot, wooden aqueducts burned, nothing left. It wasn't safe around here after that. Guardsmen patrolled in threes, foursomes even.

"'Fore that, there was stores here, and the Registry Office was twice the size of the new one," Chalker said. "Heard you were going to expand that?"

Sandry nodded. "You hear more than I do." Which was true. Peacevoice Hall rang with rumors, and the senior troop leaders always knew what was going on, more than the Lords and Younglords who were their officers. Everyone knew that.

"Maybe," Chalker admitted. "Hear tell they'll start just after the caravan comes. If it comes."

"If it comes?"

"Late, isn't it, sir? I believe that Feathersnake Wagonmaster said they'd be back before the Devil Winds came."

True enough, Sandry thought. *But they'll come! She said they would.* "How is it better now?"

"Less fighting," Chalker said. " 'Fore we had that Two Burnings year, there was more disputes over who controlled what. Nothing really settled. After everything burned down, nobody cared, of course, but before that, this was valuable territory, and every Lordkin wanted to gather here. Took a lot of guarding to make it safe." Chalker looked around the Square. "Now, that Wanshig chap has things under control. Nobody gathers here, and the kinless can get on with their work."

A wagon came across the square. A kinless trash collector. But the two kinless ponies pulling it were larger than Sandry remembered. "Are those things growing?" he asked.

Chalker nodded. "Yes, sir. They tell me it's the magic coming back."

"You say that with a straight face."

"Well, sir, we both know magic works," Chalker said. "Sometimes."

"Dangerous, though," Sandry mused. Dangerous enough that for a long time, there wasn't any magic in Lordshills. The Lords had paid wizards to cast some kind of spell that used it up, or so Aunt Shanda said. But they hadn't done that for years.

Magic never came back. It was a basic truth known to wizards and common folk alike: when magic is used up, it's gone. But magic was coming back to Lordshills. The pond fish were showing wild colors, and Lord Quintana's big table map now updated itself: it showed tiny changes to match the tides and the water in the rivers, smudges of soot to mark the smoke of fires.

Where was it coming from? Dust blown from other lands? Rain? Certain objects could be made to carry manna; there was a growing trade in such talismans. Maybe new manna rode the fumes that bubbled up from the Black Pit. Anyone who saw the tar pits would know they held magic, evil magic. The pits held a god turned myth.

"And the old, old days?" Sandry asked.

Chalker smiled in a way that older people often did when they remembered times long past. "This place was alive then," Chalker said. "Big bonfires to Yangin-Atep, and they'd play at a Burning, but about half the time it was a setup, a block of houses used as junkyards for a year or two. Made good stories for the tellers! Matter of fact, that's what brought me here, the tellers talking about the Burnings. Sounded like fun. Only I couldn't get in on any of that—only Lordkin allowed. So I joined up with the Lordsmen."

And you've been one ever since, Sandry thought. "Did you like that?"

"Not at first," Chalker said cheerfully.

"Sit down; have some tea." Sandry said.

"Thank you, Lord, but I think not." He grinned faintly. "Wouldn't do for me to get too friendly. Way it is, them Lordkin see somebody like me takes orders from you, it makes it easier for them to work for you. With you," Chalker corrected himself. "No, I didn't like it at first, but the job grows on you. Did on me, anyway. I was

Samorty's batman his last year as a Younglord, and I liked him. Mostly I worked with good officers. Like your father. He didn't turn out in armor every time it was his watch like Samorty did, and he had a temper, he did, but he was a good man, worried about his men. If he made a mistake when he was mad at you, he'd admit it later, and make amends. I'd have followed him anywhere." Chalker filled Sandry's cup with fresh tea. It smelled of sage, with only a tiny hint of hemp. "And you stop worrying about that Lord Regapisk. Nothing you could do, and he didn't get nothing he didn't deserve."

Sandry guessed that both those statements were probably true, but it bothered him anyway. The Council meeting hadn't seemed like a trial, not at first. Just hours of "Reggy stories," as Sandry thought of them. Everybody seemed to have one . . .

"Fish have parasites, see," the Harbormaster said. Inviting him to testify was Reggy's doom, right there. "We work a spell to persuade them to crawl out of the fish, and then we wait a few hours . . . but Younglord Regapisk, he came to get his fish, and he was in a hurry. He just told his men to pile them in his cart, and he went. Lord Warrand, you remember what happened? But it could have been worse."

"All I know is my cook was screaming. She made me go down to the harbor myself and find you. The cart was *crawling* with what came out of those fish. See what you mean, though. If Reggy'd got there before the spells were spoke, those worms would have been still in the fish. What would they have done to us?"

Reggy stories. Sandry didn't tell the one about him

and Reggy and the mirror, he didn't dare, but that was as funny as any he heard. Reggy and the mer people. Then suddenly this wasn't an informal meeting at all but a Congregation of Lords Witness to Decide in the Matter of Certain Complaints Lodged against Lord Regapisk, and they'd come down hard. Harder than Reggy deserved? It cost Sandry a night's sleep, and cost Regapisk much more, but there was no help for it. A Lord had obligations.

"Nothing he didn't deserve," Chalker repeated. "Here, have some more tea."

"Fear! Fear and foes!"

The shout rang out across the square. "Fear and foes! Alarm!" There was a clatter of hooves. Sandry's tea splashed over his wrist.

The Lordkin guard who protected the inn looked up, startled. The kinless owners rushed to gather up anything valuable and get it inside.

"Fear and foes! Alarm!" A chariot raced into Peace-given Square.

"From the north road, Lord Sandry," Chalker said. "That's Younglord Maydreo."

"Right." Sandry leaped to his feet. "Fullerman! Turn out the guard! Maydreo, *stop*! Report!"

Maydreo reined in. "Can't stop, My Lord! The border station has been attacked. Have to warn Lordstown and Lordshills."

Now Sandry could see that the frothy sweat on the righthand horse in Maydreo's team had a pink tinge, with some bright red spots. And there was blood trickling down Maydreo's forehead.

"How many?" Sandry demanded.

"And how armed, Younglord?" Chalker asked from behind him. "Your pardon, Lord Sandry."

Pardon, hell—I should have thought of it. "And how armed?"

Maydreo was babbling. "Monsters, a dozen of them, monsters. Two-legged, not men, bigger than men. Teeth and spears. Three men down, maybe more. Bordermaster Waterman and his collectors are barricaded inside the tollhouse. I have to go, My Lord. We have to turn out the guard and close the gates to Lordshills."

"Get hold of yourself, Younglord," Chalker said. He kept his voice low and calm. "Doesn't do to let the Lordkin see you're scared."

"Right," Sandry said. "All right, go warn the town. Take it easy on those horses! They won't last if you run them as fast as you came here. No more than a trot, Younglord, or you will never get there. Do you understand that?"

"Yes—yes, sir."

"Good. Hold them to a trot all the way to the Black Pit relay station, and get a fresh team there. We'll see what we can do here. If there's only a dozen—"

"Only twelve," Maydreo said. "But they aren't men." He managed to keep his voice down. "Bigger than men. Swords grow out of their hands! And watch out—the horses can't stand them. All our horses panicked."

"How many chasing you?" Sandry asked.

"Seven, I think. The rest are still up there. After Waterman. And the caravan."

"Caravan? What caravan?" Sandry demanded.

"Feathersnake caravan. Didn't I tell you? My Lord, I

have to go warn the town." He flicked the reins, and his chariot clattered off toward Sanvin Street, the horses at a run. After a moment, he halted them, then resumed at a trot.

The Feathersnake caravan! They were here, and would Burning Tower be with them? She said she was coming back. Sandry felt a warm glow over his whole body. Burning Tower. Maybe she was here, right now! "We have to go help Waterman and the caravan," Sandry said.

"First things first," Chalker said, "My Lord."

Chalker was right, of course. This was his territory, his responsibility. *To protect it from fire, he thought. Monsters aren't a fire. But it's still my territory.*

There was commotion in the stables behind, and Sandry knew Peacevoice Fullerman was getting the chariot ready and his men in armor. *Only seven enemies coming here,* Sandry thought. And he had a chariot and a dozen Lordsmen. How bad can that be? "Chalker, what do you make of that? Swords growing out of their hands?"

"New kind of armor, sir? Big men, good armor? I remember when that Arshur came to the city, a dozen like him in full armor would have panicked me. Maybe that's it. . . . What the devil is that?"

Someone was ringing a bell. The Peacegiven Square fire bell, one ring, then three. Dibantot. The Lordkin who lived here to protect the Firesale Inn. He had climbed up onto the platform under the bell and was ringing it. *Bong!* Pause. *Bong! Bong! Bong!* Three alarm fire at Station One, which was Peacegiven Square. But there wasn't any fire here!

But what harm would it do? Sandry thought. *Maybe do some good. Couldn't hurt to have some armed Lordkin, at least ones who'd listen. Better the Fire Brigade than anyone else. When they get here, I can go see about Bordermaster Waterman—he'll need help. And the caravan . . .*

There was a flash of green and orange at the north end of the square. The kinless artisan who'd been working on the fountain looked up the road and screamed in terror. He pushed his boy up onto the fountain. "Climb! Climb to the top!" Then he ran across the square toward Sandry. "My Lord, My Lord, save my son, save me!"

And five monsters burst into the square. Two kinless were in their way. A flash of green, and the monsters didn't even slow down, the kinless were dead and trampled. The five came on, five abreast, blood dripping from their arms. One monster had a spear in its side, but that didn't seem to bother it.

And swords grew out of their arms. It was true.

"Yangin's pizzle! I never saw anything like that!" Peacevoice Fullerman shouted. "Form up, form up! Lock armor, lads! Lord Sandry! What do we do?" He ran up leading Sandry's chariot. He'd hitched up Blaze and Boots, a stallion and a gelding, both big horses, Sandry's favorites if there was trouble, but the horses were already rearing at the sight of the monsters and the smell of blood.

"Hold on, good boys," Sandry said soothingly. He leaped onto the chariot. Chalker jumped in beside him. The kinless artisan was right in the path of the monsters.

Birds! They were birds!

They were feathered birds the size of a big pony, armed with blades where a bird has wings, and a beak big enough to swallow a prize hog. A beak full of teeth. The horses panicked, tried to turn away. Sandry wrestled with the reins, hauled them around by main force, and shouted. "Go! Go, you beauties!"

Training held. The horses darted forward toward the running kinless. Sandry brought the chariot as close to the man as he dared, hoping Chalker could handle the situation. Chalker was old, but he wasn't weak. And there wasn't anything else to do. Sandry hauled back on the reins, slowing the horses and causing them to rear.

"Inside, inside, man—get in!" Chalker was shouting.

Sandry felt someone beside him. "Go!" he shouted. They clattered back across the square to the assembled troopers. "Off!"

The kinless man leaped off, shouting thanks and begging them to help his son.

Son.

The boy was high up on the fountain, and the bird monsters weren't paying him any attention. The boy was safe enough. The birds wanted something else. They wanted Sandry.

Or—

"They're after the horses!" Sandry shouted. And they could run as fast as horses too. Maybe not quite. These were fresh horses—panicked but fresh. Maybe— "Go!" Sandry shouted. He led the monsters away from the inn, across the square. They followed. At the far edge, Sandry turned, rode north again. The birds followed. *I'll lead them back up the road, back to the border station,* Sandry thought. Only he couldn't. The north road was cluttered with people trying to tend to the fallen. For a moment Sandry cursed them for being in his way, but that was unfair; the wounded needed attention.

He rode straight past the north road to the opposite edge of Peacegiven Square and turned again. The monsters followed, five of them, their beady eyes fixed on the chariot. *Now,* Sandry thought. He led them down the square and past the formed-up troopers.

"Throw!" Chalker shouted as they rode by.

"Stand ready! Aim! Throw!" Peacevoice Fullerman shouted. Spears arced out toward the monsters. Three penetrated the lead bird, and it stumbled.

"Throw!"

Another barrage of spears, and that would be all of them. Fullerman shouted to the knot of kinless huddled behind the shield wall. "Get me spears! There's more in the barracks! Steady, lads, don't break ranks! You, innkeeper—get me spears!"

The pretty kinless waitress was the first to understand. She rushed toward the lean-to Fullerman's troops used as a barracks.

"Hurry, lass!"

Her hair bounced as she ran. A pretty picture. "We live through this, she'll make a soldier's wife!" Chalker shouted.

There wasn't going to be time. The birds had followed Sandry's chariot, but when the lead bird stumbled, they turned back toward their tormentors. The Lordsmen drew swords, but without spears they weren't going to be able to hold that shield wall and still fight. The birds would tear through or around the line and be among the kin-less—

Dibantot screamed curses and leaped off the fire bell platform. He ran toward the downed bird, still shouting, and hacked at it with his big Lordkin knife. The monster fell in a shower of blood.

Now the others had seen Dibantot. They turned away from Fullerman's line and charged. Dibantot looked around, saw there was nowhere to go, and took a fighting stance. He shouted defiance, a Lordkin to the last, but he never had a chance. He hacked at one and then he was down, speared with those great swords the birds wore in place of wings, his body torn by kicks from their clawed feet. They turned toward Fullerman's group. The pretty waitress and the innkeeper were handing out spears.

"Hold steady, lads! Get behind us, Miss!" Fullerman shouted. "Squad, kneel! Ground your spear butts!"

Training again, Sandry thought. *Training*. The guards-men knelt, shields still locked, spear butts to the ground and points held ahead of them. The birds charged. One man screamed in terror and left his post, running away. The others held, and one of the birds impaled itself on a spear. It ran right up the length of the spear to strike down the man who held it. The other three broke past the Lordsmen to pursue the running guard. One leaped onto the man's back, and he was down, torn apart by kicking feet. The birds turned again.

All of the Lordsmen were busy finishing off the impaled bird. Two more men were down, but they seemed to be moving.

Sandry wheeled the chariot and charged at the birds. "Be ready!"

"Sir!" Chalker said. He hefted a throwing spear. "Ready, sir."

"Now!"

Sandry wheeled the chariot to the left so that Chalker was facing the birds. "Away!" Chalker shouted.

"Go!" The horses had no problems with that order. "Go, Blaze! Go, you beauties!"

"Pulling away," Chalker said. He took another spear from the rack. "One's not running very well."

"Need another chariot out here," Sandry said.

"Firegod's piss, we need twenty!" Chalker said, but there was a lilt to his voice.

He loves this, Sandry thought. *Come to that, so do I! Hoofbeats on the square, wind in my face, and a monster chasing behind. Fighting fires is important work, but I was born for this!*

Wheel again. Lead them around the square. Hope Fullerman has the troops formed up and ready again. He could spare a moment to look. The innkeeper and his waitress daughter were carrying the wounded inside. Fullerman had the remaining troops formed and ready. Everything was all right. "We'll take a run past Fullerman's troop."

"Make ready to throw!" Chalker shouted.

"Make ready. Steady lads, hold on. Ready now—throw!" Fullerman ordered.

There was a cheer from the guards, but Sandry couldn't look back. The horses were flecked with foam now, and they were harder to control. "Steady, Blaze.

Steady, Boots." Horses liked to hear their names, and to hear a calm voice from a human. "Steady, you beauties."

"Another one down," Chalker said. "Two left, one's wounded, and all that running has slowed them a bit."

"About time," Sandry said. "Okay, what?"

"Turn up ahead, and slow down. I'll throw the last spear. When I throw, move again, sir."

"Right. Good tactics." *Maybe he knows what these things are?* "Turning. Slow, slow, you beauties, slow."

The horses didn't want to slow to a trot. They wanted to run flat out. It was all Sandry could do to slow them.

"I'm ready—here it goes. Go, sir."

The horses leaped ahead without waiting for orders. They could sense the urgency in Chalker's voice.

"Got him!" Chalker shouted. "And here come the Lordkin! They're on the wounded one! Hacking him up!"

"Where's the last one?"

"About twenty feet behind us, sir."

"Get a rope out."

"Sir?"

"Rope. I'm going to wheel. Try to lasso it."

"Don't know how."

"Blast. Me either," Sandry said. *But I thought you knew everything!* He continued to lead the remaining bird in a wide loop. "What are the Lordkin doing?"

"Distracting the bird," Chalker reported. "You can look back."

Sandry slowed the horses to a walk and looked behind him. The Lordkin were challenging the bird.

"We need it alive!" Sandry shouted. No one listened. These were Lordkin. Ah. There was Ilthern, some kind of relative to Wanshig, young but clearly a leader. "Ilthern! As a great favor, we need that one alive!" Sandry shouted. "We'll pay a bonus."

That got some attention. One Lordkin stripped off his shirt and waved it at the bird.

"It's confused, I think," Chalker said. "Too many targets. I don't think them things are any too smart."

Maybe it will chase us until it's exhausted, Sandry thought. He wheeled again and dashed past the bird. The sight of the horses set it off toward them, but faster than before, and Sandry had to let the horses run to pull away from it.

"Sir, I can lay the rope in a loop out behind us. When it steps in, you go. It's falling behind, it's not as fast as it was. Tiring out, I think."

I hope so, Sandry thought, as he watched the buildings of the square flash past. *The horses are tired, but they've still got some spunk.* "Okay. Get ready. Tell me when to stop."

"Got the rope. . . . Got a loop. . . . Okay, sir, anytime."

"Whoa!"

The horses were startled. Stop? Here? But he hauled on the reins, and they slowed, stopped, quivering.

"Laid out. Move at a walk; I'll lay out line. Here it comes."

Sandry wanted to look back, but it was better to look where he was going— He felt Chalker jerk hard on the rope. "Got him! Ride!"

"At a trot," Sandry called to the horses in as calm a voice as he could manage. "Trot. Go." He kept light pressure on the reins to keep the horses from pulling too hard.

"It's down, sir."

Sandry turned hard left, whipping around in a circle. "Wrap him up."

"Doing that. Here come the Lordkin."

"We want it alive!" Sandry shouted. Now he could look. The beast was down.

The Lordkin stood back, then one ran in and threw his shirt over the bird's head. Another came up to do the same and was slashed by one of those wing-spears. He fell back, cursing.

"There's Chief Wanshig," Chalker said carefully. Then he shouted, "Yes, sir!" and leaped out of the chariot with another rope. Chalker ran up to throw the rope over the beast's neck, then hauled in the direction opposite the chariot. "Chief Wanshig, if some of your laddies could help here?" Chalker shouted.

Wanshig laughed and came over to take hold of the rope. A half dozen others joined him.

The bird was trapped. *And now,* Sandry thought, *all I need is a cage to put it in.*

Chapter Five

Wagon Train

"Maydreo said seven more coming," Sandry said. "Only five got here."

"Yes, sir. Maybe they went back to the border station."

"Waterman's in trouble," Sandry said. "And there's a caravan. A Feathersnake caravan."

"Yes, sir," Chalker said. "I understand, we have to look into all that. But you better let Fullerman change horses first. You'll need fresh. No point in going until you get them."

Which was true enough. The sudden spurts of flat out running had tired the horses quickly. Better to have new. "See to that, and load up with spears," Sandry said. "And have Fullerman choose us a good spearman to ride up with us."

"Right." Chalker led the chariot toward the stables behind the inn, where the soldiers were clustered around the innkeeper's smiling daughter.

"And hurry!"

The square was alive with people. Kinless stood in knots, watchfully eyeing the Lordkin, but speaking in agitated tones. When Sandry came near any of them, they cheered. Some were even cheering for the Lordkin Fire Brigade.

The fountain artisan was talking to Wanshig. "Your men, Lord Wanshig—" He glanced hastily at Sandry, who pretended he hadn't heard. "They saved my boy—I saw them. That man waved his shirt when the beast was running toward the fountain. Ask anything. A new fountain for your meetinghouse? We will build it for you!"

Wanshig looked amused, but he nodded. "Thank you, Master Artisan. We accept." He turned to acknowledge Sandry. "Lord Sandry."

"Chief Wanshig. Your men have earned a bonus."

"Lost four," Wanshig said. "And two more will be out for months. Lord Sandry, what were those things? I never saw anything like them."

"Me either," Sandry said, but then he stopped. Actually, he thought, *I have. Burning Tower was wearing a costume made out of feathers like those when she did her high-rope act. The wagon people must know what those things are.*

Wagon train. There were seven more of those birds, and the wagon train was in danger. "What's keeping those fresh horses?" Sandry shouted. "Peacevoice Fullerman, if you please. . . ."

The road north to the border was strewn with bodies. The creatures had killed at least a dozen kinless. Further north a kinless woman hugged two children, while a teenage kinless laid a blanket over a body.

"Lordkin," Chalker said. He pointed to the dead man.

"We'll have to tell Chief Wanshig," Sandry said.

"Not one of his," Chalker said. "Flower Market, I'd say. What you think, Yiler?"

The borrowed spearman sucked his teeth. "Yeah, reckon so from the tattoos, but you don't expect to see Flower Market Lordkin killed protecting kinless."

"You reckon he was doing that?" Chalker asked.

"Had to. Why else would that kinless kid be covering him?"

"Is it unusual for Lordkin to protect kinless?" Sandry asked.

"Used to be you never saw that, but lately it happens in Serpent's Walk," Yiler said. "But Flower Market is different—"

"Trouble ahead, sir," Chalker said.

A cluster of Lordkin surrounded a monster. One of its legs was gone at the knee, but the bird seemed able to stand and even to hop forward. Whenever it did, Lordkin would attack it from behind, rushing forward to chop at its remaining leg. Sandry didn't recognize any of the Lordkin, but they seemed to have the situation in hand.

"That's the missing two," Chalker said.

"Two?"

"Yes, sir. One of them Lordkin was standing on a dead one."

"Oh. All right—if Maydreo counted right, there's five left." *And,* he didn't say, *just us to deal with them.* Peacevoice Fullerman would be marching up the road, but only about half of his troopers were effective. Two troopers dead, three wounded. "Let the Lordkin deal with that one, then. How many troops at the border station?" Sandry asked.

Chalker shouted through clenched teeth. It was hard to talk as the chariot jolted over the rutted road. "Standard group if they didn't send for more when they heard a caravan was coming."

"Would they?"

"Being it's Feathersnake, probably not," Chalker shouted.

Sandry nodded to himself. That made sense. The border post collected taxes, but it was a welcoming committee too, now that there was actually traffic on the old forest road. Before Yangin-Atep went mythical, the forest fought back against traffic, and the Toronexti who'd held the border station were Lordkin. Lordkin had been no more willing to work at keeping the road open than to work at anything else. There hadn't been real traffic for generations. But the Toronexti were gone, and Master Peacevoice Waterman had become Bordermaster Waterman and would be learning his duties as he went along. Keep the roads open, keep the streams clean and fresh, store plenty of fodder for the beasts. Serve good meals, dishes they wouldn't have found out on the Hemp Road. Don't drive the caravans away—we need the business.

Don't gouge on taxes, make this a safe place to stop, and have lots of kinless ready to do any services needed at reasonable prices. Welcome to Tep's Town and Lordshills.

Beyond the tollhouse was a long, narrow road winding north and west through the forest and out to the main north–south trade route. Sandry remembered that Burning Tower called it the Hemp Road. He could still hear her voice. But that wasn't quite it. The section here was called the Hemp Road, but that was part of a greater road stretching far to the north and south, farther than Tower or any of the Bison clan had ever traveled.

The road connecting Tep's Town to the Hemp Road was already known as the Greenway. Between the creepers and the muddy stream crossings nothing traveled fast on the Greenway. Nothing could sneak up on the border post, so there wasn't any reason to keep a lot of expensive troopers out there. The whole Lordsmen army could come to the tollhouse at need. Otherwise, it was sufficient to have enough troops to keep order, a Younglord messenger, kinless stable hands, and some kinless foresters to keep the road clear of vines.

It had all made sense when his uncle explained it to him. But nobody expected monsters! Sandry's whole heart wanted to ride like the wind. But racing ahead would mean getting there with tired horses, and those birds were fast. Sandry took a deep breath and tried to look calm, but he couldn't get rid of the metallic taste of fear in his throat.

They rounded a bend in the road, and there was the border station, a brick two-story building with a rail fence corral and brick-walled courtyard, paved road for a couple of hundred feet on each side of the gate. It looked neat and clean, as it was supposed to, but there were signs of a fight: torn bloody clothing near the main entrance, a green-and-orange heap in the center of the courtyard. *Dead bird,* Sandry thought. *Waterman got one.*

Someone shouted, and a moment later Waterman came to the upper window opening. His head was bandaged and his left arm was in a sling. Bordermaster Waterman was a decade younger than Chalker, but just now he looked older. "Careful, my Lord Sandry," Waterman shouted. "There's a whole bunch of them things left!"

"How many did you kill?"

"One, sir, and the Feathersnake guards got one."

"Three left, then," Sandry said. "Assuming there were a dozen to start."

"Hoo!" Waterman sounded impressed for the first time that Sandry could remember. "You killed seven of them things? Hoo-haw!"

"Not just me," Sandry said. "The Lordkin got a couple, and I had Fullerman's troops to help. Where are the monsters now?"

Waterman shrugged. "They was here a few minutes ago. They smell those horses, they'll be back. Seems like they really have it in for horses."

"Where's the caravan?"

"Just ahead, sir, on the road up around the bend. You can't miss it."

"How many effectives do you have, Bordermaster?"

"Three, sir. And no more spears."

Sandry nodded. First things first, then. He wheeled the

chariot toward the dead bird. Two spears stuck out of it, and another lay on the ground nearby. Sandry gestured, and Yiler leaped down to gather the spears. As he did, the dead bird convulsed, and its beak fastened onto Yiler's leg.

Chalker leaped down with a curse and ran a spear through the bird's neck. The beak opened and the head flopped over. Yiler drew his sword and hacked at it again and again.

"You can stand on that; you ain't too bad off," Chalker said. "But I think we let him deliver them spears to the toll house, Lord Sandry. He's bleeding."

"Right." Another lesson learned. Just because the birds looked long dead didn't mean they were. Take Yiler and the spears back to the tollhouse. Stand ready while they open the barred door and let Yiler in. *Do I want another spearman, one of Waterman's people?* Nobody seemed to be volunteering, and Sandry didn't know any of the troopers except Waterman. "Just you and me again, Chalker."

Chalker grinned narrowly. "Yes, sir."

They saw the birds before they rounded the bend. All three of them, running back and forth. Then the caravan became visible, a circle of wagons. Big rectangular wagons with high wooden sides and gray tentcloth roofs, drawn into a tight circle with little space between them. Men with slings stood on the wagon seats, and men and women with long spears crouched between the wagon wheels among sturdy wooden boxes that exactly fit the empty spaces. Inside the wagon circle was a circle of hairy beasts, shaggy with big horns. They stood in a solid ring, their horns out. Bison. Sandry had never seen one before the first Feathersnake caravan came to Tep's Town. He still wasn't sure he believed they were domesticated animals.

There were horses inside the bison circle. *No,* Sandry corrected himself, *not horses.* They'd be kinless ponies if they weren't so big! And they had horns growing out of their foreheads. Boneheads, one-horns. Some of the seaman traders had stories about one-horns. Could they be true? Everyone said they were true.

"They see us!" Chalker shouted.

The birds were coming.

"It's the horses," Sandry said. "They want to kill the horses. Ruby! Steady there!" Ruby and Rose, two mares, not as fast as the stallion and gelding team he'd had in Peacegiven Square. "This is going to be tricky," Sandry said. "Keep an eye out to the caravan. See if there's going to be any help there."

"Looks like they've got a gate and people ready to open it," Chalker said. "We could run inside."

"And be trapped like they are," Sandry said. "Maybe when the horses tire. The birds have been running; they can't be all that fresh—"

"They look fresh enough to me!"

They did. The birds were coming fast now. Sandry wheeled the horses. Lead them up the road, get them close to Waterman's tollhouse. Lead them to the spears—

"They've opened that gate!" Chalker shouted. "Something's coming out. Something, somebody."

Sandry didn't dare look. The road was none too straight, and the birds were getting closer, and the mares were terrified—

"It's a girl, riding one of them boneheads," Chalker shouted.

Now Sandry had to look behind. It was Tower, Burning Tower, long hair tied behind her, trousered legs astride a white stallion with a gleaming horn, her perfect feet bare and appealing as always. She was shouting in a language Sandry didn't know.

And that got their attention! The birds wheeled, abandoning the chase to turn after Tower. *Not too bright, easily distracted,* Sandry thought. *Remember that—they run for the nearest victim.* And they were running after Burning Tower!

"Whoa! Turn! Gee! Gee!" Sandry shouted. He wheeled the horses to the right. "After 'em! Chalker!"

"Ready, My Lord!"

He pushed thoughts of the girl from his mind. *Steady,* Sandry thought. *Steady.* He pulled up close to a bird. It started to turn, and Chalker thrust the spear directly into its chest just where the neck came out. The bird leaped and Chalker let go.

"That's one," Chalker said with satisfaction.

The bird ran on, squawking horribly, blood gushing out around the spear. Chalker held on with one hand and worried a spear out of the spear pod with the other. "Ready, sir!" Chalker shouted.

Sandry stole a glance. Chalker might be ready, but he was tired, gray, breathing hard, and no wonder. *I should have got another spearman from Waterman. I should have.*

"Pull up on him," Chalker said. "Little closer, sir—"

"Heay!" Sandry flicked the reins. "Go!"

A spurt of speed, and Chalker thrust at the bird. The spear

went home, and the bird dropped, pulling Chalker out of the chariot and onto the ground. He made a loud *thud!* as he fell heavily to the ground beside his victim. The bird flopped around, spurred feet kicking, toothed beak opening and closing, and Sandry had to look to his driving.

The last bird was closing on Tower and her mount. She led it directly toward the wagons. At the last moment, she turned the pony and leaped from its back onto the wagons. The one-horn put on more speed . . .

And the bird crashed against a wagon. As it did, a dozen stones flew. Some hit it. A wagoneer, big, big as a Lordkin, leaped off the wagon. Another, smaller, jumped down waving a blanket. They spread out, taunting the bird. It turned toward the smaller one with the blanket.

Sandry urged the horses forward. They didn't want to close with the bird. "Can't blame you," Sandry said through his teeth. "On! On, ladies!"

The wagoneer threw his blanket. It settled over the bird's head. The big one—Green Stone, that was his name, Tower's brother, Sandry remembered. Big, big as a Lordkin. And nearly as strong. He had a big knife, like the Lordkin knives but better made, sharp, and he swung it at the bird just as Sandry's chariot reached the scene. Sandry hurled a short spear into the bird, but it wasn't needed. It was down.

He looked back. Chalker was limping, but he was upright, and that bird wasn't.

Down. All down.

And there was Burning Tower. Here. And she'd been riding a one-horn, and everyone knew what that meant. Sandry was ready to cheer.

Chapter Six

Twisted Cloud

"Welcome," Green Stone said. "We have not set up facilities for receiving guests, but we freely share what we do have."

It sounded like a formal speech. Was that because Green Stone was speaking in the Lordkin dialect of Tep's Town? He'd have learned that from his father, but it could hardly be the language he used most. There'd be no need for that along the Hemp Road. But there was more to it than that. Someone had told Sandry that hospitality offered was a big deal to the wagon people.

"Come in, come in!" Burning Tower was jumping excitedly, chattering. "It's good to see you! I told you we'd be back. Did you come to meet us? Did they tell you I was here?"

She was wearing a leather skirt over the leggings she'd

worn when she rode. It was tattooed leather, painted over with suns and tents and wagons and exotic birds, all painted in colors, far too fine a garment to be worn fighting. Sandry was certain she couldn't have been wearing that when he first saw her. Her long brown hair was flowing free now. Brown, but it flashed red in the sun when she turned. She'd had it in a queue when she was riding. She was wearing soft leather slippers, beaded with tiny shells, over her perfect feet.

"You are a gracious host, Wagonmaster," Sandry said. "We will return your hospitality as soon as feasible, and all is ready for you at Peacegiven Square. Or—well, it's not my place to invite you, but I'm sure that if you would care to bring your caravan farther toward the harbor, we can find accommodations nearer Lordshills. Tower, it is great to see you!" He knew he was grinning like a fool. "I was hoping you would come, we waited, but then we thought you would not be here this year, the caravan was late. And I didn't know you were here, I learned that when I learned the monsters were attacking, then I came as quickly as I could, it is great to see you—"

Green Stone looked from Sandry to his sister and back again and sighed. "We were late because this is the fourth attack of terror birds we've had to fight off, Younglord Sandry."

"Lord," Chalker said carefully. "Your pardon, Wagonmaster. Lord Sandry has been made a Lord since you were here last. He is chief of the Fire Brigades."

"Oh, good!" Burning Tower said. "Was it the battle with the Toronexti? You were wonderful then!"

"You were too," Sandry said. She was glad to see him!

Really! "You burning the old charter, that's what won the war."

"Are the terror birds all defeated?" Green Stone asked.

Sandry nodded. "As far as I know, there were twelve. Eleven are dead and one is in a cage. Do you think there were more?"

"No, that's more than we counted," Green Stone said. He ushered them toward a place in the shade, where carpets had been spread to sit on and a fire blazed in a big ceramic bowl. There was a tea kettle on the fire.

The wagoneers clustered around them. They all seemed young, older than Burning Tower but younger than her Wagonmaster brother. Most were dark and short, with a queue hanging down their backs, some to their waist. Sandry was average height for a Lord, but much taller than the wagoneers. Sandry had learned that most people outside the Valley of Smokes looked alike, like these who called themselves the Bison Tribe. There were other tribes, but there was no way to tell them apart except by paint and ornaments and feathers, which Sandry didn't know how to read. But they were all one kind of people.

Then there were the others who were not. Green Stone, who was as big as any Lordkin but bore the ears of a kinless. Not surprising, given his ancestry, Lordkin father and kinless mother, no kin to the Bison Tribe people at all. But Burning Tower didn't look much like her brother. She was much shorter and smaller, more kinless than Lordkin, but she could also pass for one of the Bison Tribe. Why not? Sandry thought. Bison Tribes and kinless had to be related, they were both here when the fair-skinned Lordkin giants came following a fire god and wandering southward seeking a land they had been promised but might never find. A land of perpetual green with no winter snow. A land where gathering was good and one never had to work.

Well, we found that for them, Sandry thought. And from the stories, it had been a good life: kinless did the work, Lordkin lived by gathering from kinless, and Lords governed. Lordkin were convinced the kinless wouldn't work without the Lords, kinless convinced the Lordkin would slaughter them all if the Lords didn't prevent it. And the funny part was that it was all true, Sandry thought. *The Lordkin really would take everything if we didn't stop them, and then the kinless would just stop making anything and everyone would starve.*

"Old charter," Green Stone said. "The one that gave the Toronexti rights to steal. Burning Tower set fire to it."

Sandry nodded. "Yes. Magnificent. It was law. Written, witnessed, and sealed."

"I never understood why that was important," Green Stone said. "Please to be seated, My Lord. We will have tea served. And your—" Green Stone gestured. *Get your armsman seated before he falls over.*

"Well, thank you," Chalker said. He was still gray. "With My Lord's permission—"

"Please," Sandry said. *You look awful, and I won't say that.*

They sat on the spread carpets, the Bison Tribe men easily, with legs crossed. Sandry sat stiffly, his legs out in front of him. It seemed awkward to sit without furniture. Chalker reclined like a bag of oats, smiling cautiously.

"It is important because without law, there is nothing but chaos," Sandry said. "If each does just what he wants to do, does what seems right in his own eyes, nothing works. Surely you know that?"

"Maybe, but we don't write it all down and act like it can't ever change," Green Stone said.

"Sometimes we do," Burning Tower said. "Some things never change, never will change, and they may not be written down, but they might as well be."

"Like what?" Green Stone demanded.

"Like—like girls having to harness a one-horn before a wedding," Burning Tower said. Then she blushed.

So it is true, Sandry thought. *True, true, it's all true, and she was riding that one-horn. She wanted me to see her ride it. It's all true, and it's wonderful.*

"Well," Green Stone said, "so you're inviting us to bring the wagon up to Lordshills? Reckon not. Peace-given Square was good enough for my father; it'll be good enough for us."

So, Sandry thought, *that old quarrel, and they haven't forgotten.* "Fair enough," Sandry said. He waited as Tower poured tea. It smelled of sage, with just a twinge of hemp and wild honey. "Terror birds, you called them. You have a name for them. Are they common?"

Burning Tower looked to her brother.

"Didn't used to be," Green Stone said. "Used to be you wouldn't see even one most years."

"You had a costume—"

"Yes, yes, I still have it. I'm glad you remembered," Burning Tower said. "It was Mother's. My father killed that bird on his first trip north with the wagon train.

Mother wore it as long as she was performing, then she gave it to me."

Performing. That was the first time I looked at her, Sandry thought. On a high rope doing somersaults. She'd fallen, and he caught her. He tried to imagine Roni or any other Lordshills girl doing that, and he couldn't. *They might learn how, but they'd never put on a show, and they certainly wouldn't talk about* performing. *And I never thought about that sort of thing before.*

"But this year we've seen more terror birds than I saw all my previous years put together," Green Stone went on. "Bunches of them, five, ten, a dozen this time, all trying to kill anything that moves."

"They seemed to be after the horses," Sandry said. "Do they attack yours?"

Green Stone looked thoughtful.

"We don't have horses," Burning Tower blurted out. "No one does. Yours last year were the first horses I'd ever seen."

"But you can ride!"

"Boneheads," she said. "They're rare too, but there are some for sale up and down the Hemp Road. But no horses."

Green Stone looked as if his tea had gone sour.

His sister grinned. "Rocky doesn't want me to tell you things like that. He wants to trade for information."

Sandry frowned. "Like tellers trade stories?"

She grinned again. "See! I told you the Lords don't do things that way," she told Green Stone.

"Well, no," Sandry said. "We don't have many secrets."

"Actually, I'm surprised you didn't know already,"

Green Stone said. "But then who would have told you? We were the first real wagon train into Tep's Town."

Sandry nodded. Any sea captain might have said something. Maybe one did and no one thought it was important, because what could anyone do about it? They sure couldn't ship horses out on boats. "So you'll be buying horses," Sandry said.

"Maybe. If the price is right," Green Stone said. "Lord Sandry, here is Twisted Cloud, Shaman of this caravan."

Sandry stood. Twisted Cloud was dressed in a leather skirt decorated with whirlwinds. Her hair was in two dark braids that hung below her shoulders. Sandry guessed her to be Aunt Shanda's age, although it was hard to tell, because there was no gray in the stark black hair, and no wrinkles on a face dark as well-tanned leather.

Visiting wizards had described caravan shamans in contemptuous phrases: hedge wizards specializing in minor spells such as food preservation and divinations, in contrast to the real wizards, who could build palaces overnight and create armies of the dead. So they had said, but Sandry had never seen a wizard *do* these things. There was never enough magic in Lordshills or in all of Tep's Town. A few wizards had brought fetishes and talismans, a few could heal hurts that weren't serious—itches, a boil—and one had made rain from early morning fog, but for the most part, the tales of great magic were only stories.

When Sandry bowed, Twisted Cloud caught his hand. She stared at it for a moment, then grinned slightly.

"Wise one, what did you see?" Burning Tower asked eagerly.

"Little," Twisted Cloud said. "My father read secrets better than I, and my daughter better than Hickamore ever could. But this one has few secrets to read. All his names are known, and his wishes are plain to all. Green Stone, you may forget your fears."

Sandry felt himself blush. "Only Lordkin have secret names in Tep's Town," he said. *And that's silly. They know that—Whandall Feathersnake is Lordkin himself.* "Lords have little need for secrets. As I said." *And as they must know, so why bring their wizard to me? And what fears did Green Stone have? Oh—*

Green Stone clapped his hands. He seemed much friendlier as he said, "Bring food for our guests. Welcome, Lord Sandry, to the lesser Feathersnake caravan."

"Thank you," Sandry said. "But duties call. Bordermaster Waterman may need help."

Burning Tower smiled. "Why? You've won, the terror birds are all dead, and from what I remember of Master Peacevoice Waterman, he can take care of himself." She glanced significantly at Chalker. "Do rest a while and have some refreshment."

Sandry glanced up at the sun. Incredibly, it was not yet noon.

Green Stone nodded. "We'll have plenty of time to pack up and get to Peacegiven Square before dark," he said. "And even if we hurried, we couldn't be there in time to set up a market today. Be welcome, Lord Sandry, be welcome."

Very friendly. *He must have really been worried. That we'd rob him?* "Thank you, then." Sandry sat on the carpet again. "Leading a caravan must be hard work."

"It can be," Green Stone said. "It's the details to keep track of. And now these terror birds."

"No idea where they come from?"

"No."

"From the south," Chalker said. "When I was a boy, I had a hat with terror bird feathers, and my father told me he bought it in Condigeo off a merchant from further south. Down the Golden Road," he said.

"Outside Coyote's lands, then," Twisted Cloud said. "I believe that. I can't think Coyote would be silent if they came from his turf."

"Coyote—the god, not the animal? He talks to you?" Sandry asked. He tried to keep the skepticism out of his voice.

"To my daughter, to Clever Squirrel," Twisted Cloud said. "Sometimes to me, since he fathered my child."

Sandry looked at her in wonder. No one else seemed startled or surprised. *These people are strange,* Sandry thought, and felt a shiver. Then Burning Tower laughed, and he forgot his fears, and the hour passed too quickly.

CHAPTER SEVEN

CHIEF WANSHIG

They were packing the wagon train. Boxes of boxes, everything designed to fit into the wagons for moving, or under them as defensive walls, or outside the wagons to form the elaborate nests the wagoneers lived in. *A craft of great skill,* Sandry thought. *It would take a long time to learn all the details of that nomadic life.*

But if a *Lordkin* had learned that, so could a Lord.

And even if— He snorted. *Horses, I know. Not bison, and I'm no merchant. And where would I get a wagon?* But he kept watching Burning Tower as she helped her brother pack the carpets into the wagon boxes. *She knows this life, and I don't, and—*

"The horses are rested, Lord," Chalker said. "Reckon it's time we got back to our duties."

Sandry nodded. "Right." He turned to Green Stone. "My thanks for your hospitality. We will see that everything is ready for you in Peacegiven Square. Water, hay, kinless to shovel and carry . . ." Amazing how much water the bison could drink, and how much waste they made.

Green Stone squinted at the sun. "We'll be there before dark," he said.

"May I invite you to dinner? At my house. You and your household," Sandry said.

"Oh, yes, please," Burning Tower said, but her brother cut her off.

"Not tonight," Green Stone said. "We'll be all night setting up the market. Maybe tomorrow."

"Tomorrow then," Burning Tower said eagerly.

Green Stone scowled at her for a moment, then relented. "Oh, all right, dinner in Lordshills tomorrow night, then. If we can get there. That wizard Morth says kinless ponies can't get up your hill."

"They can't," Sandry said. "But horses can. I'll have teams and wagons waiting. And of course you'll stay the night; I'll have rooms ready for you. How many will come?"

"Just us, I think," Green Stone said. "Me, Blazes, and Twisted Cloud."

"And Nothing Was Seen," Burning Tower said. "I know he'd like to come."

"Oh. All right," Green Stone said.

Sandry caught the odd note in Green Stone's voice. What was that all about? "Wonderful. I'll have four rooms ready, then. Mother will be pleased to meet you."

Green Stone and Twisted Cloud exchanged glances.

* * *

The ride back to Peacegiven Square seemed to take forever. Then there was a fire in the Grey Falcon territory, and Sandry had to go to make sure that the Dirty Birds and Snakefeet didn't get into a turf war. Wanshig's Firemen were shorthanded because of the losses to the terror birds, and it took all afternoon before they were sure it was completely out and the kinless cleanup crew could be left to finish the job.

"Bad one," Wanshig said. "Cold drink?" He indicated the door of the Serpent's Walk guild hall.

"Thank you, yes." He followed Wanshig inside. Few Lords had ever seen the inside of any Lordkin building. Of course not many would want to. "Tough one, all right, and it's going to get worse when the Devil Winds whip up," Sandry said. "You're going to need more men."

Wanshig shrugged. "Yes, Lord, and I can get a few, but . . ."

He didn't have to finish the sentence. It wasn't all that hard to find Lordkin who wanted to be Firemen. The tough part was finding Lordkin who wanted to be Firemen but wouldn't use the position to steal, and would fight fires outside Serpent's Walk, and . . .

"Falcon Chief said he's got men who want to be Firemen," Sandry said casually.

Wanshig nodded. "I know."

"Even says his people would work with yours," Sandry said.

"I'll think on it, Lord."

And so will we, Sandry thought. There were advantages to having Lordkin bands work together, but too much cooperation among the bands might be dangerous too. *Reggy would have leapt at the chance, but it's too big a decision for me.*

"A favor, Lord," Wanshig said suddenly.

"You've earned anything within reason." *Not something to say lightly,* Sandry thought. He had learned to trust Wanshig as much as you could trust any Lordkin, but that wasn't very far . . .

"Secklers. He's the man who used his shirt to help catch that bird. He's got a kinless girl pregnant," Wanshig said. "He still cares about her." Wanshig said that with a note of disbelief. "I guess he does too, since he asked me to help. But I can't. Her people will throw her out, and he can't bring her home either. Maybe you could find her a job in Lordshills?"

Sandry thought about that. It wasn't an unusual situation, but that was the trouble—it happened often enough that there wasn't room enough in Lordstown and Lordshills put together to hold all the careless progeny of the Lordkin. But this was an opportunity to have a powerful Lordkin leader in his debt. "Yes, I think that can be arranged," Sandry said. "It won't be easy."

"Thank you, Lord."

It was impossible to read Wanshig's expression. Sandry had learned that the Lordkin were good at playing games with the Lords Witness. They even had a term for it: *messing with the lordheads.*

"Will there be more of those birds, Lord Sandry?"

"I don't know. The Wagonmaster says there have been more this year than in all his years before. So probably."

"Could cost us some," Wanshig said.

Sandry nodded.

"Anyone in the wagon train know what those things are?"

Sandry shook his head. "Not that they told me. But thanks to you and your man—Secklers?—we have a live one. Maybe a wizard can tell us something about it. Or the wagon train shaman, the woman who . . ." He stalled.

"Lord?"

His mouth had run away with him. "Claimed to have mated with a god."

Wanshig looked impressed. "Happens, sometimes. Outside."

And was Wanshig putting him on? The Lordkin looked serious. And he'd been outside the basin, two or three years at sea, before coming back to Tep's Town, so he knew more about the world than Sandry. Gods didn't mate with humans in Tep's Town or Lordshills.

"Not to change the subject, but when do we expect Lord Regapisk back?"

"Never."

"Ah?"

"The Lord Chief Witness has found other duties for Lord Regapisk," Sandry said formally.

"Vanished him, did they? And what's the blood price for a Lord?"

"High, and I didn't say what assignment they gave him," Sandry said. "But it's not likely you'll ever meet him again."

Wanshig's smile grew broader. "Manning an oar, then. His skills may be up to that."

"Just make sure none of your people try that on me," Sandry said.

Wanshig looked at him sharply. "Try what? Well, okay, but when the gold fever takes a man—"

"Gold fever be damned," Sandry said. "There was no magic in that gold. How could there be? Every bit of manna was used up, by Morth to keep up his speed, by the water sprite chasing him, by Yangin-Atep himself! There's no magic in it. It's no more than precious dust." Sandry reached into a bag—two sets of warriors tensed—and pulled out a fist-size ball of scorched glass. "Do you recognize this?"

Wanshig considered; then: "Magicians have been turning up everywhere since Yangin-Atep went myth. One sold me this. Someone gathered it before I could use it. Where did you find it?"

"In the ashes near Glegron's body. It's magic, isn't it?"

"It's supposed to make gold dust cling to itself, into one glop. Like to like. I never had the chance to try it."

"It wouldn't work," Sandry said. "I don't know a lot about magic, but I know that much. Once the magic is gone, charms and ornaments and magic tools don't work."

Wanshig shrugged.

A year ago, Whandall Feathersnake had drawn maps all over the floor of the big dining hall. Now, Sandry was startled to see something tiny in motion on one of the maps. When he looked directly at the map, nothing happened, but if he looked away and then back again, something had changed.

"The wagon train," Sandry said. "It's moving into town. How long has your map been doing that?"

"Always did since Whandall drew it," Wanshig said. "Or at least since Yangin-Atep's been gone."

And I'll have to talk to the Lordshills wizards about it, Sandry thought. Could this be dangerous? But Lordkin were never wizards. Learning wizardcraft took years of study and hard work, and Lordkin didn't do either. Not much danger they'd start now.

The wagon train came in late afternoon, accompanied by a cloud of chattering kinless and some hulking Lordkin looking for a chance to gather. They were escorted by Younglord Maydreo, and Lord Hargriff, and Peacevoice Fullerman with a fresh squad in newly polished armor.

Sandry watched them from the comfort of his outside table at the inn. Order in confusion. Boxes came off the wagons to form living quarters, storefronts, goods tents. Cookfires were lit, and a cooking pot bubbled with the smell of red meat as they cooked the terror birds. The feathers had already been collected and stored away. Wagon traders wasted nothing.

How long would it take to learn how to be a part of that? Too long. It would never work.

Could she live here? What would Mother say? Nothing—she barely notices if I come or go. But Aunt Shanda!

A flat board from a wagon's side was laid on a box to become a wide table. Travelers spread it with tiny glass bottles, scores of them, too tiny to be of use, but pretty. Bordered around them, the travelers laid small, burned-looking stones.

* * *

"May I have some tea, please?"

She had startled him, but Sandry was already grinning when he turned. Before he realized what he was doing, he jumped up and took her hand as if he were first meeting her, and then they were both grinning. But he'd have to let go to clap for tea, and he didn't want to.

But the kinless waitress had heard and went inside with a knowing smile. Neither Lordkin nor kinless were ever supposed to know anything about the private lives of Lords or even that they had private lives. And Sandry couldn't make himself care despite what Aunt Shanda would say if she'd seen this.

"Finished setting up?" he asked.

"For a while. My brother wants me to get into costume and do a performance before dark, get the crowds wanting to come to the market tomorrow."

"No danger they won't come," Sandry said. "I don't think there's anyone doesn't know the caravan is here." He grinned. "But don't let me stop you. I love to watch you, but I'm scared for you. It looks dangerous."

She shrugged. "Not as dangerous as it looks. Ropes don't usually care. I mean they do if you don't take care of them, but we're always careful. They're *our* ropes; my cousins made them."

Sandry looked at her carefully. She was chattering, just as he had been, but about what? His mind caught up. "You mean the hemp."

"Yes, the hemp."

Hemp was harmless in Tep's Town. But the magic was leaking back into Tep's Town, with blown dust from other lands, and wild hemp tried to strangle people. Sandry's folk would need years to get used to a world where everything was like the chaparral, potentially sentient and malevolent. . . .

Tea and cakes arrived.

"You said you have one in a cage," she said.

"One—oh, you mean the terror bird we captured."

"Yes! I've never seen one that wasn't trying to kill me. May I see it?"

"It will be halfway to Lordshills by now," Sandry said. "Lord Quintana sent for it as soon as he heard we had it. He wants our wizards to examine it."

"Oh."

"But you can see it tomorrow before dinner."

"Oh, good. And Twisted Cloud too."

Sandry nodded. Of course it wasn't likely that a Hemp Road shaman would learn anything not obvious to a professional wizard. "I'll arrange it, and I'll make sure the wagons are here early for you tomorrow."

"Good. I want to see where you live."

Burning Tower nibbled a cake, finished her tea, made her excuses, and went. A young kinless stepped out of her way; she smiled at him. No sense of rank. Sandry grinned.

And now he was left with enough bean cakes for two. He brushed one off and ate it in two bites, wolfishly hungry.

The kinless kid seemed frozen, staring at him. Sandry looked back . . . kinless? "You're with the caravan," he said.

The boy started to speak, stopped, then said, "Yes, Lord. We have met before."

Last year, then. But the boy didn't seem familiar at all. "Join me. Have a cake. I'm sorry—I don't seem to remember you."

The boy grinned. "Few do. My name is Nothing Was Seen. They call me Lurk." The boy sat. He brushed ants off a cake and ate it.

"I remember now. You were poisoned by the chaparral, and that Atlantean Morth had me chasing antidotes. But you look different now. Hah, that's a good act. It's not just the right clothes—you *act* right. What were you staring at?"

"Ants, Lord."

Well, they were a nuisance. "Don't you have ants on the Hemp Road?"

"Not to be seen." The boy actually shuddered.

"Then why didn't Burning Tower . . . " Good manners. She just picked up that cake and ate it. The lady had excellent manners and nerves of pure copper.

Lurk said, "Lord, I think Twisted Cloud could help."

"With ants?"

"Yes, Lord."

Practicing, Sandry thought. *Practicing the elaborate deference the kinless used. Why would he want to learn how to be kinless? But he certainly couldn't pass for Lordkin!*

"I will find her, Lord. She will not charge much. Have the innkeeper find honey and parchment."

Chapter Eight

The Caged Bird

He hadn't begun preparations for his dinner party when Roni came into the kitchen from the back garden.

"Hi," Sandry called. "No time. Unless you want to help—"

She grinned slyly. "Want me to play hostess?"

"Tep's Teeth! No!"

She giggled. "Your face. Sandry, I'd love to help—it would be good practice—but you don't have to worry about dinner."

"What?"

"Mother says she will be pleased to have you and your guests to dinner tonight."

"But—"

"The Lord Chief Witness has asked her to be hostess,"

Roni said. "So it's a big deal, and you don't have any choice."

Not that I would, given that it's Aunt Shanda. "Tell Lord Chief Witness Quintana there will be four," Sandry said. "The Wagonmaster, whose name is Green Stone, his sister Burning Tower—"

"Ah-*hah*."

"Twisted Cloud, a shaman. And a young man who may look like a kinless and may look like Bison Clan, and I won't know until we see him."

"Lurk!"

"You know him?"

"We met last year," Roni said. "He's been here to Lordshills before, didn't you know?"

"No!"

"Well, he has. I don't know how he got in, but he was here. I didn't see him then. He told me over tea in Lordstown."

"That boy gets around," Sandry said.

She nodded and changed the subject. "Four, then. And we will have Lord Chief Witness Quintana, Lord Qirama, Egmatel the Sage, and two of his assistants. We hoped Father would be back in time, but he's still in Condigeo."

"Any progress on that treaty?"

She shrugged. "Nothing in his letters. Mother has me read them to her. Sandry, the wizards keep promising to make her eyes better, but they never do."

Sandry nodded. "They always give the same reason—not enough manna in Lordshills or even in Tep's Town. Maybe it's true. Who's entertaining, Momus?"

"I wish. There's no entertainment. Mother requests

that the guests tell stories about terror birds, and Egmatel will tell us what he has found in his studies. He's got his assistants watching the bird full time."

"No entertainment. A strange dinner party," Sandry said.

"Will your mother be coming?"

"I'll ask, but I don't think so. She's not doing well today."

"Oh, Sandry, I'm sorry. Should we have Egmatel look at her?"

"He's looked." So had Tasquatamee. And the only thing that came of that was the expense. Not enough manna here, or in town, or anywhere else.

Sandry was pretending to read in his library when a servant came in. "Your guests are coming up the hill now."

"Thanks." Sandry walked briskly to the main gate. He tried to look calm, but it was all he could do to keep himself from running.

She was waiting at the gates with the others. She wore a short woolen skirt, elaborately embroidered. From the knees down, her legs were bare and tanned before they vanished into ankle-high moccasins with silver and turquoise trim. Some of the symbols matched patterns on her skirt and short jacket. At least one seemed to be her naming symbol, a silver-and-turquoise tower enveloped in red flames. Rubies? Surely not—that would be too costly even for a merchant princess. *Carnelian,* Sandry thought. His mother liked carnelian.

Her hair was full and brown but shone red when the

sun fell on it. Her jacket was decorated with elaborate beadwork, symbols of sun and birds and another name symbol over her left breast. The thin cotton blouse under the jacket was cut into a V that didn't go nearly far enough down. He realized he was staring and looked up to see her watching him. She smiled. Warmly, he thought. Finally he looked at the others.

Nothing Was Seen dressed like a trader's porter, but the others wore exotic finery. Some of the jewels on Green Stone's jacket were definitely rubies, and there was a wealth of malachite stitched onto the garment. It was all a bit out of place here, but no one would say anything. Sandry grinned like an idiot. "Welcome to Lordshills. Peacevoice, these are my guests."

The four gate guards had held them up for a bit of gossip as they waited for Sandry. Now they swung the gates open and bowed. "Welcome to Lordshills," the Peacevoice in charge said.

"Smooth," Green Stone said when they were inside. "You have them well trained."

Sandry nodded. "Lord Quintana insists on good manners."

"Even as they put a knife in your ribs. Where's the bird? I'm curious."

"Me too," Burning Tower said. "Is your man all right? He looked gray. I was worried about him."

"He's all right," Sandry said. "I gave him the day off and ordered him to take it. Thank you for asking. The bird is here, behind the guard barracks."

He led them to a stone house with a barred window in a strong door. A face looked out, then there were the sounds of bolts being withdrawn. They passed into a stone guardroom with four guards all in armor and all alert. There was a boy, perhaps twelve, seated in one corner. He had a waxed tablet board and an iron pen, and unlike the guards, he didn't stand when Lord Sandry came in.

Sandry recognized the guards, four from Fullerman's detail, survivors of yesterday's battle in Peacegiven Square. He acknowledged their courtesies with a wave. "Carry on, lads. Good work yesterday."

"Thank you, Lord," the oldest guard said.

An iron barred cage on wheels stood against one wall.

"Cold iron," Green Stone said. "Good. Magic won't get them out of that! How'd you happen to have that cage?"

Sandry shrugged. "Henry?"

The oldest guard said, "I think we have always had that Lordkin cage, Lord Sandry. Don't use it much."

The caged bird was huddled like a brooding hen. The feathers didn't seem so bright, but that might have been the light. Guard Henry asked, "Wagonmaster, you've fought these too, haven't you?"

"All year, and yesterday," Green Stone said.

"Hope we don't see too many of them," Henry said. "We lost some good men yesterday."

"Agreed," Green Stone said.

Twisted Cloud stood close to the cage, peering in. "Too close," Green Stone said sharply.

"Mind your own business, child. This is mine," she said.

Guard Henry asked, "Is it magical?"

The shaman frowned. "You'd think so, wouldn't you? But nothing I can detect, anyway. How long do I have, Lord Sandry?"

Sandry said, "I've allowed plenty of time. Dinner is after lamplighting."

The shaman sat on the ground and stared at the bird, her eyes gradually closing, first to slits, then all the way. Finally she stood. "Nothing. Maybe the wizards know something."

"We'll find out tonight." Sandry turned to the boy. "You know anything, Wale?"

The boy grinned slightly. "My Lord, I—"

"Yes, I know—you report only to your master. Well, carry on."

"Who was he?" Burning Tower asked when they were outside.

"Apprentice to the Sage Egmatel," Sandry said. "Don't you have apprentices, Twisted Cloud?"

"Our craft runs mostly in families. My daughter was my apprentice. Now I learn from her. We may as well go to your house, Lord Sandry. I can't learn any more here."

Burning Tower walked beside Sandry as he led them into the City of Lordshills. She kept glancing at him. He was much taller than she and carried himself so that he seemed even taller. Long brown hair combed neatly back. Plain kilt of good cloth, plain jacket, a gold brooch. One gold ring. Nothing elaborate, everything quietly expensive. His eyes seemed to miss nothing, and he looked at her often.

"It's not far," he said.

She looked around eagerly, not trying to hide her interest. So this was how the Lords lived! Like the great merchant princes at Road's End, or the Captains of Condigeo. Those were the only palaces she had ever seen, although she'd heard of others farther along the Golden Road, at the Great Bay in the northwest, and in the burning hills far to the south of Condigeo.

But I've never been to those places, she thought. *I've seen Condigeo only in sand paintings. And this is wonderful enough.* She was aware that others envied her home, New Castle, which Whandall Feathersnake had built not far from Road's End, but it was unpretentious on the outside, more like a permanent wagon nest than a castle.

The houses stood each in its own grounds, with walls between them. The walls were not very high, certainly not high enough to challenge anyone who wanted to climb over. They seemed pointless, unlike the high walls that surrounded the entire town. All the houses were big, most two stories with a balcony running around the second floor, red tile roofs, and thick white walls. The second-floor balconies provided deep shade for the verandas underneath.

The most wonderful thing was the water. Streams ran through the lots, passing under the walls, filling ponds. Dark shapes swam among flowered plants in the pools, and there were fountains everywhere.

"It's beautiful," she said.

"Yep," Green Stone answered. "Father said it was like this. I never expected to see the place."

"Welcome," Sandry said. "That's my house just ahead on the right."

"It's beautiful!" Burning Tower said. "The garden is wonderful." *Actually, I guess it's not a lot different from the others,* she thought. *But all those flowers! But there should be a flower bed over there, and I don't see rosemary and thyme . . .* "Hummingbirds!"

Sandry looked to the roses. "Yes, we have a lot of them here."

"They always look so angry!" Tower said. "I'm glad they're so small. Imagine all that rage in something big enough to hurt you."

"Like a terror bird?" Sandry asked. "*They* seem to have plenty of rage."

Tower nodded, and looked breathlessly around the garden. *Lords live well,* she thought. *Better than Father in New Castle. And Lord Sandry is one fine-looking man, as Mother and my sisters would say. And he can't keep his eyes off me!*

Three servants led by Chalker stood in the doorway to welcome them.

"I told you to take the day off!" Sandry said.

Chalker grinned. "I did, My Lord, and much enjoyed it. This is evening. Ladies, may I take your wraps?"

Father does this sometimes, formal parties with servants, but this doesn't look put on, Burning Tower thought. *And Chalker looks like he's enjoying himself. They all look happy to be here, not like hired servants at Road's End or even poor relations in New Castle. They look like they want to be here, and I know Chalker doesn't have to be. How do these Lords do that?*

They were ushered into a pleasant room. The far wall wasn't a wall at all, just some columns leading to a large area paved with flagstones. Chairs with little tables were arranged just inside the room. A young man was already seated in one corner. He wore a black robe with a red trim and a purple sash around his waist. A wizard.

Burning Tower was busily distracted by all the furniture, tapestries, carved ivory on the mantelpiece, but she thought Sandry was surprised to see him. The man rose and bowed, not low . . . like a man older than he looked, Tower thought.

"The Sage Egmatel," Sandry said. He made introductions.

Egmatel nodded to each of them, and asked if they had a pleasant journey, but he moved across to be next to Twisted Cloud. "I've heard of you," he said.

"More likely of my daughter," Twisted Cloud said, but she was smiling eagerly.

"I hoped we could compare notes, Madam Shaman," Egmatel said. "Did you discern what bespells those birds?"

"No, Sage," Twisted Cloud said deferentially. More deferential than Burning Tower had ever heard her. "I could sense no magic at all. The shields must be very powerful. Perhaps if I knew what to look for?"

Egmatel smiled thinly. "We have had only a few hours to study this creature, and I want to be very sure before I say anything. I must say I am not surprised that you sensed nothing. The creature's origins are well shielded indeed."

Twisted Cloud nodded.

"And with that, My Lord Sandry, I must depart. Lady

Shanda has requested my assistance, and I must make preparations. I will see you again this evening." He bowed perfunctorily.

Sandry nodded. "Elani will show you out, Sage," he said. He watched as the wizard left, then turned back to them. And he's got that silly grin every time he looks at me, Burning Tower thought. Good!

Chalker ushered them to chairs and asked about drinks, while Sandry excused himself and went out.

He returned with a frail lady, splendidly dressed. She wore a large necklace of bright gems and polished gold. They all stood as she entered. She walked slowly, clutching Sandry's arm, but her eyes were sharp as she examined each of them in turn.

"Mother, our guests," Sandry said. "Wagonmaster Green Stone, Shaman Twisted Cloud. The pretty one is Burning Tower. And this young man has the improbable name of Nothing Was Seen."

"Colorful," Lady Whalani said. "An interesting name. Welcome to my home. Is it difficult to be a Wagonmaster?"

"It is not always easy," Green Stone said.

"No, I wouldn't have thought so." She turned and looked closely at Burning Tower. "Shanda keeps telling me about a girl with your name. I can't imagine that could be anyone but you. Sandry said you were pretty. Yes, definitely, he's not mistaken there. Lovely, and you don't use too much paint. How did you get that name?"

Burning Tower blushed slightly at the scrutiny. "My mother had a dream before I was born, My Lady. And thank you."

Lady Whalani turned to Sandry. "Very pretty. Polite,

too. Good manners." She turned back to Twisted Cloud. "A shaman. That's like a wizard, isn't it?"

"Yes, ma'am." Twisted Cloud moved to her and took her hand. "May I?"

"Certainly, but you won't see anything. None of them can."

Twisted Cloud stared for a moment, then fingered a feathered stone hung round her neck. She stared again at the frail hand, then nodded.

"I haven't long to live, of course," Lady Whalani said.

"Longer than you think. You will live to see your son face a great trial."

"My. Will he be successful?"

Twisted Cloud shook her head. "That is never revealed, not to me and I think not to anyone. But you will be proud of him no matter the outcome."

"That sounds frightening. But you have told me more than the wizards have." She smiled thinly. "Of course, it is not startling that a mother would be proud of her son no matter the outcome of his trial."

Twisted Cloud looked amused.

"Well. I would like to be a wizard. I wouldn't know how to start, but I think I would be better than the ones we have hired. Of course they don't let women be wizards here. We're supposed to be quiet and let the men do everything, until they make such a mess of it that they need us. Sandry, I'm very tired tonight. I hope our guests will excuse me if I don't join them?"

"Of course, Mother."

"It has been very pleasant meeting you. Burning Tower, you're very pretty and very young, and I see why

Sandry likes you. I think I like you, too. I hope you're determined enough. You'll have to be. Now if you will all excuse me."

Everyone stood as Sandry led her out of the room. Burning Tower felt her knees shaking as she sat again. Determined? I'll show them determined!

Sandry came back alone, looking sad. "I'm sorry Mother can't stay," he said. "She's not very strong."

"No," Twisted Cloud said. "But she works hard at overcoming it."

"Did you see anything in her palm?"

"What I told her. And that she spent the entire afternoon preparing to receive your guests."

Sandry nodded. "She does that, but of course it tires her."

"No," Twisted Cloud said. "Not as you think."

Sandry looked thoughtful.

"I like her," Burning Tower said. *Now why did I say that?*

Sandry smiled.

That's why.

Sandry said, "I didn't want to ask in front of her, but did you see any way to help her, shaman?"

"We grow old, if we do everything else right. There's not enough manna to work a youth spell here. They are difficult to maintain in any event, more so in my lifetime than in my father's. I fear I can do nothing. Perhaps the Great Wizard."

"Egmatel? A Great Wizard?"

"He wears the amulet and sash of a great one," Twisted Cloud said. "Everyone knows their meaning."

"Oh. He has never said that. So he would believe we know also?"

"Of course. You're more isolated than I thought."

"Anyway the Great Wizard has seen my mother," Sandry said. "I learned no more from him than you, but it cost me."

Twisted Cloud shrugged. "The great ones have their ways," she said.

"Yes. Shaman, will that spell rid my house of ants also?"

"Your house and any other, Lord Sandry," Twisted Cloud said. "It is no great magic."

"So why hasn't Egmatel done that for us?"

"It's like knowing how to make soap. Something to make roadside life easier. Perhaps it is beneath his notice. Much of the small magic of the Hemp Road is not known to the great ones."

Maybe they're so busy calling themselves great they don't have time to learn, Burning Tower thought. *But Cloud is really impressed by that wizard. . . .*

"Do you have parchment and honey?" Twisted Cloud asked.

"Oh yes," Sandry said. "Oh yes."

"Then if you will bring them here—"

"Wait," Sandry said. "If you please. Until we are in Aunt Shanda's home."

Burning Tower noted the sly grin Sandry was wearing. *This may be fun,* she thought.

Chapter Nine

The Dinner Party

A well-dressed girl, no more than twenty, came from the back gardens and entered without knocking. The girl was fair, with light brown hair elaborately waved, and Burning Tower wondered how that yellow linen would look with her own coloring. The girl looked at each of Sandry's guests, then smiled at Lurk as if greeting an old friend.

Roni, Burning Tower thought. She had seen her only once, a year before, when she accompanied her mother to Peacegiven Square. *She looked like a child then. But so did I. Neither one of us looks like a child now.*

"Aren't you going to introduce me?" Roni said.

Sandry stood. "My cousin Roni," he said. "We grew up together; she lives next door. One of my oldest friends. Some of you met her last year."

"Hi," Roni said. She inspected Burning Tower closely. "Well, hello. I don't think we were able to talk last year."

"Not that I remember." *Cousin. Are we rivals? Do cousins marry in Lordshills? They do in Tep's Town. Mother has friends who married cousins. She's pretty. Fit too. I wonder how she got those calf muscles.* "Of course we were busy with the fair, and I had to help Morth."

"And walk a rope," Roni said. "Eight feet up." She grinned. "Sandry saw you too."

"I take it dinner is ready?" Sandry said.

"Well, dinner isn't, but Mother says you should come over now."

Sandry nodded and started toward the back garden.

"No, not that way! Through the front door."

Sandry eyed Roni with a frown. "All right."

What was that about? Burning Tower wondered. *Something about hospitality rules? But good—I'll get to see another Lord's house. It can't be nicer than this one, though.*

The door was massive. The servant puffed as he manhandled it aside. Sandry unobtrusively held his guests back until it was fully open.

Tower let Green Stone take the lead while she tried to guess who was whom.

A woman swept toward them with the power and mass of a wagon and team of bison. She moved slowly, for the sake of her elderly companion. Lady Shanda would have been formidable commanding a travel nest. She was formidable now. Her eyes raked the four merchants, judging.

Tower felt herself dismissed, and Lurk too. Shanda

extended her hands unerringly to Green Stone. "Welcome to Lord's Town, Wagonmaster! This is your host, Lord Quintana."

Her companion didn't have her strength, though he had certainly been a warrior once.

Green Stone looked like a big Lordkin. He dressed in stiff leathers: armor. "Lady, my brother leads the main caravan this trip. These are Burning Tower, my sister . . . Twisted Cloud, our shaman . . . Nothing Was Seen."

Quintana's eyebrow went up as his eyes brushed Lurk in his porter's garb. Quintana introduced Lord Qirama and the wizard Egmatel, but not his two apprentices.

Lady Shanda led them down into a . . . travel nest, Burning Tower guessed, though it looked very different. A rectangular pit three shallow steps below the main floor. Blankets, cushions and little tables, and a fireplace. A place to relax, talk, eat a variety of interesting little mouthfuls, drink tea, make deals, run civilization.

Tower sipped a tea moderately rich in cannabis. She'd have to watch her tongue, she thought. Green Stone sipped, then proffered a small package. "Lady, Lord, we also brought tea. Would you taste something exotic?"

Lady Shanda made to speak; Lord Quintana caught her eye. Instead she clapped her hands and gave quick whispered orders to the servant who appeared. The servant took Green Stone's tea away to be prepared.

There was to be no suggestion that a guest might poison his host.

"I hope you like it. I've tried it myself, of course," Green Stone said. "The Spotted Coyotes got it from halfway around the world. I was ordered—no joke,

Blazes—*ordered* to buy it at the price they set, on instructions from Coyote himself." He grinned at his sister but spoke for his hosts. "The Spotted Coyote tribe—that's a few hundred people who live twelve to fifteen days north of the Firewoods in a wild place ordained for them by Coyote."

Lady Shanda asked skeptically, "That's the god? Not the animal?"

"The god, yes, though he can act through the animal. The Spotted Coyotes sell hospitality to passersby, mainly to caravans. Well, Coyote commanded them to sell us an entire batch of tea that came their way via Carlem Markle, and told them what price we'd pay!"

Lord Quintana asked, "Can they do that?" and didn't ask, *Can we?*

"Not often. If the Spotted Coyotes overstep, everyone regrets it. Remember the Toronexti? It would be like that." Green Stone grinned. "But we paid. We don't want to offend Coyote, and he doesn't demand much."

Of those present, Sandry had met only Burning Tower and Nothing Was Seen. He asked after others he'd met. Some had been killed by wounds inflicted in the battle with the Toronexti. Others had recovered, had retired, or were with the main caravan. Had married . . .

It was not a subject you could avoid. Roni's amusement was evident. She asked Green Stone about marriage customs, and Green Stone spoke of dowries.

My brother's mind is never off money, Burning Tower thought. She said, "The caravans always keep a few bonehead ponies around—"

Lady Shanda and Green Stone tried simultaneously to

change the subject but got confused. Into the resulting silence they heard Roni telling Burning Tower, "Sandry isn't spoken for. Believe me, I'd know. I'd hear it from my mother."

"I see. What about you?" Tower asked.

Roni named a handful of eligible males. Lady Shanda and Lord Qirama discussed their merits, to Roni's annoyance, until Sandry praised one man's behavior during the Pizzles' attack. An animated discussion of firefighting ensued.

Tea arrived, with a pyramid of honey cakes.

An apprentice whispered to Egmatel. Egmatel said, "Wale is right. The manna is drifting back to Lordshills, one way and another. We know little of Coyote here, but—he could not come while the fire god was in place, but might he visit us now?"

Twisted Cloud smiled. "He is here if he wants to be, Sage."

Burning Tower caught Egmatel's sneer, instantly hidden. The man didn't believe in Coyote, or perhaps in Twisted Cloud.

And he must have seen something in Tower's face and Green Stone's. He said, "Spells involving Zoosh protect me from interference from other gods. I've wondered sometimes what that has cost me. A god may not consider the welfare of the human being he rides—"

"But he leaves knowledge behind," Twisted Cloud affirmed. "Whandall Feathersnake carried Coyote the night we conceived Clever Squirrel. He brushed cheeks with death that night, but Whandall can tell tales and lore known only to Coyote."

For an instant, Egmatel gaped like a boy seeing his first bull roarer. Then his eyes lowered and he was himself again.

The guests and hosts sipped Green Stone's tea and praised the flavor. Sandry held his peace while several chose honey cakes and brushed off the ants to eat them. Then he said, "Aunt Shanda, why don't we get rid of these ants?"

Shanda, Quintana, Egmatel and both apprentices, and two servants gaped at Sandry. Sandry smiled, but he caught Green Stone's glare.

So did Twisted Cloud. "We're guests, Wagonmaster," she said reprovingly, "and this is common enough. No great proprietary secret."

Lady Shanda was holding her peace with some difficulty. Egmatel . . . what was he thinking? Tower couldn't tell.

Lord Quintana asked, "You can get rid of ants?"

The shaman said, "Not rid. Can you find me a sheet of parchment? And pass the honey."

"I'll get parchment," Roni said. She stood with conscious grace.

They awaited her return. Then Twisted Cloud mixed honey with crushed charcoal and wrote in tiny letters, extensively. She painted honey around all four edges of the parchment and set it on the hearth, next to the honey cakes and squarely in the path of the ants.

Sandry held any ridicule out of his voice, but Burning Tower sensed his disbelief. "You're making them a gift?"

"For the queen ant, and sending her a message. Your ants, they've been deaf and mute for too many years, while Yangin-Atep was consuming every trace of local magic. They need reminding."

Roni laughed, "So do we!"

Twisted Cloud looked at her doubtfully, then at the Sage Egmatel, who was holding a perfect poker face. "Well. The god was Logi or Zoosh or Ghuju, depends on who's speaking. His tribe didn't like to clean up after themselves. Men tired of the women's complaints, and leftover bones got too much attention from coyotes and other predators. Logi made a tiny creature to clean up after them, to carry garbage away. But ants are supposed to stay out of sight, and they're not supposed to swarm over food that's ready for the evening meal!"

Roni said, "So you send a message. And what if they don't take the hint?"

"I send a stronger message," the older woman said grimly.

Sandry asked, "Will you write me another of these ant-messages? For my mother?"

The ants were all over the message, but of course they were still on the food too. The caravaners brushed them off as Sandry did, but those who weren't annoyed were amused. Burning Tower noted that Lady Shanda was not amused at all. Guests had criticized her hospitality for, of all things, ants!

She'd given some kind of signal. Now servants took away the honey cakes and other delicacies, then brought a cauldron of beef and vegetables cooked with corn. A silence fell while they wandered among the guests, serving them. Caravan folk carried their own bowls, but Shanda's servants were offering fine, fragile ceramic. The meat dish was unfamiliar, touched with spices Burning Tower couldn't identify. Caravan cooking would have been different: less bland.

Hunger appeased, the guests relaxed and sipped a wine Green Stone would have sold cheap. Lord Quintana said, "I have not had a chance to visit the market myself. Green Stone, do you carry carpets? And those little bottles?"

"Oh, yes. Here, I brought these. I hope they please you." He distributed them among those present: tiny bottles of glass blackened by cold iron, the side effects of Morth's year-old war. "They sold well last year."

"And you have an interest in horses?"

"If the price is right."

"Horses are expensive," Quintana said. A bit defensively he added, "Ask around; you'll find it's true."

"Pity." Green Stone's face gave nothing away.

Burning Tower suddenly noticed that Lurk was gone. She tried to catch Green Stone's eye, gestured with her nose at his empty place, and got a grin. Then Quintana asked, "Wagonmaster, how did you find the Gate facilities at the Deerpiss?"

Green Stone said, "Much changed," and laughed aloud.

The corners of Quintana's mouth twitched upward; they were both remembering the battle with the Toronexti, the Lordkin tax collectors Waterman had replaced. Now he asked, "Have you dealt with the Captains at Condigeo?"

Hesitation. "My brother has. He'll be in conference with them now."

"The Council of Captains rules Condigeo. They rule the trade routes too, of course; it's their major interest. They still control whatever reaches Tep's Town by ship. Before the caravan came here through the firewoods, they owned us. Now they don't, quite. I'm very serious when I ask you: Do you have any complaints whatever about what you found at the Gate? You're Waterman's first real test."

"Ah. Well, he took out some birds for us. That counts for a *lot.* His men were badly battered, not up for much, but they had water and fodder for our beasts. Otherwise, we dealt with Lord Sandry and his men, and they gave us some help at Peacegiven Square."

"Everything all right there?"

"Very nice. Everything was in place yesterday evening. We've had a profitable day, sir."

"Good! Now, I know everyone around Lordshills who raises or keeps horses. Is there anything else you'd like to find? Anything marketable, I mean."

"I would like to find those cursed birds gone," Green Stone said.

Sandry grunted agreement.

"I don't want to be misunderstood, Lord," Green Stone said. "I know how much effort goes into tending boneheads. Bison aren't much better. *Of course* horses will be expensive. If you ask too much, we'll buy something else. Whatever you're selling, we'll take it or buy something else and count our costs at the end of the year and make our decisions.

"But our costs this year include damage done by flocks of terror birds, and four men dead, and a girl.

They've never come in flocks before. They seem to come from the south and east. We approach Tep's Town and Condigeo from the north. If the birds are . . . well, migrating . . . some of my wagonmasters are thinking of opening new routes further north. We can't keep losing people to the birds."

When Quintana didn't speak, Lady Shanda said, "Qu'yuma is in Condigeo negotiating a new trade agreement. Any such contract would involve wagon as well as sea traffic between us. If the birds make it impossible for wagon traffic—are there birds in Condigeo too? What are they going to tell my husband?"

"It could be even worse there." Lord Quintana nodded vigorously. "Very well. Forget trade goods for the moment. Let's talk about monster birds. Egmatel!" The wizard jumped. "Sage, what have you learned?"

Egmatel hesitated. "Nothing," he said. He observed the shock effect. "Of course that tells us quite a lot. Aren't we all thinking the same thing? Great massive beasts don't multiply this suddenly, be they dragons or bison or mammoths or birds. Ants do that, and mice. This is no sudden increase in reproduction. Somewhere there's a wizard. He's moving birds by the score, sending them our way."

Shanda demanded, "Egmatel, do you *know* this?"

"No, Lady. I surmise. Now two wizards of very different schooling—Twisted Cloud and myself—have studied Lord Sandry's captured bird. Shaman, you found nothing." Egmatel waited for her nod. "I found nothing. No trace of wizardry. The spells that sent the monster birds to ravage our land are very well masked.

"What may we conclude? He or she or they—call them the Black Wizards—they hide from us because they already see us as enemies. Negotiation would be pointless. We must fight."

Lord Quintana asked, "Can you work spells to fight such a thing?"

Egmatel spread his hands helplessly. "I don't know what I'm fighting. We might try a Warlock's Wheel on that bird and see if its behavior changes." He perceived Twisted Cloud's puzzlement, rightly or wrongly, and said, "A very old spell. It burns all the manna out of its surroundings, renders all spells null, kills any magical beast. We use it seldom."

"Worth a try," Twisted Cloud said. "But first I'd like my daughter to see this terror bird. She's at Avalon."

Egmatel flinched. "At the Folded Hands Conference?"

"That's right. She travels with Morth of Atlantis."

They'd seen his distress. Now they saw his anger. "*I* wasn't invited to Folded Hands!"

"I wasn't either," Twisted Cloud said. "Sage, Morth is perhaps the last surviving Atlantis wizard, and Clever Squirrel is *Coyote's daughter.* Unless there's a god in your background, she will always have more power than you or me. It's why we must show her this monster bird, and soon, before the cursed thing sickens and dies."

Green Stone said, "Yes. I can't go, but—Shaman? Will you fetch your daughter?"

Twisted Cloud looked at the serious faces about her. "If she'll come. Folded Hands is supposed to be important."

"The first Conference on Conserving Manna!" Egmatel snapped.

An antic whim took Burning Tower. She said, "You can't travel alone, Shaman. It would be unfitting—and dangerous too. Sandry?"

"How long a trip is this?"

Lord Qirama said, "Twenty-six miles across the sea. Boats can be hired. A full-day trip, but you could come back the next day. We pay enough to keep the pirates suppressed around our harbor, and Avalon has its own defenses." He grinned slightly. "I shouldn't think wizards need to worry about the weather."

"Tep's Town can spare me for a day," Sandry said. "Very well, Twisted Cloud, allow me to escort you."

The shaman grinned. "Travel in the company of a handsome young man? Too tempting, Blazes. Unless . . ." She turned to Burning Tower. "Unless you'd come along?"

Tower struggled to keep the glee out of her voice. "Brother, would that be acceptable?"

Green Stone, smiling, shrugged.

"I'd be delighted," Burning Tower said.

Chapter Ten

Sea Passage

It had been a splendid evening. Green Stone insisted on going back to Peacegiven Square in the night so that he would be there when the market opened. Lurk had vanished. Burning Tower and Twisted Cloud each had a room.

Sandry offered to show Green Stone the accommodations, but Stone hadn't bothered. That seemed to puzzle Sandry, to Tower's amusement. The Lords didn't really understand about one-horns. . . . That would change, now that the kinless ponies were developing. Burning Tower wanted to explain, but her brother wouldn't forgive her if she did. Lords were free with information that the Bison Tribe kept as trade goods.

But she was free to dream. Living in this house with Sandry—that made a fine dream, a bit rough at the edges.

How would she relate to the other Lords? Would the servants like her?

Or traveling with Sandry on the Hemp Road, an ornate wagon—she could expect that as her dowry and with Sandry's wealth, they could have horses, not just bison. Their own wagon train, with this house as their winter home . . .

Her room in Sandry's house was large and airy, with a small washbasin and flowing water that vanished into a stone-lined pool on the floor. The walls had tapestries, and there were drapes to cover the windows, although Burning Tower had no need for them. Servants laid out fruit juices and snacks before she went to bed. When it was time to wake, a girl about Tower's age came in with hot tea and fresh baked biscuits.

Tower grinned at her image in the large mirror. *I could get used to this—Sandry as master of a wagon train. I'd manage it—he doesn't understand those things—but . . .* She was grinning as she went downstairs to breakfast.

A wagon and a chariot waited in the road in front of Sandry's house, each pulled by a team of horses. Servants were already loading the baggage into the wagon. Chalker held the chariot reins.

Burning Tower was fascinated by the horses. They were more friendly than one-horns. Full-grown one-horns loved young girls, but that wasn't friendship, it was some magical effect. And they hated married women, and most men. Tower watched as Sandry greeted the horses and gave each a small carrot as a treat. The horses clearly liked him.

"Ladies, chariot or wagon?" Sandry asked.

Twisted Cloud chuckled. "How long is this trip?"

"Half an hour, no more," Sandry said.

"Thank you. With no place to sit in your chariot, I prefer the wagon."

"Right," Chalker said. "I'll drive the wagon, then."

"I don't mind standing in the chariot," Tower said.

"But you have to stay inside it." Sandry was laughing. "No more climbing out on the wagon tongue!"

"Oh, all right." *Of course you were supposed to remember I'd done that,* Tower thought. *Hah! Most men don't remember things they're supposed to.*

"No showing off," she said. "I've seen you drive, and I know you're good. And we don't want Cloud telling Mother it's not safe."

"Sure," Sandry said. He helped her board, although they both knew she didn't need help. His hand lingered on her forearm after he helped her up.

"It's beautiful in your town," Tower said. "Waterfall and flower beds—it must take a lot of work to keep up."

"Yes, but what else would the gardeners do?"

They passed through the gates with a wave to the Lordsmen guards, and Sandry shook the reins. The horses broke into a trot. The wagon lurched, and she used that as an excuse to grip Sandry's arm. He didn't look at her, but she could see his grin.

The road down to the harbor was broad, gently curved, and lined with houses far less splendid than the palaces inside the walls, but considerably nicer than in Tep's

Town proper. At intervals were squares, with shops and pleasant places to sit, and shopkeepers and shoppers sitting in the shade. *Not buying much,* Tower thought. *Maybe the customers with money have gone to our market fair.*

Most of the squares had fountains that worked better than the one in Peacegiven Square. *We were in Lordshills, and this is Lord's Town. Now I've seen both. . . .* "This is nice," Tower said.

Sandry nodded.

"Much nicer than Tep's Town. Why?"

Sandry seemed disturbed by the question. He looked away. Finally he said, "Well, there aren't any Lordkin gathering here. Just kinless."

"No Lordkin here at all?"

"Well, we let a few live here. A very few. And there are descendants of Lordkin, but they're raised by kinless. Mostly these are kinless. Some lookers, a few foreign merchants, but mostly kinless."

"There are kinless in Tep's Town."

"Sure. But they work for the Lordkin. Why work hard for yourself when some Lordkin can gather everything? In these parts, the kinless belong to the Lords."

"Like slaves?"

Sandry looked uncomfortable. "No, not really. But—actually, I suppose so, at least technically. A long time ago, the Lords and the Lordkin together defeated the kinless and took this land. The kinless surrendered, but they weren't sold into slavery. They were allowed to go on living here, but they have to support the Lordkin."

"And the Lords?"

"Yes, of course, but we pay for what we gather. Lordkin don't." He looked uncomfortable. "There's a charter. Most of the kinless live in the Lordkin areas, and the Lordkin gather when they want to, but the charter lets us have this area where only the Lords can gather. Lordkin have to agree to that or they can't come in here. I guess technically you could call the kinless here slaves to the Lords' Council, but look at them—they don't act like slaves! Everyone in Tep's Town wants to live here! The problem is to keep them out."

Tower nodded. Her Lordkin father and her kinless mother had wildly different ideas of what life in Tep's Town had been like. Neither one made it sound like much fun growing up there, and both had nice things to say about Lord's Town.

"Oh!" she shouted. "That's the ocean!"

"Yep."

"It's *big*!"

Sandry smiled. "I'd forgotten you never got down to the shore last year."

"Everything happened so fast. Sandry, it's beautiful!" Sandry gave the horses their head, and the beach came up fast. Sand and palm trees, big waves crashing onto the sand. Blue skies, blue water. Big white birds soaring along the shore. Dark heads in the water. A family of eight stripped down and ran for the water in a mob. An enormous bird seemed to just fold its wings and fall into the water, to come out with a fish in its huge bill. A big fish rode an enormous wave to the shore. As the wave crashed, the fish leaped up and became a man, a young man with long blond hair and no clothes.

"Did I just see that?" Tower asked.

"Got to me first time I saw it happen," Sandry said. "Before last year, before Morth and your father drove Yangin-Atep mythical, we'd only see the mer people in fish form. They never came here as humans. Now—"

The young man stretched. The change caught him in the middle of a yawn: he was a great fish balanced on its tail, now toppling, now fallen in a spray of sand.

Swimmers pointed. Sandry stopped the chariot to watch. Children and adults emerged from the waves and began to roll the wriggling fish across the wet sand toward the water. When a wave hit him, he was a man again, just long enough for his legs to carry him out to sea.

Sandry drove away. He said, "Seawater carries manna. So Egmatel tells us, but there's not enough yet in Tep's Town. The mers catch fish for us. And here's the harbor."

The harbor was small, a patch of water walled off from the sea by big rocks and logs. Waves crashed against the sea walls.

"It's smaller than I thought," Tower said. "Condigeo—I've seen sand paintings, and the harbor there looks huge."

Sandry said, "But they have a big enclosed bay. Our harbor is artificial, and the sea wants to tear down the walls. It takes a lot of work to keep even this much protected."

There was a barge in the harbor. Men stood chest deep in muddy water. They used buckets to scoop out sand and dirt from the bottom, then they emptied the buckets into the barge.

"Like that," Sandry said. "The harbor fills up if they don't dredge it out. We keep hoping the wizards will figure out some way to make it less work, but they never do."

"That looks like hard work for strong men," Tower said. "Lordkin?"

Sandry laughed, then looked embarrassed again. "Tower, nothing against your father, but Lordkin don't work! A few of those are experts we hire from Condigeo and Black Rock, but mostly those are kinless from Lord's Town. They're well paid too."

"Is that our ship?" She pointed at a boat drawn up alongside a wooden dock. It was hard to tell how large it was, but it was bigger than any wagon, longer than several wagons put together. The front and back parts of the ship were decked over, and there was a cabin built over the deck on the front end. The middle part was open, with what looked like benches. The mast was tall, many times taller than she was, with ropes from the top down to the decks. Other ropes hung in orderly disarray.

"*Angie Queen.* That's her," Sandry said. "Got in two days ago. They were supposed to sail to Condigeo tomorrow, but the council arranged to hire it for a couple of days to take us over and get Clever Squirrel."

It didn't look quite safe, but Tower wasn't going to say that. She eyed the ship more carefully. At least four times longer than a big cargo wagon, and maybe a wagon length across at its widest point. People were moving about, on the ship and on the docks. *Like setting up a market,* Tower thought. *Everyone knows what to do, so there's no need for orders and instructions. They just do it.*

They watched from Sandry's chariot. No one paid them any attention at all. Finally the wagon pulled up behind them. Chalker jumped off, bowed in the general direction of Twisted Cloud, and boarded the ship over a long, narrow plank. Twisted Cloud studied the ship without expression, but from time to time she glanced up at the blue skies and wispy clouds. *We should have good weather,* Tower thought.

Chalker came back down. "All's ready, My Lord, Ladies. You can go aboard now. I'll see to the baggage."

"Thank you, Chalker," Tower said. "Will you be coming with us?"

"No, more's the pity," Chalker said. "Never seen Avalon. Not many in Tep's Town have." He grinned. "You'll take good care of my young master. I'm sure he'd rather have you than me for company!"

"I hope so."

Chalker grinned.

Sandry was too far away to hear what Tower and Chalker were saying to each other, but when they glanced toward him it was pretty certain what the subject was.

And the more I see of her, the more I like her, he thought. *Smart. She can be silly, and serious, and she gets along with everyone. And Mother liked her.* He smiled softly to himself as he remembered her touch. Her hand was warm when she gripped his arm. . . .

A sailor came up and made a gesture, putting his knuckles to his forehead. Sandry had noticed sailors did that when talking to their superiors. An odd custom. "Welcome aboard."

Sandry eyed the narrow plank over the sea. *No more unstable than a chariot platform, and only water to fall into, so why am I nervous?* Tower grinned and skipped across, and he followed, Twisted Cloud behind him.

The sailor led them up to the front end of the ship. "This is called the foredeck," he said. "That end is the bow, and you go forward when you go in that direction. The other end is the stern, and you go aft when you go that way. Might be useful to remember that." He paused. "Sir. My Lord. Ladies." Not used to dealing with passengers. A young man, certainly not older than Sandry, and proud of his abilities.

Sandry nodded. "Thanks. I'll try to remember."

There was a small cabin with the door on the back—aft, Sandry remembered—side of the foredeck cabin. Inside were seats for perhaps a dozen at a small table with benches on each side. Other passengers came aboard and were led to a cabin under the stern deck. Sandry frowned. "I thought we chartered this boat," he said.

Twisted Cloud shrugged. "Doesn't do us any harm to have other passengers. And we get the little cabin with the seats."

Sandry nodded agreement. It seemed much too confined inside the cabin, so they stood on the foredeck making conversation while the crew set about making the ship seaworthy. This involved moving an infinity of rope and a lot of shouting. After a while, a group of men came aboard and took seats in the belly of the ship on the benches Sandry had noticed before. Oars were put in place. He couldn't see what else was happening down there, but there were the sounds of hammering and clinking metal. Everywhere else men moved purposefully. One climbed the mast and did something with the ropes up there.

"They're very particular about getting things exactly right," Burning Tower observed. "You're like that, Sandry."

Absently, Sandry said, "Well, maybe I am." Had he forgotten anything? This trip made him nervous. He'd met few magicians in his life. Morth had been a maniac. Egmatel was something of a fraud. What would scores of wizards be like?

Burning Tower said, "The sailors, they're keeping lists in their heads, aren't they? Do this, do that, or the boat doesn't go. It's like that in the caravan too. Everything has to be just so, or the beasts misbehave, things fall off, a wagon rolls down a hill. What I noticed about the people who serve you in Lordshills . . ." Burning Tower's hands moved, reaching for words, concepts. "They're not following a list. They follow orders. They do what it takes to make you—us—comfortable.

"Sandry, the people who do the work at Road's End . . . they don't travel. Sometimes they resent it, that they don't have a wagon or a piece of one. Why are your servants so . . . ?"

"A good servant gets to thinking that he runs a household, and *that's* what drives *him.* Her. Aunt Shanda's chef. Chalker. The others . . . well, they want us happy," Sandry said.

"Right! Why?"

Sandry wasn't used to thinking in these terms. He said, "I guess they don't want to go back where they came from."

"And?"

What was she getting at? "I'm tasked with finding a place for a kinless woman who got taken pregnant by a Lordkin lover who cared enough to ask for a favor. Maybe I can . . . anyway, a lot who serve us are like that. Something drove them away. They don't always tell us. The rest . . . if they lose their place in Lordshills . . . they're either kinless or Lordkin. If they're kinless, they'll be back in the hands of the Lordkin. If they're Lordkin, that can be bad too. Lordkin women do all the work they can't lay off on kinless. Lordkin men maim and kill each other. Didn't your father tell you—"

"Well, I know he left, and he rescued Mother. They don't talk about it much."

"And," Sandry said diffidently, "I don't *really* know how they think. We have to guess. Tower, tell me about your half sister."

Burning Tower laughed. "I'll let her mother speak for me."

The Bison Tribe shaman was watching sailors swarm over the decks, but she'd heard. She said, "Clever Squirrel was Bison Tribe's shaman a year ago, when I couldn't travel. Early this year, she traveled west with the Pumas to visit Morth. She wants the spell that unravels failed spells. Had to follow him to Avalon to get it." She looked around. "Squirrely's powerful. More than me. Much more than me. Why not? She's Coyote's daughter."

"How does that work?"

Reluctantly at first, Twisted Cloud told of the wild night her father Hickamore, the Bison Tribe shaman, led his fifteen-year-old daughter and a twenty-year-old Lordkin into a hillside thick with raw gold. Hickamore died when wild magic renewed long-forgotten spells. Coyote possessed Whandall Placehold. The god dazzled and seduced Hickamore's daughter. The next morning, Willow claimed Whandall as her man before Bison Tribe.

"She might have thought *I* was going to claim him," Twisted Cloud said. "We conceived Squirrely that night. She and Blazes are half sisters because Coyote was riding Whandall."

"I didn't hear this story until I was pretty old," Burning Tower said, "and I didn't know why Twisted Cloud never claimed the gold in the hill. She's the only one who knew, barring Father—"

"Hush, child," said Twisted Cloud.

"Sorry."

Sandry grinned at them both. "There's a story here?"

Sails rose aloft and caught the wind. There were shouts from the stern deck. People on the docks did things with ropes, then shouted again.

"Well. Raw gold carries manna, you know, but the magic is uncontrollable," Twisted Cloud said. "Wizards go crazy at the touch of gold. *Spells* go crazy. Not many can handle it. Still, even wild manna may heal or rejuvenate or—anyway. What I told Burning Tower, in an incautious moment—"

"We're off! We're sailing!" Burning Tower exclaimed. The docks were flowing past them. "Sorry."

"Please," Sandry said, "go on."

Twisted Cloud thought a bit before she spoke. "People give raw gold to a shaman. Payment for spells, services. A shaman uses the manna and leaves refined gold behind. I found out that night that raw gold makes me horny. I always get pregnant when I'm around it. After five children, I knew I didn't want any more to do with raw gold. The gold stayed put, and my father's skeleton too, until Whandall needed it twenty years later.

"My oldest child is Clever Squirrel, and she is Coyote's daughter, sure enough. She'll find what that cursed bird is hiding if anyone can."

For a time they enjoyed the view of land sliding past, waves growing larger, the sails belling over them, the to-and-fro surge of a ship cleaving water. Sandry's belly grew uneasy. He thought he was hiding it until Twisted Cloud laughed and touched his ears with her fingertips, and then it was all right. *Hah! Wagons must wobble too.*

At midmorning, the sails hung slack and the ship slowed. Shouting wafted up from belowdecks.

"Curse," Twisted Cloud said quietly.

"What?" Tower asked.

"The oarsmen. They hate. They can't do anything about it, so *I* have to feel it."

Sandry looked into the midships pit where twenty oarsmen were at work. Two rows of men manned the oars: not enough to manage a decent speed. An oarmaster was cracking air over their heads with a lash. "Without them, the ship doesn't move," he said. And then he sucked air.

The girls looked at him. Sandry said, "Regapisk."

Regapisk, no longer Lord, was second on the port side, nearly naked, sitting on a yellow cloak or blanket. A mottled blue bruise marked his face. Regapisk snarled; his muscles bunched. He pulled, then lifted the oar, then pulled. The oar surged, lifted, dropped, surged in tandem with the rest.

Regapisk was better at rowing than Sandry would have guessed.

The women were looking at him. Uncomfortably, Sandry said, "Skip it. Twisted Cloud, what can you tell me about this wizards' gathering?"

"No magic," she said. When Tower and Sandry both laughed, she said, "I'm the one who has to remember. The locals are very hard on anyone who uses flagrantly powerful magic."

"What do they do?"

"I don't know," the shaman said. "Nothing esoteric, I'd guess. Drowning, maybe."

The wind picked up an hour later. The ship heeled over at a different angle and seemed to be struggling, and the shelter of the small cabin was welcome. Wind whistled through the small round windows carved into the side of the cabin.

Servants had been setting the table in the forecabin. Now they took out little wooden rails and set them into holes in the table so that the food and drink wouldn't slide off. "Lunch is served," a white-coated crewman said. He bowed. "Ladies. Lord Sandry, the captain would like a moment with you back aft, if you please." He pointed to the rear of the ship.

There was a narrow walkway on either side of the oar pits. The sailor had indicated that Sandry should take the walkway on the right, the high side of the ship as it leaned far over. The oars had been brought into the ship now, and the oarsmen were slumped in place, not looking up. All but Regapisk, who looked around warily. Sandry didn't think he'd looked up at him.

The captain and two officers were at the back of the ship. There were two more men holding wooden bars thicker than spears. These were attached to posts that went down on each side of the ship.

"Steersman, bring her up, there!" the captain shouted. "Lee steersman, haul in hard!"

"Aye aye." The man on the low side of the ship was straining. "Maybe need some help here, skipper."

The captain nodded, and another crewmen went over to help. They strained at pulling on the wooden contraption.

The steersman on the high side of the ship seemed relaxed. "No bite on the windward side," he shouted.

The captain nodded. "Stand by. Okay, lads, steady as she goes. Ah. Lord Sandry."

"Captain Saziff. Are we in trouble?"

Saziff grinned. A big man, gold earrings, a bright red shirt of what was probably silk, and a dark wool coat with gold lace on the sleeves.

Sandry nodded to himself. He could understand dressing to impress the men. . . .

"Trouble, My Lord? Not in this little blow. Not trouble, just delay. How bad do you need to get there before dark?"

"Well—we were told we'd be there with plenty of daylight."

"Wind, My Lord. Not from the usual direction today.

We'll get there, but we'll have to tack a lot. Be surprised if we're there before dark."

"Have we choices?"

The captain nodded. "For four gold, I can hire mers to help us." He shrugged. "Ordinarily I'd just do it and eat the cost, but we just had a bad run up the coast, and I can't afford it. I told your harbormaster this is a tricky time of year for the Avalon run. Usually the wind is steady from the west, but it's backed around southerly now."

Whatever that means, Sandry thought. "Isn't this your regular run?"

"Bless you, no, sir. There's not enough traffic from Tep's Town to Avalon to support a regular run! I'm headed to Condigeo and Black Warrior and then on further south to Two Capes. May even run right on around and up north on the inside, if I can get cargo. No, we were chartered to take you over and bring you back, and we'll do that, all right, but we won't make the harbor tonight without help from the mers."

"And they charge four gold?"

"Might be less, but once you hire them, you'd better have the money," Saziff said. "And I don't have it, My Lord." He grinned. "Tell you what, though—for four gold I can get you into the harbor ahead of time and we can have a bit of a show for the ladies as well."

Four gold. Sandry doubted they'd paid more than ten gold for the whole passage. But there was no way to know if the captain was telling the truth or not, and it would cost more than four gold to stay an extra day in Avalon, from everything Sandry had heard. "All right." He dug into his pouch. "Four it is."

The captain took the money without expression. "Raililiee, take over," he said.

One of the officers said, "Aye aye. I relieve you, sir."

"I'm going forward to negotiate with the mers. Stand by to trim sails."

"Aye aye, skipper."

Saziff led the way forward again. Sandry looked down at Regapisk. By both law and custom, they shouldn't speak or even recognize each other. Sandry remembered, years ago, some older boys were pounding on him. Reggy made them stop and helped him clean up his clothes. There were probably other things Reggy had done for him over the years, but that was the incident Sandry remembered best.

They reached the foredeck. "Ladies," the captain called. "Come see something you've never seen before!"

Tower and Twisted Cloud came out to watch. The captain leaned down over the bow rail. Sandry leaned over too and was surprised to see a big fish swimming there.

A big fish, as big as Sandry, maybe bigger.

The captain shouted something, and the fish stood up on its tail, most of its body out of the water, and skittered alongside the ship.

"Oooh!" Tower shouted.

The captain shouted something else, and then threw a rope over the side. There was a big loop woven into the end of the rope, and the other end was tied to a big post on the deck. The fish made strange noises. Its toothy mouth was grinning widely.

Another of the big fish came up and put its bill into

the rope loop. It began to swim, and the boat heeled over even more.

"Trim sail!" the captain shouted.

Crewmen did things to the sails. The boat came more upright. The big fish pulled, and the captain threw more lines off into the water. Other fish put their bills through them and began to pull.

"On course now," Saziff said. He clapped his hands.

More fish leaped from the water. They would charge at the boat as if they would hit it, then dart off just at the last moment. Others jumped right over the ones pulling the boat. Tower and Twisted Cloud cheered.

"Smart fish!" Tower said.

"Not exactly fish, My Lady," the skipper said. "They're mers, of course. Lots of names for them, I guess dolphins is the most common. They breathe air like you and me."

Twisted Cloud was staring at them. "Magic, lots of magic, but only the ones that are pulling, not the others. The others don't seem to be magic at all."

Saziff shrugged. "Don't know, My Lady. Used to be no one would take ship without a wizard aboard, but last ten, twenty years now, they're mostly just passengers, nothing for them to do. I never did know much about magic anyway."

Chapter Eleven

Avalon

An hour later, they could see a dark shape looming up out of the water, and gradually it became an island. As they got closer, the wind died out entirely, and they took the sails down. The dolphins pulled them closer, then dropped the ropes. The Oarmaster shouted, and they rowed into a horseshoe-shaped harbor. There were docks built out from the shore, rows of them. A half dozen ships as large or larger than *Angie Queen* were tied alongside the docks, and there was room for twice that many more.

They came alongside a dock, but the ship stood off from it a good ten feet as the sailors passed lines back and forth. Sandry and the women stood at the rail and looked in fascination at Avalon.

He saw a sandy beach, with children playing, some

half-clad, some naked. Sea animals with dark fur and flippers frolicked with the children. Half-grown dolphins played in the waves just off the shore. Here and there, adult humans lounged in hammocks. Blond youths with deep tans and muscles that any Lords officer would be proud of brought the loungers tall colored drinks. Teenage boys and girls played at some kind of game with a large leather ball.

Behind the beach was a row of brightly colored shops mostly set as storefronts into buildings that looked like warehouses. There was a warehouse built onto one dock, and the gaudy building on the dock next to it was clearly a restaurant.

"It looks—magic," Burning Tower said.

"It *is* magic," Twisted Cloud said. "The most magical place I've ever perceived."

"And, I've been told, the most expensive," Sandry said. He pointed at the dock. All along it were small stalls selling art objects, hats, clothing. "Prices in gold and silver, not shells."

Brightly painted shops crowded to left and right on the main street. Beyond those, and above them on the hills, were less gaudy structures: houses. They were charming in their differences, Sandry had thought as he watched them grow larger as the ship neared the docks. But they had certainly not been made by magic. The houses—even the oversize one that must be the hotel—showed all the crudity of human workmanship.

"I'd hoped to see one of the magic castles the wizards are always talking about," Sandry said.

"Not here," Twisted Cloud said. There was awe in her voice. "Thank you for sending me, Sandry. I never expected to see this place."

Burning Tower clapped her hands. "Me either. The Condigeo captains come here, but I don't think I ever met anyone else who did. But it feels magic even if we don't see any. Why is that?"

"It's because you don't see anything big and magical," Twisted Cloud said. "Other places, the wizards did their spectacular tricks and used up all the manna. Condigeo. There's a whole city under silt and mud where their harbor used to be. No one can get to it, not even the mers. Ran out of magic and just settled into the muck. I know of other cities with collapsed castles. But there are places south and east along the Golden Road that still have big magical palaces."

"How?" Sandry asked.

Twisted Cloud shook her head. "I don't know. I've never been south or east of Condigeo. But there must be a supply, a way to renew the manna." She grinned. "And this time I'm not holding information to trade. If I knew I'd tell you. You've earned anything I know just for bringing me here!"

"Look up there!" Burning Tower shouted.

Color flashed across the hills. A tremendous bowl was set below the highest hill. Colors played in the rock and spilled out like liquids along the hillside. The bowl looked as if it had been blown like a huge rainbow bubble, then trimmed off like the top of a soft-boiled egg.

"Magic shaped that one," Sandry said.

Twisted Cloud said, "That must be Meetpoint, where they hold the seminars. It's old."

* * *

The sailors hauled on ropes and pulled them to the dock. The crew laid a gangplank, then barred the passengers from reaching it. They waited until another ship tied up to the other side of the dock and a dozen passengers stood at its rail.

Presently a man robed in purple strode aboard, escorted by Captain Saziff. Sandry couldn't help staring. He must have weighed four hundred pounds. He was not just tall, but billowy, a smooth curve of a man. Within his hood, his face was white rimmed in black, split by a wide, wide grin.

"Orca," Twisted Cloud whispered.

Sandry nodded. Whale. Clearly those were not the colors of a human being, but of an orca.

He clapped thunderously, waited for silence, and said, "I'm Schoolmaster Wheereezz. If you're lookers or tellers, welcome to Avalon! We take most forms of money. The exchange is that gray building left of the last dock. If you're wizards of any kind, welcome also! We only impose one special rule," the sage said. "Whatever you know of magic, don't use it here. If you've come to learn magic, well and good, but don't practice it. This island is a refuge for mer folk. Here we can be human, as long as the manna holds out. Magicians also reside here, particularly elderly ones who need rich background manna to survive."

The captain called, "Be aboard at the third hour tomorrow. We leave when it suits My Lord Sandry, and if you miss the ship, you'll forfeit your fare and have to make a deal with some other captain less generous than me." Then the passengers were allowed to spill ashore.

They were joined by passengers from the other ship, where Wheereezz had repeated his speech.

When the crowd thinned, Twisted Cloud said, "Let's get to Meetpoint. I can't attend the seminars—I'm not an invited guest—but maybe Squirrel's there."

"We should book rooms," Sandry said.

"It's the same direction. Lord Sandry, these wizards tend to arrange their own housing. Squirrel's staying at one of the houses. The hotel's expensive. They'll have rooms. We can take our time."

"Shops," said Tower.

So they walked north toward the bowl. Tower tripped over a loose board. Sandry caught her hand, and they walked that way for the rest of the block. They passed along the warehouses, then along a line of shops.

Goods were arrayed facing the street, unguarded, stealable. Guarded by magic? Sandry wondered. Or was it only that a thief would have to escape the island? And there were no Lordkin guards at all. No one was armed. He could walk the street with a pretty girl wearing expensive jewelry and never worry.

A shop built into a huge conch shell sold kitchenware made of shells or decorated with shells, a thousand kinds of shells. Burning Tower bought two fragile-looking geegaws. Another sold household tools. "Wizardry supplies," Twisted Cloud said of a shop that sold dolls and doll-making equipment. A produce market . . . expensive. A bakery. Fish . . . absolutely fresh, and cheap, prices in shells rather than metal. And another building: buckets hanging on the wall, a large bell in a tower, bored-looking men sitting at a table playing a game.

"Avalon Fire Station," Sandry read.

"Oh!" Tower said. "Will you talk with them?"

"I don't know." *How? Introduce myself as the fire chief from Tep's Town? I might learn something, but I might just make a fool of myself. Learning something could be important, but letting people know that the Lords Witness of Lordshills have fools for officials would be terrible.*

A restaurant. Sandry's stomach rumbled approval, and the ladies agreed. There were plenty of tables, and the waitress led them through the large room to a deck outside. There was a good view of the harbor, but Tower sat across from Sandry, and he kept looking at her, ignoring the flashing water and cavorting dolphins and the bustle along the beach.

They ate deep-fried swordfish (cheap) and slivers of potato (expensive) under a hot sun. It was a good day not to think about Tep's Town, or terror birds, or Regapisk chained to an oar. A day to think about how good Burning Tower looked wolfing swordfish, then fresh oranges (expensive).

They walked on. Where the shops ran out, they turned uphill toward the bowl.

At the entrance they found a young man, robed, with his hood thrown back to free long blond hair. He looked them over dubiously. "Sigils?"

"We're looking for my daughter?" Twisted Cloud said with a question in her voice. "Clever Squirrel? She's attending."

The man smiled. His teeth came to needle points; there looked to be too many. Either he filed them or he was a mer. "I know her. She wouldn't be interested in this. It's Hedjeraa talking about how to walk and talk and dress like they can really do magic."

"Seriously? But where shall we look?"

"It's a big island. Let me try a find." The youth looked at the palm of his outsize hand. "Right. Try uphill, up that path—see it?—then along the ridge. Tell her Borush sent you."

They climbed.

Looking down into the bowl-shaped gathering place, Sandry saw that Hedjeraa had drawn a good crowd, fifty or sixty. Something above them had attracted their attention: he saw arms pointing up.

The path switchbacked as it rose. Before it reached the crest, it forked. "Curse Borush," Twisted Cloud said. "Which way?"

Sandry said, "We have to find her before tomorrow. Shaman, could you find the house where's she's staying?"

"If that boy can do a find . . . well, I won't try it yet. They seem very picky about who does magic. Let's keep climbing, get a view. Left or right?"

"Right."

They climbed. Below them, a score of wizards and apprentices were climbing too. That was Morth of Atlantis in the forefront, in the sober robes of a mage. He'd been more flamboyantly dressed when Sandry saw him last. Trailing the rest was a vast purple shape, Schoolmaster Wheereezz.

Twisted Cloud paused at the crest. "Let's see which way they go," she said.

"Why? They're not—"

"I know my daughter."

At the fork, the wizards straggled into the right branch. Reassured, Twisted Cloud set off again. Tower and Sandry followed. Wherever they were going, they were ahead of the wizards.

A young woman looked up, saw them, waved frantically from the bottom of a sheer drop.

They found switchbacks that led down. The Meetpoint gathering place was far below them. When she judged them in earshot, the young woman shouted. "Mother! Blazes! What are you doing here?"

"Clever Squirrel, meet Lord Sandry of the Burning City. We have a mutual problem."

"Curse it, Mother, I'm here to learn! I've already got—oh, well, come on down. Hello, Lord Sandry, pleased to meet you. Aren't you the one Blazes—right. What do you think of this?"

They had reached the bottom of the cliff. Clever Squirrel waved up, and Sandry saw that a human face had been carved into the face of the cliff.

Burning Tower clapped her hands. "Oh, Squirrely, it's Father to the life!"

"It's a little crude yet. Let me—" Clever Squirrel picked up a slender tree branch. She waved the tip over the cliffside. Dust and pebbles flaked off and fell, accenting a lifted eyebrow.

A shrill voice cried, "Stop!" And then a dozen more bellowed down at them.

"What are you—"

"The rules!"

"Young woman, you've been told the price of wizardry here!"

"Stop that at once!" A lean old man with good lungs.

"Don't hurt her!" That last cry came from Morth of Atlantis. It was barely audible; he was trailing now, and fairly winded.

The wizards descended. There wasn't room for them all in the space below the cliff. They bunched, reluctant to approach. The women were behind Sandry. Sandry hadn't consciously prepared for battle, but this lot would reach the women only if they got past him.

Now came Schoolmaster Wheereezz, somehow keeping his balance on the narrow path while he forced his way around cliff-hugging lesser acolytes and wizards. Once clear, he pulled back his hood—revealing a smooth bald black-and-white head—and looked up at the cliffside, smiling widely. "Beautiful!" he said. "Clever Squirrel, this would be your work."

Sandry followed his gaze. Though Squirrelly had dropped her wand, the face of Whandall Feathersnake was still changing, a fall of sand refining its rugged look. A mad delight looked out of the rocky face, an expression Sandry had not seen in Whandall Feathersnake last year.

"We're told that the god Coyote is your father," Wheereezz said. "Is this Coyote? And is he improving his portrait?"

"Yes, Sage," Squirrel said.

"And," Wheereezz roared, "have you any idea how much power your magic has used?"

"Yes, Sage—"

"Let's find out." Wheereezz clambered up the slope toward the vast face. Sandry distinctly saw the eyes in the portrait move. The big man stood just beneath, his robes billowing in the wind.

"This girl is under my protection!" wheezed Morth of Atlantis. He was still edging his way down.

There was a flash of color: the eyes of the god blazed and pinpoints of light played across the robes of the accusing wizard. Sandry thought he heard a laugh.

"Although she may not need it." Morth spoke quietly, but they all heard him.

"Not much gone," Wheereezz said. "Not much power gone at all."

"That's silly—forgive me, but it's not plausible," the lean old man exclaimed. He moved away from the dots of light, but they followed him. He frowned. "Even gods must obey the rules here! This cursed cliff has been ready to fall on Meetpoint for a generation already. Now she's used up most of the manna in it!"

"If she had, I'd be rolling downhill in fishy form," Wheereezz said, "and no god would be able to function here at all." He grinned up at Coyote, then laughed. "Go ahead, Conal. Test it."

Conal's jaw set hard. His hands wove a complicated series of passes. Pale rainbow fire spurted from between his fingers, in a spell that had been powerful enough to blind enemy armies a mere hundred years ago.

Conal glared at the apprentices around him. If any were thinking that they now had permission to try a few spells, that stopped them. "The magic's as strong as it ever was," the Sage Conal said, biting down on his words. "She's used almost nothing. Girl, how did you do it?"

In a small, frightened voice, Clever Squirrel said, "But there's no great magic here. Rock wants to fall. The cliff is already crumbly, can't you tell? I just tell it where to crumble. You don't have to be a mighty wizard if you're making things do what they want to do anyway. Rock sculpture is easy. We in Bison Tribe use it to mark a trail."

Conal was aghast. "Can all caravan shamans do this?"

"Anyone can mark a crumbly rock, sure, or tell a tree to write a sigil with its branches. Main Man is a better artist than me, but he can't work this large."

"Very well," Wheereezz said. "Can you prepare a lecture on your style of magic? We have a slot open day after tomorrow—"

Before she could answer, Sandry said, "No. I'm sorry, really, but we need Clever Squirrel in Tep's Town as soon as possible."

Rage ran across Squirrel's features, and Sandry suddenly perceived the young woman's power. "Who do you think you are, Lord Sandry of the Burning City? Remember where you are!"

Burning Tower spoke up. "Squirrel, it's true. You're needed. We came all this way to get you."

"I might have a solution," said Schoolmaster Wheereezz.

Chapter Twelve

Clever Squirrel

Squirrel chattered as they made their way back down the hill. "Morth was already gone when I got to Carlem Marcle. I stayed at Rordray's Attic for a night while I waited for a ship to Blackhawk Bay and Avalon. I sent Seshmarls to Whandall with messages. No point trying to get you a message in the Burning City!"

"No," Tower said.

The bird Seshmarls was a magically endowed crow. Magic still ran thin in Tep's Town.

"But the idea was to meet the caravan in Condigeo, two weeks from now! Blazes, I've never seen Condigeo! And the wizards here have invited me to lecture!"

"Well, that worked out," Twisted Cloud said.

"Oh, yes. They'll get a better look at roadside shaman technique if you do the talking. You've been at it a lot longer, Mother. And they'll have to give you a sigil and let you attend the other lectures. It all works out very nicely for *you*. How will you get home?"

"With Morth."

"Uh-*huh*. Watch out for raw gold! But *I'm* missing classes, and Blazes, you never saw Condigeo either. Wouldn't you jump at the chance?"

Burning Tower shrugged. "Someday."

"But what's this all about?"

Sandry didn't seem ready to speak, so Burning Tower said, "Terror birds."

"What about them? They're trouble, but you don't see them often."

"We do now."

"Where?"

"They attacked us just before we got to Tep's Town. And before that. You went west, we went south," Tower said, "along the Hemp Road. We were past Last Pines when three birds attacked us."

"Three?"

"Three, then four, then five. We'd reached the Firewoods by then. You know, it's lucky we had the practice. We were just through the Firewoods when *twelve* hit us. We circled for defense and held them off. Some of the birds charged off down the road into Tep's Town. Sandry killed them all but one, and caged that one."

"They killed more than thirty people," Sandry said. "They're bigger than horses and better armed than most Lordkin. We killed six and captured one alive, Lordkin Firemen and Waterman's tax squad and my boys all working together. The Bisons got the rest. A couple of our wizards—" He stopped for a moment. Tower too had seen Squirrel's momentary grimace. "Such as they are," Sandry said carefully, "they looked the bird over and couldn't find what's made them enemies. Twisted Cloud looked—"

"I can't either," Cloud said.

"The birds are a threat to Bison Tribe and Tep's Town both. Now, you know that birds that big won't hunt together. They'd never get enough to eat," said Sandry. "It has to be magic, doesn't it? They're *sent.* And if expert wizards can't find a wizard's tracks in this matter, then he must be very good at his job, yes? So the thing is, we want you to look this bird over quick, before it dies or escapes on us. We want the best, and that seems to be you."

The inn was on a hill overlooking the harbor. There were a dozen and more rooms, all different. One was a cave. Another was built on a platform at the top of a tower. Three stood side by side off a patio with a view of the harbor. Sandry booked all three. "I'll take this one," he said, pointing to the smallest. It was decorated with red lace and red hearts, and its usual purpose was obvious. Tower blushed slightly as Clever Squirrel suppressed a grin.

Dinner was served on the patio. Morth eagerly accepted an invitation to join them. Sandry sat next to Twisted Cloud, across from Burning Tower. He kept looking at her, and seeing that the others were watching him look at her, and feeling the warmth come to his face at the realization. All his life he had been taught to hide his emotions, from the Lordkin especially, but from the servants and kinless and the soldiers too. Lords didn't have private lives.

But they knew love. Even Aunt Shanda, formidable Aunt Shanda, was in love with her husband. His father had loved his mother, and when he died, part of her had died. *We can love. . . .*

Before dinner, there were tall drinks, mildly alcoholic, with a trace of hemp.

"Nothing strong, nothing to overwhelm the food." The proprietor was a thin blond man of indeterminate age. His staff called him Wolf. Sandry wondered if he was a were. "This I learned from Rordray himself; it is the drink served in his Attic," Wolf said.

"So it is," Morth agreed.

"You are familiar with Rordray's Attic!" The proprietor jumped up and down. "I only met him once; I went to Carlem Marcle just to meet him. He was most gracious as a host."

"And a bit stingy about sharing recipes?" Morth prompted.

"Yes, yes, of course, but I stayed three days and I tasted many of his plainer dishes. I was interested in the most plain because I thought I would learn them more easily. On the third day, Rordray himself joined me at table. 'Learn to know what you like,' he said. 'If you like it and you have good taste, your customers will like it also.' It was good advice, and now this is all I have left of the cuisine of Rordray's Attic. But I think you will like what I have."

"Then I will let you choose my dinner," Sandry said. "With thanks."

The others agreed, and Wolf scuttled away happily.

"It's pleasant here," Clever Squirrel said.

"Oh, yes," Tower agreed. "I'd like to stay a long time." She looked at Sandry when she said it.

Sandry laughed. "I can keep the ship over another night, but not longer. How would we get back?"

"Ride the mers," Clever Squirrel said.

"You can't mean that!" Tower laughed. "It would be cold and wet!"

"But what a ride," Squirrel said.

"There are boats to rent, and mers to hire," Morth said. "Cheaper than the ships humans use, actually. And faster."

"How did the mers get to be fish? Or dolphins?" Sandry asked.

Morth of Atlantis shook a head of red hair and laughed.

"Funny? I suppose so," Sandry said. "You're looking well, Morth. Much younger than the last time I saw you." The last time Sandry had seen Morth, the wizard looked to be a hundred years old, and dying of it, hair falling out in patches. Of course he had just done battle with a god and a water elemental and used the one to defeat the other. . . .

"And older than the last time Twisted Cloud saw me," Morth said. "I have more manna available in Carlem Marcle than they will allow me here." He shrugged. "So I age a bit here. It's worth it for what I learn."

"They're vicious about manna rationing here," Twisted Cloud said.

"Yes, well, they have to be," Morth said. "There's a small source here on the island. Hot springs. And some comes in currents in the sea. Enough to sustain the mers so long as they are very careful."

"All this so they can turn into fish!" Tower said.

"No, no," Morth said. He sipped his drink. "Refreshing indeed. Burning Tower, you have it backward. The mers are dolphins and orcas and swordfish who can turn into human beings. Not the other way around. Without manna they would be animals, not human."

"So that's what Wheereezz meant up on the hill," Tower said.

Morth nodded. "Clever of you to have noticed. Yes, precisely."

"How do they enforce this?" Sandry said.

Morth laughed. "You grew up in a land without magic, Lord Sandry, so you have never had to face a wizard in his wrath. I assure you, your sword will do you little good against real magic in a land where there is manna."

"His sword is cold iron," Burning Tower observed.

"Yes, yes, that will help," Morth said. "But he is not made of iron."

"I hope not!"

Clever Squirrel laughed. "Well, well. Have you two come to an understanding, then?"

There was an awkward silence.

"No words have been spoken," Tower said finally.

"Perhaps none need to be," Twisted Cloud said. "You're awfully quiet, Lord Sandry."

"Yes, ma'am."

"Your mother likes Burning Tower," Twisted Cloud said. "I saw that she did. So did you."

"And she told me to be determined," Tower said. "And I will be."

Sandry looked down at the table.

"Lord Sandry is not entirely his own master," Morth observed. "I lived among these people since before Sandry was born. Their ways are not the ways of any other people I know." Morth shrugged. "But I can say this. The magic is coming back to Lordshills and Tep's Town, and that will change everything. Your old ways are doomed, Sandry."

"And if we don't manage to deal with those terror birds, so are ours," Twisted Cloud said. "Squirrel, you have to go back in the morning and look at that bird. It's not just for the Lords Witness of Tep's Town. If we don't do something about those birds, there won't be any more wagons on the Golden Road."

Chapter Thirteen

Oarsmen and Oarmaster

The twilight was long and the sunset glorious. A magical place indeed, Sandry thought. He felt Burning Tower near him even after it became too dark to see. *Determined,* he thought. *She said she will be determined! And so will I be. If her people won't accept me, and mine won't accept her, the world is a lot bigger than I thought. We only have to be determined.*

He paused, startled at his own thoughts. *I have decided,* he thought. *I want to marry this girl. Will she accept? She said she would be determined. . . .*

The sky was clear and black and full of stars, the way it sometimes was when the Devil Winds blew hard across Tep's Town. Morth and the girls had names for some of the stars. "And there's the Bear," Burning Tower said. She stood next to Sandry to point to a group of stars. "That's his tail." She moved closer so that he felt her warmth next to him. Her hand found his.

"Bears don't have tails," Clever Squirrel said. "But still we call that the Bear. Morth?"

"We called it the Bear in Atlantis." Morth shrugged. "There's probably a story that goes with that, but I don't know it."

A trail of fire streaked across the sky to vanish behind the island. "Close," Sandry said. He didn't let go of Tower's hand but used his left hand to point.

Morth laughed. "A hundred leagues, I would wager," he said. "But I shouldn't laugh. I once thought as you do, that falling stars were close. We went looking for them on the plains in Atlantis. Found some, too, always much farther away then we thought. There's high manna in a falling star, even a small one. The king took half, and the guild took half of what was left, but even so, it was worth finding one. I once had a duel with a chap who thought he could claim a big one even though I reached it first. . . ."

"Did you win?" Clever Squirrel asked.

They sat at the table and Sandry reluctantly let her go.

"I wouldn't be here if I hadn't," Morth said. "The loser went to the minemasters."

"Wizard slaves?" Twisted Cloud asked. "How?"

"There is always wizard work in the mines," Morth said. "Keeping the shafts open. And losing a duel loses a lot of power."

"I would think so," Clever Squirrel said.

"Why?" Burning Tower asked. "Do you—did you do something to him after he lost?"

It was too dark to see Morth's expression. "No. I didn't, and neither did the guildmasters. They didn't *sell* Sorel to the minemasters; they found him a position there. He was happy to have it, a place where he had others to back him up if he miscast a spell."

"Then what happened to him?" Tower asked.

"Think about it, Blazes," Clever Squirrel said. "Suppose you had your doubts about ropewalking. Could you do it if you didn't think you could?"

"Oh."

It was thoroughly dark now. "I suppose we ought to turn in," Morth said. "Squirrel, may I walk you to your boardinghouse?"

"Thank you," Clever Squirrel said. "Good night. I'll be down at the docks in the morning." A porter appeared from nowhere. He carried a small lantern, which he offered to Morth. Twisted Cloud chuckled as she watched them go down the stairs to the streets. "That's a sight you would see only on Avalon, Coyote's daughter and an Atlantean wizard using a lantern in a land alive with magic. . . . I guess it's time for me to turn in too. Blazes?"

"I guess. Good night, Lord Sandry." She didn't move from the table, and they sighed at the same time.

He thought of his gaudily decorated room and blushed slightly, glad that she couldn't see him. He stood. "Good night, Burning Tower."

It was a bright and glorious morning. When Sandry came out to the patio, Burning Tower was already at breakfast.

He sat next to her. After a moment, their hands touched. "Good morning."

"It's a wonderful morning!"

"But you're alone. Not that I'm sorry."

Burning Tower grinned. "Aunt Cloudy said they have breakfast at the conference, but I think mostly she couldn't wait to show off her new sigil."

There was a long silence. He looked at her, to see her quickly look away. *I need to say it,* he thought. *But not now.* It was awkward eating breakfast with one hand, but neither wanted to let go.

Maybe nothing needs to be said, he thought. Not now.

Clever Squirrel, a porter, and an astonishing quantity of luggage were waiting on the docks. Everything was stowed away on the *Angie Queen,* and Sandry paid off the porter. Captain Saziff welcomed them aboard, and if he had any questions about one passenger being replaced by another with mounds of luggage, he kept them to himself.

Oarsmen rowed the ferry out of the bay. There a wind met them, blowing straight toward the mainland. Sails went up, and the oarsmen were allowed to put up their oars.

"There's something I need to do," Sandry told Tower. "Do you see any stairs down into the oar pit?"

She looked at him oddly. "No. No, I don't."

"They must be inside."

"They don't let passengers in there."

"I know. Excuse me."

* * *

Sandry approached the nearest sailor and offered him wine.

The man refused. "That's okay for you passengers. We get caught with that on our breath—"

"Sorry."

"That's all right, sir."

"I'd like to talk to someone about buying one of the oarsmen free," Sandry said.

The crewmen looked him over. "Tastes differ. Hey, you're from the Burning City, are you?"

"From Tep's Town, yes."

"Uh-huh." The man looked down into the pit, to pick out who might be this looker's brother or uncle. "Well. I don't sell oarsmen mysel'. You wait for shore, then you wait for tomorrow because the office is closed by the time we get in. Then you talk to someone there."

Sandry nodded. "I'd like to talk to the oarsman first."

"Why?"

Sandry kept his temper. "He might like it better here."

The sailor was amused. "Yeah. Right. Come with me." He turned away, turned back, and said, "Try not to be noticed." He went to a low door marked with a rune: CREW ONLY.

A ladder let them out behind the Oarmaster's podium. The man jumped, dropped a loaf of bread, and reached for his whip.

Sandry held up his hands, *peace*, with a refined gold coin in the fingers. "I have the urge to talk to one of your slaves, sir." He gave the coin to the man who had brought him here. To the Oarmaster he offered two.

The man didn't take them. He asked, "Now why

would you want to do that? They're not a talkative bunch. Any particular oarsman?"

"Second on the port side."

"Reggy? *Lord* Regapisk. *He's* talkative. You'd better talk fast, sir. That one'll be gone when next you look." He took the coins.

"How so?"

"I don't like the way he talks. He doesn't think he's getting his due. He's disrupting the oarsmen. I'll tell the pursers, come next chance we get, he'll be off across the wide world on another ship. Relative?"

"Not quite," Sandry said.

"My sympathies. Climb on down, but don't get too close to anyone. These are bad men."

Sandry climbed a ladder down into the belly of the ship.

Some of the slaves were sleeping. Some were eating bread and dried fish. Sandry moved quietly between the two rows. Legs and arms didn't withdraw to let Sandry past, but no man threatened him.

He shook Lord Regapisk's shoulder. "Reggy," he whispered. When Regapisk didn't stir, he tried, "Your Lordship."

"Too early. Lemme sleep."

"Too cursed late," Sandry said.

"Sandry?" Reggy snatched at Sandry's wrist and sat up, then yelped, "Owoo," on a rising note.

"What?"

"My back. Sandry, you've got to get me out of here."

Sandry saw pink ridges crisscrossing Reggy's back.

"Sandry? You testified against me. I saw you."

Regapisk's whisper broke into a whine, then a whisper again. "What did I ever do to you?"

You cost me kinless houses, Lordkin lives, Lords' tribute, and my own broken word, Sandry thought. But eyes had opened in the dark, and he just didn't feel like arguing in front of an audience of slaves. You couldn't win an argument with Reggy anyway.

"I'll buy you loose," he said.

"Good," said Regapisk. "Thank you. I'll pay you back when I can."

"Sure." Sandry was mentally adding up his funds. On his person: enough for bribes, enough to be taken seriously. What could he sell to actually raise the price of a man?

"As soon as I get home," said Lord Regapisk. "They barred me from my own home, Sandry. How could they do this to a Lord?" He was still clutching Sandry's wrist, as if it were his only hope of safety. "*Why?* It was those cursed Lordkin who let the fire get past. I think I even figured out why."

Had he really? "Morth's gold?"

"What? No. They're practicing, Sandry. They're planning to burn down Lordshills, and they need to know how to handle fire. Nobody in Tep's Town is used to fire. Somebody has to tell Lord Witness Qirama. The old man should have seen it himself!"

"Reggy, what were you told, before they put you here?"

"Told?"

"Were you told, 'Don't come back'?"

"Curse it, Sandry, they didn't know! *They hadn't thought it through!*"

"There's a lot of that going around. When I buy you loose, what will you do, Reggy?"

Regapisk hadn't thought quite that far. Sandry watched him mull it. "I could hide at my father's house, but that wouldn't get anything done. I have to see Qirama! Qirama's men might not let me in if I try to see him at home. At the office, they'd just arrest me. Sandry, if I could stay with you? and you invite him to your home . . . ?"

"Good-bye, Reggy." Sandry pulled his arm loose.

"I want to think about this. I'll see you tomorrow?"

The Oarmaster was asleep on his perch. Sandry knocked, and watched to see the man jerk awake, before he climbed the ladder. He gave the man another gold piece and returned to the passenger spaces.

To release Regapisk now . . . he'd be crabmeat within days. Sandry sighed. Another broken promise.

Chapter Fourteen

A Natural Host for Gods

Chalker was waiting with the chariot and a wagon. "Good to have you back, My Lord." He gave a warm smile to Burning Tower. "My Lady. And you'll be the new wizard?" he asked Clever Squirrel. He didn't say that she looked too young, but it wasn't hard to guess what he was thinking.

"Yes, but I'm not a wizard," she said. "Just a caravan shaman."

Chalker's fixed grin relaxed a bit. "Good to see you, Lady Shaman. You'd best come quick, though."

"Why?" Sandry asked.

"Bird's doing poorly," Chalker said. "Won't eat. Getting droopy. Maybe the cold iron cage, but we've been a bit nervouslike about letting it out of there!"

"Don't blame you. We'll go directly there, then." Sandry leaped into the chariot and invited Clever Squirrel up beside him.

Burning Tower climbed into the wagon beside Chalker, looking disappointed.

Sandry clucked the horses into motion. Dusk was falling, and he had to pay attention to the road. When he glanced over at his passenger, he could see that Squirrel was studying the houses of Lordstown and missing nothing.

"We're here," Sandy said. He waved to the guards at the Lordshills gate and the chariot clattered inside to the guardhouse where they kept the bird. "Still alive?" he asked when the door was opened.

"Yes, My Lord. It won't eat. Don't think it will drink anything either. We even tried a live rat, but it wouldn't touch it."

The room smelled like a chickenhouse. No one had cleaned up the bird's droppings, but Sandry couldn't blame them for that.

Clever Squirrel nodded to the guards, and went over to the cage. She squinted, then, as her mother had, she sat in front of the cage with half-closed eyes. Finally she stood. "You'll have to let it out," she said.

"Ma'am?" the guard was incredulous. "Ma'am, you know how much trouble we had getting that thing in there?"

"I can appreciate that," she paused, "Henry son of

Eric." The guard looked startled. "But it's important that I examine it without the cold iron around it, and before it is dead."

"Yes, ma'am," Henry said. "Taric. Lief. We got work to do."

Whenever one of the guards got close to the cage, the bird would shake itself out of its lethargy and snap at him. Eventually, by working in pairs on opposite sides of the cage, they managed to get a rope around the bird's feet. They tied it off to hobble the bird, then they passed more ropes in until they had a pair of them over its neck. "Want us to take this show outside?" Henry asked.

Sandry considered it. "If it gets loose, better it just kills us than runs around in the town," he said.

"Well, yes, sir, but there's not a lot of room to work here," Henry protested, but he ran over and took out the toggle holding the cage door shut. The door swung open, and the guards tightened the ropes. The bird looked outside at freedom, stood still for a moment, then darted out. Its jaws snapped on air a foot from Henry's nose.

"Perks up something wonderful," Henry said, "My Lord."

Clever Squirrel gestured. Nothing happened. Sandry looked the question at her. "Calming spell Morth taught me," she said. "Didn't work. Let me think." She gestured again.

That really set it off. The bird pulled, hard, so that Sandry took the rope alongside one of the guards. They held it as it tried to get at Clever Squirrel.

"It hates Coyote," she said. "It really wants to do something to hurt Coyote." She gestured again. "And it hates you."

After a while she nodded. "You can cage it again. Or kill

it. There's nothing else to learn." She looked puzzled. "There's just nothing there. Blazes? It reminds me of your father. Most human beings have a natural trace of magic, but Whandall never had anything. Just a blank ready to be filled."

The Congregation was held in the Registry Office at Peacegiven Square. Lord Quintana himself presided over a dozen Lords Witness in their dark robes and tight caps, with more clerks and servants than Sandry had ever seen outside the main courthouse in Lordstown. Five squads of Lordsmen stood guard outside with a dozen chariot-class Lords and Younglords with horses harnessed and ready, spears and spearmen standing next to the chariots.

"Putting on a show to impress my brother?" Tower asked.

Sandry shrugged. "Could be, but we don't usually do things that way." *And more likely to impress the Lordkin with how seriously we take all this,* he thought.

Green Stone spoke first, telling the Lords all he knew of the birds. "They have never been common," he concluded. "Until this year I had never seen more than one at a time, and never more than one in a year."

Burning Tower was next. Sandry was proud of her. She was respectful but firm. Her deference could as easily be because of her youth as because of her station. "When Twisted Cloud examined the bird, she found nothing," Tower concluded.

Lord Quintana nodded. "Thank you, young lady. And we have heard the testimony of the Sage Egmatel to the same end." He nodded to the clerk.

"Thank you, lady," the clerk intoned. "We now call the learned sage Clever Squirrel."

Sandry grinned without showing it as Burning Tower came down to sit next to him. *Young lady* sounded enough like the proper title for a Lord's daughter of Tower's age, and *learned sage* was impressive. Sandry could hear the absence of capital letters in the clerk's voice, but none of the kinless and Lordkin present could. They were treating the Bison Tribe leaders as visiting Lords, near enough, and making a show of it at that.

"Welcome, learned one," Quintana said. "And the thanks of the Lords Witness for your help in this matter. You examined the bird closely?"

"I did, Lord," Squirrel said.

Tower nudged Sandry. "Never heard her be that respectful before," she whispered.

Her breath was sweet. He wondered about his own, and grinned slightly at his own concern. "Not much choice," he whispered. What else could Squirrel do? Which was the point of all this, he supposed. The Lordkin and kinless were watching. . . .

" . . . and after it was removed from the cold iron cage, I could feel its rage," Squirrel was saying. "Rage against my father Coyote, rage against the wagon trains, and rage against you, My Lords. That last was harder to determine, but it was there. The birds hate you no less than they hate me."

"Or that one did," Lord Quintana observed. He said it carefully—a conclusion, not a contradiction. Clerks wrote furiously.

"I think all of them," Clever Squirrel said. "I can't be sure."

"And their origin?"

She frowned. "Desert. Meat that hides."

"Surely they are creatures of magic?"

"A fair guess, but again I do not know," she said. "There is no trace of their origin, no trace of magic about them. Only the hatreds."

"All gods welcome at the Feathersnake Inn," Burning Tower whispered. They were sitting close enough to the witness stand that Squirrel heard her.

Clever Squirrel nodded. "My kinswoman repeats a phrase our father sometimes uses. I believe it came originally from Morth of Atlantis."

The Lords Witnesses looked at each other, then back at Clever Squirrel.

" 'All gods welcome,' " Squirrel said. "There's no natural wizardry in the birds. It makes them a natural host for gods. That is the way of our father, whom you knew as Whandall Placehold."

There was a stir among the Lordkin in the back of the room. Someone muttered something obscene. "Quiet," Wanshig said sharply.

"As Lordkin were often possessed of Yangin-Atep," Squirrel continued, "although they are not themselves magical. I believe these birds are possessed of the will of—someone, god or great wizard—but if there is any magic to the birds themselves, no trace of it remains for me to find." She drew herself up to stand straight and proud. "And my Lords, I tell you, if anyone could find such, it would be me."

Chapter Fifteen

Girl Talk

The hearings were continued to the next day, to the great delight of Green Stone and the Bison Tribe merchants. A full Congregation of Lords Witness and their entourage guaranteed shoppers.

Quintana was thorough. Everyone who had anything to say about the birds either testified to the main hearing or was taken to a smaller room to speak with the clerks. By afternoon, everything anyone knew about the birds had been heard and written down. Then the Lords adjourned. A clerk announced formally that the Lords Witness would take this matter under consideration. The entourage packed up, and in solemn procession the Lords, their clerks, and their soldiers rode back to Lordshills.

* * *

Burning Tower watched them go with amazement. "That's it?" she asked her brother. "All that, and—and nothing?"

Green Stone shrugged. "You've heard Father say that the Lords are strange."

"Strange, yes. Idiots, no," Burning Tower said. "And where's Sandry?"

"In his chariot," Clever Squirrel said. "Leading his soldiers." She pointed to a figure vanishing in the distance.

"Yes, but—"

Clever Squirrel chuckled. "You don't know much about men, do you?"

"Not as much as you. But I can ride one-horns without yelling at them!"

"Tsk. No need to be angry," Squirrel said. "What I should have said is that you'll hear from him soon enough. He's got some man game to play, and men always take those things seriously, but he hasn't forgotten you."

"I don't care if he does forget me!"

"Sure. Now stop giving Stones false hopes. Not that I blame you much. Very handsome lad, and a lot nicer than any of the boys we know."

Green Stone growled. "City Lord. What use would he be on the Hemp Road?"

Clever Squirrel grinned. "You don't know much about girls, do you?"

Chalker found her an hour later at her wagon nest. "Lord Sandry's respects, Lady." He looked around to be sure they were alone. "The high and mighty ones are going to summon all you wagon folk to a big meeting tomorrow up in Lordshills," he said. "Lord Sandry was hoping he could see you sort of more privatelike before that, but they want him at their council tonight."

"What do you think will happen?"

Chalker looked serious. "I don't know, and that's the honest truth. Them Lords talk a lot and put on big shows, but they're taking this as serious as anything I ever saw."

"What do you think of them?" she asked.

He eyed her carefully.

"I mean—"

"Yes, ma'am, I think I know what you mean. And bein' honest again, I don't know if you can fit in with them or not. But they're a pretty adaptable bunch. We both think a lot of our Lord Sandry."

"Well, yes!"

"Thing is, so do the high and mighty ones. It may be that what he wants will count for a lot one of these days, and like I say, the Lords are pretty adaptable, all things considered. More so than the Captains of Condigeo, that's for sure." He bowed. "And I reckon I'll see you tomorrow."

Chalker was barely out of the wagon nest when Squirrel came in from the other room. "Well."

"You heard?"

"Sure. Told you he hadn't forgotten you."

"But what did he really say? Squirrelly, I get so mixed up! I just can't stop thinking about him."

"Do you want to?"

"Sometimes yes, sometimes not. I never see you mooning over boys!"

"You won't, either, but it doesn't mean I never did it. Or never will again, for that matter."

"You?"

She shrugged. "You're the one who keeps pointing out that I have to shout at the one-horns."

"Yeah—what was that like?"

Squirrel grinned. "Now, now, you'll find out. Overrated, I'd say, but then I wasn't really all that in love with—well, with the boy. Maybe it's different when you're in love, married, or going to be."

"Oh."

"Don't get crazy ideas," Squirrel said. "Look, I have my place. Like my mother. Five kids and no husband, but she doesn't need one. Neither do I. Nobody really expects Coyote's daughter to mate for life. But it's different for you." She chuckled. "Hang in there, Blazes. If you really want that boy, you'll get him."

"And then what? A Lordkin's daughter in Lordshills? Or—" She changed her voice to sound like her brother's. "A city Lord on the Hemp Road."

Squirrel shrugged. "Whandall Feathersnake was a city Lordkin who did pretty well on the Hemp Road." She took Burning Tower's hand in hers and stared at the palm, then shook her head. "Nothing. I'd say it was the low manna, but I never have seen anything. I think our paths are too close. You and me, Sister."

The invitation came later that evening: a parchment written in a neat hand with embellishments and illuminations. The Lords Witness would be pleased if the Wagonmaster would attend the announcement of the findings of the Congregation and the requests and instructions of the Council regarding the matter of the beasts known as terror birds. There was a separate invitation to the Learned Sage Clever Squirrel. They were delivered by Younglord Maydreo, accompanied by Peacevoice Fullerman, and read by a clerk in dark robes.

After the delegation left, Green Stone frowned at the document. "They read it to us. Does this mean they think we can't read the local language? That might be useful."

"Notice where they were going," Burning Tower said. "To the Lordkin lodgehouse. They'll know Lordkin can't read no matter what language it's in. What happens if they read it to them but not us? Might be insulting to the Lordkin."

"Or an honor they don't want to give us," Clever Squirrel observed. "One thing I've noticed, these Lords don't do much by accident." She grinned. "Think you can live that way, Blazes? You've always been pretty spontaneous."

"I don't know. But Sandry isn't that way!"

"Not with you, maybe, but think about it," Squirrel said. "Every story I've heard told about him—all of yours, even—he's always looking ahead."

"But that's good!"

"I can agree there," Green Stone said. "People who just do things without thinking, they can be dangerous." He chuckled. "Sometimes it works out, though."

"Like you with Morth?" Tower asked. "Running off with the wizard, and just barely married at the time!"

"Yes. But it worked well, better than we ever hoped,

and I sure couldn't have planned it. And you! You weren't supposed to be with my group last year! Stowed away! Good thing too—you wouldn't have been there to climb that pole to burn the Toronexti contract. Nobody could have planned that!" He sobered. "But usually it's better to think ahead, and those Lords sure do that."

"Lordkin don't plan," Clever Squirrel said. "But Whandall learned to. Not just as a Hemp Road merchant prince, before he ever left Tep's Town. So it's not in their blood to be foolish, and I doubt it's in the Lords' blood to be wise. Blood can count—look at me, Coyote's daughter, but look at you two, half Lordkin and half kinless and not like either." She grinned. "I wonder what your children will be like?"

Green Stone shook his head. "If we don't do something about those cursed birds, she won't have any kids, or any dowry either, for that matter."

"I don't think Sandry expects a dowry," Blazing Tower said.

"Maybe not, but anybody out here will," Green Stone said. "And given the way them Lords think, it won't hurt if you have your own means just in case it doesn't work out, you know."

"I don't care about that!"

Clever Squirrel's voice was affectionate and only half amused. "I know you don't. Girls in love never do. Most of the girls who want to talk to me before they marry don't care a bit and they're angry because their fathers and brothers insist on getting all the contract details right. But nothing makes a marriage last like the husband knowing you own the wagon and team!"

* * *

In the morning, the Lords sent horses and wagons for Green Stone and Clever Squirrel. Burning Tower wanted to go, but they hadn't sent anyone she knew well enough to ask, and no one responded to hints. In bitter disappointment, she watched them go, then brooded until they returned in the evening.

"Well?" She demanded.

"One thing at a time," Green Stone said. "How were sales today? Particularly out of Wagon Six?"

"Six? That's stuff we bought at First Pines to take to Condigeo. Why?"

Stone grinned. "Because I sold the entire wagon, cargo and all, to the Lords, at a good price too. Sight unseen."

"What did they want with a wagon full of goods for Condigeo?"

"They don't want the goods; they want the wagon," Stone said.

"Brother, I am going to strangle you!"

Stone grinned again. "It will be the traveling quarters for their officers," he said. "They're sending an escort, chariots and footsoldiers, and even a couple of Lordkin."

"Who? Who? It's Sandry, isn't it?"

"Yes, little sister. They're sending the only officer they have who's ever fought terror birds. Of course."

"He's coming!"

"Yep." Stone looked serious. "You just don't forget—your job on the road is to take care of the one-horns."

She made a face at him, and they both laughed. *He's coming!*

Book Two

The Hemp Road

Chapter One

Deniable

Redwoods stood tall as gods. Chaparral ran round their huge bases like belligerent servitors. Burning Tower knew their danger and tried to instruct the escorts, but mostly Sandry had to learn for himself.

Sandry had brought six Younglords with three chariots, ten Lordsmen with Peacevoice Fullerman, and two of Wanshig's Lordkin. They seemed lost in that vast forest.

"It's not enough," Sandry had told Lord Chief Witness Quintana. "Your pardon, sir, but . . ."

The corners of Quintana's eyes and mouth wrinkled slightly. "I always encourage the junior Lords to speak their minds," he said. "Although given your heredity, I am astonished that you need encouragement." He glanced at Lady Shanda with a slight smile, which she didn't acknowledge. "But the fact is, we have no more to send. Not and give them proper equipment."

"I'd rather have troops than equipment," Sandry said.

"I'm sure you would. But the Lords of Lordshills aren't going to send any delegation to Condigeo looking like it came out of a poor Lordkin stronghold! This mission must impress the Captain's Council."

"We won't impress them much if we're all dead," Sandry protested.

"You have more troops than you needed to defeat twelve of the birds. And capture one alive at that," Quintana said dryly. "Sandry, I never met an officer who didn't honestly believe he needed more troops, but I can't spare any more!"

Sandry nodded. He knew it was true enough. Tension ran wild among the Lordkin bands, the kinless were terrified, and there were no more Burnings to attract the lookers and storytellers. For as long as anyone could remember, the Lords had held the balance between Lordkin and kinless and directed the economy of Tep's Town. Now everything they had learned in centuries was probably useless.

"Tactics," Sandry said. "The best way to fight terror birds is to have the Lordsmen lock shields, and use the chariots to draw the cursed birds into range of their throwing spears. But that takes tricky driving. I need a driver and a spearman in each chariot, but if I hold out enough Lordsmen to make a shield wall, there's nobody to put in the chariots with the Younglord drivers."

"You'll think of something," Aunt Shanda said. And Lord Chief Witness Quintana nodded sagely. "You'll have to."

So now the Younglords were doubled up two to a chariot, one driving and one as spearman and observer. When they'd found that out the first morning, they'd sent Maydreo to protest, but Sandry cut that short.

"I have twenty volunteer Younglords. I've picked you six, but it isn't too late to change that. You still want to make that protest?" Sandry said.

Maydreo had a very sly grin. "What if I say Younglord Whane wants to protest?"

Sandry snorted. Whane wasn't popular with his peers. He spent much of his time reading books and lost in his own thoughts. He was also Regapisk's first cousin, and while Sandry hadn't actually seen it, he suspected there was a lot of Reggy in Whane. "Not an option," Sandry said, and left it at that. Anyone could see the fine hand of Aunt Shanda in the decision to send Whane. Surely Maydreo could?

And he did. "Sir, can we request that you assign Whane to your chariot?"

That was the trouble with just being promoted above your classmates, Sandry thought. They knew you too well, thought they could get away with things they'd never think of trying with a more senior officer.

"A tempting offer, but I'm used to working with Masterman Chalker," Sandry said. And enjoyed the look Maydreo gave him. None of the others had been allowed to bring a valet.

Sandry had had independent command rarely in Tep's

Town and never for more than a few days. Now he was in charge, and that would last for weeks.

Quintana had come to Peacegiven Square just before the expedition was to leave. He had dinner served to him in the Registry Office, then summoned Sandry. Sandry expected to find the whole council, but Quintana was alone, no guards, no one at all. His greeting was perfunctory. Then: "Something's been on your mind," Quintana said. "Ever since you came back from Avalon. Want to tell me?"

"No, sir."

"Well, you will anyway. Spit it out."

Sandry frowned, then shrugged. "Lord Regapisk was on the boat. As an oarsman. Chained to a bench."

Quintana nodded. "I knew that—forgot it would be on that boat. He tried to get you to buy him free, of course."

"Yes, sir, and I promised I'd do it, only—"

"Only what?"

"He started talking about what he'd say to you."

Quintana nodded.

"So we both know what you'd do to him if he came back," Sandry said. "And I don't want him dead."

"Neither do I," Quintana said slowly. "Not that it would keep me from feeding him to the crabs. Sandry, when we give an order, it has to mean something. If we say, 'Don't come back,' it means *don't come back,* and that has to apply to Lords as much as to Lordkin and kinless. Lordkin put up with our rules because they see them as fair, mostly, and we treat our real kin the same way as Lordkin."

"At least it has to look that way," Sandry said.

"Precisely. So you did the right thing. Reggy won't be on that bench forever. Your Aunt Shanda has made arrangements. They'll take him a long way off and arrange that he gets paid as long as he stays there. And maybe the trip will teach him something."

"Yes, sir . . ."

"And you're right, that isn't why I wanted to see you." Quintana inspected him closely. It was impossible to guess what the Lord Chief Witness was thinking.

"You're young for this," Quintana told him. "The council would rather send someone with more experience. You do have connections with the Wagonmaster, and that's all to the good. But do you know why I'm putting you in charge?"

"I'm the only one who ever captured a terror bird."

Quintana nodded. "Yes, and that's the public reason. Now I'll tell you the council's real reason. You're deniable."

"Sir?"

"Sandry, you're smart enough to see that we're in trouble. Yangin-Atep is myth. The Greenway is open. Kinless can leave when they want to, and more and more will want to when they hear how well they can do outside."

"Can't blame them, sir."

"I can't either, but the Lordkin won't like it. They'll try to stop the kinless from running away. And what do we do then?"

"I don't know, sir."

"Neither do I, yet, but I have to decide. One thing is sure, the old balance between kinless and Lordkin is over. Right now everyone's scared of us. Everybody on the coast wants to hire trained Lordsmen. But Sandry, we don't have—we can't afford—a big enough army to fight off the Lordkin if they ever get organized."

Sandry nodded. “I’ve thought of that.”

“So. Right now we run things because we always have. We have to find better reasons than that if you want to keep that home of yours from being a Lordkin clan house.” Quintana shrugged. “We’ve always been pretty good at trading up and down the coast. Now we have to learn more, learn to be master traders. That girl you’re smitten with could be important to us.”

“Sir? What does that mean?”

“I think you know. If you’re both still interested in each other when you get back, come see me. I’ll handle Shanda.”

It was hard to suppress the foolish grin Sandry felt creeping across his face.

“When you get back,” Quintana said. “But understand, Lord Sandry, if you do get in big trouble and get your command wiped out, we can say, ‘Well, he was young; we sent him to keep the traders happy,’ and maybe, just maybe, we won’t lose so much of our reputation that the whole damn city comes down around our ears.”

“Oh.”

Quintana smiled faintly. “On the other hand, if you do everything just right, we can say that even our junior officers with a few troops can do things nobody else can. One more thing. That was the reasoning of the council. It’s not mine.”

“Sir?”

“It’s not my reasoning. I’m sending you south with everything I can spare because I damned well think you’re the best man I could pick. Dismissed.”

Chapter Two

Bloodberries

And now the three chariots rode ahead, partly on watch but always very much in training. Whenever the Greenway ahead was wide enough, the lead chariot would drop a target and the next would charge forward and wheel past it, and the Younglord spearman would throw or thrust his spear into the sack of hay. The last chariot would recover the spear and target and take over as lead. Peacevoice Fullerman rode in the first bison-drawn wagon and kept score.

Sandry and Chalker rode just ahead of the lead wagon. Sandry worried about his elderly valet, but Chalker seemed content enough. He leaned against the chariot side, but that seemed to be the only concession to his age.

Burning Tower rode alongside Sandry's chariot. She had her bonehead pony, a new one bought from a kinless in Tep's Town, for more gold than a kinless might see in five years. As they moved up the Greenway away from Tep's Town, the pony grew larger, changed from gray to white, and the bump on its head became a horn. The growth was noticeable after the first day, more so the next morning.

It also became more noticeably a stallion. She called it Spike, and blushed a little at Spike's obvious interest in the mares among the horses Sandry had brought. Today Sandry's chariot was drawn by his favorite team, Blaze and Boots, a stallion and a gelding. Spike ignored the gelding, but his challenge to Blaze was obvious.

Another problem, Sandry thought. But it would be good to learn how horses and one-horns acted toward each other. Tep's Town had always bred horses, and now that they understood the real nature of the kinless ponies—now that magic was somehow coming back to Tep's Town—the opportunity was clear. One-horns were in demand all along the Hemp Road. Sandry smiled slightly at the thought. *I worried about finding a career. Now I'm a Fireman and troop leader, and I'm learning to be a horse and one-horn breeder.*

Sandry had heard of mules, but he'd never seen one, because although donkeys were supposed to be common in the mountains to the east, no one had ever brought one to Tep's Town. Mules didn't breed. Horses and kinless ponies never seemed to notice each other before Yangin-Atep went into the tar. What would happen if they interbred? Could they? Would their colts be fertile? There was only one way to find out, and it was clear that Spike was interested in the mares, and they didn't dislike him either.

There was a shout from the lead wagon. "Well done, Younglord Whane," Peacevoice Fullerman shouted. There was surprise in his voice. "Well done indeed."

"He's learning," Chalker said. He had a way of saying such things half under his breath, so that Sandry could choose to hear them or not.

"Slowly," Sandry said.

"Your pardon, My Lord, but I remember another young cadet couldn't ever get worked up about spear practice."

"I could drive, though," Sandry insisted. "Whane won't ever make a driver."

"Agree there, My Lord," Chalker said. "He's too distracted. Tries to do too many things at once. But he notices things others don't always see. Knows he's got limits too, not like his cousin." Chalker didn't name Lord Regapisk. He didn't have to.

Turns out I did the right thing there, Sandry thought. *It will be a bad year for Reggy, but he'll come out all right. Wonder where he'll end up?*

Burning Tower couldn't quite hear what Sandry and Chalker were saying. Men often did that, or at least Sandry and Chalker did. *He's known Chalker a long time.* She felt a tinge of jealousy and dismissed it quickly. "Time for more lessons," she shouted.

Sandry nodded. Chalker blew on a small whistle to get Peacevoice Fullerman's attention, then signaled with his arms, three circles of his right arm overhead then pointing to Burning Tower. *Circle them near her.*

Fullerman nodded to his assistant. Horn signals

sounded. The Younglords brought their chariots back down the Greenway. Sandry's men rode uneasily, trying not to touch any plant anywhere. As much as they must hate showing fear to their officer, they were thoroughly intimidated by the god-size trees and the deep shadows they cast.

Tower didn't want to frighten them further, but they had to *know.* She pointed: "That's Lordkin's-kiss. It can be a vine or a bush, but the leaves are always that five-pointed shape. Sometimes they turn bronze. You don't touch that! You don't touch bison after they've waded through it either.

"And look there, that patch off in the chaparral. Those bloodberry bushes are poison. They pull you in. Don't get too close or you'll be too hungry to resist. Bison can eat them, though."

"Ponies?" Whane asked. "Can they eat them?"

"Yes. The spell doesn't seem to work with them," Burning Tower answered.

"We'd better find out about the horses," Whane said. "Drive over to that bush and let's see."

Today Whane's driver was Maydreo. Whane tended to get distracted far too often to be the driver on a patrol. Maydreo hesitated. He wasn't going to take orders from his spearman, particularly not if that spearman was Younglord Whane. . . .

Burning Tower could see the emotions flickering across Maydreo's face. Curiosity. And the red berries looked inviting, and they couldn't be poisonous or the bison couldn't eat them, and . . . He flicked the reins and sent the horses left toward the cluster of red in the chaparral. Tower turned Spike right around and dashed toward the wagon train. "Clever Squirrel! We're going to need you, Wise One! Hurry."

Boneheads hadn't wanted anything to do with Clever Squirrel for over a year. Tower had wondered who the boy was, but Squirrel wasn't telling. Green Stone had bought her a large stallion from the Lords' stables. Lords didn't ride horses. They weren't big enough for an armed man to ride. Greyling was a big horse, and he didn't seem to mind carrying Squirrel. Tower's bonehead stallion reared and shied away as Squirrel came out of the wagon compound riding Greyling.

"Over there," Tower shouted, and pointed off to the left of the Greenway. "Steady, Spike. Steady."

Two chariots were in the thicket of red berry bushes. Four Younglords were stuffing themselves as fast as they could eat. So were four horses. Sandry's chariot was a good fifty feet from the red berries. Chalker was dismounted, holding the horses by their bridles, as Sandry shouted at his entranced Younglords—who paid him no attention at all.

Clever Squirrel giggled loudly.

Sandry looked up at her in irritation. "It's not funny!"

She nodded. "If you didn't have me here, it sure wouldn't be," she agreed. "But you do. Chalker, can you hold Greyling? I don't want him any closer to those berries."

"Yes, Wise One. Don't mind saying I'm glad to see you."

"Me either," Sandry said. "You can do something?"

"Sure." Squirrel dismounted and walked slowly toward

the red berry patch, her face an impassive mask of concentration. She muttered something, and her hands moved slightly.

Whane looked startled and doubled over in pain.

"Come to me now, Younglord Whane," Squirrel said.

Whane straightened slightly, then bent over to puke.

Squirrel gestured again. "Come to me now, Younglord Whane."

Whane lurched toward her. With every step, it seemed easier, until he was running. "Thank you, Wise One," he shouted as he reached her.

"Go get me the rope from Sandry's chariot and bring it here," she said. She hadn't lost the look of concentration and spoke softly without opening her mouth. "Now."

"Yes, ma'am!" Whane wobbled toward Sandry's chariot, still retching.

Squirrel muttered again, then spoke aloud. "Come to me now, Younglord Maydreo." Maydreo turned slowly and began to move toward her.

"Come to me now, Younglord Qirimby. Maydreo, what's the other one's name?"

Maydreo looked up from helpless vomiting. "Bentino."

"Come to me now, Younglord Bentino." When all the Younglords were near her and puking, Squirrel turned to Burning Tower. "Do you remember how to resist those?"

"Yes."

"Good. Take the rope and ride in there, tie it to the bridle of the nearest chariot team, and bring the end to me."

"Right." Tower whispered. "Spike." She pointed. The bonehead walked toward the thicket. When it reached the nearest bush, it looked up at Tower, then tore off a mouthful of berries and ate them.

They looked good! I should try one— A shout from Clever Squirrel woke her to her task. Bridle. Tie the rope to the bridle. There. "Spike, out. Back to the horses . . ."

The bonehead nickered and walked out again. The pull of the berries weakened, died . . .

She had to go in once more to tie the rope to the second chariot, then they were done, everyone rescued.

Sandry's face was an emotionless mask. "Younglord Maydreo."

"Sir!"

"And what have you to say, Younglord Maydreo?"

"No excuse, sir!"

"Sir, actually it was my fault," Whane said. "When Tower said the bison and one-horns weren't harmed by the berries, I thought we ought to learn what they did to horses, and I suggested it, and—"

"And Maydreo takes orders from his spearman now?" Sandry said.

"Sir. No, sir," Maydreo said.

Sandry's face relaxed a bit. "No harm done, and yes, it is a good thing we learned this when there was someone around to help. But did you go there just because Younglord Whane suggested it?"

"Sir, I don't know. It seemed like a good thing to do. And those berries looked good. I can still taste them. They are good."

Sandry looked to Burning Tower. "Is it always like this?"

"Yes, a little, but it's only this strong here in the Greenway, and they weren't this bad last year, either. Squirrel?"

Clever Squirrel nodded agreement. "Out on the Hemp Road, we've pretty well burned out and destroyed the strongest bloodberry thickets, and the bison keep eating them anyway. In here, they've been protected for generations. Your fire god would have eaten most of their manna, but now he's myth." She shrugged. "They're powerful, all right. Even I could feel the call."

"One more thing to worry about," Sandry said.

"The only ones to worry about are those near the road," Squirrel said. "Until we get out of the Greenway and back to the Hemp Road, Tower and I will ride ahead to watch out for them."

Sandry nodded. "But not too far ahead. Don't forget the terror birds, and there might be bandits. And can you teach us how to resist those berries?"

Squirrel frowned. "Blazes, how long did that take you?"

"I don't know. I learned on my first trip away from the New Castle, but I never felt any this strong. Sandry, you think about being full, so full you want to puke. At least that's what I do."

"It doesn't hurt to imagine yourself tied up with their vines while they smother you," Squirrel said. "Or how you'll smell after a couple of days."

"Ugh," Whane said.

"All right, no harm done," Sandry said. "And we all learned something. Chalker, see that Master Peacevoice Fullerman tells his troopers. And maybe you can have a word with the Lordkin?"

"Yes, sir," Chalker said. "Reckon I need the morning off tomorrow to help with that."

"Good idea. Do that," Sandry said. He squinted up at the sun.

Burning Tower nodded. "Another hour to lunch. I'll go scout ahead for more bushes."

They made a big circle of the wagons, but they didn't unhitch the teams or unload the wagons for the lunch break. Bison were fed where they stood. Horses and one-horns were hobbled and turned loose inside the wagon circle. There was one big central cookfire. Soup was served as soon as it was hot.

"You must make this up in advance," Sandry said. He slurped his soup. "Good stuff."

"We do. We make big pots of it," Tower said. "Sometimes Squirrel can keep it hot all day."

"Easier just to keep it from spoiling," Squirrel said. "Takes a lot of manna to keep soup hot all day, and there are plenty of bison chips for a fire."

Tower finished her soup and daintily licked the bowl. Then she stood. "Time to get moving. I'll scout ahead for bloodberries."

There weren't any bloodberries near the road. Tower walked Spike alongside Sandry's chariot. He kept looking around, at the tall trees and malevolent chaparral. The Firewoods held Sandry fascinated. He asked, "How did your parents ever get through this? They were on foot, weren't they?"

"Father said they gathered a wagon and some boneheads at the wine farm, and Father could still throw fire. Even so, it was difficult, and they had children to take care of. They talk about it sometimes. Mother was afraid the whole time. Lost in this forest with only a Lordkin to protect her!"

Tower looked back at Trebaty and Secklers, the Lordkin Wanshig had given them, and Peacevoice Fullerman, selected by the Lords with Sandry's enthusiastic seconding. Fullerman usually rode in the lead wagon, his troopers marching along beside. The wagon held their shields and heavy equipment, and frequently Fullerman held drills.

"Alarm! Fear and foes!"

The men scrambled to get their equipment on, shields up and locked. Two boys from the wagon train opened boxes of throwing spears, then stood ready to pass them out.

In addition to throwing spears, there was another kind, heavier, with an odd shape to the spearhead. Tower pointed it out to Maydreo during one of the drills.

"What is that?"

"Sandry's invention," Younglord Maydreo said. "He calls it a birdcatcher. See, the first time they fought the birds, one ran right up the spear and killed a trooper. Sandry and Fullerman invented those crossbar things to hold the bird out at the end of the spear."

"Oh. Will it work?"

Maydreo shrugged. "Let's try it on a bird."

And Sandry thought of it! She grinned. *And he'll be surprised I know about this. . . .*

The two Lordkin walked close alongside the lead

wagon, careful to avoid plants, dodging them as if they'd been doing it all their lives, although Tower knew they hadn't known about them until she told them. Her father was like that, learned fast when it interested him.

Gradually the redwoods gave way to other trees, and the vines and creepers stopped growing aggressively. The Greenway widened hourly.

Chapter Three

Firewoods Town

On the morning of the fourth day, they emerged at Firewoods Town. They stopped and talked to people, showed a little of what they'd collected, traded stories. They left a heap of their cargo to be guarded by the mayor. Maybe they'd return for it; if not, next year's caravan would.

"They treat you like Lords," Sandry said.

"Maybe a little." Burning Tower sipped tea. "I never thought about it. It's just the way things are—Feather-snake wagons are welcome everywhere."

Someone scratched at the entrance to the wagon nest. "Yes?" Tower called.

Green Stone came in. "One of your Lordkin tried to rob a merchant."

Sandry got to his feet.

"It's all right," Green Stone said. "No emergency, anyway. I paid, and this close to the Greenway they're used to Lordkin thinking they can gather anytime they like. They see those tattoos, they watch their merchandise. It's not like the Lordkin are sneaky about it. Anyway, the mayor gave Lordkin Trebaty the standard lecture. That's what they do here, reparation, lecture, and another chance." Green Stone looked serious. "That's here, Lord Sandry. Farther down the road, it won't be like that."

"Make sure all the townsmen know I'll pay," Sandry said.

Green Stone shook his head. "It won't be necessary. Or you can pay me, because Feathersnake always makes good. But it won't be enough."

"What's enough?"

Green Stone shrugged. "Depends on where. Some places will want free labor to forget it. In Meculati, they'll want blood."

"I'd better go talk to Trebaty and Secklers." He paused at the nest door. "Thank you for lunch, Burning Tower." He bowed.

He found Trebaty and Secklers sitting by themselves. Chalker was not far away, and beyond him was Peacevoice Fullerman, trying to be inconspicuous despite his four fully armed troopers. Trebaty was fuming.

"The way he talked to me! Secklers, they're puny! Twenty Snakefeet and we can burn the place out, teach them some respect."

"Greetings, Lord Sandry," Secklers said.

Sandry nodded in acknowledgment. "Understand you had some trouble with a merchant."

"Yeah, I forgot," Trebaty said. "I know what Lor—Chief Wanshig told us. I know we're not supposed to gather out here, but I forgot, and it wasn't much anyway, just a ring I was going to take back to my old lady."

Sandry nodded.

"And the next thing I know, the mayor is yelling at me," Trebaty said. "Him and those lord's lace guards of his."

"So you think you could raid this place with twenty of your Serpent's Walk comrades," Sandry asked.

"You're cursed right I could!"

"Do you think you would kill everyone, or would some get away to tell who did it?" Sandry pointed to the serpent tattoos Trebaty and Secklers both wore.

"Hey, we're not like that! We don't just kill everyone!"

"So the rest would tell their friends. And then what would happen?" Sandry asked.

"Depends on how many friends they have, I guess. How many would that be?"

Sandry shook his head. "I don't know either. Probably all the wagon trains, to start with. Maybe the Condigeo Captains? I don't know. Neither do you, Trebaty, but there could be a lot of them. What will Chief Wanshig do if you get him into a war and you don't know who you're at war with or how many you're fighting?"

"He won't like that, Treb," Secklers said. "That's for sure."

"Yeah, I guess."

"And then there's the Lord Chief Witness," Sandry

said. "The Council is trying to promote trade along the Hemp Road. Burning out the towns probably won't help that a lot." Sandry shrugged. "You heard what happened to Lord Regapisk?"

"Heard rumors," Trebaty said.

"I hear the Condigeo Captains are paying well for oarsmen," Sandry said conversationally. "I expect Chief Wanshig would know."

Secklers snorted. "So if the High Lords don't sell you, Lord Wanshig will. I told you, Treb."

"Oh, shut up."

"Sure I will."

"No harm done," Sandry said. "This time. But they tell me the merchants farther down the road aren't used to Lordkin. You think gathering, they think robbery."

"Yes." Trebaty said. "I told you—I forgot."

Sandry smiled. "I sure hope your memory gets better."

Secklers laughed. His hands moved in circles: rowing motions.

The Hemp Road led east until they were out of the redwood forests, then turned sharply south. Now there were pine trees and chaparral, villages with small farms, green fields with water trenches in the middle of brownlands. The line between green and brown was as sharp as a knife.

CHAPTER FOUR

MORE TERROR BIRDS

This part of the road was new to Burning Tower. She had never been south of the Burning City. Green Stone was too busy to play guide, so Tower hung out with Mouse Warrior.

Mouse Warrior was a small man, injured at birth, so that he'd never married. He was small enough to ride a bonehead pony. He'd been to Condigeo four times. He and Tower rode with the Younglords and Lordkin behind the wagons, and Tower listened as he instructed them.

"Water management gets you through alive," Mouse said. "Never lose your hat." He had a constant stream of advice, all good.

Tower tuned him out. She'd been hearing this for half her life. The terrain was sparsely forested, richly green valleys separated by dull brown hills, but sometimes the hills had pine forests. There was a sudden storm of small birds and a hawk in their midst. The Lordkin ducked, then laughed at each other.

This was easy travel. Sandry and his men had no trouble adjusting to the caravan style of living: pack everything, every time. To the Lordkin this was almost strange . . . but not quite. "You're all like the boss—like Chief Wanshig," said Secklers. "Is that because he sailed on a ship? A place for everything and everything in its place."

"That's the way we live," Tower assured him.

"It's a pain."

"You can live with pain. How did you get that scar?"

Secklers grinned and told a harrowing tale of a raid on Howler turf.

The days passed. The Lordkin learned a little, and, hey, you could put up with just two of them. Sandry tried them out as scouts. They were a token, Tower thought, sent to even things out. Peacevoice Fullerman was the Lords' eyes and ears.

A caravan did more than move. The wagons carried grain to cook, and various kinds of tea, but any variety in diet had to come from the land. The hunting grew better as they moved south, but predators grew more numerous. Tower taught them to see fruits and roots that could be eaten.

On the fifth morning, they passed a terror bird. It left them alone. Later that day, another attacked them. Sandry distracted it, and as it turned to chase him, Maydreo drove up from behind to let Whane drive a spear into its back, just where the neck came out of the torso. It ran a few more paces and fell dead, the battle over before Peacevoice Fullerman could get more men into armor. Trebaty found a clutch of three huge eggs. The bird and its eggs served as their dinner.

"This is odd," Sandry said to Squirrel. "This one attacked us when we came near her nest. The other stayed clear. Are there two kinds of terror bird?"

Squirrel said nothing.

On the eighth day, the road gently turned to southwesterly.

"Aren't we getting closer to Condigeo?" Burning Tower asked.

Squirrel nodded. "We'll be in Condigeo by noon tomorrow, earlier if we make good time today. It should be safe enough from here on. Never heard of terror birds this close to the sea."

Sandry nodded in relief. "I'll keep scouts out to both sides and ahead just in case," he said. He waved to the Younglords in their chariots. "Be alert," he said, but it was hard to stay alert this close to the end of a journey.

An hour later, they topped a low hill. A wide valley stretched out to the east and west, a sluggish stream in its middle. There was a fortified town just south of where the road forked to the west. Guards waved from their watchtowers as the caravan went past without stopping.

There were loud bird cries, and a half dozen seagulls glided over, wheeled to inspect them. This was the first time since leaving Tep's Town that Sandry had seen gulls. He pointed to one of the graceful sea birds. "I'm surprised we didn't see more of them. Aren't we close to the sea?"

"Getting there now," Clever Squirrel said. "But the Hemp Road stays on the other side of the hills from the ocean. The coast road is dangerous. Pirates in the Flea-bottom Creek area. Robbers in the Greyswift Hills. Too many to fight. There's a big patch of manna in the Greyswift Hills. I've never been there, but I'm told there's a nice town there if you can get to it. But we stay away from the coast until we're close to Condigeo."

"Fear! Fear and foes!" The shouts came from Sandry's scouts to the east. Maydreo, shouting the same words he'd shouted in Peacegiven Square, but with confidence and defiance now, a lot less fear.

"Fear! Fear and foes! Alarm! Make ready!"

Someone in the watchtower in the town behind and to their left sounded a conch shell horn. The guards outside the town gates scrambled inside. The gates slammed shut in haste.

"No help from them," Peacevoice Fullerman said. "To arms, lads, to arms. Full kit. My Lord, I have four men under arms. It will take a bit to get the rest equipped."

"Right." Sandry had been riding in the wagon with Fullerman, his empty chariot tailing the wagon. "My team's rested. Chalker!"

"Coming," the old man shouted. He ran up from the second wagon where he had been riding and climbed into Sandry's chariot.

Sandry gathered throwing and thrusting spears and dropped off the wagon. Clever Squirrel loosed the chariot reins from the wagon as Sandry jumped into the chariot.

Sandry looked around for Burning Tower. Nowhere. He waved to Clever Squirrel, and caught the reins as she threw them.

Maydreo was closer now. "Fear and foes! Alarm! Lord Sandry, it's birds!"

"How many?" Sandry shouted.

"Twenty, I counted," Maydreo answered.

"Twenty-one," Whane corrected. "And all bunched up."

Sandry wheeled the chariot to face east. There they were, a quarter of a mile or less down the valley, birds bigger than horses and coming on fast over the grassy fields. A stock fence slowed them momentarily, then they jumped, a graceful echelon of green and orange.

Beautiful, Sandry thought. *Damned deadly, but they're beautiful.* "Maydreo, walk your horses," Sandry shouted. "Let them rest up a bit; we'll need all the speed you can get. Fullerman, hurry it up!"

"Fast as we can, My Lord."

It wouldn't be fast enough.

"Call in the other outriders."

"Aye, My Lord." Fullerman's trumpets sounded.

"Tep's balls!" Trebaty and Secklers ran up, their big Lordkin knives ready. They had their woolen ponchos over their left arms as shields. "That's a lot of them buggers!" Trebaty looked around. "What do you want us to do, Lord Sandry?"

What to do with stray Lordkin? "Please stay with Peacevoice Fullerman," Sandry said. "Keep him alive so he can direct his men."

"Right!" Trebaty said. "We'll do that."

A pledge. One less thing to worry about, Sandry

thought. He flicked the reins and sent his chariot hurtling toward the oncoming green-and-orange wave. "Steady, steady . . . get ready, Chalker."

"I been ready!"

"Steady—haw! Haw!" The chariot wheeled to the left, so that Chalker, to Sandry's right, would have a clear shot. As the chariot wheeled, Chalker threw forward and to the right, forward so that the chariot's momentum would be added to the strength of his arm—

"Score!" Chalker shouted. "The leader's not down, but he's slower. They're after us, My Lord."

"Good." *Now if the horses hold out and don't stumble* . . . "Gee! Gee!" The chariot wheeled to the right. The wounded bird was trailing now, clear of battle. Its plumage flared, gaudy, a rainbow of colors. The rooster? And the rest were hens? The terror bird hens surged after the chariot.

"Are those town watchtowers manned?"

"Yes, sir."

"Good. I'd rather be on the road than in this field."

"Better slow just a little—they're wavering."

"Right." It was a balancing act, staying far enough ahead of the birds that they couldn't catch him, not so far that they lost interest. Last year Sandry had done this dance with a wave following him, a water elemental flowing uphill in the wake of his chariot. Birds were nothing. Here was the road now—follow it down toward the town.

"They're no help," Chalker shouted. "They're cheering you, but they ain't throwing nothing from those towers."

"Blast."

A trumpet sounded.

"Fullerman's ready," Chalker shouted.

"Right. Here we go."

Fullerman's troops stood ready, shields locked, thrusting spears leaned against their shields as they held their throwing spears loosely.

The birds were strung out in a line following Sandry's chariot. The one Chalker had hit trailed well to the side. The others were in fine shape, and the horses were tiring. "I'll lead them close," Sandry shouted.

He guided the chariot on a path parallel to Fullerman's line and no more than ten feet away. The birds followed.

"Hey, Harpy!" The shout came from the lead wagon. Sandry stole a quick glance at the wagons: There was a wagoneer with a sling on top of each, half a dozen on the wagon closest to Fullerman. Mouse Warrior was calling. "Hey, Harpy!"

As the birds closed with Fullerman, a shower of stones flew from the wagoneer slings. The lead bird was hit several times, stumbled, another bird crashed into it from behind—

"Throw!" Fullerman ordered. Spears arched out.

Three birds went down. Another flight of stones pelted them. The other birds held up short, looking at these new dangers.

"Thrusting spears!" Fullerman ordered.

The line of troops sprouted a bristle of points. Two of the birds charged into the spearpoints, impaled themselves. One of the guardsmen was thrust backward as the bird pushed onward.

Secklers ran up behind the guardsman and pushed him

back into the line. The bird struggled for a moment, then fell in front of the guards.

Now Maydreo charged from behind the wagon line. His chariot brushed past the birds, and Whane thrust his spear, a perfect thrust. Another bird down, and the rest were chasing Maydreo, but the slowest two fell to flying stones from the wagons. Trebaty and Secklers rushed out to slash at the wounded birds, chopping at their necks, then dashed back behind the shield wall. Mouse Warrior shouted in triumph.

Sandry brought his chariot to a halt behind the shield line. Chalker leaped out to brush the foam from the horses' necks. "Steady there, beauties, steady. Take a rest now, steady . . ."

And Maydreo led the remaining birds in a big circle, back to where Fullerman's troopers stood with throwing spears, and the cries of "Hey, Harpy!" sounded from the wagon train.

They were all babbling like fools. Twenty-one dead terror birds. One guardsman lightly clawed, and one bruised from where Secklers had shoved him into line with thirty stone of bird held on the end of his spear. No horses harmed, and twenty-one heads to be carried on pikes, feather trophies for the wagons, Green Stone serving up Golden Valley wine . . .

And at noon of the ninth day they saw houses on the high bluff ahead. "Condigeo," Green Stone said. They went along the valley road to the lowland port area in triumph, knowing that the Captains in their great houses on the bluff above would be watching, noting the heads on pikes and the green and orange feathers flying from each wagon.

"But why?" Sandry asked Clever Squirrel. "Groups of them attack us, hate the horses and bison, go for the wagons. Then there are the others who couldn't care less about us unless we disturb them. Why?"

Clever Squirrel said, "I don't like it one bit."

Heads turned to look at her. She said, "It's a god."

"A god?"

"A god can't pay attention all the time. Coyote doesn't. When the god's not there, they're just empty-headed birds. They defend their nests. If they're hungry, they find something to kill; otherwise, no. But when the god is in their heads, they do what he tells them."

"But why is he telling them to fight us?" Tower asked for all of them.

Squirrel said, "The god of terror birds wants more turf. You want reasons? Gods aren't reasonable. They're powerful, and they're crazy."

Chapter Five

The Welcome

The wagon train came down the river valley. Condigeo was spread out ahead of them. A low wall with gates stretched across the valley between them and the city. Where the city was elegant, the wall was crude, made of newly turned earth and stones and green wood. The road they were on was high enough that they could see beyond the wall to the city itself.

The city of Condigeo was built in two parts. There was a cluster of buildings large and small on lowlands around the docks and wharves. Beyond the docks were channels cutting through swamps until they reached the sea. High above the lower city was a line of great houses on a bluff. They all faced west, looking across the lower city and its docks to the ocean. The city and harbor were much larger than Lord's Town, but what really caught Burning Tower's eye were the houses on the bluff above.

"They're grand!" Burning Tower said. "If I hadn't seen Lordshills I'd think that the grandest sight I've ever seen."

"There's a couple pretty big even for Lordshills," Chalker said. "Great view of the sunset too." He frowned. "They got some kind of troopers up there too. No chariots, but there's men with spears."

Clever Squirrel rode up to the lead wagon. "Circle," she said.

"But we just got here," Tower protested. "Why?"

"We'll find out when we need to, my lady," Chalker said. He looked to Sandry and got a nod, made hand signals to Peacevoice Fullerman. Trumpets sang out.

Fallen Wolf gestured for them to sit inside the wagon circle. When they were all there, Green Stone came out. He was wearing his best clothes, buckskins painted with symbols, a great feathered serpent with malachite green eyes dominant on his chest.

He looks splendid! Burning Tower thought. It was the first time she had really thought of her brother as a Feathersnake Wagonmaster.

Green Stone spoke conversationally, his voice audible inside the wagon circle but not beyond. "I called you here because there's something different ahead," he said. "Fallen Wolf."

"I've been here many times," Fallen Wolf said. "And there wasn't never a wall across the valley there, no gates, no troopers on watch. Every time before, we get this close to Condigeo, there's wagons with merchants and greeters, maybe one or two armed shoremen, but that would be it. Now they got a wall, and marines—that's what they call their soldiers—and look up there on the bluff where the Captains live. There's more of them marines watching us. Not like Condigeo used to be."

Green Stone nodded grimly. "Feathersnake has property in the city. A warehouse at the docks, and a hospitality office. They know who we are, they know we belong here, but nobody's come out to welcome us. I'm going in to find out why."

"Shall I come with you, Wagonmaster?" Sandry asked.

"Thanks, but I think not. I don't think we'll need your army to get out of here, but if we do, they'll sure need you!"

"Stone!" Burning Tower blurted out the name, realized she was babbling, but no one else would ask him. "You can't mean that—Condigeo turned bandit?"

He wagged his head. "Don't know, Burning Tower. I don't know anything except that this isn't what you call a proper welcome." He smiled. "I'm sure it will be all right, but if this is the way they welcome us, they can't blame us for not just rushing in."

"Let me drive him in, My Lord," Chalker said. "I'll use Younglord Maydreo's chariot and team so you'll have yours. I can bring in the Wagonmaster in style, so to speak."

"Good idea," Sandry said. "If that's acceptable, Wagonmaster?"

Green Stone looked pleased. "Generous of you, Lord Sandry."

"Good," Sandry said. "And with your permission, Wagonmaster—Fullerman, full armor, but polished. I want the troops looking like they're on parade. Whane, that makes you my spearman until the Wagonmaster gets back."

Green Stone nodded.

"Chalker, I'll need my armor too. Maydreo can help me dress. Then I want all the Younglords in armor."

"Ours won't be polished," Whane said, "sir."

"Mine won't either," Sandry said. He turned to Green Stone. "I haven't had the charioteers in armor because that slows the chariots down, and against birds speed is more important than protection."

"Against birds," Green Stone said.

"Yeah. And we'll want bowcases and arrows too."

"Bows," Green Stone said thoughtfully.

Sandry nodded grimly. "Bows aren't much use against birds. Hard to get through the feathers, and they move too fast to hit them at any range."

"Against birds. But good against men."

Burning Tower felt a chill. She'd never seen Sandry this way before. A warrior commander, grim. And all his men looked the same way, determined.

Green Stone frowned. "All right, armor and bows. But all of you listen. They're acting scared in there. Scared of us, which doesn't make any sense, but it sure means we don't give them any reason to be scared of us." He grinned, tried to seem friendly. "When we get inside, no shortchanging the customers. Don't promise more than you have. Make them glad they bought from you. And I don't have to say *No gathering*." He came over to Burning Tower. "You're the family member in charge, then," he said. "Lord Sandry, if anything happens here, get her home to her father. Lordsman Chalker, if you're ready, I guess I am."

Burning Tower clambered atop the wagon nearest the Condigeo gates and watched as Chalker drove her brother toward the city. Green and orange feathers fluttered from the spears in the spearcase, and a terror bird head topped the longest spear.

"All those spears," she said.

Sandry looked up with a grin. "Throwing spears with feathers tied on, thrusting spear with a bird's head on it. Even an idiot can see this is for show."

"Oh."

Sandry nodded. "But an idiot can also see that those are real spears, and that's not the only war chariot we have." He touched his bowcase. "And we are the Lords of Lordshills. They've heard of us."

Aha. And Peacevoice Fullerman's men were in shining armor, but it was armor, and they marched in perfect step, trained men. She watched as the Younglords strained to string their bows. The bows were odd looking, curved the wrong way, nothing like the simple bows Tower had seen among people along the Hemp Road. "Chalker didn't take a bow," she said.

"He's a Lordsman, not a Lord," Sandry said absently.

"Don't Lordsmen use bows?"

"No." Sandry hesitated. "Lords only," he said. "Chalker's got spears and a shield. Better at close quarters anyway."

She nodded in agreement, although she didn't really understand. *And once Rocky gets inside those gates . . .*

The gates swung open. Someone in a bright red jacket came out of a guardhouse to speak with Green Stone. Tower couldn't hear what he said, but the chariot drove inside. The gates swung closed.

And up on the bluff above them, a dozen armed men looked down on the wagon train. Gulls wheeled overhead.

Chapter Six

Condigeo

It was two hours past noon when the gates opened again. Chalker and Green Stone rode out. Their chariot was followed by wagons, decorated wagons. Girls perched on the sides of the lead wagon. There was no sign of armed men.

Green Stone was gesturing. Fallen Wolf watched, and turned to Burning Tower. "He's signaling to move into line and go into town, Mistress. Shall I?"

It looked all right. She turned to Sandry. "What do I do?"

Sandry was watching from the lead wagon. "All's well. See how Chalker is standing? He'd have a different pose if there was something wrong."

She nodded to Fallen Wolf.

"Heads up. Move out!"

Sandry turned to Peacevoice Fullerman. "Sound stand

down," he shouted. He grinned at Burning Tower. "So it's all right after all."

She answered his smile with her own, glad to be near him.

Green Stone rode near her in the lead wagon. "Get ready to put on a show when we get to the Feathersnake office buildings," he called.

"But what—?"

"No time. Put on Mother's costume, that'll wow 'em. Lead us into town, Lordsman!"

Chalker was grinning like a Lordkin.

Sandry drove his chariot behind Green Stone. The other chariots followed, then Peacevoice Fullerman with his troops in their shining armor. All the wagoneers were grinning. Feathers and bright cloths appeared. Girls rode one-horns bareback. The wagon train became a parade before they reached the gates.

They rode through the gates and down toward the harbor. People came out of their houses to watch them. Whane waved to the crowd, caught a thrown bunch of grapes, and shared them. Some cheered, then more, and before they reached the docks the streets were lined with cheering people. Others fell in behind them to follow the wagon train. Tower dashed into her wagon. She quickly put on her mother's costume, the one made from terror bird feathers. As soon as they reached Feathersnake Square, she shouted to her assistants. "Get the poles up!"

They set up her tightrope. She climbed to the top and grinned down to Sandry. "Catch."

"Sure, if you give me a minute to get out of this corselet." He let Chalker strip off the heavy leather and bronze armor, then moved to be under Burning Tower, to catch her if she fell, and they both remembered another time. . . .

And that drew a bigger crowd. She ran along the tightrope and did somersaults until curiosity overcame her and she spiraled down the standing pole to applause.

Sandry and Green Stone caught up with her inside the Feathersnake offices.

"All right," she demanded. "All right!"

"Yes, it is," Green Stone said. "It was the birds."

"Birds?"

"Yes. This is the first wagon train to get here in weeks. The birds drove the others off. Condigeo has been cut off from inland for more than a month."

"So why were they suspicious of us?" Tower demanded. "Oh!"

"Yep. They saw all those feathers—they thought maybe we owned the birds," Green Stone said. "Once we set them straight on that, it was the biggest welcome we ever got."

"Which settles one question the council had," Sandry said.

"Sandry?" Tower asked.

"Whether Condigeo was sending the birds," Sandry said. "Think on it. We're negotiating trade treaties with the Captains; it was possible they were using the birds to help their trading position."

Green Stone grinned. "I think your council has a lot to learn about trading," he said, and chuckled. "Think of the cost! But the birds are coming from the east. I found that much out already."

* * *

The Captains of Condigeo met in a large roofed pavilion near the sea. The walls could be removed, and some of them had been, so that there was plenty of light without torches. Thirteen Captains sat on a high dais at a curved table. Parallel and a step below them was another curved table with clerks. Marines in scarlet tunics, shields brightly polished, stood along one wall.

The center of the room was tiled, with a table for those having business with the council. Behind that were seats for the public. Half of Condigeo seemed to be crowded into the building.

There was another pavilion just beyond the council chambers. This one was smaller, roofed, but also open on the sides, filled with long tables. Enticing smells came from a kitchen on the docks behind the banqueting hall.

Twelve of the thirteen Captains stood as Green Stone led a dozen of his wagoneers and guests into the chamber. The thirteenth was hoisted onto the council table by two burly marines. His legs were mere stumps, but it didn't seem to bother him. "Welcome, Green Stone of Feathersnake!"

"We thank you, Commodore Pergammon," Green Stone said in fluent Condigeo. "I present my sister, Burning Tower of Feathersnake. Our friend and ally Lord Sandry of Lordshills and Yangin-Atep's City. The Wise One Clever Squirrel."

"Welcome all," Pergammon said. Pergammon was thickly bearded, and his dark eyes darted over them, daring anyone to notice that he was set on the tabletop rather than standing behind it. He gestured toward the banqueting hall. "A feast is being prepared. We trust you will join us."

"With great pleasure," Green Stone said. He beckoned, and three wagoneers came in with bundles. "And it is our pleasure to offer you these gifts."

Bundles of green and orange feathers, including sword-wings from the terror birds. Burning Tower suppressed a smile. That message was clear enough. *We have these, and we can get more. We don't hide behind walls. We go where we choose, and if the birds get in our way, it's too bad for the birds.*

The captains all bowed. Pergammon introduced them in turn, his marine attendants turning him toward each captain as he was introduced, but there were too many for Burning Tower to remember. They were all different, but there was something about them that was the same, a stance and an attitude. They were all stout men, well fed but not fat, and their eyes never rested in the same place for long. Pergammon stood out even among that company. When he spoke, everyone listened.

"Impressive," Sandry muttered.

Burning Tower nodded. And everyone in the big room had stood when the captains stood. Everyone, including cripples and children, and they were all quiet when any of their leaders spoke.

"We thank you," Pergammon said. "I don't mind telling you, those birds had us worried." He looked to his fellow captains. "We're masters of the sea, but it's a long way by water to the inner seas. Protection bets grow more costly with each voyage. Can you open the Golden Road again?"

"We can try," Green Stone said. "That will be costly."

Protection bets?

Pergammon fingered his beard. "Indeed. Well, perhaps between us we can afford the cost. We can discuss the details later. For now, there's a banquet, and Condigeo welcomes you!"

The room exploded in applause and shouts.

They seated Burning Tower with the women. Other tables held both men and women, but not the captains. The captains' table held only men, including Green Stone and Sandry. Peacevoice Fullerman and his men sat with a group of marines, and the Younglords and Lordkin were seated at another table with well-dressed young men and women. Burning Tower found herself next to a richly dressed lady twice her age. She glittered with jewels, and Tower wasn't surprised when she was introduced as Pearl, wife of First Captain Granton. The First Captain was deputy to Commodore Pergammon. No one was introduced as Pergammon's wife.

"We're so glad to see you," Pearl said. "I was really getting worried when the wagon trains stopped." She fingered her cheeks. "Wrinkles. I feel them. They don't show yet, but another few weeks . . ." She touched her large turquoise earrings. "But there, you'll get through and I can charge these again, and everything will be fine. Aren't you going to open your present?"

She indicated an ornate small box on Tower's plate. It seemed to have a tricky fastening, and the women all watched with wry amusement as Tower tried to puzzle it out.

"The silver stud," Pearl said. "Press that."

The stud moved inward at her touch. There was a sensation, warmth and something else, in her thumb. She felt her skin tingle. The box opened, to reveal a small bit of polished stone shaped like a tower. Tiny carnelian flames ringed the stone tower. The tower stone had grain and looked like wood, but it was stone to the touch.

Petrified wood, refined, polished, and, from the sensations she felt, charged with magic. Burning Tower couldn't imagine the price of such a thing. Her mother had a similar charm box, but not carved to her naming vision. They must have done this quickly. But how?

"It's wonderful!" Tower said. "Oh, I thank you!"

Pearl looked pleased. "I'm glad you like it. You don't know about these?"

Tower felt bewildered. "No, Pearl."

"I'm sorry, I thought you would. It's magic, of course. Close the box without touching the stud. Don't touch it again until you're ready to use it; there's still enough charge. Next time you use it, be with your man, kiss him while you feel the glow. Not that you need a glamour."

"Not now," an older lady said. "I'm Grandin, Captain Wartin's wife. You don't need that charm now, but there comes a time when we all do."

Tower grinned. "You don't! And I hope this will long be useless before I need it."

"Oh, it will never be useless," Grandin said. "You can get it recharged just the way Pearl gets her earrings charged."

"Oh. We don't deal much in magic," Burning Tower said. "But Clever Squirrel will know about these things. She's Coyote's daughter."

"Umm. Impressive," Grandin said. "Pity they sat her with our Wise Ones. It would be fun to talk with her. Pearl?"

"Well, I thought she'd want to be with them," Pearl said. "And, well, they can tell us what they learn!"

Tower grinned. "I'm sure they'll learn something, but Squirrely may learn more than they do."

Grandin's eyes wrinkled in laughter. "Coyote's daughter. I expect so! We had a girl here who was Jaguar's daughter, but she went south and never came back. We see a little of Coyote, but of course we're mostly in Cormorant territory."

"Does Jaguar come here?" Burning Tower asked.

Pearl shrugged. "I've never seen him, but I've never seen Coyote."

"I've heard they avoid each other," Grandin said. "Jaguar and Coyote, they don't fight, but they don't share either."

Dinner was all seafood. Fried strips of something delicious that Tower later learned was squid. Three kinds of fish, each in a different sauce, one wrapped in seaweed. Crystal glasses, with three kinds of wine. Tower tried to be careful of how much she drank, but she still felt the glow from the box, and whenever she sipped at any of the wines, someone came up behind her and refilled the glass, so it was impossible to tell how much she was drinking. And it tasted wonderful.

Across the room, Sandry and Green Stone were engaged in earnest conversation with the captains, particularly the legless Pergammon, who sat at the center of the table, his marine guards at rigid attention two paces behind him. Tower wished she could listen. Sandry looked handsome in his dress tunic. From time to time, he looked over at her and smiled when he caught her eye.

Pearl began to tell her about the fish and the mer people who caught them.

"I saw mers at Avalon," Tower said excitedly.

"Yes, a wonderful place, especially in spring," Pearl said. "Do you go there often?"

"Just once."

"Only once! Well, you should do something about that! It's a wonderful, magical place. And now, of course, it's going to stay that way."

"No more magic exports from Avalon," Grandin said. "None at all. And with those birds blocking us from the east, we're going to be in real trouble. Or would be. But I'm sure it will be all right now." She smiled at Tower.

"Morth of Atlantis was at Avalon," Tower said.

"I was told that you know Morth of Atlantis. Do you really?"

Tower looked up. Lady Hartta, wife of another of the captains, but Tower couldn't remember which. "Yes, I helped get him to the sea after he drove Yangin-Atep mythical," Burning Tower said.

"Oh! The last Atlantean magician—he must be very old. How does he look?"

Tower smiled. "Well, just then, he looked his age and then some. But he was gallant even then! He said I should stay with him—there was magic in a young girl's smile. Then they took him to the sea."

"But he was at Avalon?"

"Yes, and he looked just fine. Much younger."

Hartta smiled. "Younger. Burning Tower, when you see Morth of Atlantis again, tell him that the Captains of Condigeo would be more than pleased if he would visit. Or if he wishes a new place to live, we can build him a palace."

The other ladies at the table nodded enthusiastically.

It was nearly midnight when the dinner ended. Torch-bearing marines guided them to the wagon camp in the Feathersnake compound. Burning Tower saw Sandry going into the factor's office and followed. Green Stone was already there.

"Did you miss me?" Tower asked.

"Of course," Sandry said.

"Not much," Green Stone said. "Too much work to do. The captains don't give much away."

"What do you mean?"

Stone shrugged. "Well, you know, they keep their trade secrets. But I think we learned some things. The trade with the interior, that's important to them. Really important. I wish we knew why, but we'll find out when we go across."

"But I know why," Burning Tower said.

"Eh?"

"It's no secret at all," she said. She showed her box. "It's magic. They get magic items from the interior. Their wives use them to stay pretty."

"Really?" Sandry sounded incredulous.

All right—there won't ever be a safer time with my brother here . . . She pressed the stud on the box, held it a moment, then grabbed Sandry and kissed him.

* * *

"Enough! Stop." She felt her brother's hand on her shoulder.

"Wow."

"Wow, huh," Green Stone said. "You all right?"

She nodded breathlessly.

Sandry was standing like a stone.

"Is he all right? Sandry?"

Sandry said, "Tower? Was that magic?"

She held up the box.

"And not just you?" Sandry smiled. "Wow. No wonder they were desperate to get the trade going again! Green Stone, can you can give consent for a marriage—"

"Yes!" Tower said.

"No. Not just now," Green Stone said. "You both know it would be a bad idea. You're not thinking."

"Who wants to think?" Tower said.

"Who wants to think? About what?" Clever Squirrel stopped at the door. "Whooo! That's strong manna!" She looked from Tower to Sandry and back. "Well, no problem guessing what you're thinking about!" She looked at the box. "May I see?"

Tower reluctantly handed over the box. "If you press the silver stud, it will use up all the manna," Tower said. "Please don't."

"Silver. Manna flows through silver," Squirrel said.

"I didn't know that," Green Stone said.

"Flows, but doesn't stay. Silver won't *hold* magic. Never any reason you should have known it. We don't get much silver," Clever Squirrel said. "This box is interesting. Did you see what it's made of?" She took out an iron knife and used that to press the stud to open the box.

"Made of the same thing as what's inside, but all the manna is drained out of the outside stonewood. Makes a good insulator. Tower, they *gave* you this?"

"Yes. It's wonderful." She looked at Sandry, who was still staring at her. "I mean, really wonderful."

"I believe you," Clever Squirrel said. "Now why would they give you something so valuable?"

"That's obvious," Burning Tower said.

They were all frowning at her. "Maybe not to me?" Green Stone said.

"Look, it only has maybe one more charge in it," Tower said. "And I sure want it to have more. So does Sandry. Don't you?"

"Oh, yeah."

He looks like a teenage boy, she thought. *And I like that.* She grinned. "So they made sure I'll want it. Rocky, if your wife had been along, they'd have given it to her, I think. But Lilac stayed home, so they chose me. They want our help getting more. They want us to *want* to help."

"Stonewood," Clever Squirrel said. "It comes from a long way off, and that's all I know about it."

"Me too," Green Stone said. "Not very common trade goods anyway, and nobody who sells it ever tells where they got it."

"Well, we know now," Burning Tower said. "East. At the Inland Sea. That's where it comes from, and that's where we have to go." She caught Sandry's eye. They both grinned.

And he'd asked her brother to consent to a marriage. It wouldn't be fair to hold him to that, not after she'd charmed him with the glamour in that box. Would it?

CHAPTER SEVEN

THE CAPTAINS' COUNCIL

The Captains' Council offices were on the third story of a tall building near the docks. Sandry grew impatient as the others got ready for their meeting, and walked ahead to the harbor. The conference room was on the sea side, with a balcony running all around the building. The view across the harbor was perfect. Sandry stood at the balcony rail and watched the activity below.

The harbor was large. There was an inner harbor, then channels through the swamplands, then a larger bay protected by what looked like a narrow sand spit. There were ships at anchor in the bay, some wide—they looked fat to Sandry—with sails and few rowing benches. Others were more narrow, with lots of benches. One of those might have been the *Angie Queen.* It looked enough like her, two masts, fore and aft cabins, lots of oars, but the ship was too far away to read the name on her stern.

The harbor bustled with activity. Dockhands loaded and unloaded ships at the nearby docks. In the anchored boats, sailors brought cargo up to the decks or carried it below from the decks to the holds. There seemed no pattern to all this activity, but everyone worked purposefully.

He saw half a dozen girls skimming across the water. Mers? When one came closer, Sandry could see she was standing on a board, longer than she was tall but not very wide, and she held a feathered sail. The way she held the sail steered the board. It looked like fun. She was graceful, and clearly having the time of her life.

Another girl swooshed past. Her sail was green and orange, and as she came perilously close to the docks below where Sandry stood, she waved. The sail was definitely made from a terror bird wing. They must have worked all night on it.

Two narrow ships with no masts were patrolling near the harbor entrance. Marines in bright red tunics stood on their foredecks. The oarsmen were all dressed alike, cotton tunics with horizontal stripes, and there was no sign of chains or men with whips. A drummer beat the pace, and in one of the warships the men were singing. The war galleys sailed in a big oval pattern that brought them close under the balcony where Sandry stood.

"Impressive, isn't it? Of course it's meant to be. They put this show on for me the first time I came here."

Sandry turned to see Lord Qu'yuma. Aunt Shanda's

husband, Roni's father, he thought automatically. A stocky man with no beard. He wore a miniature shield of office on a necklace, and his clothes were radiantly clean and ornately decorated. "Sir. I'd heard you were here," Sandry said, "but last night at dinner they said you had already left."

"And so I had," Qu'yuma said. He stood next to Sandry. "Might be best to keep our voices low," he said conversationally. "Some of their clerks have very good ears." He grinned. "They sent a dolphin mer to tell us you'd arrived, and when I heard, I insisted on coming back. Rowed all night."

"Oh. Well, sir, good to see you . . ."

Qu'yuma grinned wider. "Now, now. I haven't come back to steal your triumph! The fact is, we weren't getting too far with our trade negotiations, and what I heard made me think you'll get more from them than I did. Only you have to know what to ask for."

By all accounts, Qu'yuma was the best negotiator in Lordshills. Persuasive. Roni had said once her father could talk you into anything if you listened to him long enough.

"So what are we asking for?" Sandry asked.

He stared back out at the harbor. Gulls wheeled overhead. Huge birds with big yellow bills, looking far too big to be able to fly, soared above the water, then dropped like stones, vanished beneath the water, and came up with fish. Smaller long-necked birds swam, then vanished for longer than Sandry could hold his breath before popping back up a long way from where they had gone under. After a while, he realized Qu'yuma hadn't answered.

He turned to see the older man still looking out across the harbor. He lowered his voice again. "What do we want?"

Qu'yuma moved closer. "First, a little background. For all our history, we've been cut off from the interior. The only trade in Tep's Town was by sea, and that meant we were pretty well at the mercy of Condigeo."

"Aren't there other merchant ships?"

"Some. We even own a couple. But Condigeo controls this coast, and they're powerful enough to make it tough on anyone going against their wishes. We were pretty well at their mercy until last year when that Morth of Atlantis sank Yangin-Atep in the tar and opened up the Greenway. Now that we can trade with the interior, we've got some bargaining power."

"Good. Okay, so what *do* we want?"

"Well, a lot of things. The right to have our own merchant ships go anywhere they like, carry any cargo they can find. Protection of our merchants from pirates. Better prices for our hemp ropes and our tar. Better prices for other stuff the kinless make. I got pretty good terms on most of that. Where I didn't get anywhere at all was getting access to the magic trade."

"Sir?"

"They don't like to talk about it. The Captains of Condigeo have a monopoly on trade in magic items," Qu'yuma said. "Especially now that Avalon has banned export of talismans. Some manna items come in from the north, but not very many, and the pirates at Castle Rock Bay charge so much for protection that we can hardly afford anything from up there.

"Now that Yangin-Atep is myth, we've got no god to protect us. We've got the best trained army on the coast, and pirates are too scared of the Lordkin to invade the city—"

"With good reason."

"But without Yangin-Atep, we have no protection against magic at all."

"Oh! So if an invader comes armed with magic, it might be hard on Lord's Town."

"Precisely. It's no secret that we're in great need of talismans in Tep's Town. We're buying, and Condigeo's the only one selling, so the prices are steep. Only now they don't have anything to sell, and they won't tell us why." He waved to indicate the war galley approaching them again. "But they care enough to put on that show for you. They want to impress you. From what I've heard, you've got a way past those birds. I think they need that. I never did put any stock in the idea that Condigeo was sending the birds."

"No, sir. They're as afraid of the birds as we are."

Qu'yuma nodded. "Good. Later you can tell me why you're sure. And Sandry, I think the magic items they sell come from inland."

"Yes, sir. So do the Bison Tribe. And after last night we're pretty sure of it. The trade comes from what they call the Inland Sea, but it comes over land."

Qu'yuma nodded. "That's close to what I had deduced," he said.

"But sir, if they can reach that area by sea, why do they need land travel?"

"Costs, I'd say. It's a long way." Qu'yuma pointed

southward. "Their charts are secret, but I bought one off a merchant skipper. It's interesting. There's a long neck of land they call the Forefinger, not more than forty leagues wide, but it goes five hundred leagues, maybe more, straight south. No wind and no water most of the way down, so the only way around it is to row, only oarsmen need fresh water. If you carry enough water to keep oarsmen alive, there's not much cargo." He shrugged. "So it's a thousand leagues and more by sea to get fifty leagues straight east, and then you have to come back again. Much easier by land."

"But they're blocked by the birds," Sandry said.

"Precisely. And you can deal with those?"

"So far," Sandry said.

"Is it easy?"

"Well, it's not simple."

"Good. Make sure the captains believe it's very hard to do. No false modesty." Qu'yuma turned and waved. "Here come the others. Want me to sit in on this conference?"

"I wish you would. Thank you for offering." *And for asking, for that matter, since you can pull rank on me anytime, and we both know it.*

"There's a lot to learn about these captains," Qu'yuma said. "And not much time. The main thing is dignity. Their leaders think they have earned their positions through hard work."

"And have they?"

"Sometimes. Usually. They've all been successful ship captains, and that's something. Even so, sometimes it's influence and bribes. They'll promote anyone. We put more stock in breeding than they do."

"And sometimes end up with Regapisk in charge," Sandry said under his breath.

"Look what happened to him."

"Uh—sorry, I hadn't meant you to hear that."

"I have very good hearing. It is one of the qualifications of a diplomat," Qu'yuma said. "Condigeo finds us odd. We find them strange. But we are more alike than they believe. Aha. Your people are arriving. And I do believe that must be my daughter's rival." He looked down at the street below.

Green Stone and the others arrived in a wagon drawn by bison, but Qu'yuma was watching Burning Tower dismount from Spike and tie the one-horn to a rail in front of the building.

"Rival, sir?"

"Well, her mother put it that way," Qu'yuma said. "I've known for years you were never going to be my son-in-law. Roni's going to grow up to be like her mother, and it takes a special—well, let's say that you don't have the temperament to be married to someone like your Aunt Shanda."

"Yes, sir. I thought I did, once, but now I'm sure you're right."

A horse-drawn wagon arrived. Marines carried Commodore Pergammon into the building. It was time for their meeting.

There were only five captains, including Commodore Pergammon and First Captain Granton. Pergammon was placed in a chair at the center of the table. Another man, darker and in wizard's robes, sat behind Pergammon and between Pergammon's ever-present marine attendants.

Clerks with parchments and pens sat at each end of the table. The captains sat side by side on both sides of Pergammon. Sandry and Green Stone sat opposite Pergammon, with Burning Cloud and Clever Squirrel to Sandry's left and Lord Qu'yuma to Green Stone's right. The two groups eyed each other suspiciously.

"Greetings. It's not our way to have ladies in our meetings," Pergammon began bluntly.

"Burning Tower is my sister and one of the owners of the wagon train," Green Stone said. "And Clever Squirrel is our shaman. It is our way."

Not really, Sandry thought. *They don't always bring women to their meetings.* We *do, sometimes, but often as not, the Bison Tribe leave the women at home just as we usually do.*

Pergammon shrugged. "As you will. Welcome back, Lord Qu'yuma."

"Thank you, Commodore. When I heard my nephew had arrived, I thought it best to return."

"Your nephew," Pergammon said. "You Lords all seem to be related."

"Indeed, it is true," Qu'yuma said. "Difficult to keep track of all my relatives sometimes." His smile was disarming.

The clerks wrote furiously. Clearly they were recording everything said, but Sandry didn't think they were as good at this as the Lords Witness clerks were. They certainly didn't write as much.

"Well. It's pleasant chatting, but there's work to be

done," Pergammon said. "Lord Sandry, I have a proposition for you. But do I put it to you or Lord Qu'yuma?"

"Perhaps to both," Qu'yuma said. "Lord Sandry is a highly competent officer, but perhaps not overly experienced in matters of commerce."

"All right. To both of you. We want to hire your wagon train to go to the Inland Sea and back."

"It's not my wagon train," Sandry said.

"No, but it's not much use without your army, is it?" Pergammon demanded. "What we need is to get wagons to the Inland Sea and back. We'll pay well."

"Bison Tribe does not usually hire out as carriers," Green Stone said. "We prefer to be traders. But we often have partners in our adventures."

"Partners. And what would that be, partnering?"

Green Stone smiled. "We share. Each of us owns half the cargo. Each of us pays half the costs."

"Half the cargo. And what would that cargo be?"

Green Stone's smile broadened. "Why, Commodore, you would know far better than I what the most profitable cargoes are! I think I know what I wish to buy at Inland Sea, but for the most part, what I buy here and what I will take there for exchange will duplicate what you send and buy."

Pergammon snorted. "Qu'yuma, are all your people like this?"

"They're not my people," Qu'yuma said. He looked from Burning Tower to Sandry. "At least not quite yet. But yes, I think you will find there are few fools here."

"What do you think you'll be buying at the Inland Sea?" Pergammon demanded.

"The ladies of Condigeo gave my sister a wonderful present last night," Green Stone said. "A magical box. I am sure I could make enormous profits on such a cargo. But perhaps you know of even more profitable items. We would be pleased to learn."

"You're doing all the talking," Pergammon said. "But it's the Tep's Town Lords who have to do the fighting. Qu'yuma, what's your price here?"

"Oh, we're content to learn. And perhaps, say, a tenth part of the value of the cargo that returns here. Of the whole, of course."

"A tenth! That's ruin!" Pergammon said.

"I thought it generous," Green Stone said. "Without them, there will be nothing at all. I can't fight the birds. And it's clear you can't either."

"So you'll give them a tenth of your share if we'll do the same," Pergammon said. "We'll have to confer about that."

The other captains gathered around Pergammon. There were whispers, but Sandry didn't understand any of what they said. Finally they took their seats.

"A tenth, then," Pergammon said.

"Clearly we asked for too little," Qu'yuma said politely.

"But we pay the protection bets before we divide," Pergammon added.

"Half," Qu'yuma said. "Pay half from the undivided profits, then you will pay the rest from your share alone."

"Robbery," Pergammon muttered. He glanced at the other captains. Clearly they had anticipated this, because they all nodded. "All right," Pergammon said. "Now, as to how we do this: much of the best cargo for the Inland Sea is large and heavy, heavier than you will like for your wagon train. We propose to send part of that by ship. It should arrive not long after you get there."

"And I own half of that cargo too?" Green Stone said.

"If you buy it, you own it, yes," Pergammon said.

"You buy it. I pay half. When it gets to the Inland Sea, your people divide it, and I choose which half I take," Green Stone said.

Pergammon conferred with his captains again. "Done."

Now they tediously dictated every part of the agreement, and each clerk wrote it down. The two accounts were compared and the documents passed around for inspection. Sandry couldn't read Condigeano, and he didn't think Green Stone could either, but Qu'yuma examined the parchments and nodded approval.

"It is done. So say I. So say you all?"

The four captains said, "Aye," in unison.

"It is agreed, Green Stone of Feathersnake?"

"Aye."

"Qu'yuma and Sandry of Lordshills, is this agreed?"

"It is."

"Then it is done. Witness Jaguar and Cormorant."

"And Coyote," Clever Squirrel said. The look in her eyes that usually appeared when Coyote was present wasn't there. It was a bluff, Burning Tower thought, but nobody called her on it.

Chapter Eight

Protection Bets

First Captain Granton led them down the stairs to the docks. Green Stone dropped back a few steps and, when Sandry and Qu'yuma followed, asked, "What is a protection bet?"

Sandry shook his head.

Qu'yuma said, "I hope to learn a little more about that. My best information is that captains bet against themselves to reduce the risk of a voyage."

"How does that work?"

Qu'yuma answered with a shrug.

First Captain Granton led them to a teahouse. The sign above the door showed a ship superimposed over a large bell. The ship on the sign looked like one of the wide, fat ones Sandry had noticed that morning. Granton led them inside and up to the second floor.

To their left was a public room. Men and women sat and talked in low tones as they drank tea and ate cakes and dried fish. *Captains and merchants,* Sandry thought. *Mostly. And who are these others?*

"Ladies, it is best if you wait here," Qu'yuma said. He indicated the public room.

Burning Tower started to protest, but her brother's frown cut her off. Sandry smiled faintly as Tower let Clever Squirrel lead her to a table.

Granton led the men through a doorway to the right. Two burly guards sat just inside. They waved greeting as Granton came in. Qu'yuma, Green Stone, and Sandry were waved in only after Granton said, "We have business here."

"Certainly, Captain." A young lady, pretty, expensively dressed, came to greet them. "Will you want your own table?"

"Yes, that will be best," he said.

The room was about the size of the public room, but with fewer tables. Like the public room, it faced onto the sea, but there was no balcony outside the window, only thick thatched eaves jutting out below the windows. It would be difficult to hear anything said in this room down in the streets below, and when he looked out the window Sandry saw armed marines. No one would be listening down there.

Their table was near the window. A liveried waiter brought a pot of tea and cups. Sandry sipped. Mild tea, no hemp flavor that he could detect. He had seen wine bottles in the public room, but there were none here.

After a moment, a plainly dressed man in his thirties left

his own table and came over. "Captain Granton," he said. "Do we have business?" He bowed.

Granton and Qu'yuma stood, so Sandry and Green Stone did as well. "Betting Master Calafi, I present Wagonmaster Green Stone of Feathersnake and Lord Sandry of Lordshills," Granton said. "You already know Lord Qu'yuma."

"Indeed I do. May I join you?" The voice was smooth, educated Condigeano with only the tiniest trace of an accent. *Perhaps it is no accent at all,* Sandry thought. *I haven't met all that many Condigeanos. But this man has never been a captain—I'm sure of that.*

"Please do." There was already an empty cup at Calafi's place. Granton filled it from the teapot. The waiter quietly came and retrieved the pot, replacing it with another.

"I understand you killed three score of the monster birds," Calafi began. He smiled softly at Sandry.

"Not quite so many as that," Sandry said. "We had good luck."

"I trust luck had nothing to do with it," Calafi said. "I don't believe in luck." He looked to Green Stone. "So you two will be taking the wagon train to the Inland Sea."

"Yes."

"Going yourselves, both ways?"

"Yes," Green Stone said.

"Good. I always feel better about these bets when the owners are going along. But I understood there is to be a ship as well?"

Captain Granton nodded. "The *Angie Queen* will sail

in the morning. Here's her manifest." He took parchments from a pouch he carried.

"And half of this is owned by the captains, half by Feathersnake? Plus, of course, the ship herself."

"Correct."

Calafi studied the parchments. "Of course you have no objection to inspection and seals on the cargo."

"Of course not," Granton said.

"Good. Let us consummate this simple transaction before we study the matter of the wagon train," Calafi said. He looked over the sheets again. "Yes, I believe we will have an offer for you. Excuse me." He stood and carried the parchments to another table, where he was joined by four other men. They all looked alike, plain tunics and trousers, black hair cut straight at shoulder length, dark eyes in almond-colored faces.

"Would someone explain this?" Green Stone demanded.

"Protection bets," Captain Granton said. "You don't do this in wagon trade?"

"I doubt it. I don't know what you're doing."

"He will offer to pay the value of the ship and cargo if it does not arrive safely at Inland Sea," Granton said. "And he'll name a price paid to him before she sails. In my experience, that will be close to one part in sixteen of the value of the cargo and one in twenty of the value of the ship."

"I'm not paying for any protection of a ship!" Green Stone said.

"You'll have to, to get a protection bet on the cargo. But the ship owners will pay part of it too."

Green Stone frowned. "What's to keep the ship owners

from sailing the ship somewhere and selling it and then claiming it was lost?"

"It would not be wise," Granton said. "The bets never cover the whole value of the ship. And if the story comes out, the captain and owners would regret their actions. It would not be wise."

They sipped tea and waited until Calafi came back to their table. "We have an offer for the *Angie Queen* and her cargo," he said. "I regret I can make no offer regarding the wagon train and its cargo."

"None at all?" Granton said frostily. "Yet Bell's of Condigeo boasts that it will make protection bets on anything."

"And so we can," Calafi said. "But it will take time. We have no history of such journeys since the monster birds appeared. Without history, we must make guesses. Such guesses lead to offers that you will not like, for they will be very costly." He shrugged. "No one of us wants any large part of such a bet. It will require the entire resources of this establishment, and it will take time to assemble all the partners and allocate the risks. I understood you were in a hurry."

"I need no such protection to begin with," Green Stone said. "My protection lies with Lord Sandry's chariots and our Lordsmen allies, and I think that will be protection enough."

"So be it," Calafi said. "Here is the offer for the ship."

Chapter Nine

Preparations

Green Stone and Qu'yuma were engaged in inspecting documents. Sandry found this tedious. He took Qu'yuma aside. "The troops will want to be paid extra for this," he said. "Maybe a lot."

"I know," Qu'yuma said. "Make the best deal you can, but be generous rather than stingy. This will make our reputation. It may make our fortunes as well."

"You see it as that important?"

"To bring the Condigeo Captains a cargo they can't get for themselves? Sandry!" Qu'yuma said. "Just get there and back. Leave the rest to us."

"All right." He turned to the table where Green Stone was still talking to Captain Granton. "Lord Qu'yuma can speak for me. I'll wait for you with Tower," he said.

Green Stone nodded without expression. "We should not be much longer."

Maybe, maybe not, Sandry thought.

Burning Tower and Clever Squirrel were sitting with two men. One was stout and short and moved slowly. When Sandry reached the table, he saw that the man was old but dressed well, and carried a cane of black wood with gold mountings. The other man was a giant. Sandry thought he was at least forty. Up closer, he looked to a dozen years older or younger than that. His hair was blond and his eyes were Lordkin blue. The ears were Lordkin, but he did not act like a Lordkin, and his accent was not of Tep's Town.

Neither stood as Sandry came to the table.

"Sandry! This is Tras Preetror, the teller. He knows my father. And his companion, Arshur."

Sandry nodded. "I heard you sing the story of the fall of the Toronexti. Last winter, in Lord's Town."

"Indeed I did," Tras Preetror said. "To an appreciative and generous audience. You and the lady had a prominent part in the song. As her father figures in the story of Tep's Town. An unfinished story, I think."

"He was telling us how Father got his tattoo!" Burning Tower said.

Tras shrugged. "It is only a tale. When you tell your father of me, say also that I say it is only a tale, and one well known to many others."

"Tell them I'm going to be king," Arshur said. He had a wild look, battered and mad.

Clever Squirrel frowned. "With your permission." She took Arshur's hand and studied it. "It may be true, but your reign will not be long. This old scar, this slash, changed the pattern."

"Long or short, I'm going to be king," Arshur said. "I have always known it. Even Tras believes it now."

"I understand you travel east," Tras Preetror said.

Sandry looked blank.

"Surely it is no secret," Tras said. "And anyone can follow a trail of bison chips. A long and slow journey, east to the Inland Sea."

"You've been there?" Sandry asked.

"Years ago. I went there by ship, a long passage south and around the Forefinger—dull for the most part, but sometimes there are wonderful things to see. Whales feeding their children. Fish that fly across the water, other fish with swords for beaks, great sea monsters with a hundred arms and eyes like giants. Crocodiles three man-lengths long. I came back by wagon train."

"What was that like?" Burning Tower asked.

"Wilder than the Hemp Road," Tras said. "Long stretches where there is only wilderness. A day's passage across blowing sands that rise into hills that walk. Towns in valleys, towns of people who have never gone a league from the place they were birthed, and never will. Wonderful songs in strange languages." He sighed. "I am minded to go again. Have you room for passengers?"

Sandry shook his head. "It's not entirely up to me, but I'd vote no."

"But why?" Burning Tower said. "The stories—and he is an old friend of Father's."

"I have not claimed that," Tras said. "It is true that your father and I have known each other since he was a boy, but our relationship is more complicated than friendship. Tell me, Lord Sandry, why would you not want me on your journey?"

"One more thing to worry about," Sandry said. "We don't know what we're facing. Never been there, and we know we have the birds to fight. That's enough for me."

"Birds to fight. You came to town bearing trophies," Tras said. "Tell me of that fight. Leave nothing out."

He's good, Burning Tower thought. *Tras Preetror is getting more details than Sandry ever told me.*

"The trooper was pushed back," Tras asked. "That would have been serious."

"Yes, it would, if the bird could get among the troopers. Those things can kick a man to death in seconds. But Secklers saw what was happening and got his shoulder on Manneret's back and pushed him right back into the line."

"Ah," Tras said. He sipped tea. "And you were right there when that happened."

"Yes, we were resting the horses, while Maydreo led the birds around the circle."

"Resting the horses—is that important?"

"Sure. Tired horses can't outrun the birds, not pulling a chariot with two men in it. Everyone knows that."

"Perhaps not everyone knows as much of horses as you," Tras Preetror said. "So you were resting the horses. Then what?"

A waiter came to the table. "There is a boy here who wishes to see wagonmaster Green Stone," he said. "But the Wagonmaster is in the Betting Rooms. I noted you were of his party; perhaps he could wait with you?"

"Certainly," Burning Tower said. "Bring him here."

Tras Preetror hid his unhappiness and tried to be interested in the newcomer.

Burning Tower guessed the boy was about twelve. He wore buckskins similar to the travel clothing of the Bison Tribe, but the fetish painted on his chest was a mountain goat. Distant cousins to the Bison Tribe, then. No relation to Feathersnake at all.

The boy stood politely at the table, waiting for someone to speak to him.

Good manners, she thought. "I'm Burning Tower of Feathersnake," she said. "My brother is Wagonmaster Green Stone. And you are welcome."

"Thank you. I am Spotted Lizard, of the High Trail. They say that you are going east along the Golden Road." His speech was slow, breathy Condigeano.

"That story sure gets around fast," Sandry said.

Tras Preetror nodded. "There are few secrets in Condigeo."

"And what can we do for you, Spotted Lizard?" Tower asked.

"Take me with you. I fell ill when my father's wagon left here to go east. That was three moons ago, and no one has heard from him since. I know something of the road. I have been across to the Inland Sea and back three times now. I can help you. And . . . and . . . I don't have anywhere else to go."

Sandry hardly saw Burning Tower for the next two days. She was busy with the details of buying provisions for the wagons and cargo for both the wagons and the ship.

Meanwhile, Sandry was burdened with details of the military expedition. Buying spears, fodder for the horses, leather and bronze for repair of armor. And keeping Secklers and Trebaty out of trouble. For that he employed Nothing Was Seen, to follow them and keep track of anything they might gather, to offer to pay before there could be difficulties.

Surprisingly, there were none. Secklers bought a necklace and some perfumes, and Trebaty bought a dress, paying with the wages they had earned as wagon guards.

"How?" Sandry demanded, when Lurk reported to him that evening. "I didn't think they were that, well, smart."

"Sea chanties," Lurk said. "I learned a rowing song from Tras Preetror, and I sing it whenever they are in a shop."

"I didn't see you anywhere around when I had that talk with them," Sandry protested.

Lurk grinned.

"You leave in the morning," Qu'yuma said.

"Yes. Do you have instructions?" Sandry asked.

"Only that you get there and back—alive, if possible," Qu'yuma said. "Learn what you can of the conditions at the Inland Sea. You have a right to know, I think, but don't get accused of being a spy. Things may be different there."

Sandry frowned.

"Some places keep secrets," Qu'yuma said. "We don't usually allow strangers inside the walls of Lordshills."

"But that's not to keep secrets," Sandry said.

"No, merely privacy. And outside those walls, we

don't care. We invite lookers and tellers. But that is—or was—because it was better that people knew how things were in Tep's Town than if they guessed. That we had no great wealth, and a good army, and fierce Lordkin ready to gather from anyone we considered enemies. And the protection of Yangin-Atep."

"That wasn't much protection."

"More than you know," Qu'yuma said. "Think. Buildings would not burn unless Yangin-Atep wanted them to burn. Fires would go out. Magic weapons would not work against our army, while swords and spears worked just fine. And now that we don't have that protection, we have to rethink our policies. Do we want the world to know what things are like in Tep's Town?" He shrugged. "Condigeo is open. Many towns are. But there are places like Swallow's Nest in the hills north of here, whence no stranger returns alive, and the only traders are their own and won't talk."

"The Inland Sea is different. We have a boy who has been there three times."

"What does he know of the towns?"

"Little," Sandry admitted. "He always stayed with the wagons. The town traders came to their wagon camp."

"And have you met anyone who wandered freely in the Inland Sea towns?"

Sandry shook his head.

"Nor have I." Qu'yuma shrugged. "Learn what you can. Information is valuable. But be careful. I don't have to tell you how successful you've been already. We already have a better reputation with the captains than we've ever had before. And now they've seen how useful horses are, they'll want some. So will the Bison Tribe. Sandry, we don't know the wagon trade, and we don't know the sea trade, but we do know horses."

"Burning Tower knows the wagon trade," Sandry said.

Qu'yuma grinned. "I'll be sure to put that in my report to the council and congregation," he said. "She's an heiress too."

"That's not—"

"Of course not, but it doesn't hurt, either. We train armies, we train horses. All good, but it won't hurt us to have the Lords involved in the wagon trains too."

Sandry nodded, as if in agreement.

"Thing are changing fast," Qu'yuma said. "We always thought we were adaptable, we Lords, but we never had to face changes like these."

"Interesting times," Sandry said. "Wasn't that an old curse?"

"Yes, from our ancestors," Qu'yuma said.

Later, alone, Sandry thought about his conversations with Qu'yuma, and with the Lord Chief Witness before he left Tep's Town. *They're assuming I will always be a Lord of Lordshills, and that anything I do will be for the Lords. That I can't possibly just go off on my own, be a wagonmaster or a horse trader.*

Then he chuckled. *Wagonmaster? I think wagonmaster, but I'd be lucky to be a wagon owner, and then it would be Tower's skill that keeps us from starving. But I do know horses.*

And I am a Lord of Lordshills, and these are interesting times.

Book Three

The Golden Road

Chapter One

Departure

"We're all set, then," Green Stone said. "Everyone ready?" He looked around the circle of men and women standing by their wagons and mounts.

"All ready, Wagonmaster," Fallen Wolf said.

"Clever Squirrel?" Green Stone asked.

"I have no visions at all," she said. "But I believe we are ready."

"Lord Sandry?"

Sandry inspected his troops: Younglords in their chariots, Peacevoice Fullerman with his Lordsmen, looking pleased with themselves. *As well they might,* Sandry thought. *They're getting a year's pay for this. Be generous, Qu'yuma said. But it is to be paid in Lord's Town on their return. No point in letting trained men go find out what they could earn on their own.*

There were ten of the Condigeo marines as well, with an officer cadet named Gundrin in command. Gundrin and his men were more or less equipped like Lordsmen, with shields and spears, but they carried good-quality bronze short swords that Peacevoice Fullerman much admired. The captains had insisted that their own guards accompany the wagons, but Sandry knew their real mission was to study tactics. Well, let them. They'd find that horses and chariots were needed too, and they didn't have those. Condigeo's marines knew nothing of horses, and less of one-horns.

They didn't have compound bows, either, and Sandry wasn't going to show those. No point in giving away more than he had to.

"Junior Warman Gundrin, are you ready?" Sandry said.

"Aye, aye, Lord Sandry."

Behind the marines were Secklers and Trebaty. The Lordkin weren't needed, but there was no way to send them home either. And they did make good bodyguards.

"We're ready, Wagonmaster," Sandry said.

"Eastward," Green Stone said. "Let's do it."

Sandry waved. Maydreo drove ahead, then the other Younglords in their chariots. Then the first wagon behind the plodding bison, followed by the Lordsmen and the marines. The other wagons followed, and Younglord Qirimby brought up the rear, keeping his chariot well back from the wagons and their trail of bison dung.

As they passed the gates, they saw Commodore

Pergammon sitting impassively on the guard platform above the gatehouse. Pergammon waved to them. "Good luck," he called.

"Thank you," Green Stone answered.

An hour later, they saw a dozen terror birds. The birds divided into two groups and tried to flank the column, and they had to circle the wagons. Sandry gestured to his charioteers, and Fullerman deployed his men, while the wagoneers climbed high to ready their slings.

Sandry was pleased to see that Junior Warman Gundrin was careful to follow Fullerman's instructions on where to put his men, and Secklers and Trebaty stood behind Fullerman like guards.

Our first test, Sandry thought. *We're organized.* He studied the birds as they approached. They seemed more cautious than the last group had been, each group hanging off to the side of the wagon train as if waiting for opportunities. Finally Sandry nodded to Chalker and charged the group approaching from the left side of the wagon train. "Try to get the lead bird, the big gaudy one. I think that's the rooster."

"Aye, My Lord."

Chalker's throw was good but not perfect. The bird took the spear full in the chest, staggered, then charged toward the wagon train, ignoring Sandry and his chariot and horses. The others followed.

"Never saw them do that before," Chalker shouted. "But if they're ignoring you, maybe we can come up behind them." He hefted a stabbing spear.

"Right. Let's do it." Sandry wheeled the chariot and

charged. This time Chalker's thrust was perfect, just where the neck joined the body. The chariot wheeled.

"They're turning toward us!" Chalker shouted. "They're chasing us."

"Right. Let's lead them to Fullerman." *And that's the way it should be,* he thought.

As he led the birds toward the waiting spearmen, he heard Mouse Warrior's triumphant shouts from the wagontop. "Hey, Harpy!"

The marines cheered. They had killed two of the birds, with one marine clawed badly.

Sandry examined the wounded marine. "I think you'd better go home," he said. "Maydreo, take him back to the gates and leave him with his comrades. With three in the chariot, walk the horses most of the way there. Trot back."

"I don't want to go back," the marine protested. "I'll lose my pay."

"Squirrel?" Sandry said.

She shook her head. "I can keep him alive, but it will take time and magic, and we don't have either to spare. He'll be a lot better off back in Condigeo."

"Right. Maydreo, you and Whane help this trooper home. Sorry, lad, but not much we could do." He waited for a nod from Gundrin, then waved Maydreo on his way. Sandry waited until the chariot was well away and turned to the others.

"Now. How did he get clawed?"

"Broke ranks to finish a wounded bird," one of the marines said.

Sandry nodded. "Lesson learned?"

"Sir. Yes, sir!"

"Good. Carry on." Sandry touched the reins. They rode back to the front of the wagon train. "We can move out now," he said. "Maydreo shouldn't have any problem following the trail."

Green Stone nodded. "You win again," he said.

"Easy enough fight," Chalker observed.

Sandry nodded. "Two groups of six are a lot easier to fight than one big group. I wonder why they tried it that way."

"The god is experimenting," Clever Squirrel said. "Learning. But we're learning too! He can only control a few at a time, maybe only one. I don't know how fast he can shift attention from one bird to another. May depend on how far away he is."

"Hmmm," Sandry said. "Maybe that's it, then. That first column, we charged, and Chalker put a spear in the bird's chest, but they kept on going toward the wagons. Fullerman was scrambling to get in front of them before they could get at the bison."

"Bison!" Green Stone said. "If they start attacking bison instead of following the horses, we have problems, I think."

"Yes. And I think that's where these were headed," Sandry said. "But since they were ignoring us, I could come up behind them. Chalker got the last one in line, and the lead one he'd put a spear into stumbled, and then they all charged after me the way they're supposed to."

Squirrel looked thoughtful, then nodded.

"What makes you think the god's not right here?" Burning Tower asked.

"I watched the fight," Squirrel said. "If you watch close, it's pretty easy to see what's happening. If I could have watched from the wagontop and given orders to each bird, I could have won that battle no matter how good Sandry's men were. At least I think I could. But it didn't work that way. I think the god can only see through one bird's eyes at a time. He can jump from one bird to another, but he's not overhead looking down on the battle, so he's not close. I think he's a long way off."

"Long way?" Sandry asked.

She nodded. "I don't feel any presence of a god here at all. Not a trace."

"Well, that's good," Sandry said. "I'd hate to fight them if they were all getting orders from someone watching what happens. But Squirrel, usually they chase horses when we get close, even if that's not smart."

She nodded again. "That's their nature. If the god could stop them, he would. He cobbled things here. He could control that one group, but while you were playing with them, Bentino was leading the other group by the nose. So then the god left your group to try to guide the other one, but they were already chasing horses in a circle. That's why I think he's far away."

"So when we get closer, the birds will act smarter?"

Squirrel nodded.

"That's scary. Anything we can do?"

"A god is making war on us. I'm as scared as you can imagine," Squirrel said.

Maydreo caught up with them in the evening. "They wanted to send a replacement, but I'd have had to wait for them to find him, and I didn't really fancy trying to catch up with three in a chariot anyway," he said.

"Good decision," Sandry said. "We have enough troops. And now we have some extra rations."

In the afternoon, they came to the Great Fork. The north branch was the Hemp Road to Firewoods and farther. The other fork went east: the Golden Road that led to the Inland Sea and beyond. Rumor said it went on from there, south and deep into Jaguar territory. No one of Feathersnake or the Bison Tribe had ever taken the Golden Road east even as far as the Inland Sea, and their only guide was the boy, Spotted Lizard.

The road was easy to follow. It had once been well traveled, with wide ruts in the low areas, rocky ledges carved in the hillsides when the road climbed to cross over hills between the valleys. Streams ran through the valleys, and there were farms everywhere, but few farmhouses. The villages were all walled, not the hastily made walls of Condigeo but older walls, stone and earth as well as timber, with suspicious guards staring out at them as they passed. Men and women worked in the fields, with more armed men standing watch nearby. It was not a peaceful land.

They camped that night in an open field, not cultivated despite a small stream. The sky was clear overhead. The River blazed across the night sky. About midnight someone shouted: a dozen falling stars, one after another, all coming directly at them before they vanished.

It all looked vaguely magical, but Clever Squirrel said nothing.

CHAPTER TWO

ABOARD THE *ANGIE QUEEN*

DAY 1

A wind was rising. Above the oar pit, Regapisk could glimpse sailors moving at a run. Sails rattled as they rose. The Oarmaster signaled: Stop oars.

Regapisk settled his oar across his lap. To the man across, he asked conversationally, "How long d'you think this'll last?"

The man's mad eyes rested on Regapisk, promising murder; then drifted away. He never said anything to anyone.

The man behind Regapisk murmured, "If you don't stop poking the Ghost, Lord Reg, it isn't me he'll remember the day he gets loose."

Regapisk was tired of hearing Fethiwong abuse the title he'd lost. How would *Sandry* put an end to that? "One day, Fethiwong," Regapisk murmured, "the Oar-master will hear you call me Lord."

"Naw, he won't. What was your turf?"

It dawned on Regapisk that Fethiwong thought he was a Lordkin tribal leader.

That was funny. Should he claim Serpent's Walk? His firefighters had come from there; he'd learned a little, but Fethiwong might know enough to catch him out. Regapisk hadn't yet placed Fethiwong's accent.

He waved it away. "That's all in the past."

Waves played with the ship. Oarsmen murmured. Above, sailors shouted. When they stopped, Regapisk could make out softer voices. Passengers. You rarely saw passengers; they never looked down into the pit after the first day.

Regapisk liked the quiet, but he didn't need the rest. The *Angie Queen* had been in Condigeo for at least eight days. Oarsmen ate well when a ship was in port. They carried cargo under careful supervision—hard work, but a change from rowing.

Eight days? Ten? Regapisk wasn't sure. He'd started a count on the day he woke, battered and confused, head ringing, to find himself chained to an oar bench. He tried to keep track of the days: a training period, layovers, trips to Avalon and Houseman's Beach. He'd heard about San-barb Island, had always wanted to see it—still did. Seeing a mushroom shape, then bluffs and a beach through an oarlock didn't count. He'd seen a lot more of Avalon. They actually went ashore and slept on real mats in

Avalon. Across to Tep's Town harbor again, where Sandry had abandoned him despite his promise. Why had he done that?

Afraid of the congregation. Sandry wasn't afraid of much, you had to give him that, but he was afraid of the council and congregation, as if they'd do anything to Sandry. Sandry's aunt Shanda was the First Lady of Lordshills! She was only cousin twice removed to Regapisk. That's why she didn't help! Sure. But Sandry? He had money; he could have bought him loose. They were right there in the Tep's Town harbor. But nothing happened. Cargo was put on board, and they were off again.

Then three days to Condigeo, sailing with the wind most of the way. A long layover, and rumors. A barracks to sleep in, plenty to eat, not all that unpleasant at night. Daytimes, they scraped the sides of the ship or of the docks, or swept streets. The *Angie Queen*'s captain never missed a chance to make a few coppers renting out his crew. Eight days? Ten? That's where he had almost lost track of the time.

Rumors said that Feathersnake wagons and a Tep's Town Lordsmen army had beaten the birds and gotten through. Their next move would be to open the wagon trade again. What birds? Fethiwong told him an implausible tale of horse-sized shrieking demons with daggers in their wings. . . .

But if Tep's Town had sent Lords here, then Sandry would be with them, and Sandry would use the chance to free him. Regapisk stopped making marks alongside his bench.

Ten days waiting. They'd left Condigeo this morning. Regapisk resumed his count, a mark on the wood next to his head, made with a jagged fingernail. *Day One: depart Condigeo.*

DAY 2: SOUTHBOUND

In thirty days or so at sea and in harbor, Regapisk had learned an oarsman's pace and was earning the strength.

In his youth he had admired the muscles on Lordsmen. He'd hoped to grow up that way. He was getting his wish. His arms and shoulders had never looked this good.

It was all thanks to Lord Sandry.

Regapisk's mind darted about his skull like a rat in a cage, seeking any escape from what he most wanted to avoid knowing. Sandry's testimony had put him here. Sandry had promised to buy him free . . . but the *Angie Queen* had left Condigeo, hugging the coast, keeping the dawn on the left. Down along the Forefinger, Regapisk thought; but he knew little of that land. In Avalon they'd been housed ashore, and in Condigeo too, but at sea they slept in their chains. There was no chance of escape.

It wasn't that he liked Sandry. They'd played together, and fought sometimes, and broken rules and been caught sometimes . . . but they were nearly cousins. You didn't sell a cousin into slavery; you defended him.

But Sandry wasn't going to buy him loose.

Two passengers were staring down into the oar pit, talking, laughing.

Lookers, Regapisk thought. Two old men, one still brawny, one lean and stooped, maybe not so old. Hard to tell. They were both twisted by old injuries. Fighters, Regapisk would have guessed, but what was their interest in the oar pit?

When foreigners came to Tep's Town for entertainment, Tep's Town called them lookers. They used to come to watch the Burning. Tellers were lookers who told tales for a living. Sometimes they traveled great distances. When the Burning didn't happen on time, lookers were only disappointed, but tellers could end up sleeping on the beach.

There hadn't been a Burning—a wholesale riot through Tep's Town, wine aflow, theft and rapine, buildings alight—since the fire god went myth. Tellers had become rare.

Entertainment was in short supply for *Angie Queen*'s oarsmen. The men about Regapisk had become proficient at guessing about passengers. Of course they had no way to test their guesswork. On the day trip to Avalon, there had been a few Lords, a few kinless, twice that many lookers, and a dozen tellers lured by the Folded Hands gathering. The *Angie Queen* was more crowded on this trip south; she rode low and sluggish, heavy with cargo and passengers and barrels of fresh water. Regapisk hadn't seen any Lords, and the only kinless seemed to be lookers' servants. Several families with children had boarded at Condigeo.

Lookers and kinless looked once into the oar pit, mesmerized, maybe horrified. Thereafter their eyes slid over or past the chained men at their oars. Lookers and kinless didn't like slavery. Lords and soldiers observed the oar pit as if they bought and sold oarsmen. Oarsmen hated Lords. Children and tellers looked down in frank curiosity. . . .

"Tellers," Regapisk said.

"Bet. Next bread," Fethiwong said. "Soldiers."

"That one's a teller. That one's his bodyguard, with scars and no shirt. Next bread?"

"Hah! You knew their faces, you son of a thousand rats!"

Regapisk laughed, because Fethiwong was right. He called, "Tras Preetror!" and braced for the whip.

The Oarmaster had already given up trying to tell Regapisk whatever it was he had done wrong. He just laid on the lash and let it go at that. It was how he had taught Regapisk to row. Regapisk took the line of fire across his back, wriggled a bit, and then grinned up at Tras Preetror and Arshur the northman.

They grinned back, both of them, and walked away.

"They'll want to talk to me," Regapisk said. "Next bread, Fethiwong."

"Hah. When?"

"While we're still southbound." He was guessing that the *Angie Queen* would go south as far as the tip of the Forefinger, and maybe a lot farther. Weeks, maybe moons.

"Done. Next bread."

Next bread was all you ever had to bet with. You couldn't bet your cloak, after all. Who needed two cloaks or could keep track of them? And how would you sleep without one? But anyone could eat a little more bread or survive a hungry morning.

CHAPTER THREE

ABOARD THE *ANGIE QUEEN*

DAY 6: SUMMONED

Rumor said that there was no fresh water along the barren shore of the Forefinger, and no wind. You rowed all the way. Gods help the oarsmen if a greedy captain stowed extra cargo instead of extra drinking water.

The sails stayed rigged and ready, just in case. Today there had been a long afternoon breeze. Oarsmen could doze. When daylight went and the breezes died, sails came down and oarsmen slept. Regapisk had never slept better before boarding the *Angie Queen.*

But he woke, on his sixth night since Condigeo, when a lash fell across his shoulders. Not a whipstroke, he realized after that first spasm and gasp, but just the lash sliding along skin.

Still dark. It felt as if he'd just fallen asleep.

"You're wanted," the Oarmaster said. "Make one wrong move, and we'll be one oar short."

Naw, Regapisk thought as he watched the Oarmaster open his chains. *You'd row in my place if you lost me this way. What kind of bribe did they offer?* Uncharacteristically, he didn't say any of that. Up close, dark against starlight, the Oarmaster was scary. His shoulders and arms were huge and ridged with scars. He must have been an oarsman himself.

Regapisk stood, his legs badly cramped, and moved as he was directed.

Up a ladder to the Oarmaster's perch. Up another ladder to the deck, then into one of the better rooms. The Oarmaster left him there, but Arshur the northman loomed.

The huge old man said nothing. Despite a twisted body and lavish scars, dark mottled scalp, and sparse white hair, the barbarian was still a tower of muscle, an accident waiting to happen. Very clearly he was Tras Preetror's bodyguard, if Regapisk proved untrustworthy.

Tras Preetror remained seated. "Next bread you're a Lord," he said.

"I want half your bet," Regapisk said. "Have you worked the oars, or do you just listen good?"

"Both," the teller said. "I have to listen or the tales don't come to me. Tell me a story. I saw you talking to the oar behind you, and he's Lordkin."

"That's Fethiwong of Dirty Birds. He robbed a clothing shop and had some *won*derful luck. He got most of the gowns for Lady Tzarbon's wedding. Worth a fortune, they were, and he gave a few away to friendly women. All he had to do was not tell stories in dockside. She's married a captain from Condigeo, you know?"

Tras Preetror chuckled. He patted air: "Sit. Tell me stories."

Regapisk sat. He nibbled pastry filled with meat paste, as if he weren't prepared to devour it in a mouthful. Manners. "I know some of *your* story," he said. "Where you were when the Toronexti were burned out at the Deerpiss Meadow. How Whandall Feathersnake put you both in a tree so you'd live through it. You must have missed some of the battle, but I've heard the rest."

"What I didn't see, I got from witnesses." Tras Preetror dismissed the matter, a tale told too often. "The little girl, Burning Tower, who burned the manuscript of the laws? I saw her in Condigeo."

"She was on this ship twenty days ago, with my cousin, Lord Sandry."

"Curse, I'm sorry I missed her! But what I want to know about is the birds. Have they got as far as the Burning City?"

Birds?

A little desperately, Regapisk said, "Big killer birds? I only heard about the birds in Condigeo port. I do know tales a teller wouldn't hear unless he talks to Lords' children. And you can tell me about birds. It's your turn." Tellers traded tales; everyone knew that.

Tras waved, expansive generosity. "You first. What was it like to be a Lord's boy?"

So Regapisk told him about Lord Sandry and the mirror.

Mirrors were expensive. Outside Tep's Town, they might be magical. Regapisk had been twelve, Sandry had been ten, when Regapisk talked Sandry into trying to enter the mirror world. "I told him I'd already been inside," Regapisk said.

At a walk, Sandry only bumped his nose. At a run, he knocked over Lord Fesk's mirror and cracked it. He was caught trying to repair it with chicken fat.

And Regapisk got the blame. He'd never understood that.

"Maybe you had a reputation by then," Tras suggested.

"Nah."

Tras Preetror told how he'd learned to bet with next bread, in a galleon's oar pit, after he tried to talk his way into Lordshills with the aid of a Serpent's Walk boy. "That was Whandall Placehold. A lot of these scars are from when he caught me later."

"Caught you doing what?"

"Well . . . yes." Tras laughed. "Invading his privacy, he said."

The child Regapisk had hidden on balconies and spied on Lords and their ladies, and learned nothing Lord Regapisk thought interesting. But Tras probed for details: how they dressed, what they ate, how they talked, schooling and schoolmasters, and what children did when they weren't around. . . .

"Now, the birds," Regapisk said. "It really is your turn."

"Lots of them off to the east," Arshur said. "Not so

many up north. In the high north country, we had three in cages until it got too expensive to feed them meat, then we ate the birds. Taste like chicken, but the meat's red like bison."

"You never told me any of this," Tras protested.

"You never asked."

They talked to each other that way, Tras and Arshur. Regapisk wondered why. But Tras was asking the questions now, so Regapisk need only listen.

"Did the birds up north attack wagon trains? People?"

"Not more than once," Arshur said. "They were just birds. Took more than one man to kill one, unless it was me. I figured out a way to kill one by myself. Most times you got six or eight guys to surround one with spears and lassoes."

"One," Tras said. "The stories we're hearing are about a dozen and more birds attacking people and wagon trains and towns. They've closed down the Golden Road."

"Never heard of them doing anything like that," Arshur said.

They got Arshur to tell a story of theft and battle in the far north. *Lordkin in a land of ice and peaks,* Regapisk thought, and was captivated.

Then the Oarmaster was there, wanting his oarsman. Regapisk went without complaint.

"Keep your bread," he told Fethiwong loftily. "I ate better than that." Maybe the sails would go up and he could sleep away the morning. He'd been taken away in the middle of a tale. Maybe he'd be summoned back.

Chapter Four

Aboard the *Angie Queen*

DAY 7: SOUTHBOUND ALONG THE FOREFINGER

Tras summoned him again the next evening.

Regapisk had heard Lordkin's tales of thefts and turf wars. He tried to tell of Whandall and the Suitors, but Tras had heard it from Whandall himself, and told it better too.

Regapisk told a tale he'd heard in Serpent's Walk, of the brothers who could read. Tras knew where one of the brothers had wound up—bookkeeper for the tax collectors.

Tras spoke, like Fethiwong, of huge birds running through Condigeo, leaving a trail of destruction. Tras had followed the monstrous flock until four were killed and the rest escaped into the countryside. Had they reached Tep's Town? Not that Regapisk knew; but he remembered the caravan girl, Burning Tower, who danced in a costume made from a terror bird's feathers. Arshur told how he had fought the terror bird single-handedly, strangled it with his bare hands. Watch for the wing daggers; keep pulling the bird off balance so it can't claw you with a foot. . . .

Regapisk was yawning before the Oarmaster came for him.

DAY 8: SOUTHBOUND, WITH THE WIND

He'd been summoned three nights running. Regapisk was getting enough to eat, but not enough sleep.

He knew sailors' stories, but so did Tras. But Regapisk knew stories the mers told. There was a mer who tried to claim his landborn daughter when she'd reached a proper age. The man realized in the nick of time that she was drowning. The magic goes away. . . .

Tras had been in the heart of at least one Burning, and maybe started it. Of course he hadn't participated. No looker dared be caught gathering property that Lordkin rightly considered their own.

"They never stopped *me* from gathering," Arshur said. Both men laughed, and neither answered.

When Regapisk ran out of stories, he talked about himself.

Tras asked about kitchens and cookery. The kitchen in Lord Fesk's house was huge, and Fro Hassic, the cook, was excessively territorial. Regapisk told them about the Great Race, when he and several other boys ran a route through the old house. When they charged through the kitchen, Fro Hassic tried to chase six of them at once. She caught Orsith, Lord Minder's son. Regapisk waved a shaker to get her attention, then began to scatter black pepper around. Hassic dropped Orsith. Regapisk charged for the dining room, still on the path—

"Idiot," Tras laughed.

"But she had Orsith!"

"But you hadn't done any damage yet!"

"That never stopped Hassic," Regapisk said.

"Would the cook whip a child?"

"No. She'd just tell Lady Fesk."

"You didn't have to stop Hassic. If Hassic has something to tell Lady Fesk, *then* you get whipped. Like if you wasted black pepper and ruined their dinner! Did you get whipped?"

"We both did. But that was just Hassic. She didn't catch us, but she knew who we were."

Regapisk normally liked telling stories about himself. The trouble was, too often Tras would notice something Regapisk hadn't. He'd see why it was all Regapisk's fault. Regapisk grew tired of Tras knowing more about himself than he did.

One night he said so.

Chapter Five

On the Golden Road: the Undead

Sandry kept his chariot just ahead of the lead wagon. Chalker pretended to watch diligently, but his eyes closed from time to time. Sandry said nothing. He'd chosen Chalker for convenience, and now he'd have to watch for both of them. It was worth it.

Besides, the road was well marked, and despite the cautions of the villagers and farmers, they had seen no dangers since the attack of the birds not far outside Condigeo. Now there were no more farms, just thickets and wildlands.

The next morning Sandry kept his forces together at the wagon train, sending one chariot out ahead to scout. He rode alone in another, shuttling back and forth between the scouts and the wagon train itself, while Chalker kept another chariot ready but with no load. If there were trouble, Sandry could rush back to the wagon train to fresh horses already hitched and ready.

The road led steeply down. There was a thicket ahead. This looked like good land gone wild, once cultivated but now covered with bushy scrub and vines and brambles. Idly he wondered why no one claimed it to build a farm village here. There was certainly enough water to keep all the vines green. He reached the bottom of the valley and crossed a small stream no more than a foot deep.

On the other side of the stream, a small road led off to the right. Signs in some unknown language pointed south down the fork. Sandry found Maydreo and Whane staring at the signs.

"What's this?" Sandry demanded. "Why stop here?"

"Well, it's a road fork," Whane said. "You said to wait at crossroads."

"Crossroad?" Sandry pointed off to the right. "Doesn't look like much traffic went that way. It's clear that this is the main road."

"Yes, sir, but look." Maydreo pointed to one of the signs. It depicted a wagon train in a circle, pots of stew in the center, crudely drawn wagoneers wearing crudely drawn smiles.

"So?"

Maydreo asked, "Aren't you hungry?"

Suddenly, he was. Good food, hot food. The letters on one of the signs seemed to swim and change, and now said "EVERYONE WELCOME!" Another sign changed from unreadable words to a picture of a rapidly flowing stream, clean fresh water flowing through a field of grain and fodder.

But I just crossed that stream, Sandry thought. *And it won't flow over there where those signs are pointing; that fork goes uphill. There's no water over there!*

"Reminds me of those berries," Whane said.

Maydreo was getting angry. "Fallen Wolf tells us about hospitality towns along the Hemp Road. We haven't seen any here. Think this is one? Did we bring enough rations to make it all the way without buying some decent meals once in a while?"

"No idea," Sandry said. "It might be a hospitality town; it might not be. Wait here. Can you do that? Wait—don't explore—just wait."

"Sure," Maydreo said.

Sandry wheeled the chariot and drove back to the wagon train. "Wise One," he called, "if you would come with me . . . and Bentino, you drive my chariot. Take Chalker and follow."

"What's the matter?" Burning Tower called from the lead wagon. "I'll get Spike and come with you."

"Might be a good idea. And Spotted Lizard, if you'll come also . . ."

The chariots weren't designed for three, and Clever Squirrel had trouble keeping her footing as the small car lurched over the rutted road. Spotted Lizard clung to the chariot sides, his face twisted in fear each time they hit a bump.

Sandry explained what he had seen. "Whane said it reminded him of bloodberries," Sandry said. "But Maydreo was wondering if this leads to a hospitality village. Spotted Lizard, you know of one here?"

"No. This is an unfriendly stretch," the boy said. "They tried to set up toll gates here, and the Condigeo marines came and burned out the whole town. My father told me—it was maybe five years ago. That's why there aren't any farms here."

"So what will this be?" Sandry asked.

"I think I know," Clever Squirrel said. "But let me see first."

Maydreo and Whane were arguing as Sandry drove up.

"He said to wait," Whane was saying.

"Sure, but we could go have a look . . . oh. Sir. You're back."

"And just in time," Clever Squirrel said. She examined the signs carefully. "Well, it's certainly true that everyone is welcome," she said. She grinned. "A feast, and everyone is invited."

"So!" Maydreo said. "A feast! I am tired of the rations we brought, I'd love a proper stew."

"Not from inside, you wouldn't," Clever Squirrel said. She gestured, and the letters on the sign swam again, to form new words that Sandry still couldn't read.

"All right, fine, but what does it say?" Sandry asked.

"Everyone welcome to Vic's Vampire Feast."

Spotted Lizard turned pale.

Sandry and the Younglords looked at each other. "What does that mean?" Sandry asked.

"Ah. No undead in Tep's Town? Not so far, anyway."

"Undead?" Sandry demanded.

"I'll explain later. It's enough to say that your scouts did well not to go have a look." She looked up at the sun just past overhead. "I don't know what you'll find up there in the daytime," she said. "But I know what you'll find at night." She got off the chariot. "And I'm staying here until everyone is past, well past. Just in case. Now, you scouts, go on ahead, keep looking, and if you see anything else like this, come straight back to me."

"What about the birds?" Maydreo said.

"I would be very surprised to find any terror birds on this part of the trail," Squirrel said. "Or any other big, meaty creature. Now move along, Younglords. I'll explain tonight."

Sandry left Chalker and a chariot to wait for Clever Squirrel and rode ahead. He shook his head slowly. *Too much* to learn, he thought. *But Green Stone and Tower don't seem to know any more than I do about this . . .*

Chapter Six

Aboard the *Angie Queen*

DAY 26: THE NAIL IN SIGHT

Regapisk had been eighteen days at his bench. He was well caught up on sleep. Tras hadn't sent for him—or else the Oarmaster refused. They'd been rowing steadily for the full eighteen days.

But tomorrow some of them would rest. Some would row the little boats. Springs of fresh water were to be found at the southern tip of the Forefinger, the Nail. If he could get some sleep in the afternoon, the Oarmaster might let him see the teller.

He raised the subject when the Oarmaster came for him.

Laughter. "Naw, what gave you that idea? That teller,

tonight he wants you. He tips good. He can have you whenever he says. This last week or two, he didn't. Did you say something he didn't like, Lord Reg?"

"I was polite."

"Uh-huh."

"We were trying to get Halfania drunk," said Regapisk. "I think she was keeping up with us, but you know, she works in a saloon, she's used to being around wine. That idiot Sej started chasing her around the dining table and while I was trying to talk sense into him, she just ran. So we were alone in the saloon. So I decided to tend bar—"

Tras laughed.

Arshur said, "I've done that. Got my arm broke for it, and my tailbone when they threw me out. That hurts. Takes forever before you can sit again."

"I was just trying to help out. I tried to collect for the drinks, but nobody took me seriously. When the wine tender came back . . . yeah, he broke some heads."

"Collect in advance, if that ever happens again," said Tras. "And keep a big friend with you."

"Yeah. Your turn."

Tras told of a teller who didn't know when to shut up, and another who wanted money not to tell a secret, both fools who came to bad ends. Regapisk told of the Year of Two Burnings and Aunt Shanda's dragon bone jar. Tras didn't know about that. He spent half the evening asking for details.

Regapisk found himself remembering things he'd tried to forget, events he'd never linked as cause and effect, telling far more than he had ever wanted known. "The problem is, Tras, I never got any responsibility. I don't *think* like a Lord. People I work with like me, but they don't work *for* me. I thought working with Lordkin would be perfect, but I couldn't get them to *do* anything."

"Nobody else can either."

"Sandry can."

"Tell me about Sandry."

"He's younger than me, but they put him in charge of the Fire Brigade."

"Why did they do that?"

"He's First Lady Shanda's nephew, that's why."

Tras sucked his teeth. "That the only reason?"

"Well, he was lucky. He's always been lucky. Like when we raced through the kitchen that time, Sandry hung back until Hassic was chasing the rest of us and just walked through. He won the race, and he never ran!"

"And said something nice to Hassic on the way," Tras said.

"Yeah. Okay, I see that. So it wasn't just luck."

"Your friend Sandry is in charge of the Lordsmen with that wagon train," Tras said. "You may see him in Crescent City. That's the Inland Sea harbor we're going to."

"Sandry? And he was in Condigeo when the *Angie Queen* was there?"

"Sure, he owns part of this ship's cargo. Or the Lords do. Qu'yuma—do you know him?"

"He's Lady Shanda's husband."

"You said she's First Lady," Tras said. "But Qu'yuma is only an envoy. He's not First Lord or whatever you call him."

"Lord Chief Witness," Regapisk said. "Qu'yuma is Lord Chief Witness Quintana's nephew. He doesn't have any living children. His wife is dead, so Qu'yuma is his heir, and that makes Lady Shanda Lord Quintana's official hostess."

Tras laughed. "And that's simple to you, is it? And Sandry is her nephew?"

"Sure, that's why they keep promoting him." Regapisk paused, and said reluctantly, "I guess he's done all the jobs they give him. But he's lucky!"

"Luck helps," Tras said. "Sometimes a lot. Sometimes it's hard to tell the difference between luck and magic."

"Magic? Luck is magic? Magic doesn't work, not usually."

Tras nodded. "Where you grew up, there was a fire god sucking up all the manna. Of course magic didn't work very well."

"We tried bringing in manna! Lady Shanda bought dragon bones, and we ended up with two Burnings in one year." Regapisk gave a sudden smile. "We were never very lucky with magic."

"Good phrase."

Regapisk grinned wider.

When Regapisk recognized the Oarmaster's footsteps approaching, he said, "Tras, I want to persuade you to buy me loose."

"I don't have any reason to do that," Tras Preetror said.

"I know, Tras. I'll try to give you one," Regapisk said. Then the Oarmaster was at the door.

Chapter Seven

On the Golden Road: Deadlands

They saw the dark hills from a long way off. First Mouse Warrior called from his perch atop the lead wagon. At the next rise, they all saw them: barren, drifting sands, blowing spiral towers of dust. They lost sight of the deadlands after they crossed the ridge and went down into a valley, but when they climbed the ridge on the other side, they were closer. Brown sand, blowing in complex patterns. Hills of sand that shifted even as they watched.

There were no farmlands here, just low scrub. The plants faded out as they approached the sands.

Clever Squirrel shivered.

"Cold?" Sandry asked. It was a very warm day.

"Not the way you'd be cold," Squirrel said. "This is a desert."

"Well, yes," Burning Tower said, looking at the blowing sand.

"Not just dry," Squirrel said. "I can't feel Coyote. I can't feel anything—it's like being blind. There's no manna. Something terrible happened here."

"When?" Sandry asked. "Ambush?"

"More like a war of gods, long ago," Squirrel said, "and all the manna eaten, all the gods gone myth. I'll ask Coyote when I can. But I'm no help to you as long as we're in this place."

The road stretched on. They could see green on the other side of the deadlands, and everyone hurried. Even the bison seemed eager to get past that dead place.

The next day, a calf was born. Bison calves born on the trail were a burden, and most were not permitted to live, but this one was a spotted bull, and Green Stone shouted his thanks to the heavens.

"It's good luck, a sign of fortune," Burning Tower told Sandry. "Look at the herd; we don't have a spotted bull. In two years, we will have."

Sandry nodded as if he understood, but Tower thought he was pretending. In an hour, the calf was on his feet, and he trotted along after his mother. The wagon train moved eastward.

CHAPTER EIGHT

ABOARD THE *ANGIE QUEEN*

DAY 27: TAKING ON DRINKING WATER

With all her oarsmen rowing for all they were worth, the *Angie Queen* made anchor before noon. The oarsmen rested and joked and slept while boats put ashore with empty water barrels. Some passengers went ashore to find their land legs and visit the springs and the little village that had grown up there.

The Oarmaster came at sunset for Regapisk.

Tras had set out dinner in the cabin. The old teller looked feeble tonight, and he didn't get up. He asked Regapisk, "Are you willing to talk to passengers? Tomorrow night?"

"Sure!" Regapisk said.

"I buy my passage aboard ships like this," Tras said, "and I tell stories and pass the hat. This time was a mistake, maybe. The trip's too long. Passengers don't want to run out of money, and all my stories start to sound alike after a while. We're at anchor now, and they're ready for something different. Even if it's one of the oarsmen."

"I'd love to talk to the passengers," Regapisk said. It wasn't just a break in the routine—it was a chance to catch the attention of someone who might buy him free.

"You'll have to stop stalling," Tras Preetror said bluntly.

"Stalling?"

"It's been driving me crazy. I know how to draw out a story," Tras said. "I also know not to do it too much. I don't stall. I can lose an audience that way."

"I haven't been stalling. I've been building suspense," Regapisk protested.

"You can see the marks want to hear an ending, right? Finish the story. Tell them where it all went. And that means you've got their attention, right? So they'll keep listening as long as you don't finish. But a good teller always has another story behind that one, so he doesn't need to stall, and if someone else wants to talk, that's *good.* Nobody will listen to you twice if you hog the podium. I'm a teller, Regapisk. Only a teller would put up with your stalling, and it's only because you actually know things. You buying this?"

"I'm listening."

"Good. Do more of that. Now, tell me the tale of Sandry and the mirror. I want to see what you leave out."

DAY 28: AT ANCHOR, THE NAIL

There was fresh gopher meat at dinner in the main salon. Regapisk was summoned afterward, but Arshur had saved him a bit.

Tras introduced him. He told the tale of the mer's daughter, then Sandry and the mirror. Then he and Tras talked while the passengers listened. Tras asked questions that led Regapisk into stories he'd already told, and back into Regapisk's past. Regapisk told of fighting the brush fire, the tale of how he'd ended up an oarsman. Tras broke in from time to time. He knew a little more about fighting fire in other cities, and details of Lords' jurisprudence. The way it came out, Regapisk had let the fire spread. Regapisk held his temper. This was a new sensation for Regapisk: the audience was listening.

Chapter Nine

Aboard the *Angie Queen*

DAY 41:
NORTHBOUND, SHORE IN SIGHT TO BOTH SIDES; CALM WATER, NO WIND

"There was a ship that went down just outside the harbor, and its cargo was all barrels of wine. You listening, Ghost? The mers all got roaring drunk. They danced on the beach and played pushing games on the sea. Pushing games, that's two mermen trying to push each other off balance. The girls don't do that. Come dawn—"

Maybe the Ghost was listening; his mad eyes never left Regapisk's. Fethiwong certainly listened, and laughed or winced in the right places.

"Lord Reg." The voice behind him was the Oarmaster. Regapisk flinched, then turned.

The Oarmaster leaned on the rail of his lofty podium. "If I'd known you could tell such tales, I'd have put you on a closer bench."

Regapisk considered a biting answer, but he said, "I can speak up, Oarmaster."

"Much obliged. Meanwhile, the wind is dying. Oars up!"

Regapisk rowed and wondered why he hadn't been summoned.

It might be Tras had got everything he wanted. Not only had he heard every story Regapisk had been able to give him, he had entertained the ship's company too—and taken the fees.

Regapisk's dread was that he had run out of stories, or else that they sounded too much alike, or were too long, or too whiny. He had really hoped to find something Tras needed to know more about. Armor and arms, maybe, or the uses of Lord Samorty's map, or some way a teller could get into Lordshills without getting beaten half dead and sold for an oarsman. Something!

Regapisk was barely aware of rowing. His arms and shoulders and belly were like boulders now. If his legs matched, he'd have thought himself the equal of Arshur. Rowing was automatic. Just a glimpse of water through the oarlock was enough to warn him where to dip the oar to avoid waves and eddies.

Here was a new thought: money. Regapisk had never been trained to conserve money. What he needed, and much of what he took a whim for, had come from his family until recently. His elders moved wealth around in big masses, but he took no part in that. All children are poor. Now his inheritance was next bread and a cloak and a chance to wash out the wastes beneath his bench. Nothing to conserve or lose.

But a teller on a ship must arrive in port with something to buy his next meal and a room. Maybe not even a room, if he knew of someplace to bed down. He'd asked Tras to buy him free because Tras was richer than an oarsman. Maybe he wasn't rich enough?

In the last rays of sunset, the captain made anchor and the men shipped oars. Regapisk slipped easily into sleep, then jerked awake when the whip draped itself across his back. The Oarmaster liked doing that. It showed his skill.

"Teller wants you," he said. He followed close behind as Regapisk climbed the ladders, and he asked, "What happened to those mers?"

What? Oh. "Not much. They were the town's whole fishing industry. What could the mayor do? He got them to clean up some of the mess and the damage, but hey, most mers are like Lordkin. They turned it into games and then drifted back to the beach. Mers can't stick with anything." Regapisk suddenly wondered: *Is that why they like me? Because I think like them?* But there wasn't anyone to ask.

"I wanted to give you time to think up more stories, or remember them, or see new ways to tell them. I know *I* need that sometimes. And I was sick, Regapisk."

"Sick how?"

"My guts back up on me. I'm old." Tras said, "There's another thing. I'm out of money for bribes."

His heart sank. "So buying me free isn't an option?"

"Oh, we could talk about it."

"That could be depressing."

"I've got *some* money. I'd have my ship's fare back maybe five times over, except some of that went to the Oarmaster. But I don't have the price of an indentured man! So I need to know, have you hidden out anything?"

"What?"

"Did you hide any silver, gold, jewels?"

"How?"

"Well, I don't know, Lord Reg. Some people swallow gems or small coins, and get it back later—"

"That's disgusting."

"I've got some jewels sewn into this coat, if a thief lets me keep the coat. I know of a woman who bound up jewels in her hair, and another—anyway, what I'm getting at is this: if we pool our money, I could buy you loose. You'd be my servant for a while, but hey, you could learn to tell stories, and it beats rowing."

Regapisk's heart felt like lead. "And all it takes is anything I might have hid on my person?"

Tras shrugged.

It was a scam. Tras had taken his stories, and now he wanted . . . imaginary loot. Regapisk laughed. "A Lordsman hit me on the head, and when I woke up, I had just this loincloth, a cloak, and tomorrow morning's bread. And this ripped earlobe where I had an earring."

"Mph." Tras closed his eyes. His voice was weak, feeble. "There's another thing. Arshur."

Arshur didn't react. He was out of earshot, half asleep. Regapisk said, "Arshur?"

"Somebody needs to take care of Arshur. He's been hit on the head too often, or maybe he grew up that way, but he needs someone to bail him out every so often, or just tell him *no.* I'm a twisted old man, Lord Reg. I can free you both when we get to Crescent City. Will you stick with him?"

"Gods, Tras, I'll still be at the oars."

"I'll make an offer," Tras said. "If the Oarmaster says you're worthless, maybe the captain will sell you cheap. Will you take care of Arshur?"

"He won't say that. I'm better at rowing than at anything I ever tried, unless it's telling stories."

"You haven't answered me."

Regapisk looked at the barbarian giant. Was that the price of getting free of this ship? Certainly saying so was easy enough. "Yes, I'll take care of him."

"Good. I won't summon you again, Regapisk. I want to save the money. Tell me a story."

"Do you know about Lord Samorty's map? Hah! I thought not. It used to be magical. . . ."

CHAPTER TEN

ABOARD THE *ANGIE QUEEN*

DAY 50: SMOKE TO STARBOARD MIGHT BE A TOWN

It dawned on Regapisk that posing as a Lordkin chief was a bad idea. Wherever he went, he'd be thought a gatherer. He told Fethiwong the tale of Sandry and the mirror, loud enough that the Oarmaster could listen. Maybe he'd be believed, maybe not.

And he told of Tras the teller, proud of the truths he could ferret out the hidden places he'd penetrated, who overreached himself at the Lordshills gate. People need their secrets. A tale that comes as a lie is at least the property of the teller; the truth is not.

Lord Regapisk was a dead man; but Lord Reg the oarsman was learning. Tras had taught him to listen. He'd taught himself to tell the stories he heard. Regapisk the storyteller lay still in the future. Some day he'd be loose from these chains.

DAY 61: RUMOR—CRESCENT TOWN IS NEAR; WIND BLOWS NORTH; SHORE TO THE EAST.

The Oarmaster unchained him at sunset. Regapisk went without asking questions.

As on previous evenings, Arshur let him in. Tras, seated at his desk, didn't even look up. The Oarmaster went away.

"I thought you weren't going to summon me again," Regapisk said to Tras Preetror.

"He's dead," Arshur said.

Somehow it wasn't a surprise. Maybe it was the way Tras sat, hunched over, all bones. Regapisk whispered, "He die that way?"

"Yeah, at his desk, making those chicken footprints and little cartoons that're supposed to tell him how to tell a story."

Regapisk stepped around to look. Tras Preetror's writing was readable, but it didn't say enough about anything. It was just notes, not stories, and the pictograms weren't in any style Regapisk knew.

"You haven't told anyone? The Captain?"

"Way I see it," Arshur said, "I don't want to turn over

what he's got. The captain or the mate, they'd just take it and say it's for his heirs. Even if he's got heirs, I don't know who they are or how to get to them. There's not enough to be worth a search."

Regapisk found a dark amusement in the situation. "You can't dump him overboard. If they don't see him when the *Angie Queen* docks, they'll want to know you didn't hit him on the head."

Arshur mulled that. He said, "Let's jump ship. Can you swim?"

"Sure. You too?" It was an unusual skill.

"Yeah."

"Be better if we could steal a boat."

"Too noisy. Here, get into these." Clothing. Tras Preetror's would have been too small by half. Old Arshur's were loose around the belly but fit him otherwise. These weren't a Lord's clothing, but they weren't cheap, and they had a style. Regapisk suddenly felt much better. He tied soft boots around his neck, knowing they'd be too big.

"What else? We can't carry too much," he said.

"He hasn't got much. Here, take this stuff." Gold coins. A jeweled box. Regapisk didn't see what Arshur had packed in a rolled blanket. Something lighter and more valuable, like . . . "Jewels," Regapisk remembered aloud. "Sewn in his shirt."

"I took them. Go!"

Arshur dove in silently. Regapisk lost his balance and raised a mighty splash.

The water was startlingly warm. They might drown,

but they wouldn't freeze first. They trod water beneath the swell of the hull until they were sure nobody had heard. Then—the land west was a waterless wilderness. They struck east.

He'd worried that gold coins would weigh him down, but the water was buoyant. It tasted brackish, salty. The shore was a long way off, a shadow along the horizon. They aimed for the nearest point of land. It didn't come closer for a long time. Regapisk was worn out, and Arshur barely had breath to mock him, before they heard the splash of waves.

But Arshur wasn't making for shore. And the water that had seemed startlingly warm was getting colder.

Regapisk didn't have breath to shout. He followed. The chill had his teeth chattering . . . but a pale hairball was afloat in the nightbound ocean. A minute of staring allowed Regapisk to make out a man's white hair and beard and a big crooked nose peeping through.

Arshur called cheerily, "Out for a swim?"

"Quiet," the man croaked.

Arshur's voice went soft. "Why?"

"You can stand here," the man said in passable Condigeano.

Regapisk's toes found bottom. Now his head and shoulders were out of the water. All his tired muscles cried in relief. Arshur asked again, "Who's listening?"

"That's my farm," the man said, waving toward shore. "And those are bandits. We'll have to wait for them to go away."

"How many?" Arshur asked.

"There were four. One gave up already. They think

I've got money, so the rest are still searching. I don't know why that rumor doesn't die. If I had money, I'd buy talismans and get myself young again!"

"We'll take care of it," Arshur said.

"Hold up a minute."

Arshur started walking toward shore and was afloat again.

"Curse. That other one went for help," the old man called. "Can't you see them? That makes six. You better wait with me."

"I'm tired of waiting. I'm cold," Arshur said.

"They went for friends who can swim," the old man said. "Boys, I'm glad you showed up."

Arshur was halfway to shore. He shouted, "Come on, Lord Reg. I hope you can fight!"

"Sure," said Regapisk. He noted that the old man hadn't come with them. He noted that the two men wading toward him had swords, and he and Arshur didn't. But the rest were hanging back. These must be the ones who could swim.

The waves were a handsbreadth tall. The water was armpit deep. The bandits hesitated; but Arshur didn't, and the bandits weren't inclined to back away. Regapisk tried to stay just behind and left of Arshur, as he'd been trained. He'd wrapped a shirt around his left fist. His right gripped Tras's tiny eating knife. Maybe he could grab a blade and get in a punch.

Arshur laughed.

One of the bandits stumbled behind a wave. There was a gentle sound like a ship knocking against a dock. Then Arshur had a sword and was splashing toward the remaining swimmer. The bandit lunged away from him, whining, found shallower ground, and turned to fight, waving his sword like a child. Arshur killed him, dipped below the water, came up with the man's sword, and tossed it to Regapisk.

Regapisk remembered his training . . . and what he remembered was being knocked down, disarmed, bruised, beaten. Years of that. The Lords trained all their boys to fight, but Regapisk hadn't been very good at it. He was good at jeering. He called, "Gentlemen! The owner wants to know your business here!"

The bandits shouted obscenities Regapisk had never heard. Arshur seemed familiar with them: he laughed and bellowed back. The four were standing in an arc on the beach, holding Arshur at the focus. Then one cursed and ran at them, sword held high, like a total idiot.

That was the most awesome part of that whole night. Regapisk *knew* how good a swordsman he wasn't, but these fought like six-year-olds. The unfamiliar sword felt light as a feather in his hand. He cut at extremities, notching a wrist, above a kneecap, tip of a thumb, then running a man through when he bellowed and charged. The living man he'd left in the ocean crawled out and ran at his back. Regapisk whipped around in an elegant circle and beheaded him and was back in guard before the remaining two could move.

Arshur had killed one, but now he seemed to be just playing around.

The two men dropped to their knees and threw away their swords.

* * *

"My name is Zephans Mishagnos," the old man told them, "and I'm a wizard of sorts. This is not a good place to be a wizard, but not a good place to leave either."

They were in a pointy-topped one-room hut, crowded close around a fire in the center. Regapisk had stopped shivering. He said, "Even at night, this is odd for a farm. Where do you get fresh water?"

"You swam through it."

"That's salt."

"Yes. I'll show you tomorrow. You want to help me run this farm? It's coming on toward harvest, such as it is. We'll eat like kings, at least." He looked at them. "You're big men, but we'll have more than enough."

CHAPTER ELEVEN

THE SALT FARM

For the first few days, they'd had to make the old man repeat everything. He didn't speak much Condigeano. Now Regapisk was learning his language; Arshur already knew a little. It was Aztlani, Zeph said.

"I was already an old man when word of the Warlock's Wheel spread here from Asia. That makes me a hundred and sixty or seventy years old," Zeph told them. "There's no manna hereabouts. Not even in Crescent City, barring a market in shielded talismans. If I tried to walk out of here, I'd turn to dust."

Regapisk and Arshur continued picking squashes and fruit in the twilight. The watermelons were big. Lord Reg was surprised at how light they were. He asked, "Where's Crescent City?"

The parrot on the old man's shoulder screeched, "Where's Crescent City?"

Zeph jumped. Zeph's deafness seemed to come and go. The parrot helped. Zeph said, "Oh, northwest along the shore by ten leagues or so. That's by canoe. Further by road, you have to go north a ways to get past the delta. I got here forty years ago, running from Aztlani soldiers, in a wagon I stole from a farmer. Full of seeds, it was. I had this talisman too. They gave up on me when I got into the badlands. I never was good at taking a hint. I used up the manna in the talisman, and that left me as a farmer. Look . . ."

The irrigation trough ran downhill from a pond that fed the crops. Regapisk hadn't seen how Zeph kept the pond filled. The old man scooped water from the trough in cupped hands. He offered it to Regapisk.

Regapisk sipped. It was fresh. Regapisk dipped up more in his own hands, sipped and spat. "Salt," he said. "What's going on?"

"You tell me."

"You're turning brackish water to fresh. It's the only way you could farm this land. *How?*"

"There's currents of manna in the sea," said Zeph. "You can see 'em if you've got good eyes. The currents are piss-poor here, but there's enough to make fresh water and get it up here to the reservoir."

The old man gestured down at the shore. Waves humped a little higher. Waves ran uphill along the main irrigation channel and stopped halfway to the field.

"Curse," Zeph said without much emphasis. "Can you see the manna, how it streamed in and then out a little too quick for me?"

"No," said Arshur.

"Just sun-glitter," said Regapisk.

"Well, there's manna in sun-glitter," Zeph said, "but cast your eye north along the strand. See, where it's just a bit brighter?"

The water of the Inland Sea was mostly brown. A thread of brightness ran through it. "Yeah . . ."

"Now, south, there's a pool of it going into the waves, where it's no use to me. Farther out, the main rivulet—"

"Yeah."

"Right, then. Shall I summon it?"

"It's nowhere near the channel," Regapisk said.

Arshur bellowed, "Hah! You are the match of Tras himself!"

"No, really—"

"But you can fight. 'Lord Reg,' they said, but not like they meant it. I wasn't sure. But Tras could make a man believe anything!"

But Regapisk was sure he could see something. If he wasn't trying to look, they were there: bright lines in the water, dim patches here and there, and bright current lines. The water was mud colored everywhere, and it flashed with momentary sunlit reflections, but in places there was a pervasive tinge. . . . "Down the middle, there's nothing," he said.

"Down the middle, there's nothing!" the bird shouted.

"Yes, that is where the Rainbow River runs in. The Rainbow carries some manna, but not much, and it gets used up at Crescent City. People pray in temples and courtrooms and do business in tearooms—you know how it is. Everybody's a little bit magician. They use up the manna. See where the current is moving past the channel now? See if you can bring it up."

"What do I do, wave at it?"

"Like this. Can you feel what I'm doing?"

"Nothing. Wait, it's getting brighter."

"Getting brighter!"

"Not your arms. Your whole body . . . mph. Just 'cause you can see it doesn't mean you've got the talent."

But the water was pulsing up the channel in little waves, flowing into the pond that fed cabbages, yams, squashes, and a maize patch. Zeph was tangled in the lines of brightness, though he was here and they were way out there. . . .

They didn't eat like kings. Meat was short. When stoop labor got to be too much, Arshur and Regapisk went hunting for prairie dogs and turkeys and such.

Kings would have better manners than Arshur, Regapisk thought. The old swordsman watched Regapisk using silverware improvised from two sticks, and laughed. "Lord Reg!"

"You should be learning this. Weren't you bragging that you were going to be a king?"

"I am. That old sorceress said so, and the young Feathersnake shaman, she said so too!"

"Kings don't eat with their fingers."

Arshur shrugged, but he began to study the way Reg used his implements. The next day, he made his own.

Chapter Twelve

The Salt Sea

There was food and language instructions done with magic and a safe place to sleep, all three in the common room in an arc around the fire. They wore clothing they'd taken off bandits, the dead, and the two they'd set naked on the road to run for their lives.

The house was a cone with a northward-facing entrance. Zeph taught them to enter to the right, depart from the left. The parrot lived outside. Zeph's people did everything in fours, when they could. Indoors, the hogan itself was one of the four.

Life was good. From time to time, farm wagons came down the road. Regapisk learned to sell produce. What they grew was always bigger and looked better than what the farmers had in their wagons.

*   *   *

The old man had some stories to tell. “The Warlock’s Wheel was the great discovery of that age. Manna, the power that makes magic—it doesn’t grow back once it’s used up. The Wheel was a way to use it up fast, leave a sorcerer with no defenses. I can’t even draw a Wheel. The drawing would suck me dry and leave me dust.”

“You could leave here if you could buy a talisman.”

“Yes, a powerful one.”

“Where would you go?”

“Aztlan,” Zeph said promptly. “Manna flows there. It’s in the air, in the river, everywhere. I’d take these crops to Aztlan, and then I’d stay awhile. In Aztlan they pay through the nose for fresh produce. Nothing grows around there. There’s nothing but the talismans and the trade routes. Arshur, how bad do you want to be a king?”

“Who do I have to kill?”

“Well, there’s that. You might have to fight.”

Arshur laughed.

“And nobody’s king in Aztlan very long. On the other hand, there’s more or less interesting places to be a king, and Aztlan is the most interesting of all. We can talk about it in the morning if you like.

“The berries will be ripe in a week. We’ll want to take what we’ve got to Crescent City to sell. You’ll see some Aztlani folk there.” Old Zeph looked hard at his laborers. “Be careful then, boys. They’re wizards, and they’re not always nice people.”

Chapter Thirteen

Lordsman Bane

After the deadlands, the road seemed endless. Hills and valleys, small streams, plenty of fodder in abandoned farmlands where patches of wheat and oats grew unattended. The hills were chaparral. There was plenty of forage along the road, a sign that few wagon trains had been here. Even with the new spotted calf slowing his mother, the wagon train made good time through the chaparral and low grass.

Bandits skulked in the dry brush, but none approached the well-armed wagon train. Every few days there was a terror bird or two. None attacked.

One bird followed at a distance. It never got close enough to kill, and when chariots were sent after it, the bird ran off into wild country where horses couldn't follow. This would be a rough place for an ambush, and Sandry got little sleep.

A month and more past the deadlands, the road climbed steeply. There was a small river far below as they made their way along a road that became little more than a ledge wide enough for two wagons. On their right, it sloped upward too steeply for wagons, although Sandry could just scramble up it on foot. To their left wasn't quite a cliff, but no bison-drawn wagon would ever get down it. The road led steeply upward.

For most of the route, the hillsides were too steep and rocky for horses or chariots off the road. Sandry sent Secklers and Trebaty up among the rocks to scout. "Below doesn't bother me," he told the two Lordkin, "but I worry about bandits up there, ready to roll boulders down on us. If anyone lives up there, they've seen us coming all morning."

"I never saw bandits here," Spotted Lizard said. "And this is a big wagon train, with all these soldiers."

"Never hurts to know what's ahead," Secklers said.

An odd thing for a Lordkin to say, Sandry thought. *But they aren't stupid.* "If you see anything, signal. Don't try to fight on your own. I need you tomorrow and the next day, not just this morning."

Secklers grinned. "Sure. I bought a ring for my woman—I don't need some bandit woman to get it. Let's go, Treb."

They were gone half an hour when the boy Nothing Was Seen—Lurk—came to Sandry. One of the Lordsmen troopers followed behind the boy, obviously not happy to be there. Sandry searched for the name. Bane, he called himself. An unusual name. Bane spoke in the dialect used by the Lords of Lordshills, without an accent. That was unusual too.

"We need to see you, Lord Sandry," Lurk said. "And Burning Tower as well."

"What's this?" Sandry asked, but he waved for Burning Tower to join them. They walked together, a few paces from the wagon train, where no one would overhear. "What?" Sandry demanded.

"I caught Lordsman Bane spying on Burning Tower," Lurk said. "Two nights ago."

"And you waited until now to tell us?" Sandry said. "In any case, it's a matter for Peacevoice Fullerman, not me."

"Maybe not," Lurk said. "Listen to his story first."

Sandry inspected Lordsman Bane. "How long have you been a Lordsman?"

"Four years, My Lord. Since I was twenty-three."

"Where are you from?"

"The records say from Houseman's Coast."

"You don't sound like it." Sandry noted the copper armbands Bane wore, two on his left arm, one on his right. "Good record, I see. One major and one minor decoration in only four years. All right, trooper, why were you spying on the lady? You weren't likely to see anything."

"Wasn't trying to—nothing like that, sir. Just wanted to see how she lives. How wagon people live."

"Hmmm. Thinking of joining a wagon train when your hitch is over?"

"Thought of it, sir, but I probably won't. I belong in Lord's Town. I grew up in Lordshills."

Sandry frowned. "You didn't get a name like that in Lordshills."

"No, sir. My given name was Firegift. I went to sea when I was sixteen. Sailed up and down the coast. Then I settled in Houseman's Town for a year, and decided to go home. When I came back to join the Lordsmen, I brought a new name with me."

"Does Peacevoice Fullerman know you grew up in Lordshills?"

"No, sir. Not officially, anyway."

"And the officer who let you join up?"

"Don't know what he knew, sir. He was your father, sir."

Sandry walked on in silence for a while. It would be easy enough to check the story with Chalker, but there wasn't any reason to doubt it. "So, Nothing Was Seen, why did you wait this long to tell us?"

"Wanted to wait until the Lordkin wouldn't hear," Lurk said.

"You're kinless, then, Bane?" But of course he had to be kinless, even if he didn't look it. That would be why the record showed him coming from outside Tep's Town. Kinless were never recruited directly into the Lordsmen ranks. The Lordkin wouldn't stand for it. Kinless were slaves, bound to Lords or Lordkin, depending on where they lived, defeated enemies who wore the noose to show their servile status. . . .

"My mother was kinless. My father was a Lordkin of Serpent's Walk. I was conceived during a Burning, My

Lord. That's why the name. There's lots of kinless in Tep's Town named Firegift. Mother was lucky. She found work in Lordshills, in Lord Jerreff's household. You might remember me. When you were about eight, you went on a picnic with Lord Jerreff's boy. I carried the baskets. You wanted to know how baskets were made, and I tried to tell you. I was named Firegift then."

"Maybe I do remember," Sandry said. Half kinless, half Lordkin, officially kinless—but a dangerous combination. There had been more than one attempted kinless revolt led by a kinless with a Lordkin father. Usually halvers lived in Tep's Town and were a problem only for the Lordkin. Male halvers who managed to be born in the Lords' territories were generally encouraged to go seek work in other cities. Not many came back.

"But it doesn't explain why you were spying on Burning Tower."

"And what does it matter if he was?" Tower demanded. "I don't mind if people watch me when I'm outside my nest. And he wasn't inside—I'd have known that!"

"He wasn't inside," Nothing Was Seen said.

"All right—he wasn't inside," Sandry said. "And the lady doesn't mind, so I see no reason to disturb Peacevoice Fullerman, but I still don't see why you're interested in Burning Tower, other than the obvious reason that she's the prettiest girl in the world."

"Why thank you," Tower said. They both laughed.

"I think you're my sister," Bane said.

"W-what?"

"My mother recognized your father last year when the wagon train came in. She made me take her down to

Peacegiven Square, and she knew him. Whandall. Told me she hadn't, that it wasn't him, and made me swear I'd never tell anyone, but I think she did, the way she acted. She died last winter. Never was very healthy. And maybe you're my sister, and maybe you aren't, but I wanted to see, that's all."

"So what do you want?" Sandry said.

"Sir? I don't want anything. I haven't asked for anything. I just wanted to know. I wouldn't have told Lurk, only he threatened to tell Peacevoice Fullerman I was spying, and I didn't want that. And I'm sorry I bothered you, and now I want to get back to my duties."

"You like being a Lordsman?"

"Sir. Yes, sir. My mother's kinfolk threw her out. My father's people don't admit I exist. I was a pretty good sailor, but I don't like the sea, and I never fit in at Houseman's. I fit in just fine at Lord's Town. Got a nice kinless wife, apprentice cook; we're looking to have kids."

And his children would be free to live in Lord's Town or leave Tep's Town altogether, as they chose. "Carry on, trooper," Sandry said. "I won't talk to Fullerman about this. You don't talk to the Lordkin."

"Sir. Yes, sir."

"Just a moment," Burning Tower said. "What was your mother's name?"

"She called herself Lottie in Lordshills, ma'am. I never knew her kinless name."

"Or any of her kin?"

"No, ma'am. Will that be all?"

"Yes. Thank you."

* * *

They walked along in silence for a while. Lurk discreetly vanished.

"Conceived during a Burning," Tower said. "His mother was raped, in other words. By my father!"

"If it was him," Sandry said. "It was the Lordkin way. Twenty-eight years ago, your father would have been what, fifteen? It was the Lordkin way."

"But Mother could still harness the one-horns when they were married," Tower said. "She's proud of that, and so is Father. And they met during a Burning."

"Your father isn't like most Lordkin," Sandry said. "From what I have seen, Whandall Feathersnake isn't like anyone but himself. I'm a little nervous about meeting him again, you know."

She giggled. "You! Scared of Father?" She lost the giggle and walked along in silence for a while. "Maybe he was different when he was fifteen."

"Well, he probably was," Sandry said, remembering. "Boys that age have some, uh, well . . . have trouble controlling themselves."

"Did you?"

"Did I what?"

"Well, I notice you can't get near the one-horn mares."

"Uh . . ."

"Who was she? Not all of them, just the first."

"You really want to know?"

"Yes."

They walked on for a few steps. "A kinless girl. One of the cook's daughters. We were both sixteen," Sandry said. "And I don't like to talk about it."

"What happened to her?"

"Zemmy? She's married to one of Rasatti's gardeners. Has two kids now, neither mine. She got a big wedding present from my mother."

"Does your mother know?"

"I don't think so. She gives wedding presents to all the servant children."

"I bet she knows. What would have happened if one of the children was yours?"

He made himself look at her.

"Come on, Sandry, it has to happen—a kinless girl gets pregnant by a Lord. What happens to her? And to the child?"

"I don't know."

"You must know."

"I must avoid knowing. You hear stories, *rapid* weddings between a groom and a household girl, and then there's an early baby. But I wouldn't really want to know, and neither would the father."

"So you'd let your son be property?"

"Kinless aren't property. At least not in Lordshills they aren't, except in theory or when we're talking to the Lordkin. And I never heard of a Lordshills girl being sent into Tep's Town to have a baby. Never. Why are you asking all this?"

"Well, we have to do something about Bane, or Firegift, whatever his name is."

"No, we don't! Everything is all right there," Sandry said. "He's satisfied."

"But if—if he's really my brother, we have to do something, because Feathersnake always makes things right," she said. "We have to. It's the way I was brought up."

"Tower, you can't know! His own mother said she didn't recognize Whandall. And that boy looks nothing like Whandall Feathersnake. Not the same features at all."

"That doesn't mean anything, and you know it. All the Lordkin look alike at least a little, and once you look at him that way, you can sure tell he's Lordkin even if he's not as big as most of them. I have to find out. Maybe Squirrel can find out."

"You're going to make trouble," Sandry warned.

"So you're telling me not to try?"

Sandry laughed. "I know better than that. But think: you sure don't want to get the Lordkin interested in this. They might not see him as any kind of Lordkin at all, just a kinless with weapons, and that really would burn the stew!"

"What would they do?"

"How would I know? I know Lordkin better than most of my relatives do, but that's not saying much. Maybe they'd challenge him. Then Fullerman and the other Lordsmen would stand up for their comrade, and they'd ask me to take sides too. Or Trebaty might go to Chief Wanshig, and Zoosh only knows what he'd do."

"But Wanshig's Whandall's brother!"

"And Bane's uncle, if he wants to be. Or an aggrieved Lordkin band chief, if he wants to be that," Sandry said. "All I know is that I sure don't want to be part of stirring up a mess between Lords and Lordkin over a half kinless who says he's satisfied with his life!"

"Oh. Well, I guess you're right."

"So you'll forget all this?"

"Yes," she said thoughtfully.

Sure you will, Sandry thought. *Sure.*

Secklers and Trebaty returned about two hours before sunset. "Nothing up in those hills at all, nothing we could see," Secklers said. "Except coyotes. Lots of those."

"At the pace you're making," Trebaty said, "you'll get to the top with just a little daylight left. There's a place to camp up there. No water, not much growth. Some dead wagons you can use for firewood."

"Dead wagons. How long dead?"

Trebaty shrugged. "Weeks. Weathered pretty bad, bones but nothing stinks. Weeks."

"Any sign of what did them in?"

"Sure—them birds did it. Big teeth marks on some of the wagon boards, and some of the bison bones are cracked wide open, bit clean through," Secklers said.

"And then something human come through," Trebaty said, " 'cause there's nothing worth gathering up there. But first they was done in by the birds. Then someone gathered what was left."

"But it's a good place to camp," Secklers said. "If you keep a good watch."

"We'll certainly do that," Sandry said. "Thanks."

CHAPTER FOURTEEN

THE HILLTOP

The place smelled dead. Most of the bodies were mere bones, and those scattered. You wouldn't have expected them to smell. There must have been pockets of still-rotting flesh wedged in among the rocks, in places inaccessible to the sarcophagus beetles and other scavengers of small dead things. The smell wasn't everywhere, and it wasn't so strong that Burning Tower couldn't get used to it, but it was an unpleasant reminder of their danger.

The trouble was, there was no other place to make camp for the night. The hilltop was reached by a road far too narrow for camping, and far too vulnerable to rocks rolled down from above. Beyond the hilltop, the road wound steeply down into another valley they had not scouted. It would be dark before they got down there.

Sandry and Green Stone conferred. "I don't like it," Sandry said.

"And you suggest . . . ?"

Sandry shook his head. "I don't see any other choice."

"That's probably what they thought too," Green Stone said. He waved expressively at the wreckage surrounding them. The boy Spotted Lizard was moving about, examining the wreckage with a look of dread. Nothing Was Seen followed him silently.

"Which way were they going?" Sandry asked.

Green Stone shook his head. "Can't tell. There's dung on the road in both directions. None fresher than this, though."

"So there's been no traffic along this road since this happened?" Sandry asked.

Burning Tower noted his frown. Sandry was worried.

Green Stone nodded. "I think they were the last to come here. Whichever way they were going, I'd guess they circled the wagons, but even that isn't certain, the way things have been thrown about." He stared for a while and shook his head again. "I'd guess they were hit by birds, a lot of them. Then a bandit gang; birds wouldn't care about cargo. After that, the coyotes and crows got their chances."

"Maybe Squirrel can tell what happened," Burning Tower said.

Sandry shrugged.

"It doesn't hurt to ask," Burning Tower said. Sandry had to believe in magic—he'd seen enough of it—but he never thought of using it. Burning Tower beckoned to

Clever Squirrel. "Can you tell which way the wagon train was going?" she asked. "Before it was attacked."

Squirrel said, "Coyote would know, but I can't seem to find Coyote. This place is pretty dead—I mean magically."

Sandry said, "So we're on our own."

Green Stone frowned. "At least there's plenty of firewood."

"Fires will blind your slingers," Sandry said.

"Sure, but what can we do?"

"Build fires outside the ring as well as inside. As you say, there's plenty of wood. For one night, anyway. I sure wouldn't want to stay here two."

Green Stone nodded agreement again. He caught Spotted Lizard's attention and beckoned him to come. "Was this your wagon train?" he asked gruffly.

"No, sir. That is, I don't know. It might have been. I don't see anything I recognize, but there's nothing to see!" The boy's voice rose there at the end.

"All right. Do you remember this place? Did you camp here before?"

"Yes, sir. There used to be a little spring just over there—not enough to water the stock after that long climb up, but enough for people and some stew. And there was, well, not a village, but a couple of hogans and two or three families—maybe ten people, mostly men—who lived up here in summer. They earned a living hauling water up from the stream down in the valley ahead."

"Hogans?" Sandry asked.

Burning Tower stifled a smile. There was a lot Sandry didn't know.

Spotted Lizard corrected him: "Hogans," using the male suffix. "Made of logs standing on end. Over by the spring, but that's all gone now. Don't know where the logs are. Burned, I guess. Who'd carry them off?"

"I don't know what a hogan is," Sandry said stiffly.

"A house," Green Stone said. "I've never seen one, and what Lizard described isn't what I was told about. But it's what the people east of here call a house. They say they're alive."

Spotted Lizard said, "A hogan talks to you."

Burning Tower could read nothing on Clever Squirrel's face. *I wonder if she already knew that.* "Do they leave ghosts?" Tower asked.

Spotted Lizard looked startled, almost offended. "No! You don't leave a hogan alive. You tear a wall open, let out the spirit. Hogans too," he added, using the female suffix. "There isn't much left of the two that were here."

"Show me," Green Stone said.

They followed the boy across the hilltop to a corner sheltered by boulders. "The spring came out between those rocks," he said. "The hogans were about here."

"No ghosts," Squirrel said. "I don't feel a thing. There is some running water down below here somewhere. You might get some if you dig in that sand pit there."

"Looks like a lot of work," Green Stone said.

Sandry climbed to the top of the boulders and looked over to the other side. "Safe enough here," he said. "Long climb up these rocks; nobody could do that without some noise. Probably why they put their houses here. Just in case, we'll put one team on watch here." He waved to Chalker.

"Sir."

"Ask Junior Warman Gundrin to join me here, please."

"Sir. Yes, sir."

Sandry grinned. Ever since they left Condigeo, Chalker had been trying to outdo the marines in military manners. So had Peacevoice Fullerman.

Junior Warman Gundrin was about twenty, the son of a Condigeo captain, a member of the Captains' Council. Clearly he was a Younglord under a different title, even if the captains didn't inherit their positions. More than a chief, not quite an officer. Sandry hadn't seen much of him on the journey. Gundrin stayed with the Younglords most of the time.

"Gundrin, we'll want guards in teams of four. Two of yours, two of mine. Two stay awake, two can rest, but I want two of them alert. If they have to stand watch with a spearpoint under their chins, I want two awake."

"Yes, sir."

"One team here," Sandry said. "With a fire, and two fresh torches ready to light. I don't think anyone can climb up those rocks without us hearing them, but you never know until it happens. This post is a reserve. If anything happens anywhere else, they're to light a torch and throw it over the boulder here, then look down the other side. If there's nobody coming and nothing down there, they can join the fight on the other side."

"Yes, sir."

"And keep that fire shielded. In this pit will do. Now let's go see where we'll put the other guards," Sandry said. "Green Stone will see to setting up the wagons and cook fires. When he's got the fireplaces laid, I want to set up some fire sites outside the perimeter. Let's go see where." He strode off, still barking instructions, as Gundrin scrambled to keep up with him.

Burning Tower sat up, startled by a dream that faded before she could remember it. Coyotes howled in the distance. There was a dull glow from one corner of the camp, but that was all. Sandry had insisted that fires be laid ready to light, but then all fires were put out.

She got up silently and stood to stretch. They hadn't built a proper travel nest. Instead the nesting boxes were used to fill in gaps between wagons and boulder. Sideboards had been lashed to the wagon wheels to fill in the gaps under the wagons. All the animals were in a rope corral inside the circle, which was more like a rectangle because of the boulders and cliff side that formed one base of the camp. They hadn't put up any roofing, so Tower's nest (such as it was) was open to the night sky. The stars were bright, and the River was a gleaming silver stream across the sky. The Hunter blazed in his glory.

Was that the Hunter? She could never be sure which star patterns were which. If you stared at any of them long enough, you could see any picture you wanted to. Stories about heroes and gods in the starry sky were just stories. She went to the nest entrance. That faced inward, of course. She went around the corner toward the outside wall.

"Is all well, My Lady?"

A Lordsman in full kit, sword at his belt and two spears and a shield grounded next to him, was standing at the corner of her nest. There was an opening no more than two fingers wide to the outside, and after turning toward her for a second, he went back to looking out. She thought she recognized the voice and its accent. "Bane?"

"Yes, My Lady. I'm not spying. This is where the Peacevoice stationed me tonight. I'm on watch for another hour."

She giggled. "I'm not a lady," she said. "Or at least I'm not 'My Lady'!"

"Yes, ma'am," Bane said stiffly.

"And don't get huffy with me. Are you really my big brother?"

She couldn't see his face in the starlight, and he was turned away from her anyway. There was no expression in his voice as he said, "I might be. I hope not."

"Why? Would I be so bad as a sister?"

"Ma'am, if you marry Lord Sandry, you will be. What do I do then? What would my wife do? We'll have to leave Tep's Town, go somewhere else. So, no, My Lady, you're not my sister, and you never will be. And I'm on watch."

"Marry Lord Sandry," she said. "You think I will?"

"Ma'am, every one of us thinks so!"

She smiled to herself. "I'm going for a walk."

"Not outside, you're not!" Bane said.

"No, of course not. I'll stay inside."

"Yes, ma'am, but you be careful. Some of the troopers are pretty nervous; one of them might brain you before he figured out who you were. And I can't come with you. The Peacevoice would have my hide for leaving my post. Ma'am, I can't tell you what to do, but I'd sure be grateful if you'd go back in your nest and stay there."

She sighed and went back into her nest. There was a small opening in the wall that faced outside the wagon circle. She removed the cover and stared out. There was nothing to see, just stars and a few clouds scudding across the sky. She stared out for a long time, then lay down again.

"Fear and foes! Alarm!"

Bane, she thought. She looked out but couldn't see anything.

"Alarm at Post Four!"

The camp was stirring. She heard scuffling on the roof of her wagon. Bandits? But Mouse Warrior slept up there; it had to be him. Didn't it?

She briskly combed her fingers through her hair; she reached for moccasins—

"Hey, Harpy!"

That would be Green Stone alerting his wagoneers. She had slept in her leggings and jerkin in case of alarm, so she was dressed as soon as she put on her moccasins. Outside her nest was a confusion of activity, but everyone seemed to know what to do. Green Stone's slingers were climbing atop the wagons. Peacevoice Fullerman and his men were in full armor, already forming up near her nest entrance.

"Lordsman Bane! Report!" Fullerman was shouting.

"Sighted four men outside the perimeter, sir!"

"Mouse Warrior, what do you see?" Fullerman shouted.

"Maybe something was out there," Mouse Warrior said.

So. That was him on top of her wagon.

Sandry ran up, Chalker just behind him. "Fullerman?"

"Intruders sighted outside the perimeter," Fullerman said. "No other information, sir."

"Right. Mouse Warrior, do you see anything?"

"No."

"Shaman? Anything?" One of the Condigeo marines.

"No gods, no magic," Clever Squirrel replied from behind her.

Secklers and Trebaty came up yawning. Secklers was carrying a bright torch. Sandry winced, but didn't say anything. "We'll have a look," Secklers said.

Sandry doesn't like that, Burning Tower thought. *But he can't tell them what to do.*

"Open a passage for them," Sandry said. "Fullerman, four men with spears at that gate before it opens. Secklers, don't go far. This could be an ambush; it could be a way to get us to open a gate so they can rush us."

"And it could be a bad dream," Secklers said. "Anybody seen anything?"

"I did. Four men," Bane said.

"I mean other than you," Secklers said.

"You men, back to your posts!" Fullerman was shouting. "Don't all come look over here! Warman Gundrin, I'd be obliged if you'd check that hogan area for us."

"Right." Gundrin ran across the compound to the far wall, where there was a glow from the fire. A moment later he was on top of the boulder wall with a torch, which he threw over.

"Clear below," he shouted.

"All right," Sandry said. "Secklers, you want to have a look outside?"

"Yes, Lord. Treb?"

"Yep. Let's do it."

They carried their torches to the gate, waited until four Lordsmen faced the entrance with shields and spears, then stamped impatiently until the wagoneers opened a gap. It was dark inside the perimeter without their torches.

"Praster, go relieve Bane," Fullerman said. "Bane, tell us again what you saw."

"Four men, Peacevoice. Sneaking. Some kind of head-dress, feathers anyway, on two of them. I just saw them for a second—it's dark out there—but they were on the skyline with the Star River behind them. I could see their outlines."

"Weapons?"

"Couldn't say, Peacevoice."

"Hello inside!"

"Secklers!" Sandry shouted.

"We found something. Nobody out here now, but there was somebody here, all right."

"What?"

"Bringing it in now. It's a funny thing, glows—"

"Glows?" Clever Squirrel shouted. "Leave it alone! Stand away from it. How big is it?"

"About the size of a crow," Secklers shouted.

"Stay away from it! Sandry, if can you bring some men? Lurk, you too, come with me. Tower, get the cook pot."

"Cook pot?"

"The small iron one. Bring it along. And everyone, keep a good watch. This isn't over."

Tower ran over to the kitchen area. The big stewpot

was filled with leftovers of last night's stew. The smaller one was empty, still dirty because there wasn't enough water to clean it properly. She emptied it onto the ground and ran to join the others.

"All right. Fullerman, four troopers ahead, four behind. Full kits, all," Sandry was saying. "We ready? Open the gate. Everyone keep a sharp watch."

They could see the torch a few yards away. Secklers and Trebaty were standing well back from something that glowed.

It looked like a stone bird, smaller than a crow or a chicken. A softly glowing stone terror bird.

Squirrel took the iron pot from Tower. "Lord Sandry, may I borrow your sword? Thank you." She used the sword blade to push the object into the pot. "Did you bring the lid? No? Too bad. All right, everyone back inside and keep watch." Squirrel lifted the pot and held it high above her head, the open top to the sky. "Inside, inside—quick, quick," she was saying. "Tower, run and get the iron lid to the pot. Run, girl."

Tower sprinted in to find the lid. When she got back to the gate everyone was already inside except Squirrel.

"When I lower this, you put the lid on," Squirrel said. "Don't look inside."

"All right." As Squirrel brought the pot down to just above eye level, Tower clapped the lid on. "Done."

"Good."

Tower used a scrap of rope to tie the lid down. Then they brought it in.

"But what is it?" Sandry demanded.

"I don't know," Squirrel admitted. "But if it glows, it's

magic, and if it looks like one of those birds, it's not *our* magic. Maybe it summons birds. Maybe it lets the god see through the eyes of anyone who looks at it. Maybe anyone who has already looked at it, but I hope not. Do you feel anything? Any of you?"

Tower thought about it. She had looked at the bird, but only for a moment. "I don't feel different," she said.

Secklers laughed. "Me either, but you're giving me the shivers."

Squirrel nodded. "I think that's safe now, but I don't know." She looked thoughtful. "Something else not good. We're fighting something more than birds, more than birds and a god. Bane, you said you saw headdresses?"

"Feathers, ma'am. Like crowns of feathers, but I just got a glimpse—didn't really see anything."

Squirrel nodded thoughtfully. "Spotted Lizard, you ever hear of anything like that?"

The boy shook his head.

Squirrel sighed. "I don't think we'll get much sleep tonight."

Chapter Fifteen

The Last Ridge

No one wanted to sleep. As soon as there was enough light, they broke camp and loaded the wagons. Lordsmen and marines stood ready and never complained about sleeping in their armor.

The road led steeply down into a green valley. Spotted Lizard studied the way ahead, and said, "I think this is the last valley. That's Sundusk Ridge ahead. When we get to the top of that, we'll see Crescent City and the Singwah Sea. I think so, anyway."

"What's in this valley?" Sandry asked.

"A village. Fresh water," Spotted Lizard said. "Stream crossing's got a toll gate, but they don't charge much and the water's good, and they have hot soup. It's a day's trip up to the next place to cross; better to pay and cross here."

Green Stone nodded sourly. There were a lot of places like that. "Nibbled to death," he said. "Pay and pay and pay and pretty soon, there's no profits."

"I'll be glad to pay for some good soup," Burning Tower said.

Sandry grinned at her and got a smile in return. "Ours has gotten a little thin lately," he said. "Let's do it."

The road was narrow and twisty. When they rounded a bend, Spotted Lizard stared ahead, then frowned. "I thought this was the last valley," he said. "But you should be able to see the village from here. And smoke from cookfires—we should be seeing that."

Sandry ordered, "Maydreo, ride ahead but be careful. First sign of trouble, you turn around and come back at full gallop."

"Yes, sir. Whane, want to come with me?"

"Sure." Whane clambered into Maydreo's chariot. They waved and went ahead at a trot.

An hour later they were back. "There's no cookfires because there's no village," Maydreo said.

Spotted Lizard frowned deeply "I sure remember—"

"You remember right," Whane said. "There was a village, but it's gone. Nobody there, house walls knocked down. It's gone."

There had been ten houses in the village. There were remains, foundations, crumpled logs. Part of a log corral. The road ran through the center of what had been the village, and across the stream. A human skull grinned at them from the streambed. There were bones farther downstream.

Burning Tower took Sandry's hand and stood close to him. "What happened here?"

Sandry shook his head. "I think they ran. Or some of them did."

"Houses," Spotted Lizard said. "They knew they'd have to run, so they knocked out a wall on each hogan. To kill the house before an enemy could use it. They had time for that."

Sandry felt Burning Tower's shudder. "Let's move," he said.

"Please," Tower said. "This is an awful place." She went back to her wagon.

Sandry and his troops stood watch as the wagons crossed the stream. The water came up to a standing man's knees here where the stream broadened. Farther down it narrowed again, and was deeper. As the wagons crossed, Maydreo and Chalker poked among the ruins of one of the houses. Maydreo came out with a bone, a human shinbone with bite marks.

"Terror birds," Chalker said. "I've seen bones gnawed by coyotes. These are different. That murderin' beak."

Sandry nodded. "When we get across, fill the water bottles," he said. He looked ahead. The road ran straight up and over the next ridge. He thought he saw a wisp of smoke far ahead in that direction. The last ridge, Spotted Lizard had said. "I hope so," Sandry said aloud. Chalker looked at him, puzzled, but he didn't ask.

When the last wagon was across and the water bottles were filled, Sandry urged his horses into a trot. The road here was easily wide enough to let him pass by and get ahead of the wagon train.

The last ridge lay ahead.

They'd crossed the valley by two hours past noon. Sandry waited until the lead elements of the wagon train were approaching the hilltop, then rode ahead to see what was beyond. He topped the ridge.

Ahead was a broad basin, mostly water. A river snaked across the basin to split into scores of mouths emptying into a sea. *Not quite a sea,* Sandry thought. He could see across to the other side, except to the southeast where the water went on to the horizon. Below, in a crescent shape along the edge of the closest branch of the river delta, was a city, the river, and then the sea along its east side. Sandry counted more than a hundred houses, some large and some small, but all curiously alike, conical, their doors facing in any of four directions depending on what part of the city they were in. Smoke rose from openings in many of the roofs. A few buildings near the water were different, squares and rectangles alongside the docks. These were larger than the other buildings.

It was a city under siege.

A wall ran around the landward edge of the city. For forty paces around an ornate gate, the wall looked like something Lordsmen might build. To left and right, it was no more than a mound with stakes on the top. Men might have done that with their hands.

A broad road ran from the gate and crossed another broad road in the center of the city. There stood a large round building, taller than any of the others. Next to it, what looked like a staircase rose in a spiral, twenty paces or more, up to nothing at all at its top.

Outside the wall were the remains of houses. They'd been cones, like the ones inside, but each of them had at least one side ripped open. In every case, it looked as if a crew of men in a hurry had torn part of the wall out and left the logs and rubble where they fell.

Bright flashes of green and yellow moved among the ruined walls.

"Terror birds," he said.

"Aye, My Lord," Chalker said. "I've counted more than fifty and I haven't gotten started good. Count on near two hundred of them down there."

Sandry nodded. The birds were running in and among the ruined buildings, along the crudely built wall that held them out of the city, wandering in flocks of twenty or more.

Maydreo brought his chariot alongside Sandry's. "Tep's pizzle! That's a lot of birds!"

"Astute of you to notice, Younglord Maydreo," Sandry said.

"What do they eat?" Whane asked, as much to himself as anyone else. "What keeps them there? There can't be enough around here to feed that many."

"Reckon they get fed," Chalker said. He pointed.

Four birds were coming from the north down the stream. Two of them carried deer carcasses drooping from their huge beaks. The other two carried something large and unrecognizable between them.

"Never saw any bird do that!" Maydreo said.

"Crows can cooperate," Whane said. "Sometimes. And birds feed their young—"

"They've seen us," Sandry said quietly. He pointed. Four of the birds had stopped their aimless roving and were staring in their direction. Two more were running toward them. "Maydreo, go alert Peacevoice Fullerman, and get all the chariots ready for battle. I don't think we have very long. I want all the wagons over the top of the hill. Make them come uphill to get us. Get moving, Younglord Maydreo, and maybe we'll live until dark . . ."

Chapter Sixteen

The Battle of Crescent City

"I think they're organizing," Clever Squirrel said. She stood next to Sandry's chariot and watched the birds below. Four of them had approached to within fifty yards of them, then dashed away again. Now the birds were milling about down in the valley.

"They know we're here," Sandry said. "How smart are they?"

Squirrel shook her head. "I can sense . . . well, *him.*"

Suddenly curious, Sandry asked, "Could the terror bird god be female?"

"A *hen*? A god making war usually goes with the top male—the rooster, the bull . . . In Rynildissen, the god of bees goes with the queen, they say."

"If they all come at once, we've had it," Sandry said. "We don't have enough troops to fight all of them at once. And if we circle the wagons, they can starve us to death right in sight of the city."

Squirrel nodded. "It looks like the city is safe enough if we can get into it," she said. "That's the gate there, and the people sure see us up here. Maybe if we run for it, they'll let us in."

"I wouldn't," Sandry said. "Open that gate without a proper shield wall, and you might as well not have a gate. And I don't see any shields down there at all. Spears, swords . . . "

"All bright and shiny too," Chalker said.

"Bronze," Sandry said.

"Expensive," Whane said.

Sandry nodded, thinking, *Now what? We need to get inside that city. To do that we have to make it safe for them to open the gates, safe enough that they know they're safe. Which means we have to kill a lot of birds.*

So how do we do that? Two hundred birds. He turned to Clever Squirrel. "Can you do anything with magic? What about that thing we found at the hilltop?"

"It's calling the birds," she said positively. "It would have called them down on us. I'm pretty sure that if you open that pot, they'll come to it."

"Fire," Sandry said. "Can you make fire? Quickly?"

"There has to be something to burn," Squirrel said. "Wizards can make fire out of nothing, but I never learned how, and besides, well—"

"Besides, there isn't enough manna," Sandry said. "I know." *Never enough troops. Never enough provisions. Right.*

"There's some," Squirrel said. "And I can draw on that love charm they gave Tower, if she'll let me."

"Enough to burn up those birds?" Sandry asked.

"No. But I can make fires if you have firewood."

"Sagebrush? Logs, what's left of those houses outside the wall?"

"Sure, I can make those burn."

"I'm getting an idea." Sandry looked up at the sun. "Four hours of light. It will take us an hour to get down there. That leaves three hours to kill all those birds."

"You are joking," Green Stone said.

"I hope not," Burning Tower said. "You don't make that kind of joke, do you, Sandry?" She looked at him with wonder in her eyes. Wonder and hope and faith.

"I'm not joking, I just don't know if I can do it. Green Stone, we need to talk. I hate complicated plans. I'm really going to hate this one, but I don't know anything else to do. First thing we have to see is what happens if we move closer to them. . . ."

They moved cautiously down the hill. Some of the birds stood watching the wagon train, but the others continued to move around outside the city wall.

"Control," Clever Squirrel said. "The god is waiting to see what you'll do. I can't read its mind, Sandry—I wish I could—but I think he's a little afraid of you."

"Of me?"

"Well, of us. He's got to know that we're the ones who've been killing birds from here to Tep's Town to Road's End. He won't know quite how we do that. Maybe we have big magic. Maybe we have a god on our side."

"Do we?"

She shook her head. "Coyote's nowhere. I felt him watching while we were on that hilltop, but he didn't tell me anything. I think he knows what's happening here, but if he wants to help us, he sure hasn't given me any sign. But the bird god might not know that."

"Would birds be afraid of Coyote?"

She shrugged. "These are *big* birds. Coyote's a long way off, and there's not much manna around here."

"So he can't control the birds very well?"

"Not one at a time. He could tell them all to charge, though. Send them into a frenzy. They'd follow the top rooster. Sandry, the easiest magic makes things do what they want to do already. These birds are hungry and they want to kill us and eat us, and eat the horses, and eat the bison, and eat anything they can tear apart."

"Does it take magic to *keep* them from attacking us?"

"The closest ones," Squirrel said. "They want to attack. Others want to go hunting. They're not doing that."

Sandry nodded. "Then this just might work. Here we go. Chalker, have the trumpeter sound engage."

"Yes, sir." Chalker signaled. Notes sang out in the warm afternoon.

Maydreo and the other chariots charged toward the birds. As they came closer, they wheeled. Spearmen threw, and the chariots raced away from the road, across the open fields.

"First test passed," Sandry said. "They're following."

Each chariot was followed by a group of birds. For the

moment, the way down to the abandoned hogans was clear. "Green Stone! Now!" Sandry shouted.

"Heeyah!" Green Stone urged the bison forward. At their fastest, they were slower than a man can run, far slower than the birds. Sandry rode ahead, ready to attack any birds that hadn't followed the charioteers. So far the way was clear.

As the wagons reached the gaps between the ruined hogans, the wagoneers urged their bison through, so that the wagons plugged the gaps. These hogans had been built in nearly converging parallel lines with a street between them. With the wagons filling the gaps between the abandoned houses, the street became an extended wagon camp, irregularly shaped but sturdy.

"This wouldn't work against an army," Sandry said. "But maybe with birds. And if we're fast enough before the horses tire."

"It'll work."

Chalker sounds confident, Sandry thought. *I wish I were that confident.* And Burning Tower was looking at him with no doubt in her eyes at all. He grinned at her and got a flashing smile in return. *She should be scared,* he thought. *We're all depending on her. But she thinks it will work, because I told her it would.*

His heart pounded. *And if I'm wrong? She'll be dead. We'll all be dead.*

Thin notes sounded from far away—Maydreo, signaling that all was well. But the horses would be tiring now.

"Ready!" Green Stone shouted.

Sandry nodded to Chalker. More trumpet notes

sounded, signals to the charioteers, and to Burning Tower.

Burning Tower sat astride Spike and whispered to the one-horn as the trumpet notes sang in the afternoon. "We can do it," she whispered. "We can." She clutched the cookpot against her chest.

The one-horn nickered and tried to turn around to lick her hand. The monster birds made him nervous, and that showed. Around her, the wagoneers worked frantically to fill in the gaps between the houses, unhitch the bison, and get them clear. And now it was too late—it had to work.

Of course it will work, she told herself. *Sandry knows what he's doing!* She looked around for him, but he was busy giving signals.

New trumpet notes from both sides. The charioteers were coming. Burning Tower touched Spike's ear. "It's time," she whispered. "Let's go!"

At a gallop. To the right, there was Maydreo, followed by the birds. The chariot horses were lathered, straining to stay ahead of the birds. Tower urged Spike ahead, toward the oncoming chariots; now, turn, run behind the chariots, between the chariots and the birds. She shouted, "Run, Spike," and looked back. Most were following her. Most but not all. Was it time?

She slacked the loop of rope that bound the iron pot. She lifted the lid for a long moment, then slapped it down again. She whiffed rotting meat: they'd never had the chance to clean the cookpot. Have to boil it out later.

But the nightmare birds were following her. She led the train of birds across, toward the other chariots, around, opened the pot, averting her eyes from the glow, slapped the lid down. Now for the next, riding at a gallop; no time to be afraid. "What am I doing?" she shouted, and laughed, then galloped toward another group of birds, the pot held ready. . . .

"She's doing it," Chalker said. His voice was unnaturally calm. "She's got every bird out there following her. Chariots are all clear."

Sandry nodded. His men were safe for the moment. Now for Tower. "Sound recall."

"Sir." Chalker signaled. More trumpet notes.

"What do you see?" Sandry shouted up to Mouse Warrior on the wagontop.

"Too much dust."

Dust and confusion. Maydreo trotted past Sandry's chariot, wheeled, and stood ready, letting the horses rest. On the other side of the corral they'd formed out of wagons and ruined hogans, the other charioteers would be doing the same thing, waiting, resting.

"Here she comes!" Mouse Warrior shouted.

"Ready all!" Sandry called. It was hard to keep his voice clear. *Tower! Be safe!* There was no point in screaming—screamed orders were never understood—but he wanted to scream just the same.

Hoofbeats. Now he could look up the line between the hogans. Dust, and out of the cloud of dust a white horse—not a horse but Spike, looking huge—with a tiny girl in brown on his back, her hair flying out behind her, her bare feet flashing in the afternoon light. And behind her, gaping beaks and bright feathers. Close. Too close!

But not too close. She galloped past Sandry, to the end of the corral, to the barricade they had built higher than a man, and Spike leaped, an arc against the sky. The birds came on, the lead one made its jump—

And jumped onto a spear point. Another bird tried to jump the fence, and the wagon train blacksmith smashed at its head with his big hammer. The bird fell back into the corral, and two more stumbled over it to crash into the fence.

The birds were in a frenzy trying to reach Burning Tower. Sandry shouted, "Tower, throw . . ."

Throw the cookpot at the birds! But they'd discussed that, and she remembered. She threw. The lid was still on, curse it! Then the pot bounced into the middle of the corral, and a bird snapped at it and the lid rolled free, and then the glowing stone inside.

And the birds became a seething, shrieking storm of feathers, claws, and beaks. They were ripping each other apart, all trying to reach the glowing stone statue of a bird. Sandry screamed, "Now! Squirrel, now!"

Fire blazed across the fence line, then everywhere in the corral. Wood chips, brush, logs from the ruined hogans, all burst into flame as Squirrel danced on top of the wagons. Green Stone's slingers shouted in triumph and hurled their stones into the mass of green and orange feathers.

Birds turned, frantic to get out of the corral, but across the end of the corral stood Fullerman and his shield wall, while Gundrin and the marines ran along the sides of the corral to thrust spears at any bird attempting to get out.

The first wave of birds struck the spears and shields.

One man was down, but Secklers rushed in to fill his place, the big Lordkin knife swinging murder.

Squirrel danced faster. Flames rose, until there were no more green and orange feathers, only smoking black ruin, and the screams of the birds faded. Mouse Warrior chanted in triumph.

And there was Tower, still mounted on Spike. He couldn't go to her. The one-horn pranced and reared and wouldn't let anyone near. But she was there, mounted, tears and laughter mixed. She waved to him.

He ran as close to her as the one-horn would let him. It looked at him, and its rage seemed to turn to something like fear. "Marry me!" he shouted.

Spike reared high, stood on two legs, and danced, fear and rage. "Down, Spike," she shouted. She was just able to look at Sandry. "Of course!"

And now everyone was rushing to them, Green Stone and the Younglords, everyone shouting in triumph. Green Stone came up to Sandry.

"You heard?" Sandry demanded.

"I have expected this for a year," Green Stone said. "So has she. I expected it first with dread, but for weeks I have hoped. Welcome, brother found."

Spike was rearing again, but Burning Tower was able to dismount. She led the one-horn stallion to a wagon and tied his bridle to it, then ran to Sandry. They looked at each other, held hands, and stood at arm's length for a moment—then she was in his arms. She looked up at her brother, saw his smile, and clung to Sandry.

Chalker came up with two goblets of wine. He handed one to her, one to Sandry.

Sandry's eyes met hers. He lifted the goblet. Burning Tower was confused for a moment, but Sandry was sure of himself. He sipped from his goblet, then held it out to her. She drank. Then she sipped from her own and held it to his lips. He smiled broadly.

Chalker was grinning like a Lordkin. "Congratulations, My Lord, My Lady. On a good day's work, and a long life together."

CHAPTER SEVENTEEN

FEAST AND FAMINE

The wagon train rolled along a wall that was no more than rocky earth pushed into place. "Primitive," Sandry said.

"They used magic first, and craftsmanship too." Squirrel waved at the gate. It was tall and ornate, made of vertical copper bars. It stood in a long ridge of granite, a civilized stretch of wall until it abruptly became little more than a ridge of earth and stone. "Maybe saved their talismans for something more urgent."

Tower tried to picture what could be more urgent than keeping terror birds out of a city.

Men, women, and children were crowded up against the bars, looking out through the gate. They spoke in whispers; they sounded like a wind full of ghosts. Now someone was shouting orders. Now the crowd edged away from four tall men in armor polished to a glitter. As Sandry and Green Stone and their entourage reached the gate, the gate swung wide.

Sandry had never seen a besieged city before. He waited for Green Stone to announce himself.

The wagonmaster shouted in Condigeano. "Are you hungry?"

A laugh, then a small, ragged chorus answered.

"There's fresh-killed bird meat up there!"

A jumble of voices rose. Only a few must have understood Condigeano, but they were translating for the rest, and the wind carried smoke and roasted meat.

What followed then resembled a stampede. Sandry held back his men, and Green Stone his wagons, as a horde of pale brown robes and a few armored, shouting soldiers streamed out and uphill.

What remained were a great many soldiers and a handful of what must be merchants and dignitaries, judging by their dress and elaborately coiffed hair. One, then the rest bowed low. A tall man straightened first. His robe was wonderfully ornate. A garden splashed across the front, worked in colored thread: yellow corn, red peppers, a rainbow of flowers, tall trees in black and green. He announced, in oddly flavored Condigeano, "Gentlemen and ladies, you have broken the siege. We thank you. Crescent City is yours. And I am Mayor Buzzard at Play."

"You do us much honor. I am Green Stone of the Feathersnake wagons. This is Lord Sandry, who leads our fighters." Green Stone wondered what would happen if he accepted the gift of the city; he decided against. "We come in trade."

"Good! Our water source comes from outside the gate but was never contaminated. You will camp along the West Bank, where the other caravans are. And when you can . . ." The Mayor hesitated, then: "We hope you'll tell us how to deal with the nightmare birds."

"They make a formidable enemy, Mayor. Today we had some luck. We hope to hear the tale of what happened here. First we should get the caravan settled, and then—I trust there will still be stewed bird meat. We came hungry."

The streets were filthy with trash and sewage. Feathersnake's wagons and Sandry's men hesitated. In that moment, the mayor sighed, then shouted, "Wait here."

"For what?" Green Stone asked.

"I'd hoped—never mind. Move off the avenue, I beg. Off to the side. Then wait. Gentlemen?" He spoke to the local merchants in alien speech.

Green Stone set to moving the wagons off the filthy street. There was room among the conical houses. Meanwhile Mayor Buzzard at Play and a score of dignitaries—and two lines of soldiers—marched down the avenue to the main square.

The Lordkin jogged to catch up. Spotted Lizard and Burning Tower hesitated, then joined them. The Lordkin grinned, welcoming; they bracketed the woman and child for safety.

Flower gardens partly converted to fruit trees and truck gardens surrounded a palace and a stairway. The palace was big, a cone of vertically mounted logs that glittered like a rainbow . . . petrified logs, tree trunks turned to stone and garnet and chinked with mud, leaving vertical chinks for windows. It seemed to Burning Tower that the palace had once floated—that the stairs ended where the triangular front entrance would have been. The mayor climbed the broad stairs alone, leaving his little cluster of officials and merchants below.

He stopped, puffing a bit, above a crippling drop. He looked about him.

Now he reached inside his wonderful robe and pulled out a crude metal pot, opened it and set it at his feet. In the garden embroidered across his chest, the trees and the corn whipped in an unseen breeze.

Turning his back on the gate, the Mayor began to dance above nothing, chanting in a language Tower didn't know. She caught phrases from Squirrel's secret languages, given in a twisted accent.

Secklers asked, "What's he doing?"

The merchants had been keeping their distance from the Lordkin, but one answered: "Stand clear. This is well past due."

Burning Tower saw motion down at the far end of the main avenue.

Garbage and sewage rose in a great stinking wave. It flowed toward the palace and stairs. Burning Tower coughed and then held her breath as it went past. Some of the mud spilled off into the gardens. Most of it kept moving, high and higher yet, up the street toward the gate and Feathersnake caravan. The Bison Tribe merchants and Sandry's men fell back among the houses as a tidal wave of garbage spilled through the gate and on into the countryside.

The dignitaries applauded. Burning Tower and the Lordkin joined in.

The mayor strode down the stairs. His dignity held for a moment; then he looked at two Lordkin, a child, and a woman, and laughed. He said, "I wanted witnesses! You sent them away!"

Secklers asked, "Mayor, why did you let it get so dirty here?"

The mayor wasn't angry, only curious. "You're a Tep's Town Lordkin? And you ask me that?"

"I'm Secklers, Lord. I follow Chief Wanshig of the Placehold. *He* wouldn't have let the streets around the Placehold reach this state."

Mayor Buzzard at Play spoke above the dignitaries' angry grumbling. "Well, Secklers, it's our usual practice to dump our trash outside our homes. Every few days we summon up scavengers to deal with it and then send them away again. Every thirty or forty days, I use the greater spell and send it all out to the farms. And that's the way it was until the birds came. The nightmare birds come wherever there's magic! Now what would you have done?"

Secklers grinned into the mayor's rage. "I'd ask someone smarter."

"We locked up all the talismans."

"Good."

"I was a caravan shaman for half my life before I became mayor. This city runs on the talisman trade. The birds cut me off from my living and the city from its life! Now I can make magic again, and the streets have got to be cleaned for your thank-the-gods caravan, but there's nobody to *see* but you and these few friends. My citizens have all gone away."

Burning Tower had learned a little from her brother. She said, "Follow them."

Lurk saw no reason to hide his origins from the churning citizenry of Crescent City. He was Nothing Was Seen, a bandit's child adopted by the Feathersnake wagons, come all this way to return the boy Spotted Lizard to his family. Green Stone had sent him to mingle and to see that the caravan's gifts weren't wasted. He was mildly appalled at what he saw.

Gaunt men, women, elders, and children climbed in pursuit of the delicious smells, up the hills and into the makeshift corral where the birds had died. Before they could recover their breath, they were tearing big black sheets of feathers and skin off the birds that were worst burned. They ate what they found underneath, charred or cooked or just warm. A few raked burning timbers to make fires, to further cook the meat they found. Coyotes watched from a distance; buzzards circled; none would challenge the crowd.

Later arrivals brought big pots riding on animals. Nobody made room for them, and there wasn't any water.

The scavengers wore knee-length robes of hide or wool; children ran naked. Lurk tried talking to some of them. The scavengers understood no language known to Lurk, though they were polite enough, and several men and women hugged or kissed him. Their robes were pale brown, sometimes ornamented with blue thread. A boy, better dressed, offered a thick cut of red terror bird meat, nearly cooked through. Lurk accepted with a smile and a bow.

"*Yes,* I'm a shaman, and a good one. And *yes,* I'm hungry," the boy's father told Lurk in passable Condigeano. His robe was better than those the rest wore, a faded elegance. "I haven't worked in a year. The shields hanged my apprentice because he hid a talisman from them. You don't look like a shaman—"

"I'm not."

"Warn your shaman. No magic unless you ask permission of the shields. Only . . . if the birds are gone, maybe that's over? It'd be nice to have clean streets," the man said hopefully.

The ones who understood Condigeano had other things in common. Their robes were cleaner and more brightly painted, scarlet and blue decorated with bright weaving. They were the higher ranks, the ones who had brought cook pots.

Things changed when the mayor and a score of dignitaries arrived. Glittering soldiers pushed scores of Crescent City folk aside, more or less gently, to make a place for pots. More were being carried up the hill. One big pot floated on the air, filled to the brim with water. The shaman who had been speaking to Lurk cheered.

Soldiers retrieved an intact bird from under half-stripped corpses. It was barely singed, dead of a single spear thrust. Some of the mayor's entourage gathered around it to examine their enemy, pulling its beak open, manipulating the wings, ultimately cutting it open to read the entrails.

The mayor was as elegantly dressed as Green Stone at his best. He instructed his soldiers in a booming voice and broad gestures while they continued doing what they were doing. They fired up the pots using half-charred beams that were already burning courtesy of Clever Squirrel's war. The soldiers emptied heavy pouches into the pots. They tore up carcasses and added them, more and more as more pots appeared.

The mayor used an ornately carved sword to cut a couple of birds apart. Some went to the pots, some to eager hands.

Then the mayor spoke and waved to families wearing coarse brown cloth. They nodded happily and left off eating. Men began collecting firewood while women and children, their first hunger satisfied, scattered into the fields. The fields were covered in crops grown wild, Lurk saw. Some vegetables could be salvaged. Corn, beans, tomatoes, and little bulbs Lurk didn't recognize were cut up and dumped into the pots. Soldiers were bringing more water. The mayor departed with a diminished escort.

"We were with Prairie Dog caravan," an aging woman told Lurk. "The birds attacked us. Our wagon was still hitched up, a little slow, and we beat them off while the bison dragged us as far as the wall. We climbed over. The bison were killed and the other wagons are still"—she pointed with her nose, a sweep around her—"here."

Lurk asked her, "You're not cut off from the sea, are you?"

"Almost. It's a cursed long trip to anywhere civilized, and the cost is enormous when there's a real ship, and there hasn't been one for moons. There are the little boats that run around in the Inland Sea. They don't go anywhere, but if it got any worse, I'd have tried that, farmland down the coast, anything. Now there's a real ship in port, the *Angie Queen*, she's called, but I don't have enough left to buy my way back to Condigeo." Her face brightened. "Will you have a place for us when you go back? We can work."

Lurk shook his head. "I don't know. You'll have to talk to the wagonmaster."

It was beginning to smell like a feast.

Now a procession began winding up from the city: Green Stone and his people mingling with . . . Lurk watched them come. They wore varied clothing, but rich cloth and fine colors. Most of these must be merchants who'd been trapped in Crescent City when the birds came. Some were local dignitaries, by their robes. They were in animated conversation with Green Stone and Clever Squirrel.

Sandry's men and Crescent City's glittering soldiers paralleled them in formation. Now that two hundred slaughtered birds were becoming soup and stew, the rest of the politicos were coming to take charge.

The caravan was settled. Green Stone was in a fine humor. He'd found caravans in place by the river, but they'd all been there for up to a year. They'd have nothing left to trade.

He looked about for the most efficient-looking cook pot brigade and tried their stew. It wasn't hot, yet it burned his mouth! And yet—he tried another bite—it was good. Very good. It just burned.

"I was shaman of the Road Runner caravan for twenty-eight years," Mayor Buzzard at Play told Burning Tower. "We cycled between Condigeo and Aztlan. When I got tired of the trail, Crescent City made me mayor."

"The chief at Road's End did that too," Burning Tower said. "Quit as shaman and made himself chief. Hahhh!"

She was breathing hard. The mayor asked, "Are you all right?"

"What did you put in the stew?"

"Bell peppers, potatoes . . . chilis. Just don't bite down on these." He showed her.

"Thank you, this news comes late. . . . And then the birds came?"

"I had a year of good times before that. It's magic that brings them, but why didn't they come before? Crescent City has traded in talismans and magic since gods walked among us."

Green Stone said, "That's what we came for."

"We do not permit strangers to trade in magical items," Mayor Buzzard at Play said. He sounded dangerous. "But without you, there would be no trade, and few of our animals are in condition to make the long journey to Condigeo."

"Some of us may still have talismans to trade," a lean merchant said cautiously, looking a bit like a predatory bird himself.

Tower said, "We wondered why you didn't use magic to finish the wall."

The mayor barked, "Hah! Magic pulls the birds! Spells aimed at the birds fade to nothing. Shaman—Clever Squirrel—haven't you tried magic on the terror birds?"

"We don't have the manna," Squirrel said.

"Lucky. We're used to magic. We were horrified when we saw nightmare birds gathering around wizards and hogans and any bespelled thing. They grew more powerful, on our magic! We locked all our talismans behind cold iron, and I had to hang two shamans who wouldn't give theirs up. We finished the wall with plows and our hands! That was before the birds grew so thick, else they would have killed us all. Our shamans dare not so much as heal the sick or bless a hogan. Some of us died of colds last year!

"Manna still leaks a little, not from talismans but from where they were once used. There will be more birds, I think. How can we fight them?"

Sandry said, "We can teach your soldiers, if we're here long enough. Mayor, we'll have to go back to Condigeo as soon as Green Stone is done trading."

"You can't stay to help us? We'll make it worth your time," the mayor said.

"The wagons have to go back," Sandry said, "and my men to guard them. Perhaps someone can stay to help you."

"We would be most grateful." The mayor gestured helplessly. "Our guards are mostly ceremonial or police. We've always defended ourselves with magic."

The hawk-faced merchant leaned over to speak to the mayor. Buzzard at Play nodded. "And more. The Emperor is impatient. We must send our tribute, and soon, but we dare not travel among those birds! I say earnestly, Green Stone and Lord Sandry, we need your help, and we will be generous if you provide it."

"So none of your men has ever killed a bird with spear and shield?" Sandry asked.

"No, and we don't have those chariots of yours, either. Our horses are mostly mares; we use them to breed mules."

"You have donkeys, then?"

"A few."

"Can mules draw chariots?"

"I never saw that done. Perhaps the Emperor has chariot warriors," the mayor said.

"That is twice you have mentioned an emperor," Burning Tower said.

"The Emperor in Aztlan. Very old, very wise. His dominions end east of here, but none trade on the Golden Road without his permission. We don't ever see him," the Mayor said. "No one goes to Aztlan without his invitation."

And that's fine with you, Sandry speculated. "But you don't have fighting chariots and horses?"

"No, we use donkeys to carry loads." He pointed, where what looked like a small gray horse with very long ears was weighted down with a large cook pot, and two more carried bundles of driftwood. "There are few left. We ate most of the animals during the siege. Now that the siege is lifted, more will come in from the South along the Golden Road, enough to pull wagons on the road to Aztlan."

"I thought no one goes to Aztlan."

The Mayor nodded. "True. The road goes there, but we never go farther than the trading posts. Those are big enough, one's nearly a city. Once in a while someone gets an invitation to the island, but I never have."

"Where do the birds come from?" Sandry asked.

"They've always lived here," the mayor said. "Never many. You had to be careful, of course . . . guard the children and old ones, carry a stick . . . When I was a boy, I was taught to go for the eyes. Then, suddenly, they were everywhere, drawn to magic and stronger than magic."

"A god," Clever Squirrel said.

"Our wizards thought so. *I* thought so," the mayor said. "But what was to be done? Who can fight a god? It was just an excuse to give up."

Clever Squirrel edged closer to the mayor. She held out a crude bird carved of semiprecious stone, orange and green, which no longer glowed. "Buzzard at Play, what do you think of this?"

The mayor took what she was holding. "Nightmare bird," he said promptly. "It's dead now, but it must have held power. It's stonewood, good quality, from the stone forests."

"Stone forests? Really? Where do we find those?"

While the mayor hesitated, one of the merchants answered. "Aztlan. The Island City of Aztlan. That is where they make such things."

Chapter Eighteen

Divination

Merchants had set up shops along the main road, all the way from the gate to the harbor. They arrayed their wares on blankets in front of conical tents. In one of the shops, Burning Tower bought a congealed droplet of melted sand.

You could see through it. It made things bigger. She'd heard of a lens of far-seeing, somewhere. She showed it to Squirrel and Green Stone. They took it to the Feasting Heights.

They called it that now, the Feasting Heights, the place where they'd killed the birds. It stank, and ants held territory there, but the Heights offered a wonderful view of the harbor.

Green Stone picked out the *Angie Queen,* a toy on the water. The lens made it larger.

Sandry found them there. Tower showed Sandry the lens. Sandry watched for a bit, then said, "That's Captain Saziff in the hammock."

They spent an hour watching the town, the harbor, the *Angie Queen*. Then the women went wandering while Stone and Sandry walked down to the harbor.

The mayor had pointed it out when they passed, a big square building built of stone. He called it a sweatbath house. Tower was intrigued. She and Squirrel went back to see.

The proprietor, Snail Rock, was most pleased to see them. "You're the wizards who trapped the nightmare birds!"

Snail Rock led them through a locker room with an attendant who handed them handfuls of dried moss . . . to wipe off sweat, Tower surmised, and dirt and dead skin. There were benches too, and two men asleep on them, naked.

The sweatbath house was already in use. Snail Rock took them in anyway, past half a dozen naked men. The women smiled at them in some embarrassment. The men grinned back and casually covered their private parts with dried moss.

"Your bodies accumulate poisons." Snail Rock lectured them all. "Every month or so, you should sweat them out. It leaves you feeling completely relaxed. You should nap afterward, or at least rest. Doesn't anyone practice sweatbathing along the Hemp Road?"

Tower hoped the tour went quickly. It was hot in there!

In truth, there wasn't much to see, and that was

obscured by thick steam. The bath was a single big square room with thick walls and roof. Three walls were solid granite, with benches around them. The fourth was of porous stone. Snail Rock explained that it was tuff, a form of lava. Behind the tuff was an oven. Light the oven, the tuff wall got hot, too hot to touch. A vat of water stood waist high, with several clay dippers. Use the water to wash and to cool off. Snail Rock explained that his clients threw water on the tuff to make it flash to steam, to sweat even more.

They came out dripping wet. "If you'd like to wait," Snail Rock said, "I can give you the bath for yourselves alone. Women only. Many barbarians flinch from our custom of mixing—"

"No, thank you," Burning Tower said, while Clever Squirrel was saying, "Yes, that would be delightful."

They came back an hour later. The attendant gave them cotton robes and presently took their clothes and shoes and a few items they'd bought in shops.

They sat on the stone bench, sweating. Burning Tower said, "This didn't sound like fun even when Snail Rock was raving. Are you chasing something magical?"

"Don't have to," Squirrel said. "Extreme states bring visions. This whole town is alive in manna, now that they've lifted the restrictions on open talismans. Any vision will be magical." She stretched out on the bench. "I'm going to sleep if I can. Care to try?"

"No, you go ahead. Squirrel?"

"Yes?"

Tower didn't answer.

"What's eating you?" Squirrel asked. "You have not been yourself since the battle."

Tower felt the heat seeping into her. It wasn't unpleasant—more like a new state of being. Eyes closed, she asked, "Does it show that much?"

"Not to everyone. To me, sure." Squirrel grinned. "I can see into the hearts of men and women—"

"No, you can't!"

"Well, no, but you'd be surprised at how many believe it. So what's your problem?"

"I don't know. It's just . . . there's nothing scarier than terror birds, but they were obeying me, going to their deaths. Me and Spike together. And you and Sandry and his men and Condigeo's and Bison's, all working like some huge machine. I rode the wind. With Spike to obey me! Squirrel, I never felt so alive!"

"Battles do that."

"Yes, Father always said so. But he was ashamed."

"Whandall Feathersnake was ashamed," Squirrel said. "He never enjoyed killing. But Coyote isn't ashamed."

"Coyote's *your* father, not mine. But I wasn't ashamed of anything. I was—it was wonderful, and it may be that I will never do that again." She paused. "You once told me it was overrated."

"I don't have to ask what you're talking about, do I? I said *I* thought it was overrated. But I haven't been in love, and I didn't mate for life. It will be different for you."

Tower didn't answer, and after a while she thought Squirrel had gone to sleep. But presently the shaman said, "Lick yourself."

Curious, Tower licked sweat off her shoulder. It tasted fresh. She said, "We must have sweated off a lot of salt."

"Yeah."

"How much is enough?"

"You heard Snail Rock. When you think you can't stand any more, throw water on the wall."

Heat accumulated near the roof. You could avoid it by lying down. Tower felt herself drifting off, then woke with a start. She was melting like wax!

Squirrel seemed deeply asleep.

Fine. Tower picked up a dipperful of water and threw it at the tuff wall. It hissed and was gone. She threw more water, and then she felt the wash of heat. She dipped cool water over her hair, and watched Squirrel.

Squirrel sat upright with a moan.

"Enough?"

"I dreamed," Squirrel said. "Yes, enough."

They lay on the benches in the locker room, worn out, as if they'd hiked all day. Squirrel talked in a monotone.

"I can do anything. Men and women serve me their whole lives. Every animal is my prey; nothing can escape my jaws and the daggers in my hands. But something comes down from the northwest. It falls on me, traps me, and I shrink.

"I shrink. Almost I disappear. Death would be better. The time to come would be no more disturbing than a wall across my sight, if it were only death. But I shrink to the size of a man's thumb, and I don't die. I live in endless impotent fury. My worshippers are the lowest of the low, and every one of them towers over me like a mountain, for ten thousand years and more.

"I see it coming. I have to stop it.

"I can feel the power as my beak crunches through a bison's thick bones . . . Tower, I know its *name.* The god's name is Left-Handed Hummingbird."

"You're kidding?"

"It might be an old joke. A terror bird is the opposite of a hummingbird, isn't it? Big instead of small, runs instead of flies, daggers instead of wings, tears animals to pieces for meat instead of sipping flower nectar. Left-Handed Hummingbird sees us coming."

"I didn't have any kind of dream," Tower said. "Could it be that you just went nuts from too much heat?"

"Oh . . . sure. There are other kinds of divination. Let's see what I can find."

They were directed to a shaman, a woman who reminded Tower of Twisted Cloud. Her name was Fur Slipper.

Clever Squirrel told the shaman as much as she thought she needed to know of the dream in the sweatbath. "Fur Slipper, what else might we use to see our fate?"

"Augury is my specialty," Fur Slipper said, "but I know some other work. Have you seen the Cliff Writings?"

The Rainbow River split into a thousand streams where it fanned out into the Salty Sea. A few of the streams had names. This stream, bigger than others, was named Messenger.

A tumble of dark rock spilled down to a narrow beach.

The slope ran to north and south as far as the eye could see. There were white scrawls on some of the granite blocks.

Three women and Lord Sandry stood on the beach. The women were looking up.

"I only say that you should have taken guards when you went bathing," Sandry said coldly. "And shopping, and sightseeing. You should be guarded at all times. Curse, woman, if you're shopping, it's clear you've got money! Bait for gatherers! And if you're bathing—"

Clever Squirrel seemed hypnotized, her mouth slightly open, her eyes fixed. Burning Tower turned to Fur Slipper and pointed, showing Sandry her back. "These are writings? I can't make them out."

"They're beautiful!" Clever Squirrel said. "All the mountain sheep running, spears flying . . ."

There were rows of vertical lines and dots. There were straight lines with hooks at both ends, lots of those, and vertical lines each with a small circle at the top. There was cross-hatching. There were sketches of sheep and deer. No dye had been used. Scrape away the weathered black surface, and the exposed rock was white, until it weathered and faded under a dark desert patina. You could tell a drawing's age at a glance.

"Where do you see spears?" Tower asked.

"Oh, here, let me," said Fur Slipper. She touched Burning Tower's eyelids, then Sandry's.

Now the drawings moved.

Sandry gaped. On a face of black rock, sketchy big-horned sheep ran from sketchy men. The men hurled a kind of hooked stick with a spear caught in the far end.

The spears flew fast, thudded deep into flesh. Rams fell, got up, ran again, the men threw again, round and round, while torrents of rain fell and slacked and fell.

Burning Tower was climbing.

"Watch it!" Fur Slipper called. "These rocks roll. You too, Lord Sandry—don't stand below."

"What are these?" Sandry climbed toward a faded row of hooked sticks several paces high. When he got close, they swung like whips, somehow hurling ghostly spears. "Wait, I think I see. With the stick in your hand, it's like your arm is longer. You throw harder. Tower, this is how they killed those birds we found at the last camping ground."

"Show you something," Fur Slipper said. "This boulder split under its own weight, and this side slid, and it split a drawing in half."

On the leftmost fragment, taller than a man, were cross-hatching and stick figures, and most of a set of concentric circles: a target? On the right and lower down—but that wasn't part of a target. It was horizontal flow lines, but they matched up. "It's a shooting star," Sandry said.

Fur Slipper said, "It's the Sunfall meteor. We see it in dreams, sometimes. It struck east of here, halfway and more to Aztlan. It left a place like a dish, flat, with a circular rim."

Chapter Nineteen

The *Angie Queen*

Captain Saziff was frantically busy when Green Stone arrived. There were boxes stacked on the dock, and more boxes being carried about by muscular wretches who must be oarsmen. Green Stone watched for a time. Captain Saziff looked to be dressed for a banquet, in gold earrings and a new yellow silk shirt, hair in a thousand braids.

The ship had been quite idle when they watched him from the Feasting Heights. Was Saziff putting on a show?

Sandry called from the dock. "Captain Saziff!"

A seaman Sandry remembered as Raililiee led them aft.

The harried captain left off his bellowing. "Excuse me, Lords," he said. "You'd be of the wagon folk? And"—a bit startled—"Lord . . . Sandry. Of the Burning City."

"Yes, Captain. My Aunt Shanda had a commission for you."

"Yes. Yes, of course. The money is with the city moneychanger, Lord Sandry, but that oarsman jumped ship with the teller's guardsman and left the teller's corpse behind. Excuse my distraction, Lords."

Sandry fumbled his way through that. "You don't have Regapisk?"

"No. Lord Reg is gone. As for the money that was to be his, it's—"

"With the moneychanger. Good." Not quite yet, he suspected. If Sandry hadn't showed up, Regapisk's funds would have stayed with Captain Saziff. "Was Regapisk involved in murder, then?"

"I would hate to think so. The teller, Tras Preetror—he seems to have just died. At his desk. We buried him at sea. I can get you his last words."

Green Stone spoke up. "*I* should have that, I think. My father knew Tras Preetror. He'll want to know."

"Yes. Tras was in the habit of summoning Regapisk to hear his stories. He and his servant Arshur seem to have taken everything of Tras's that they could swim with."

"Curse." Sandry noticed Green Stone's bewilderment. "Aunt Shanda had intended to pay Regapisk a certain sum every moon as long as he picked it up *here.* She hoped that that would keep him from coming home. But he wasn't to know any of that until he arrived in Crescent City. Until then, he was an oarsman. Did he drown, do you think, Captain?"

"I would think that if a man jumps ship, it must be that he can swim."

Sandry thought back to Regapisk and the harbor. "He can swim. He talks to mers."

"Can he now? Had I known that, I might have employed him differently." Saziff shrugged. "It was a calm night; it is unlikely he drowned. Might have starved afterward, though. I'm sorry, Lord. If you tried to teach him a lesson, he learned the wrong one."

"He has that habit. What of Tras Preetror's last words?"

"Raililiee, it's on my desk, if you please."

Raililiee went.

Green Stone said, "The *Angie Queen* was to carry certain goods for the Captains of Condigeo and Feathersnake caravan."

"Yes." The captain waved portside. "Do you see them two piles of goods on the dock? I was to separate them; you are to choose the pile you like."

The piles were unequal. Blocks of furniture in one; clothing in the other; bags of beans here, shoes there; other inequalities . . . Green Stone said, "It would help if I had an inventory of what's in which pile."

"We haven't done that. Wagonmaster, wouldn't you prefer to take inventory yourself?"

"I'll see to that. It'll take up more dock space. We'll have to pull the piles apart to see what's in the middle."

Raililiee was back with two sheets of bark.

Sandry said, "I can read." He took the parchments. "'How the Bonehead Got His Horn.' Preetror was telling a story. It's all compressed style. Doesn't make much sense—wait a minute . . . yes. Coyote stole a sea animal's horn—narwhale, I think—and had to hide it quick when narwhale turned man and came running after him. He gave it to a deer—I'd have said *horse*, but he's underlined *deer*—and said that it would help him run. So they've each got one horn."

Green Stone laughed. "Raililiee? These were the teller's last words?"

"These were on his desk, under his hand, and a dried-up quill in it."

Sandry read the other sheet. "'Mirandee and the Tax Collector.' You're too young, Green Stone." Sandry grinned. " 'The Emperor's Hearts.'"

"All stories?"

"Yes, but . . . 'In city Aztlan, wall of thousand hearts. Brick, stucco, jars. In jars, hearts. Emperor, heart. King for a year, heart. Felons and enemies, hearts.' He's being too concise, but—Aztlan?"

Captain Saziff spoke with apparent reluctance. "Aztlan holds rights to all the magical sources east of here. Sunfall Crater. The wood of stone. They claim title to whatever smells of magic. Caravans run between Crescent City and the trading posts. No one goes to Aztlan."

"No one?"

"Few, then. Some are invited. Of those, few return. Why would they? The Island City of Aztlan is said to be paved with gold. Warriors cast spears to the four winds, and rainstorms follow the spears. Magic flows everywhere, in the air, down the river. No one is ever hungry or thirsty there."

"And you believe this?" Green Stone asked.

Saziff shrugged. "Those who have been there say it is so." A small wave lapped at the sides of the ship. Gulls wheeled above the shallow water.

"Who says it?" Stone demanded.

"The soldiers and traders at their trading posts," Saziff said. "They live in Aztlan and are always anxious to return. Sometimes a trader has been invited and sent away again, like Ruser of Low Street. Yes, I believe it."

"So all trade is with the trading posts?" Green Stone asked.

"Yes. Caravans go northeast to the trading stations. They return with stonewood and other talismans, mainly of silver and turquoise. There are also maguey products. Rumor said that huge killer birds had stopped the caravans from Crescent City to Condigeo. I thought to make a fabulous profit. Curse! I never guessed that the birds stopped *all* caravans, even those from Aztlan."

"Why would those be spared?" Green Stone asked.

"I thought they would be protected by the Emperor," Saziff said. "The priests of Left-Handed Hummingbird serve him. He is powerful—he is the Emperor—but it may be that his power doesn't reach far from Aztlan. That is frightening."

"Frightening?" Sandry said.

"That something more powerful than the Emperor controls the caravan routes between here and Aztlan." Captain Saziff looked them in the eyes. "Lord Sandry, Wagonmaster Green Stone, I see I must speak plainly. If the caravans cannot travel to Aztlan and back, Crescent City has little worth trading for. Crescent City goods are useful, but no more so than those made on the coast. No one would come here for Crescent City meats and vegetables. There is willow bark, and there is jewelry, but it is more prized for its magic than its workmanship. Beyond that . . ." He shrugged. "Unless they have hidden magical items to sell, we are both ruined. These goods"—he waved down at the dock—"there are secrets to the way I divided them, yes, but in normal times either would be worth great wealth. Now—now they are worth more in Condigeo than here! We are both ruined."

"Speak for yourself," Green Stone said. "Feathersnake does not need trade with Crescent City to make profits along the Hemp Road." He looked thoughtful. "Tell me of the reputation of the money changers here."

Saziff nodded as if comprehending a great secret. "The city money changer, Jade Coin, is well known here and in Condigeo," he said. "A friend."

"How much of a friend?" Green Stone asked.

"He takes perhaps one part in twenty for bringing him accounts," Saziff said. "But he is honest. The city mayor keeps him that way. But they all are, here. It is the pride of Crescent City to have honest money changers."

Green Stone said, "There is little trade here. They cannot ask much for the use of a warehouse for a year. If I leave the goods in the care of Jade Coin to be held until a new caravan comes from this Aztlan, I think there may be profit enough."

"You will need a good man to negotiate," Saziff said.

"I know that. Or I can return," Green Stone said.

"I have a proposition for you," Saziff said.

Green Stone smiled. "See if you can describe it."

Saziff sighed. "We run these piles together. We leave our shares in your warehouse, and when you next come here and return to Condigeo, you divide what you have obtained for the entire heap, and I will choose which pile is mine."

Green Stone grinned. "There will be expenses. I will divide three ways, and you will choose one."

"Ruin!" Saziff shouted.

Saziff would choose two piles out of five. Sandry smiled to himself. *This bargaining—it is a skill I need to learn. . . .*

Chapter Twenty

The Merchants of Low Street

Regapisk, no longer Lord, and Arshur the Outsider rowed north through the Salty Sea. Zephans Mishagnos spent much of his time asleep in the bottom of the hollowed-out log. Just now he might have been dead but for the snoring. The parrot rode the prow, muttering to itself.

It was easier to see the glow of magic at night, whatever Arshur believed. The moon's glow was a comfort but distracting. Through the mist, Regapisk saw a change in the light.

"Pull hard, Arshur. If I angle us a little left—"

"Yeah, then what?" But Arshur pulled mightily, and

Regapisk steered, and a few hundred breaths later Zeph sat up with a start.

"Hah! That feels good." Zeph looked around him, then down into the water. He grinned. For the age he claimed, Zeph had kept an amazing number of teeth. "Rest for a bit. Regapisk, do you notice anything about this live patch?"

There were rivers in the sea, streams of unformed magic, as Regapisk thought of them, too far to reach, and a darker stream ahead. But the oval patch he'd steered into— "It's not moving with the water. It's deep."

"It's not moving!" the parrot screeched.

"Shut it, I can hear! Reg, look down."

Arshur said, "I can't see anything. Wait . . . sometimes you see fish that glow."

The outlines of light weren't moving, and they weren't fish. It was all angles and circles. "Cone-shaped buildings," Regapisk said.

Zeph said, "The sea rose when Atlantis sank. There were quakes. It must have left sunken villages all over the world. These were the Crescent City docks. Avoid that dark stream; it's the Rainbow River. We must be right on top of Crescent City. This cursed fog is hiding the watch lights."

"I see something ahead," Arshur said. "Pointed."

"The palace. Like this." Zeph's hands formed a blunt peak. "The houses all look like that."

Through thin mist, the vista looked spiky. Two glowing patches shrank to bright points as they rowed near.

"Thirsty, boys?" Zeph dipped a bowl over the side.

"Curse! They've been dumping their garbage in the water." He poured out what he had and dipped the bowl more carefully, held it a moment (Regapisk saw a darkening of the manna glow), then passed it around. Fresh, clean water.

They pulled up in a row of canoes. Zeph spoke at length to a man on guard. Then he reached toward the quiet water, and Regapisk perceived Zeph entangled with the glowing lines of manna.

Zeph told them, "I made a deal. I clean up the sewage for docking rights. We get the loan of a donkey too."

They piled half their goods on the donkey. The little beast stood patiently until they put one more load on, then it lay down and refused to budge until they lightened its burden. It got up, ready. Regapisk and Arshur carried the rest of the gear.

They moved onto the main road and followed it away from the dock. Not far from the palace, at the end of a row of tents and blankets arrayed with wares, Zeph directed them to lay out what they had to sell. Dawn was hiding the stars.

Regapisk asked Arshur, "What's got you chuckling?"

"You didn't notice? Yeah, I thought not. You never saw it from a dock. We're parked twenty paces from the *Angie Queen*. Don't look back."

Regapisk couldn't help it. The docks were a long way below them by now. Seamen were beginning to move. Regapisk couldn't pick out the ship, but he knew the captain's gaudy coat.

Arshur said, "Zeph, we have to buy some clothes. We can't go dressed like oarsmen. Someone will know us."

"Oh, all right. Six up, that's Cheprea; she sells clothes. Tell her you're with me, and ask for trade-in. Here." Zeph gave them two big yellow melons and some coins. "I'll be along as soon as I buy a good talisman."

The street looked more like Peacegiven Square than Lord's Town. Merchants sat at tables, looking up eagerly when anyone came past, then returning to staring glumly at their meager supply of trade goods. No one seemed to be buying anything.

"Gentlemen! Got a headache?"

"Only metaphorically," Regapisk said, looking into the darkened cone of a booth.

A dark, lean man grinned at them. Face and head, he was shaved clean. Great sheets of pale bark surrounded him. "Willow," he said. "The secret to surcease of pain, almost beyond price the world over. You're with the caravan, aren't you, sirs?"

Regapisk said, "I fear not. We don't have the headaches and we don't have the money."

The merchant lost his smile. The dapper man in the next booth was grinning, though. "A natural mistake," he said soothingly. "You, at least, look very like the warrior Lord who killed the birds."

Regapisk felt his belly twist inside him. "Would his name be Sandry?"

The willow merchant said, "Something like that. A relative?"

"No, it's just that I've heard of him. He learned how to kill terror birds around Condigeo."

"Did he? Well, he saved the city. We've been hard put

to find our next meal. They brought trade goods too, and I wish they'd find their way here!"

Regapisk said, "I would think that a warrior would need infusions of willow bark pretty often."

"Yes, it's excellent for wounds, or a knocked head, or blisters such as an oarsman—"

"We can scarcely buy clothes."

The willow merchant scowled.

The dapper man in the next booth wore half a dozen silver necklaces with silver and turquoise ornaments bobbing on them. He said, "Haladik's problem is good news for everyone else. The bark has been growing and thickening on the willow trees, untouched, ever since the nightmare birds came."

"Where do you find willow?" Regapisk asked.

The dapper man grinned. "Should I tell you? Yes, perhaps I should; it's not work I care for. In low areas, near water. But everything nearby will be claimed. Ten leagues upriver, it will be different."

"Not work you care for," Regapisk said.

"Perhaps Lord Sandry will want to know. They'll need trade goods. They're assembling a trading concern, I hear, around Badger Caravan. They're being almighty picky about it too."

Regapisk silently wished them joy of it, and a quick departure. "And you, sir? What are you selling?"

"Gems and talismans. Like this, and a good deal more under guard. Some are charged and some depleted."

"Depleted?"

"Yes, used up by a wizard. They'll need recharging."

"You can bring a dead talisman back to life?"

"Well . . . examine this one." The jeweler showed Regapisk a big turquoise inside a massy silver frame, without taking it off the chain around his neck. "You just take it to a place rich in manna. Silver conducts manna. Turquoise holds it. Take it into the Stone Forest, or into Sunfall Crater, paying your fees, of course. Wait a bit, then take the turquoise out of the frame—thus—before you leave, or it'll all drain out through the silver. Are you sure you're not with the traders?"

"I might join them," Regapisk said.

The jeweler nodded. "But your interest is in Cheprea, four booths that way. Tell her Ruser sent you, if you like."

The tea and bun shop was on a high platform attached to the south side of a curiously shaped building made of logs laid in a spiral. The door into the building was directly below them, but the platform had its own stairway outside. Tables faced the sea.

The stairway was steep, and Zeph was looking older again. Arshur helped the old wizard up the stairs and to a table where Regapisk was already seated.

Regapisk felt better. He had buckskin trousers and a coat woven from yarn made of some vegetable fiber and dyed a dark blue. It had two shiny buttons. According to the clothing merchant, it had belonged to some elderly merchant dead in the Bird Wars who had threatened to haunt anyone who wore his clothing. Regapisk wasn't worried about ghosts, and besides, there were plenty of beggars on the streets near the docks. He'd give the coat away if an unsettling ghost really appeared.

He was now dressed like many of the townsmen,

except for the heavy bronze sword at his side. The bandit's weapon wasn't a very good sword, not well shaped, and it didn't keep an edge well, but it was a sword. Not many in the town were armed. Regapisk felt very much the gentleman, and sometimes he even dared think of himself as Lord Regapisk.

"You don't look good," he told Zeph.

Zeph didn't react. The parrot screeched, "You don't look good!"

"Yeah. Can't buy a talisman," Zeph said. "I got good money for the melons. This was the right time to sell, gates just open, birds all driven away, people hungry and opening their pocketbooks, but there's no glow left in the talismans! I have more money than I ever had, and I can't buy a talisman with a decent charge. That wagonmaster bought everything that was for sale! Curse!"

"Ruser the jeweler spoke of both charged and uncharged talismans," Regapisk said.

"You know Ruser? I already talked to him. The wagonmaster bought every charged item in his stock. Except this." He showed a small turquoise set in stonewood dangling from a leather string around his neck. "Keeps me going, but that's all. He's got some great items, but none of them charged."

A waitress came over to take their orders. She winked at Regapisk, but she waggled her hips at Arshur. They ordered terror bird stew. It seemed to be the only meat dish they had. She brought big ornately decorated ceramic bowls, full of meat and hot red bulbs Zeph called peppers. The spoons were ceramic with wooden handles.

Arshur watched as Regapisk dipped stew and ate, then used his spoon the same way.

"So what will you do?" Regapisk asked.

Zeph shrugged. "Go back to my salt farm and wait," he said. "What choices do I have?"

"Not me," Arshur said. "I'm going to be a king, and I won't find that at a salt farm."

Zeph nodded gravely. "I expected that."

"What will you do?" Regapisk asked. Something far out in the Inland Sea splashed and blew a plume of spray. *Whale,* Regapisk thought. *Not a mer, though.* Mers never came up this side of the Finger. The last mers they'd seen were back at the Nail.

"Feeling responsible for me?" Zeph grinned.

"A little. We saved your life."

"Maybe. Say you did. I knew you weren't coming back to the farm with me." He jingled his coin bag. "I'll hire me some youngsters to help out until a caravan comes through with live talismans."

"You trust the locals?"

"Some," Zeph said. "Ruser the jeweler's an old friend. He'll know people who have honest kids."

Chapter Twenty-One

Willow Bark

"There's nothing to trade for," Green Stone said. He passed his soup bowl to Burning Tower and watched morosely as she filled it from the big pot. "I weary of terror bird stew, and there's scarcely a wagonload of magical items in the whole town. Of course there's twenty times that much in depleted jewelry, with all the power gone."

"Willow bark," Nothing Was Seen said. "I've listened. It grows wild north of here and hasn't been harvested in moons, since the birds came."

Green Stone said, "It will be, soon enough. The townsfolk want our goods, and they have little enough to pay with."

"How far north?" Sandry asked.

Nothing Was Seen shrugged. "I couldn't get too close

to them. It was a strange group, merchants with nothing to sell, and two men who walk like sailors. I've seen one of them before, in Condigeo, I think. Big man, big muscles, some gaudy scars. Looks like a Lordkin."

"And the other?"

"Looked a little like you," Lurk said.

"Regapisk," Sandry said. "Who else could it be?"

"Do you want to find him?" Lurk asked.

"Not just yet," Sandry said. "Should we gather this willow bark?"

Green Stone nodded. "It will be worth a day."

Sandry clapped his hands.

Chalker appeared from nowhere. "Sir?"

"We'll want four chariots ready in the morning, including mine. You'll come with me. The other three will each have a Younglord driver, a trooper, and one of Green Stone's wagoneers. We'll go north and look for this willow bark."

"Sir. So I'm to pick men who don't mind getting their hands dirty?"

"Hands and feet."

"I will have the cooks pack lunches for twelve, then," Green Stone said.

"Yes, sir. That be all, sir?"

"Yes, thank you." Chalker went away.

"And that's something to take back, maybe, if we're there in time and those people Lurk overheard know what they're talking about," Green Stone said. "But we didn't have to come to Crescent City to find willow swamps! We're still going to be short of goods."

"You don't sound devastated," Burning Tower said.

"No, little sister, I'm not. I've already sold half our cargo at better prices than I expected to. I have enough credit with the moneychangers to buy a full load for next trip even if we come here with empty wagons; I have more goods in the warehouses. We can't lose!" He rubbed his hands in anticipation. "And I have the one wagonload of charged talismans, the only ones for sale, but think! In Condigeo they'll be worth a fortune! The first magic in a year. With Sandry's army to protect us on the way back. Little sister, I am not devastated at all." He paused. "I am eager to be started, though. Sandry, while you gather willow bark, I will begin preparations to return to Condigeo. There is little to remain here for."

Chapter Twenty-Two

Augury

In the morning, Clever Squirrel went back to Fur Slipper, taking Tower with her.

"Crescent City has no llamas," Fur Slipper said. "We have few animals we did not eat while the birds encircled us."

Clever Squirrel nodded. "Does it have to be a llama?"

"No. Sheep, goat, calf—"

"Come with us. I know where to find a calf." She strode toward the Feathersnake wagon camp.

"Squirrel! No!" Tower shouted.

Squirrel didn't look back.

The wagon camp was a flurry of activity as Green Stone directed the others in setting up a market. Squirrel went up to him, and whatever she said dampened his enthusiasm. When Tower came closer, her brother was saying, "You can't have him."

"I can and will," Squirrel said. Tower had never seen her this way before. "It is needed."

"It has been years since we had a spotted bull calf," Stone said. "Wait for another."

"No. This cannot wait. There is need, and the time is now. Do you question my right at need?"

Stone looked at her intently. "I may question how you know of the need."

"I know," Squirrel said.

Stone stared at the ground for a long time. "Then take him. But not until the herd goes out to pasture. I will not have his mother see this."

"So be it," Squirrel said.

The bison herd was led out in the late afternoon. The two-month-old calf was kept behind until the herd was out of sight. Then Squirrel and Fur Slipper led the calf away. Tower followed reluctantly.

Fur Slipper held the calf. It was tame and trusting, and Clever Squirrel cut its throat. When it stopped struggling, she and Fur Slipper split the beast open and wrestled its lungs out of the carcass . . .

Burning Tower turned away.

Clever Squirrel was fascinated. The two shamans pored over the extended lungs, chattering in low voices.

Squirrel raised her voice. "Tower, the veins in the lungs make a map. We're going northeast. There's an island a hundred leagues and more away, right in the middle of this vast land. Left-Handed Hummingbird waits there. Here at this pucker, closer, rewards await us too."

* * *

They found the willow swamp before noon. Sandry set his men to gathering the thin bark. It was dull work, and they had surprisingly little to show for their efforts when the sun hung low and Sandry ordered their return. They reached the Feathersnake encampment at dusk, to find Green Stone surly and shouting.

"She had the right," Burning Tower was saying.

"If she is not the Feathersnake wagon shaman, she has no rights over us at all," Green Stone said. "She certainly didn't have the right to slaughter my spotted calf!"

Squirrel said coolly, "It is the patterns in the calf's lungs that tell me I must not return with you."

"Why? Are you ill luck for us? The calf was our good luck, and you've taken it!"

"What is this to you? We will find you a shaman for the return trip. I know five here who can do the task, and every one of them is willing to go. Every one but the mayor, and you would not want him anyway. Choose your shaman, Green Stone."

"What's this?" Sandry asked quietly.

"She says she has to go to Aztlan," Burning Tower said. "She has a mission there."

"What mission?" Sandry asked.

"It is not your concern," Clever Squirrel said. She turned to face them. "Go, you two, and marry, and leave me to my work."

The morning dawned bright, with a cool breeze from the sea. Sandry woke with a grin.

Go and marry. The Bison Tribe shaman was powerful in magic. She must know whereof she spoke.

I have brought the wagon train to Crescent City, I have lifted the siege, and I return in triumph. He stretched and did his morning exercises. A beautiful morning. *Go and marry,* Squirrel had said. And Green Stone's look was sour, but he had nodded agreement.

A wonderful morning, of a wonderful day and a glorious year.

CHAPTER TWENTY-THREE

WHAT MUST WE DO?

Breakfast was plain fare, boiled oats such as they ate on the trail, but Sandry had had enough of terror bird stew. So had they all. They'd eat well enough when they returned to Condigeo.

Condigeo, then north to Lordshills. Should they wed in Lordshills or go on to Feathersnake's New Castle? He lusted to see that place. Nonetheless . . . Lordshills, Sandry decided. We will marry in Lordshills and visit Avalon, and go to New Castle afterward.

The Feathersnake wagon encampment was a blur of activity. Green Stone was interrupted half a dozen times by wagon owners with questions.

By contrast, Burning Tower sat staring into her bowl. She didn't return Sandry's foolish grin. Something was wrong. But what?

He'd learn soon enough. He always did.

Green Stone, vividly busy organizing cooking gear, wouldn't look at him either. So, "Wagonmaster, what's the problem now?"

Green Stone looked around. "Where do terror birds come from?"

"Eggs. No, you mean terror bird brooders. East?"

"How far east? How many more are there? When will they arrive?"

Sandry thought about that.

"And why are they attacking us? We were sent here to find the cause of the terror bird attacks and put a stop to them. We have done neither." When Sandry began a protest, Stone waved it aside. "We've won every battle. We have opened roads to Condigeo, for now. We've learned a great deal. We'll take it all back to Condigeo and Tep's Town and New Castle. We look good! We'll make profits from this journey. But tell me, Lord Sandry, who sent the birds? And what will prevent him or her or them from sending more?"

Sandry looked to Burning Tower. She was staring into the cook fire, unnaturally silent.

"What were your instructions?" Green Stone asked him.

"To get here and return with information," Sandry said.

Tower looked up, finally. "We've done that. Or will have when we go home. All that the Lords sent you for, and more."

"Yes!" Sandry said.

"For how long?" Green Stone asked. "Yes, we seem to have cleared the way from here to Condigeo."

"The Hemp Road is safe, then," Burning Tower said.

"We have always lived on the Hemp Road. What need do we have of this Golden Road?"

"Aside from the new wealth?" Green Stone said.

"Yes, aside from that," Burning Tower said. She looked possessively at Sandry. "We have no need of new wealth. We'll breed horses in Lordshills!"

"And when the birds return to the Hemp Road?"

"Why would they?"

"Why did they go there at all?" Green Stone demanded. "Little sister, we all assumed that if we could only get here, we would know why the birds were attacking. Here we are. What about the birds?"

Sandry asked, "What do you want to do?"

Stone shook his head. "Yesterday morning, I would have said we were done. Go home with what we know and let your council, and my father, decide what to do next. But then Squirrel pissed in the soup."

"We can ill afford to lose her," Sandry said. "But *I* know no way to prevent her from traveling the road to Aztlan."

"Nor I, and I know her better than you," Green Stone said. "Even unicorns don't mess with that girl! But if anyone can learn the secrets of the bird god, that will be Squirrel." He spread his hands. "Of course it is of no use to anyone if she dies with this knowledge."

Sandry finally saw what he was driving at. "Why do you think I can keep that madwoman alive?"

"I think one of you may return," Green Stone said. "Don't you?"

"That's a year's work!" Sandry said. "I had expected to be home and married well before that."

"We don't always get what we want. And Tower will wait—"

"I will not," Burning Tower snapped, glaring at them both. "If you're going up that road with my sister, with Clever Squirrel, you aren't going without me!"

"You saw this coming?" Sandry asked her.

"I did."

The way she'd been behaving . . . Sandry wasn't being punished for any crime he'd committed yet. But people grew to know each other well, traveling in a caravan, and Burning Tower's sister looked too much like Tower and lived too much by her own rules . . . and neither she nor Sandry could be expected to harness a one-horn. Whatever happened on the road to Aztlan, there would be no way for Tower to know.

And she would brood. Sandry nodded to himself. So would he, in the same circumstances. But for him, there was tattletale Spike.

Sandry said, "I don't want to risk you. We still can't guess what danger lies east of us." He knew at once that Burning Tower would not be persuaded this way. "You're starting to like that, aren't you?"

She shrugged.

"Green Stone?"

Green Stone shrugged. He wouldn't, or couldn't, force his sister to return with him.

Another year. He looked at Burning Tower and thought of Roni, and sighed. Then he turned to Green Stone. "What must we do?"

* * *

Nothing Was Seen returned at lunch time. Green Stone gathered the Feathersnake leaders into the wagonmaster's nest to hear what he had learned.

Clever Squirrel joined them uninvited.

Green Stone stood in the doorway to block her path. "Do you return to Feathersnake?"

"How could I leave?" Squirrel said. "Your Feathersnake people pulled me out of Avalon. If I'd stayed there, I'd be safe at Road's End now. I am here at the behest of Feathersnake. My father rode Whandall Feathersnake's mind the night I was conceived. Whatever drives me to Aztlan is no stranger to Feathersnake. And I believe—no, I *know* that I was conceived and born for this task."

"And you need our help," Green Stone said.

"Eh. My interest is yours," Clever Squirrel corrected. "But if you seek gratitude, brother, you have it." She smiled at Tower. "Thank you, sister." She turned to Sandry. "And brother found."

Green Stone turned silently from the door and took his place on the east side of the nest.

"Three wagon trains," Nothing Was Seen said. "They have taken every beast still alive, and those from the trains from the south, and they are sending them all. It makes three trains, but all will be under the mastery of Wagonmaster Ern. Ern leads the Road Runner train." He paused, clearly waiting for someone to speak.

Green Stone frowned, then nodded. "Mayor Buzzard at Play was shaman of that train before he retired to politics."

"Shaman and then owner," Nothing Was Seen said. "Now he has partners, but he is owner still."

"Like Father with Bison Tribe," Green Stone observed. "Well enough. So it is with the mayor that we must negotiate. Sandry, what will you need to provide protection to that train?"

"From what?"

Green Stone shrugged. "How would I know?"

"Then I don't either. Every Younglord and Lordsman we have couldn't protect against a hundred birds at once."

Clever Squirrel spoke. "Until this year, there were never more than a dozen," she said. "I think Left-Handed Hummingbird sent all he had to destroy Crescent City. We slew them. Even a god takes time to hatch and grow more birds."

"He is a god," Green Stone said. "And there are wild birds aplenty."

"No," Burning Tower said. "Brother, think, wild birds do not cooperate any more than wild one-horns. Without the god to restrain them, they fight; they claim wide hunting grounds. Before the god sent these birds, we scarcely saw one a year on the whole Hemp Road! How many can there be on the desert roads to Aztlan?"

"It's not all desert," Clever Squirrel said. "But Blazes is right: there can't be as many wild birds here, and the god will have claimed most of those already."

"He claimed them; we killed them," Sandry said. "So. Not so many on the way up. I believe I can teach Mayor Buzzard's troops to use spears rather than rely on magic. Enough so that we can get through to the trading posts. Of course the return may be a different story."

"Ah," Green Stone said. "I hadn't thought of that. Tell me: how many of our people will you take with you? Only they will be your concern on return."

Sandry frowned.

"We can write an agreement that ends when you reach the trading posts," Green Stone said. "Indeed, they'll insist on that. Crescent City wants none of us on the road to Aztlan. They will be expecting us to demand the right to send our own wagon trains north and east. They won't permit that except at great need. So take only those you need, and only they will be your charges for the return."

Sandry stood and paced for a moment. "A chariot, four horses. Enough for a spearman, say Younglord Whane and myself. Tower will have Spike."

"And I have my stallion," Clever Squirrel said.

"You will want a wagon for the journey," Green Stone said.

"Two," Clever Squirrel said. Tower nodded agreement.

"Two wagons, then," Green Stone said. "I will ask for four and settle for three."

"Three?"

"We must look to our profits, little sister. If you must have two wagon nests, there must be one wagon for cargo. A thing you easily forget, but I do not."

"And if we must abandon the wagons?"

"Cargo to Aztlan is bulky," Green Stone said. "What returns is small. A chariot can hold magical items to buy three wagons twice over." He sighed. "That is with Burning Tower negotiating the sales. Would I were going, I would double that."

Chapter Twenty-Four

Jade Coin

Regapisk, no longer Lord, beamed a smile at the pretty waitress. Her name was Laughing Rock. He'd learned she was the proprietor's daughter and would sometimes give a free breakfast to a handsome young man down on his luck. Regapisk thought he fitted that description well enough. She'd already brought him flat corn cakes and a hot drink of herbs and sage honey even though he'd made it clear enough that he couldn't pay. Regapisk sipped at the hot sweet drink and smiled again.

"Lord Reg." A man's voice. Behind him.

Regapisk leaped to his feet, his hand on the hilt of the bronze sword. Laughing Rock shrieked.

"Steady, Lord Reg," Captain Saziff said. He grinned nervously. "I see you have found new clothing." Saziff spoke in the language of the Tep's Town kinless dock-workers. No one here would understand that.

Laughing Rock and her father stood at the kitchen entrance, their brows furrowed. Regapisk thought briefly of sending her father for help. He owned this place; he ought to have influence with the local watchmen. But he'd also made it clear that he had his doubts about Regapisk as a suitor. Better to keep this private for the moment. "And I heard you were sailing this morning," Regapisk said. He looked around for friends but saw no one but the girl and her elderly father. *Where's Arshur when I need him?*

"I'd planned that," Saziff said. "But I have one last errand to perform before I can safely return to Condigeo and Lord's Town. I have looked for you for the past three days without success."

Regapisk nodded warily. "I know." He had seen the Oarmaster and several sailors from *Angie Queen* going through the town, and they'd asked Ruser the jeweler if he had seen anyone from Lord's Town. "You're not armed," Regapisk said.

Saziff laughed. "No, and I'm alone. I haven't come to take you back! I couldn't, you know, even if I wanted to. I've had to keep all the rowing crew in chains the whole time we've been here. If one of them gets outside the dock area, he's free. It's the law here—didn't you know that?"

"No."

"Well, it is! You, sir, do you speak Condigeano?"

"Some." Black Stone kept his arm around his daughter. "What is all this?"

Saziff explained.

The old man nodded. "It is as he says. Crescent City has no slaves and allows no one else but the Emperor to hold slaves beyond the docks. You are safe here. If anyone tried to take you by force, we would send for the watch." He eyed Regapisk coldly. "I had wondered where you gained those muscular arms."

Regapisk ignored that and turned to Saziff. "Then why were you looking for me?" He could afford to scowl now, and did.

Saziff chuckled. "Why, man, you're rich!"

"Rich?" Regapisk and Black Stone spoke together.

"Well, not rich, then, but you won't starve. Your relatives in Lordshills sent money for you. I gave it to the money changer in your name, but now I have to introduce you to Jade Coin so that you can collect. Come on, man, you're making me miss the tide!"

The money changer's hogan seemed different from the others. The entrance faced north, and logs formed a kind of anteroom to the main part. Saziff led Regapisk past the armed men who sat at the entrance, but two stopped him to relieve Regapisk of his sword. Then they waved him on.

Jade Coin had almond-shaped eyes, and his coloring was different from that of the citizens of Crescent City. He looked like a Tep's Town kinless. He listened quietly as Captain Saziff spoke.

"This is Regapisk. I have left money and goods in his name."

Jade Coin nodded and turned his half-closed eyes on

Regapisk. "Do you understand the terms?" he asked. His voice was smooth like old cloth.

Regapisk said, "Only that you have money for me."

"I do," Jade Coin said. "Not to be paid all at once, and not to be paid at all when there is a ship in harbor or a wagon train forming to go west."

"You can pay him for all of me," Saziff said. "I'd as soon have a loose rattlesnake aboard as a former oarsman for a passenger."

"I understand. There is also a caravan departing for Condigeo."

"They'll never let me on that!" Regapisk protested. "And I sure can use some money. Clothes, food . . ."

"As to that, I have no problems," Jade Coin said. He took a small bag of coins from somewhere beneath his table and poured them out. A dozen copper coins and two small gold. "That will be more than enough to buy clothing and food. Come see me when it is exhausted."

"So how much am I worth?" Regapisk asked.

Jade Coin shrugged. "Over your lifetime, possibly quite a lot. Not all is here. Some was sent in obligations of money changers in Condigeo, to be exchanged another time as I need. But however much, you will never have it all at once. Such are my instructions."

"I am done here," Saziff announced. "Lord Reg, it has been my honor to know you. Perhaps we will meet again, but not as shipmates."

Regapisk considered this. He was rich but he couldn't claim the money! Who had done this to him? How had Sandry accomplished this? But in any case, now he could do better than charm a silly girl for bread and hot tea. *Very nice girl,* he added to himself, *but silly.*

Regapisk bowed. "Good morning, Captain. And a pleasant voyage. Give my regards to the Oarmaster, and . . ." He paused, then selected four of the copper coins. "And use these to buy extra rations for my benchmates."

Saziff regarded the money with a slight smile. "I'll just do that, Lord Reg. I'm sure they'll be grateful." He made an economical bow that took in both Regapisk and Jade Coin, and left.

And with luck, I'll never see you again, Regapisk thought.

"There is one more matter," Jade Coin said. He struck a metal rod held in place by small clay supports. It rang with a soft tone, and a girl, almost certainly Jade Coin's daughter, came in. "That box the captain left with us," he said softly. "Bring it, please."

The girl nodded. Minutes later, she returned with two boxes, one long and slender. "I presumed you wanted both."

"I did. My thanks." Jade Coin waited until she had left. "This first item you may not have until you have left this establishment. The other is yours immediately." He pushed the smaller box across the table.

It held treasures. A small mirror. A carved ivory fork and spoon, and a pewter bowl. A salamander brooch of the kind that Lords wore when traveling away from Lord's Town. A sigil stone cylinder seal, his own, that had been taken from him before he joined the ship. Regapisk quelled a powerful urge to weep.

And a rolled-up letter.

Regapisk opened it carefully. Aunt Shanda's handwriting leaped out at him.

"My dear Reggy,

This is best for all of us. Understand, dear, this is all we could do and all we will ever do. Your exile is witnessed and signed, and if you ever return, the Lord Chief Witness will not even learn of your death until it has been accomplished. I speak bluntly because I know that that is the only way I can get your attention.

I have begged you the privilege of saying that you travel on orders of the Lord Chief Witness. You may send reports to him, but I trust you will send them in my care. You do not wish to annoy Quintana. And do not try to make agreements in his name. He bears you no great ill will. Do not give him reason to regret that.

And do not return. Let me say it again: this is Witnessed and signed.

Grandnephew, I do hope you will make something of yourself. I always thought you were smarter than many of my relatives, and you always worked at proving me wrong. Please change that, my dear. You remain a Lord of Lordshills—at least until you try to come back—and I expect you to conduct yourself as a Lord. You've been taught well enough to know how.

"With kindest regards,

"Shanda, First Lady."

Reggy read it through twice. That was Shanda, all right, and she meant it. Witnessed and signed.

He wasn't ever going home again. It began to sink in. This was no adventure from which he would return. His life as a Lord of Lordshills was over. He wouldn't be in the army or become a Witness or conduct a business or marry a wealthy girl and manage her estates. He wouldn't be a leader in the Fire Brigades or return to his duties at the harbor. He would never go home again.

Regapisk, now Lord again, put on the brooch Aunt Shanda had enclosed, and bowed. "My thanks, Jade Coin. I believe we may have further business to conduct."

"As you say," Jade Coin said. His smile was unreadable.

Lord Regapisk bowed again and left.

Chapter Twenty-Five

Partners

The jeweler's hogan faced east. Master Ruser lived alone, and had invited Regapisk and Arshur to share his quarters—whether out of pity or for companionship, they didn't know.

It was a bare place. Ruser had sold nearly everything he owned to stay alive during the siege. Now he had barely enough to live on himself, yet he shared with Arshur and Regapisk. He said it was because they had been kind to his old friend Zephans Mishagnos.

Regapisk found Arshur and Ruser at the table in the hogan's main room.

"Rejoice," Regapisk said. "We're rich."

"Rich," Arshur said. "How rich?"

"Indeed," Ruser the jeweler said. "I would never have expected that."

"Well, I don't have it all yet," Regapisk said. "But I'm rich enough to buy us a good dinner, and food for the week. And look, I have a new sword."

He handed it over to Arshur. It had a tooled leather grip, and the scabbard was thin wood bound in tooled leather. The blade was leaf-shaped.

Arshur hefted it thoughtfully. "Good balance. Nice grip," Arshur said. "I think I know the kinless who forged it. I like iron better than bronze, but this is good bronze. Should hold an edge." He swung it experimentally. "Yep, a good one. Where'd you buy it?"

"I didn't. It was a present from Aunt Shanda," Regapisk said. "It was on board the *Angie Queen* all the time." He explained the arrangement with Jade Coin. "So I have money, but I have to stay here to collect it. Master Ruser, my gratitude for your hospitality, and we can pay our share now."

"I'm not staying," Arshur said. "I'm going to Aztlan to be king."

Ruser nodded. "You are determined, then?"

"I've always known I would be a king," Arshur said. "And I will be."

"How do you propose to get to Aztlan?" Ruser asked.

"I'll hire out as a sword for Ern's caravan! That will get me to the trading posts. From there?" Arshur shrugged. "Leave that to my fate."

"I know the way to Aztlan," Ruser said carefully. "I am minded to go again."

"Yes! You've been there," Regapisk said.

"I have been to the caravansary that stands next to the Palace of War," Ruser said. "While I was there, a boat arrived. From Atlantis!"

"A long time ago, then," Arshur said.

"Half a lifetime," Ruser agreed. "But I was not invited inside the city itself. My brother Flensevan was invited in. I have scarce heard from him since. Is he married? Does he prosper? I would see him again before I die—not to mention that he owes me money. He will not leave Aztlan, but perhaps he will come to the gate to speak with me."

"Can you take me to that gate?" Arshur demanded.

"Perhaps. If I had any way of going." He gestured to indicate the empty shelves that should have held his goods. "I have uncharged talismans. If I sell them to buy a wagon, I will have nothing else."

Regapisk fingered his brooch and touched the cylinder seal sigil now bound to his wrist. *I am a Lord of Lordshills. Without assignment, without duties, except to act like a Lord. And what does that mean? Arshur is ready, eager, to go to Aztlan. What will happen to him there, or on the way?*

He sighed, remembering a promise he had made. Whatever else Lords did, they kept their obligations and paid their debts. *Tras Preetror gave me an obligation, and I accepted it: look out for Arshur. A nearly impossible task. The outlander barbarian does as he wills.*

"I'm coming with you," Regapisk said.

Arshur nodded as if there had never been any doubt about that.

"In what capacity?" Ruser asked with amusement.

"He's not bad with a good sword," Arshur said. "Better than any bandits we've met around here."

Regapisk still found that astonishing, but it was true.

"I'll fight if it's needed," Regapisk said. "But I had something else in mind. Master Jeweler Ruser, I'd like to be your partner."

Jade Coin was willing enough, provided that the caravan was not going west. He seemed almost enthusiastic when he learned that Ruser of Low Street would be a partner. Regapisk left the details to be negotiated by Ruser. Haggling was not a skill a Lord was expected to know.

Presently, he found they had two wagons for the three of them. "I could have had more," Ruser told them, as he led them toward the wagon camp. "You have more credit, and Jade Coin decided he would invest his own resources after he saw Arshur." Ruser shrugged. "He doesn't know your friend won't be coming back. But two wagons is just right. My talismans don't take up much room. We don't have bulky cargo: my uncharged talismans, and gold from Jade Coin to pay our taxes at Sunfall."

"So what now?" Arshur demanded.

"You must meet Wagonmaster Ern," Ruser said. He sighed. "And usually we would buy provisions for the trip, but those will be very dear."

"Plenty of terror bird jerky," Arshur said. He spat.

"Better than starvation," Ruser said. "Yes. And you lads can hunt. We should manage."

"Hunt better with a chariot," Regapisk said.

"A chariot. You continue to surprise me. You know how to drive a chariot?"

"I do," Regapisk said. "Lords are taught these things."

"A chariot," Ruser said again. "Would Arshur be your spear man?"

"I know how," Arshur said.

"There are horses here?" Regapisk asked.

"Mules," Ruser said. "Not as fast as horses, but horses are very rare here. There are also mares. Perhaps something can be arranged to take mares to Sunfall and return them to foal. The Emperor demands that all stallions be kept in his dominions, and since the terror bird attacks began, no mares have been put to stud. There is a tax for breeding horses, and it must be done there in his domains."

Regapisk pointed toward the corrals where the wagon train was forming. "Those are horses, and that is a stallion." He paused. "Oh."

Ruser looked the question at him.

"It's Sandry's team," Regapisk said. "I suppose that means that Sandry will be going on this wagon train."

"You have reason to dislike your countryman?" Ruser asked. "I believe you told us once that you did not know him at all."

Regapisk opened his mouth to speak but thought better of it. "He broke a promise to me once. It was a long time ago."

"I suggest you mend your quarrel with him," Ruser said. "We will be on that trail for a long time."

"I'll do that," Regapisk said. "Let's go have a drink while I think how."

BOOK FOUR

AZTLAN

CHAPTER ONE

TWO WAGON TRAINS

Wagonmaster Ern seemed distracted. Sandry found that understandable. This wagon train was larger than the Feathersnake train commanded by Green Stone, and there was far less organization. Feathersnake's wagoneers had all traveled the Hemp Road together many times and did what was necessary without being told. This group was different, and every dispute was brought to the wagonmaster for settling.

Two wagoneers bickered over precedence. Ern listened to both, then casually assigned each a place in the order of travel. There was no dispute or quarrel. The wagoneers wanted someone to decide for them. Sandry thought that most of the wagon train disputes were like that, no real substance, but they had to be settled by authority. Eventually the wagoneers were finished, and Ern could turn to Burning Tower, Sandry, and Clever Squirrel. They had waited through much of the afternoon.

"At last," Ern said. "My apologies." He was a serious man, stocky, around forty, and wore leather clothing decorated with symbols that Sandry didn't understand. A painting on his chest depicted a long-legged bird pursuing a snake. His hair hung down his back in a long queue. "Admit no more of them today," Ern told the guards at the entrance to his nest. He gestured for his guests to sit, then clapped his hands for tea. He served fragrant tea in small cups, and waited until everyone had a sip. Sandry recognized the flavor as one brought with Green Stone's wagon train.

"So," Ern said, "it is settled. Lord Sandry, you will command all the wagon guards. Younglord Whane will be your second in command. When there is danger, you will have direct command over all the wagons. When there is no immediate threat, you will come to me first."

They all nodded. Whane grinned widely.

"Good. And one of your duties will be to instruct the others in how to fight the terror birds."

"As much as I can," Sandry said. "It's not part of my duty to teach chariot warfare. I couldn't anyway—we don't have enough chariots or horses." *And no decent bows except mine,* he thought, but there was no reason to tell these people about compound bows.

"Yes. But you will fight as needed."

"Of course," Sandry said. "I have my armor and weapons, and I am bringing chariot horses."

Ern sipped tea. "I confess curiosity about your ways of

war, how you use those chariots, but there will be time enough to discuss that on the trail when there is little else to talk about," he said. "For now, let us be sure we are agreed on more important details. Lord Sandry, you will instruct the guards in the use of weapons without magic, and you and Younglord Whane will aid in defense against both bandits and birds.

"Clever Squirrel, you will share the duties of wagon train shaman with Fur Slipper, who will be chief shaman and receive the chief's shares and privileges. This is agreed?"

Clever Squirrel agreed without enthusiasm.

"So. You may choose your own place in the wagon line. What more is there?" Ern asked.

"Well," Sandry said, "there will be others. Mouse Warrior believes it is his destiny to travel to Aztlan. He can train your wagoneers in better use of the sling. And Burning Tower has a servant boy who will accompany her."

Ern nodded. "I am pleased that Mouse Warrior comes with us. I have heard that he killed four birds in the final battles. Of course your lady is welcome, but I was not certain she was to come with us. She brings the one-horn?"

"Of course."

"We know little of such beasts," Ern said. "They are said to be difficult."

"Burning Tower won't have any trouble with Spike," Clever Squirrel said. "Sandry, what of the Lordkin?"

Sandry shrugged. "We will know when we leave. They haven't said, and no one gives them orders."

"I have mixed feelings," Ern said. "They are formidable warriors, but I have heard . . ."

Sandry grinned. "We know."

"Feathersnake will pay, if payment is needed," Burning Tower said.

"So I have also heard," Ern said. "So. We are agreed—"

One of Ern's sons scratched at the entrance to the wagon nest. The boy was about twelve, and Sandry knew him as Small Condor. The boy was eager to learn about throwing spears and other weapons and often followed Sandry around the wagon camp.

Ern frowned. "Did I not say I was not to be disturbed?"

The boy smiled nervously. "It is Master Ruser of Low Street," he said. "He wishes to join the wagon train."

"Can he not meet me another time?"

The boy grinned more widely. "I thought it important that he meet Lord Sandry. He has brought two warriors with him. One is a giant."

When Wagonmaster Ern stood to greet Master Ruser, Sandry got to his feet as well, so he was standing when Ruser's companions came in. Sandry recognized the giant who had been with the teller Tras Preetror in Lord's Town and Condigeo. And—

"Hail, Cousin," Regapisk said. He held out his hand.

Regapisk. Sandry noted the salamander brooch and the tooled leather handle of a quality sword made in Lord's Town. "Hail, Lord Regapisk," he said formally. He stepped forward to grasp Reggy's forearm. "I'm glad to see you in such good circumstances."

"Thank you. Better than before, thanks to Aunt Shanda."

Wagonmaster Ern watched curiously, but most of his attention was given to Ruser. "I am told you wish to join our wagon train, Master Jeweler. And you bring these two as guards?"

"Two wagons only," Ruser said. "And they are both guards and partners."

"Partners," Ern said slowly. "Interesting. Will they fight?"

Arshur struck a pose. "Who needs killing?" he demanded.

Regapisk shrugged. "I am a Lord of Lordshills; we are all trained in war crafts," he said.

Sandry smiled to himself, remembering Reggy in sword practice, Reggy at spear throwing. Reggy's hopelessness with a bow. He had spoken the truth, but . . .

"I will also have a chariot with two teams, mules and mares," Regapisk said. "Arshur will be my spearman."

Sandry nodded with more enthusiasm. Reggy could drive. As to Arshur, Sandry asked, "Do you have any skill with a spear thrower? They call it an atlatl."

Reggy looked blank. Arshur frowned slightly. "Yes, if I understand what you mean."

Sandry made gestures of placing a spear onto a stick, then throwing it.

Arshur laughed. "*Assilima,* we called them in the north. Sure, but you don't do it that way! They're a little tricky, but I can show you."

"I never saw one," Reggy said quickly.

"I'll teach you both," Arshur said. "But why are you interested in those things? They're not much good for fighting from a chariot!"

Sandry said. "We'll only have two chariots, counting yours, and no trained Lordsmen either. I'm sending everyone but Whane back with Green Stone's wagons to Condigeo. We'll have to defend ourselves with the help of locals who aren't too well trained at fighting without magic. I was hoping these spear throwers would make up some of the difference; they look like they'd give you a lot more range."

"More range, more power," Arshur agreed. "Not as accurate. You pay by losing accuracy. But at close range, they'd sure help green troops against those birds. Good thinking . . . I forgot your name."

"Sandry. Of Lordshills."

"Sandry. We've met before, but I don't remember where."

"There was a tea room in Condigeo."

"Yes. Sure was," Arshur said. "I was with Tras Preetror. Been with Tras for twenty years, more. But he died, you know. On that ship. Tras died, and I'm going to Aztlan to be king."

Going to be king, Sandry thought. He found it no more likely now than when Arshur had said it in Condigeo, but he noted that neither Ern nor Clever Squirrel laughed or even looked incredulous. "Congratulations," Sandry said. He must have sounded as if he meant it, because Arshur looked pleased.

Younglord Maydreo tried to keep a straight face, but he was having trouble hiding the big grin that kept breaking out.

"You've earned the right, but not that grin," Sandry said.

"Sir?"

"I'm putting you in command because I think you can do it, but that doesn't stop me from worrying about you," Sandry said. "Remember the bloodberries?"

"Yes, sir—"

"And Vic's Vampire Feast?"

"Yes, sir, I understand—be careful about magic."

"Precisely," Sandry said. "You've had good training with weapons, and you got some good experience fighting birds, not that I expect you to run into very many birds on the way back. But that's just the point, Acting Lord Maydreo."

Maydreo suppressed another wide grin.

"Without the birds, the bandits will be more active."

"Oh. So I should keep the chariot men in armor?"

"You'll have to decide that yourself," Sandry said. "Certainly at least one team ought to be armored with bows."

Maydreo nodded, suddenly sobered. "Bandits. Yes, sir, I'll be ready for bandits."

"Bandits, yes. But you'll have to be alert for what the shaman called undead. And all kinds of horrors we don't know because we don't know much about magic," Sandry said. "The worst of it is that Chalker and Peacevoice Fullerman won't know much about magic either."

Maydreo frowned slightly.

"I think you're smart enough to realize that the real secret of leadership is to listen a lot before you say anything," Sandry said. "I sure hope you learned that, anyway."

"Yes, sir—"

"So they can tell you about bandits, but your best people won't know any more than you do about magic. That leaves Green Stone and the shaman."

"Yes, sir. I'll listen to them."

"Chalker can help you with Trebaty," Sandry said. "He may or may not be the biggest problem you have." Sandry stood. "I'm not following my own advice," he said. "I'm talking too much. You'll do fine, Acting Lord Maydreo." He held out his hand to grip Maydreo's forearm. "You'll do fine."

The wagon train was formed and ready. Sandry and Burning Tower stood close together as Green Stone stood on his wagon and looked at his charges. He turned to wave at Tower, then turned back. "Whenever you like, Acting Lord Maydreo."

Maydreo raised his spear to Sandry, then turned to Chalker, who stood as his spearman. "If you please."

Chalker looked one last plea at Sandry. Sandry turned his eyes away. There was a long pause, then trumpet notes sounded. The wagons began to move. Peacevoice Fullerman shouted, and the troops began their steady march. Lordkin Trebaty ambled behind them. He turned to wave to Secklers, who waved back. Secklers had decided to go with Sandry to the Aztlan trading posts.

The Feathersnake wagon train moved west, down the road through town and out the gates.

Burning Tower looked very serious.

"Worried about them?" Sandry asked.

"I'm more worried about us," Tower said. "I wish we were going with them."

"You still can. You can grab all your things and still catch up before they top the last ridge."

"And leave you here with Squirrel? Never." She tried to say it as a joke, but it came out serious. "But I do wish we were going home. To be married, to live at Road's End or Lordshills—I don't care." She looked east and shivered.

"Premonition?"

"I don't have premonitions," Tower said. "My father has less talent for magic than anyone I ever met, and I don't have a lot more. But I don't need premonitions to be scared. Squirrel's scared, and she has premonitions enough for all of us."

She turned away to see the boy Spotted Lizard staring after the wagon train. "I thought you would go with them," she said.

"It was kind of Green Stone to invite me," the boy said. "But maybe my people are hiding somewhere. They were coming here; I'll wait for them here."

"How will you live?"

"I have found work."

Sandry and Tower left the boy staring after the wagon train.

The next day it was their turn. Ern looked up and down the wagon train, asked if anyone needed more time, got no answer, and waved forward. The lead wagons moved out the east gate and up the road through the valley.

Regapisk rode alone in a roughly made chariot drawn by sturdy mares that looked more accustomed to pulling a plow than a chariot. They wouldn't be fast, Sandry thought. Faster than the mules that trailed behind Ruser's wagon, but not much, and the chariot was heavy—spokes too thick. It wouldn't be fast even with good horses. They didn't make good chariots in Crescent City, and they didn't seem to know much about using them. Something to remember.

Arshur drove the first of the jeweler's pair of wagons with Ruser sitting beside him looking relaxed and unworried. Ruser had hired two young men from neighbor families as drivers and helpers, and between them they seemed competent enough in the second wagon.

Burning Tower rode Spike. He was larger now, bigger than any horse, blazing white with a big spiral horn. The big one-horn seemed docile enough so long as Burning Tower was near, and he would follow their wagon if she sat at the tailgate, but if he couldn't see her, he could be difficult despite the stoutest harness and bit. He clearly disliked Clever Squirrel, but he also seemed afraid of her. Sandry wondered at the wisdom of bringing Spike, but Tower insisted.

The road led across the wide valley through green fields. There were crops and pastures on both sides of the road, all well watered by the river that cut through the valley but neglected during the siege of the terror birds. Farmers were cautiously returning to work. It would be harvest time soon enough, and the food was needed. The farmers waved at the wagon train and watched it go by.

Sandry wore his lightest armor. Speed would be more important than armor out here. His chariot was well equipped with weapons, four throwing spears, a thrusting spear, and a light shield, and most important, the bow case held his compound bow and forty arrows. Now that the Younglords were gone west there was not another bow like it. At least he had never seen a good bow outside Lordshills. The Feathersnake and Crescent City bows were simple affairs hewn from springy manzanita, the sort of thing a Lord's child might use for training. They were not difficult to draw, and the arrow wouldn't penetrate a shield. Or a terror bird.

Sandry's bow had taken a dozen years to construct, and cost more than his chariot. It was made of thin layers of wood and horn bound together by sinews and glues. Stringing it took nearly all his strength, but it could send an arrow much farther than a man could throw a spear. Chariotmaster Lords all had such bows, and they were one of the reasons the Lords had held Tep's Town against invaders and Lordkin revolts. An armored archer in a chariot was formidable, with enough speed to keep away from swordsmen and spearmen, and enough range to hold at risk as many lives as he had arrows. Add the disciplined Lordsmen soldiers and the wild Lordkin, and there had never been an army that could face the Lords of Lordshills.

But bows and armor were nearly useless against terror birds. They moved too fast for multiple shots, and they had few vulnerable spots among their thick hides and layers of feathers. It took the mass of a spear with its heavy bronze blade to stop the birds, and often that wasn't enough. The bows had stayed in their cases for the entire journey to Crescent City.

Now, with fewer birds, there might be other dangers. Sandry stood tall in the chariot. What was out there?

The river went roughly north. The road angled straight to the northeast, and as they went farther from the river, the green fields thinned out—fewer crops and more pastures, and no trees at all. Hillocks were covered with scrub brush.

They topped the first ridge. The ridge top was nearly bare, flinty soil with chaparral but little grass. From the top Sandry could see far ahead.

The road stretched northeast across a broad flatland. Near the road was mostly tall grass. Countless wagon trains had trampled out the sagebrush for a hundred paces and more to each side of the road. Grass grew there. With no wagon trains to graze it, the grass was tall and lush.

"Good foraging for the horses," Sandry said aloud. He clucked his horses into a trot and caught up with the Wagonmaster. "How long until camp?" he asked.

Ern looked up with a start, as if he'd been dozing. He stood on the wagon bed to look ahead, then looked to the sun to estimate the remaining daylight. "Another hour, Lord Sandry. There is a small pond and stream, with a corral if the birds didn't destroy it. There was a small village there, but the villagers are back in Crescent City hoping we'll find it's safe for them to go back."

"I think I'll ride ahead and have a look," Sandry said.

Burning Tower rode closer to him. "Premonitions?" she asked.

"No. It's the obvious place to camp," Sandry said, "so it's the obvious place for an ambush."

"Ambush by what?" Wagonmaster Ern asked. He concealed his smile, but some of the indulgent look came through. "And this close to the city?"

"The day before we reached Crescent City, there was a hilltop camping place," Sandry said. "And in it was the wreckage of a wagon train. Men able to summon birds were waiting for us to camp there. It never hurts to have a look."

"I'll come with you," Tower said.

Sandry nodded. "Ride with me. Let Spike follow," he said.

She frowned but dismounted and climbed into the chariot. Spike followed close behind. "I'm glad you like my company."

"I very much like your company. I also like having you on a fresh mount," he said.

"Oh." She stood close to him. Then closer.

He chuckled. "Keep that up and Spike won't be following us," he said.

"Squirrel says it's overrated."

"What is?"

"You know . . ."

"Oh. Maybe she's not doing it right."

"But I think she's wrong." She moved even closer to him. Spike snuffled his lips. Tower giggled. "Did you think it was overrated?"

"I wasn't in love."

"That's what Squirrely says—she wasn't in love and I am—so it will be different for me."

He bent over to kiss her. Spike snuffled again. Sandry found it wasn't easy keeping his eyes on the road and paying attention to Tower at the same time. Finally he straightened. "We don't have to wait, you know."

"How's that?"

"No one is going to make you harness a one-horn if we're married in Lordshills."

"Mother will."

"Your mother? Blazes, you told me yourself, she's kinless, she was long away from Tep's Town before she knew anything about one-horns!"

"Yes, but she learned, and she's very proud that she could harness hers the morning she married Father. And there's Father, I don't know what he thinks, but he's always said marriage is important. It's not just property, either."

"Well—but aren't you even a little impatient?"

She laughed. "As much as you—maybe more—but think, there's no one else here who can ride Spike or even harness him! What would we do with him?"

"Bugger Spike," Sandry said, but he mumbled it so that she wouldn't understand.

"I'm going to have a proper wedding," Burning Tower said. "Your people can add whatever you do—what do you do for weddings? Lordkin don't have marriages, and I know what Mother tells me about kinless, but I never heard about Lords."

"Mostly it's contracts and witnesses," Sandry said.

"Contracts. Witnesses. Well, fine, but I'm going to have Bison Woman and Coyote, and a great feast with all my friends, and one-horns. A proper wedding!"

Sandry sighed. "Yes, my love."

The campsite stood in a circle of broken hogans that ringed a small pond of clear water. Fences had been set between the hogans so that the entire pond was encircled. They drove into the village. "No one gathered here," Sandry said. "They just walked off. Except for the houses."

One wall had been opened on every house. *The village looks dead,* Sandry thought, *but it would be easy enough to revive. If the birds don't come back,* he added.

A small running stream trickled out of the pond and ran eastward. It grew visibly smaller as it ran through the dry rocky land, but the line of green marking its course continued a long way. The pond had been divided into pools—a small one, then a much larger one down where it flowed into the stream. Wagon trains could water the animals in the large pool without muddying the water in the smaller one upstream.

Tall grass grew all around the campsite. Sandry left Tower with Spike at the pond and drove in a big circle through the tall grass around the campsite, noting that the grass hadn't been broken down and that the only wheel tracks on the road were his own. There were some confused animal tracks, and one footprint that might have been made by a terror bird running along the dry stony road, but it might have been anything else. The ground wasn't soft enough to hold tracks.

No tracks, and nothing hiding in the weeds. It looked safe enough. When he was satisfied, he joined Tower at the spring.

"Nothing," he said.

"I thought I saw . . ."

"Yes?"

"I'm not sure. I thought I saw a terror bird, far out along the road, almost too far to see."

"Terror bird. What was it doing?"

"Nothing. It's gone now. It was so far away, Sandry, that I'm not sure I saw anything at all."

"And I thought I saw a bird track. But just one. We'll watch for it, then," Sandry said. He took a last look around the deserted village. "They left a lot of stuff behind. Secklers may like that."

Tower grinned. "Not our problem this time. How will he carry it all?"

He led Tower back to the wagon train.

"All clear," he told Ern. "And good grazing all around the spring."

Ern nodded. "I hardly expected bandits."

"If you expect them, you probably won't find them," Sandry said. "But Tower thought she saw a bird watching us."

"So did I," a voice said from behind him. Arshur. "Just when you started to ride out, it was ahead of you. Ran along the road in front of you. Just one," Arshur said. He grinned. "Lord Reg and I can handle one without bothering anyone else."

"I'm sure you can," Sandry said. "But if there's one, there may be more." He turned to Wagonmaster Ern. "When you get to the campsite, please let the women set up camp. I want all the men for an hour's spear practice. Arshur can teach them to use the atlatl."

Arshur nodded amused agreement. "Soon as I remember how they work. Been a while."

Chapter Two

The Road to Aztlan

The drills continued every evening, two hours in light and another hour in twilight. The men complained, but once they got started, Arshur was an eager teacher and no one wanted to challenge him. Sandry wondered what he would do without the giant acting as a Peacevoice, then shrugged. He had Arshur, and that was enough.

There was another reason to learn quickly. Whenever anyone looked far ahead on the road, they'd see the gaudy bird.

"Rooster," Clever Squirrel said. "And I'm sure it's just one."

"Sure. Why are you sure?" Sandry asked.

"Coyote thinks it's just one," Squirrel said.

"Ah. This is his territory, then?"

She shrugged. "Not really. He comes to me seldom. There are other gods here also. Many gods claim this territory, and there will be more as we come closer to the Island City of Aztlan. Sandry, there's so much power there! Each night I dream of it, a small island that burns bright with manna. Gold, and jewels, food and power, everything you could ever want." She grinned. "That's what I see in my dreams. When I wake up, we're still here." She indicated the rolling hills covered with sagebrush and grass stretching endlessly in all directions.

At dawn and dusk, they could see jagged shapes in the rising and setting sun, and sometimes they passed great buttes and mesas, but mostly the road led gently uphill through nearly level rocky ground covered with scrub and grass, dotted here and there with springs and small streams that never ran more than a league before vanishing into the rocks at the bottom of the stream bed.

Every evening Sandry held drills. Crescent City armor wasn't very good, but they did have stout shields. Armor was more useful against humans than birds anyway.

Sandry taught them to use shields and stabbing spears together, to stand close together and march with shields held in covering position and stabbing spears thrust forward, throwing spears held in place against the shield. Then they would halt and lean the thrusting spears against the shields as they prepared to use throwing spears.

Arshur taught them to use the atlatl, and Sandry took his place in the ranks for the lesson, motioning Younglord Whane to join him. The atlatl was new to them, but Sandry could see its value, something to teach the Lordsmen guards when he got back home. He was startled to see Regapisk take a place beside him as Arshur began his demonstration.

At first it was awkward to juggle thrusting spear, several throwing spears, shield, and atlatl without dropping one. They learned to stand the thrusting spear and spare throwing spears against their bodies, then bring the shield in to keep them from falling down. Then they would use both hands to load a throwing spear into the atlatl, and be ready to throw and reload.

Sandry analyzed each motion, having them do everything in slow motion until they had it right, then slowly speeding up the pace, making sure that everyone was keeping up. In three weeks they looked good, not as good as Lordsmen under a trained Peacevoice, but better than they'd ever expected to be, and proud of using a weapon of their ancestors, one that was new to this stranger officer from Lordshills.

And among the best was Regapisk. Reggy's overmuscled arms became supple enough for smooth throwing motions, and now they added strength.

"He's graceful," Burning Tower said as she watched Regapisk at atlatl practice. "I think he's as good with that as you are."

"Better," Sandry conceded, and wondered if Reggy could use a bow now that his arms were so strong. He could sure throw a spear. . . . "Not that either one of us will be doing a lot of atlatl throwing. Comes to a fight, we're more valuable mounted up. But yes, Reggy's pretty good with an atlatl. Come to that, so are you."

She grinned. "Surprised?"

"Yes, actually. I never knew any girls who could use weapons."

"Ever see anyone teach them how?"

"No."

She grinned again.

The road continued northeast, climbing steadily out of the Crescent City valley. Two weeks out, the climb became noticeably steeper, and a week later they reached a high plain. Everywhere along the road there were ruins, the remains of villages and campsites. In the Crescent City valley, the villages had been built of logs, but now they mostly saw rectangular houses of woven brush covered with mud. A few were stone, with flat roofs. Most had been damaged or destroyed, but nearly all had all four walls.

"Not alive, like hogans," Sandry observed.

Clever Squirrel agreed. "These are not the same people. But I don't know who they are."

Survivors who had crept back and lived in fear of the birds occupied a few of the village sites. They spoke little. None had seen any birds for weeks now, and they were slowly rebuilding, but warily, ready to run again, and no one had any food for sale.

As if in compensation, there was good hunting along the road. The grass had grown high enough that their animals could graze with little effort, and not far from the road were rabbits and quail. Springs were frequent. Day followed day.

It was the twenty-eighth day. They camped near a village of ruins where a dozen men and women struggled to survive. They needed tools, and Ern gave them some, although the villagers had nothing to trade. "On account," Ern said. "You can pay when we come back through."

That night at camp, Ern reminisced about previous travels on this road. "A village every two days, three days at most between them. Hot food. Fodder and forage all gathered and ready for sale, and good prices, because if anyone charged too much, another village would open close by. And it was all peaceful and orderly, patrolled by soldiers." He shook his head sadly.

Sandry said, "I hear a lot about the Emperor, but he sure hasn't been able to protect these people."

"We are not in his lands yet," Ern said. "Not in the lands he rules directly."

"When will that be?"

"Ten days," Ern said. "Understand, the Emperor takes tribute here, and in Crescent City as well. There we have our mayor, and our tribute to the Emperor is light, but tribute there will be. Here there is a king who pays tribute. The king's soldiers kept order." Ern shrugged. "Now we see no signs of soldiers or king."

"And none of the Emperor," Sandry reminded him.

"No, and I do not know why. Surely he has noticed that all trade to Crescent City has ceased."

"And that he's not getting any tribute," Clever Squirrel observed.

"Surely he knows that!" Sandry said. "Why hasn't the Emperor sent his army to look into the matter?"

Ern shrugged. "No one knows the ways of the Emperor. He does as he wills. Who can question him?"

On the thirty-fifth day, Ern pointed to the horizon. "That large rock, red like blood," he said.

Sandry frowned at the distant object, staring until his mind realized how far away it was. It was big, and flat on top.

"There will be a village and factory at its base. The Emperor's lands begin there," Ern said. "He will have soldiers there, and his people maintain the roads. From there to Aztlan, the wagons should be safe enough. I confess that I am relieved that we have not had to fight terror birds."

"They were all at Crescent City," one of the wagoneers said. "None left to devil us here."

"More than enough," another said. There were mutters of agreement.

"We're not there yet," Sandry said.

"Four days," Ern said. "Perhaps five."

Clever Squirrel and Fur Slipper sat together, their eyes closed. They sipped strong hemp tea, and rocked back and forth in time to a wordless song. The whole wagon camp fell silent as everyone watched. Presently Fur Slipper opened her eyes. When she did, Clever Squirrel awoke with a start. She stared around without understanding, then saw Burning Tower.

"Ugh. That was vivid," Squirrel said.

"Did you share a dream?" Tower asked.

"Yes. A strong one. Lord Sandry!" Squirrel called.

"Right here, Wise One."

"There are bandits near," Squirrel said. "I recognized them in my dream, but now I don't know who they are."

"The survivors of Dust Devil village," Fur Slipper said. "They had a caravan stop a day's travel ahead. Then the birds came."

"Refugees from the birds," Sandry said. "The birds attacked them and took their living, so they turned bandit?"

"Worse," Clever Squirrel said. "The birds attacked them, yes, and killed some, but then . . ." She shuddered.

"I can't tell. They may have joined with the birds," Fur Slipper said. "Their village remains. Perhaps they will invite us in for the night, but then they will summon the birds."

Sandry digested this information and frowned. "Doesn't every wagon train have a shaman?" he asked. "How would they expect to befool anyone?"

"Perhaps not," Fur Slipper said. "I would not have seen this vision."

"And I would not have known its meaning, I think," Squirrel said.

"Coyote's daughter," someone muttered.

"No, Coyote is far away," Squirrel said. "This is not his land. This land belongs to the birds. I think it has always belonged to their god. This was my vision. Coyote is not here."

"We heard coyotes last night," Sandry said. "And I saw three of them today. There are coyotes all around us."

Squirrel said, "But coyotes are not Coyote. Coyote lives in the spirit world, and here the spirit world belongs to other gods. Coyote has a place here, but it is not so grand."

"I don't think I understand," Sandry said.

Fur Slipper smiled thinly. "I would not expect you to understand," she said. "But know this: Clever Squirrel and I have shared a vision. There is danger beyond the next ridge at the stream crossing. There will be a village there, and they will smile and smile. And then the birds will come upon us."

"Did you see them do that? See them bring the birds?" Squirrel asked.

"Plainly."

"But I did not. In my dream, bandits crept on us at night to cut our throats in our sleep. There were no birds."

"So this vision wasn't shared," Burning Tower said. "Not really." But she said it in a whisper so that only Sandry heard her.

"Ah, but I saw birds, and people bringing them. Headdresses with feathers. Men carrying talismans." Fur Slipper signaled for her cup to be filled with water, and drank heartily. "Dreaming is thirsty work. Daughter of Coyote, I saw a little of that dream. You saw more than I. But I saw other wagon trains, and there were birds enough."

"Have you seen what will be?" Sandry demanded. "How can it be, since we certainly will not sleep in that village?"

"Dreams are but dreams," Fur Slipper said impatiently.

"So is it certain that Dust Devil has made common cause with the birds?" Ern demanded. "They have been at the crossing as long as I remember. They are said to have power over the wind. Perhaps the rain as well."

"They served good stew," one of the drivers said. "Lots of plants in it. Hate to miss that stew."

Fur Slipper asked, "Would you ignore our warning?"

"We know well enough how to deal with bandits on the Hemp Road," Burning Tower said impatiently. "How many will there be?"

"Squirrel, how sure are you of this vision?" Sandry asked. "How sure are you that these are enemies?"

Squirrel and Fur Slipper answered in chorus. "Very sure, Lord Sandry." They looked at each other and smiled thinly.

"The shamans are certain," Sandry said to Ern. "Why should we let them attack us? Better we attack them."

"No!" Ern was emphatic. "Although this is outside the lands of the Emperor, it is still within his protection. We may defend against bandits, but if we attack a village, the Emperor will know."

Sandry said nothing.

"And if the Emperor knows only that we have attacked his village, he will never listen to us. He will send his army, and we will all be killed."

"He has sent no army to defend the ruined villages behind us," Sandry said.

"I know," Ern said. "And I don't know why. But Lord Sandry, we dare not earn his wrath! His vengeance can be terrible! Those villages"—he waved toward the road they had come up—"are behind us. This is close to his border, and now we go into the heart of his domain! And he will know, Sandry. He knows everything. He will know if we defend ourselves—and he will know if we attack unprovoked."

"That makes it a bit harder," Sandry said. Burning Tower looked at him quickly. "Quite a lot harder, actually."

Chapter Three

The Dust Devils

"Will we fight men or birds?" Secklers eyed Sandry's heavy armor and noted the bow case and quiver in the chariot. Then he fingered his big Lordkin knife. "Looks like you expect men."

"I do," Sandry said. "But I don't know. The shaman said there would likely be birds as well."

"So the lady can lead them around," Secklers said. The big Lordkin waved at Burning Tower in her place on Spike. "I'll stay with the wagons. Lead them to me, Tower!"

When they left Tep's Town, Spike was a large gray kinless pony. Now he was a white stallion, larger than any horse Sandry had ever seen, and armed with a formidable spiral horn growing out of his forehead. When he was younger he had seemed attracted to Sandry's mares, but now he paid them no attention, to the enormous relief of the stallion Blaze. At one time Blaze had challenged Spike. Spike was much smaller then, and they were evenly matched until they were separated. Now Blaze avoided the one-horn, and Spike did not deign to notice a mere horse.

It was Sandry that Spike hated now.

"If there are birds," Sandry said. He shaded his eyes to peer up the long gentle slope to the Dust Devils village two thousand paces ahead. The road ran right through the village, and the soil here was dotted with big chunks of crumbling black rock. Vegetation was sparse except for the high grass in the cleared areas on both sides of the road. It would be bad country for horses to run in, worse for chariots. Birds would have far less trouble.

Next to the village was a large fenced corral, also full of tall fresh grass. Smoke from cook fires rose straight up to the sky in the windless afternoon. There was no breeze to waft smells of stews and soups toward them, but it wasn't hard to imagine them. A stream ran invitingly along the far edge of the village. The village gates were wide open. A perfect place to stay.

As they drew closer, Sandry saw that the corral and much of the village fence was made of living plants, big broad-leafed plants, leaves as long as a man and nearly as broad at their base growing from a central stalk. Each leaf had a sharp spike at the end.

"Maguey," Ern said.

"What's that?" Sandry demanded.

"They make mescal from it," Fur Slipper said. "A drink fit for the gods, full of manna and strong with fire. A cup of that will make anyone see visions."

"But there won't be any here," Ern said.

The wagon train moved onward toward the town. No one had come out to greet them.

"Why not?" Sandry asked.

"This is the first village outside the Emperor's land that has been given the right to grow the maguey," Ern said. "I remember when they earned that right." He paused. "Another name for the maguey is the fifty-year plant. It produces the pulque only when it blooms, and it blooms every fifty years. Those plants are no more than a dozen years old."

"How does it grow?" Mouse Warrior asked. "Will it grow anywhere?"

Ern shook his head. "I don't know. It grows only with permission of the Emperor. How they make it grow after he gives his permission is not anything I would know."

"Maybe we can find out," Whane said. "We have excellent gardeners in Lordshills, and the Emperor doesn't rule there. I'll see if I can find out."

"Maguey may not grow without a spell," Fur Slipper said. "Certainly the mescal will not be the same."

"Is there manna here?" Sandry asked.

Regapisk had been listening quietly. Now he shaded his eyes and squinted toward the village. "Not much," he said.

Sandry nodded indulgently and looked to Clever Squirrel. She shrugged. "As he says. No more than along other stretches of the road. Nothing special."

"The road narrows. There's no way around their village," Sandry said.

Ern agreed. "We would have to clear a path. The ground is too stony for wagons."

And for chariots as well, Sandry thought. "If we're going to fight, I want to do it here, with the sun behind us."

"We can't just attack them," Ern insisted.

Secklers grinned. "Let me go in and look."

"And if they kill you?"

"I'll sure take some with me," the big Lordkin said.

"I will come," Arshur said. "How can they kill me? I will be a king."

Secklers chuckled. "I'll be glad to have you with me, Majesty. Let's do it."

"You won't speak their language at all," Ern reminded him.

Secklers shrugged. "I can sure look around. And Arshur here knows some."

Arshur was already striding ahead of the wagon train. Secklers scrambled to keep up.

Sandry took the big compound bow out of its case and strung it with an effort. He motioned to Whane to join him in his chariot. "Drive," he said. "At a walk. Stay about fifty paces behind those two. If anything happens, we'll try to rescue them. Just get to them, let them get aboard, and run for the shield wall. Stay on the road; that's leg-breaker turf out there."

"Yes, sir. It looks pretty quiet in the village," Whane said.

A boy no older than Lurk came out of the gates and waved in welcome. An older man stood in the gateway. He shouted a greeting that Sandry didn't understand, but Arshur answered and laughed. A puff of wind whisked smells of hot stew toward them.

"Stop short of the gates," Sandry ordered.

They halted. Moments later, Regapisk plodded by in his heavy chariot pulled by two mules. In the wagon with him were Mouse Warrior and one of the Crescent City youths Regapisk and his partners had hired as drivers. Sandry took in a breath to shout at him, then thought better of it. "Whane, if they try to close those gates, I'll use my bow to stop them. If I can."

"I think you're worried about nothing," Whane said, "My Lord."

"We had a warning."

"Sir. Yes, sir. Two women babbled a lot after drinking hemp tea," Whane said.

"The shaman was right about the berries," Sandry said.

"Sir. Yes, sir. And maybe about the undead or whatever she called them. And she was good with the fires in the big battle. But we all felt something was wrong, we all saw what was happening. This is just dreams." Whane shrugged. "Sir, I dreamed we found a city of gold, and a lot of times I dream I can fly."

Regapisk was well inside the gates now. His driver began to chatter excitedly with the villagers. There were more villagers now, and they weren't just women and children and old men. There were young men too, some armed with knives or axes but none of them in armor, and they were all mixed in with the women and children. Sandry frowned. "They sure look glad to see us."

"Sir. Yes, sir."

"You can omit the sarcasm," Sandry said.

"Yes, Lord Sandry. But they do look glad to see us. If they're trying to fool us, they've done a good job on me."

A pretty girl brought Arshur a bowl of soup. He drank

heartily and offered it back to her. She blushed and drank more daintily. Another girl gave Regapisk a flask. Reggy drank deeply and smiled at her.

"And me too," Sandry said finally. "Let's go back and get the others."

They camped in the corral area. Sandry inspected the fence: a sturdy palisade of wood between stone pillars, and outside that a thicker fence of the spiky plant Ern called maguey. Each of the plants had more than a dozen leaves that tapered in thickness from as wide as a man's forearm at the base down to a finger-length hard thorn at the tip. It wasn't hard to cut the plant, but nothing large could come through that fence until a passageway had been cut.

For a moment he had visions of being trapped in there and burned the way he'd trapped the birds, but the ground beneath them was hard dirt cleared of the rocks. Nothing to burn there. Bales of fodder had been piled in one corner of the corral, and fountains poured water into basins, one large enough for animals to drink from.

"This is how I remember the Dust Devil village," Ern said.

"Pleasant," Sandry said. "Do you trust them?"

"Why should we not?" Ern asked.

"The shamans said—"

"I heard them," Ern said. "And I always listen to the advice of our shamans, just as I listen to you. But I ask again, why should we not trust them? You see their young men, some armed, some not. Mouse Warrior has stood on the wagontops and searched and sees nothing. What is there to fear?"

Clever Squirrel had come up behind them. "I wish I knew," she said. "But I agree, all seems well."

"Do you often have false dreams of warning?" Sandry demanded.

"Seldom, and never shared with another. Such a thing would have to be *sent*."

"We'll keep watch," Sandry said. "The men will hate it but we'll do it, anyway."

Supper was excellent. Visitors and villagers ate from the same stew pots and drank from the same pitchers. The stew was goat meat, strongly flavored, and a welcome relief to terror bird jerky. Afterward many of the village men joined them to sip tea and talk. Sandry understood none of the local languages but was surprised to see that Regapisk was conversing with the locals.

"You speak Aztlan, cousin?" Sandry asked.

"I do." Reggy paused. "I learned from the wizard on the salt farm. I've always been good with languages."

Sandry nodded, remembering. "So what are they saying?"

"We're the first wagon train from the south in a long time," Regapisk said. "Several have gone south through here, but none have come back for nearly a year, and that's unusual. When we told them about the birds, they seemed surprised."

"Surprised. Of course they'd say that," Sandry said.

"Yeah, but you know, Sandry, I think they really were surprised. Anyway, they're glad to see us because there's been nobody to trade with, and they're afraid they'll get behind on their tribute payments. I gather that's not a good position to be in."

"But everybody south of us will be behind," Sandry said.

"Yep."

"Don't these people know that not two days south of us the villages are all burned out?"

Regapisk frowned, and turned to one of the village headmen. They talked for a while. Then Reggy said, "Nah, they didn't know. Their place is here, so here they stay. They paid their taxes, the Office sends rain, and they waited for caravans to come through. Not their job to worry about why they don't come."

At dusk Mouse Warrior mounted the wagontop to stare into the sunset. He saw nothing, and the night was peaceful. At dawn when he awoke, he shouted. "The bird!"

"Same one?" Sandry asked.

"Think so."

They had seen the rooster every day since they set out. One huge bird spreading inadequate wings, always at a distance, and always on the road ahead of them.

Chapter Four

The Endless Road

Fifty days out from Crescent City, Sandry began to keep a journal.

We are climbing steadily now, toward a rim above us that runs across the world as far as I can see in either direction. We should reach the top by noon tomorrow.

Burning Tower and I had a quarrel. It was about nothing, but I'll have to be careful for a while. We both want to get married! And soon.

Another imperial post today. We are very welcome, and everyone was astonished to hear that birds are attacking wagon trains to the south and west. This post has no clerks and no tax collectors, and only five soldiers. They serve a year here before being allowed to go back to the city, and I don't know what they are here for. I don't think they know, unless it's a punishment detail. They're all bored. One wanted to come with us to tell the next post about birds attacking wagons, but his officer wouldn't let him. They asked us to tell the story up the line, and we will.

I'm not impressed by the Emperor's soldiers. Crude, simple bows, as I expected. No concept of chariot warfare. Good spears and decent shields, but not much discipline even when turned out on parade when they're supposed to be impressing us. But Ern says they have magic weapons, and all the manna they could want, and the Emperor's army will have wizards.

I've talked to their officers, or Ern and Reggy have anyway, and none of them has ever been in a battle. They don't have to be. Everyone is afraid of them. Maybe with good reason, but I haven't seen any reasons.

I'm going to ask Reggy to teach me Aztlan. Maybe Squirrel can help. Surely a wagon train shaman has spells to help learn languages?

Fifty-six days since Crescent City. Burning Tower and I made up after our quarrel. I don't know what's worse, fighting with her or having to wait until we're married. That cursed one-horn of hers wants to fight me.

We have reached the top of the rim. The land east of us seems flat now, with a few jagged rocks rising out of the plains.

As usual we saw that bird out to the east today. We

haven't seen any bandits since we crossed into the Emperor's lands—not that we saw many before that. We're at a larger post, bigger village, more civilians. Better buildings too. Important-looking civilians—tax collectors and clerks, I'd guess. Maybe a score of soldiers and two officers. The barracks area looks comfortable, but there's an air about the place, temporary but fixed up the way troops do when they have to be there for a while.

No one had heard about the birds attacking wagon trains. The officer here said he'd let everyone know up the line. I don't know how he will do that. No one knows, but Ern tells us they can send messages to the Emperor, fast, if they really want to. They don't do that much. It's as if they're afraid to get his attention, and I guess I can understand that. But the officer here thought it might be important. He'll tell his superiors up the line, and they'll tell theirs, and then there are some officials who supervise the soldiers, and they'll tell someone at the capital, and they'll tell their bosses, and eventually someone will tell the Emperor. I think that's how it works.

I am studying the Aztlan language. Reggy is a good teacher, and Squirrel does have some spells that help me learn while I am asleep.

I'd never have thought Reggy would be a good teacher, but he is. He's pretty good with that atlatl thing too. Better than me, but I have my bow. Reggy can string my bow now, but when he tried to shoot a prairie dog, he missed by a long way. I have to say I like him better now than I did back home. Maybe he learned something from his experience. But he can never go back.

The village has a maguey factory. There are hundreds of the maguey plants. Some have been used to make the pulque. When a plant is about to bloom, it sends up a stalk from the center. Before it can flower, they cut the stalk out, and the center of the plant fills with the sap they call pulque. They suck that out and spit it into jars, and I don't know what they do after that, but it turns into mescal. They gave us some last night. Fur Slipper is right: anyone would see visions after drinking that.

After the plant stops producing pulque they cut all its leaves off and pound on them, and that makes fibers a lot like hemp. They weave those into rope and cloth, but they wouldn't let us see how they do that. Burning Tower says one of her uncles is a rope-walker and makes rope from hemp, but she won't tell me much about how he does it. I don't think she knows. Ropemaking is a big secret in Tep's Town, and Tower's family are all Tep's Town kinless. Maybe it's a secret everywhere.

Lurk has been collecting little maguey plants. He had some hidden in the wagon. I made him throw them out. We don't need the Emperor getting mad at us over some plants! If we need to learn how to grow maguey, we can send a wagon train to the Dust Devil village.

Squirrel and Fur Slipper had that vision of theirs again, stronger this time, but now it's about some other village up ahead of us. They're sure it's a warning, but I'm not. I was all ready to start a fight at Dust Devil! And that would really have been bad. It would be worse now that we're in the Emperor's lands!

Why are they having these visions? And they both have them. They're confused, but they all point to the same village—Dust Devil before, then another we've passed. Nothing happened at either place. Now there's another one ahead. I feel like a fool getting the men in armor and standing watch every night, but those women are so sure! And I know magic works, sometimes.

Sixty-first day since leaving Crescent City. No trouble at that last village. I don't trust my shamans anymore. Just outside the village, we found a stone head taller than any of us. It looks west, back toward Crescent City. Its face is carved in lines of terror. Clever Squirrel sat before it while we made camp. She says she talked to it. She tells a wild tale. Sometimes I think Clever Squirrel is testing my gullibility.

Sixty-second day. We've reached another of the Emperor's posts. This is a small one, four men, a little squared-off house, a little round chamber with a fire pit. Their speech is hard to understand, but I'm learning. They're all very glad to see us. The old captain tells us that Clever Squirrel's stone man was next to the fort when he first came, thirty-one years ago. He lives here, and one of the troopers is his son. He says it's a good life, a little lonesome lately because there haven't been any wagons from the south. When I told him why, he was shocked, so I guess that last village didn't pass the word up the line, or not faster than a wagon can travel anyway. He said the Emperor would do something about it. I told him I already did something—I killed the cursed birds.

There's colored sand available. The imperial troopers will sell charged talismans, prices cheap compared to what we'd have to pay in Condigeo or Crescent City. Tomorrow Squirrel will talk to her mother.

Chapter Five

Sand Paintings

Clever Squirrel had assembled her working materials the previous evening. At dawn she painted her mother's portrait by drizzling various shades of sand from her fist. When the painting was done, it had a cartoonish look.

She waited. Regapisk pestered her until she sent him to find more black sand. Warriors and traders of three civilizations came to watch, grew bored, and went away.

Regapisk came back. Squirrel used black sand to outline her mother's face. From time to time, she added detail to wrinkles around the eyelids or the curve of a lip or a fall of black hair.

Burning Tower brought her corn bread. "Still nothing?"

"Do you imagine you see motion?" Squirrel's tone was acidic.

"It's a very good painting of her," Tower said.

"Thank you. I was taught to paint the essence and leave it at that, but how can one not fiddle? *Mother!*"

The sand stirred in a fitful breeze.

The lookout post was on the tallest of a cluster of rocks. The kneeling guard was watching Squirrel's painting, not the world outside. Secklers squatted, waiting with uncharacteristic patience.

Squirrel muttered, "Call at dawn, we said. I haven't lost track of the days; I checked the stars last night. Today is Coyote's name day. . . . Hello, Sandry. Have some bread."

"Thank you. I grew impatient."

"I'm ready to kick this painting apart. Wait—did you see—*Mother!*"

Twisted Cloud's painting twisted in a delighted smile. A voice in the wind said, or perhaps only suggested, "Daughter! You still live!"

"I was worried too. Where have you been?"

"It's only just past dawn. I can't paint in the dark," Twisted Cloud's image said. The voice was distant but clear.

"It's well past dawn!"

"Is it? Wait—now I think I understand. 'The east sinks to reveal the sun,' my father Hickamore used to say. He taught that the world is a rolling ball. I'm west of you. The world's shadow—"

"Oh. That explains—*Yes,* Tower. Mother, Lord Sandry of Tep's Town has asked Burning Tower to wed. She needs to ask her parents."

"Excellent news! Hello, Tower!"

"Can you see me?"

"I'll pour more sand. Tell her I'm at Road's End, but Willow and Whandall are at home, at New Castle. I will go and tell them. Daughter, we speak again in a moon or so, don't we? On your birthday?"

"Yes."

"I'll visit them then. What other news? How goes your voyage?"

"Green Stone should be arriving in Condigeo even now," Clever Squirrel said.

"With great wealth! New trade!" Tower shouted.

"And Burning Tower reminds me that we have discovered new items to trade. There is wealth on the Golden Road."

"Whandall Feathersnake will be pleased. And the birds? But why are you not with Green Stone?"

The images rippled.

"The manna is falling," Squirrel said. "Mother, we pursue the source of the birds, but we've cleared the Hemp Road for at least this next year. We've seen two moons of nothing much happening, and one to go before we reach Sunfall Crater.

"That is a place of high manna, and we can talk as long as we like there."

"And fight a god," Sandry said.

Squirrel waved him away. The portraits were losing animation; they looked like sand. "Mother, we will magic a wagonload of old talismans at Sunfall and come home rich. We've seen more of desert than we care for. There's water enough, most days, and forage for the bison. We eat mostly prairie dogs. Every so often a terror bird turns up, and then the Crescent City soldiers get some practice and we get soup. I've gotten good at finding mustard greens and such."

"Oh, daughter, you're seeing territory I never will!"

"Well, yes. Huge piles of sand shaped like crescent moons. Great squared-off mountains of red rock. A rim that stretches across half the world. We climbed it. Wonderful plants, like huge pincushions trying to become trees. The maguey plant that may be more useful than hemp. Things to remember the rest of my life. Oh, and yesterday was interesting—"

"*There* you are, Tower. Hello, dear! Is Sandry with you? Let me paint him as he was on the boat."

"Hail, Twisted Cloud! Not green, please!"

"He says, 'Hail, Twisted Cloud!' and requests that you don't turn him green." Squirrel grinned. "And yesterday, Mother, we found a stone man wading neck deep through the earth. We saw only the head and the churned wake from his passage. I talked to him. He's running away from two disasters, running very slowly. Fire falling from the sky almost got him, he says, but that had to be thousands of years ago. He's running away from a god's rage to come. Given who he is, it might fall any time in the next ten thousand years."

"Do you know what god?"

"No. Only that the stone man fears him."

"With good reason," Sandry muttered, but no one was listening.

Another moon passed.

Chapter Six

Sunfall

Sandry wrote:

Eighty-four days since we left Crescent City. The days are growing shorter now, and have for a moon, but day is longer than night. Clever Squirrel says day and night will be equal soon, and the day after that will be her birthday. I don't know if it's really her birthday. It's all mixed in with Coyote.

Ern says we near the end of our journey, and Fur Slipper and Clever Squirrel are beside themselves. They feel the manna.

I know the manna grows stronger, because Spike is grown awesomely large and Burning Tower spends more and more time with him. She says she has to, to keep him calm, but I am afraid. I think she loves him as much as she loves me, and soon enough she's going to have to choose one of us. I think she will choose me! But as the manna grows stronger, her bond with that cursed animal grows as well.

And I—but no, others will read this account. I do not like this.

About midmorning, Fur Slipper pointed with the prow of her nose, right of their course and dead east. "There!" She waved her arm to catch Ern's attention on the lead wagon. The Crescent City wagons began to turn.

Sandry rode up in his chariot. "I don't see anything," he said. "Just more desert. The ground rises a little?"

"Yes, but follow the road around. Expect guards."

"I see a tower. There's someone in it."

"There would be," Fur Slipper said. "I'm blinded. I see a line of light glowing in a sea of nothing."

Off in the distance, several terror birds watched them. One was the rooster they'd come to know. The birds didn't approach, but they watched.

"That's more than we have ever seen on this road," Sandry said. "Be ready, all!"

"This close to the Fallen Star? Birds will never attack there," Ern said.

They came to a gentle rise of ground gradually curving off to their right. The road the caravan had followed since Crescent City continued around it. A league of following the curve of the road revealed that the tower stood seven or eight manheights, with an armored man on the platform at its top. A little farther and they could see over the rim of the crater.

There were buildings below the tower: blocky squared-off structures, housing for more than a hundred people, Sandry thought, set down into the pit itself.

This must be the Emperor's main trading post. The main gate and the buildings it served were just below the crest. There was a wall of logs and maguey plants around the post, but the plants were not thickly planted, and the wall in places was lower than a man's height. This post did not depend on walls for defense.

Above the walled town, and around the part of the crater rim that Sandry could see, there were odd statues, man-high and higher, of grotesque heads stacked one on another. They were made of bright colored—wood? No, it was stone, though it had the texture of wood. The eyes of these monsters were jewels, and they glowed brightly. The statues were set about a hundred paces apart, ringing the trading post, then extending along the crater rim in both directions.

"Protection stones," Ern said. "You would not wish to pass between those without permission!"

The ground was rocky and dangerous, but Regapisk drove his chariot off the road and over to one of the stones, carefully staying outside the ring they formed. "Ugly!" he shouted.

The road led to a gateway wide enough for wagons bigger than these, and the big double gates stood open. A pair of the ugly protection stone statues faced each other across the gateway opening, multiple carved faces with bulging eyes and protruding tongues staring at each other. *And at us?* Sandry wondered. The eyes seemed to follow them as they approached. An illusion?

Sandry watched a handful of men assembling: a force of twenty, four groups of four men, and another group of four officers.

They wore bright armor and carried bows. The armor was thin plates of polished bronze over leather. The bows were simple wooden bows and probably couldn't penetrate that armor. Sandry smiled to himself. His bow would outrange those things by double, perhaps more, and even at long range his arrows would penetrate that feeble armor. With a chariot and fast horses, he could fight all twenty and win. Fifty Lords with chariots and a thousand Lordsmen and Lordkin could defeat any number of such men.

If this was the best of the Emperor's army, why would anyone fear the Emperor?

They followed the road uphill. On the flat, the road continued, but greatly changed. Thenceforth it ran straight as a spear's flight at a constant width of about nine paces, and a line of logs ran right up the middle.

Fur Slipper shouted, and all heads turned. "Nothing must profane the High Road! Set foot on it only at the invitation of the Emperor! Beasts are not to touch the High Road at all!"

They followed the—low road?—up the gentle rise. Ahead were the main gates into the town itself. There was no more to be seen until they neared the top of the crest.

Then the crater seemed to appear magically out of the desert. It was a bowl hundreds of paces across, tens of manheights deep. It was all rubble, barren of life. To Sandry it looked weird beyond understanding . . .

"A mountain fell out of the sky." Clever Squirrel whispered in his ear. "It smashed this hollow into the earth. See here, where rock melted and splashed, where a fiery wind lifted the surface and peeled it back. Pristine magic, never drained by the world's gods or wizards. Can you feel the power? It's making me drunk!"

Burning Tower said, "I don't feel a thing."

Sandry shook his head.

Regapisk and Arshur rode up. Reggy shielded his eyes from the crater. "It's bright!" he shouted.

Arshur laughed.

"You can see the manna?" Clever Squirrel asked.

"Sure, can't you?" He cupped his hands around his face to shade his eyes, then peeped out to examine the crater. "There," he said. He pointed to discolored rocks near the crater floor. "That's a really bright spot."

Arshur laughed again.

"You don't believe him?" Sandry asked.

Arshur shrugged. "Lord Reg is learning the craft of Tras Preetror, and learning it well," the giant said. "Since I have known him, he's seen a lot of things I didn't."

Regapisk looked hurt.

"He's right about that spot," Clever Squirrel said. "I don't see it as brighter than the rest, but I can feel the manna flowing."

And Reggy probably saw where you were looking, Sandry thought.

Ern brought his wagons to a halt. The twenty bowmen blocking their path stepped to left and right. Other men and women waited beyond. Sandry glimpsed a formal garden of amazing extent, but Clever Squirrel exclaimed at sight of a blocky house. "They've got sweatbaths!"

The governor was a woman named Hazel Sky. Her dress was awkward and beautiful, with a huge and spiky headdress. "Fox," Squirrel whispered, though the woman didn't look much like a fox to Sandry. But the burly man next to her was unmistakable in his costume. "Terror bird," said Squirrel.

Hazel Sky squinted, then smiled thinly. "Greetings, Ern of Crescent City. We have met before. It has been too long since your city brought the Emperor his due."

"The way was closed, Great Mistress. Our city was besieged and was nearly destroyed. Has it not been long since any wagons came from the west?"

"It has. We have noted this, but my Master has sent no instructions." She shrugged. "So we have done nothing."

"Did you tell Emperor no wagons long time?" Sandry asked.

Hazel Sky frowned. The Terror Bird man hid a smile.

"Great Mistress, this is Lord Sandry, of Lordshills," Ern said. "He comes from lands far to the west of Crescent City, lands that lie on the Great Western Sea. He begs your pardon. He does not know the proper forms of address."

"Let him learn them," Terror Bird said. "One does not slight a Great Mistress!"

Sandry bowed.

Hazel Sky nodded in acknowledgment. "I see stallions, and the great one-horn. It has been long since a one-horn was brought to Aztlan! We thank you. And the stallion is splendid. What other gifts have you brought for the Emperor?"

"We have the customary gold, Great Mistress," Ern said. "And we beg the privilege of provisions, and the customary gifts of manna."

She nodded. "The Supreme One will be greatly pleased with gifts such as those," she said, indicating Blaze and Spike with a wave. "Have you counted out the customary tribute?"

"Yes, Great Mistress."

She smiled. "Then nothing else is needed. Welcome to the place of the Fallen Sun! In the name of the Supreme One, I bid you welcome."

The Great Mistress and the other costumed priests retired. Lesser officials were sent to welcome them. Ern explained his caravan's needs. Fodder was brought. The wagons were led down a steep road into the crater itself. No water supply was to be seen, but when Regapisk asked about that, there was general laughter.

The women made it clear that they wanted to bathe. "At once, Mistress," a servant girl said. She was no younger than Burning Tower, but she knelt to her. "At once. I will go to heat the stones myself."

"Best welcome I ever had," Ern said.

Burning Tower looked to Sandry, with both question and fear. Sandry nodded. "Not the time to talk about it," he said quietly. She looked unhappy but nodded agreement.

There was plenty of room for visitors. Only about forty people were in the fort.

They spoke the Crescent City tongue with a raspy accent. Twenty were warriors armed with spears or simple bows, led by a Captain Sareg. Six were officials of the Office of the Emperor's Gifts.

The chief of these was called Regly. Tax man, Sandry thought. Toronexti.

Ern laid out a blanket and covered it with goods. There was some gold, but there were other items, manufactured in Crescent City. Fruits and melons preserved by Fur Slipper's spells. Pots and dishes. Sandry frowned. Except for the gold, little of this would have brought a decent price in Peacegiven Square, and most would have been worthless in Condigeo. Aztlan was rich! Why did they want crude goods?

Regly examined the items. "Acceptable. When will you deliver the stallion and one-horn?"

"Soon," Ern said. "All our beasts are needed to draw the wagons and chariots into the pit, and I think you have no one here who can harness the one-horn."

"That may be true," Regly admitted. "Good. Your gifts are acceptable."

Ern explained after Regly left. "There is no trade with the Emperor. We bring gifts, and the Emperor gives gifts in return. His gift is the privilege of using the crater.

"Over there are traders, with goods." He pointed to a line of stands, like any market. "They buy and sell. There will be stonewood, every kind of stonewood, carved and crude, charged and depleted. There will be jewelry talismans of turquoise and silver. And rain arrows, to make the trip back much faster. With rain arrows, we do not have to follow the streams."

"Are the arrows expensive?"

"Not very. But each is accounted for, and its use is taxed, and all of that takes time."

Nine officials and six clerks belonged to the Office of Rain.

Rain was a good deal of the post's business. Hundreds of rain arrows with turquoise heads were stored, waiting to be used here or carried away to other lands. The luxuriant vegetable garden was testimony to their effectiveness. Rain arrows, charged in the crater, traveled all over the Empire. Each one was accounted for by documents meticulously kept by the clerks.

The Office of Rain was a circular sunken room, a *kiva,* inside a blocky building that wasn't much bigger. The head of the Office of Rain was Thundercloud, a burly, powerful man in middle age—he who had been dressed as an archetypal terror bird. He looked more comfortable in black robes.

Ern said to him, "We are ready for water now, Lesser Master."

Thundercloud stood and summoned a clerk, who produced a document. The clerk asked questions, got answers from Ern, and wrote. Then he asked more and wrote more.

It took most of an hour. Finally the clerk was satisfied.

Thundercloud selected an ornate arrow tipped with turquoise. He brought that to the clerk, who recorded something on the document. Thundercloud took his seal cylinder from his wrist and rolled it in fresh clay dripped at the bottom of the document. The clerk did the same.

"One gold bit," the clerk said.

Ern produced the gold, not much larger than a speck. The clerk noted that on the document, and dropped the gold bit down through a slot on his desk. "All in order," the clerk said.

Thundercloud took a bow from the wall and strung it with an effort. Sandry suppressed a grin. It was only a simple bow, and it couldn't be that difficult. But it was ornately carved.

Thundercloud took the bow and the rain arrow outside. "I will do this myself," he told Ern.

"We are honored," Ern said. Thundercloud nodded agreement.

He nocked the arrow and sent it upward, almost straight up, chanting as it rose. Tiny sparkles of lightning followed it up. It rose until it was nearly out of sight, then fell, still trailing brilliant sparks, to just short of where Ern had placed his wagons.

Upslope from the wagons, it began to rain. A junior clerk rushed down the hill to retrieve the arrow. Soggy and dripping now, he brought it back to the first clerk, who examined it and added notations to the document. They went back inside out of the rain.

"We recharge arrows using these." Thundercloud showed them a line of thumb-size frames of silver. "I won't demonstrate. I don't want to get wet."

Chapter Seven

The Wizard's Bathhouse

There was a line of sweatbaths not far from the Office of Rain, but the servant girl led Burning Tower, Fur Slipper, and Clever Squirrel past those to a smaller area fenced with maguey. Inside the enclosure was a rose garden. Hummingbirds were everywhere. One frantically tried to drive the others away, but there were far too many roses for one bird to defend.

Like the other baths, this one was placed at the crater's rim. Mats placed outside, for relaxing after the sweatbath, would have a wonderful view. The building was made of petrified logs aglitter with garnet and other semiprecious stones.

Hazel Sky, no longer in robes of office but dressed in a

simple gown, joined them. Burning Tower was afraid to speak to her, but Fur Slipper greeted her by name and introduced them to her.

There was no sign of the imperious Great Mistress. Now she was friendly.

"Welcome," she said. "We have many baths here at Sunfall, but this one is reserved for the enlightened and their guests."

Burning Tower frowned, and Clever Squirrel suppressed a laugh. "My sister is not favored," Squirrel said. "But she is certainly my guest."

Clever Squirrel examined the stonewood walls and looked questioningly at Hazel Sky.

Hazel nodded agreement. "All depleted," she said. "A place where those burdened with magical talent can relax."

Burning Tower looked puzzled. Fur Slipper explained, "There's no manna left in these logs. This building would make a dandy insulator if you wanted to avoid a curse. It's also a shield from visions. Hazel, did you use the magic in the logs to heat the thing? Easier than getting wood, until it ran out."

"Likely," Hazel Sky said. "But that was long before I came."

The way inside led to a smaller room where they removed their clothes and hung them on pegs. They turned left to another small room, right to yet another, then left into the bathhouse itself. Each room had a stonewood door.

Clever Squirrel smiled at Burning Tower's look of puzzlement. "As Hazel said. This is a place of refuge from magic. Manna flows in straight lines. By turning those corners, we have escaped all the cares of the world." Squirrel lay on a bench and sighed. "I think I have never been to a place like this," she said. "Not even Tep's Town before Yangin-Atep went mythical was so devoid of manna. So *clean*."

"You were there when the god was . . ." Hazel searched for a word. "Retired?"

"No."

Hazel took another bench and sprawled out contented. "Your friend has no talent at all?" she asked.

"None," Tower said. She thought it would be impolite to add that her family had never needed any. "I saw Morth of Atlantis after he sent the god mythical, but I wasn't there when it happened. No one was, except Morth and my father."

Heat filled the room. The source was hot rocks along one wall, and a small brazier held a wood fire far too small to have heated all the rocks. Tower moved around restlessly as the talented ones—*enlightened,* she thought, and sniffed—relaxed on benches with contented smiles.

The brazier sat in a small fireplace. The stone floor had no soot or any other indication that a fire had ever burned there. Tower could feel a mild breeze going up the chimney, which was just big enough that she could have scrambled up it. No light came down it.

Clever Squirrel was watching her with a lazy grin.

"All right," Tower said. "That fire isn't big enough to heat this place! And those stones are hot!"

"Of course they're hot," Hazel Sky said. "The servants heat them and bring them in for us. The brazier is for scents and powders, not heat." Hazel laughed. "Do you think we use fire to heat rocks here? With wood so precious and manna so cheap?"

"Ah," Clever Squirrel said. "So you use magic to heat the stones."

"Of course. The Supreme One has commanded that guests be treated properly. How could we heat stones enough for all your wagon train to enjoy a bath if we did not use manna? It would take everyone here working full time to bring in enough wood!"

There were eight sweat lodges heated, but to Sandry the sweatbath sounded like an exercise in discomfort. He gave orders that the bath kettles be heated at the wagon train. That too would be done with magically heated stones. Wood was precious.

Then he turned to Ern with a frown. "There are no walls here. No protection for the wagons," Sandry said.

Ern shrugged. "Nor need."

"We saw birds not a league from here," Sandry reminded him. "We saw the rooster that has tracked us since Crescent City. Why is there no need to protect ourselves from the birds?"

Ern laughed. "We are in the Emperor's stronghold! The priesthood is here, in a place of great manna! Protection stones ring the crater and this town as well. This is the safest place I know, safe against any enemy." He paused. "Any enemy save the Emperor, and there's nothing we could do if he decided to rob us."

Quintana would say that we could sell our lives at a price to teach him to leave others alone, Sandry thought. "We saw half a dozen birds, more than we have seen for days," Sandry said. "How long would it take for them to kill us in our beds? Circle the wagons and put up the barriers."

Ern glanced at him nervously. "Would you insult our hosts and their protection?"

"If we needed the protection of those soldiers, we'd be in real trouble," Sandry said.

"The Emperor's might rests on far stronger shoulders than those soldiers'." Ern shrugged. "But as you will. I confess I remain troubled by the visions of our enlightened ones. But Sandry, if they ask why we camp behind barriers, I will say it is your outlandish customs, and I have no choice because your backers own this wagon train!"

Sandry shrugged and signaled to Mouse Warrior. "Circle the wagons."

The diminutive fighter grinned.

"You expected this?" Sandry asked.

Mouse Warrior grinned again. "I have won a bet with the Lordkin."

Sweatbaths didn't appeal to Sandry; he wanted a bath.

A water bath required hot stones, and many had been needed for the sweatbaths. While he waited for more stones to be heated, Sandry walked the garden with a few of the soldiers who tended it. He saw edible plants, beans and corn, fruits and nuts. There were great gaudy flowers and plants he didn't recognize.

One entire garden patch was devoted to maguey, with plants grouped by age. Some were blooming. Some had tried to bloom and now had a large hollow where the central stalk had been. Those were filling with pulque.

They pointed out the garden where the Great Mistress entertained her guests. Sandry saw roses. Hummingbirds swarmed, zealously guarding their territories among the blossoms.

Another garden held fruit trees, including some Sandry had never seen before. He tried new fruits. The center of the garden was a pond; he washed his face there, nosed by big gaudy fish.

Then Sandry persuaded Captain Sareg to escort him up into the tower.

The view was awesome.

The sun was setting behind a glory of orange clouds. North, a scattering of flightless terror birds dipped in and out of flying cloud shadows. One—gaudier than the others, ablaze with rainbow colors when the sunlight struck it, the bird they'd been calling the rooster—gave over displaying his plumage and burst into speed, chasing something small until it ran afoul of one of the hens.

East ran the Emperor's Road, broad and amazingly straight, never deviating as it crossed hills and dips.

South, the crater itself was an incredible artifact, a bowl big enough to feed all the gods who had ever lived. Far enough below to exercise Sandry's fear of heights were the cook fire for dinner and the plumes of steam from the sweatbaths.

CHAPTER EIGHT

FEAST

The banquet tables were large slabs of wood held up by stonewood trestles. A feast was laid out, and the room was filled, nearly everyone from the imperial offices and the wagon trains. Servant girls rushed about.

Burning Tower had ceased noticing the rich smell of men who had not bathed in many moons, but she noticed its absence at dinner. She herself felt clean and fresh. There was only water to drink, but a wonderful variety of food. It was as if the company grew drunk on the feast, and on fresh viewpoints.

Sandry was dressed in silk. He had found someone to smooth the wrinkles, and Tower thought him the handsomest man in the room. He stood tall and spoke freely. His Aztlan wasn't polished, but he didn't seem to care. Polite but proud, and she was proud of him.

The soldiers laughed at Sandry's caution in setting up the wagon fortress, but they didn't seem offended. None had ever seen the sea. They kept after Sandry to tell them more of the Great Ocean, and waves, and mer people.

Whatever story Sandry told, Arshur had another. Arshur was a natural storyteller, though imperial soldiers twitched at his tales of banditry.

"You have been many places," Captain Sareg said. "So, Arshur the Wanderer, why have you come here?"

"I have come to be king. I am destined to be king," Arshur said simply.

The room grew quiet. Captain Sareg beamed. "Destined to be king! This is wonderful news. I will tell the Emperor before I sleep tonight," he said.

Clever Squirrel asked, "How?"

"We have our ways," the captain said.

Sandry watched all this without understanding. It was clear that they didn't see Arshur as a threat. Instead, they believed him. . . .

Fur Slipper developed an interest in Thundercloud. The burly rainmaker told her, "We folk worship a number of gods. My mother named me for a storm, and I followed my name to my fate. But I am a priest of Left-Handed Hummingbird in addition to heading the Office of Rain."

Ern said, "We could have used your help at Crescent City," a phrasing Sandry considered nicely diplomatic.

"Dry, was it?"

"No, I meant your terror birds have blocked off all trade," Ern said, "for over a year, until Sandry and his warriors came to rescue us. You could have driven away the birds."

Captain Sareg said, "That explains why all the wagons stopped coming. The Office of Gifts has been most puzzled. We're most glad you've arrived."

"So you will tell the Emperor that the birds are attacking the wagon trains?" Sandry asked.

"I will certainly report that," Captain Sareg said. "My superiors will be interested. And of course the Office of Gifts will demand a full report. I will send a clerk to call on you in the morning; you can give him all the details."

"But you won't report that to the Emperor tonight?"

"No, of course not. That is news for the officials, not for the Supreme One."

But, Sandry thought, *you will report that Arshur has come to be a king.*

"The birds attack wagon trains all the way to Condigeo," Sandry said. Sareg looked blank. "Far to the west of Crescent City, all the way to the Great Sea."

Sareg nodded. "So you fought from the ocean to Crescent City?"

"Yes." He looked to Thundercloud. "I wondered if you would forbid us to kill terror birds," Sandry said cautiously.

"Oh, no," Thundercloud said. "It isn't birds we worship; it's the essence, the god, the symbol of the Emperor's might. Gods don't take much note of individual worshippers, you know. If the birds have become a nuisance, feel free to discourage them."

The rest of the company didn't even seem particularly

interested in the conversation. Captain Sareg said, "My officer and I had to kill a terror bird once. It got into the crater and attacked our stocks. I was only a foot soldier then. Two men can generally kill one, or drive it off, but that was scary."

Regapisk shouted from far down the long table. "Ever been attacked by a dozen?"

"What? No. They stay apart."

"Not anymore. They've been ganging up," Regapisk continued. "Lord Sandry had to kill two hundred at Crescent City!"

The imperials seemed politely dubious, and Thundercloud actually laughed out loud. Otherwise Regapisk couldn't have pulled a reluctant Sandry into telling stories. Terror birds attacked in strength? And Sandry knew how to fight back? Crescent City soldiers were growing angry. They knew what they'd seen! Sandry had taught them his techniques, and they'd used them on the way here, cursed right!

Fur Slipper and Thundercloud began discussing magic, cautiously, not eager to reveal secrets. Clever Squirrel got involved. They were a buzz of conversation against a background of men discussing war, until Thundercloud exclaimed, "You were at the Folded Hands Conference?"

"How did you hear about that, this far east?"

"Oh, Red Rock was invited. He's our high priest in Aztlan, and the Emperor needed him; he couldn't go. But Clever Squirrel, do I understand right? Threescore wizards gathered at Avalon to find ways to restrict the use of magic?"

"Yes, to conserve what's left in these days of dwindling manna."

"I see. Then tell me this, shaman: why are you supporting a trade in talismans, in charged turquoise and petrified wood?"

"Why . . . I never thought of that."

"You encourage waste. The days of the great gaudy floating castles are over. Gods are going mythical for lack of manna. What will happen if we keep sending what little we have all over the world? Wizards will live as if there were no end to wealth, until it's all gone in a day."

"Well, but talismans aren't *free,*" Squirrel said. "We learn to conserve magic just to save wealth. Some of us become very good at it. Meanwhile there are civilizations that would die without the trade."

Fur Slipper found the argument very amusing. "What would you do, Thundercloud? Shut down the trade in talismans? Magic drives the trade routes. Nothing else would be traded either, you know, not even ideas. Every culture would grow in isolation, turn inward, grow mad."

"And no one would bring gifts to the Emperor," Ern added softly.

CHAPTER NINE

NIGHTMARE

Burning Tower watched the full moon from her window. Theirs was a tower room on the rim. The same full moon illuminated a ring of wagons deep in the crater, and the barren land around.

Squirrel was fast asleep.

Tower saw something coming down the High Road, something like a streamer of mist a-sparkle in the moonlight. Where the row of petrified logs ended, the mist moved up the crater rim and in, purposeful, seeking the guardhouse.

"Locusts," she told herself.

Crescent City sometimes used locusts for exploration or to carry messages. She'd heard of such practice from other tribes. It couldn't be more difficult, could it, than persuading ants to keep to their places?

Tower lay down and was presently oblivious.

Squirrel dreamed.

She knew it was a dream by its clarity, the glare of color and the sharp edges. Manna was strong in the crater.

She stood on a butte, a great spur of rock above a vast flat plain. A manlike shape stood on the ground far below, stood so tall that his vast mismatched face was level with her eyes. Dressed in a feathered robe, he was divided down the middle: one side a living, laughing, well-muscled man; the other a skull, fingers of bone, white ribs showing through decaying feathers.

"The world is endangered," he said. "Clever Squirrel, you must join us."

"Who are you, then?"

"We are the conservators. Human beings are natural magic users. There is magic in our very being. With no trace of magic left, who knows what our descendants would be like? They would be no longer human. We must save the magic for generations to follow."

The intruder was seeing into her mind by a little bit; she was seeing into his.

She asked, "Thundercloud, do you send terror birds to kill for you?" and knew at once that it was not only Thundercloud. She sensed a pair of adversaries, Thundercloud and a more powerful personality, his mentor. She perceived his name: Vucub-Caquix, Seven Macaws.

"We do," the composite said. Both were speaking the

truth as they saw it. "We must, to block the flow of trade. Tell me how you kill the nightmare birds."

It was pulled from her, what little she knew. Sandry fought without magic, in ways Squirrel didn't understand, with chariots, atlatls, the many-layered bow, a stone bird gathered from the enemy, and by making patterns with armed men. She sensed her adversary's disappointment.

"Do you rule the god, or does he rule you?" she wondered, and she knew. Both. The god's own purpose was to evade its fate. Trade must be stopped because traders were coming to destroy Left-Handed Hummingbird.

She'd learned enough. Now she tried to wake up.

Her adversary said, "Sandry fights the nightmare birds. Who else has learned from him?"

All he had trained, his own Younglords, the Condigeo marines, the Crescent City soldiers, Arshur the wanderer. She gave them all to the half-skull giant, and knew that all must die. She whimpered.

"Sleep," said her adversary, and velvet blackness took her. She woke in midafternoon, in the midst of battle.

Chapter Ten

The Battle Begins

Starting at first light, the merchants began charging their cargos of silver-and-turquoise talismans. Clever Squirrel was still asleep. She would be sorry she'd missed seeing this, Tower thought.

Actually the process looked simple. Ruser's own collection was typical. Carved turquoise objects, figures and faces of gods known and obscure, were worked into cages of silver. The silver frame was there to charge the blue stone. The stone would hold magic until a spell released it. It had to be dismounted from the silver before it left the crater, or the manna would leak away. Then the charged talismans were put into boxes of magic-depleted stonewood.

So Regapisk and Arshur took loads of Ruser's talismans into the bottom of the crater and strung them on lines. They'd be left there all day. Ruser supervised. Secklers the Lordkin helped. He seemed to enjoy the work. The others watched him pretty closely. Tower opened her hope chest and removed the birthname talisman the ladies of Condigeo had given her. The central charm was removed and wrapped in silver wire, and Burning Tower herself carried it to the crater. After a moment's thought, she climbed the central pole that held up the wires the other talismans were strung on, and put her charm at the very top. No one would gather it there unless they could climb like Burning Tower, or fly.

Captain Sareg came down to watch. He beamed when he spotted Arshur. Tower heard him; the whole circle of wagons was meant to. "Arshur the Wanderer! You are to be king!"

"What you say?"

"A reply from the Emperor arrived last night. The Emperor has accepted you as king. We're all very glad: we've been without a king for most of a year. You'll be taken by the High Road to Aztlan as soon as transport arrives."

"High Road . . . when? How shall I dress? Act? May I take companions?"

"Soon, I would think. Dress? Your servants will dress you when you arrive. Act as you've always acted, it's worked for you so far. Some of your companions have been invited to the city, but they'll come by their own path. My congratulations, Majesty." And he bowed.

* * *

So it came about that the entire wagon train was busy at hanging jewelry. Sandry and his minions were guarding the jewelry against gatherers, but there didn't seem to be any of those. The imperials were spending their time watching them, even the man on the guard tower. Nobody was seeing what was outside the crater, except Arshur, who abandoned the lines he'd been stringing and went scampering up the walls of the crater to watch for what was due to arrive on the High Road.

Around midmorning, he began shouting.

Then the man on the guard tower was shouting too. He was using some military jargon. Burning Tower couldn't understand him, but she saw soldiers scampering up the crater slope. She climbed laboriously uphill to look.

Terror birds surrounded the crater, close up against the rim, just outside the ring of ugly stone statues that surrounded the crater. They were widely separated and behaving like flightless birds, but they wouldn't find much prey this close to civilization. The gaudy one, the rooster, had placed himself farther back.

Behind her, Mouse Warrior ran among the wagons crying, "Hey, Harpy!"

Sandry heard the shouts from the guard tower. "Birds! Terror birds! Alarm! Call the wizards!" the soldier was shouting.

Birds. Alarm! Call the wizards. How many birds?

"Call the wizards!" the guard repeated. Someone on the ground heard, and took up the shout. "Close the gates!" someone else called.

Sandry looked at those gates with contempt. They wouldn't keep out determined terror birds. Neither would the low walls and broken maguey fences. Enough birds and—

"Terror birds!" the tower guard shouted again.

"How many?" Captain Sareg shouted from below the tower.

"Hundreds!"

Hundreds would be more than enough to overwhelm the imperial soldiers and the wagon train as well. That many birds could be stopped only by magic.

"Wizards! Call the wizards!" Captain Sareg was shouting.

The birds came to the crater rim. They lined up along its lip, held in check for the moment by the stacks of stonewood heads with their glowing eyes. *Foolish,* Sandry thought. *If they rushed us now, we wouldn't have a chance.* "Younglord Whane!"

"Sir!"

"Get everyone you can into armor; turn out with weapons. We'll make a stand on the road down from the rim."

"Sir." Whane ran off, afraid but under control. And the birds gathered at the rim, more and more of them.

"What are they waiting for?" Arshur demanded. "A fair fight?"

"It almost looks that way," Sandry said. "Or some way through that ring of statues." The eyes of the guard statues were burning fiercely now, making lines of light wherever dust blew past. The birds would not cross that line, but more gathered behind it.

"The light's dimming, I think," Younglord Whane said conversationally. "When it's gone, will they come through?"

Sandry looked around for Clever Squirrel. No sign of her. Sareg had summoned his own wizards, but not Squirrel. Burning Tower was rushing up toward the rim. Sandry went to her.

"Where is Clever Squirrel?"

"Asleep," she said.

"Wake her. Run!"

She ran. Sandry smiled to himself, watching her. If they lived through this . . . "Fur Slipper?"

"Down in the pit. I've sent for her." Ern had put on thick buckskins and brought his spears. "What are those things waiting for?"

"I don't know, but the longer they wait, the better I like it," Sandry said. "I want my armor. Gather everyone you can. Arshur, you and Whane get some kind of battle line set up while I get my stuff."

"I'll get it!" Wagonmaster Ern's boy looked eager. "I know where you keep everything! Let me get it."

"Go," Sandry said.

"Now what?" Arshur said. "Look."

A half dozen of the imperial soldiers were running down the hill to them, with Captain Sareg puffing behind them. "Majesty," Sareg shouted. "We are come to defend you." The other soldiers laughed nervously.

"Defend me?" Arshur demanded. He whirled his great sword and laughed. "Defend me or stand behind me?"

"If you die, we die," Sareg said quietly. "I'd rather be killed by a bird than impaled by the Supreme One."

"Know how to fight those things?" Arshur demanded.

"No, Majesty."

"Magic? Wizards?" Sandry asked.

"The Great Mistress is trying to ready them," Sareg said. "She keeps the Ring of Protection strong, but she says something, or someone, is fighting her."

"An enemy wizard?" Ern demanded.

Sareg shrugged helplessly.

"Can the Great Mistress blast those things?" Arshur demanded.

"No, no—that kind of magic belongs to Thundercloud," Sareg said. "And no one can find Master Thundercloud. Most of his apprentices are missing too. So are many of the rain arrows, and all his robes of office."

"What does that mean?" Arshur demanded.

"I don't know, Majesty."

"Betrayed," Arshur said positively.

"So what will the Great Mistress do?" Sandry demanded.

"She's casting the spells she knows," Sareg said. "Sleep and calm and fear and nightmares. And she sings songs to the Protection Stones."

"Is that what's holding those things back?" Sandry asked.

Sareg shook his head. "I don't know. I'm not a wizard."

"I think the eyes are getting dimmer," Younglord Whane said.

Squirrel's sleep was so deep that Burning Tower feared for her health. She didn't stir when Tower patted her cheeks, or rubbed her hands, or pulled her hair. Tower lifted her by her ankles and dipped her head in a basin of water.

Squirrel stirred. Her eyes vacant, she whispered something under her breath. Then, "You're strong," she said.

"You're little. What's the matter with you?"

"Nothing now. That crazy wizard put me under a spell of sleep." Squirrel still seemed dazed. "Tower, I went to Avalon to get a spell from Morth. I ever tell you how my grandfather died?"

"Father did."

"He walked into a gold field with Mother and Whandall. Wild magic all around him. All the old failed spells he'd made in the past started coming true. If he'd known how to unravel a spell, Grandfather could have saved himself. I asked Morth how to do that. I expect he'll want a heavy price some day—"

"Good, good. Now what do we do about the birds?"

"What birds?"

Chapter Eleven

The King at War

Lord Regapisk was panting as he ran up from the pit. A dozen and more merchants and wagoneers and guards were strung out behind him, all gasping for breath.

"Good to see you," Arshur shouted.

Arshur stood in a battle line across the access road, imperial guards to either side. He was flanked by the others. Sandry had arrayed every soldier in ranks just below the crater rim. Some had bows. Some carried atlatls and spears. Ern's boy was just finishing the task of hitching the mules to Regapisk's chariot. Sandry's chariot stood ready, but there was no one in it. Regapisk understood. This wasn't good terrain for chariots. There was no room to maneuver, and the boulder fields on each side of the access road were better than walls. The birds might work around behind Sandry's roadblock to get to the wagon laager, but it would take them time, and they wouldn't do it unseen.

Regapisk hadn't thought this way in years, not since the nearly forgotten lessons taught by the Peacevoice assigned to his military education. It always came hard to Regapisk, as it was easy for Sandry, and it had never seemed important before.

Chariots were no use here, but up on the plain above the rim it would be different. Up there was rough too, better ground for mules than horses. It would take a skilled charioteer to keep his chariot upright. *And I'm out of practice.* Would that be important? There was no way up there now. The birds were gathered tight against the crater rim, clustered just beyond the flashing-eyed statues. Hundreds, Regapisk thought. They'd number several hundred, maybe a thousand, and more coming from far across the plain. There were frantic shouts from the guard tower.

Sandry was in armor. Whane tightened the last of Sandry's laces and began struggling into his own. For the first time since they left Crescent City, Regapisk regretted not buying armor, but Arshur wasn't armored, only wrapped in thick wool leggings and a leather jacket. The merchants weren't armored either.

Most of the merchants took up arms and joined the ranks. It didn't look very safe with them. Regapisk drew his Lord's Town sword and went to join Arshur.

"Regapisk," Sandry said crisply. "I need an object in Clever Squirrel's possession. Can you find her room?"

"Sure, the women all bedded down in the same complex. What do you need?"

"There's an iron pot *this* big. In it there's a statuette of a terror bird in petrified wood. The statue is magic. It attracts terror birds. Get it."

"Why not just ask the shaman?"

Sandry looked at him for a brief moment. There was time, Sandry judged. He said, "Look down. Follow my finger. What do you see?"

Regapisk looked. "That's Squirrel and Tower."

"They're halfway up here. I could wait for them to get here, then send one back for the bird statue, but I want it faster than that, and I want them both *here*. How much more of my time are you going to waste, Reg? You're the man I can spare best. Get me the stonewood bird."

Regapisk ran. It came to him that he should have said something—*Sir* or *Aye,* as if Sandry was his superior officer? Or as if the men around him thought he was? Too late. He ran. He noticed that Burning Tower had turned back to the wagon laager. He turned to tell Sandry, shrugged, and ran down the steep path.

He passed the shaman on the way. "Clever Squirrel!"

She ignored him. He persisted. "Where's the statue of the bird? Lord Sandry wants it."

"Oh, curse, I should have brought it—"

"I'll get it. You go to Sandry."

"It's in my big bag."

* * *

Regapisk found a bag. He dumped its contents on the sleeping blankets. Something heavy rolled. He picked up an iron pot, tightly bound. He opened it and found a bird of glittering striated stone.

He picked up the bird and ran.

Clever Squirrel arrived puffing. Sandry said, "Shaman, I'm glad you're up. You would have missed all the excitement."

"I was ensorcelled. I've had dreams!" She was shouting, and heads turned. "I know our enemies now. They're the priests of Left-Handed Hummingbird, Master Thundercloud among them. They're trying to stop the trade in magic."

"They tell me he can cast terrible war spells," Sandry said. "I've never seen a war spell."

"Me either," Squirrel said. She squinted up at the statues.

"Worry about war spells when they happen," Sandry said. "Right now, what we're fighting is birds. I thought we could use that stonewood bird as a lure. Pull the birds up over the cliff edge, twenty at a time, and shoot them when they're silhouetted against the sky. How's it sound?"

"I'm not a warrior, Lord Sandry. I wonder if the bird needs to be recharged."

"Curse!"

"The manna's thick as mud here. It should work fine. Sandry, look!"

One of the statues blazed for a moment, then its glowing eyes grew dark. Sandry watched in horror as the great pillar of heads collapsed into dust. A score and more birds spilled over the crater's edge like a dark wave. Sandry shouted over their screeching. "Ready! Throw!"

Terror birds were coming over the rim as Regapisk climbed toward Sandry's fighting men. A wave of spears and arrows answered them. Birds fell thrashing. Birds behind them came on.

Regapisk called, "Sandry!"

Sandry looked around. "Squirrel, take that." He went back to directing warriors while Clever Squirrel climbed down toward Regapisk.

She took the stone bird from him. "Where's the pot?"

"Pot?"

"The iron pot. We need it for shielding." Her eyes went big and round. "Without that, the birds will all come at once!"

Regapisk absorbed that. *I wasn't told,* he thought. *It's not my—* Instead of speaking he drew his sword and stepped in front of the shaman.

"Arm! Ready!" Sandry bellowed. He waited until a number of the men had put throwing spears onto their atlatls and stood comfortably. The birds thundered forward. "Throw!" Spears flew straight, not in an arc. Plenty of power. A line of birds screamed, and several fell. Others stumbled over the falling bodies.

"Arm! Ready!" But the stone bird was pulling them in, sure enough. Some were getting through the hail of spears and arrows. It would be down to swords too soon.

"Throw! Arm! Ready! Throw! Mouse Warrior, to me!"

The little man scrambled to his side. Sandry said, "Gather twenty warriors and get them to the Office of Rain. Get all their rain arrows. We need them for ammunition. Kill anyone who tries to stop you. Kill anyone who's wearing terror bird feathers."

Arshur laughed and used the atlatl to launch another spear. One of Sareg's troopers had laid down his own weapons and was loading for Arshur. Sandry grinned. Every time Arshur launched a spear, a bird fell, and the only thing slowing the blond giant was loading.

But he'd soon be out of spears. They all would. Spears and arrows, and then it would be swords.

But there was a barrier ahead now. Dead birds, some still twitching. And up above, Hazel's magic was channeling the birds, keeping them coming through the narrow gap between two of the ugly statues.

Fire blazed high on the lip to the left. A pool of fire washed across the protection stones, spilling over the rim and down, but it died as it fell.

"War spells!" Captain Sareg shouted in Sandry's ear.

"Doesn't look effective."

"Someone hit it with a counterspell," Sareg said. "The Great Mistress. She's still fighting."

"Fighting who?"

"I hate this!" Sareg shouted. "She's fighting Master Thundercloud!"

More birds leaped down the hill. Arshur's spear impaled the first one, and two others fell over it. As they struggled to get up, something white flashed past Sandry.

Spike, carrying Burning Tower. The one-horn charged up the hill. It reared high, then brought hooves down on the struggling birds. Tower was carrying a stone axe. Its handle was nearly as long as a spear. She brought the heavy axe head down on a bird to crush its skull.

"Back!" she shouted. Spike reared again and turned and dashed back down the hill, but he wouldn't get close to Sandry.

"Tower!" Sandry shouted.

Her reply was meaningless, a loud shout of triumph. Arshur took another loaded atlatl from the imperial guardsman and shouted as he hurled the spear. Another bird died.

He turned for another spear and got a helpless gesture. No more spears. Arshur lifted his oversize sword and charged uphill. Regapisk and Secklers whooped and followed. Two or three birds had gotten ahead of the rest. The three men converged on the leader.

The flood of birds seemed endless. Sandry had to learn how many were left. He sprinted for the observation tower. A bird saw him and turned toward him, and Arshur wheeled and whacked off both its feet. It came at Sandry anyway, wobbling, thrusting its dagger-tipped wings ahead of it.

Sandry reached the ladder and climbed. Even over the screeching of terror birds, he could hear Arshur's laughter.

From the top of the tower he looked out into a sea of terror birds. The gaudy one, the "rooster," was just outside the rim, hidden from everyone but Sandry and the imperial lookout—who had shouted himself hoarse and had nothing left to say.

Sandry could imagine that the rooster was trying to get the other birds into ranks. If he'd brought his bow—no, it was beyond bowshot, even for his compound bow. Did it know how far the Lords' weapons would shoot? And how?

Regapisk was fighting a terror bird, sword to beak. They danced. They looked ridiculous and deadly.

Clever Squirrel lifted the stone bird. The terror bird turned to look, and Regapisk sliced through its thick neck. It fell kicking. He had to dodge the claws.

An idea struck her. "Regapisk!"

"Yeah?"

"Got your breath back?"

"Sure. Hooff!"

"Take this. Take the bird into the sweatbath! The one in the rose garden!"

"Why the—?" Regapisk shook his head. "Close the door on it?"

"Right!"

Regapisk took the bird and ran.

Eleven men and Mouse Warrior climbed uphill with armloads of rain arrows. Sandry watched them approach the imperials. Good thinking: they would be familiar with the weapons.

The imperials seemed dubious, but some of them began firing into the mob of birds. Lightning sputtered along the tracks of the arrows.

Burning Tower was riding Spike, and they were in the thick of battle. With magic all around him, Spike was at the peak of his form. Sandry saw Tower ward off a huge stabbing beak as Spike dodged under it and sank his horn deep in feathers and flesh. The bird wrenched loose and ran. Four more converged on it, beaks jabbing.

Tower looked for another target.

She was driving Sandry crazy. He was mightily relieved when Clever Squirrel shouted at her, summoned her back. They gestured and shouted. Then both women shouted at some of the warriors, distracting them.

Burning Tower galloped Spike downhill, away from the battle, toward the sweatbath house. A couple of Sandry's warriors ran after her, losing ground. Sandry's impulse was to fume at losing warriors in the midst of battle . . . but it was too bizarre. It had to be magic, and magic was not Sandry's business. Meanwhile . . .

Where the rain arrows fell, birds were attacking each other.

The terror bird rooster was on the rim now, dancing in rage, screeching commands at his minion hens. It did no good. Terror birds attacked magic, even when it was a rain arrow embedded in another terror bird. Now the birds outside the crater seemed to slow, losing interest.

Mouse Warrior looked around him and spotted Sandry on the tower. He shouted an inaudible question.

A bird broke through. Sandry pointed. Mouse saw it. He whirled his sling a breath too slow. Mouse was dead, torn apart, when Secklers slew the bird.

Sandry saw Clever Squirrel climbing the ladder. She pulled herself up and looked about her. She asked, "How goes it?"

"We'd be fine if there was an upper limit to these

birds. They're too many. Squirrel, stop distracting my soldiers."

"Could you deal with the rest of the birds if I take out the rooster? And the god?"

"And the *god*?" She just looked at him. He said, "Yes. What have you got in mind?"

She looked east toward the bathhouse.

Burning Tower tied Spike, then jogged into the bathhouse. She came out with Regapisk. Two more soldiers came running up. They talked briefly. Then they tore the door off.

"I hope they get it right," Squirrel said. She started climbing down.

The terror bird rooster wasn't dancing in rage. He was looking about him, studying the war. It made Sandry uneasy. The birds were too many. If the rooster organized a charge, they were doomed.

Chapter Twelve

The Wizards' War

It looked like Sandry was holding the birds. Clever Squirrel walked rather than ran, conserving her breath.

Tower and Regapisk and two soldiers were working on the bathhouse, making good progress. They'd enlarged the bathhouse doorway and were fitting in a much bigger block of petrified wood, part of the floor of the cooling-off area, using the same hinges that had served the little door. That setup wouldn't last the ages, but it didn't have to.

She looked inside. They'd broken a hole in the tuff wall into the chimney beyond. Of course the bathhouse was stone cold, but Squirrel had wanted to see that for herself. And the hole into the chimney looked big enough.

"We're ready," Squirrel said. "Blazes, take the statuette and go." Burning Tower jogged into the bathhouse and came out with the stone bird. "Regapisk, stay. We need you to bar the door. Lurk, put that inside. The rest of you, back to battle. From here on, it's just us."

Spike surged uphill like nothing on Earth could stop him. Burning Tower clutched the petrified wood bird hard against her ribs.

A thousand terror birds were running toward her. That number never seemed to decrease! Tower guided Spike up toward the rim—and there, that was the rooster, and now he was in the lead.

Tower turned Spike and fled.

She took a moment to wonder how she would protect Spike. The new, bigger door would admit a one-horn—but then he'd be trapped inside with a terror bird! No, she'd just have to jump off the bonehead and count on the statuette to keep the rooster distracted.

The birds flooded toward her, but, drawn from hundreds of miles around to fight in battle, they were tired. Warriors hacked at the dawdlers, hurled arrows and spears. The rooster was far in the lead.

Clever Squirrel waited in the doorway. Doubts riddled her, but she shrugged them off. There was nothing left to do. And here came Spike and Burning Tower. It was far too late to change plans.

She was counting on walls of depleted petrified wood to shield the interior against magic. Putting the bird statuette inside had worked well enough: its influence cut off, the hens had danced in confusion, and the rooster had come closer to take command.

So. Regapisk was on the bathhouse roof, possibly safe, possibly not. Tower jumped off Spike, shouted at the bonehead, and ran for the bathhouse. Spike kept moving. The rooster ran after him.

Tower dashed inside, came back to stand in the doorway. She screamed at the rooster, waving the statuette. The rooster thought it over, then charged the bathhouse.

"Remember, you first," Squirrel shouted.

Tower nodded. As the bird came up, she ran into the bathhouse. She dropped the stone bird. The hole in the foamed rock wall was just big enough. She scrambled into it, through ankle-deep ash, up the chimney and out. Squirrel followed her through the hole and stopped there.

The bird hadn't stopped to kill Spike or Regapisk. It shouldered through the enlarged doorway and stopped suddenly in the sweat room. Squirrel heard the big new door slammed shut and barred from outside.

Regapisk had better be back on the roof, before a thousand more birds arrived . . . and here they were now. Squirrel could hear them thumping against the thick stonewood walls.

Squirrel began to chant.

There was no magic in her words, other than that she was speaking a tongue the gods understood. Magic wouldn't work here anyway. She was taunting the god, hoping to drive him to blind rage.

The bird's response was a beak thrust into the chimney. Squirrel leaped up, caught herself, and kept climbing. Up and out of the chimney, with a bird's beak below her smashing big chips out of a stonewood wall. And Regapisk to lift her free.

Regapisk asked, "What's happening?"

Squirrel said, "It's the god's decision now."

Regapisk looked blank.

Poor Regapisk, always out of the loop. Squirrel said, "The god is riding the terror bird rooster. The rooster is in the box. It can't even call for help; see how the birds are milling around? No magic gets in or out. When the walls have absorbed enough manna, the god goes myth."

"He doesn't need to call," Regapisk said. He pointed to a distant figure. Thundercloud, resplendent in his robes of office, surrounded by a host of apprentices, was running toward the bathhouse door.

Chapter Thirteen

Arrows

"He'll break the door down," Squirrel shouted. "Stop him."

"How?" Regapisk demanded. "You stop him."

Squirrel sang. Little happened.

"What are you doing?"

"It's a slowing spell, but it's not working," Squirrel said.

"I knew it would come to this," Regapisk said. He leaped down off the roof to stand in front of the door. He fingered the salamander brooch. "Tell Aunt Shanda."

Squirrel looked around for help. "Tower! Get Sandry! Get Arshur! Bring help!"

Burning Tower whistled, twice, and Spike jumped over a bird he had been fighting and ran to stand next to the roof. Tower leaped on his back, and they galloped toward the guard tower.

Sandry could see the roof of the bathhouse but not the door. Something was happening there. And now Burning Tower was riding Spike, coming toward him. She needed help.

He signaled to Younglord Whane down on the road below the rim, his arm circling over his head then pointing down to the base of the guard tower: *Come here with my chariot. Now.*

Whane waved and leaped into the chariot. *Good driving,* Sandry thought, as Whane wove between two squabbling birds. Squabbling. The birds were fighting each other as well as humans. They weren't working together at all.

A flash of lightning from near the bathhouse. He caught a glimpse of green and gold robes, a high headdress, a flashing arrow followed by lightning. Thundercloud was coming. Thundercloud the traitor.

"My Lord!" Whane was shouting from below the tower. He looked pleased with himself.

Sandry came down the ladder too fast, knocked his breath out landing, and climbed painfully into the chariot. "To the bathhouse," he wheezed.

"Sir?"

"Follow the lightning. Ride to the lightning."

"Sir!"

The chariot wheeled. Here in the compound, the ground was clear enough, nothing for the horses to stumble on. Tower was coming, though, and the horses reared to avoid Spike.

"Sandry," she shouted. "Squirrel needs you! Over here!"

"I saw." He was getting his breath back. He took his bow, already strung, from the bow case and selected a stout bone-shafted arrow. A flight arrow, for range.

The chariot clattered between the low buildings of the compound, past the common bathhouses, toward the rose garden. Lightning flashed among the roses, then there were flashes of green and ruby red. *Hummingbirds,* Sandry thought. *Afraid of the lightning.*

Lightning. From where? And it was pouring rain now, rain in bucketsful. The bow string wouldn't last long in this.

Another lightning flash, this time just next to them. The horses reared from the thunderclap. "There!" Whane shouted.

Master Thundercloud, splendid in his robes of office, running toward the bathhouse.

"Stop him!" Squirrel was screaming from the roof.

Burning Tower shouted, and Spike dashed forward and stopped as if he'd hit a wall. The beast screamed in agony. One of Thundercloud's apprentices was holding up a sigil, and whatever it was, it was more than Spike could bear. The one-horn screamed again, an eerie sound in the driving rain.

Thundercloud ran toward the bathhouse door, bow in hand. Whane whipped the horses forward, but they were confused by the thunder. *We're too far,* Sandry thought. *We'll never stop him. . . .*

And Regapisk dashed out, sword raised. He waved it in Thundercloud's face, struck at him clumsily, missed. Another flare of lightning and Regapisk was down. Thundercloud raised his arms in triumph, nocked another arrow.

Sandry's arrow was already in place. He drew the arrow to his ear, held steady, released . . .

Thundercloud screamed in pain and outrage. He turned toward Sandry and shouted curses. A wave of pain ran through Sandry's head and body. Another wave of pain in his arm. His arm was heavy, too heavy to hold the bow.

"You can bear it." His mother's voice, speaking in his ear. His mother? Or Squirrel, who was singing in a language Sandry did not know but was at the edge of his understanding, soothing, easing the pains. He gestured for Whane to turn away from Thundercloud, turn away, turn away . . .

"Away?"

"Go! Now!"

"Sir!" The chariot wheeled. An arrow fell behind them and the horses reared again from the thunder, leaped forward.

"Now stop. Turn," Sandry said quietly.

"Aye."

His arms ached, and Squirrel's song was softer, but he could lift his left arm. Another arrow, bone-shafted, a flint arrowhead, gull feathers. Sandry noted every detail of the arrow as he drew it. Thundercloud laughed and turned away contemptuously, nocked an arrow to fire at the door of the bathhouse.

Slow. Aim. Smooth release. The arrow took forever to fly. It struck Thundercloud in the back. The priest screamed and dropped his bow. Lightning struck, knocking Thundercloud and two apprentices to the ground. Another apprentice turned to run, but now Spike was free of whatever had held him. He ran forward to batter the boy to the ground, and danced on him with sharp hooves.

Whane had already started forward when Sandry's arrow struck. "Drive!" Sandry shouted. Thundercloud was thrashing on the ground, trying to rise. Spike turned toward the priest, but the apprentice with the sigil managed to get to his feet, and Spike was driven away. Thundercloud shouted another curse. Sandry felt his strength begin to drain. "Drive!"

"You can bear it."

But I can't. I can't stand up—there's no strength in my legs. His mother's voice was blended with Squirrel's wordless song: "You can bear it."

Thundercloud was shouting. Squirrel's song rang out above the shouts. Whane was urging the horses forward. Sandry struggled to find the strength to raise his bow. They were close enough now to hear the frantic shrieks from inside the bathhouse, furious pounding on the doors as the rooster god tried to batter his way out.

Thundercloud struggled to get to his feet. Blood poured from wounds in his shoulder and back. "I come, I come."

"No. You will not." Tower stood in his path. She raised her war hammer. Sandry felt a rush as his strength returned, and now it was Tower who fell helpless to the ground.

"Enough," Sandry said. He leaped off the chariot and seized Thundercloud's arms. "Whane."

Whane was already there. They held the priest's arms behind him. Whane stuffed something into the priest's mouth so that he couldn't talk. Sandry felt the priest's struggles dying away.

The clatter inside the bathhouse stopped. There was a long and ominous silence.

"The birds have stopped attacking," Whane said quietly. "They're milling around."

"And running away." Clever Squirrel had come down from the roof. "Blazes, you all right?"

"Yes," Tower said weakly. "Whew. What was that?"

"It will pass," Squirrel said. She listened. "Quiet in there."

"What does that mean?" Sandry asked. He held Thundercloud tightly, but the priest had ceased to struggle.

"I think the god is myth," Squirrel said.

Thundercloud spit out the ball of waste that choked him. "He cannot be dead," he shouted. "He cannot die. But—"

"But what?" Squirrel demanded. She put her hand on Thundercloud's forehead. "What?"

"Did you not dream it?"

Squirrel looked puzzled. "I dreamed of a transformation, of a god made small and angry." Suddenly she stood straight and laughed hysterically.

As she did, a hummingbird rose out of the chimney.

It flew straight at Clever Squirrel's face, then veered off as if abruptly realizing how *big* she was. It circled once, and then buzzed off toward the garden.

"Left-Handed Hummingbird," Squirrel said. "Now I know what that means."

"Is it over?" Regapisk struggled to sit up. He was favoring his right arm. Something wrong there, the shape . . .

"It's over," Squirrel said.

"Welcome back, Cousin," Sandry said.

CHAPTER FOURTEEN

THE RED SEEDS

The station's visitors lined the crater's rim to watch the Emperor's messengers appear.

Regapisk clutched his cloak around him. His arm itched. Ruser the Jeweler eyed him suspiciously. "You fought alongside us," Regapisk said to Ruser. "Everything's changed. The Emperor might invite you in."

"No."

Regapisk waited. Ruser was troubled. There was a story here . . .

"No. Even if he did, I wouldn't dare. I have had enough of Aztlan to last my life. I will send you with signs and sigils that will prove you to be my partner."

Ruser took a small stonewood box from an inner pocket. He opened it. "Here. Hold this." Ruser held out a small crude statue a fingerlength tall. It was dressed in a small silver loincloth. Crude as it was, the statue was clearly of a naked male.

"Hold that. Think about women. Think about the last time you had a woman. Think about the most exciting woman you ever had."

"Why?"

"Just do it. Are you aroused yet?"

"Yes, curse you. She was a mer."

"Good. Now take that silver off it and put the statue in this box." He gave Regapisk the stonewood box. "Don't open that box until you're with Flensevan in a place with manna. Anywhere in Aztlan will have enough."

"And then what?"

"Flensevan will know what to do. It won't work except the first time you open the box. Remember that."

"All right."

"So. Ask Flensevan about the boat. We are wealthy, you and I," the jeweler said. "As is Flensevan, if he wishes to be, which I doubt. With what I can take to Crescent City, we have enough to rebuild our business, even to rescue Zephans Mishagnos from his salt farm. Return when you can."

"What's keeping you out of Aztlan? I go with Arshur—he's demanded it—but I can meet you at the gate. As king's companion. Or even with an invitation from the king."

Ruser shook his head. "They come," he said. He pointed to a rapidly growing dot on the high road. "They come."

* * *

Four officials rode in a woven basket that flew just above the High Road along the line of petrified logs. They left the basket at the end of the road, still afloat above the last log. They climbed to the rim through windrows of dead terror birds and dead men. It didn't shake their dignity.

Regapisk had to depend on rumor for the rest.

They didn't give names. Tall, narrow-headed, lean, and bony, they seemed to consider themselves as interchangeable, even though they were garbed very differently. "Road Runner, Jaguar, Bighorn Sheep," Fur Slipper whispered, "by their headdresses. I don't know the bareheaded one. Maybe he was supposed to be Left-Handed Hummingbird."

They interviewed Arshur where he reclined in the infirmary. It took over an hour. Regapisk watched with mixed emotions. The old warrior had actually become a king. Was he still under Regapisk's protection? Could a king ruin himself by not knowing how to use cutlery? Regapisk wondered if he was only jealous.

Barehead and Jaguar spoke to Hazel Sky in the infirmary. She was too exhausted to tell them much. Then Captain Sareg took them into the main building, and only rumor followed.

Rumor came in bits and droplets:

The Office of Rain had numbered nine. All of them were priests of Left-Handed Hummingbird. When the terror birds attacked, the Office of Rain had been found empty but for scattered robes, and those were weirdly changed.

At least half a dozen priests had fled out onto the

plain. They must have been sure they could control the birds, and they must have been wrong. Birds tore them apart.

"Jaravisk didn't run. He was Thundercloud's chief apprentice. We've got him downstairs," Manroot told them at the noon meal. Manroot was an imperial of no great rank. "The messengers want to interview him, and I'll be on duty."

At the evening meal they all found themselves facing Jaravisk, the imperial messengers, and Hazel Sky. "We have seen great changes," Hazel announced. "It is best we come to terms with them. Jaravisk, tell us what you told the messengers."

Jaravisk didn't bear marks of torture, but he wobbled as he walked. Perhaps he'd been chewing coca leaves. Below coca's induced calm, he seemed scared out of his wits. He didn't speak until the bare-headed messenger showed him something pinched between two fingers. Then he blurted, "Left-Handed Hummingbird is no longer a terror bird. The god of war has become a h-h-hummingbird."

The hall rang with amazed laughter.

"A hummingbird," Jaravisk repeated. He seemed ready to cry. "The feathers of my cloak changed. I was casting *ilb'al* to learn more—"

"For our visitors," Hazel suggested.

"What? *Ilb'al,* the red seeds of the flute tree, what we use for seeing." Jaravisk blinked about him. "Seeing other times and places. Captain Sareg found me, but I learned a little first. Our god of war is cast out of power for ages to come, ten thousand years or more. I couldn't learn my own fate, but what I have to tell the Emperor—

please, Jaguar, please, Voice of All Gods, don't bring me to the Emperor. Kill me now."

"Tell them about trade."

"What if I laugh at the Emperor? The Emperor's cloak, symbol of his might, that must have changed too. He'll be wearing a cloak covered with little teeny feathers." Jaravisk's high-pitched giggle ended in a hiccup. "Trade? I followed Thundercloud's orders and I obeyed my god. What do I know of trade? We sent the birds to attack people and horses on the roads that link the western cities. The god watched and guided them. Now it's over. We'll use up our magic or sell it away, and one day our folk will be gone and our city will be blowing dust and roofless ruins to be picked over by lookers. I have seen it in the pattern of red seeds."

CHAPTER FIFTEEN

SAND PAINTINGS

A large canopy covered the reception area and courtyard outside the gates to the crater. Where the canopy ended, rain beat down on the High Road. The basket floated above the High Road, bright against shadow, just caught by the rising sun shining in bright skies to the east. The basket was wet, but the rain ended a few hundred feet away. The ground around the gates and down into the crater was frothy pink, but much of the blood had already washed away.

A day and a half had passed since the battle, and Arshur was only now setting off to meet the Emperor. Arshur the Wanderer, now Arshur the King, walked under an umbrella held by a soldier. Another imperial spearman held a large umbrella to cover the other three in the king's party. Two more soldiers followed behind. Arshur was slow to climb into the great floating basket, and so were his companions.

They were all wounded, the three who boarded the great basket with the Emperor's Jaguar-headed emissary. Arshur was marked with bloody gouges. The birds had scored him again and again while he twisted, turned, danced, so that claws and beak tips almost missed. The merchant Regapisk, Sandry's cousin who had once been a Lord and thought himself Lord again, was walking a little crooked, looking uncomfortable and favoring his right arm. Hazel Sky was unmarked save by a strange torpor.

Imperial guards brought them blankets and cloaks and saw to their comfort. When all four had settled themselves in their finery, Jaguar gestured. The basket slid away, slowly at first, but faster with every breath.

Burning Tower watched them go, but she was also watching Squirrel work with her meticulous, somewhat exaggerated portraits of colored sand.

The sand grains rippled. Twisted Cloud's portrait smiled. "Daughter! Happy birthday. Are you well?"

"Mother! I've defeated a god!"

Sand rippled; the smile became an *O*. "Anyone we know?"

"*Long* story, which I will be pleased to tell *at length*." Rain pounded on the leather awnings above the sand paintings. "Have you got Whandall and Willow?"

Two more paintings stirred. Willow's said, "Squirrel, what have you gotten yourself into?"

"It's all over, Aunt Willow. Mother, do you know of Left-Handed Hummingbird?"

"Barely. God of big flightless birds?"

"Not anymore! We trapped it—we trapped the bird that was its avatar in a bathhouse devoid of manna. I thought I'd mythed it. But a hummingbird got in from the garden—fated, I guess—and the god took that form. It's a hummingbird!"

"What if it switches back?"

"No, it'll be that way for ten thousand years and more! Visions are easy here, Mother."

Willow's image asked, "Are you hurt?"

"I'm the only one who isn't! Sprained every tendon in my body, but that's nothing. Tower's that way too, really limping. Arshur's got scars on his scars. We had to leave Hazel Sky—the governor here, and a wizard—had to leave her in the bathhouse to keep her isolated while we worked healing spells on her. She spent the whole battle blasting back spells from that damn traitor Thundercloud until she fainted. And Regapisk—" Squirrel giggled.

"Who's Regapisk?"

"Sandry's cousin. I shouldn't laugh. He really fought a battle! Killed a dozen terror birds, moved a magic statuette to where it could do some good—that's how we mythed the god!—and then he went up against Thundercloud with just a sword, poor bastard. Hahahaha!"

Whandall Feathersnake's image was gaudy. It asked, "Brave or stupid?"

"Brave! Without him, Sandry would have run out of time. And Thundercloud hit him hahahaha! Hit him with a spell, and it ran from his sword right down his arm and torso and both legs and out his sandals, and hahahaha!"

Her arm waved in circles while she tried to find her voice. "Left a trail of little green and red feathers winding up his arm and down his chest and both legs, and that's all I've seen."

Whandall and Willow were looking at each other.

Squirrel prattled on. "And we fought thousands of terror birds, but they're mostly dead, and the rest fled. We're making unearthly quantities of soup—can you hear the pelting of the rain? It's to get us water for the pots as well as to wash the blood away. And we'll send home feathers for hundreds of cloaks. There's an empire three hundred leagues east of you, an empire of trade, and we've brought their new king!"

Whandall Feathersnake's image spoke. "May we speak to our daughter?" At New Castle, an image must have moved. "Burning Tower, are you well?"

"Yes, cursed near exhausted, Father, but very well! Spike and I fought birds and a god and won. Sandry—"

"Spike?"

"My bonehead." Perhaps they saw her face fall. These sand portraits exaggerated any emotion. "The Emperor will take him, and I'll miss him. Father, Mother, I want to marry Lord Sandry of the Burning City."

"Hello, Sandry. Will you have my daughter?"

"With all my heart."

"I remember your courage, Sandry. You've mythed your second god now, haven't you? A dangerous habit."

"Yes, sir."

"Our accustomed dowry would be a wagon and a team. Is that acceptable, or are you planning to settle somewhere? We can deal. A house?"

"Who could scorn a Feathersnake wagon?" Sandry asked.

"Will the Lords accept a girl of her ancestry?" Willow asked.

"They have said they will," Sandry said. "And that is another reason for a wagon and team. I know your people will accept me."

"Good." Whandall's image stirred. "A trade empire. New trade."

"Yes, sir," Sandry said. He hesitated. "Father found."

Whandall's image smiled.

Tower said, "Locusts arrived from Aztlan while we were setting up the sand paintings. We have an invitation from the Emperor."

"How big is this empire?"

Sandry: "Ten thousand citizens and a bigger number of slaves, but that's a wild guess. There are questions they just don't answer. We haven't seen anything but the outposts. They're impressive."

"They have magic," Burning Tower said excitedly. "Squirrel says more manna than she has ever seen."

"I feel that," Twisted Cloud said.

"A trade empire of magic," Whandall Feathersnake said. "It makes me wish for youth, for time to explore."

"Morth of Atlantis knows how to bestow youth," Tower said. "Father, you could come this far. But few are allowed to go farther."

"And you?" Whandall asked.

"We've been invited into Aztlan itself," Sandry said carefully. "The core city. A signal honor. Tower and I have been invited to marry there, the Emperor officiating."

Whandall absorbed that. "I'd thought you'd marry right away. How long must we wait?"

"Another five cursed days. I sense that the Emperor's suggestion is law."

Tower said, a bit woodenly, "The Emperor accepts our gift of paired bison and a bonehead. And Sandry's stallions. That was in the message."

"Did you offer?"

"No."

Whandall's image asked, "You're to give him Spike?"

"Hand him over personally."

Neither Whandall nor Willow remarked on their daughter's continuing proximity to a one-horn. Whandall asked, "Giving up two bison, can you still pull all the wagons?"

"Yes, but Wagonmaster Ern isn't happy. Those are our spares! Now, only a few of us are invited to Aztlan, so Ern will go back with a fortune in talismans, and some of those are ours."

"Do you trust your trading partners?" Whandall asked. "With a fortune they will carry without you?"

"Father, they are afraid of the Emperor, and they have good reason to want to be in Sandry's good graces. Feathersnake's goods are safe here."

"Good."

"They'll be happy to see those goods in Crescent City, and beyond. Sandry says they need rain arrows in Tep's Town! You know about Green Stone? *He* went back—"

"Called us from Three Pines. He's on his way home."

"Oh, good!"

"I was pleased to learn of the new route to Crescent

City," Whandall said. "That will require new wagon trains, new crews. Now I must think of this Aztlan as well. Do we need it? Sandry, Blazes, you have all done very well. You trust your partners, but can you not return with your wagons? We can hold the wedding this instant, while the manna is strong. Willow?"

"Indeed I am ready, if our daughter and our new son are willing."

"I would with all my heart, Father found," Sandry said. "But we are in the midst of the Emperor's power. No one dares offend him. They whisper of terrible things he has done in his joy. No one wishes to think of his wrath."

"I never heard you show fear," Whandall said. "Even riding against a god!"

"I fear this Emperor more than I ever did the angry god," Clever Squirrel said. "Even Coyote respects this Emperor."

There was a pause. "I wish you could just cut and run," Whandall said. "But I agree it would not be wise. Are you dealing with him, or just some flunkies?"

Sandry said, "I don't know. Doesn't matter. We're facing serious power."

"Right. Who's going?"

"We have brought them a king. Do you remember a looker named Arshur? Traveled with—"

"With Tras the teller. *Him?* But he always said he would be a king."

"And he will. They are very serious about this," Burning Tower said. "Their soldiers risked their lives for him."

"So how will you go?"

"They've taken Arshur the King directly on the High

Road," Tower said. "We must travel another way, but they haven't told us how we will go."

The colors in the sand began to fade.

"Their manna is failing," Squirrel said. "The manna here will never fail, but it takes manna at both ends to work these pictures. Say your good-byes."

At lunchtime they were joined by Captain Sareg. "Rejoice," he said. "You are summoned to Aztlan, and you will take the High Road."

"What of our companions?"

"They are free to return to Crescent City and beyond," Sareg said. "I suggest they take all your property."

"My chariot and weapons?" Sandry said.

Sareg frowned. "We had thought you might offer those to the Supreme One."

Sandry recognized the command in that suggestion. "Of course. But for my return?"

Sareg smiled. "You have the favor of the Supreme One. If you need weapons or an escort, you will have them, and he will provide transportation to any place in the known world."

The rest of the day was spent organizing. The wagon train would return to Crescent City, with Younglord Whane as military commander. "With Mouse Warrior dead, you will be in command of everything," Sandry told him. "But I doubt you have much to fear. The villages along the road were peaceful before; they will be more so now that they know the Emperor's aware of their problems."

"What about your chariot? Your bow?" Whane asked.

"They will be sent along with my horses." Sandry clapped Whane on the shoulder. "You are in command, Acting Lord Whane. Act like it, and try not to daydream when you are on duty."

"But as commander—"

"You will always be on duty. Yes. Remember that." *And that sounds pompous,* Sandry thought, *and Whane knows it, but I had to say it.*

And one final expedition to be organized: a caravan to carry the visitors' gifts to the Emperor. These fit easily into an imperial wagon, all but the animals. Spike and two stallions must go, and two buffalo pulling the wagon. Sareg and two emissaries, No Face and Bighorned Sheep, would go with them.

"And a virgin," Tower said. "Someone has to lead Spike."

In due course Sareg introduced her to a fourteen-year-old apprentice baker, and Tower introduced the awestruck girl to Spike. She left them together in the kraal. Her heart was breaking.

Chapter Sixteen

The King of Aztlan

With the sun setting behind them, the king and his entourage skimmed through a city that was all squares and circles. The line of logs stopped at the edge of a great winding river. The basket skimmed across the water, brown roiling water with bright ripples and streaks of power. The basket was flying free . . . not falling . . . lifting toward a tremendous butte.

The flight had lasted all day. Regapisk, indisputably Lord, had endured, trying not to know how easily death could take him. Lord Regapisk was no coward, but none of his training had prepared him for this. He was flying at unnerving speed, a tall man's height above the ground, in a wickerwork basket! If he didn't want wind blasting in his eyes, he could look through the weave, squinting a little, to see land he might one day have to traverse on foot, if his fortunes continued their accustomed wild swings.

Hazel Sky watched him in amusement. Arshur barely noticed him. Jaguar . . . who could tell what the shaman was thinking behind the slits in his mask? He pointed at the butte and said, "Temple Mesa Fajada. Our major rites are performed on the peak. You'll compete to be king there."

Arshur said, "Compete?"

"You'll kill a terror bird before you go up. It's one of the rites. Don't worry, Majesty, the bird will be drugged."

"Drugged? I forbid it! Am I to cower before a bird?"

For now Regapisk was the king's companion.

And the king was having a wonderful time! Arshur stood up and braced himself as the basket rose up the wall of stone toward the rim of the butte. Four baskets already in flight converged on them as escorts. Each carried an armored guard.

The king's basket paused two thirds of the way up the butte. Here an arc of ledge sprouted from the vertical stone, and on it, a single round building, a *kiva*. A bareheaded man in a kilt watched them set down.

Odd to be seeing it that way, Regapisk thought, when the ledge was actually thick with people. Warriors on alert: four. Cooks tending an arc of hot stone and big haunches of broiling meat: also four. Four women bracketed a heap of clothing in wildly brilliant colors. One man in a mask . . . a mask of the god Coyote. With a tail, a splendid tail that waved like a part of the man. And beyond him, one ageless man in a wonderfully embroidered kilt.

* * *

Arshur was first out; he helped Hazel Sky down. Regapisk rolled over the side, hampered by his cramping legs. Jaguar's priest emerged last. He and Hazel flattened their foreheads against the stone floor as the man in the kilt strolled up. Regapisk prudently did the same.

The man's belly looked like knotted cables: it bore deep old scars. His face was ageless—certainly not young, but there were none of the wrinkles of age.

"Get up. You are Arshur?" He spoke slowly, spitting his consonants. Regapisk had no trouble understanding his Aztlan speech. "It's good to have a king again!"

"I was to translate," said Coyote's priest. He was lanky and blond, with a long waist and short legs and a sharply pointed nose: a little like a coyote, mask or no. He'd taken his mask off to eat, but the tail remained. Regapisk still didn't know if it was real or a magical bit of costume. It waved from time to time. "We didn't know you would both speak as we do," Coyote said. "How did that come about, King's Companion?"

"Call me Regapisk. There was an old man, a refugee from Aztlan. People don't leave Aztlan by choice, do they?"

"Why would they, Regapisk? Wait until you see Aztlan in daylight." He was smiling, though the tail swished angrily. "Tell more about this man."

"Not much to know," Regapisk said. *And why is Coyote interested in old Zeph? Is it Coyote the god or Coyote's priest, loyal servant of the Emperor, who wants to know? Best to find out before I say much more,* Regapisk thought.

The king and the Emperor were talking. Arshur wasn't showing any kind of diffidence, and both men were enjoying themselves hugely. Regapisk wasn't the world's greatest diplomat, but even he knew better than to interrupt them. Meanwhile the four women were stripping Regapisk of his travel-worn clothing and draping him in finespun, marvelously decorated kilts and robes. They exclaimed at the feathers along his arm and down his legs.

"We saved Zeph from the sea. He taught both of us," Reg said. "He knew a little wizardry, and he taught me that too, and something about raising crops."

"Only a little wizardry?"

Reggy shrugged. "More than I'll ever know, but it didn't do him a lot of good."

"Did he know Atlantean magic?"

Regapisk snorted. "I know little of Atlantean magic, but I do know Atlantis was powerful. Zeph was an old man living on vegetables. Tell me, is there a story to go with the Emperor's scars?"

"There must be, but none knows it. Some great secret is there. We know only that the Emperor has ruled for nearly a thousand years."

Regapisk carefully didn't smile. "Do the kings live that long too?"

"No, only the Emperor." Coyote's priest picked up an ear of corn. Regapisk took one and gnawed it, imitating the shaman's technique.

He asked, "Is it easy to become king here?"

Coyote looked to be swallowing a laugh. That was irritating. "Not so difficult," he said. "Some cannot avoid it."

"Then why were you so long without?"

"In his third year of rule, the old king choked to death on a chicken bone," Coyote said. "Nobody had any idea what to do about that. We don't like to choose a king from ourselves, so we waited for a stranger. No stranger came."

"Nothing else came either?"

"Hah! Nothing. We knew bad luck would come from the lack of a king, but we never guessed our own priests would revolt! It was the cursed birds, wasn't it? Blocking off the trade routes."

"Until Sandry broke the siege."

"Not Arshur?"

"King Arshur is a mighty warrior, but Lord Sandry is a thinker and fighter. He found a way to kill two hundred birds at Crescent City. We killed more than a thousand at the crater, and we couldn't have done it without my cousin. Coyote, how could you not know that you were cut off from the world?"

"This is the world. Even so, we knew," Coyote's priest said. "But without a king, there was nobody to tell the Emperor."

"I don't understand," Regapisk said, but Coyote's priest only smiled and went on eating. Baskets rose from below bearing more food, and the women served them exotic dishes, describing what Regapisk found unfamiliar.

Regapisk said, "I know Coyote's daughter."

"Is she really?"

"Oh, yes. The story's famous," Regapisk said, and he told how Whandall Feathersnake, possessed by Coyote, had loved Twisted Cloud, the shaman's daughter. "Their child is Clever Squirrel, and she'll be coming here with Sandry."

"I'm eager to meet them both, and Burning Tower too. Is she a mighty fighter?"

"Riding her unicorn, she is mighty enough."

"I yearn to meet her. And Coyote's daughter. Is she a beauty?"

"Many would say so," Regapisk said. "But not many think of her in that way."

Coyote's priest grinned knowingly.

"Even the one-horns fear her wrath," Regapisk said.

The grin widened. "Now tell me more of Sandry," Coyote's priest said. "And I will tell you how we will cure you. Or try to cure you. You have been afflicted by the curse of a transformed god who has no love for you. A cure will not be easy. But first, tell me more of Sandry. Do you admire him?"

Their quarters were at the base of the canyon walls: a rectangular house with a *kiva* and several rooms.

Arshur had asked for four virgins to serve them that night. "I wanted seven. Lucky number in Atlantis. Then I thought—"

"Not so young anymore?"

"I thought: everything comes in fours here."

Three of the girls were young, a bit thrilled, a bit scared. The fourth was a woman in her thirties: an instructor. She wasn't expecting to be chosen, and none of them were expecting to be seduced.

The older woman's name was Annalun, and she was

the daughter of a king. She sat with Regapisk and poured wine over ice for both of them as she watched her charges tease Arshur.

"The king is more mannerly than we had been given to expect," Annalun said. "You have known him a long time, King's Companion?"

"Call me Regapisk. Long enough, and we have shared adventures enough. But not so long that he can't surprise me."

"He is not of your land?"

"No, from the north lands somewhere," Regapisk said. "I'm not sure even he knows how to get back there now."

She smiled as if Regapisk had made a clever joke.

"I cannot believe someone of your beauty can still saddle a one-horn," Regapisk said.

She smiled again. "There is a great deal of manna in this place, and with enough manna all things are possible. The girls, now"—she indicated the three, who were making a complicated game of undressing Arshur—"have always been able to ride the one-horns, because we have had no king for a year. They have grown impatient for this night. As my mother was impatient the night I was conceived." She poured more wine. "Bring your drink, Lord Regapisk, and come with me. I see my ladies have nothing to fear, and we can find more pleasant work than watching them. I doubt we will either of us be missed."

Regapisk hesitated.

"Your heroism at the crater has been told," Annalun said. "I will not laugh at the marks of a hero. But the girls will want to see. Come, Feathered Lord."

Chapter Seventeen

Islands

At dawn outside Sunfall Crater, the emissary who wore the mask of a road runner boarded a floating basket. Sandry, Burning Tower, and Clever Squirrel climbed after him, wincing at stiffness and bruises, flinching from the wobble of the basket and the strangeness of what they were doing and what was to come. The emissary, impassive in his mask, watched them settle themselves. Tower could not have said when the basket began to move; but they were drifting down the line of logs, faster and faster. A wind picked up. All ducked their faces beneath the wicker rim, all but Road Runner, protected in his mask, with slits for eyeholes.

The road on both sides of the High Road was very broad. It ran straight as an arrow's flight. Tower found she could watch the road unreel behind her, wind whipping her hair around her cheeks. For a glimpse ahead, she could brave the wind for a few seconds at a time.

Sunfall Crater was hours behind them. As the basket reached the top of an uphill slope, Clever Squirrel told them, "It looks like islands scattered across a sea."

"No, it doesn't," said Sandry. "It's a jumble out there. Wilderness. Plants that reach out and stick you with needles."

"I can see manna glowing in spots and lines. Flickers of light in a sea of darkness. I can't make you see it. Fur Slipper had that talent. There—close up—Sandry, do you see twin spires of light?"

What he saw, when they drew closer, was two great petrified trees standing upright. Lesser stone trees began appearing along the High Road, many fallen, many still upright. They glided through a forest of stone. From time to time, armed men showed between the trunks.

"Our priests have dreamed, aided by the *ilb'al* seeds," Road Runner said. "Stone men lived in a stone jungle until gods fought a war here. They fled south until doom overtook them. Clever Squirrel, magic once gone doesn't return. That may be what happened to the stone men, and the trees too. They no longer grow."

"What do you guard?"

"What the Emperor holds, we guard," Road Runner said.

Sareg said, "We guard the stone wood from thieves. People who know nothing of magic would steal it for its beauty alone. The Emperor sells it to far lands."

* * *

Near day's end the High Road ran through a canyon. The great road still ran straight as a rain arrow's flight. Dusk was coming on. Shadows marked out a maze of rectilinear structures. There was a pillar of light ahead, an enormous fluted tower far too large to be made even by wizards. The view of the tower was framed by impressively tall gates leading into the city. This side of the gateway were big, ornate wagons laid out with travel nests, blocky buildings, and a stream running through meadow.

"Aztlan?" asked Sandry, and "Aztlan," said their guide.

There were sentries on the cliffs. Smoke from signal fires rose in puffs.

"I was expecting a sea," Sandry said to Road Runner. "Aztlan is thought to be an island."

The basket slowed, stopped, and settled almost to touch the stonewood log. The Emperor's emissary said, "Whatever an island may be, this is Aztlan. We may not enter tonight. The Emperor will have ceased his duties for the day. Come, we'll find meals and blankets below." He shooed them over the side and followed them down.

At that day's dawn, Regapisk woke to squabbling voices.

The girls had prepared them a meal of potatoes, corn, and flatbread. Arshur was already up and trying to eat, but a dozen men were waiting to talk to him; four guards were keeping them in line. The official talking to Arshur was getting frustrated and trying to hide it. He talked slower and slower, as if dealing with a fool.

Arshur wasn't having trouble with the language, but

the concepts were odd. "But how could you keep such a thing secret! Whole towns are deserted or dead, and nobody's doing anything about it. Somebody *had* to tell the Emperor."

"None would risk his life. None but the king would be safe," the official said.

"Why not choose a new king, then, or a king for the day?" He noticed Regapisk. "Welcome! How's your head?"

"Pounding. How's yours?"

"I did not see why anyone would not want to be king until this moment! Well, Swarm of Hornets, find me a map so that I may know which villages have not paid tribute, so that I may tell the Emperor. Is the army prepared to ride out and deal with these matters?"

Regapisk said, "I need to go out into the city."

The king grimaced. "Better there than here, friend. What do you need? A chariot?"

"That would be handy. I want to talk to my new partner."

The river that wound through Aztlan was bounded by three- and four-story structures that leaned over the water. The streets were narrow and shadowed.

Reg's charioteer drove them unerringly to Flensevan's shop.

Flensevan was small and burly, older than Ruser. He bowed low before the king's markings on chariot and charioteer. "I am Flensevan and your servant. What would Your Lordship want with me?"

"I bear a letter from your brother and partner, Ruser." Regapisk gave the man a parchment roll.

Flensevan read. “Ruser lives, then.”

“Healthy and happy and busy, with a new scar healing along here.” Regapisk drew a diagonal along his shoulder and chest. Flensevan’s eyes bugged as he saw the feathers inside Regapisk’s wide sleeve. “I last saw him at Sunfall Crater. He would come no closer to Aztlan.”

“Hardly surprising. I take it you are my new partner, then,” Flensevan said with little enthusiasm.

“Shall we speak inside?”

“Enter.” Flensevan led the way.

“Rejoice!” Regapisk said when he judged they were out of earshot of the charioteer. “Our first business dealings have made us rich! Or will, when Ruser reaches Crescent City.”

“Ruser was too optimistic when I knew him. The letter says he was penniless when you came along.”

“Yes, and I came as a pauper, and he took me into his house, and Arshur too. Arshur the new king,” Regapisk said pointedly. “And I am king’s companion, and we owe Ruser. Partner, you could have done worse.”

He could see the wheels turn in Flensevan’s mind. “What are you to King Arshur?”

“He was placed under my protection by our employer. We’ve fought together since.”

“And how do you know the language of Aztlan? Did Ruser teach you this?”

“Refinements. I learned from an old wizard, Zephan—”

Flensevan cut him off. “I see. Welcome, then. Will you have tea, Regapisk? Or wine?”

“Tea. Don’t threaten me with wine today, Flensevan. The king and I drank half our life’s allotment last night. . . ." Regapisk stared as Flensevan led him through the jewelry shop. Stonewood stood in great slabs; turquoise, jade, and treasure Regapisk couldn't name was heaped in bins and on shelves. Aisles ran between. He saw wealth on display in a fashion never seen anywhere in Tep's Town.

A wicker screen covered one wall, and hand weapons were mounted on it: spears and atlatls and swords. He asked, "Do thieves bother you much?"

"Not much," Flensevan said.

The only man on duty was half-grown and lightly built. His beard was just coming in. His eyes followed Regapisk mistrustfully as Regapisk bent over a bowl of deep purple gems without quite daring to touch them. Flensevan set the young man to closing up shop.

"What's to stop somebody"—*some Lordkin,* Regapisk didn't say—"from just walking off with a handful of this?"

"The Emperor," Flensevan said.

"Not personally?"

"No, but a thief would lose his heart to the wall."

The young man was Pink Rabbit, Flensevan's eldest. He prepared their tea, and then remained in attendance while his father and Regapisk explored each other's pasts. Regapisk named his home as Tep's Town and was relieved when Flensevan showed no sign of recognition. He described his financial arrangements with Jade Coin, tacitly admitting that his people didn't expect him home, ever. Ruser, of course, couldn't go home either. Regapisk hinted that he would like to know why, but Flensevan did not respond.

* * *

Regapisk waited until the boy was out of the room before he said, "Ruser told me to ask about the boat."

Hot tea slopped over Flensevan's hand. Flensevan's face did not move. "Boat?"

"Boat. He said not to speak of this until we were alone."

"Mmm. Rabbit?" He didn't raise his voice. Pink Rabbit appeared. Flensevan asked, "Where is the charioteer?"

"Guarding the chariot. He hasn't moved."

"Were you able to hear us in the kitchen?"

"Yes, Father."

"Stroll with me, Regapisk. There is a place where we will be harder to hear, even by an Emperor's servant. But first—" He held out his hand.

Regapisk took the small crude statuette in its box from his pocket and gave it to Flensevan. Flensevan opened the box and held the statuette to Regapisk's forehead.

The statuette grew an erection. So did Reggy.

Flensevan nodded. "Come with me, partner."

In an inner room, two of Flensevan's servants joined them. It took them both to lift and move a table, exposing a rug. Then the rug had to be rolled up to expose a wooden floor. Then—not the trapdoor Regapisk was expecting. Four heavy timbers in the floor had to be slid along their length, and then eight steps led down by a man's height, down to water. Boards bordered a sluggishly moving pool.

Flensevan reached to touch a fist-size blob of jade, raddled with stony intrusions, hanging on a rope. It lit up in garish green. He lowered it into the water. By its light Regapisk could see a boat tapered at bow and stern, nine or ten paces long. The mast lay along the length of the boat, dismounted. There was no room for oarsmen, a thing Regapisk was inclined to notice. The boat was tilted on its side on the mud, and the bottom had windows in it.

"My brother must trust you amazingly," Flensevan said. "Then again, that may be how he lost the money he was given—"

"No, it was the blockade. Lots of people in Crescent City lost everything. They were starving when we came," Regapisk said.

"Ah? Good. In any case, the boat is a secret. It's our means of escape if politics turns nasty. It was Atlantean, of course."

"It's very dark," Regapisk said. "I mean it was dark underwater before you lowered the gem. There's no manna down there at all, and you'd have to float that thing with manna."

Flensevan grinned thinly. "You're a wizard?"

"No. I can see manna. Sometimes."

"Ah. There's manna. It's shielded."

"Well shielded, then. Good. Is it provisioned? And you'd have to get it to the river."

"We're on the river. There are barrels of water. I leave them open, so it's always fresh river water. If we get time, we could add stores of food, but starvation won't be our most urgent problem if we need this boat! Let me show you." Flensevan walked along the boards to what should be the river side of the house, if Reg hadn't got confused.

"Here. Throw all your weight down on this beam, then that one across, then this in the middle. It's a puzzle, so get the order right. The whole front of the house slides aside, and that's your access to the river."

"Then what?"

"Well. Ruser and I began stowing talismans nineteen years ago, and I've kept it up. There's a king's ransom in the hold, in charged turquoise, silver bars and filigree, jade, some gems. But the first thing we did . . . mmm. First an Atlantean sold us the sunken boat in return for a getaway. He wanted to leave Aztlan quick."

"An Atlantean. Zeph?"

Flensevan looked wary. "What do you think?"

"I didn't think Zephans was any kind of great wizard," Regapisk said. "But I never heard of anyone better at using tiny fizzings of manna."

"That's what the best Atlanteans did. As to Zeph's powers, he never claimed to be more than a journeyman. But he could see the future well enough to know to get out of Atlantis. And out of Aztlan."

"Mm-mmph," Regapisk muttered. "And why was he in such a hurry to leave?"

"You're king's companion and you don't know?"

Regapisk kept his stern face. "Ah. So how did you get him out?"

"So we got him in a basket in a mask that wasn't his, and he took our secret with him. Then we built the shop over and around the boat. We bought some logs of depleted petrified wood and we sawed them into slats. We surrounded the cargo bay with slats. They're all tied together with cables, completely surrounding the cargo bay." Flensevan was leading him around the pool. "*Then* we could put magically charged talismans in the cargo bay without the boat popping up out of the water. Dismounting the mast, that was a challenge too. I learned how to swim like a fish."

He whacked a pulley mounted on the wall. "Here, you reel this in and the slats roll up inside the bay. Now the treasure's exposed and radiating manna. The old spells come alive. The boat pops up as far as the second story, and if the mast was up, you'd break it. You get up this ladder. Look straight up, do you see the ramp from the second story? Cross that and you're aboard, and so am I, because that's where I'm waiting."

Flensevan looked straight into Regapisk's eyes. "Remember that we can only use it once, and it's treason."

"Why do this? What were you expecting?"

"Ruser got away quick and easy, and if he won't tell you why, neither will I. But they watch me more closely now. What happened to my brother could happen to anyone. Now, Regapisk, I can't stand it anymore. Tell me how you got feathers."

Regapisk returned to the palace in midafternoon, bringing Flensevan. "You should meet the king," he told his partner.

They found a mob of officials waiting outside their building. The guards led them past.

A woman was trying to tell Arshur about kitchen supplies gone undelivered for a solid year. Arshur gestured her silent. "Lord Reg! The Emperor wants to see me, but only once a day. I saw him at noon. It's all bad news, and it's all months old. He . . ." Arshur hesitated, but the guards wouldn't know Tep's Town speech, would they? ". . . raved. He didn't want to hear any of it. Tomorrow I'll have three times as much to tell him. I've got two secretaries rotating duties. Who's this?"

"My partner Flensevan." Flensevan's forehead was against the rug.

"Greetings, Flensevan. Welcome. Get up. Treat Regapisk nice, he's simple. Look, Reg, I can't get loose to meet Lord Sandry and the girls. Greet them and make them welcome."

"Shall I bring them here?"

"Curse, I don't know. Let them lodge outside tonight. The Emperor may wish to welcome them outside. He may not."

"Is he changeable, then?" Regapisk asked.

Arshur shrugged. "Lord Reg, I can make nothing of the man. He is one of the Great Ones, and they live as they will. Greet our friends tonight, and return here."

"It's a long journey to the gates and back," Regapisk said.

Arshur grinned. "And a short one to the wall, Lord Reg. Take what you need. Go to them this evening and see that they are made welcome. Return here tonight."

"What shall I tell them?"

Arshur looked distracted. "Tell them—" He caught himself. "Tell them they will be invited inside, and they'll have suitable quarters in the city. If no one tells you different, I can find them a place in this palace; there are more rooms than I'll ever need. The Emperor has a huge ceremony planned, wedding, something else about my coronation, a big public holiday where he'll show himself to the people, but it's not for four days yet. It'll take that long to bring the beasts. As to when they meet the Almighty One, he didn't say. Perhaps tomorrow, perhaps another day."

Chapter Eighteen

The Gates

At dusk Regapisk rode through the streets of Aztlan. Stonewood logs ran to his left, separating two lanes of traffic. Flensevan's wide eyes and white-knuckled grip made it clear that the man had never ridden at the speed a king's chariot could make with all other traffic scattering to give it room.

Regapisk had hoped to meet Sandry's basket, but the streets of Aztlan were a puzzle. It was near dark when the great gates appeared before them.

The great gates were not gates in a wall. They stood alone, and if they could be closed, it wasn't obvious how that could be done. They seemed symbols only.

Regapisk asked, "What's to stop anyone from just driving around the gates?"

"Guards," Flensevan said. "You don't come in without

invitation, unless you want your heart cut out and set in the wall. A lot of business gets done outside anyway."

"You're going to have to tell me about that wall."

"North of the shop, under the Great Mesa. You will see it soon enough. But it is ill luck to speak of it." The chariot lurched as it went through the gates, and Flensevan stopped talking.

There was a city outside the city: a few big blocky buildings, and several circular buildings of the type usually associated with religion—*kivas*. The wagons were impressive even to a man who had seen the Feathersnake caravans. Regapisk asked, "We're looking at considerable wealth, aren't we?"

"Oh, yes," Flensevan said.

"The High Road is over there," Regapisk said positively.

"Why, I believe so, but how do you know?" Flensevan braced as the chariot rounded a turn to go south.

"I see it as a bright line," Regapisk said. "I'm surprised you can't see this; the power in it blazes even at dusk. And there it is."

The guards at the High Road terminal saluted the king's chariot.

"I am king's companion," Regapisk said.

"Yes, Lord, how may we serve you?"

"I seek the visitors who arrived today."

"Certainly, Lord. In the Caravanserai." The guard pointed. "They will lodge there for the night."

The Caravanserai would have been a palace in any other city. It was built in a manner Regapisk already thought of as Aztlan public building style: a multistoried building nestled against the cliff face, with a broad, flat patio in front. Inside the city, many of the buildings were faced with tiers of seats for the public, but this one had nothing obscuring the patio's view of the High Road and the long stretch to the west, flatlands with mesas, lightning storms above high mountains to the northwest.

An elegantly dressed servant led Regapisk and Flensevan to a table on the broad patio. The table was set in a pit, with a bench around the pit's wall for seating. In the center of the table was a large, shallow, round bowl of red clay. It held a fire that at first looked like burning brush, but the brush blazed away without being consumed. The fire sparkled with magic, and what little smoke it emitted obediently avoided the eyes and noses of everyone around it.

"Visiting Ladies and Lords, the king's companion and his friend," the servant announced.

Sandry stood and bowed. Regapisk thought his cousin was doing a good job of hiding a grin. "Hail," Sandry said. "Please join us."

"Yes, we have much to discuss," Regapisk said. "This is Flensevan, my partner."

"Welcome to Aztlan," Flensevan said. "No doubt you will receive a more formal welcome tomorrow." He lowered his voice. "As to discussions, in Aztlan it is well to be careful of what is said. The Emperor's servants are everywhere."

The bench around the table was surprisingly comfortable. Conversation ran up and down the table with the wine.

The wine was from someplace far south, and it was

old. It had to be. No caravan had come near Aztlan in nearly a year. Flensevan spoke rumors of treason by priests who served the nightmare birds. Yes, they were true. What, then, of the rain?

It evolved that the priests of Left-Handed Hummingbird had infiltrated deep into the Office of Rain. The Emperor and his servants would have to separate out those blameless among the apprentices. Weather might be dry in Aztlan until those became proficient in the work.

Now Flensevan was urging Regapisk to speak of his past. Reg couldn't lie in front of Sandry. "I am a Lord of Lordshills and Tep's Town, sent to explore. I have farmed," he said, "and trained with weapons and fought terror birds. I know the sea. I can speak to mers, but I don't suppose there's call for that here."

"Mers?" Flensevan asked, and Regapisk laughed and explained, aided by Sandry. The port at Tep's Town, the tales of Lordkin sent to sea for crimes. Flensevan listened, not quite believing.

"Then here's to my new partner," Flensevan said presently, and drained his cup. A servant refilled it, but Flensevan set it down untasted. When the servant retired to his place along the wall, Flensevan said, carefully, "We are outside, but so are the Supreme One's servants. Wine loosens the tongue, and that can be dangerous."

"Dangerous how?" Regapisk asked. "Dangerous to the king's companions?"

Flensevan smiled thinly. "You may know less of that than you believe," he said.

"Does everyone fear the Emperor?" Burning Tower asked.

"Fear him or love him," Flensevan said. "The wisest love him in fear."

"What must we fear?" Clever Squirrel asked.

"You are a shaman. Have you had visions of a long wall?"

Squirrel frowned. "I have dreamed of a wall of stucco, and heard a sound," she said. "But I don't know what it means."

"What sound?" Burning Tower asked.

"Almost like rain. Or a thousand drums. Or a million butterfly wings—"

"A thousand hearts," Flensevan said.

"Hearts?"

The jeweler said, "The Wall of Hearts lies under the Great Mesa. You will see it tomorrow, or when it pleases the Supreme One to invite you into the city. There are niches in it, bricked up. Each holds a heart. At least a thousand hearts have been placed there."

"Hearts," Sandry said with disbelief. "Hearts without bodies, but they still beat?"

Flensevan shrugged. "Your shaman hears them. And I assure you, Lord . . . Sandry? I assure you they were beating when they went in."

"Whose hearts?" Burning Tower asked.

Flensevan shrugged. "Mostly enemies of the Emperor, of course. Those who blaspheme against the gods, those who oppose the will of the Supreme One, or the bureau chiefs. Thieves. And a few others, who are sent to the gods for the good of Aztlan."

"What others?" Clever Squirrel asked. "And to what gods? I know no gods who wish for such gifts!"

"Not gifts," Flensevan said. "Messengers. Doubtless those who know more of this will explain it all to you." He shuddered and would say no more.

It was well past dark when Regapisk and Flensevan took their leave. Two soldiers carried torches to light their way. Like the cook fire at the table, the torches gave light but no smoke and were not consumed.

More servants with glowing torches led Burning Tower and the others to the large building and up winding stairs through corridors and small rooms. Tower was soon lost.

Their sleeping quarters were three spacious rooms with windows that looked out to the city gates and beyond into the canyon that held Aztlan.

All the beds were in one room.

"Aztlan has different notions of privacy than we," Sandry said when the servants were gone. "I can move my bed."

"No," Squirrel said. "If they expect us all to sleep in one room, we should do that."

"Three to a room," Tower said. "Isn't three bad luck in their world?"

"And this may be an oversight, or it may be an insult," Squirrel suggested. "Their ways are not our ways, and our only safety now lies in not offending them."

"Squirrel, are you afraid?"

"Of offending them? Yes," Clever Squirrel said. "There is power here. The manna is not as . . . as dense here as it was at Sunfall, but there is more than anywhere else I've been, and it is all under control. It is as if I could reach up and seize manna from the air because they have put it there for my use. And if that is so, they can take it away again. Tower, Sandry, this is a place of great magic, and I feel very small."

"Coyote will protect you," Burning Tower said.

"Perhaps." She opened a bag and began to pour sand, building a crude stick figure that might have been anyone of any sex. It came alive. It spoke.

"Squirrel?"

"Greetings, Mountain Cat," Squirrel said. "Mother said someone would be watching."

"Yes, but talk fast."

"I will. Tell Mother that I'll give as much warning as I can, but the wedding is at the convenience of the Emperor, and he hasn't told us when. Days, I think. From now on, I'll try to call in the mornings."

"All right," the figure said. "You know what it costs to keep this painting ready? Talismans are expensive!"

"I know," Squirrel said. "Tell Whandall we'll bring wealth enough to replace them. Good night." She swept the black sand into its bag without waiting for a reply.

In black moonless night, Clever Squirrel cried out, "It *is* an island!"

Sandry woke. "What?"

She was at the window. "Sorry. Lord Sandry, it's an island of magic in a sea of nothing, a big island with a blazing peak. Mesa Fajada? A burning tower. You don't see it?"

"No. Even when there was light, it was just a city in a desert . . . impressive enough, though."

Clever Squirrel said, "It's not that kind of island, Sandry. Wait for daylight. You'll see a butte. To me it's ablaze with manna, with sparks of brighter magic flying around it."

Sandry took the shaman very seriously, but he didn't always believe her every word. She'd been fooled once before.

Chapter Nineteen

The Wall of Hearts

"Reggy! Wake up, Lord Reg!"

"My head hurts," Regapisk complained.

"Awake! Now! I need you." Arshur's shouts couldn't be ignored. Regapisk noted that there was no one else on the mat with him. Whatever her name, she'd gotten up before he woke.

"Regapisk!" Arshur's voice had a snap to it.

"Coming, Majesty," Regapisk called. He pulled on a gown, hardly noticing the supple fibers and rich colors that would have made the garment worth a fortune in Lordshills. He found Arshur seated at breakfast. A dozen scribes crowded around him.

"Yes, Majesty."

Arshur grinned. "The Emperor asks a favor."

"Instantly," Regapisk said.

Arshur nodded, and Jaguar's priest said, "The Emperor finds that his duties today are more extensive than he anticipated."

Arshur laughed. "Everything's going to hell, and I haven't finished telling him the half of it! There are situations to deal with to the north as well as the west. We'll be all day planning this stuff!"

The Jaguar-headed priest nodded and continued, "And thus the Supreme One asks that the king's companion greet the new guests who arrived last night. I believe you have already seen them yesterday at dinner."

"I did, priest."

"They were invited by the Supreme One, and they must be conducted into the city by a suitably important official," Jaguar said. "Come to the window, if you please, King's Companion."

"Sure."

Jaguar pointed. "You see the Imperial Palace, and the great Temple Mesa Fajada to the north there."

"Yes."

"Now look west, across the river, beyond the merchant homes. You see a palace against the cliff there. That is reserved for important visitors. Your friends would be lodged there, and all was made ready for them, but now King Arshur has invited them here. They may choose as they will. The servants expect them."

"Bring them here, Lord Reg," Arshur shouted.

"As the king commands, then," Jaguar said. "Bring them here." He bowed formally. "The Supreme One requests that you go to the gate and in his name welcome his guests and conduct them into the city. Chariots await you outside."

The roads were clear and the horses—all mares, Regapisk noted—were fresh, but it took over an hour to get to the gate from the king's palace. He found Sandry, Tower, and Squirrel in the dining area of the Caravanserai.

"You again?" Sandry said.

Regapisk grinned. "Not just me. I am here as king's companion to welcome you to Aztlan in the name of the Supreme One. Welcome, guests. I am to conduct you inside."

The effect was startling. Everyone nearby bowed, not head to the ground but low.

They passed through the gates. Burning Tower held Sandry's arm tightly. "Four days, then," she said. "And then we'll be married. Finally!"

"I can't help wishing it were all done and we were headed for home," Sandry said.

"But think of what we will see! And the stories we will tell," Tower said. Her eyes darted everywhere. People stopped whatever they were doing, scampered for the road's edge, and then bowed as the chariots passed. She examined their mode of dress. Their skin color varied, but she thought she could pass as one of them. If she had to.

Her thoughts toyed with notions of escape. Traders on the Hemp Road did not like to be so restricted, and trading partners could turn in an instant.

But mostly she thought of the coming wedding. How

would she look? What gowns did they have for her? The Emperor would preside. It would be magnificent.

And then he would claim Spike. She tried not to think of that, to concentrate on Sandry and her wedding day.

The way led through the city. Regapisk pointed out the military barracks and training ground, the stables, a hospital. He turned down the river road to show them the jewelry shop in the house by the river. There was a market beyond that.

Squirrel was sniffing the air like a dog, catching scents, no doubt, but manna traces too.

The road led to the Imperial Palace, and the great Temple Mesa. It gleamed in the prenoon sun, tiles of all colors, awnings and shades above the balconies.

"Mesa Fajada," Regapisk said. "You saw it from the High Road."

"Impressive," Tower said. "That may be the most gorgeous thing I have ever seen."

The road led up the river directly toward the Mesa. Regapisk pointed to his left. "The Imperial Palace."

The palace faced the temple. There was a huge raised flat plaza backed by an arc of multistoried buildings, rows and rows of narrow windows facing the plaza. The plaza itself faced the Temple Mesa. The walls behind the buildings were bare, no windows or doors at all. All windows faced the plaza, and across it, the Mesa Fajada.

"The Emperor lives there?" Sandry asked.

"I think not, Cousin," Regapisk said. "The Supreme One lives where he chooses, of course, but I believe he has his apartments up there." He pointed upward to a great wooden balcony that ringed Mesa Fajada.

"That's high," Sandry said. "Twenty manheights?"

"I am told thirty. It felt that high," Regapisk said. As they came closer to the Mesa, they could see a continual line of baskets flowing up and down along the mesa sides. When they were closer still, Regapisk pointed. "The Wall of Hearts. Slow, driver, that our guests may see."

It wasn't that impressive, just a big old stucco wall with a checkerboard pattern, crude compared to the newer structures around it. A more ornate tiled wall rose high at the base of the mesa. A bridge crossed over the wall from the landing platform for baskets to the Imperial Palace itself, actually bridging over the old wall, which wasn't high enough to be seen from the palace courtyard. The wall was old and dusty, but ornately dressed guards stood post at either end, and the air was full of a fluttering sound just at the edge of Tower's hearing. Sandry watched the wall with brooding intensity. He did not suggest that they stop.

"Old blood," Squirrel murmured, "and murder. There's manna in murder, did you know that? There's a special name for wizards who get their power that way."

Their way led past the wall and around the Imperial Palace, which was even larger than Sandry had thought.

The sun was still high when they reached the king's palace. There was time for a sweatbath. Sandry again declined in favor of a pool. He was relaxing in the warm water when a servant came.

"Come," the man said urgently. "You are requested. The Supreme One himself will greet you. Come!"

Chapter Twenty

The Welcome

They dressed hurriedly and were whisked away in large wagons. Three passengers and a driver in each wagon—they were called by the same word that Aztlan used for chariots, but to Sandry they were far too unwieldy to deserve that noble name—and each drawn by four mares. The driver wore brilliantly polished bronze armor that shone in the sun, and there was a case of spears next to him, but the spears were also polished, with black wooden shafts that gleamed without signs of ever having been held by human hands. There was no bow.

The driver was competent on the paved roads. Sandry wondered how good he'd be in a war formation.

They drove up to the Imperial Palace, and through an arched door into gloom. This part of the palace was a bewildering series of walls and small rooms, not well lighted, with no windows. Statues stood lonely in some of the rooms. Others were empty. They turned a corner to see bright daylight coming down a broad staircase.

They climbed the stairs to what Sandry had thought was the palace roof, but instead it was the immense tiled plaza built high above ground level. The plaza faced the great Mesa Fajada temple and was high enough that from its center they could not see the Wall of Hearts at the mesa's base. The flat plaza surface was marked by four large circular openings, each ten manheights across. *Kivas,* Sandry remembered. Ceremonies were carried out in there. Some were secret.

Behind the plaza facing the mesa were tiers of seats built against the multistoried buildings. The seats were just filling with people. People streamed in, some from the *kivas,* some from other stairs onto the plaza, many from inside the various palace buildings.

They were led to the center of the plaza. There was a great *kiva,* and they were led down a stairway into it. As they vanished, there were cheers from the crowd behind them.

The *kiva* was a large circular pit three manheights deep. It was partially roofed over by silk tapestries held up by an elaborate arrangement of spars and hoops projecting from the walls. The tapestries were too thin to provide much shade, but they were brilliantly colored and decorated by drawings and strange complex symbols. Sandry could not make out what they represented.

A bench ran all around the walls, broken only by the

entrances. There were two entrances, steep stairways barely wide enough for two abreast to enter or leave.

Down on the floor of the *kiva,* ornate tables and chairs stood in the bright sun. Servants held umbrellas, and despite the blazing sun, the guests felt cool when they sat at the tables in the shade. More servants brought stone cups of fruit juices.

"Ice," Clever Squirrel said. "Ice."

"You sound impressed," Regapisk said.

"I am impressed. Do you know how much manna is needed to make ice here?"

Regapisk nodded sagely.

Servants came and bowed. A great gong sounded from deep inside the palace. The umbrellas were lowered, and another gong sounded.

The *kiva* filled with thick white smoke, so thick that Sandry could barely see his drink on the table, but the smoke had no smell and did not sting his eyes. More like fog than smoke, he thought.

Shapes appeared, and as the smoke cleared, the guest saw masked priests. When the cloud was gone, the priests spread their arms high above their heads to the great cheers of the crowd behind them. Sandry wondered just how many of the people could see into the *kiva*. Enough, he supposed.

"The stairs aren't wide enough," Regapisk muttered. It took Sandry a moment to understand. Then he nodded. He counted sixteen priests plus attendants. That many priests could not have come in by the stairs. There hadn't been enough time. There was another way into the *kiva*.

A secret entrance, or else magic, Sandry thought.

The priests bowed to their guests, then took places at the tables. When they were all seated, servants brought food.

Clever Squirrel regarded the array of priests and tried to pick them out. Turkey was easily recognized. And Bison Woman, looking very much the same here as back on the Hemp Road. As Squirrel watched, Bison Woman came over to them and bowed to Burning Tower.

"Welcome to Aztlan. You are to be married here. Is this the fortunate man?"

Burning Tower blushed. "Yes."

"We have our customs and requirements, of course, and anyone married by the Emperor is married indeed throughout all the worlds, but the Supreme One commands that all be done according to your customs as well as ours," Bison Woman said. "And we have little time. Would you come with me to speak of the necessary details?"

"Of course." Burning Tower stood.

Bison Woman smiled thinly. "And you as well, Lord Sandry. If you please."

Clever Squirrel chuckled to herself and regarded the other priests. Road Runner's priest had escorted them to Aztlan in a flying basket. That gorgeously dressed bareheaded man was another of the four priests who had come to Sunfall Crater; she'd wondered if he was Terror Bird's priest. That—her heart leapt. The man who stepped to meet them wore Coyote's mask. She knew it, however unfamiliar. It felt like coming home.

The mask exposed his mouth, and she could see his grin. "I am Coyote's priest," he said. Confronting Regapisk and Clever Squirrel, he did not bow.

Regapisk made introductions. Coyote's priest said, "Coyote's daughter? Clever Squirrel, I've been eager to meet you. Have you seen Coyote yourself?"

"Not seen. Sometimes I feel him in my mind. He was in my father's mind the night I was conceived."

"I don't see him either. I sense him in my thoughts when matters around me become most amusing or most confusing."

"Such as?"

Regapisk had moved down the table and was eating ribs. Sandry and Tower had been led away. Squirrel was effectively alone with Coyote's priest. He said, "Things have turned wonderfully active since you people turned up. A dozen priests are all in detention, awaiting the coronation ceremony on Mesa Fajada with no great eagerness. The Emperor is not expected to appear in his formal cloak, the one covered with terror bird feathers. There's speculation and rumor. Can you tell me—"

Squirrel nodded. "The cloaks at the crater all turned to hummingbird feathers. Enough to cover a small blanket."

"Then the Emperor's great cloak must have too!" Coyote's priest barked laughter. "Try this—it's rattlesnake. Chili for dipping. What can you tell me about the war against the birds?"

Squirrel described the battle at Sunfall and its end at the sweatbath. "And a hummingbird tried to kill me. It must have been possessed." It wouldn't be good if the Emperor's servants learned too much of Sandry's tactics, she thought; but what would a shaman know about that? Squirrel could sense a watching presence behind her eyes. Coyote was with her. Was the god with his shaman too?

Coyote's priest asked, "Have you questions, Clever Squirrel?"

"To ask a question, one must know most of the answer. We just got here."

"Start somewhere. Ask a bad question."

"We're sleeping three in a room. Is that normal?"

"I expect the concierge thought you'd want to guard each other. Besides, three in a room makes a visitor welcome, because four is lucky. Would you prefer your own rooms? Something about your marriage customs?"

"Exactly. Sandry has enough to put up with without that! . . . Tell me about the priest with no mask."

"He stands in for all the forgotten gods. You thought he stood in for Left-Handed Hummingbird? No, that one waits with the rest of the bird's priests. We must have four fours of gods, though, and some entity must be chosen to replace the bird. Ask again."

"The wall," she said, "What's it for?"

For an instant, she glimpsed an answer; and then Coyote's priest said, "For the hearts of the enemies of the Empire, and certain heroes too. Ask again."

He'd slipped aside from something important; she knew that. It struck her that she was being invited to display her ignorance. Change directions? "When do you take off your mask?"

He grinned. "Do you really want to know?"

She grinned in return. Then the gongs sounded.

"Follow me," Coyote's priest said urgently. "Watch me and be careful."

"But—"

"Come."

Everyone rose, quickly, and climbed the stairs to the plaza level, where they stood facing Mesa Fajada. Sandry, Tower, and Buffalo Woman hurried across the plaza to join them. They all stood, waiting, and Squirrel didn't dare turn to see, but she thought that all those in the stands behind them, hundreds, perhaps thousands, were standing also. The silence was awesome.

The sun burned hot, and there was no wind. Squirrel lost track of time. Then the gongs, and now trumpets, sounded from all around them, from in the *kiva* and from the plaza itself, although there was no sign of musicians or instruments. The gongs and trumpets rose to a crescendo.

Brilliant fire flashed from the top of Mesa Fajada. All looked up. A man stood there, a big man on a tiny balcony jutting out from the big circular balcony. He wore a cloak of fine black fur and a long, wonderfully embroidered kilt. He was bareheaded and shirtless and scarred along chest and belly. She squinted to see him. He was terribly far away.

"Welcome, our guests from afar!" His voice rang; it filled the plaza and the city beyond. It might have filled the whole earth, Squirrel thought, and knew she was being silly. But the Empire threw magic around as if there were no tomorrow. Squirrel remembered an argument out of a dream. The priests of Terror Bird did have a point.

"People of Aztlan, we welcome Lord Sandry of Lordshills and the City of Yangin-Atep. Welcome, Burning Tower, heiress of the House of Feathersnake, a great one of the far lands of the Hemp Road. Welcome, Clever Squirrel, Daughter of Coyote."

The crowd stirred at that announcement, a short sound that might have been pleasure and might have been amazement, cut off quickly as the great voice continued to boom. "Welcome, Lord Regapisk of Lordshills and companion to our new king, Arshur. Welcome all!"

There was a short pause, then the priests began to cheer. The cheers were taken up by the crowd behind them. "Hail and welcome! We greet you, guests from afar! Welcome to the king and his companion. The king! The king!"

Squirrel looked up. There was another man standing with the Emperor, blond and taller even than the Supreme One. Arshur the Wanderer, at home at last.

"The king!"

"I would come to be among my people this night, but that the king has laid massive obligations on me," the great voice boomed. "And now we prepare the coronation feast, and other wonders for my people."

"I can barely see him," Squirrel whispered. "He's glowing like the sun in my eyes!"

And suddenly the Emperor was not far away at all. His image grew and grew until he was nearly as large as Mesa Fajada. His presence was immense.

Tower winced. He looked like he'd been gutted like a trout.

Sandry's look spoke for him: grim, and a little sick. "Those scars!"

The priests looked at Sandry with alarm, and Squirrel

felt fear. Her eyes pleaded with Sandry, but he didn't need the reminder. He fell silent and waited.

There was a long pause as the enormous image showed itself to the people of Aztlan. Then the gongs sounded, the image faded, and the balcony was empty.

They were silent as they went down the stairs to the stables under the plaza, and there was little conversation as they returned to the king's palace. The banqueting hall seemed small and familiar compared with the glaring open plaza and the great mesa above.

"Are you all right?" Burning Tower asked.

Squirrel smiled without warmth. "He was—impressive."

"Frightening, you mean," Tower said.

"Very."

"But very generous," Tower said.

Squirrel could hear the excitement in her sister's voice. And why not? She was to be married soon, and unlike Coyote's daughter, Tower would mate for life, coupling with a man she loved. "Are your wedding plans set?"

"No, we are to meet with Bison Woman again. And Jaguar's priest, and of course Coyote's—they'll all take part." She turned serious. "I'm going to miss Spike."

"Nothing you can do about that," Squirrel said.

"No. I do want to be married. But it will be hard saying good-bye to him." Her mood brightened. "Bison Woman says we can go anywhere we like in the domains of the Emperor. There are wonderful places here. Maybe we'll see some of them, but mostly, I want to go home with my new husband."

Squirrel smiled agreement.

Bison Woman came to collect Burning Tower for another conference. Tower and Bison Woman and Sandry went to a table in the far corner of the room, where they were instantly surrounded by a host of scribes.

Squirrel felt lonely. Then she felt a presence behind her.

"He is awesome," Coyote's priest said. "Even to you and me. Think of how he appears to those not blessed with Coyote's vision."

Night came. The walls glowed with soft light, and the banquet tables were filled again with food. Regapisk sat at one place from the center of the high table, to the right of where Arshur would be, only Arshur wasn't there.

"Lord Regapisk, may I join you?"

Regapisk grinned. "Certainly, Cousin. And welcome. Has Bison Woman done with you?"

Sandry poured a cup of wine and sipped. "Yes. Her scribes wrote out the contracts, and they'll be witnessed and signed in multiple copies, so Quintana and Aunt Shanda will be satisfied. They'll have to be."

"But not through with Tower," Regapisk said. He pointed to the corner table where the scribes were writing furiously.

Sandry laughed. "And never will be, I think. She keeps coming up with other details, things she remembers from some other girl's wedding, or things her mother told her, and she wants it all."

Regapisk grinned. "The Supreme One can afford it."

"That he can," Sandry said. "How's the king holding up?"

Regapisk laughed. "He's still Arshur. He likes everything about being king but the work itself."

"What work is that?"

"The king is the only bearer of bad news," Regapisk said. "No one else can tell the Emperor anything bad, because he might be blamed, or he might be sent to the gods as a messenger to tell them."

"Sent to the gods. You mean his heart goes in the wall?"

Regapisk nodded. "So everyone tells things to the king and the king tells the Supreme One. Only there hasn't been a king for so long that a lot of bad news piled up." Regapisk shrugged. "So far it's gone well, though. King Arshur has sent off half a dozen expeditions to deal with minor tax revolts. He said something about asking your advice, maybe asking you to take charge of something."

Sandry grinned. "I'm getting married, Cousin, and I will have more pleasant things to think about than leading an army to beat up tax delinquents. And then I'm going home."

Regapisk nodded.

"Sorry. I guess that's a delicate subject," Sandry said.

"Yeah. Okay, I figured out why you didn't buy me loose from the ship. It was because I talked about going back, wasn't it?"

Sandry nodded.

"I know better now." Regapisk grinned. "But I'm still a Lord, and I'm rich, I can make my home anywhere I want except Lordshills, and who needs that place anyway?"

"That's the spirit."

Regapisk watched Coyote's priest and Coyote's daughter. He said, "It looks something like a seduction and something like a duel. Sandry, what do you think?"

"Something like a game of solitaire too," Sandry said.

"They serve the same god, but one serves the Emperor. They may not know themselves what they're looking for. Ah. They are finished with Tower." He stood.

Burning Tower came over, her eyes blazing with excitement. "It's going to be wonderful," she said. "They are making a wedding robe. I think I'll look beautiful!"

Sandry smiled. "You will always be beautiful."

"I hope so."

"Doubts? Misgivings?"

"No, not really." She looked around the banquet hall. "Who are the girls?" she asked.

"They serve the king for the evening," Sandry said.

"You sound wistful."

"No, my love. Impatient, but not wistful."

Tower looked again. "Pretty. But *eight*? Arshur is magnificent, but he's a bit old."

Regapisk blushed.

"Oh. They reward both the king and his companion, then." Tower picked at her dinner. There were a dozen dishes, enough food for a hundred, delicacies that few Lords and no Lordkin or kinless could ever afford to taste, all set out for the visitors and the priests. "All this," Tower said. "What will happen to it all?"

Regapisk and Sandry looked at each other and smiled. "Servants always dine well," Regapisk said.

"Oh. Yes, I suppose they do," Burning Tower said. "We have servants at home at New Castle, of course I knew that. I guess I got used to being on the roads with the wagon trains."

"It has been pleasant, but I will be glad to go home again," Sandry said.

"Will we be welcome?"

Sandry smiled thinly. "Lord Quintana was ready to welcome us both if we returned alive from Condigeo. Now—"

"Now," Regapisk said, "you will stand so high that you can ask any favor you like of the Congregation of Lords Witness."

"Not *any* favor," Sandry said.

Regapisk tried to smile. "No? I bet you could. We can talk another time."

The chief servant of the king's palace came to their table and bowed. "The king asks in what rooms you wish your beds."

"I'll stay with Clever Squirrel. Put our beds in one room, and Sandry's in another. I think." She looked down the table to where Clever Squirrel was still lost in conversation with Coyote's priest. "We won't disturb her. Yes, put her bed in a room with mine."

The majordomo bowed. "When you are ready, I will send a maid with a light to guide you to your rooms. This palace can be confusing."

"I'll go now," Tower said. "It has been a very long day."

"As you wish, mistress," the majordomo said. "I will send the maid."

The servant had one of the ever-burning torches that gave no smoke. Tower stood.

"Good night, love," Sandry said.

She smiled dreamily. "Good night. Not long now!"

"No."

She lifted her face to be kissed. Sandry made their good night a lot shorter than he wanted it to be and noted Regapisk's barely concealed amusement. He wasn't the only one. Why did people always think it was funny to watch two people before they were married? But they did.

"How's the arm?" Sandry asked.

Regapisk winced. "The feathers, you mean."

"Well, yes." Sandry grinned.

"They itch," Regapisk said. "And so far, no one has been able to cure them. The Many Gods priest thinks he has cast a spell that will get rid of the damn things if I ever get to a place with no manna. It takes a lot of manna to make feathers grow on a man. Or so they say."

"So you can take a chariot and go off into the desert for a while," Sandry said.

"Maybe. King Arshur is talking about sending me off with an army." Regapisk laughed. "Me. The only guy to flunk out of military class!"

"Well, not the only one," Sandry said. "But you didn't last long."

"And I still know more than anyone else here! They have so much manna that they never learned how to fight. That's what I think, anyway. They use magic because they can, and they don't need to know anything else."

Sandry nodded agreement. "Sounds right to me. But it's not my problem."

"No, you can go home again," Regapisk said. "I can't, so maybe it is my problem." He put his hand inside his robe. "Cursed thing wouldn't be so bad if it didn't itch. Women find feathers fascinating."

There were giggles from the other end of the table—Clever Squirrel, amused by something Coyote's priest had said. She answered, and both of them laughed.

Chapter Twenty-One

The King's Duties

Sandry found Tower at breakfast in the banqueting room. Tower scowled and said, "Clever Squirrel was gone when I woke up around midnight. Any idea what happened to her?"

"I haven't—Tower? I slept alone."

"Sorry. Just—pay no attention."

Squirrel came in while they were piling shells with corn, potatoes, and bird meat. Sandry pointed with his nose. "Shall we ask?"

They didn't have to ask. Squirrel was bubbling. "There's a face behind the mask. Good-looking man, with some tattooing that makes him like a coyote—but no name. They all give up their names when they turn archpriest. The one with no mask, you don't name him at all. Coyote is Coyote, even in the blankets. A lot like my mother described the god."

"How?"

"Well . . . vigorous, of course, but . . . vain. Playful. He's playing games, and he knows I know it, and that's part of the game. Hey, so am I. I learned a lot, Tower, and I think I didn't give up much, but—Sandry, I don't understand war, or the kind of bloody games you play, and that's a good thing. He asked about you a *lot*. I didn't have to hide anything . . . ?"

"Right," said Sandry. She seemed to need reassurance. "What I know can't be taught with just words anyway. It takes years of practice."

"I don't know why he's so interested in you when he doesn't give a curse for the terror bird priests we've been at war with."

"What else did you learn?"

"Middle of the night, we broke to take a sweatbath. It was wonderful. Just right. We've got to build some sweatbaths when we get home."

Sandry and Tower exchanged edgy looks.

"He asked about you, Tower. I tried to explain why . . . approaching you would be a bad idea—"

"I'd kill him," said Sandry.

"I explained that. Sandry won't accept excuses, I said. Being Coyote is no excuse; being drunk wouldn't be either. He might do it anyway. Coyote loves danger."

Tower was staring.

"What, sister?"

"He was Coyote! And Coyote was your father!"

Squirrel looked serious. "Burning Tower, I have told you before, Coyote's ways are not meant to be followed by everyone!"

"Well—"

"Think on it," Squirrel said urgently. "Your father was Lordkin, and as a Lordkin acted in ways that the Bison Tribe would never accept."

"Bane," Burning Tower remembered. "Firegift—"

"Bison Tribe, men and women, always acknowledge their children," Squirrel continued. "Lordkin don't. They don't even believe in fatherhood. And the Lords! They are very concerned, but mostly because of inheritances. And in Bison Tribe, hasty marriages are hardly unusual."

"My mother harnessed the one-horns on her wedding day!" Tower insisted.

"Your mother was kinless, and takes such things even more seriously than ever did the others of Bison Tribe," Squirrel said. "My mother has children by four men she never married, and it was Whandall Feathersnake that Coyote rode when I was conceived." Squirrel laughed. "I am Coyote's daughter and Coyote's bride, and our ways are not your ways, little sister."

Sandry frowned. "Nor mine. Make certain Coyote knows that!"

Squirrel grinned. "He knows."

Tower continued to brood.

Sandry frantically tried to change the subject. "All right," he said. "What else did you learn?"

"The Emperor knows things have been going wrong. He doesn't do much about details. That's up to the bureaus. When everything comes apart, then a whole bureau can be executed in a public ceremony. The bodies are eaten and the hearts go in the wall."

"It gives me the creeps, that wall. I think we should

have looked at it closer. I'll ask Reggy to take me back," Sandry said.

"Bad idea," Squirrel said earnestly. "People who get curious about the wall—something bad can happen to them, particularly outsiders. The wall is one place where the Emperor does look at details. Taking care of the king is another. And when I wanted to know more, Coyote laughed. We're missing something obvious, something very funny."

"Something Coyote's priest thinks is funny?"

"And Coyote too, and he won't let me know."

Sandry said, "Ah."

"What?"

"He doesn't even hide it!" Sandry gathered them in his arms, Tower's and Squirrel's heads against his, his mouth concealed in their hair. "This is not to be told to anyone else. We all saw the Emperor's belly—"

"It's awful. Scarred," said Tower. "But he doesn't . . . hide it."

"But *I've* seen corpses after a battle," Sandry said. "After we killed the Toronexti, we walked the field, and some of the older soldiers . . . pointed out . . . But *my* point is, there are organs missing inside the Emperor's torso."

He released the women. They drew back as if he'd turned into a snake. "I want to see the wall," he said.

The king's hospitality included the stables, where a dozen of the big four-wheeled chariots were ready at all times. After breakfast that day, their second in Aztlan, they used the chariots to visit Flensevan's shop. It faced the River Road, away from the Little Rainbow River. Flensevan and his two sons showed them around. Sandry, Tower, and Squirrel all bought gifts, magical items that weren't for trade. Willow would have a talisman like Tower's, a tiny carved turquoise tree. Twisted Cloud would have a tiny tornado.

They still had time to visit the wall. Markings on the king's chariots got them past the guard, but before they could approach the wall, three more ornately dressed guards and an officer appeared. The soldiers did not speak, but they watched.

They walked its length, always aware of the following eyes. The wall was old and often repaired. The Emperor was supposed to be a thousand years old, wasn't he? And the wall assuredly was, and some of the niches. None of the niches were marked in any way, except that new bricks were obvious and randomly scattered. There were open niches, lots of them, each a little bigger than a man's two fists. They too were scattered in no apparent pattern.

"I'm no wizard," Sandry said later, his voice lost in traffic noise, "so I'm asking. Squirrel, if you took out a man's heart, could you enchant it to make it beat forever? And he'd go on living too, wouldn't he? Unless someone found where he hid it."

"I couldn't do it. No one I know could. But there are old stories like that," Squirrel said. Old stories of magic were generally true, though many had become impossible in an age of fading manna. "Would we be looking for just a heart?"

"At least the heart. Maybe kidneys and a liver in separate niches. But would it be safe to look?"

"Not to look, not to ask, not even to be curious. Drop it, Lord Sandry."

"Squirrel, is that you or Coyote speaking?"

"Both. Forget the wall. Never mention it again."

"Done. I'm glad Reg isn't with us. He might get the wrong idea."

Arshur went daily to meet the Emperor and came back to plan strategy with Regapisk and the masked priests. At breakfast on the third morning, he and Regapisk found time to ask Sandry's advice regarding military matters.

"I know too little," Sandry protested.

"That is easily changed," Arshur said. He clapped his hands.

Captain Sareg appeared. He bowed to Sandry.

"Your escort," Arshur said. "High Captain, show Lord Sandry the King's Guard. Listen when he comments."

"With pleasure. And with my personal thanks, Lord Sandry."

"For what?"

"You brought King Arshur to the realm, and because of you, we survived the battle at Sunfall. And from that came my promotion to High Captain in the King's Guard." Sareg smiled warmly. "You do not know it, but now my rank is sufficient that I may court a Great Mistress."

"Aha!" Regapisk said. "Hazel Sky."

"Of course, Lord Companion," Sareg said. "I can say now, it was a great strain to be captain of her guard but unable to tell her of my feelings. Nor could she speak of the matter. Not then, and this went on for months! Now, we are together, in Aztlan."

Arshur grinned. The grin faded when another official came forward with reports of tax delinquencies.

Sareg's chariot, like all the chariots of Aztlan, was too heavy. The increased weight made it more comfortable to ride in, but slow and less maneuverable. Sandry pointed this out on the way to the barracks.

"But how would you fight?" Sareg demanded. "They must be heavy to hold four."

"I fight with two. Why do you need four?"

"A driver, a shieldsman, a wizard, and his apprentice. Do you not do things that way in . . ."—he fumbled for the words—"Lordshills?"

"Magic is costly," Sandry said. "We find other means."

He spent the day at the barracks. He worked with the Emperor's soldiers. He did passably well at mock fights, yucca sword, chariot duel, horseback, and barehanded. He never tried to compete at archery. The Aztlan bows were simple bows crudely made. They'd have little accuracy. Sandry thought of his own bow in its case on his chariot, even now coming to Aztlan with Spike and the other animals. The emperor expected presents, but perhaps he wouldn't be interested in a bow.

The Emperor's officers wanted to talk. Sandry tried to trade stories, but the Emperor's men had few. Their tales of combat were all older than they were, and there were no tales of defeat. For a thousand years, they had kept the Emperor's peace. The Battle at Sunfall was the greatest battle in their lifetimes, and they made Sandry and High Captain Sareg tell it over and over. Sandry noted that each time the story was told, Sareg made Sandry a greater hero. It was always Arshur and Sandry who had won the battle.

"High Captain Sareg is too modest," Sandry said. "He stood with Arshur the king and faced the birds without magic. If the birds broke through there, it would have been all over." Sandry paused. "And that's the lesson, you know. Battles are not won by a few heroes. When everyone stands together and does his part, then you get victory." *And don't I sound like an old Lord!* He recalled a class. Everyone wanted to laugh at the elderly instructor, but they didn't dare, not under the watchful gaze of Master Peacevoice Waterman . . .

They asked other details of the battle. They were curious about the bow he'd used, and how it outranged the Thunder Bows of the Office of Rain, but they never asked how it was made. From what Sandry could see, the Empire didn't really care about military technology. They had magic.

And each time he told the story, no matter how he tried to minimize his part in it, the officers looked at each other excitedly; then, led by High Captain Sareg, they bowed to Sandry. That was what they did in the presence of Arshur, and the bowing made Sandry uneasy, but he couldn't have said why.

Tower had better luck.

A woman seen with a guard *must* have wealth. She could go anywhere, and there was more to shop for than gems. She tried on wondrous garments that shaped themselves to her, and had to reject them: she was sure they'd disintegrate where there was no manna. Half sure. Where was Squirrel now that Tower needed her advice?

On the fourth day, they walked about the city. Sandry and Tower attempted to dress like natives. Their clothing was too rich for that. They didn't stand right; they gawked at wonders that must seem commonplace to those around them. They still enjoyed themselves.

Squirrel was off somewhere with Coyote's priest.

Word reached them that the animals had arrived. Tower and Sandry arrived at a kraal below Mesa Fajada. Sandry's chariot stood in a thicket of apprentices and cadets. They were cleaning and shining every part. Sandry smiled to himself. Polish wasn't the secret.

Or was it? Gleaming armor impressed people, and sometimes that was enough, much better than fighting. How much of magic worked that way?

Two stallions, two bison, and Spike: all combed and groomed, all well fed and watered. The Emperor's minions had been told to treat the animals well, and they knew how. Four young girls attended to Spike, who seemed larger than ever in the manna-rich air of Aztlan. Burning Tower bade a long farewell to the one-horn. Tomorrow she would see him only to give him away.

Coyote's temple was a hole in the ground, a hidden place whose entrance was just inside the city gates. It looked like the entrance to a basement below an inn. Crowds passed it every minute of the day.

Inside . . . it wasn't big, but it was magnificent. Daylight came through from somewhere overhead, and a brushfire burned without smoke. On the stone altar stood offerings: two fat prairie dogs in a cage, and a closed urn. Not just a temple, but a lair. Clever Squirrel was in awe.

Two lesser priests attended. They didn't wear masks; their faces were tattooed with the nose and whiskers of Coyote. Coyote's priest sent them elsewhere, into the city, and then he and Squirrel were alone in the temple.

"Where?" she asked.

"I'll throw some blankets on the altar," he said, "but not yet. Do you know what this is?" He opened the urn.

She knew the smell. "Pulque."

"Have you ever—"

"Yes, we found some in a village at the edge of the Empire. It's strong stuff. Dear, I'd better call before you get me drunk."

"Call?"

"Feathersnake doesn't know that the ceremony's tomorrow. May I use the altar? I brought some colored sand." She moved the cage and the urn to the ground, and then began drizzling sand onto the altar. "This will tell Coyote too."

Coyote's priest watched quietly, amused, while Clever Squirrel called Mountain Cat. Afterward, she brushed the sand off onto the floor. She asked, "Now what?"

"Have you eaten prairie dog?"

"Sure. What, do you mean raw?"

"Squirrel," he said soberly, "this is Coyote's ceremony before tomorrow's official proceedings. Other masked priests are holding other ceremonies. You don't have to participate, but you are Coyote's daughter."

She laughed, over a thrill of fear. "What, would you lure another woman down here if I refused you?"

"Sure. They know me at the inn."

"Well, what kind of weirdness are we talking about?"

"Eat, get drunk, make love on Coyote's altar."

"Sounds good. May we cook the animals? You have a fire. Or are you locked into some specific format?"

Coyote's priest grinned. "I weave my spells just the way my own god has these past ten thousand years. I'm making it up as I go along."

"Squirrel? Clever Squirrel, dearest, please pay attention."

"Nnn," Squirrel said. Her mouth was numb. She could barely move. The altar was hard and cold beneath two blankets, but she felt wonderful.

"The pulque is hitting you much harder than I thought it would. I should have known: magic never touches the stuff they make in the border towns, not until it reaches the Crater for blessing. This stuff is blessed up to the eyeballs." A wild giggle. "I'm used to it and it still knocks me on my ass."

"Mmm," she said urgently.

"Marriage, yes, tomorrow. I don't know any way to sober you up. It would help if you could walk around. Burn it off. Can you stand?"

"Nnn."

Coyote's priest started to speak, then stopped. Then the blankets on the altar were suddenly thrown to cover Squirrel. The priest's voice was muffled as he called, "This place is sacred. Enter at your peril."

"Peril relieves boredom," said a voice that rang within her skull.

She heard a wood-on-stone *thunk* below her. Coyote's priest had knocked his forehead to the floor, and this was the Emperor. But wild colors flowed in the dark below her blankets, and Squirrel was drifting off into dream.

At the name *Sandry,* her attention flew back. Coyote's priest was hiding a woman's presence, and he was talking fast.

"Sandry is a mighty warrior. Sareg is in awe of him. Regapisk says so, and Regapisk doesn't like him very much. I've watched King Arshur come to Sandry for advice. He sent Sandry to investigate the readiness of our military, and he accepted what he heard. Sandry is very fit to rule.

"We can send Arshur to the gods now," said the earthly voice of Coyote. "Sandry is wonderfully qualified to be king. Not only an outlander but also a true hero."

"I like that," the Emperor said. "The news they brought made hard hearing. Let them suffer a little of what I suffered. Do you think King Sandry might be distracted by the women of Aztlan? Would Burning Tower seek revenge? With you? Even you would not be safe from the king."

Wild chittering laughter. "Coyote loves danger more than I do. . . ." And Squirrel faded into Coyote's laughter.

CHAPTER TWENTY-TWO

THE BIRD

He woke alone. He would not see Burning Tower until he was led to her at the wedding. The king's servants dressed him in bronze armor copied from his own but inlaid with lapis and jade. It had tooled leather straps, and the breastplate was polished bronze. *No iron at all*, Sandry thought. *It's probably magical.*

He didn't trust magic.

His iron sword was nowhere to be seen, and there wasn't a bronze replacement. It didn't seem worth commenting on. High Captain Sareg led him outside. Arshur waited there, in an imperial chariot. The giant grinned and waved. A kneeling servant offered Arshur a golden goblet, and the king drank heavily.

"He'll be too drunk to fight that bird," Sandry said.

Sareg grinned. "The bird will be no more sober."

Sandry's chariot had been cleaned and decorated, but it looked small and mean compared with the magnificent royal and imperial chariots. There were spears, all polished, and each spearhead covered in jewels and leather. The bowcase had its own cover, also jeweled. No one said anything, but it was obvious: only those sworn to the Emperor's service carried weapons anywhere near the Supreme One.

Blaze the stallion and Boots the gelding stood in harness, their tails braided, red ribbons in their manes. Soon to be gifts to the Emperor. There were escorts in the heavier war chariots of the Empire.

Arshur led the way. People came out of their houses to cheer, and many followed in a procession to the palace. The sun was two hours high, still low enough to cast long shadows. The cloudless sky promised a hot day, but for the moment there were cool breezes from the west along the river banks.

"Where does the river go?" Sandry asked.

"Ten leagues west, it joins another river, the Rainbow," High Captain Sareg said. "And that flows south and west through a most magnificent canyon. I have been there. It is amazing! I am told that it then turns south and flows into the great sea at Crescent City, but I have never been there. The Emperor's domains end at the canyons."

The road led along the river. The water seemed fresh and cool. "Do all the rivers lead to the great sea?" Sandry asked.

Sareg shook his head. "We are at the roof of the world. A few leagues into the rising sun, there are other rivers that flow eastward to places no one we know has ever been."

Sandry smiled thinly.

"You are amused?"

"I am," Sandry said. "The world is huge even to you. Think how large it is to me. It was only a year ago that I first traveled beyond the borders of Tep's Town basin!"

They came to the base of the temple and drove into a tunnel below the great piazza of the palace. They could hear the cheers of the crowd above. Music swelled, trumpets and drums rising to a climax as the crowd sounds grew more frantic.

"He comes, he comes!"

There was a long hush, then more trumpets and drums. Then for a long moment there was silence, then the scrambling sounds of thousands falling to their knees.

"Rise and rejoice, my people! I bring you a king!" There was no mistaking the sound of that voice, or the joy of the people of Aztlan at hearing it. Thousands cheered. The trumpets and drums began again.

Arshur's chariot led the way up the ramp to the piazza. A wall of smoke seemed to form ahead of him. Then as his chariot went out onto the piazza, the smoke swirled away and the great voice boomed. "People of Aztlan, Arshur the king!"

The crowd went frantic. While they were yelling, Sandry drove out behind Arshur onto the piazza. Few seemed to notice. All attention was on the king.

"This way," Sareg said urgently. He directed Sandry toward a high dais. It was flanked by two others not quite so tall. The flanking platforms were filled with costumes and masks and guards, cloaks and wizards and priests, a riot of magic and color. The central high dais held only one man. At Sareg's urging, Sandry left the chariot and went up the stairs onto the raised dais. At the top, he knelt and touched his head to the floor in deference to the Emperor.

"Get up, Sandry. It's your wedding day. Stand beside me. Look happy. Rejoice."

The Emperor wasn't wearing armor. He was dressed in silken kilts and a bright blue and green silken tunic that hid his scars. He wore a high crown of intricately carved gold, and a cloak of flowers. Thousands of flowers, all tiny, all woven into silk netting. It flashed in the morning sun as he lifted his arms to show himself again to the crowd. Sandry found the cloak was impressive enough, but disappointing compared to what he had been led to expect. The Emperor moved back into the shade of the dais.

The crowds continued to cheer as Arshur rode around the piazza in his great heavy chariot.

"Let them cheer the king," the Emperor said. "He looks like a king, your giant."

"Yes, Supreme One."

The Emperor smiled. "Impatient?"

"I have attempted patience for a year, Supreme One."

"And it palls," the Emperor said. "At my age patience is natural, but I can remember youth."

"You look as if you have never lost it, Supreme One," Sandry said with sincerity.

The Emperor grinned. "So. It will shortly be your wedding day."

"Not precisely as I had foreseen it."

For most of his life, he'd known how it would be. "I've been to a hundred weddings, Great One," he told the Emperor. "I knew a dozen girls who might grow up to marry me. Now I'm with a foreign woman in a land strange to both of us, following customs—"

The Emperor waved dismissively. "Burning Tower told Buffalo Woman the essentials. We'll follow the woman's custom. Isn't that always best? But first, the king must earn his crown. We can't get animals up to Mesa Fajada," he said, "so the bird must die down here, and after you're wedded, we'll come down again to present the beasts and other gifts."

Sandry nodded. There was a good view of the long Valley of Aztlan from the dais. Behind him were the wall and the great Temple Mesa Fajada. Baskets rose and dropped constantly between its base and the wooden platform near its summit. His eyes flicked left, right. Left was the river, broad and shallow, somewhat muddy, cleaner than rivers in Tep's Town or Condigeo. It flowed on to the west and out of sight. Downstream and across the river was the king's palace. Not far beyond the bridge to the palace was Flensevan's shop, now hidden by houses.

Downstream and to the right, nestled against the walls of the canyon, was the palace where he and Burning Tower would spend their wedding night. They'd been shown all this before, in what wasn't quite a rehearsal.

Out on the Great Plaza, Arshur had finished the first of his circuits in his chariot. He was passing by the kraals, carefully separated, but the animals were aware of each other. Spike, alone in his kraal, faced two terror birds. Sandry's chariot was led over there. The stallion and the gelding stood in harness, but they'd been given food and water and shade. They'd be all right. They seemed very aware of the birds and Spike.

The crowds were still cheering. Arshur's driver looked up to the Emperor, got a sign in the form of a minute wave of the ringed and jeweled right hand, and took another turn around the piazza. As he did, the music rose and swelled. Sandry looked for its source, but it was hidden. Magic? Or artists hidden in the *kivas* let into the piazza? He couldn't tell.

The chariot came around to the dais. The Emperor stepped forward again. "People of Aztlan, Arshur the king!" His voice boomed through the piazza and the stands above, through the five hundred rooms of the palace beyond. It wasn't so much loud as all-pervasive, impossible to ignore, and it seemed to Sandry that it would be heard in Crescent City and Condigeo.

The Emperor gestured, and priests came forward. They wore cloaks of tiny feathers, and long-billed masks. Hummingbirds, Sandry thought. That should be funny, but there was no humor in this. Arshur, urged by his guards, stepped down from his chariot. One of the priests knelt to him and handed him a golden goblet. Arshur took it impatiently and drank.

The other hummingbird priest knelt and held out a great bronze sword. Arshur took it and grinned, balanced it on extended fingertips, swung it in practiced moves. His scarred muscles rippled in the sun. They'd dressed him well, leather and silk kilts, leather harness holding a jeweled breastplate more symbolic than protective, a lot of Arshur's scars and tattoos showing.

"He's drunk," Sandry muttered.

"Well, of course," the Emperor said. "He drinks more than any king in my memory." He stepped forward into the sun and raised his arms. The music stopped and the crowd fell silent, an eerie silence across the entire piazza. One of the stallions nickered.

Arshur looked around to see that he was alone. He waved the great bronze sword and shouted something Sandry didn't understand. Ten manlengths away, a cage door swung open and a terror bird came out blinking into the sunlight.

The bird didn't look drugged. It looked hungry.

Arshur shouted and waved his sword. He grinned widely, but he no longer looked drunk. The bird approached him warily, and they eyed each other. Then the bird rushed at Arshur.

Arshur pivoted on one foot, turning and leaning just far enough that the bird's gaping teeth snapped on empty air. Then Arshur laughed and struck at the bird with his sword, hitting it on its back just behind the neck. Feathers flew, and blood. As the bird ran past, Arshur leaped after it, slashing at its leg.

The bird was limping now, and frightened. It looked around the walled piazza. The gates, both those into the *kivas* and those into the seating stands, were all closed. Men with spears ready stood at the base of each dais. There was no place to run. The bird turned back toward Arshur.

"Interesting," the Emperor said.

"How, Supreme One?"

"Well, we've always had the priests control the birds. This one's just drugged. Not too well drugged, at that," the Emperor mused. "Good thing your giant is a warrior."

Arshur feinted toward the bird. It dodged, then darted forward to snap at the king. Arshur whooped. The bird ran past as Arshur pivoted again, and when the bird ran on to smash into the wall beyond, it no longer had a head. The crowd went mad with cheering.

Chapter Twenty-Three

Anticipations

Burning Tower was surrounded by priests and girls and attendants, but she felt alone. Butterflies in my stomach, she thought. This is the day. She forced herself to stand still.

She stood on the platform at the top of Mesa Fajada and watched as the Emperor, far below on the piazza, showed himself to his people and proclaimed the new king. Arshur appeared in a cloud of smoke, and then rode his chariot around the piazza.

There was Sandry. She was too high above him to see his face, but his armor twinkled. Everyone was watching Arshur, but Tower kept her gaze on Sandry as he mounted the dais to stand alone with the Emperor. She frowned and turned to Buffalo Woman. "Why Sandry? Why isn't anyone else with the Supreme One?"

"Who can know the ways of the great?" Buffalo Woman asked. She was older than Burning Tower's mother, and said to be very wise. Burning Tower hadn't seen evidence of her wisdom. But she was kind, and the only friend Burning Tower had up here on this high platform among all these strangers.

They were in full view of the huge crowd in the piazza. "Will we look enormous, the way the Supreme One did when he welcomed us from up here?" Tower asked.

"I think so," Buffalo Woman said. "We haven't done a wedding from here in a long time. The last time was one of the Emperor's sons when I was much younger, and yes, they used the vision then." Buffalo Woman sniffed. "You are being very highly honored."

"Yes, I know that," Tower said. And why? But there was no point in asking; she'd only be told not to question her luck. And they'd be huge! She was aware of every flaw, the tiny blemish on her left cheek, the fading bruise from the combat at Sunfall. There were bruises on her thighs too, but no one would see those. No one but Sandry, and that much later. . . .

Everything seemed ready. Tower was dressed in thin white silks, so thin and so light that any breeze lifted her sleeves and cloak like wings. She'd admired herself in the mirrors at the palace. She'd never been so beautiful.

She had been awakened before the sun rose, and in the dark they had come to the Great Plaza. It was just dawn when, under the watchful eyes of Buffalo Woman and her apprentices, Burning Tower had bridled Spike, choking as she realized that she would see him only one more time.

Then he would be a present to the Emperor. And after tonight, he would hate her.

It was early morning when they ascended Mesa Fajada in those flying baskets. Now the sun was high, but not yet noon. It was hot up here, despite the wind that blew through the canyon and billowed her white silks.

The platform circled the mesa. It was wide and high, as high as she had ever been in her life. It was large enough to have rooms, each room walled in screens of flowers. They were shaded by another flower screen above them. Everything smelled of blossoms and sage. Music welled up from the piazza. Now it was triumphant.

She couldn't see Sandry any longer. He was lost in shadows with the Emperor as Arshur rode around the piazza. It was very bright down there, and she looked away.

Here on the platform, just out of the sun, there was a table, a great wooden slab, on short legs so that the top was at knee height. Bags of sand were lined up around it. Her parents would be here through sand paintings. But where was Clever Squirrel? She hadn't come back to the palace at all, last night or this morning, and neither had Coyote's priest. They'd left together, and it was obvious what they'd been doing, but Tower was worried. Where were they? But when she asked, she only got knowing smiles.

There was more cheering down on the piazza. Arshur had ridden around the Great Plaza and was stopped in front of the Emperor's dais. A priest knelt to offer him something, a drink, then a sword. A cage opened, and a bird charged out.

Tower held her breath. The bird was much bigger than Arshur. But the fight didn't take long, and then the bird was headless, running around the piazza menacing everyone with the great blades that tipped its wings until grooms wrapped its legs with ropes and dragged it away, wings still beating.

And the crowd was cheering wildly again, and she couldn't see Sandry and the Emperor any longer.

"Soon," Buffalo Woman said. "They come now."

Clever Squirrel giggled.

She was riding in one of the floating baskets. Coyote's priest rode with her, and he wore a dreamy, tranquil smile. He'd had as much of that stuff as she had, but he must be used to it.

The basket rose high. She vaguely remembered being brought to the base of Mesa Fajada in a chariot, held up by Coyote's priest and two of his tattooed assistants.

In the basket ahead, she could make out Sandry, High Captain Sareg, and the priests of Prairie Dog and Mammoth in their elaborate formal masks. It was accompanied by a basket of four guards.

Those two baskets rose together, and above those were three baskets all together. One held Arshur the king with his attendants: Sandry's cousin Regapisk and the Aztlan jeweler dressed in his finest, and a burly young guard or servant. The king's basket was flanked by two others, each with four guards. And in the basket above that, the Emperor, blazing with magic, with an older man dressed in kilts, and, greatly favored, the Great Mistress Hazel Sky. Beside Hazel was Jaguar's priest in a towering headdress. The great mask turned down to her for an instant, and Squirrel felt the oppressive mass of tradition settle on her.

"Great Mistress," Clever Squirrel giggled. "Does it mean what I think it means?"

Coyote's priest snorted. "There was a time when Hazel Sky shared the Supreme One's couch. Then she was sent to govern his most important possession. Now she returns after a glorious victory and the discovery of treason." He shrugged. "A bright woman, a woman of power. Who is to say where she spent last night? We know where we were!"

Squirrel laughed loud, so loud that others in the rising baskets turned toward her. "Too right." The memories were warm and delicious. *Not overrated at all,* she thought. *I'll have to tell Blazes. Not overrated at all.*

Baskets traced shadows against the Mesa Fajada. The blazing forenoon sun turned it into a burning tower. Could this be why the Emperor had commanded this wedding be here? Squirrel tried to recall the details of Burning Tower's naming vision. Her mother had dreamed of those great Burnings in Tep's Town in the days before Morth of Atlantis drove Yangin-Atep mythical. And Sandry had assisted Morth in that; did the Emperor know?

Sandry was guarded, and there were two baskets of guards for King Arshur. The Emperor had none at all. "Who is the man with the Supreme One?" she asked.

"Doentivar. The Grandson of the Sun."

"The heir?"

Coyote's priest looked around warily. "Perhaps. If the Supreme One continues to choose him. You and I are not concerned with such matters, and it is best not even to think of them."

Why? Squirrel wondered. The giggle bubbled up.

A voice whispered in her head. Coyote? An old memory? *"For there to be an heir someone must die. Some detest such thoughts."*

Even the gods?

"Especially the gods. Gods have gone myth. The Supreme One is no god, but there are gods who are wary of him."

Squirrel's head was whirling, and the higher they rose, the dizzier she became. Up here everything glowed with manna. Power glared from the valley below, from the cheers of the people—she became aware of the music and the shouting and waves of euphoria from ten thousand and more below.

She could see out onto the piazza now. The crowds in their seats, processions of masked and costumed priests coming from the *kivas*. Sandry's chariot standing near a pen where a young girl dressed in bright flowers stood with her arm around the neck of a bridled white one-horn. Spike, stamping in impatience. Another pen held a live terror bird.

There had been death below, and the manna of sudden death mixed with the excitement of the crowd. Near the kraal a crew was dragging what looked like green rags off through a gate. It trailed blood.

"The king's conquest?" she asked.

Coyote nodded. "I thought it best you stay below."

He's too polite to remind me just how drunk I am, she thought, *or too embarrassed.*

Coyote handed her a flask. She sniffed warily. Pulque was wonderful stuff, but she'd had enough. This was water, and she drank eagerly before realizing that it too was suffused with manna, nearly as intoxicating as pulque. She still felt the ecstasy of the pulque, hours later, with a glow of sex and magic in her, and a knowledge that must have been in Coyote's priest's mind: something wonderful was going to happen today, even beyond the marriage of Sandry to Burning Tower. All would be put right. If only she could remember what she'd dreamed.

CHAPTER TWENTY-FOUR

THUNDERCLOUD

Lord Regapisk, king's companion, held the side of the basket and hoped that Arshur wouldn't make any more sudden gestures. His last wild swing had almost swept Flensevan's son Egret out of the basket.

They were rising up the side of Mesa Fajada, the Emperor ahead, Sandry himself behind. It would be Sandry's wedding, and as his cousin's only countryman, Regapisk would have a prominent part, but he was more—he was king's companion. Of course he and Flensevan and Egret weren't supposed to be in this basket. They were major dignitaries, but there were dozens who outranked them. But Arshur had seen them in their seats in the piazza after the ceremonies and sent the King's Guards to make way for them to follow him, and when they reached the baskets, Arshur had let them assist him into the basket and pulled them in with him. No one disputed the king's whim.

Flensevan and his son were bursting with pride, but there was fear beneath that. Everyone in Aztlan felt that way: joy, pride, fear. Regapisk looked down from the rapidly rising basket to see the old wall. The Wall of Hearts, where anyone might be taken at the whim of the scarred Emperor.

Doentivar, Grandson of the Sun in his place beside his father: straight back, blank face, no emotion visible. He'd be the wariest of all.

Lord Chief Witness Quintana might sell you to sea or send you to the crabs for a mistake, but not just for a whim.

The baskets rose higher. Mesa Fajada blazed. The whole valley below blazed with manna. There were bright threads in the river below, silver streaks that wound out past the gates and beyond the Aztlan valley into the far west. Above them the sky was clear and dazzling blue.

The basket halted, and guards drew it onto a wide platform built right around the mesa. The basket was almost steady, but still it hovered a finger's breadth above the wood. Regapisk and Egret leaped out to assist the king, leaving Flensevan to dismount on his own.

Flowers everywhere. The walls were flowers. And songs and music welled up from the piazza. *They do things right here,* Regapisk thought, remembering shows and circuses the Lords had put on for Lordkin and kinless. The Emperor was rich and spent money and manna, more than the Lords of Lordshills had ever had to spend on anything. And the day was just beginning . . .

* * *

The Emperor had gone first. He was standing at the edge of the platform now, and the crowd was going wild.

And there was Sandry, just catching sight of Burning Tower in her white silk robes. She was beautiful, no question about that, and Regapisk felt a twinge of envy despite last night's attentions from Annalun and one of her young ladies trying to hide her joy at being with Regapisk rather than Arshur.

Guards ushered them off the landing area as other baskets arrived. Regapisk noticed how many of the Emperor's guards there were, even up here. They stood in fours, in identical kilts and shoulder capes, carrying identical clubs embedded with chips of obsidian. They were there to protect the king's companion and partners as much as for the rest of these worthies, but Regapisk remembered the Lordsmen at the docks in Tep's Town. Those had not liked Younglord Regapisk one bit, even before his fall from grace. He grinned at a knot of soldiers, but there was no response at all.

The part of the platform that faced the Great Plaza far below shone with an unnatural light. The Emperor stood there. Guards gestured Arshur and Regapisk into the light, and when the king was illuminated, the crowd cheered wildly. The light was dazzling, and Reg felt strange. Arshur bowed, then he and the Emperor backed away into the shadows, leaving Regapisk for a moment alone in the bright light. A lesser priest gestured urgently for Regapisk to move back, and when he did, a guard was there. The priest was masked, but there was no mistaking the guard's unfriendliness.

The priest was watching the Emperor. When no sign came, he gestured the guard away. "Do not again spoil the Supreme One's exit," the priest hissed, and then Regapisk remembered how the Emperor's image had grown enormous on the first day they saw him.

Tower and Sandry were standing together now. She looked radiant. Sandry looked terrified.

Clever Squirrel was led in from the landing platform. Two of Coyote's apprentices were holding her up, and Regapisk thought she needed the help. There was a low table with bags of sand just out of the lighted area of the platform, and she bent over it.

Coyote's priest took her hand. "Not yet," he said. "You would not wish the bride's parents to see what comes next."

Burning Tower had overheard. "What? What comes next?" she asked.

"Think happy thoughts," Coyote's priest said.

Four of the guards dragged out Thundercloud.

The Terror Bird's priest had been stripped of all his finery. He wore a white loincloth. He was not fighting the guards, but he was not drugged. His eyes fixed on Sandry, Tower, Flensevan, Hazel Sky. No help there, and his eyes kept moving.

In the lighted area, there was a big slab of rock veined like wood. The Many Names Priest came forward. "People of Aztlan! You have heard of the high treason of the former priest of Left-Handed Hummingbird. You have heard of the transformation of this god! The gods show their favor to the Supreme One! See now the fate of the priest who defied the Sun!"

It happened fast. The Emperor strode forward and spread his arms. His four guards laid Thundercloud on the slab and tethered his wrists and ankles.

The maskless Many Names Priest came forward, accompanied by Coyote's priest and another in the robes and mask of Jaguar, and a fourth with the thin bill and bright colors of a hummingbird. Thundercloud's whimpering stopped; he stared at that one in fathomless horror.

The hummingbird priest struck Thundercloud's chest with an obsidian dagger. Blood spurted everywhere. The Emperor himself reached into the chest cavity and drew out the still-beating heart. He held it high, then placed it into a small, floating basket. The basket vanished over the side of the platform, then Thundercloud's body, still twitching, was rolled off the platform to fall fifty man-heights to the dry ground at the wall far below.

The crowd below had stood in silence. When the body hit the ground, they cheered. "Live a million years, Son of the Sun!"

CHAPTER TWENTY-FIVE

SAND PAINTINGS

"Now," Coyote's priest said. Clever Squirrel felt his hands gently guiding her to the low table. His voice was urgent as he said, "The Supreme One is ready."

The death of Thundercloud felt like a nightmare; she wasn't sure how much was real. She poured sand with unsteady hands.

The image didn't look much like Willow. It was all angles and arcs, distortions and shiftings, and the colors were off: she'd misjudged the bags of sand. She touched the sand with her fingertips, moving the patterns.

It wasn't coming out right. The image wouldn't come alive. She tried again. Whandall Feathersnake's picture emerged like Willow's, like a face slashed in straight lines, ear and eyes and nose jumbled almost at random, a style that wouldn't be seen again for fourteen thousand years. She heard a laugh quickly suppressed.

She poured fresh sand into the distorted image of Whandall Feathersnake. Lavender sand trickled up the figure's forearm, upper arm and shoulder, and splashed across his face. Then red, yellow, green, a shape growing clearer, shaping itself: the gaudy image of Whandall's Atlantean tattoo, a great feathered serpent that wound from his eye down his arm. The serpent's eye was coincident with Whandall's, and as she added detail, Whandall's eyes opened. Then Willow's opened too.

"Hail!" Whandall said. "Great One, we see only the image of Coyote."

The Emperor nodded with understanding. "Bid them welcome," he said.

Coyote's priest spoke in imperial tones. "Welcome to Aztlan, Willow and Whandall. The House of Feathersnake is known even here, and the Supreme One bids me tell you that you need only appear at the gates to be welcomed into the city.

"And today we have tasks of great joy. The Supreme One himself has consented to marry the lovely daughter of your house of Feathersnake, Burning Tower, sister of the daughter of Coyote, and Lord Sandry of Lordshills, Fire Commander and Great Officer of the City of Yangin-Atep! Rejoice, people of Road's End and New Castle. Rejoice, people of Aztlan!"

Chapter Twenty-six

The Day of the Sun Dagger

Regapisk stood in the shadows, well out of the blazing light at the center of the platform. Over on the rock wall of the mesa itself, a sliver of sunlight approached the shadowed center of a spiral carved into the rock. The Sun Dagger, one of the priests had explained at dinner last night. Today that dagger would touch the center of the spiral, making this a day of great fortune. Jaguar's priest had explained their great fortune to Sandry and Burning Tower. "It is the Day of the Sun Dagger in the Year of Jaguar."

"People of Aztlan, witness the bounty of your Emperor," Jaguar's priest proclaimed.

"People of Aztlan, the gods are pleased!" The maskless priest bowed to the Emperor, then to the sun.

"Coyote is well pleased."

"Blessings on this union of an heiress of the Bison Tribe!" Buffalo Woman shouted. "I bear witness: this morning Burning Tower placed a golden bridle on the great stallion one-horn, according to the customs of her tribe."

One by one, all the priests of all the gods blessed the marriage.

"Hail to a great warrior prince," Arshur the king shouted. A priest knelt to Arshur and handed him a bronze goblet. It wasn't large. The king drained it in a gulp, handed it to the priest to be refilled, then handed it to Sandry.

Regapisk smiled thinly. Sandry had no choice but to drain that cup, and when it was given to Tower, she did the same. He glanced at Clever Squirrel, who was trying to stay awake at the sand-painting table, and wondered if they'd get Tower that drunk today. No one seemed to be offering him anything to drink. There wasn't even food up here. The feast would be down below, in the *kivas,* he supposed.

The Emperor said something, and there was a laugh from Whandall Feathersnake's image. Arshur roared with delight.

Then there were contracts, read to Whandall and Willow, signed by Burning Tower and Sandry, witnessed by Regapisk and Clever Squirrel. Squirrel's signing was a crooked squiggle that would never have been accepted by even a junior Witness Clerk. Regapisk was going to mention that, but Sandry gave him a hard look. This could be corrected another time. Sandry looked as if he wanted to scream, *Get on with it!* Regapisk gave him a look of sympathy, but Sandry wasn't watching.

Then Whandall and Willow Feathersnake spoke of the joys and hopes they held for their youngest daughter. *Youngest,* Regapisk thought. *Are they making it clear that she is not the heiress?* Lords thought that way. Lordkin never thought of such things at all. He didn't know the ways of kinless.

And none of it mattered. *Sandry is rich; they're both rich.* Wagonloads of charged talismans would be a good way toward Crescent City now, and Green Stone was already on the Hemp Road. Sandry and Tower would never want anything.

I'm rich too, Regapisk thought.

When Whandall's image spoke glowingly of the wagon and team that was Burning Tower's dower gift, Sandry smiled. Regapisk nodded. It was clear that Whandall Feathersnake was more Bison Tribe than Lordkin now.

"Squirrel, dear, did your mother give you something for the wedding?" Willow asked.

Clever Squirrel blinked in the sunlight, frowned, and dug into the pouch at her waist. She took out a roll of willow leaves. "Yes, Willow."

"I gave it to your mother when she left with Burning Tower, in anticipation of a wedding I both hoped for and feared. Give it to the couple now. It is the tears of a mother, shed for her wedding."

Squirrel held herself in an iron grip, clearly determined not to spoil this moment. Somehow she got across the platform to Burning Tower to deliver Willow's gift.

Tower burst into tears. She held the willow leaves until Sandry gently took them from her and put them inside his breastplate.

As Burning Tower took her place in the glaring sunlight of the platform, the walls of flowers on both sides turned to mirrors. She could see herself, gossamer white silks floating in the bright sun. *I'm really pretty,* she thought.

Her world changed, like a dream. She was enormous, standing on the great piazza below and looking down at the people of Aztlan in their seats, but she was here on this platform, standing beside the man she loved. *I do love him. I do.* And around her were the priests and Clever Squirrel and that strange cousin of Sandry's—*my cousin now*—and in front of her was the Emperor, the Son of the Sun. He looked like a twisted god. To one side was Arshur the king, on a golden throne, looking like a great king. They were all there on the temple platform with her, but they were not in her waking dream. That she shared only with Sandry and the Emperor.

The crowd gasped as her image grew. She could feel herself getting closer to them even though she hadn't moved from the heights of the Temple Mesa. She stood with Sandry and the Emperor, towering above the crowd.

And they were all looking at her. She felt ten thousand and more eyes on her. The mirrors showed what they saw. The silks billowed. *I'll never look this good again.*

Sandry took her hand. She guided his hand to his breastplate. *Mother's tears. I never knew,* Tower thought.

Music swelled from below. Voices now, choruses in

languages she didn't quite know, the languages of the gods. We've been blessed by all the gods. Witnessed and signed, the Lords say. There has never been a marriage more witnessed than this!

"The Dagger of the Sun!" a priest behind her was shouting. "The Sun Dagger! It is time, it is time!"

The crowd cheered again.

The Emperor stood before her.

"Sandry, Fire Chief of Lordshills and the City of Yangin-Atep, Lord Witness of Lordshills, warrior and advisor to King Arshur, guest of Aztlan, will you have this woman, Burning Tower of the House of Feathersnake and the Bison Tribe, as your wife, according to the laws and customs of the Lords Witness?"

"I will!"

"Lord Regapisk, companion of King Arshur, companion and countryman of Lord Sandry, do you witness this marriage and swear to bear witness to all who shall ask it of you?"

"I shall!"

"Burning Tower of the House of Feathersnake, you stand before the people of Aztlan. Do you choose this man Sandry of Lordshills to marry, according to the laws and customs of the Bison Tribe?"

"I do!"

A gentle wind came up from nowhere, and from the walls of flowers came butterflies of every color. They settled on Tower's gossamer sleeves and cape and veils, until she was a swirl of living color.

Sandry! His face beamed. He'd never looked at her this way before. Had any man ever looked at a woman that way? Love, astonishment. And the Emperor smiled. Burning Tower felt her heart would burst.

"Burning Tower of the House of Feathersnake; you now know the favor of the Emperor and gods of Aztlan, of all the tribes of gods! At this moment you may choose anything you desire. Is it your wish that you be married to this man, Lord Sandry?"

Far below she heard a familiar nicker. Spike. He could see her. Everyone in Aztlan could see her. And soon she'd have to give Spike to the Emperor, and after tonight, he would have nothing to do with her. Her friend and protector.

And Sandry looked afraid! He was really scared!

And this was cruel. "Son of the Sun, it is my greatest wish to be married to Sandry," Tower said.

"So be it," the Emperor intoned. "So be it known to all, in the presence of the gods, in the presence of the people of Aztlan, in the presence of your father and your mother, throughout our domains and throughout the world, you are now married. Join forever, Sandry and Burning Tower."

The music swelled and filled her heart, as Sandry gathered her to him, gently, fearful of crushing butterflies. Butterflies swirled about them, and the people of Aztlan, ten thousand and more, cheered.

Chapter Twenty-Seven

King Sandry

Sandry stood with Burning Tower. His vision blurred as they seemed to grow enormous yet stayed in place.

In Lordshills, this would all be over. In Lordshills, the contracts were all that mattered, disposition of land and houses and wealth and servants, what the heirs would have and what would be forfeit if the couple separated, what would pass to sons and what to daughters. When that was settled, all was settled. But Lordshills was a city without gods and magic, and this was a far different world.

Buffalo Woman spoke: Burning Tower had bridled the bonehead. *Yesss.* That was Sandry's triumph too, and it had been hard! A year with this girl, a year of wanting her. Now that was over. *Thank you, gods!* And that too was a strange thought. The Lords believed that the gods existed for others, but they had never had much importance in Tep's Town.

Tower seemed recovered from the shock and horror of the execution. Sandry frowned. She had hated that, but they'd made her watch. Why today? But Buffalo Woman had said this was an important day, the day the Dagger of the Sun pierced the center of that spiral. Another of the customs of people who had gods, and would such things come to Lordshills now that Yangin-Atep was myth?

Then she grew more beautiful than he had ever seen her, as the butterflies covered her. Her face shone.

"Burning Tower of the House of Feathersnake, you now know the favor of the Emperor and gods of Aztlan, of all the tribes of gods! At this moment you may choose anything you desire. Is it your wish that you be married to this man, Lord Sandry?"

He held his breath. In the silence, he heard the nicker of the one-horn and suppressed a grin of triumph over that rival. But the silence stretched on, and fear clutched his heart. Burning Tower looked at him, lovely and wonderful, and said nothing. That moment stretched forever.

Then she spoke, and the Emperor proclaimed the marriage, and he held her close as the butterflies swirled around them, and the world was wonderful.

The images of Willow and Whandall Feathersnake shouted in joy. Burning Tower stood so that her mother could see her, but suddenly the images faded and were no more than sand. As they did, Clever Squirrel collapsed across the table. Coyote's priest gently rolled her aside and swept the sand into a bag. "There is no more manna at New Castle," he said.

Tower looked disappointed, but she was surrounded by jubilant priests.

"Can we go now?" Sandry asked.

Coyote's priest looked at him with a strange expression. "Not yet."

They were married, but it would be a long time until the night and until they would be alone. Sandry put on his best military expression and prepared to wait.

The Emperor stood in the sunlight. He was joined there by Jaguar's priest. "People of Aztlan!" the masked priest shouted. "It is the Year of Jaguar and the Day of the Sun Dagger!"

There were no cheers now. The crowd below was still, waiting for something. Two priests led Arshur the king out onto the platform. Arshur swayed unsteadily. A lesser hummingbird priest knelt to Arshur and offered the golden goblet. Arshur took it and drank, and then two other priests urged Sandry out to stand next to the king.

"I show you a great prince, Sandry of Lordshills!" Jaguar shouted. "A great warrior from a far land."

Behind him he heard Tower. "What is happening?"

And Clever Squirrel stirred behind him, trying to say something he didn't understand.

The Emperor took the cup from Arshur's hand and held it out to be filled. He gave it to the hummingbird priest, who turned, knelt, and offered it to Sandry.

Sandry hesitated. That first cup was already dizzying him. He saw disapproval in the Emperor's eyes. The

Emperor's son was there too, staring intently. Everyone waited.

"My congratulations on your wedding on this day," the Emperor said. "This is the cup of my blessing."

And everyone stared. Behind him Squirrel said, "Nnn."

"Do you refuse the gift of the Supreme One?" Coyote's priest said. His tone was low and urgent. "The favor of the Great Ones has its dangers, but they are nothing compared to his disapproval! Quickly, Lord Sandry, lest you anger the Son of the Sun."

Sandry took the cup and drank.

"He accepts!" the Emperor shouted.

The crowd shouted approval.

The drink was pulque. Sandry tried to resist its effects. The world swooped around him as Jaguar's priest raised his arms. "People of Aztlan! This is the Day of the Sun Dagger in the Year of Jaguar, the day when we send the king to plead with the gods for us! And the gods have favored us, they have sent us Arshur the King who came following his fate! And with him they sent a mighty warrior prince.

"More than a year ago, we lost our King Halenon of the Great River, and we have been without a king, and evil has besieged Aztlan. Great wizards have wrought treason against the Son of the Sun! Cities and tribes have sought to rebel, and there was no king to deal with these evils.

"Now we send King Arshur to the gods, and we bring you King Sandry to punish the rebels!

"People of Aztlan! Rejoice! King Arshur goes to the gods!"

And the four guards hustled Arshur out to the great slab of rock. Arshur blinked but didn't resist. Whatever was in the last drink had overcome him. Listlessly he allowed himself to be spread-eagled over the slab. He looked up, saw the hummingbird priest coming with his obsidian knife, and almost tore loose from the grip of the guards.

The small priest was too fast. Before Arshur's arms tore free from the soldiers, before Sandry or anyone else could move, in one great slashing stroke the priest plunged the knife into Arshur's chest and ripped it upward. The Emperor reached into the chest cavity to remove the beating heart. He held it high for the people to see.

"King Arshur bears our messages to the gods!" The Emperor's voice roared out above the buzz of thousands cheering, and the tiny thread of an agonized scream—Regapisk.

A basket, this one silver and gold, floated to the Emperor's hand. He put the heart into it. Another basket, large, coffin shaped, covered with flowers, was brought in. The soldiers laid Arshur into it. That too floated free, down the side of the great Mesa Fajada, sinking fast. Arshur dead was still a big man.

And below, the people of Aztlan shouted their welcome to King Sandry.

Chapter Twenty-Eight

Hail to the King and Queen

His part in the wedding had been small enough, but he thought he had played it well. Regapisk, Lord and king's companion, stood in the shadows as the butterflies swirled around Sandry and Tower. He was glad of the shade. King Arshur sat on his golden throne in full sunlight.

The king was very drunk. With Arshur, it was hard to tell, but Regapisk had been with the northman long enough to recognize the signs. Drunk and trying to pay attention. In that condition, Arshur could be struck by the whim to do anything, say anything, and Regapisk wasn't close enough to stop him. He tried to move closer, but guards and lesser priests barred his way.

The wedding was done, and Arshur hadn't embarrassed himself. Regapisk felt relieved. This would be over soon, and he could turn Arshur over to Annalun and her virgins to let the king sleep it off.

They weren't done with Sandry. Sandry was pushed out to kneel beside the king. They gave Arshur another drink—big mistake, that—then the Emperor held out a cup to Sandry. "He accepts!" the Emperor shouted. And the crowd screamed approval while Arshur blinked in the bright sun, then seemed to slump down on his throne.

Regapisk didn't like the pattern he could almost see emerging.

Jaguar's priest stood in the center of the platform. His voice boomed loudly, but echoes made it hard for Regapisk to understand what he was saying. "The day when we send the king to plead with the gods for us!" What did that mean?

It became all too clear.

"People of Aztlan! Rejoice! King Arshur goes to the gods!"

And they dragged Arshur out to that slab. Regapisk reached for his sword, but he didn't have one, and the guards stood all around him, watching him, not watching the king.

For a moment Arshur seemed to come alive. Arshur always came through! He was Arshur the Magnificent. No one could—

Regapisk screamed as the black obsidian knife flashed in the sun and the Emperor tore out the king's heart.

One of the lesser priests put his hand on Regapisk's

shoulder. "It is done," the priest whispered. "Your friend is with the gods. Rejoice."

Rejoice. Regapisk stood mute, his knees ready to buckle under him. There was nothing he could do! Nothing! And he knew it was true, but it didn't seem to help.

The crowd was cheering for King Sandry. Burning Tower looked horrified. *Well she might,* Regapisk thought. He turned to the lesser priest and asked, holding his fury in check, "How—how long before they send King Sandry to the gods?"

"At least four years," the priest said. "Always in the Year of Jaguar. Perhaps eight. We have known kings who reigned well. Hessinge of Bird City held the throne sixteen years before there were troubles that only the gods could repair. Your Sandry looks to be another such.

"Will you be his companion?"

"If he'll have me," Regapisk said.

They led Regapisk out to stand next to Sandry, Burning Tower on one side, Regapisk on the other. The Emperor himself drew back in the shadows.

"Take the king to his throne, King's Companion," Jaguar said. "King Sandry, will you have Burning Tower as queen?"

"She's my wife forever," Sandry muttered.

"King Sandry proclaims a queen," Jaguar shouted. "Hail Burning Tower!"

The crowd roared again.

Sandry looked warily around. No way out. He let them lead him over to the throne. Burning Tower sat at his feet, and Regapisk stood to his right behind the throne, where he'd thought he would stand for King Arshur, only they'd pushed him aside.

Eight guards had carried the great stone slab away. All the blood was gone. There were flowers and butterflies everywhere, and the sun shone down from clear blue skies. Joyous music, joyous shouts from the crowds. Great tears rolled down Burning Tower's cheeks. Regapisk, Lord and king's companion, felt his own tears come.

"Hail, King Sandry! Hail to the king and queen! People of Aztlan, rejoice!"

CHAPTER TWENTY-NINE

THE WEDDING CHASE

Sandry sat quietly on the golden throne and tried to ignore the shouts of the crowd and the buzzing in his head. Out on the platform, the Emperor and various priests were making proclamations, but they'd left him here with companion and queen, in open view but with no one nearby. He had time to think.

Burning Tower was crying. Sandry didn't blame her, but that wasn't going to help. What could they do?

"You'll have four years." Regapisk's voice was low and urgent. "At least four, maybe eight, and one king lasted sixteen."

"This happens to every king?"

"I think so."

"How long have you known this?"

"Less than a breath." Regapisk sounded hurt. "Do you think I wouldn't have saved Arshur? Or tried?"

"Sorry, Cousin. I was distracted."

"They were all over me. Anyway, Arshur always gets away. You know the stories . . ."

Burning Tower looked up at him in fear. "Sandry, what will we do?"

"For now, nothing," Sandry said. "Let me think. Shut it, Reg."

"I have a way out of here," Regapisk said.

A flash of hope, then reality. *Another Reggy story.*

I am king. I'll have soldiers, and I can go out of the city. And they've got to have thought of that. This has been going on for hundreds of years; they must have had kings who tried to run away.

"I have a way out," Regapisk said again.

"Tell me."

"It's under Flensevan's shop. You were there."

"The Emperor proclaims this a day of rejoicing!" Jaguar was shouting. "And the new king and queen have gifts for the Son of the Sun! We go now to receive them."

The animals. Sandry had forgotten the animals.

"What is this way out?" Sandry demanded.

"A boat. An Atlantean boat," Regapisk said.

"A boat. How many can it hold?"

"I don't know; it's a big boat."

A boat, Sandry thought. What had he heard about Atlantean boats? But it ought to be fast, as fast as the river, and that river ran fast. *As far as Crescent City! Get us to Crescent City ahead of the Emperor, and we're safe enough—I know the way back to Condigeo. We just need a head start.*

The Emperor and his son were leaving the platform, headed toward the baskets. The Emperor would go first. Then the king. *That will be me, and Tower, and Regapisk—*

"Regapisk. Get Squirrel to that shop."

"Sure. When?"

"Now. As soon as you can."

"Sandry, the boat won't move without us. We can go anytime."

"Maybe," Sandry said. "And maybe not. Can you get Squirrel there now?"

"I'll find out," Regapisk said. "I'll have to see to Flensevan and his son. It's their boat."

"No one will care what they do," Sandry said. "Tell them to go home while everyone is watching the next ceremony. You go with them, with Squirrel."

"Right now?" Reggy whined.

"No better time," Sandry said. The ghost of a plan formed in his head. "We'll give you as much time as we can. Now see to Squirrel."

The Emperor had left the platform, and everyone was waiting. Sandry stood. "My queen." He kept his voice low so that it wouldn't be picked up by whatever magic was making them heard throughout the city. "I am concerned for your sister." Sandry gestured toward Clever Squirrel, who lay babbling in scattered sand on the big table.

"I will see to her, Majesty!" Regapisk said.

"If you please, Companion," Sandry said. "Bring her now."

Burning Tower held his arm. "What do we do?" The tears were gone, but she sounded scared.

She should be, Sandry thought. "I may have a plan. It depends on Reggy."

"It depends on Lord Regapisk?" She sounded more frightened than ever. Sandry nodded grimly.

Reggy carried Clever Squirrel like a rag doll. Her head rolled back and forth, and her arms twitched. As he carried her toward the basket, he came close to Flensevan.

"Go home. Now," Regapisk said. "Take Egret."

"Lord Reg—"

"No time. Just go. Is Pink Rabbit home?"

"Yes, watching the shop."

"Get home—stay there. Keep both your sons there," Regapisk said urgently.

"Poseidon protect us," Flensevan muttered.

Regapisk followed Sandry and Burning Tower. He had to elbow some of the lesser priests out of the way.

"Do you wish assistance?"

Coyote's priest, his mask under his arm. He looked concerned. "The king told me to take care of her," Regapisk said, "so I will."

"Admirable. You will miss the ceremonies on the plaza."

"There will be others," Regapisk said. "I'll take her to the river. She needs water."

"Water?" Coyote's priest sounded puzzled.

"Flowing water. Don't you know about such things? I'll explain it all tomorrow," Regapisk said.

They were at the basket. Two guards leaped in with

Sandry and Burning Tower. Two more baskets were filled with guards, then all three were lowered. The next basket was filled with priests, then the next.

Regapisk gestured to Flensevan. "Come." He turned to the apprentices who controlled the baskets. "I carry the queen's sister," Regapisk said. "Give me a basket. I will be accompanied by my friends."

The apprentices looked around. No one contradicted Regapisk. "Certainly, King's Companion."

Squirrel stirred and mumbled. "King. Goes to the gods. Tell Sandry."

"He knows," Regapisk said. "Be quiet just for a bit, please, Squirrel. . . ."

The trip down the side of Mesa Fajada took forever. The great Temple Mesa still glowed like a burning tower in the afternoon sun. *Omen,* Regapisk thought. *An omen foreshadowing what?*

But below stood the king's chariot, and next to it, a chariot for the companion. Everyone was following the Emperor and the king up to the Great Plaza, and no one cared when Regapisk claimed the companion's chariot. Flensevan and Egret held the babbling Clever Squirrel upright as Regapisk drove down toward the river, then, when no one followed, along the deserted streets to Flensevan's jewel shop.

Flensevan had been silent until they were well out of the palace. Then he asked, "What are we doing?"

"Sandry is going to run for it. In the boat."

Egret looked startled and almost lost his grip on Clever Squirrel.

"Why am I not astonished?" Flensevan said.

"All right, why not?" Regapisk said.

"It happened before, you know. We used baskets to get Zephans out of the city. I think they have been suspicious of me ever since," Flensevan said. "So. It is time to go. You say we will have wealth in Crescent City?"

"Fabulous wealth, and welcome in other places."

"I have always wanted to travel," Egret said.

"Yes, and I never did!" Flensevan said waspishly. He shrugged with his shoulders, his hands occupied with bracing Clever Squirrel against the side of the heavy chariot. "Seven, then. An auspicious number. You, Sandry, the Queen, my two sons, the shaman, and myself. In Atlantis, seven was lucky. This may be fated."

"Will they pursue us?"

Flensevan laughed. "Of course. They will seek to keep the king alive, to capture him without harming him. As for the rest of us—" Flensevan shuddered.

The Wall of Hearts, Regapisk thought. *I just hope Sandry knows what he's doing.*

And he must be thinking the same about me!

Burning Tower held tightly to Sandry's arm as the basket dropped down the side of Mesa Fajada. She felt crowded by the two expressionless guards. Emperor's guards, humorless, not the friendly guards who had served King Arshur.

As if that made any difference. All these soldiers served the Emperor no matter what colors they wore. She didn't understand Aztlan, but she knew that much. When they named the Emperor the Supreme One, it was simple truth.

And Sandry was going to defy him. She didn't know what he would do, but Sandry would never submit to this.

Would he? She'd overheard enough of the stories, of Arshur and Regapisk and eight virgins, of the accomplished lady Annalun. Was Sandry tempted? He was king now, as well as her husband, and he could do anything he liked. *But he's not like that! He's still Sandry.*

She held that thought as the basket descended. *He's still Sandry.*

Four years, Regapisk had said. *Four or eight or sixteen.* But Sandry wasn't going to wait. She wished she could talk to him, but the guards stood close by.

Hah! They wouldn't understand. "My husband," she said, using a word that a kinless of Tep's Town would use.

"Yes, my love? Do you think these Lordkin sons of donkeys will understand?"

"They think—"

Sandry sprawled at ease. "They think it's our wedding night, and they're right, and that's what they think we are talking about." He put his arm around her and peered suggestively at her breasts. Butterflies stirred restively.

"So what will we do, my love?"

"I'll tell you in this tongue when I know," Sandry said. "Until then, you are the frightened bride of the king."

"A part I have no difficulty playing," she said.

The Wall of Hearts loomed up before them as the basket touched the ground. Burning Tower shuddered.

The Emperor and his priests waited impatiently at the stairway to the Great Plaza. Everyone smiled and was pleasant. The only malice in those smiles was the common cruelty of a wedding day, when everyone schemed to keep the newly wed couple from being alone for as long as possible. They treated Sandry as king, but always there were fours of guards, impassive and unsmiling, armed with clubs and leather cords. Though they said nothing disrespectful, it was plain they would never allow a king to leave the city.

"We'll get this over as quickly as possible," the Emperor said. He leered at Burning Tower. "The king will be impatient. I don't suppose you'll want the services of a Great Mistress tonight, Majesty?"

"I will have more than my share of happiness," Sandry said.

"Discreet. I trust the ceremony was satisfactory?"

Burning Tower started to speak, but Sandry gripped her hand tightly. He said, "So far, indeed, Supreme One."

"So far? There is more? What more?" the Emperor demanded.

"It is only a small part," Sandry said. "We come from far away in a land of hunters and barbarians. Has the Son of the Sun ever heard of Lordkin?"

"No." The Emperor was impatient.

"The Lords have retained ancient customs that originated among the barbarians," Sandry said. "You may enjoy this."

They emerged onto the Great Plaza. The crowds were still in the stands. Vendors moved through the stands with buckets and dippers, and food rolled in corn shucks. From the sounds, the buckets contained intoxicants. Someone shouted a raucous obscenity, and everyone laughed.

Spike stood next to Sandry's chariot. He eyed the stallion with contempt, but when he saw Sandry he stamped and reared. "He doesn't like me," Sandry said.

The Emperor smiled.

"And now the bride mounts her one-horn," Sandry said.

Burning Tower hesitated only for a second. Two hands and an athlete's leap put her aboard Spike, settling like a feather. Spike turned to look her in the eye.

"And I stand in my chariot—" Sandry mounted the chariot. A guard jumped in with him.

"Careful of those gifts," someone said importantly. The Emperor frowned.

"Now, Tower," Sandry said. He used the kinless language. It sounded like he was chanting. "Ride to the shop, ride to my cousin, ride fast. Ride now!"

Tower shouted. Spike shook himself free of the young girl who had acted as groom, and darted across the plaza, long white veils streaming behind her, and a rainbow cloud of butterflies. The crowd roared.

"And I must capture the bride!" Sandry shouted the language of Aztlan. "I must do this without assistance! Hee-ah!"

Blaze and Boots darted forward at the command. At the same time, Sandry pushed the already unsteady guard. The guard lost his footing and fell off the back of the chariot, and rolled as if he'd practiced it, and came up smiling to watch Sandry drive his war chariot across the Great Plaza of Aztlan in pursuit of Burning Tower on her great white unicorn. It was easy to follow the trail of butterflies.

The people of Aztlan shouted encouragement as first Tower, then Sandry clattered down the steps into the palace stables below, then out through the tunnels to the streets of Aztlan.

Chapter Thirty

Flight

She was squiffed, but she was swift: Clever Squirrel ran as if she were flying, upright as long as Regapisk and Flensevan were holding her arms and running alongside, with Egret leading. She fell once, scaring Regapisk and amusing herself, before they reached the chariot. Then Regapisk drove while Egret and Flensevan kept her from falling out. Squirrel was having the time of her life . . . and then she went to sleep.

She wasn't heavy. Egret carried her into the shop.

Pink Rabbit was there to greet them.

Flensevan spoke a few words to his sons. Pink Rabbit bleated like a goat facing the butcher. Then all three scurried toward the back of the shop. Reg followed. Squirrel was out like a blown candle.

The boys paused in the main display room. They

pulled the wicker weapons display off the wall and rolled it up, a tube with spears and blades inside.

They all streamed down to the pool beneath the shop. Egret began turning the crank in the wall. Regapisk perceived a growing magical glare from the black water.

Squirrel's eyes opened. "Ooo," she said.

The King's Guards would never catch Spike. *He'd* never catch Spike! Sandry swayed as the chariot swung from side to side down the streets of Aztlan. An occasional butterfly showed he was on her trail, and he'd just have to trust that Tower was riding in the right direction. It would be a disaster if she were actually riding for the palace.

As he left the plaza, he saw that Sareg was boarding another chariot. Sandry laughed. Those clumsy excuses for war chariots would never catch him. By the time they got off the piazza, he'd be out of sight, and they wouldn't even know where he was going. They might assume the wedding palace, or even the king's palace, and either guess would be wrong.

If they did catch him . . . Sandry began to arm himself, removing the jeweled covers from spear points. His bow was unstrung, of course, and he'd never be able to string it while riding at a gallop, but it was there, and so was a full quiver of flight arrows. If it came to a fight, it would take only a moment to string that bow, and there wasn't a weapon in Aztlan that could touch him as long as the arrows lasted.

Not only his arrows, but some others. Dark arrows, the kind Thundercloud had used, dark shafts with turquoise heads. The Emperor must have planned some spectacular for his people, something he was going to do with Sandry's bow.

Then he had throwing spears and the atlatl. He'd seen no sign of atlatl practice in Aztlan.

Spears, arrows, but there were more guards than he had weapons.

His sword! They'd put his iron sword in its place. He buckled it on, almost falling when the chariot lurched, but he felt better with the familiar weight hanging against his left hip. So. Arrows, spears, then cold iron. He careened into a large public square. To the left was the bridge leading across the river to the king's palace. There were butterflies straight ahead. She hadn't taken the wrong turn.

He stuffed the weapons into the largest spear case. Rope. Had they put the lasso in the chariot? He found it and wound it around the weapons and the case so that they made one bundle.

Drive with both hands! How often had Masterman Chalker shouted that at him when he was learning? But he needed one hand to drive and one to bundle the weapons and one to hold on to the chariot. He compromised by laying the reins across the chariot bulkhead and shouting orders. He could do that with these horses, so long as the street was straight.

There was enough leather rope to make a neat bundle of all the weapons. It made a heavy package. *Boat?* he thought. *I'll never swim, not with armor and all these weapons.*

And with all his weapons, there were still too many guards. Would they try to kill him? He didn't know. Probably they didn't want to kill him, and that might give him an advantage, except that he didn't want to kill them either! *Curse!* And they wouldn't hesitate to kill anyone who assisted him, or to hold Tower as hostage.

And of course they could follow butterflies as well as he.

The city was empty, almost abandoned. An old woman was crouching fearfully in a doorway; there were loaves of bread scattered in the road, and two baskets. *Hah!* Tower had passed. She must be headed for the gem shop. "Hee-ah! Go, you beauties!"

Tower tumbled off Spike. Regapisk was in the shop's doorway; he shied from the beast's horn. "Come on in," he said. "Where's Sandry?"

"The gods know! He told me to come here, and he was following when I left the piazza. If he's fast enough, he won't be bringing guards down on us. What have you got? Is there really a way out?" She'd kill him if there wasn't. Sandry had never trusted his cousin.

"I'll wait here for Sandry. Go on in."

The bonehead was glaring at Regapisk. Tower turned him forcefully away. Tower fondled his ears and whispered into them, then stepped back. "Good-bye." She swatted his flank, and he went. He kept looking back. They'd see him! But there was nothing she could do about that.

"Inside!" Regapisk ordered. "In and down."

She tried to resent his tone, but he was right—there was no time—and she'd just have to trust him. She darted into the shop.

* * *

There was a boat down there. A *sunken* boat, in a pool surrounded on three sides by a stone floor just higher than the water level. The fourth side of the pool, the south side, was separated from the river by a heavy-beamed wooden wall.

The boat glowed faintly down there under the water. Tower gawked. *Regapisk,* she thought. *I might have known. A sunken boat.*

Clever Squirrel, cross-legged on the stone floor, watched her with her jaw hanging. Her eyes didn't follow Tower's fingertip. She giggled.

Flensevan and Egret were there.

"Does this thing float?" Tower demanded.

"Of course," Flensevan said. "When we are all here. And this had better be worth it! It's the second time I've been imp-implicated in a king's escape. Zephans was worse. The Emperor actually put a crown on him! Where's King Sandry?"

"I left him—"

"You *l-left him*?"

"He's a big boy. Who's Zephans?"

"Zephans Mishagnos was a wizard of Atlantis. He came as a trader, but the Emperor named him king. They must have expected him to run, nearly half of the kings have tried to, but they thought he'd use a boat. Atlantis, right? And he *had* a boat, only we made it disappear while Zeph played king. Then we got him into a basket and away he w-went off with Ruser. My brother says he got as far as Crescent City. So the Emperor forgot about the boat . . . gods willing."

Pink Rabbit appeared on a balcony, his arms loaded with clothing and jewelry. He dropped it all in a heap on a balcony high above the water-lapped stone floor.

"But—but it's sunk!" Tower said. "Flensevan, how do we get it outside? Does the roof open?"

"It will rise," Egret said. He indicated the low ceiling. "It will rise above the water, so all this has to go before we can raise it."

"Above the water." She remembered, Morth of Atlantis had said something about boats flying above the water, but she hadn't believed it. "Are we going over land?"

"Oh, the ships of Atlantis prefer water under them. Anyway, what do you want under you when the magic goes away? We'll go out through"—his hand slapped thick wooden beams—"here."

Regapisk bellowed through the halls. "I can see him!"

Flensevan and Egret lifted a wooden beam in the south wall. "Give us some help," Flensevan grunted, and Tower added her strength to theirs. Squirrel was asleep, still sitting on the stone floor.

Rolling and bouncing down toward the river road, Sandry saw Spike coming up at him. The bonehead paused to stare down the stallion, then brushed past. Sandry threw up a shield to fend off the horn, and turned, ready to do it again, but Spike was disappearing upslope.

Sandry could hear chariots and horses behind him in the winding roads. He kept riding. He could glimpse a sparkle of water between the houses.

There. Flensevan's combination house and jewel shop. Butterflies marked its door. Butterflies and Regapisk.

"Sandry! Hurry!" Regapisk was shouting.

"Help me with the weapons!"

Regapisk ran out as Sandry leaped from the chariot. "Tep's teeth! You have enough weapons here to fight an army!" Regapisk paused, then grinned. "Inside. Inside and down. Go, Your Majesty!"

"You son of a dog," Sandry said, but he said it under his breath. Reggy was Reggy, and just now he could say anything he liked.

Stairs at the back of the house led down into a dark pit. There were lights down there. Sandry ran to the lights. Regapisk clattered down the stairs behind him.

CHAPTER THIRTY-ONE

LITTLE RAINBOW

There was a boat down there, but it was underwater. Everyone was straining at moving beams. It was a nightmarish scene that made no sense at all.

"King Sandry! Lord Regapisk!" Egret was shouting. "Help with this." He was turning a drum, some kind of winch. A rope led from that up and into the house above. "Help me!"

Regapisk threw his weight onto the winch handles. "Here, Majesty! Help!"

"You call me that again and I kill you," Sandry said.

Regapisk laughed. "If you don't help us, you won't have to—your guards will do it for you."

Trust Reggy. Sandry took one of the winch handles and threw his weight into it. The winch turned, slowly. The house groaned.

"Heave!" Egret shouted.

Sandry strained. The drum turned, and daylight seeped into the dank basement. More. The ceiling was rising, folding up against the upstairs north wall. Flensevan and Pink Rabbit were hauling on another rope. Suddenly the entire south wall of the house fell away and floated downriver. The afternoon sun blazed into the basement as the ceiling came free to fold against the still-standing north wall.

"Now!" Flensevan shouted. He gripped ropes that led down into the water. Pink Rabbit seized another, and Egret rushed to join them. They pulled. There was a flash of blue light, bright enough that even Sandry could see it. Squirrel was startled awake and mumbled something.

The boat rose. Up through the water, higher, until it was floating above the river, the decks just level with the wooden balcony high above the stone floor. Egret swung a gangplank across to it.

Regapisk didn't wait. He grabbed Clever Squirrel and carried her up to the balcony, then across to the slippery decks. Water streamed off the decks.

The boat was floating, *flying.* It was all curves, like Sandry's bow. There were windows in the bottom, set flush.

"Welcome to *Little Rainbow,*" Flensevan said. "Quickly. Quickly."

The river was ten manheights wide here. There were people across the river. They stared and shouted as Sandry and the others scrambled aboard. Flensevan's sons threw bundles of goods to the deck.

"Cast off," Flensevan said.

Egret was grinning widely as he loosed the last ties, and let *Little Rainbow* drift out into the current.

Witnesses were not an issue. The only folk in town were a few servants who had not gone to see the king's death, resurrection, and wedding, and the dozen guards now pouring through the winding streets toward Flensevan's shop. Now they halted, staring at a flying boat as it wafted downstream. Now they were scrambling over walls and into houses, dodging a bonehead's lethal horn.

"Seven," said Regapisk. "It's an Atlantean boat. It'll hold seven. The mers all know that the Atlantis numbering system is base seven."

"And I wouldn't have left without my sons," Flensevan said firmly. "Some of us will be sleeping on deck, I suppose. We're loaded with trade goods, mostly charged talismans. Plenty of manna to keep us afloat. They'll still be partly charged when we reach Crescent City."

Tower asked, "Are you a magician?"

"No. I can't see manna. Ruser picked us a good partner: Regapisk can."

Tower let that pass. "I don't see any way to row."

The Little Rainbow River flowed west below them, and the boat flowed with the water.

"That's one thing Zeph forgot to tell us," Flensevan said, "how to move faster. Sails might work if you're going downwind." A horde of children was following the boat along the River Road. Flensevan smiled and waved to them. "Keep your husband below. It might help if nobody actually *sees* him aboard."

"The guards saw me," Sandry said, rising through the

hatch. "Love, we'll get little out of your sister. I only had a sip of that stuff, and I can still feel it. She must have been drinking it all night."

The stream flowed faster. Not as fast as a real war chariot, but faster than those wagons the Aztlan troops used. And he'd never taught anyone how to use his chariot.

He looked upriver. "I hope they don't take it out on Blaze and Boots."

"I was thinking of Spike," Tower said. She stood beside him at the stern rail.

"He was raising hell with the guards who were chasing me," Sandry said, "last I saw. He belongs to the Emperor now; they won't dare hurt him."

"Mmm. All right. And we're married, and there aren't any boneheads around." And suddenly she was in his arms. How had that happened? She rubbed her cheek against his beard. He held her, and looked back toward where Spike would be. *With this many people aboard a small boat,* he thought, *you don't need a bonehead.* They stood close together at the stern rail.

Little Rainbow passed the city gates and skimmed past the Caravanserai. Guards stared. Then there were trumpets, and the thunder of drums, and a cloud of locusts flew up the valley toward Mesa Fajada. For a few hundred paces, the river paralleled the High Road. That was frightening, but then the river wound northward and straightened. They drifted fast away from Aztlan and its roads and into wasteland, rocks, and sagebrush.

CHAPTER THIRTY-TWO

THE LAST BATTLE

"I think we made it!" Regapisk shouted. He was holding the stout tiller attached to the left-hand steering oar, but there didn't seem to be much work involved. The river ran swift and deep here, no rapids and few turns, and the boat drifted above it, the keel and steering oars just in the water. Regapisk gestured, and Flensevan took his place at the steering oar. "Dinner," Regapisk said. "I brought food."

Sandry realized that he was hungry. They hadn't eaten since an early breakfast. "Good."

He stood with Burning Tower, looking back through the Aztlan canyon. In the late afternoon sun, Mesa Fajada blazed against a clear blue sky. There were yellow buttons at its top. He watched them grow larger.

"Baskets," he said regretfully.

She pulled away. "Oh my gods," she said, but she was looking toward the bow.

Clusters of baskets rushed down on them from Aztlan. They were still too far away and too high for Sandry to make out faces, but he saw the flash of scarlet capes. The King's Guard. His guards, but they weren't going to be taking orders from him. He stooped to loosen the lashings on his bundle of weapons and took out his bow, caressing it for a moment before stringing it.

The baskets ahead of them, downriver, seemed to cluster together and hang high above the river.

"See if your sister can move yet," he said. While Tower went below, Sandry stepped aft to talk with Egret, who was manipulating the boat's right-hand steering oar. Both steering oars had large blades, big enough to catch a wind. Their tips dipped into the water below. *Little Rainbow* was moving at the speed of the current, and the oar tips and keel left almost no wake.

Sandry pointed out the baskets. There were only five in the downstream cluster. The upstream baskets trailed away like a comet tail: at least a dozen, maybe more coming. Both clusters were nearing fast. Both were staying above the river. Was there magic in river water, to hold baskets aloft?

Flensevan scrambled out of the hatch. "What now? Curses! Who are they?"

"Too far to tell about those," Sandry said, pointing to the downstream cluster. "But that's the King's Guard upriver."

"We're finished," Flensevan said.

Sandry ignored him.

Regapisk came on deck carrying an atlatl and a handful of spears. He looked his cousin over. Sandry was wearing the same ornamental armor he'd worn for his marriage. Reg asked, "Flensevan, did you pack anything like armor aboard?"

"No. Am I a warrior? The Emperor doesn't favor armed merchants. I had a few weapons for fighting off thieves."

"I feel naked. . . . All right, cousin, those behind will be the Emperor's, but who's chasing us from in front?"

"Sunfall Crater is that way," Sandry said.

Tower did her best. Clever Squirrel would walk, but she wouldn't climb. Tower and Regapisk had to lift her through the hatch. They settled her on a blanket, and Tower sat next to her.

Then Tower talked to her as if she could hear. Perhaps she was only organizing her own thoughts.

"Those upstream, they're the King's Guards. They may want the rest of us dead, but they want the king back. Downstream, those could be more guards, if locusts flew fast enough, or if the Emperor sent sand paintings, or . . . Squirrel, is there any way he could have sent messages to Sunfall Crater?"

Squirrel shook her head in wide slow arcs. "Flute tree seeds. *Ilb'al*."

Tower patted her shoulder. "I'm glad you're with us, sister. All right, they read the future and saw us coming, saw *something* coming. They could be more of the Emperor's people, or—"

The downstream flock of flying baskets had almost reached them. They were small, carrying two men each. Like Tep's Town chariots, she thought. Tower saw a man stand up in the nearest basket, swing a cloth sling around his head, and let go of one end. Motes drifted.

"Duck!" she yelled. She rolled her half sister into the hatch and followed her down. She heard thumping on deck.

"—or they could be the last of Terror Bird's priests throwing rocks at us from the sky. Come on, let's get back up there. You're our only magical defense."

Of those still on deck, Sandry was the only one wearing armor. That bothered him. Tower, Squirrel, Egret, and Regapisk looked very vulnerable.

More stuff was falling. Not rocks—arrows.

Clever Squirrel stood up. She waved her arms and shouted. High above the boat, arrows exploded into a network of lightning.

Then three upstream baskets confronted the five downstream baskets. Arrows crossed. Lightning flared among the upstream baskets: the King's Guards. Two fell burning.

Squirrel closed her fists in Tower's wonderful wedding dress. Butterflies swarmed. "Get me something magical!"

Regapisk used his atlatl. The spear flew farther than imagination and ticked the nearest of the Terror Bird baskets. An arrow flew in response.

Tower went below.

The arrow struck the ship's bow in a flare of lightning and a flurry of rain.

The next few of the guards' baskets held back, clustering, unwilling to be ganged up on. One of them—was that Hazel Sky?—waved at a flurry of arrows. They exploded in lightning, short of their targets.

Tower came back up carrying an armful of jewelry. "I hope this is—"

Squirrel took it, a lapful of gems. "I was taught," she said, "can't remember. Wait. Yes." She spoke another language, being abnormally precise with her pronunciation.

"Better. Ow," she said. Her diction was clearer. She chanted again. With each phrase, her voice was clearer. "Ow! There was magic in that stuff, that pulque, but Morth's spell unwrites the blessing. So much for divine madness. But it's still pulque! Ow, my head." She looked up into a maze of flying baskets and asked, "Who's with us?"

"None of them, really, but some want to kill us and some just want to take us back and kill Sandry in four years. What can you do?"

"Not kill him. Send him to the gods," Squirrel said. "I remember now." She shuddered.

The guards' baskets were still holding back, gathering into a wall. Then all five Terror Bird baskets dropped toward the boat.

Regapisk hurled a spear with his atlatl. It pierced one of the baskets. One of a pair of priests jerked and yelled. Regapisk hurled again, and the other priest took a spear through the jaw. He fell. The basket fell more slowly.

Sandry selected one of the black rain arrows, nocked it, and sent it into the basket. Nothing happened.

"The cost!" Flensevan wailed. "Do you know what those arrows are worth?"

"I expected rain and lightning!" Sandry shouted.

"Next time," Squirrel said. "Tell me before you launch it." She was still lurching drunkenly, but she stood. She chanted; her arms moved in complex curves. Tower couldn't feel a thing, and nothing much seemed to be happening. Wait, now, another of the baskets was off course, curving down.

Falling.

"I can unwrite the spell that keeps a basket aloft," Squirrel said with some satisfaction. The basket and its two priests struck the shore.

Regapisk's target basket thumped hard into the deck. A single priest tumbled out with a spear jutting up into his abdomen. Pink Rabbit popped up from belowdecks to push him overboard, into the raging water.

The remaining three of Left-Handed Hummingbird's baskets veered away, and then the King's Guards' baskets were among them. They were fighting with blades and spears. Sandry watched critically; Tower watched in awe.

"This thing's myth," Squirrel said, and dropped a glorious sapphire pectoral. "What have we got with any magic in it?" She swayed and sat down. "Maybe they'll all kill each other."

"Maybe we can outrun them," Regapisk said. He was joking, but the boat was flying through roaring white spume, between rock walls that reached to the sky.

Sandry stared ahead. The current was moving fast now, much faster than a chariot, and *Little Rainbow* skimmed over the water even more swiftly. Egret was frantically trying to steer, but it didn't look as if he was doing any good. The boat went where it wanted to go.

"Squirrel! Can you talk to the boat?" Burning Tower asked.

"Uh. I don't think so." She looked ahead and pointed unsteadily.

There were canyons ahead. Narrower than the valley of Aztlan, but much higher, spectacular colors to the walls, jagged spires of rock, monstrous shapes everywhere. *Little Rainbow* dashed down the stream into that maze of rock.

The priests of Left-Handed Hummingbird were falling. Three baskets, six priests, and none of them turned to run. They fought and died in the air, and fell into raging waters.

The baskets of the King's Guard flew lower and came near. Hazel Sky pulled alongside the boat, a pace or two higher than the deck. "Majesty," she said, "you must return."

"Hail, Hazel Sky. I thought Sareg would be among you."

"Sareg fell to a traitor priest, defending you as he should. I will mourn him."

Sandry nodded. "A good man."

"I have avenged him," Hazel Sky said. "We may not harm you, Majesty, but we don't have to. We only have to rescue you after this boat sinks. Look, the keel is already in the water, and the rudder too, and you go into waters beyond your skills."

Sandry peered far over the boat's rim. He could see that she was right. "Squirrel, can you do anything about this?"

"Curse. No."

Hazel asked, "How would you know how to renew the spell that lifts a boat of Atlantis? You're none of you Atlanteans. Your treasure trove won't help you float. You will sink. Can you swim? We'll pull you from the water before you can drown, Majesty. Then we'll rescue your bride and her sister and your companion, if there's time for that and the river allows. We will do all we can."

Sandry said, "Great Mistress, I can't sell my rescuer and his sons to the wall."

"Majesty, nothing can save them. Atlantean boat! They helped the wizard Zephans escape the Emperor's decree. They've been doomed for years, even if we didn't know precisely where that doom would fall."

Squirrel asked, "Hazel, can you swim?" She began to chant.

"Stop." Hazel raised her bow and started to nock an arrow. She stopped when she found herself facing Sandry's bow. Squirrel continued to chant.

"We need only wait," Hazel said, and then her basket plunged her into the water. She swam toward shore through a gathering current.

The river had widened. Perhaps they had reached the Rainbow River itself. The water had grown rough. It was affecting the boat, throwing it this way and that.

"Let me take the tiller," Regapisk said to Egret.

"I'm fine," the burly jeweler said. "You do good with that atlatl."

"Give me the tiller or we'll be in the water. You can't see where the magic flows," Regapisk said.

Sandry called, "Give it up, Regapisk—" A wave against the hull set him lurching.

Squirrel got to her feet. "Let me! He's right—" Another wave dropped her sprawling. "We've got to follow the manna currents!"

"But—"

"Bet on me, Cousin." Regapisk took the tiller, and Egret let him. Regapisk swung it hard over. The boat heeled and, a moment later, lifted.

The baskets followed them downstream. One came close. They recognized Coyote's mask. Squirrel began to chant. They heard a plaintive wail, but Squirrel chanted it down into the river. When it touched down, she spoke under her breath, but Sandry heard her. "Good luck. Farewell, my love."

"Flensevan," Sandry asked, "What did Zephans do to get himself in such trouble?"

"Foreigner. Wizard. Spent too much time near the wall." Flensevan pitched his voice so that his sons couldn't hear. "I always thought he must have figured out which niche was the Emperor's heart. I never asked."

Rabbit and Egret ran up a sail. Sandry wondered if a wrong wind could put them on land, but the boat seemed to want to stay above water.

It ran low. This wasn't all bad: it put the keel and rudder in the water, and then the boat steered much better. Regapisk squinted forward as if he could see things others could not. Arshur had always been sure that Regapisk was improving a tale. Sandry just couldn't tell.

The last baskets hung back, out of range even of

Sandry's bow. He grinned and selected a black rain arrow. "Squirrel!"

"Right here," she said unsteadily. "Good plan." She began to chant in the language of the gods. "Now, Lord Sandry."

He fired the arrow upstream. It trailed lightning, then a full storm. Rain fell behind them and the last baskets vanished in the storm.

Chapter Thirty-Three

Wedding Night

The last baskets were gone. The river was wild, but *Little Rainbow* stayed just above the water.

There, a bright ribbon of manna in a rash of rocks and white water. Reg steered into it. The boat lifted high above the water, and now he could barely steer. The boat drifted toward a dark patch, and Reg threw the tiller hard over to avoid the rocks, never mind the manna current. Too low, too low. If they broke a cursed window, they'd flood and sink.

"Harder than it looks, isn't it?" Egret said cheerfully.

"You'll never know," Regapisk said. "Egret, can you get me some water? Sandry, I can do without you watching me quite so closely. You can see the boat's still afloat."

"He's doing as well as Egret. We're still up," said Burning Tower. "And missing rocks is a good thing."

Sandry said, "And we're missing our wedding night."

Regapisk pointed with his nose, to the hatch that led into the boat. "Go below. Send the rest of them up here, and it's all yours. We can have the deck."

Sandry looked at Tower. She blushed. "I am as impatient as you, my husband, but you may be needed here. Squirrelly, can't they find new spells to lift those baskets?"

"They can," Clever Squirrel said unsteadily.

"It grows dark," Flensevan said.

"I can see the manna and steer to it," Regapisk shouted. "But I don't know how to see rocks at night!"

"Deep water," Squirrel said. "Make the water deep enough and the rocks won't matter."

"How?" Burning Tower said. A look of amazement came to her face. "Oh! Make storms!"

"And that's the way to stop the baskets," Sandry shouted. "Get me storm arrows!"

"The cost," Flensevan moaned. "But yes, it must be. Pink Rabbit, bring arrows."

Sandry nocked an arrow and aimed high above the stern of the ship. "Ready."

Clever Squirrel stood beside him. She sang a wild song that suggested storms and lightning in its very rhythms, and as it reached its climax she gestured. *Now!*

Sandry released the arrow. It flew straight and true, high above the river, then suddenly flashed jagged blue-white. Storm clouds grew in the wake of the arrow. Before it was out of sight, Sandry had nocked another arrow, and Squirrel began her song.

Arrow after arrow flew upriver. Lightning danced.

"Listen!" Regapisk shouted.

A rumbling sound, growing louder. Sandry stared upriver. Something white flashed in the black clouds, something white and low on the water.

"Water stampede!" Burning Tower shouted. "Stampede!"

Sandry almost laughed. Stampede. Animals did that. Not water. But there was a roaring wall of water coming down the river toward them! "Reggy! Look behind you!"

"Can't," Regapisk shouted.

Sandry felt the stern of the boat rise. It lifted higher and higher, and he was looking down the boat at a steep angle toward the water ahead of them. Rocks!

Somehow they missed the rocks. *Little Rainbow*'s bow lifted. The boat wasn't level, but it wasn't diving down the wave straight toward the bottom any longer. The roaring waves crashed around them.

Regapisk shouted in triumph. "It's working!"

Something was working. They were riding that wave, moving faster than Sandry had ever moved in his life. *No,* he thought, *not quite.* "As fast as the High Road!" Sandry shouted.

"We're faster, I think," Regapisk said. He was staring ahead into the river, paying no attention to anything but the water just ahead, making tiny movements of the steering oar. *Little Rainbow* skimmed just above the crest of that rushing flood. Regapisk shouted again.

Burning Tower huddled against Sandry in the pitch dark. Canyon walls loomed above them. She couldn't see the walls, only that there were no stars on either side.

Blackness, except for a river of stars directly overhead. The water beside them seemed almost calm, but she knew that was an illusion, that they were racing down the stream at the speed of the flood.

Wedding night, she thought. It wasn't anything like her dreams. But when other wives told the tales of their wedding nights, she'd win.

Little Rainbow raced onward.

CHAPTER THIRTY-FOUR

THE HEART OF THE EARTH

Dawn came slowly, light from behind without direct sun. It shone high on the walls that rose above them while they were still in darkness. The sounds of rushing water echoed from the canyon walls. Gradually the light filtered downward as the sun rose.

They were deep in the Earth. Painted walls rose on either side, dark at the bottom near the river, brightly lit above and ahead where the invisible sun fell on them. Up high there were colors, wild colors, jumbled together, here in patches, there in stripes. Odd shapes, pillars of rock with boulders on their tops. Arches. Burning Tower stared in disbelief. Colors everywhere. As the light grew brighter and came lower into the canyon she could see the river ahead. They were just above the water to either side, but if she looked ahead they were, two, no, three manlengths above the river! The water ahead was strewn with boulders, but the flood they rode was higher than any of the rocks, and they stayed just above the top of the wild waves.

There was color everywhere. Patches of color, blotches, stripes. The canyon walls looked layered as if a mad cook had been making an enormous cake. There were other shapes, arches and mounds and hoops and heaps, all in different colors. She had never seen anything more beautiful.

Land on either side rushed past. She had no way to know how fast they were going. Faster than Spike could carry her. As fast as the High Road, perhaps faster. The dawn light was tricky.

Then she gasped and pointed.

"The walls are getting higher!" she shouted. She pointed ahead. "Higher! Or else we're going deeper. The earth, it's swallowing us! Sandry, wake up—look!"

Sandry stirred. They had slept fitfully on the deck. Sandry had passed a loop of rope through a deck fitting and around them so they couldn't be shaken off when, sometimes, Regapisk sent the boat through wild turns and gyrations. Once Tower had wakened from fitful sleep to see Sandry watching over her. He must have fallen asleep finally. Now he was waking.

Flensevan was lying on a blanket on the other side of the deck. He woke at Tower's shout and looked ahead. "I know of this place," he said. "Zeph told me of a cut to the heart of the world about halfway to Aztlan from Crescent City."

"Halfway?" Sandry said wonderingly. "Halfway in a night?"

"An afternoon and a night," Flensevan said.

"But how far?" Sandry said. "We were moons crossing that wasteland! Now we have come halfway back?"

Tower looked back to see Regapisk still standing at one steering oar. He seemed barely able to stand, and he steered by muttering directions to Egret. "Right a little. Follow that riplet." Regapisk's voice was infinitely weary. "Straight now." He shook his head like a man afraid of sleep.

"How long can he last?" Tower asked Sandry.

"Not much longer, I'd say. Better find your sister," Sandry said, "my love."

She tried to smile. "What a night," she said, "my love."

By noon the walls were shrinking. The river twisted and turned now. Clever Squirrel and Regapisk took turns directing Flensevan's sons, who acted as steersmen. Sandry strained to see any signs in the water, but there was nothing: whatever Squirrel and Regapisk saw, he could not.

"I can't see it either," Burning Tower said. She moved closer.

"I thought Reggy was making it all up," Sandry said.

The sky overhead was clear. They had left the storm far behind them, and Sandry could see no trace of it.

They were still riding the wave, but it was tamer now, no longer the wild storm-driven stampede. Some of the wave had passed them, so that when he looked ahead, it was down a long slope of water. Far ahead he could see rocks, but the flood engulfed them long before *Little Rainbow* was in any danger. Behind them the slope of water continued upward.

"Left a little," Regapisk said. "Sandry, I'm getting hungry."

"I'm starving," Burning Tower said. "Didn't we bring any food?"

Flensevan's head appeared from the hatch amidships. "No time. I've been looking for anything we stashed. Nothing. We had some bread, but it dissolved."

"Dissolved," Sandry said. "There's water down there?"

Flensevan laughed. "One of the windows got smashed by a rock."

"So what's keeping us up?" Sandry demanded.

"It's an Atlantean boat." Flensevan's voice took on a tone of infinite patience. "Manna keeps it up. Water magic. Only we don't have enough of it."

Regapisk laughed bitterly. "We have chests and chests of magic. Enough talismans to keep us all young for all our lives! And the only thing that keeps us afloat is me, and I'm hungry."

"Reggy—" Sandry said.

Clever Squirrel looked like a pile of rags at Reggy's feet. She stirred. "He's right, Sandry. We have manna, but it's the wrong kind, and none of us knows how to weave Atlantean magic to renew the floating spell on *Little Rainbow*."

"So—"

"So the only ones here who can see the streaks of manna in the water are Lord Reg and I, and he sees them better than me. And the boat knows how to use water magic to stay above the water."

"But not to steer to it," Burning Tower said.

Regapisk looked surprised. "No. I don't know why, but no."

Clever Squirrel grinned. "Ships that sail themselves don't need wizards."

"Reggy's no wizard," Sandry insisted.

"Started too late," Squirrel said. "If he'd had proper training when he was young, he'd have learned."

"I told them," Regapisk said. "Right just a little, Rabbit. I told them I shouldn't be in that school getting beat up in weapons practice. And I never did like iron weapons even after I learned to fight. And I learned to talk to the mers. I could have been a wizard!"

"You're wizard enough for us right now," Burning Tower said. "Thank you, Cousin."

Regapisk tried to grin.

Egret, the stronger of Flensevan's two sons, had been crouched in the bow with a fishing spear. He shouted in triumph and pulled out a trout the size of his leg. He threw it onto the deck and drew his knife.

By the time Sandry reached the foredeck, Egret had filleted the trout. "It tried to talk to me. You don't think it could really have granted me two wishes, do you? But I was hungry!" He held up the boneless fillets. "I guess we'll have to eat him raw."

"No." Clever Squirrel looked horrified. "I may not be able to use the manna on the boat, but I sure know how to cook fish!" She looked down at the fish. Its eyes were open but dimming. "Why didn't you wish for bison steaks?"

Evening came. The canyon walls were gone, replaced by steep banks not much higher than the wave they rode. The water behind them was higher still, rising upward as far as Sandry could see.

He pointed upriver. "The storms must still be filling the river."

Clever Squirrel nodded. "How many storm arrows did we use?"

"I lost count," Sandry said. "A dozen, maybe."

"Enough," Squirrel said. "As long as the water is higher behind us, we'll move fast, and it's sure deep enough to cover the rocks."

"Could Reggy have become a wizard?"

She shrugged. "I never heard of anyone with real talent who couldn't learn enough magic to be useful," she said. "Of course, sometimes that's not very much. Some big wagon trains will have two or three wizard assistants to do routine spells. They never learn much more, but it's a living. No telling how good Regapisk might have been."

No telling? Sandry thought. *Regapisk won't see it that way. He'll know—*

"Getting dark," Squirrel said. "I'd better get some sleep so I can keep Reggy going."

"You mean take over finding the manna streams?" Burning Tower asked.

"No, little sister. Little married sister. Reggy really is

better at seeing water manna than I am. Do you Lords have Atlanteans in your ancestry?"

"I doubt it," Sandry said. "The Memory Guildmaster has stories about times before we met the Lordkin, but they don't lead to Atlantis."

"Well, Atlanteans can find manna when no one else can, and Reggy has a natural talent for seeing dim manna traces. He's sure better than me. I'm always scared when I pilot this boat."

"Scared? You?" Sandry was incredulous.

"Scared. Me. So what I do, I use the manna in a talisman to keep Reggy awake and inspired, and I talk to him, and he steers the ship. It works." Squirrel went back to the steersman deck.

"And you have to sleep," Burning Tower said. "So you can steer." She nestled against him. "Will this ever be over?"

"You mean, will we ever be alone?"

"Yes."

"Soon, I think."

"South! We're going south," Clever Squirrel shouted from back on the steering deck. "The river turned—look at the stars!"

Sandry looked up. It was quite dark now, and the skies were clear. There were no canyons to block the view, and the sky overhead was filled with stars, with only a faint glow of red to mark where the sun had vanished. The stars were thousands of points of varying brightness in the black, except for a mighty river of stars that cut the night sky in half.

Burning Tower was pointing. "There's the Bear, and

the Snake. The Snake's Eye is north." She pointed upriver. "So we've turned south; we were going west, right into the sunset."

"South."

"Sandry, when we went to Aztlan, we went much farther east than north!"

"Oh." He shook his head in wonder. "I'm not used to traveling this fast."

"None of us are," Burning Tower said.

The night closed around them. "Hard right," Regapisk called. "Hold. Okay, left, straight down the river."

CHAPTER THIRTY-FIVE

BEACHED

Burning Tower slept fitfully. When it was Sandry's turn to steer, Burning Tower stood next to him, sharing the warmth of his cloak. Her white wedding dress was soiled and torn in places, and she knew she looked awful, but there were no other clothes on the boat. For now she wore everything she owned, and there wasn't even a comb to pull the knots out of her hair. With no mirror, she couldn't see how awful she looked, but she could imagine.

She fingered the hard object in a leather pouch at her waist. A small stonewood box with a silver stud for a latch. *At least I have this,* she thought. *He'll love me no matter what I look like. Do I need it?*

I can still ride Spike. The thought came unbidden and returned whenever she made the effort to banish it. With it came memories. The wild ride across the plains outside Crescent City, herds of terror birds following, Sandry's men depending on her and her alone to lead the birds away from their chariots before their horses tired.

Spike didn't get tired!

And the battle at Sunfall, Spike rearing above his enemies, her war hammer smashing birds and rebel priests alike. She'd never been more alive. *Warrior princess.* Who had called her that? Sareg, the guard captain. *Warrior princess.* She liked that idea.

Now she was a queen, in Aztlan. What did they do with queens after the king went to the gods? She shuddered.

She'd had no choices in Aztlan. She could have refused to marry, but if she'd avoided marrying Sandry, she would still be prey to someone. Coyote, the Emperor, one of his sons. Spike would go to the Emperor and she would lose him forever no matter what she did. They told her that the accomplished Lady Annalun could harness the one-horns, but Tower had noticed that while Spike didn't shy *away* from Annalun, he didn't like her either. No. They wouldn't have let her keep Spike in Aztlan. She could be queen or something else, but never a warrior princess. She had no choices there. . . .

"Right! Hard right!" Regapisk called and interrupted her thoughts, part dream, part reverie.

Sandry hauled left on the steering oar. She had been standing so close to him that she nearly fell.

"Sorry, my love," Sandry said.

Casually, she thought. She knew she was being unfair. Sandry couldn't be more attentive, usually, and he had to steer the ship, and he resented taking orders from his cousin. And soon, really soon, they would be alone together.

She looked down at the ruins of her dress. The butterflies were long gone. She had never been more beautiful. But that was then, in Aztlan. Now the dress was torn and her hair matted, and her hands and feet were dirty despite washing in river water.

Would he want her, now that she wore rags and looked like grim death? She fingered the box she'd been given in Condigeo. *He'll want me all right. But would he if I didn't have this?*

The sky brightened to the east. When the sun rose, they were moving swiftly down a broad river, the crest of their wave almost to the banks. The deck was above the banks; they could see across the plains to either side. The river was a bright ribbon of green through the brown lands.

"There!" Clever Squirrel was jumping up and down. "There! The city! Crescent City ahead!"

The river broadened, and they moved more slowly. Now there were settlements to each side, the familiar hogans that the people of Crescent City built: male, female, young and elder.

"The willow grove," Sandry said. "We went there to gather willow bark, about ten thousand years ago." More than a dozen workers were stripping bark from the trees. They stopped their labors and stared as the ship went past. "It was deserted when we went there before."

"No birds," Squirrel said.

"That's for sure. The birds haven't come back," Sandry said. "Houses along here now, no walls."

"And no manna," Regapisk said.

He spoke calmly, and for a moment, no one reacted. Then Squirrel looked over the side, ahead and behind them. "Curse! They're drawing all the manna!"

The ship settled deeper into the water.

"Will it float?" Sandry asked.

Flensevan laughed. "It never would have floated, and it sure won't with the windows knocked out. The hold's full of water. Of course it won't float."

Regapisk stared ahead. "Right. Steer right. Just a little more. There. Steady on—"

"We'll hit the bank!" Burning Tower shouted.

"I sure hope we make it that far," Regapisk said. They were headed almost straight across the stream now, moving downriver with the flood but angling toward the bank, going as fast as the water flowed. "Hope the bottom's strong!" Regapisk shouted.

"It's ironwood, it's strong," Flensevan said. "Hold on!"

"Left! Turn left, hard left!" Regapisk shouted. "Work the rudder! Row with the rudder oar!"

The boat turned downriver, still angled toward the bank. The bow touched ground, carved its way into the muddy river bank. When the boat slowed, it allowed more water to catch up with them. The water behind them was higher and pushed them further inland. They were over what had been dry land, now flooded with the remnants of the rushing storm water.

"Which way?" Sandry shouted.

"Doesn't matter," Regapisk said simply.

The manna was gone. *Little Rainbow* settled onto a greasewood bush and hung there, heeling over slightly to rest on the nearly flat bottom. Water rushed past on both sides, then on the left side only, then receded. The storm waters passed, and *Little Rainbow* was at rest in what had been dry plains land only minutes before. Furious prairie dogs popped out of holes and shook off water. The river was twenty muddy paces away.

"Welcome to Crescent City," Regapisk said.

Sandry asked, "Flensevan, are we stable?"

"Looks like."

Squirrel put a hand on Regapisk's feathered arm. "You can sleep."

"Sleep?" Regapisk tasted the thought. "I'm going to fall over now." She helped him recline on the deck . . . and he was gone.

"Wedding nights are exhausting," Sandry said. Burning Tower hugged him, then giggled. Nobody else even noticed.

CHAPTER THIRTY-SIX

PARTNERS

Sandry climbed to the top of the boat rail and stared south. "Looks like about an hour's walk to the city."

"Closer if you have a boat," Egret said.

"One that floats," Pink Rabbit agreed.

"But we don't. I'll walk," Sandry said.

"We don't dare leave this unguarded," Flensevan said.

"You stay here. I'll be back. Find me something to trade. Or some money."

"Find Zeph." Regapisk raised himself on one elbow. "Take a good talisman and find Zeph. He'll need a good one to get here, but if anyone can float *Little Rainbow*, it will be Zephans."

Sandry shrugged. "I don't know how to find him."

"I do," Regapisk said. He tried to get up. "I suppose it can't wait."

"It can wait long enough for you to get some rest," Sandry said. "I'll hike into town and buy a wagon. Or hire one. Get some sleep, Reggy. Flensevan, find me some trade goods. Tower, you up to walking?"

"Not in these shoes," she said. She looked down at the shreds of her wedding dress. "Or these rags, for that matter."

"I'll go with you," Clever Squirrel said. "Tower, I can buy you some clothes."

"Find Jade Coin," Regapisk said. "Ruser won't be back yet, but Jade Coin is a partner."

"Another partner?" Flensevan demanded. "How many share our wealth?"

"Just four, now that Arshur is dead," Regapisk said. "Jade Coin is a money changer. You, me, Jade Coin, and your brother. We all have shares in Ern's wagon train too."

"If the wagon train escapes the Emperor's wrath," Flensevan said.

Regapisk laughed heartily despite his weariness.

"The Emperor is amusing?" Flensevan demanded.

"No, but who will tell him the wagon train is escaping?" Regapisk said. "King Sandry?"

"I had not thought this through," Flensevan said. "I have been in terror all the day, but you are right, there is no king! There is no one to tell the Supreme One that things did not go well in the river battle, and there will be no one to tell him of the escaping wagon train! We are safe for years to come!" He turned to Sandry and gave him a sweeping bow. "Majesty!"

Sandry grinned.

Flensevan became serious. "And there is Zeph," he said. "He'll get a share of *Little Rainbow* and anything in her."

Now Regapisk looked stern. "I never offered him any shares."

"This is his boat," Flensevan reminded him.

"Well, it's all right," Regapisk said. "I liked him. Didn't like the salt farm much."

"What about us?" Burning Tower demanded.

Flensevan looked sly.

"We never drew up agreements, but Squirrel has a right to the shaman's shares," Tower insisted. "And Sandry was the guard commander. He fought too. He gets shares."

Clever Squirrel was chuckling. "I doubt that the rules of the Bison Tribe on the Hemp Road apply here on the road to Aztlan."

"Fair is fair," Burning Tower said. "Tell you what, Flensevan: you choose a champion to fight Sandry, and a wizard to duel Squirrel, and we can settle the matter right now."

Flensevan leaned forward to stare at her. "You are not serious."

"Well, I might be."

"We should charge you for passage," Egret said. "King Sandry, Queen Burning Tower."

"We don't even know what's left," Flensevan said. "Whatever it is, it's all we have. We can never go back. I lived well in Aztlan."

"So did everyone," Egret said.

"Everyone whose heart didn't go into the wall," Clever Squirrel said. "Are we going to argue until the next storm?"

"We are Feathersnake," Burning Tower said. "Squirrel, my husband, and I. Feathersnake always makes things right."

"Why have I heard this name, Feathersnake?" Flense-van asked.

"There were legends," Pink Rabbit said. "A feathered serpent. The name gives me chills."

"No need for chills," Burning Tower said. "We seek only our own."

"There is treasure in plenty, here and on the wagon train, and we are all safe," Clever Squirrel said. "And I ask again, will we argue until the next storm comes?"

"I won't," Sandry said. "I have more pleasant tasks. Squirrel, choose some trade goods, and a talisman for Zeph." He looked to see if anyone questioned his right. None did.

Sandry and Squirrel reached the city gates at high noon. The guards shouted excitedly. "Sandry!" one called. "Lord Sandry!"

"The same. Let us in."

"We have sent for the mayor. He will wish to greet you himself."

Leaving us standing here in the sun, Sandry thought. *At Aztlan they had the Caravanserai. And in Lordshills we have the guard rooms.*

But the mayor came quickly, with a train of officials. He wore his robes of office, and all of them wore jewelry.

"Greetings, Mayor," Squirrel said. "I see you no longer fear the birds."

Mayor Buzzard at Play fingered his pectoral jewels. "Yes, things are back to normal. The birds no longer come when manna is exposed. But there is so little manna here!"

"That will change," Sandry said. "Ern is coming with a wagon train of charged talismans. And we have many with us as well."

"You are not with Ern," the Mayor said. "You left by the east Gate with a wagon train. You return on foot to the River Gate. I believe you have a story to tell."

"We do," Sandry said. "A story, and treasure to show, but all that will be later. For now, we need wagons and draft animals."

"These are scarce," the mayor said.

"We have goods to trade."

"And credit with Jade Coin," Buzzard at Play said. "I am aware." He stood aside and gestured to the guards to open the gates. "Welcome to Crescent City, Lord Sandry."

Chapter Thirty-Seven

Dreams

The inn was called the Black Stone. It faced south, and from a small balcony there was a view of the sea, calm in the afternoon sun. Burning Tower sat alone at a table on the balcony. She wore a new skirt and blouse, buckskin and cotton, nothing like the finery of Aztlan, but it felt good to be dressed properly. A pretty waitress brought her tea. Her name was Laughing Rock. Regapisk had introduced her when he brought Tower and Sandry to this place where he had insisted that they would stay.

"Lord Reg is safe, then?" the girl asked.

"Very."

The waitress smiled. "I had hoped he would come back."

Tower nodded absently. *Tonight,* she thought. *Tonight.*

"Did he have many adventures?"

"Yes."

"But he did not marry?"

Burning Tower smiled thinly as she thought of the Lady Annalun and her charges. "No, he did not marry."

"What happened to his friend?" the girl asked.

"He died."

"Oh. I guess you don't want to talk about it."

"Not now, thanks," Tower said.

"Of course not now, I am sorry. But I became very fond of Lord Reg," Laughing Rock said.

"Many have," Tower said, but she said it under her breath.

The waitress went away. Of course she wasn't just a waitress—she was the owner's daughter, and Regapisk had insisted on coming to this inn and restaurant. To repay a kindness, Reggy had said. Sandry had looked startled.

Sandry often looked surprised at Regapisk. *There's so much I don't know,* Tower thought. *About my husband, about Regapisk, about the Lords.*

"It's ready." Clever Squirrel called from below.

For a moment, Burning Tower was startled. "Oh. All right." She gathered her things and went down the stairs to where Squirrel was waiting.

"You look great," Squirrel said.

Tower tried to smile. "Not much like a bride. Not in this outfit. Maybe I should have let them buy me a wedding dress. Sandry wanted to."

"What for?"

"That's what I thought—what for? I will never look as pretty as I did in Aztlan, and no one will ever have a more lovely gown. Now it's all in ruins."

"Are you crying?"

"Maybe a little," Tower said.

"Over losing your gown?"

"Well, and everything." She bit her lip. "Will he still love me? Am I really married?"

Squirrel looked serious. "Sister, you are married. May I never meet anyone more married! Before your gods and his, before Aztlan, with the Emperor and Coyote himself as witnesses! Don't worry about what you wear. Whatever you put on, you won't be in it long! Not after you use that charm thing of yours."

"I don't want to use it."

"Oh?"

"I'm afraid. Suppose I need it?"

"You don't need it," Squirrel said. "You look great! And I never saw a man more obviously in love."

"He's not here!"

"He's not far, and you insisted on shopping and bathing alone!"

They had reached the sweatbath. Squirrel ushered her inside.

Tower lay dreamily on the bench and felt the heat of the place. The walls faded, and she was somewhere else. She had never been there before, but she could see every detail. Trees, but all in gemstone hues. Something white flashed through the stone trees.

"Where?"

"Hush." Squirrel's voice. "You rode past it on the High Road."

"Is this your doing?"

"It's your vision."

"Why am I having it?"

"Coyote sends it," Squirrel said.

Nothing seemed to be happening. Just the stone forest, and something white at the edge of her vision. After a while she went to sleep.

There was a gorgeous red sunset when they came out of the sweatbath. "Even the skies put on a show for you," Squirrel said.

Tower laughed nervously.

Squirrel hurried her along the harbor street to the Black Stone Inn. Black Stone himself stood in the doorway. "Exactly on time," he said. His grin was infectious. "Your Lord awaits you inside."

Black Stone led them through the main hall of the restaurant. Half the city officials had gathered there. "They hope to hear your tales of Aztlan," Black Stone said.

"But—"

He grinned. "They can wait." He showed Tower and Squirrel into a narrow hall. At the end of the hall was a closed door. Squirrel opened the door and pushed Tower inside. The door closed behind her.

Sandry was there. He had taken off his armor and was dressed in new clothes that didn't fit him very well. Tower thought he had never been so handsome. He stood and opened his arms.

After a while she became aware that she was hungry. A table was set for two, and everything smelled wonderful. Food and wine.

"We're alone?" she said.

"Alone, and there's another way out."

"But the mayor and all his court will want to speak with us. They said so!"

"And they will," Sandry said. "Tomorrow. There is a feast, and we'll have to go to it, but it's in the afternoon. We have the night to ourselves, and we can sleep as late as we want in the morning."

"Oh."

"Aren't you hungry?"

"I thought I was a minute ago." She fingered the charm box in its leather pouch at her belt. The air in the small dining room seemed heavy. *I don't need this,* she thought.

"I guess I should eat." She sat at the table. Sandry hesitated, then sat across from her.

Bison steaks. Vegetables, including some she didn't recognize. Honey cakes.

"Plain fare," Sandry said. "They're still recovering from the siege. This may be the best meal anyone is having in Crescent City tonight."

"Oh." She smiled. "I thought I was hungry. Now I'm not so sure."

"There will be wine and honey cakes in the room," Sandry said.

She ate another bite of the steak. "Are we really alone?"

"Reggy will stay at the salt farm tonight. We'll see him tomorrow."

She cut off another bite and chewed mechanically. *He's as nervous as I am!* she thought. *Sandry! Lord Sandry, warrior, king of Aztlan!* That made her feel better.

"Only once have you been more beautiful," Sandry said.

"That was a wonderful gown."

"Actually, I was remembering you in your costume, on the high wire, the first time I ever saw you," Sandry said.

"That's sweet." She stood abruptly. "Is that the door?"

Tower jerked awake with a water stampede roaring darkly through her mind.

It was nearly dawn. Sandry lay sprawled in exhaustion across the bed. Burning Tower rose, careful not to wake him. She pulled on a robe against the chill of the morning and went out to the balcony.

A thick fog rolled in from the sea, so thick she could not see the street below. As she stared into the fog, shapes appeared.

The stone forest. A flash of white. It came closer. Spike, running free in the stone forest. The bonehead looked at her and tossed his head, the great horn lifted high.

Tower thought she heard a soft nicker, not of rage or hatred. Perhaps wistful.

"I love you," she whispered to the beast.

Sandry stirred, and Tower looked back at her sleeping husband, then at the vision ahead. "I love you, but I won't miss you at all." She turned away from the vision.

NOTES

Much of the research for this book was done by Roberta Pournelle, who found most of the primary sources we used to build our version of Aztlan/Aztec culture, as well as the codex exhibit.

The authors did considerable research for this book. We drove the path that would have led our wagon trains to Chaco Canyon, though we didn't veer around the Salton Sea, as wagons would. We climbed around Chaco Canyon and the Petrified Forest. We skipped Meteor Crater because we'd both roamed through it years ago. With Roberta Pournelle's help (because Niven was in a wheelchair), we toured a traveling exhibit of Aztec lore at the Los Angeles County Museum of Art, a wonderful array of buildings built above the Black Pit. We collected a sizable stack of reference material on Aztecs, and it was there we found Aztec sweatbaths, an overburdened merchant with a parrot, giant stone heads, and many other wonders. The exhibit was put together by the museum, and it brought to one place materials scattered in twenty museums about the world, including a codex from Germany.

Niven was led through petroglyphs inscribed on cliffs in California, by Aleta Jackson and a host of rockhounds. He researched Navajo magic in Salt Lake City. He owes much gratitude to his guides.

As in *The Burning City,* we took what we found and made what assumptions seemed good to us. We have tried to account for many odd and seemingly contradictory twists in ancient legends, as well as the capricious character of gods like Coyote.

Of course, this book is still fantasy, and not much of it should be taken as history.

Or the reader may ignore this warning and assume that later civilizations are the heirs of magic-using civilizations of fourteen thousand years ago, when the manna was dying, most gods had gone myth, and humankind was learning to live in a magic-depleted world.

For instance: Hogans are well described in Navajo lore. If later Navajos believe that a properly built hogan was a living thing, fourteen thousand years ago it may have been so. So also with locusts used as scouts, and the rule that everything comes in fours.

Terror birds were quite real. They didn't become extinct until long after humankind was speading through the Americas. Even the skeletons found in the southwest and Mexico are scary as hell.

In Aztec myth, Aztlan is the island origin of the Aztec people. After they left the island city, they roamed for ten thousand years before certain signs allowed them to build a new home. Their war god was a hummingbird—a nasty-tempered, quarrelsome little bird, however pretty. The god was called Left-handed Hummingbird for reasons unknown; we think our explanation is as good as any.

Chaco Canyon, in the middle of the North American continent, is about where Aztlan ought to be. It's a desert now, but a river once ran through it. It was a mighty trading empire: food had to be imported from scores of miles away, and trees too—they used lumber in building. One problem: Aztlan is certainly not an island.

The Salton Sea was real enough, and it drained into the current Sea of Cortez. The Colorado emptied into it, running not as deep as it does today, but the canyons must already have been impressive.

The Petrified Forest was woefully depleted during the days of the American robber barons, so much so that there's no telling how extensive it might once have been. The servants of Aztlan's Emperor might have stripped a far more extensive stone forest.

And the Aztecs worshipped a feathered serpent.

The assumption of this series has been that ancient legends are garbled accounts of true events that happened in a time when magic was still a major force. Magic is fueled by manna, and manna is a very nearly nonrenewable resource. Today we use science to accomplish wonders; but, as C. S. Lewis once pointed out, science and magic were born twins.